Heirs to the Kingdom

Book Two

The Lost Sword of Carnac
(Revised Edition)

Robin John Morgan

www.heirstothekingdom.com

Violet Circle Publishing, Manchester, UK.
www.violetcirclepublishing.co.uk

In Loving Memory.

Patricia Lillian Morgan
Your encouragement and support meant everything
in those early days of doubt.

Know that the one sword has returned and has been hidden for all this time.

The five will remain powerless until such time as those who value them as a part of themselves come forth to claim them.

From brave Gawain, we hold Truth, and only in the hand of the one whom truly seek it, can this sword find its power.

Defeated Gaheris who grieved for his slaughtered true love gave up his sword, and Merlin made it the sword of justice. Fair should be the hand that holds it.

Brave Tor who was tireless in his defence of the realm and his king, faced with his sword many moments of peril. Courage was his gift to the swords.

Without honour there can be no ruler, and none were honoured more than the knight who lost his and repented, in the final hours of a good king's life, the sword of Lancelot brought honour back to these fair isles. FIND THE LOST SWORD AND UNITE BEHIND IT.

One more sword was forged that none knew. In the years of pain and suffering that followed the death of a king. Merlin filled the sword with the knowledge of men from the past, to be a beacon to light the flames of the future.

Upon this earth they reside and will find their true owners. When the guardians of the table's call they will come, and this land will be reborn.

The prophecy of Sequana seer of Avalonia
(Discovered by Leenard Rimmer 1998)

CHAPTER ONE

A KINGDOM WITH NO HEIR

Mason walked at a brisk pace along the hotel corridor, followed by his aides who could see the very visible rage within him. Billy hurried at his side, almost the opposite of his father, his exterior calm and cool, despite the red swollen stitched ear, which had coloured his hair, neck and shirt in blood red. His father talked fast, clutching his heavily bandaged throbbing hand.

"I want them found, I don't care what it takes, you get every man we have out there, they must be holed up somewhere close by, hunt them down and then kill all of them, do you hear me?" Billy gave a slight nod as his father's eyes stared in a cold watery blue at him. The shrill voice of one of his aides interjected.

"We have scouts out in every direction now Lord Knox; no stone will remain unturned until they are located." Mason stopped in his tracks as he stepped out through the main doors back into the cathedral square. The scene was one of chaos, as men hurriedly passed buckets of water along a line to the opposite end of the long building, to throw on the fires that burned fiercely. The pain was pulsating up his arm, driving his anger that rose swiftly as he turned to face the gathering of his officials.

"It's a bloody shame no stone was unturned before today isn't it? JUST HOW THE HELL DID THAT LEAF LOVER WALK RIGHT PASSED YOU INTO THE CATHEDRAL... WELL!?" The aides stepped back in fear.

"My Lord?" Bells rang loudly round the square, as the scent of smouldering timber wafted into Mason's nostrils, it was utter pandemonium and his anger at seeing it finally peaked, he lunged with his heavy gold bedecked left hand, and grabbed the aide roughly, dragging him forward so his face came to almost to touching his own as he spoke through gritted teeth.

"I want this wood lover and everyone who has supported him finding, they want to burn down my kingdom do they? You listen to me you snivelling worm, you bring in every one of the Cutter Brigades, and you start at the sea and head north, I want all of them to know that I am in charge, not that leaf lover. They like wood do they? Well, you move forward with the Cutter companies and you burn every house and stick you find and drive them out of their holes and from under their rocks. They say they love this hooded man, well just let them run to him, this is my country so you drive them out and kill every last one of them, and don't you rest until every man woman and child that supports him is gone." He pushed hard with his arm as his cold blue eyes burned an even greater fear into the already quaking aide. The man crashed to the floor at the feet of the others, who stepped back sharing his fear, Mason glared at all of them.

"WELL, WHAT THE HELL ARE YOU WAITING FOR? GET ON WITH IT!"

The black clouds rolled in with the wind and rain across the sea, and pelted down on to the circle of twenty stones, set high in the ground on the wild moor, below the large craggy cliffs and rocky outcrops. Tall and proud they stood, a remnant of an age almost forgotten, but there were still those who remembered them fondly, not everything from the early times of man had been forgotten. The days before the coming of the Red Death had ended, and now the Age of Dreams was approaching as humankind woke from their sleep of complacency.

Those who fought to resurrect the corpse of an old life that would destroy everything now divided the country, and the dream of one man had grown into a tide of many. This was now a time when prophecies would be fulfilled, and a new hope was growing around the countryside. All eyes were on the one man in hope he could lead them all to a better way of life, and save what the modern age had tried to destroy.

In a world that had grown up with the love of money and power, all sanctity of life had been lost, and people no longer used their ability to understand the delicate balance of their actions. Human life had become worthless, as the love of machines and the power of money had grown into a beast of destruction. Mother Nature had wept for too long, and the powers of the olden times, which had been sleeping for an age, had awoken.

The Red Death had been an incurable virus, it was swift and violent, and humankind spread it around the globe freely, and all that met it died, and those who lived, fought and killed each other, until soon the few that remained out in the wilds, turned back to their old skills and began a dream that was balance.

One man had been chosen to seek the truth, and find the lost heirlooms of a kingdom that once ruled with a fair hand. He was young and not sure if he was up to the task at hand, and yet as he began, he soon saw the truth of what was possible. Surrounded by loyalty, he had won his first battle to pave the way for the future, and now he was faced with the task of bringing together those who knew only the times after the fall of man, for any born before could be tainted by the past.

He was a simple living woodsman, who knew nothing of the old life and ways of modern man, his life was set in the garden of the countryside, living amongst the trees and the plants. The wildness of the world was his life cycle, and deep down inside his dream grew stronger. A life of love was his goal, a life that loved the world in which he lived and the woman that lived beside him. His dream was the focus of the future of the whole of mankind, it was his task now to realise it.

The kingdom was balanced on the edge of a knife, as the dark older powers regrouped, to begin again to destroy his dream and bring back the ways of death. He was a simple bowman who stood out from all the others, and had taken the lead in the fight to seek the truth and discover the true heirs to the kingdom.

The grass was almost flat as the wind blew across the top of the sea, and on to the land. Bits of twig and tufts of loose grass bounced along the floor looking for somewhere to wedge themselves, and the large heavy raindrops tried to batter them into submission. The silent stones, which had weathered the storms of a thousand lifetimes, stood silently waiting for her; they knew she would not be late for she had never kept them waiting before.

The tall slender figure came over the rise, as the wind whipped her long waist length brown hair around her face, she slid her arms up wiping the wet hair back, and smiled as her slate grey eyes saw the stones again, for this was the hundredth time this year. She pulled the pale blue cloak around her as protection from the wind, and she strolled as if on a leisurely walk on a summer's day.

Entering the stones, she felt the calmness grow within her, the power of her lord was strong here, Callanish had always been a place she loved, but with hope, today she would know if it was time to go home. She walked to the centre of the circle and raised her arms, the wind dropped and the rain eased, and silence fell across the whole island.

Holding her arms out, her eyes began to glow blue, and her breathing slowed as she closed her eyes, and the sun opened as a cloud parted, and pushed through its first rays of sunshine in weeks.

"Hear me my Mother."

"I hear you my daughter, and I have great news of joy."

"Oh mother, can I return to my homeland at last?"

"Melanie my child, come home and bring with you my granddaughter and grandson, I have missed them so."

"He has done it then, has he Mother?"

"There is no king in this land and his quest for truth starts now, as does yours my daughter. The lost sword must be found before we can reveal the one who will lead."

"I have heard things Mother, they say it has left France and is on its way here."

"Then find it my daughter before the snake does, for he has lost a crown and will

want all the swords in order to make his claim again. He craves the power, and has never understood what we all know to be true, sadly he will never be able to join as we have, where one mind becomes one for the good of all."

"I will return to my children and prepare mother, and I will wait for the time when I too am written onto the Runestone, and will be free to feel my family again."

"Come my dear daughter, I will prepare the way."

"**R**une are you alright?" Robbie looked at her as she sat on the log next to the fire; she had lifted her hand to the side of her face.

"I just had the strangest sensation, I felt someone who is a stranger to me, but that is not possible I am the centre of the circle and know all of them." She looked worriedly at Robbie. "What do you think that can mean?"

"I don't really know, but to be honest Rune, your family does seem to be a source of confusion to me most of the time, no doubt one of your family will walk through something to tell you." She smiled and leaned against him.

"You did well today Rob, look how happy they all are."

Robbie sat, and watched as they all sat round the campfire eating and talking, he lifted his arm around Rune. "I am so glad they are safe for now."

"Only for now?"

He gave her a soft squeeze. "We have taken Mason's prize from him; I expect about now he is having a tantrum and planning his revenge. I have no idea what he will do now; I just know that he will remember the name of Loxley for the rest of his days."

Robbie smiled as Hog and Bear; lifted John into a basket woven chair, and Hog gently lifted John's leg on to a box. All the others laughed and jeered as Martin shouted. "Faker, it was only a splinter." John beamed at them all.

Harry sat with Maggs and Blades, and crooned over his baby girl, the fact she was sixteen was irrelevant to him. She now had her arm in a sling to take the weight off the stitches that Alice had put in her arm. Jett was sat heavily bandaged with Jade and her mum, and the others all sat close and talked quietly. Robbie sighed. "We were lucky, how the hell we did that, I will never know."

Rune moved slightly as she turned to get comfortable beside him. "You led us in, and you led us out Robbie, and we believed in you enough to follow. I never had any doubt that you would achieve it although.... Robbie, why is everyone staring at us, and why is Rowan bowing?" Robbie looked up at the group, who all now wore faces of wonder and surprise; Rowan was down on one knee, as the breeze softly touched Robbie's cheek. "Hearne." Robbie began to realise that everyone was looking behind him.

Rune had already turned, and as her eyes flickered a pale violet, she broke into a huge smile, got up, and began to run to the forest edge where the old man of green stood with his arms open, surrounded by a white rolling mist. Robbie smiled at the joy of Rune, as she was taken into the arms of Hearne, the old lord smiled down at Rune, as he embraced her in his arms. "You are a flower of great quality my daughter, I feel great joy today towards my kin so filled with life and love of all around her."

The old man stroked her hair back from her face as she smiled with joy, and violets appeared in her braids. "Oh, my Father of all life, I am so pleased to see you again. To have you come here and let all that love you see you, will bring such joy to their hearts."

Hearne looked with love in his eyes, as he embraced Rune in his arms, and Robbie bowed to the lord of the woods. "My Lord Hearne, I am honoured and pleased you have chosen to visit here."

Hearne stepped forward keeping one arm around Rune. It sounded like the rustle of small twigs in the high breeze; he pulled Robbie toward him and placed his arm around his shoulder as he would a son. "You have shown courage and wisdom beyond your years My Bowman, it is you who have honoured me with your heart, and I thank you."

Robbie smiled at the kindly old man, who squeezed him with his long twig like fingers, and then looked up and across the camp to the others, who were all down on one knee and bowing. "Your woodland family has grown Bowman; I would speak with them." The group trembled as they saw the green lord walk towards them with his arms around the shoulder of Rune and Robbie. They stood in awe as the old man who appeared as if made by parts of the earth, came towards them smiling kindly. Jade beamed, and approached her lord to greet him.

She bowed with great reverence before him. "My Lord of the woodland you have honoured us beyond all we could hope for." Her eyes blazed green as she raised her head to him, and smiled a big happy and quite cheeky smile.

Hearne looked down and smiled with great affection. "My little green child, as cheeky as the wood nymphs and as happy as the daffodils, I have watched you with great interest, and you have proven yourself in many ways. It brings me such joy to see you have found your place in my realm."

Hearne slid his arms from around Robbie and Rune and knelt down to Jade; he pulled her into a warm embrace and hugged her. "You bring joy where there was great pain," he whispered into her ear. "My woodsman now heals for his love of you is deep my cheeky nymph, and I am pleased he has given you what for so long you have sought. Be happy my dearest of woodland children, for you deserve what you have found."

Jade looked so surprised, and Rune smiled as she saw two tears of green run down Jade's cheek. "I love you my lord and protector."

Hearne rose and beckoned to Rowan. "Woodsman." Rowan rose and came forward and bowed.

"My Lord, and Master."

Hearne put his hand on Rowan's shoulder. "I am pleased with you my woodsman, you have a place of high honour at my table, and you have served well the cause of green life."

Hearne now looked to the others and smiled, and all of them looked up in great reverence. "My children, you have shown love and loyalty to my bowman and daughter beyond the measure of hope, and today you have fought the first of many battles. I have watched you all, and I will continue to do so. You have paid a dear price recently in the loss of one of you, and I have seen inside all of you the hole left in your hearts. Be at peace my children and know he has been embraced by his lord, and is at peace in my other realm where he knows great joy."

Two huge tears welled in Big John's eyes as Hearne spoke, and the others put their heads down. Hearne raised his hand and waved it across them, it sounded like the whistle in a soft breeze, and all of them felt it brush past them. It was like electric in the air, and they felt a tug at their hearts. "Be healed in your hearts and your bodies my children, for after a short rest you will be busy." Hearne to the surprise of everyone, bowed in honour to them. "I will leave soon my children, but first I will talk to your lord."

He turned and put his arms around Robbie and Rune. "Walk me back to the trees my children." His legs seemed to creak and groan as the trees did in a winter wind, his robes that looked like they were made of flower petals and fresh young leaves, swayed with the sound of tall grass bending in a summer breeze.

Hearne turned with Robbie and Rune and walked toward the woods; everyone noticed the place where he had been standing was filled with small white daises. A perfect circle grew, and they gasped as it slowly expanded, and the small plants spread rapidly in front of their eyes, filling the whole of the campsite. Maggs jumped back on to one of the logs to allow them to fill the place where she had stood, and stared speechless as she watched them. Jett pulled the bandage from her shoulder and stretched her left arm; she opened the rip in her top and showed Maggs. "Look at that, it is gone, healed not even a scar."

Maggs lifted her glasses and slid them into her wild hair, as she stared at the smooth pale skin of Jett's shoulder. "Wow... Groovy... how cosmic is that? My darling you have been touched by a most cosmic power, all of us have had a most positive influence put on our auras, we arc all now blessed."

Jett looked at Maggs and smiled. "Yeah, Maggs whatever."

The Green Lord turned to Robbie, his kindly old lined faced smiled. "Well my Bowman, what will you do now? The crown is safe, and only the true heir to the throne will remove my arrow, and by the time he does, I think you will like the improvements we have made to the cathedral that the snake favours so highly." He smiled at Robbie.

Robbie looked up at Hearne's old lined face. "This will not end here, will it? I cannot see him just going away, he has dreams of power and wealth."

"Yet you have dreams of love and life for all, he will return and you will face him again, for now your journey to the truth has begun in earnest, I am not worried my dearest woodsman, my faith in your heart and the love of my daughter has assured me you will rise to him and meet him with honour. The snake has many lessons yet to learn."

Rune watched Robbie as he spoke with Hearne, they entered below the trees and he turned back to her. "My dearest daughter such trials you have faced and overcome, you have a power that was not expected, but she will return who is as black as the heart of the snake, draw your power from the daughters of the woods, and wait for the circle of knowledge to form, for you are of two lines and you are the centre of both circles, be prepared my child, you will have aid you did not see, have you not felt them?"

Hearne kissed her on the forehead, and her eyes blazed a deep violet. "Be at peace for a time and watch over those who carry the seeds of the future... Take care my Bowman, I will be wherever you need me." The old green man walked slowly into the wood, as a fine mist swirled out from the trees and welcomed him.

Robbie and Rune stood and watched as the mist swirled back and he was gone. Rune pulled Robbie close as she slid her arms round him. "I love him and his realm, and you are now a huge part of it." She kissed him softly as her eyes faded from deep purple and back to pale lilac. "What do you think he meant about two circles?"

Robbie shook his head. "I am not sure, maybe you should talk to your mum, one grandma walking through walls is enough for me." He started to chuckle. "If you have more family Rune, Hearne knows what they will get up to."

She grinned. "I might be better asking granddad; I will talk to him on the boat."

They walked slowly back to the camp, where everyone was either excited as Jade was, or quiet and reflective as John was. Rags looked at Robbie with a smile. "Your well in with 'The Old Man,' I'm impressed." It felt like quite a compliment, and Robbie looked down and he chuckled.

"So are you Rags, everyone has fought to save his realm, he would not appear in person as he did for any other reason. He will watch over you and all the others."

"You are a good guy Robin Hood, and you have some really nice people around you, it has felt good being here."

Rune smiled as she looked from Robbie down at Rags. "You are one of us now Rags, there will always be a place here amongst us for you, I hope you realise that?"

"I like knowing I belong somewhere; I have never really fitted in anywhere."

Robbie started to chuckle again as he pulled Rune closer. "Well, when it comes to misfits, I think that is a term that all of us can relate to, you will fit here Rags have no doubts." Rags smiled as she lowered her head, they were indeed an unusual group and yet she had found that common bond that all of them shared. All of them lived in fear of the world they loved being destroyed, and all of them felt in some way a feeling of being isolated from everyone else in the world, and they all admired, respected, and loved their leader.

The afternoon was wearing on and Robbie wanted to get clear of Canterbury and back on the boat. He was nervous as the time began to pass, he knew that Mason Knox would regroup quickly and his response would be severe, his men had fought hard and valiantly but they were also very tired, he had used many arrows, and as he looked across, he could see Rune had less than a dozen.

Everyone had swords and daggers, but close quarters combat against a large number would lead to loss, he had been able to get them all out safely; he was not about to lose anyone now. He organised his men and split the few arrows left amongst the eight bowmen, Harry, Blades, Jett, and Scarlet, preferred the sword. Bear, Skip, and Hog headed off to prepare the yacht and he now had the task of convincing Hilda she had to come with them.

Maggs had been easier to convince, she had lost Harry once and Robbie understood that no matter how odd she was, he knew that the love between Harry and Maggs was strong. Maggs tried everything, but Hilda would not leave her home or her animals, and eventually Hilda won over, and she kissed her daughter goodbye with a fierce look of determination on her face.

The group left the farm on Honey Hill with a slight air of sadness, the last five days of living in the circle had bonded everyone even closer; Robbie looked back across the fields at the circle of trees where he knew the tepee village lay hidden and sighed. Rune's bright eyes sparkled at him. "It is sort of sad, isn't it? I think it really felt like a little community up in the trees, I am going to miss it."

Robbie nodded. "Yeah, I wasn't so sure when we arrived, but it has been nice and I think it has been good for all of us to just rest up a while together." He turned and looked down the long lane to the trees up ahead, which would lead them to the harbour, and the boat home. Rags came up on her horse and smiled, she would not leave her faithful mount and was going to ride across country and meet up with them later.

"Me and Bags here, will see you back at the castle Robbie."

Rune gave her an odd look. "Bags, isn't that an odd name for a horse?"

Rags grinned and smiled. "Rags and Bags, it sort of fits... you know, postie?" She pulled on the reins. "See ya!" And kicking her heels, the horse clattered down the lane, and off over the fields in the direction of Caerleon.

Robbie watched as she rode like the wind into the distance. "Do you think she will be alright Rune?"

"Oh, I wouldn't worry about Rags, she can take care of herself, there is something about her I am not sure what, but believe me Rob, she will always come through."

The tree line was now in sight, and Robbie rested on the wall as the others passed and disappeared into them, Rowan was still some way back with Jade watching the rear, as Harry, Blades, and Maggs came level. Harry had his broad arm around Maggs who was sniffling, and Blades he noticed held Maggs hand. He smiled as they entered into the trees, and waited as Rowan came up with Jade. Jade as always beamed, and her green eyes danced under her blonde curly fringe as she held Rowan's hand tight. He smiled, his chiselled face softening, yet his eyes still watched the road and the trees ahead. "All quiet?"

She giggled. "As night."

Robbie looked at her knowingly. "What's got you so happy?"

Her eyes sparkled and she looked up at Rowan, as excitement seemed to be pushing up inside her and trying to explode out. "Can I tell them?" Rowan smiled a happy smile and nodded at her. Jade burst out with a huge chuckle. "Rowan has asked me to marry him when we get back to Loxley, and I have said yes."

Rune leapt with delight, and pulled Jade into a huge hug as she danced around with her, and Robbie and Rowan smiled as they watched. A very happy smiling Rune put her arms around Rowan, and pulled him into a huge hug. "Oh, Rowan I am so happy for you two, I really think you belong together." She kissed him on the cheek.

Jade stood smiling in front of Robbie, and he smiled at her, she squeaked a happy little burst of joy and jumped into his arms. Robbie pulled her close and hugged her tightly. "Oh Pebbles, I cannot tell you how happy I am for you."

"I was afraid you wouldn't like it; you know I wasn't sure, oh Robbie I am so happy I have never felt like this before, and I know this is really right."

"Me too," he whispered. "Pebbles he is a man of great honour and courage and I know how deeply he loves you; I really think you deserve to be together." She slid down and looked up at him.

"Thanks Robbie that means a lot to me." He smiled as he cupped her face in his hands.

"You are very special to me Pebbles, and have been for many years. Your happiness is all I could ever want for you, I am glad that you have found it with someone who is also precious to both Rune and myself." Rune turned and looked back up the road toward the farmhouse, her eyes flared deep purple as she turned back to Robbie and Jade. They both jumped, as a very loud scream brought their attention back to where they were. Robbie turned to face the direction of the scream; Maggs was struggling in Harry's arms, her eyes were wide as she stared back at the farm at the top of the hill, and she kicked and struggled to get free, yelling and wailing in fear.

Robbie looked back at the farm, and the smoke billowing out of it, Rowan was already turning to head back, when Robbie seized his arm. "Look!" Rowan glanced across the field to where smoke issued out of the trees where the tepee village was, it billowed up into the air and across the hill behind it. Robbie and Rune both pulled arrows, and fitted them to the bows. "Harry get her out of here, and on the boat." He turned and looked back as two soldiers came over the hill. "NOW HARRY!"

Harry dragged Maggs, who was screaming for her mother, back into the trees, Rune's eyes glowed violet, as Robbie took aim and fired at one of the soldiers. The arrow hit its mark, and the soldier staggered and fell to the floor. "Robbie, Hilda is gone; grandmother will guide her to Hearne, Jett is moving them faster to the yacht." The other soldier fell as Rune released her arrow; more soldiers were now starting to appear on the top of the hill. Jade and Rowan fired.

"We don't have enough arrows for this guys." Rune released another shot; Robbie looked down at the six arrows left in his quiver.

"Two more shots each and then let's get the hell out of here." A large man seemed to be directing the soldiers their way, Robbie took aim and fired, the arrow hit him square in the chest and threw him off his feet, he reloaded fast and fired again. "Ok let's move it."

He grabbed Rune's arm and pulled her, a few feet into the trees there was the wall, and gripping her quickly, he whisked her into the air and over, she squealed in surprise as he came flying over after her and grabbed her hand. "Oh, I love it when you're masterful."

He smiled as he tugged on her hand and pulled her through the trees to the next wall, on what use to be the other side of the buried road. She was ready and swung on to his neck as he lifted her, Jade squealed with delight as Rowan whipped her over at Rune's side. Both Robbie and Rowan vaulted over, they wove their way quickly into the dense trees. Robbie felt his heart pounding and his ears straining to try to work out how near they were, he darted left to right avoiding the trunks of the trees with skill. He could hear Maggs crying up ahead, as Harry bounded through the trees with her on his shoulder.

They reached the meadow of long grass and wild flowers, and he saw Harry just heading into the trees in front, they all bounded across the long grass towards the spot where they last saw Harry. Martin and John appeared out of the grass their bows loaded and raised.

The four shot past and heard John and Martin slip in behind them to cover their trail. The trees here were thinner and Harry could be seen with Blades, heading through the wide gaps between trees and sprinting at full speed, Robbie dodged the trunks, his feet firm on the leaf covered woodland floor, it was warm, and he felt the first beads of sweat form on his brow as he pulled Rune by the hand to safety.

Robbie looked back at Rune. "Give me your arrows, and let Jett know that they should raise the anchor, and get ready to leave quickly." She slowed as she pulled out her arrows and handed them to him; he dragged her into his arms and kissed her. "Now run like hell and get ready, Rowan and me will be coming in fast, have a couple of special arrows ready, as you see us fire into the trees behind us." He smacked her bum. "GO!"

Rune and Jade flew off in the direction Harry had taken, as Rowan and Robbie crouched down behind the tree trunks. Robbie wiped the sweat from his forehead; John and Martin came flying through the woods. "Bugger me there are loads of em." John panted, as he fled past, and Robbie brought his bow up. Red and black was an easy target in a sea of green, he unleashed the arrow and it whipped through the trees, before it hit the soldier, he had reloaded and Rowan's bow sung.

The ones at the front hit the floor dead as they fired constantly; Robbie pulled his final arrow still panting, and looked at Rowan who was now down to his last, he winked at him. "Ready?" He took aim and fired. "RUN!"

The two of them turned, and flew into the trees, they headed in a direct line, and Robbie gasped as he ran as he had never run before. The trees broke as they hit dense soft foliage, and the next thing they were out, and running down the harbour where the yacht was at least eight feet away from the wall, and starting to move. Robbie forced his legs forward with all of his strength, as he saw Rune and Jade light their fuses and aim. The fizzing arrows whipped past him as he reached the end of the wall, and pulling his legs and arms swinging into the air, he launched himself at the yacht with all his effort.

There was an almighty explosion behind him as his feet hit the deck, and he reeled forward landing sprawling on the side of the yacht, and rolled over the top of the cabin and into the railing on the other side. Gasping he sat up and looked at Rowan's legs waving in the air, as he had slipped and gone into the stairwell of the cabin. Flames licked through the trees in front of the harbour, as the yacht pulled away and into the centre of the large bay.

Rune and Jade laughing hysterically, pulled on Rowan's legs to get him back upright, and his beaming red face appeared above the cabin roof, and he looked at Robbie grinning broadly. "You do love your adventurous endings, don't you?"

Robbie smiled as he breathed deeply. "Can't have you bored now, can I?" He struggled up to his feet, and watched as figures staggered out of the trees, they were safe and had gotten clear, Martin and John were still crouched on the deck watching with their bows ready, but as the sails went up the masts, and the yacht picked up speed, they lowered them and sat back relieved.

"Welcome aboard My Lord, gang planks not grand enough for you two?" Skip gave them a huge smile. "Next stop Wales I take it?"

Robbie nodded unable to speak as he caught his breath, Rune came up and slid her arms around him and hugged him. "You frightened me then."

He put his arms around her and pulled her close. "Never a worry. We knew you and Jade was here waiting." She smiled and he kissed her softly. "That was worth a run and jump for," he kissed her again.

Harry sat with the tiny figure of Maggs cradled in his arms as she sobbed. With each tearful sob, there was a rattle of bangles, and her huge mop of curly hair filled with beads and feathers shook violently, Harry held her tight and softly rocked her.

Alice sat with her bag open, as she mixed some leaves together and ground them in a small pedestal of marble, Robbie sat down on the other side of the table and watched, as Steph brought a steaming mug of water in and placed it on the table.

She gave Maggs a sympathetic smile and sprinkled the herbs into the water and stirred it. She smiled at Robbie; he had watched her do this a thousand times over the years, as she had cured every cold and ailment that Robbie had ever suffered. Alice in the Lox household was regarded with high praise. It was well known that Alice had far greater knowledge of herbs and plants and their uses than Len Rimmer. She handed the mug to Harry and smiled. "Harry let her drink this and then put her in bed, it will help calm her down and make her feel a little more relaxed."

"Thanks Alice, her vibes is all over the place."

Alice came back to the table as Harry did his best to get Maggs to drink, and then shortly after he picked her up and carried her out towards the sleeping cabins. Alice sighed as Rune slid in beside Robbie with coffees, they all grabbed a mug, and Robbie shuddered as he took a sip. "Sugar!" He swapped with Rune and sipped again as she smiled.

"Sad isn't it?" Alice gave a huge sigh. "Hilda was sweet."

Rune nodded. "She was really kind, poor Maggs she was very close to her mum."

Robbie's mind drifted off as he thought about the little old woman that had a very tight bun of pale pink hair. He remembered how she wandered around the farm talking to all her animals in a long blue raincoat, and bright flowery pink wellingtons. He hadn't really spoken to her much apart from when she had offered him a coffee at the camp with a very bright and chirpy. 'Here you go darling.'

Robbie had wanted to bring her along, and yet only hours before she had been quite resolute. "You can bugger off; I am not leaving my animals here alone. Who will take care of them? They are used to their comforts." He had watched as she had slipped a hot water bottle into the pig's straw bed.

Robbie smiled to himself, she was as odd as hell, and yet he had felt a great feeling of love and peace emit from her, her animals had certainly responded well to her. A little more anger rose in him, as once again it felt like the evil hand of Mason Knox had begun to stretch out towards him. Knowing Knox was still alive and sent his men after him sickened him, he felt responsible for the death of Hilda, and he knew everyone around him or that helped him would suffer the same fate if Knox were to find out about them. Mason would be more determined than ever now to stop any one from helping him, he could see the coming days slowly mapping themselves out in front of him as Knox tried to regain his control.

"Robbie... Robbie... Hey dreamer?" He blinked as Rune's voice seeped into his mind, Alice, Steph, and Rune were all looking at him and smiling. "Hey... are you with us, or off in the land of the fairies?"

He smiled at Rune whose bright blue eyes sparkled. "Sorry guys I was miles away, what's up?"

Alice spoke softly. "We were just wondering what we do next." Robbie yawned.

"I am not sure, I need to sit and think about it, there is no king and no leader for the country, so I was wondering about talking to Bear and Skip, both of them seem to have a good grasp of government. I suppose if we can get all the local leaders talking, there might be some chance of coordinating the country."

"Rob that would be quite a move, it would at least put a halt to Knox." Alice took a large swig of her coffee.

Robbie looked at his mug. "I am a woodsman, I know nothing of these things, those two are better at that sort of stuff, I just thought that if I was able to rally everyone to help Loxley and York, by getting all the groups of woodsmen to work together, I suppose I have wondered whether we should try to do the same for the running of the country. It probably sounds daft but we already have a woodsman law, I just wondered if we could start there and get everyone to enforce it."

"The only problem there Robbie, is that Knox is still the self appointed Governor of England and backed by the Christian church, which gives him a lot of power." Steph was right and he knew it.

"I control all that is green as the hooded man, he controls the rest, I have to pull together all of the woodsmen, and then find the true king. If I can do that, we can remove Knox and replace him with a king defended by woodsmen, I think the church will back a true heir to the throne."

Steph seemed to agree. "Well according to dad, you pretty much control the west side of the country at the moment, at least as far as York. So, you have at least a third of the country behind you, which is something to build on." Steph smiled. "It's a start, Loxley, York, Gloucester and Caerleon, have very large areas of control, bring them together and others may follow Robbie, I think considering your lack of political knowledge you have arrived at a very good solution."

"I suppose if we have regional governors with the town leaders under them, we may have a chance of bringing some unity and organisation, as I say though, this is not something I want to do, I have a king to find."

Rune squeezed his hand. "Talk to Skip tomorrow and see what he thinks, it's been a long day Robbie and you look so tired. Why don't you get some rest, it will be at least dawn before we arrive at Caerleon?" She took him by the hand, and led him down the corridor to the small cabin at the end. Inside, she snuggled up beside him in bed, and he lay staring at the little porthole and softly stroking her hair. Why now did he suddenly feel the worst was yet to come?

Robbie had left Loxley only twenty-three days ago, as Lord Loxley the new hooded man. He was seventeen years old, and yet now he had a whole country looking to him for leadership. He still felt like Robbie the hunter and woodsman who could shoot a bow better than anyone shoots, and watch the girl he had been in love with for most of his life from behind the hedges.

Now his world seemed so overwhelming, he had to find a king who was hidden and he had no idea of where to begin, and there were large parts of the country that wanted him to lead them. That in its self was so daunting he felt buried under the burden, but he also had the problem of Mason Knox who wanted the country for himself, and wanted him dead. Knox was still very powerful, and his evil reign of terror for at least ten years had created quite an effect, he did run the country now, and his army was big. Robbie was under no illusions that Knox now understood he had over stretched his forces, which had cost him dearly, that was not a mistake, he knew Mason would make again.

Rune's eyes stared at him in the dark, he looked down past his chin and saw them peering at him from his chest, they twinkled and he smiled, as he slid his arm down towards her and pulled her into a hug. He felt her soft slender frame warmly curl tight around him, and her eyes came closer. "Hi gorgeous."

"Hey beautiful." She smiled and put her head on his shoulder.

"Oh Rob, this is nice... I love all our moments alone; they do seem to have become less and less since those archery lessons."

Robbie remembered the day so well, and he laughed. "You will never know how nervous you made me; I was shaking like a leaf when I first stood behind you."

She chuckled. "You were nervous, I was terrified, I kept thinking what if he doesn't like me. I was so crazy about you; I am glad it went so well I would have died if you had ended up with Jade."

He stroked her long hair down her back and she relaxed on him. "It's only ever been you Rune, and it always will be, you are now my life and my future." His whole world was wrapped in uncertainty except for one thing, about Rune he knew without doubts or worry, she was, and would forever be, the centre of his world.

CHAPTER TWO

THE FIRST HOUSE OF RIMMER

Mason Knox burst out of the doors of the archbishop's house in a fury. His eyes were narrowed, and his frowning face red, as he stormed across the church square, and on to the compound towards the huge cathedral. The two guards saluted as he approached muttering to himself, and cursing under his breath, the archbishop ran down the steps a distraught look of anguish on his lined face, as he pointed a shaking finger at the building. "Look, go on. Look what they have done, how could you let this happen?"

Knox grimaced at him. "What the hell are you whining about now?"

The archbishop recoiled at the blast from Knox, but held his ground as his shaking finger still pointed at the doors. Mason felt his contempt for the old man. "Always bloody whining about something Bishop, you lot are never bloody happy, are you? Best moneymaking racket on earth, and look at you all, miserable bunch of whining bastards the lot of you?"

Mason climbed the steps and went in through the carved doorway, into the large main entrance of the cathedral. Two cleaners scurried as they swept the ash of his burned up soldiers off the carpets; he glanced unconcerned, and headed into the main church. Was it a cathedral, or was it a forest? Tall oak trees lined the walls of the mighty cathedral, side by side; they grew to the roof, and branched out across the ceiling, meeting in the centre to form a canopy of green.

Bramble, ivy and bindweed crept up the large stone pillars bearing fruit and flowers, the pews were now raised mounds of mosses and grass decorated with fern. At the far end stood the wooden partition, now dense green, and filled with large fragrant butterfly covered lilac flowers.

Mason stared into the woodland wilderness, as two squirrels ran chattering at each other along one of the high tree branches. The walls and ceiling groaned under the strain of the pushing trees. Glass panes were starting to crack as masses of leaves pushed towards the light.

Mason walked slowly up the centre aisle looking at the growth and smiled. He saw the crown in amongst the foliage and flowers of the lilac pinned into the wall with a long golden arrow. Slowly he nodded his head and began to chuckle. He stood below the crown of England, and a deep thunderous laugh bellowed out of him, as he slowly turned to the balcony where Robbie had stood with his bow pointing down. His laugh grew louder and almost hysterical, and he wiped a tear from his eye with a blood stained bandaged hand, as he nodded to himself.

Hands on hips at the top of the cathedral Mason Knox, laughed as he had never laughed before; he raised his arms in the air as the elderly bishop scurried up the cathedral. "I like this boy Bishop, look what he has done? You cannot tell me the lad doesn't have spirit. His god seems to have kicked your Gods ass don't you think?" Mason bellowed his roaring laugh as he stared around what was now a scene of a living building.

The bishop was frantic. "This is not funny, LOOK! Look what he has done, a thousand years of work destroyed in one day. It is pulling my cathedral down; you have to stop it Knox." He waved his arms about, dancing in distress as he spun around.

Mason watched laughing harder at the dancing elderly bishop. The bishop fell to his knees and began to weep, shaking his head and shouting, "ruined, destroyed, ruined."

Mason seemed to be calming down, and as he chuckled loudly, he patted the bishop on the back. "Don't worry old man; I will kill him for you." He began to wipe his eyes on a handkerchief as he walked down the aisle towards the high doors; he stopped, turned, and shouted back. "You know what you need don't you Bishop...? A woodsman." Mason howled once again with laughter as he strode out into the daylight, and parts of the roof began to splinter and fall inside.

The sun was fading as Melanie closed the door on her small stone cottage with a roof of thatched heathers, and turning the old black key, the lock clicked. She picked her woven fabric bag off the floor, and turned to face the long stone path that led to the wild grass outside the gate, and down the rock face to the small wooden jetty far below.

Reaching the gate, she gazed at the tips of the stones just visible over the top of the bluff, as they began to turn pink with the last hour of light that coloured them. She stroked her long dark brown hair back, and slid on her old battered straw hat, and smiled at the stones that she loved so much.

It was sad in many ways to be leaving; she would miss the sense of calm that the two large circles of stone had given her over the years. All the hours that she had sat alone in the sunlight, her eyes closed as the stones had amplified her thoughts. They had enabled her to talk to Maddy, and now soon they would be together, and the stones would sit here alone for another age until a new sister returned.

Melanie walked slowly down the grassy path, the soft evening breeze patting her goodbye, and waving her long flowing blue skirt in front of her. She silently stared at the tall proud stones glinting pink. "Goodbye my friends," she softly whispered.

Friends indeed they had been in her years of solitude, her only companions with the great eagles that had circled high above her, and she looked to the heavens and saw them, her own wild children high in the sky. She opened her mouth and screeched. A large female Callanish eagle swept out of the sky, and swooped to the fence post as Melanie approached. It bowed its head to her as a mark of respect and a gesture of goodbye. Melanie's eyes flickered blue, and her mind spoke her own goodbyes to the queen of all Callanish.

"Goodbye friend, fly free and ride over my stones for me. Guard them well, My Queen."

The huge eagle let out a soft shriek, and then soared in the air as Melanie watched her fly free above the stones, and laughed with joy at the sight of her friend, riding the currents of air high into the sky.

Slowly she came down the steep bank, on to the small jetty as the old boat drifted up, and hit with a soft bump. The scruffy sea captain helped her aboard and pulled her into an embrace. "Hello Mel my love." His fat red round face beamed at the sight of his old friend, and he patted her softly as he hugged her.

"Oh Toby, at last I can return to my family, it has been a long time coming."

"They will miss you Mel love." Toby looked up the hill where the top of the stones burned scarlet. "Alright Wilbur, pull her away we are on board." Toby took the bag out of her hand. "I will put this below while you say your goodbyes Mel love." He smiled, as he knew she would not leave the deck until the stones had gone forever.

The small boat chugged slowly away from the jetty, and Mel moved along behind the cabin where she leaned on the wall and watched her precious home fade into the distance. The happy memories of the children when they were young flowed through her mind, as she remembered the picnics at the stones, and the fishing on the jetty. All the long walks they had taken around the island, and the sadness of the day they had left together with Toby. Melanie pulled her cloak around her as the wind on the sea blew spray over the rails. They were so small now, almost pin like, glowing red in the last minutes of the sun; a small tear ran down her cheek, as half of her heart was left on that wild side of the island forever. There it would remain in amongst the stones, and guarded by the queen of the Callanish eagles. The sun drifted down, and the stones were gone, and yet somehow now a blue hazy light seemed to hover above them, she knew her love was still there keeping them company through the passage of time.

Toby came around the corner and smiled, he handed her a steaming hot tea and leaned on the wall as he sipped his. "So it's time then, and your sister is coming?"

Mel gave a sad smile and nodded. "I am sorry Toby, I know how much they will miss Saff and Jaz, but it will not be for long. You will see, within the year we will all be back together." She lifted her hand and squeezed his arm. Toby sighed.

"It won't feel the same not popping up here with your supplies, or hearing the laugh of that sweet girl." He stood quietly looking out to sea. "Mind you it will be a relief to not be beaten every time I go fishing." He gave a big smile. "That bloody Jaz, he always landed a bigger bloody fish than me." Melanie started to chuckle as Toby broke into a laugh. "Its bloody true Mel love, I am sure he talked em on to his hook." The two friends stood close on the old boat talking as it chugged its way slowly into the dark, and made its way down the coast away from Stornaway heading south.

"What the hell do you mean he has slaughtered the lot? That village had four hundred people living in it." Robbie's rage was at boiling point as he yelled across the hall at the captain of the woodsmen, who visibly shrunk away from him.

Rune came running down the steps followed by Rowan. "Robbie what's happened? What is it that's got you so mad?"

"KNOX!" Robbie slammed his mug down, and coffee splashed in every direction across the table. He lifted a piece of paper up and handed it to Rune. "They were just women and children Rune; they had nothing to do with us." He flopped to the chair with a bump, and put his head in his hands.

The captain looked very white, and very nervous. "It was Cutters My Lady, most of the men were at sea fishing. They murdered the children and raped and tortured the women before killing them. That notice was pinned on every door, Knox says this is punishment for helping Lord Loxley."

Tears welled in her eyes as she read, and Rowan looked over her shoulder. He looked at the captain. "But we had no help at all, that area is devoid of woodsmen."

The captain looked down at the floor. "I know Sir, but Knox does not care about facts Sir."

"Those poor men coming home to see what had happened, it must have been terrible." Her voice was almost a whisper. "What do we do Robbie?"

He sat with his head in his hands staring at the table, a sad haunted look on his face. "How do you fight that kind of fear Rune?"

She slipped behind him, and rubbed his shoulders. "I have no idea Rob; I just know we must find a way to stop him."

"With your pardon My Lord, I must return to my men." Robbie looked up at the captain who was white, and he nodded.

"Of course Captain, I am sorry; I did not mean to shout at you."

The captain bowed. "It is quite alright My Lord; I screamed at my sergeant, nobody wants to receive news of such terrible things." The captain turned and walked out of the large hall.

Rowan came round the table, and sat down beside him, he patted his arm. "We knew this would start Robbie. Mason will draw you out by hurting the innocent; many more will die by his hand, until we find him and kill him."

Robbie turned to his friend. "They were children Rowan, just children like at Sister Mary's. How can they hurt small children like that?" Rune felt his pain, and slid down to his shoulder and squeezed him. She put her head on his shoulder, and he leaned on to her and closed his eyes. It was like remembering some distant dream from the past, where woman and children screamed in panic in his head, as they fled a brutal onslaught. He had always known what Knox was like, and he knew deep down inside that this is how Knox would retaliate.

The war for the hearts of the people had begun, and now people would be punished and shackled with fear, to prevent them bringing aid to Lord Loxley. The rowdy sound of returning men came in through the doorway, they had all been out with the other woodsmen into the large wood, and now in jubilant mood they trudged into the hall laughing. Robbie stood up. "I need some air." He walked past the happy smiling faces and down the corridor to the side gardens.

Martin looked back at him and then over to Rowan, and the pale white face of Rune. "What's going on?" Rowan slid the paper across the table, and Martin picked it up and read it, he passed it to Jade and Jett who were laughing. Their smiles faded.

Robbie stood in the rose garden as Alice came down the steps looking pale; she smiled weakly and came across to him. "What you doing out here?" Robbie sighed.

"I just needed some air, and some space to think." Robbie sat down on the bench and patted it to tell Alice to sit, he watched her as she sat down beside him. "You look pale this morning Alice; did you not sleep much?"

She stared at the roses. "No, I got some sleep, it's just... I have started to be sick in the mornings. Oh god Robbie it's horrible, I hate being sick at the best of times." He raised his arm to her and pulled her close. She slid up to him. "Looks like there is no doubts now Rob, Billy will be a daddy."

Robbie looked down at her. "You know it is not too late Alice, I know you know how to do it, I remember that Thompson girl who was raped. You helped her."

Alice pushed her head on to his shoulder. "Please Rob don't talk about it, it is not something I can do. That poor girl had been raped, right or wrong I helped her, but I cannot do it to my own, no matter who the father is." Alice went quiet for a minute and snuggled against him. "I miss being held the most."

Robbie pulled his arms around her. "I will always be here for you Alice just say the word, and you shall have your hug."

"Thanks Rob." He squeezed tight and gently rocked her as he stared at the roses, his mind alive and racing trying to find a way to stop the Cutters.

Earlier that morning just before sunrise, as Robbie and his team had slipped into bed at Caerleon Castle; a young woman dressed in all white, with a sapphire blue cloak had walked down the long stone harbour of Kilmory carrying a lantern. She had gazed out to sea with her deep blue eyes, as the breeze came in blowing her long auburn hair, and whispering in her ears. She smiled and took a long taper out of her pocket, and opening the top of her lantern, she lit it.

Saff opened the doors on the two large lamps at the end of the harbour, and lit the wicks. Two bright blue lights blazed illuminating the harbour walls, and gave a beacon to the small boat chugging its way through the channel of Jura and Islay.

Melanie was stood up front in the dark staring across at the headland in the distance; she fingered the golden talon pendent around her neck. Her eyes were fixed and staring into the dark, and then she saw them. One after the other, the two blue lights ignited, and she knew that in between them stood her daughter. "There!" She screamed, as she pointed out to sea. Toby smiled as he put his head through the door.

"I see em; soon have you with her Mel love." He grinned as he saw the excitement on her face, and watched her turn to face forward and watch the lights grow larger, as they slowly came nearer.

Sapphire saw the lights of the boat come on in the distance, and bobbed on the spot as she smiled. A huge wave of excitement grew up inside her. She could hardly wait any longer; the night had dragged minute by minute, as she had watched the clock above the old stone fire. Jaz had dozed in the chair, but she hadn't slept, how could she? It had been so long since she had seen her mother, and now she was back with her for good.

The little boat chugged onward, and Saff could now hear it in the distance. "Oh, hurry please." She jumped up and down on the spot. Melanie was filled with the same tense excitement, as the blue lights grew brighter and bigger. Then she saw her and gasped. A tiny figure in white with a blowing blue cloak waved franticly from the harbour wall. Melanie jumped up and down and waved back at her. Tears filled her eyes, as her smile grew wider. Toby came up by her side, and put his arm on her shoulder as Melanie watched her daughter grow larger. Her hands came to her mouth, the tears flowed, and she heard her daughter shouting across the water.

"Mum... Mum!"

"Sapphire my darling, I am here." She called as the engine slowed, and the small boat began to move toward the harbour wall. Toby held her steady as the young sea hand jumped on to the ladder on the wall, and scrambled up with the rope. Sapphire looked down, the tears dripping off her cheeks as she watched the young boy tie the rope hard, and the boat pushed into the wall. Toby heaved her up, and she was on the ladder going up the four rungs to the top, where her daughter stood crying and aching to feel her mother's arms around her.

Melanie cleared the top of the ladder, and felt Sapphire's arms pull her close.

"Oh Mum." She sobbed as her mother embraced her, and squeezed her as close as she could.

"I am home darling... don't cry now."

Toby watched from the boat and pointed as the young lad dropped back on to the deck. "See that lad... that's what's important that is... Family."

It was a long embrace, with whispered words of love from a mother and daughter, and as Toby climbed up the ladder with the big woven bag, he smiled as he saw a mother and her daughter reunited. He opened the doors of the large lanterns and blew out the wicks, and the blue lights died. "Come on now you two, let's get indoors; it's not that warm for May." Arm in arm the two women chatted happily, as they walked down the harbour, and onto the small cobbled street to the cottage at the end of the lane, where smiling, Jasper stood watching his mother and sister approach.

While Robbie, sat in the garden talking to Alice, and the others huddled around the table talking, Scarlet appeared. "Rune I need you and your sister." Jade looked at Jett who shrugged, and then to Rune who was already standing up. "My daughters as well." Jett looked up at the balcony where Ruby was sat with Steph, and she winked at them both.

Ruby got up and headed for the small staircase that led down to the main doorway into the hall, she came scampering down the stairs, as Rune and Jade appeared closely followed by Jett. "What are we being busted for now? I have not done a thing since we got back, well apart from dropping a few of those biting ants in the cook's knickers on the line earlier. But she can't have found out about that yet... can she?"

Jade shrugged, as Rune smiled at Ruby. Scarlet stood at the end of the long passage. Jett nudged Jade. "Hey it's the table again."

Jade smiled. "Cool I've not seen it yet." They followed Scarlet down the corridor to the very end, but instead of opening the door on the left, Scarlet took out a bright silver key and opened the door to the right. Jett looked up at her mum.

"Aren't we using the table then?"

Scarlet smiled. "That's the table of swords; our own table is in here. This is only for the daughters of the wood, and we call it the Wheel of life."

Jade and Jett, looked at each other with excited sparkling eyes, as they both turned the corner, and entered the room. Once again, there was a large circular table, much bigger than the one used for swords. It was the same white table edged in gold with a huge star of five points and five colours. This table was made of wood and surrounded by heavy carved chairs. "You know your colours girls; Rune you sit at the violet point for now, Steph will be here shortly to sit at the white." As they all moved to their seats, Jett black, Jade green and Ruby red, Steph came in smiling at her sister.

"This brings back memories do you remember?" She nudged Scarlet's arm and she broke into a big smile as she nodded, Scarlet took the seat between Rune and Ruby and waving her hands the light began to soften.

"Rune dear you would normally sit here where I am, but for today only, I need you to fill in, alright all of you, relax and close your eyes." Everyone breathed deeply. Jett opened one eye at exactly the same time as Jade, and both silently sniggered at each other. "Girls... Relax." The two girls put their heads down in silent titters, and the room began to grow a little cooler. The lights dimmed.

"Alright everybody, open your eyes."

Jett and Steph's eyes were flickering lilac, Ruby and Scarlet's flickered pink and red. Rune's eyes had already gone a very deep shade of purple. Jade's green eyes shot the first beam. The green light came out in front of her and then bent to the ceiling. Ruby's followed pink, and then Scarlet's red. Jett shot out blue light, and the colour rose to the ceiling curling and twisting like smoke. Rune looked across at Steph and as their eyes met, a flood of violet light poured into the centre of the table, and surrounded all the other beams. Golden light flowed out from Steph, and began weaving around the violet light creating a net that held the light together. It began to spin faster and faster, and then, the column of light came down to the table, in a bright mixed rainbow coloured disk that spun on the table surface. Rune watched as a figure rose up in the disk. She was hooded in white, and yet wore a sash of blue. Rune just knew it was not her grandmother, her grandmother felt different from this. Rune felt a familiar feeling that she had felt the first day in the woods, when her grandfather's power had almost blown her off her feet, somehow without knowing why, she greeted the hooded figure who bowed. "Greetings Gwendolyn White Circle, you have come a long way to speak to us."

The small figure in the middle of the table lowered her hood, and her shimmering golden hair fell down her back. "I bring greetings to you Runestone the centre of your circle, and tidings of your family from the lines of old."

"We are happy you have returned to us one more time, I feel the strain of your journey."

Gwendolyn smiled at Rune. "You have his power my child, and it brings me joy to feel him with you, tell him I wait in the outer realm for him."

Rune smiled. "He knows, he is watching."

Gwendolyn raised her hands to her mouth and tears formed in her eyes. "I do not have long Runestone, so heed what I say to all of you now." Gwendolyn slowly revolved as she spoke, and looked at each of them in turn.

"My dear sisters of the woods, you are the second house of Rimmer, and with the Runestone in your circle you are powerful, for you are all come from the union of two. Beware the Dark One grows strong as I predicted, and during my age of sleep she managed to sabotage my return. My last effort before passing into the outer realm was to wake my daughters and send them forward ahead of all, protected in circles from the power the Dark One had stolen." Everyone in the room watched as she addressed them.

"You will need them if you are to defeat the Dark One and help the bowman. They are your family and I beg you embrace them, and use your power to help Runestone join them to the circle. For my daughters form the circle of knowledge and can bring other gifts to your table, let the first house unite with the second house and use your powers to win over. They are gathering and will soon want to join with you Runestone, please welcome them for they are the line of your grandfather, which are mixed with my own gifts."

Gwendolyn turned back to Rune. "You have power none of us saw Runestone centre of all circles, your bowman has passed power of purity to you, it will aid you greatly. Protect the seeds of the future and watch over my children for me."

"I will watch over all the sisters you have my word grandmother to our line."

"Good luck my sisters." Gwendolyn slowly faded back into the revolving circle, and Rune closed her eyes and the light disappeared. The room was dark for a moment and then the lights began to slowly burn brighter and everyone looked up.

Jett beamed at Jade. "How cool and awesome was that?" Steph smiled at the pair of them. Jett looked around the table smiling at the others and then at her mum. "What do you reckon mum...? More sisters, looks like we need a bigger table."

Rune's eyes still flickered violet. "Melanie and Sapphire are already with Jasper, one third of their circle is complete." She blinked and shook her head. "That felt weird."

Later, Rune sat in Scarlet's study, which looked more like an armoury, as the walls were covered in swords and weapons and ornate shields. The three red chairs faced each other, and Steph leaned forward in her chair. "Are you sure you are alright, you have gone very pale Rune?"

"I am fine Mother, honestly."

Scarlet sat back and sipped her wine as she looked at the family tree on the wall. "Gwendolyn was quite a powerful sorceress; if her lines have any of her gifts, we will be fortunate."

Rune looked at her. "How do you mean her gifts?"

Scarlet lowered her glass. "All my father's line have the power of the stones, which has been increased by the addition of my mother, we have all been based in the powers of life and nature from the seasons. Gwendolyn was very spiritual, and brought other qualities to her line, she had power based in life and death from what I can remember... I am sure she had intelligence and health on her wheel."

Steph nodded. "Yeah, she did, and it was all linked through the spiritual, I know one of her line can talk to birds, it was a gift she passed to dad, and one I think Rune may have a little of. Although my dad only ever told me about Sapphire, she was considered the centre of the wheel until Rune was born." She looked up at Rune. "That is why you share her name. She only had the power of one even though she was very powerful. Dad saw something more in you and that is why you became the stone that everything would be written on. You were much stronger at birth. She does have quite a power in the mystical though."

Rune looked up at the family tree. "It's odd you know, because I have always known about her, but up until today I have never felt her, what do I do now Mother? Do I wait for them to contact me or should I start looking for them?"

Scarlet looked at her. "Let them come to you, they have protection only in the circles until you join them to us. If you go looking and they are not protected, the Dark One will find them and destroy them. Be patient Rune then we will know all."

Rune nodded at her aunt. Scarlet smiled and stood up. "There is one good thing about all this, Gwendolyn made the sword in Carnac, one of this lot must have the answer to where it is, and the sooner we cheat Knox out of getting it the better. The word is, his grubby little hands have been over every possible site in the last ten years, and he has not found it yet. Let's hope to hell they can help, if he gets just one of those swords, we will never find the true king." Scarlet looked just for a moment quite worried, Steph and Rune both noticed but Steph gently shook her head and Rune said nothing.

Sapphire pulled Gaynor into a hug. "Oh, you are getting big. You be good for Toby now you hear. We will not be apart for long I promise."

"But why do you have to go Aunty Saff?" Gaynor's eyes filled with tears.

"Hey." Saff pulled out a lace hankie and wiped the tears from her eyes. "Don't cry now, this is not goodbye, we will see you all soon enough. I have promised, haven't I?"

Gaynor nodded and sniffled. Sapphire turned to Will, as Jaz picked up Gaynor and hugged her. "Right my young squire, you look out for your sister and be nice to Toby, and no tricks you hear?" Sapphire smiled and hugged him.

"I will Aunt Saff; I will be good." She gave him a huge smile. "I know you will. I have every faith." She moved closer to his ear, "see if you can get Toby to show you some sword skills, he is the best around here."

"Is he?" Will did not look so sure, but Saff nodded and winked at him. His face broke into a huge smile. "Alright I will," he whispered.

She climbed down the ladder and on to the boat, as Jaz gave Will a hug and patted him on the back, and then climbed down to the boat. Melanie stood on the boat as it pulled away holding her two children. Both of them waved to Toby as he stood by the two waving teenagers on the harbour side, until the harbour was gone from view.

The three of them settled on the top of the deck and watched the sun climb, and the waves rolled across the front of the bow. Saff dabbed her eyes to clear the tears, and Mel pulled her arm around her. "They will be fine. Toby is a wonderful man and they are his family, he will protect them don't fear."

Saff nodded. "I know Mum, it's just they have been with me for so long now, it's like they are my own, I will always worry about them."

Mel gave her another big squeeze. "Let's go below and get something to drink, it's going to be a long trip, and at this speed we might as well get comfy." Saff nodded, and the little boat rose and fell in the current.

Jaz pulled out his fishing rod and baited the hook. With a sharp flick of his wrist, the hook and float fired out over the sea, and he settled down to watch the float bob behind the boat. Saff sat with her mother at the little table, in the grubby little cabin below the wheelhouse. She looked up at her mum. "What is Rune like do you know?"

Mel took a sip of her drink. "Because your grandfather has been in hiding so long, it is difficult to really know. From what little I know she is very warm, loving, and similar to you in many ways. She has the power of two lines where as we do not, I can only assume that the power of Opal, which is vast mixed with your grandfathers, must have created something very powerful indeed. Yet he seems to think that she has such a delicate balance within her that it is controlled very effectively." Saff stared at the table in thought as her mother spoke softly.

"Unlike you. Rune's powers have come earlier. She will be almost seventeen, and as you know, you were eighteen before your true powers emerged. It has been said she could replace Opal one day, and Opal is no push over. Your grandfather has always been reserved about what he tells us all. I think he feels it will protect us."

Mel stared out of the little porthole. "None of us are safe until we reach Rune. I will relax when we stand in the circle at Castleriss, and we are carved on the Runestone, I feel almost naked and vulnerable away from my stones at Callanish." Saff put her hand on top of her mums. "We will be safe as long as our power is kept hidden until we are there."

"I hope so Saff, I don't like being out here alone."

The day wore on as the mother and daughter sat in the little boat slowly chugging its way down the coast, and talked. The four years of separation from Saff's sixteenth birthday to her twentieth year had been hard for her. Her role had always been the education of the orphaned children of Toby's sister.

Sapphire now was being pulled back to the family, and asked about her aunts and her cousins. None of them had ever met, and so it was a time of excitement although Melanie was worried, she knew how the inexperienced could leak power and leave a trail the Dark One would follow to find them. Her senses were at their peak as she felt the surrounding atmosphere for the slightest changes. She knew she would not relax until the boat was at land, and they were in sight of the stone circle where they could seek protection. The day slipped slowly past.

Jaz was sat on deck watching his line dozing in the sun. The headland was in sight far in the distance as he screwed his eyes up, to peer through the bright glare of the sun above him. He smiled and pulled on his rod; reeling in his line he knew it would not be long now before they landed. He folded the fishing rod back into the bag and laid it on deck beside the pile of freshly caught fish.

Wilbur sounded the horn, and it boomed out as the boat chugged into the bay, and headed towards the stonewall that seemed to grow out of a huge forest of trees. Jaz watched as Mel and Saff came above deck, and made their way forward to his side. "I cannot see anyone Mum." He shaded his eyes and stared along the trees. It was the movement of something white, which caught his attention. Pale green separated from the trees and he realised that it was a woman; the bright white was her hair that hung down her back. She waved.

Melanie felt tense, she had not seen her twin Una since the time of their awakening, when their mother had very quickly taken them and transported them to their chosen places of safety. Their moments together had been brief after so many years of isolation, and all that Melanie had been able to do in her years alone, had been to remember a time when they had all been young teenage girls together at court, and on the farm.

That had been a time so very different from now, their sleep had crossed a span of time so vast, and yet they had not aged at all. It had taken Mel a long time to adjust in her years alone with her children, and Toby had been the one who had helped her understand the world that she now lived in.

Una smiled at her sister as the boat came alongside the harbour; she looked with her violet tear filled eyes, as she stood alone her white hair radiant in the long plait down her back. Her lime green top and skirt were bright in the sun, as the brown edged leaf designs seemed to sparkle with an autumnal feel. The bronze belt of oak leaves was a memory Mel had cherished.

Mel saw the tears in her sister's eyes as she smiled at her. She flew down the gangplank and they were reunited for the first time in over twenty years.

"Melanie." She gasped as Mel squeezed her tightly, and her violet eyes shone through the tears in the sunlight. "Mel we must move quickly there have been disturbances, we have little time to talk. Mac is already preparing at the circle; I have horses waiting under the trees."

Mel could feel the tension in Una, and she hurried Saff and Jaz up from the boat. "Saff she is looking for us we must leave now." Jaz looked up at the sky, he could sense something in the air, as the darkness seemed to gather to the north. Una ran back to the trees, and began to untether the horses, as the others caught up. Jaz helped his mother and Saff up on the horse, and sprung into the saddle. Saff looked worried.

"Jaz I have never ridden, I don't know what to do." He leaned over and took hold of her reigns.

"Hold tight sis, I will lead you." Una kicked, and the horse moved forward. Mel followed with Jaz pulling Saff; she leaned forward in the seat and gripped the horse's mane tightly. The horses gathered momentum as Una led them to a wide path between the tall trees, and with heads down they galloped through the woodland.

They rode hard for over an hour, Una leading them from tree covered space to tree covered space, as she did her best to keep them hidden from view. The dark clouds always in her sight were now moving quickly south as they passed over woods, lakes and streams. The iron hooves of the horses pounding on the shale mixed in the dirt of the old worn road. Una felt her, and knew instantly she was coming, she looked back at Mel, and she knew that her sister had felt it too, her face was determined and yet fearful, Una nodded to her and Mel knew that her greatest fear was about to be realised. She pushed her horse hard to catch up to her sister.

"Can you protect us?" She shouted to Una.

Una's face was fierce and she gritted her teeth. "I am not sure, she is the Dark One, and has mothers' power." She looked at her sister's frightened face. "It's not far Mel, and the road through the trees is straight, I will try."

Una looked up to her left where the sky was beginning to roll towards them, swirling in black brooding clouds. She knew the Dark One was coming but was still far away. "We have time." She screamed, her eyes flickering lilac. "Whatever happens do not stop, ride into the circle and protect yourself." Una leaned forward on the horse and lay her head as close as she could.

"Hear me Mother." She focused hard but panic was rising within her. *"Oh please Mother, HEAR ME!"*

Rune sat at the table laughing at John and Martin, who were both jumping about having been victims of Jade and Jett. Tiny bites made them suddenly jump, as Jett and Jade giggled from the balcony. Rune obviously had understood the minute Martin had leapt up and squealed.

Martin was now pulling his pants outward and staring down to see if he could find the source of pain. He pulled a huge fat looking ant out and put it on the table. Rune gasped, realising the terrible two had struck again; she sat giggling with Robbie who was in on the trick, as Rune had whispered about the cook's knickers. John was pulling at the back of his pants screeching, and asking Alice to look down and see if she could see anything. Alice recoiled, the thought of examining John's large hairy bottom was too foul to contemplate, her face contorted as she slid away down the bench, and Rune and Robbie howled with laughter.

John jumped up and squealed. "Oh god help me Martin." He stretched his pants forward and Martin jumped back.

"You can sod off; I am not putting my hand down there!" Jade and Jett howled up in the balcony. Rune's eyes suddenly glowed bright violet. She stopped laughing immediately, and jumped up to her feet. Robbie laughing still, looked up at her and noticed the fear on her face as violet light spilled out of her eyes. He grabbed her hand and she looked down at him.

"Oh god Robbie, she is back, and she is after them."

Rune looked up to the balcony. "Jade, Jett I need you, get Ruby to the table." Rune flew down the main hall as Steph and Scarlet came running up the corridor.

"We felt it, what's happening?" Rune did not break her pace. "She is back, and after the others, I need your powers." As they flew down the corridor, Scarlet pulled out the silver key and unlocked the door. All of them dashed in and took their seats, this time Rune took the head of the table, and Scarlet took the violet point of the star.

They were all breathing heavily, as Rune closed her eyes and the lights dimmed, the temperature lowered. Everyone began to feel the sense that Rune was passing around them, her fear mixed in with the fear from her new sisters, and as she opened her eyes, and a huge blinding purple light filled the whole room.

"Una I'm here, hear me now."

"Oh, mother is that you? I need help she is coming."

"Una this is Runestone, where are all of you?"

"Runestone... Oh, thank Hearne... Runestone please help us she is coming."

"Una please relax you are blocking the others, your sisters are here, we will do all we can."

Una was scared and the fear was rising rapidly, Rune looked around at the others. "Concentrate sisters they need us." One by one the others began to focus on Rune, as she joined their minds to hers. Colour splashed out of their eyes, although from all of them it was violet, Rune had connected and was now the centre controlling the circle. The violet light spun at amazing speed around the table, and she turned her mind to Sapphire.

"Sapphire hear me, I am the Runestone who binds you all."

Sapphire lay on her horse clinging to the mane, her eyes suddenly ignited, and violet light flowed out of them bathing all of the riders in a strange purple mist. The trees seemed to be streaking past them at high speed, and everything around her was blurred.

"Runestone, I hear you and feel you, help them."

"Sapphire you have great power I feel it. I need you to open your mind and connect to your sisters; I am here but can only help if you can join all of them together."

The black clouds were closing in, and rain began to lash down, the horses were panting heavily as they pounded up the forest road. A bright fork of blue lightning struck a tree, and it crashed, splintering to the floor behind them, exploding into flames. Sapphire screamed to her mother. "Mother connect to me, all of you connect, Rune is with me."

Mel and Una looked back, hardly hearing what she was screaming over the now pounding rain. Una could see the violet in Sapphire's eyes, and she looked at her sister. "Connect to your daughter NOW!" She screamed.

Jaz was already trying to hold to the reigns and steer his horse, he saw his mother relax and knew she was trying to bond with Sapphire; he focused on her and made the connection. "Mother Join me I am with Sapphire."

"I hear you Jaz."

"Sapphire hear us."

"I hear you and I have you, Una join me."

Una's eyes flickered lilac. "I hear you Sapphire and I am with you."

Rune gasped. "I have them, focus my sisters." Everyone sat round the table their minds now connected, and their powers mixing in the light that spun round at an alarming speed.

Una was watching as the rain lashed at her face, and she screwed up her eyes to try and focus better on the road ahead. Mel suddenly began to shake and her eyes turned violet, Una glanced back to see Jaz and Saff both had violet eyes and the colour was intensifying.

"Hurry Runestone she is almost upon us."

A huge black bird came screaming out of the sky towards them, Una's eyes glowed deep purple, and a bright purple light erupted all around them. A ball of white light exploded in the sky above them and the huge bird pulled up, and skimmed the light, screaming out in pain as it touched it. They rode harder and harder, Una knew the circle was not far away, and she clenched her teeth to flow power to Rune.

Mac stood in the stone circle and saw the violet glow in the trees; the rain was pounding as he stared down the road through the black cloud that was forming above them. Within the midst of blackness around her, he saw her large and bird like, with a face of hatred and rage. She swooped and white light flared up at her, she recoiled from the light and lightening blasted the riders.

Mac walked towards the edge of the circle, a faint lilac shimmer appeared in front of him, he stretched out his hand and it burned bright purple, as if it was a wall of light. He pulled back his hand and the light faded; he was protected but he did not know how.

He stepped into the wall of light, and there was a flash of deepest purple, and he was thrown back into the circle. A woman's voice echoed in his head. 'Stay where you are safe.' He landed with a bump and shook his head. It was a voice he did not recognise, he knew it was not his mothers, but was it Sapphire?

The trees ended, and heads down their horses gasping for air, the stone circle came into sight. "Almost there," screamed Una over the driving rain, and her horse drove up on to the stony path towards the circle. Mel saw the circle and her heart soared, the lightening was now flashing down and bouncing off the violet circle that surrounded them. The large black bird swooped down again, trying to weaken the power of the protection, but each time it tried, white light exploded upwards towards her, and she had to divert her course and fly off in another direction.

Una swept into the circle through a blinding flash of violet, closely followed by Mel, Mac jumped back as the horses reared up. Jaz exploded in a huge flash of violet pulling Saff behind him, and pulled hard on the reigns as the horses stumbled to a halt. He slid down, and ran around to Saff who was still gripping the mane with fear, violet light streaming out of her eyes. Mel was down on the floor, and ran to her daughter as Jaz slid her down. Una pulled the horses out of the way, as they stood steaming with sweat and fear, gasping for air. Saff spoke; but it was Rune's voice they heard. "Form a circle... quickly!"

Rune sat at the table, her face pale and light streaming out of her.
"Gwinne hear me."
"I hear you Runestone."
"Crystal, Amethyst, hear me."
"We hear you Runestone."
"My sisters of the wheel of life, the daughters of Gwendolyn have returned unto us, the Dark One attacks as we speak. I will open the circle to receive them, and bring the circle of knowledge within us, lend me your power for three are far away."
"We hear you Runestone centre of our circle, make haste and connect them; receive our gifts in your aid."

As Rune raised her arms from the table, her hands began to glow, and white light erupted into the spinning swirl of purple light on the table, Rune shook violently as she received a greater power than she knew, and fought in pain to control it.
"Grandmother guide me I am failing."
"Relax my child and let your fear flow away, I am with you."
Rune's arms shook as her voice boomed out in the room.

"Sisters of knowledge and sisters of life, bring together your power to one need. Join your minds and become one against the force of darkness, give me your gifts, and revolve around me for I am the Runestone, and the hub around which you all spin. Join us Melanie, Una and Madeleine. Prepare the way for your daughters and sons."

In the stone circle purple light bounced around from person to person, Sapphire shook with fear as a purple light formed in the centre, and as it spun faster, she watched the figure appear formed of the brightest violet light. The shadowy figure of Rune in pure violet stood in front of Sapphire. "Welcome my sister, join me."

Rune smiled and the fear in Sapphire subsided. She turned to Jaz. "Jasper come in to our circle and be at peace." He smiled at her as she turned to face Mac.

"Malachite enter our family, and know you are protected."

The violet image of Rune walked slowly around the circle and hugged each of them smiling sweetly at them, and then she returned to the centre and looked up to the sky.

"Citrine I welcome you, enter here in peace. Alexandrite we await your coming, and know you are now at one with us."

The Dark One flew round high above them, as if knowing she had them all in one place and was waiting to pick them off, the shadowy figure of Rune looked up at her. Rune closed her eyes and began to spin fast, and then with an almighty flash of the brightest white light, she exploded into the sky like a missile.

Up high into the air, the light streaked, there was a scream of anguish and an almighty flash as purple sparks showered out of the sky, and then it was quiet. Sapphire fell to her knees, and the black clouds rolled back, and the sun broke out above her, as she reeled forward. Mel dashed to her daughter and grabbed her just in time to stop her from hitting the floor.

The room had gone instantly dark, the scream had been terrifying and the small door burst open, and light flooded in as Robbie entered followed by Rowan. Everyone blinked in the sudden light; Rune lay out stretched on the table. Robbie seized her into his arms as the lights brightened within the room. He pulled her into his arms, as her eyes flickered violet, her face was as white as a ghost, and his heart stopped in fear. He pulled her close as tears filled his eyes. "Rune my darling, my love." A white figure walked in through the wall and came up close to him.

"Fear not bowman she is alive." Tears streaked down his face as he looked up at the white hood. The lady lowered herself to his height. "She has channelled power that would destroy all of us here, and once again she has pushed back the Dark One." She laid her hand on Rune's head, and it glowed for a second. "She needs rest now, for one so young, she used a great deal of strength. Let her rest and surround her in your love, dry your tears bowman she will not leave you."

Robbie smiled, and gasped out a sob. The white lady rose and turned to them all. "You have done well here today my family; the circle is expanded and complete, knowledge and life are one."

"I peed myself again Grandma." Jade looked down at her legs, Steph started to chuckle as Jett looked down at Jade's seat.

"Me too, I was terrified." The white lady chuckled.

"I believe it's less harmful than ants." Jade and Jett both stared together in shock, and spoke as one.

"You know?"

"I am Opal, daughter of Hearne, I see all around me my children." Both Jett and Jade swallowed deeply. Scarlet let out a mighty laugh at the sheer look of surprise and shock on the girl's faces. The white lady turned and waved her hand over Rune. "Awaken child your work here is done." She walked past Robbie and patted his shoulder as he held Rune close, and she disappeared through the wall.

Rune stirred and opened her eyes, they still glowed purple, and she gave him a weak smile. "Hi."

He smiled back at her. "Hey Beautiful." He lifted her up into his arms, and carefully carried her out of the room and up to their bedroom. Scarlet looked exhausted as she looked across at Steph who was still a little shaky.

"I think in future if we have to face the Dark One, we should bring those two a couple of buckets." Scarlet looked under the table at the puddle, as Steph collapsed in hysterics. Jade and Jett grinned looking slightly pink around their cheeks.

CHAPTER THREE

RECOVERY AND RETRIBUTION

Sapphire sat up in her bed, she had no knowledge of leaving the circle, and as Una sat beside her holding a tray of soup, her mother filled her in on the details. Sapphire now had a permanent pale blue in the whites of her eyes, as she watched her mother whilst she spoke. "After you collapsed, the sun came out and the black clouds dispersed, we knew Rune had pushed the Dark One back to wherever she had come from. Mac carried you back here, we are only a short distance from the stones, but now we are all in the circle of our family we are protected and safe anywhere."

Una nodded as Mel spoke. "Rune is more powerful than any of us expected, I felt only a small amount of her in me, and it was a greater power than I have ever known. Her power is greater than that of my mothers."

Sapphire's eyes flickered blue as she looked at Una. "Rune pulled you together through me and her power frightened me, when she appeared before me and I saw her for the first time, then I realised she truly was the power of goodness. I was so afraid of her power at first, it was terrifying."

"So young and yet already filled with such force, how can she channel that kind of power without being destroyed?" Mel's quiet question had been on all of their minds since it had happened. Saff ate her soup thinking of Rune. In many ways she had always felt a little cheated, she had thought that she would be the centre of her circle. When her grandfather had announced the two circles must join, Saff had been bitterly disappointed to find that her younger cousin had been selected to centre both, and Saff now began to understand why.

The previous day Rune had tapped into Saff's power that was in itself great, but when she had connected to Rune, the force that began to come through her had really scared her. She remembered the panic that had risen inside her as she had fought to focus, and it was only when Rune realised her fear, that she put a barrier around the force to protect Saff. That allowed Rune to channel through her; Saff now understood she did not have the strength to control such a force. In many ways now, she felt glad that she did not have to be at the centre of the circle of knowledge. Saff looked up at her mum. "She stayed with me last night. She was drained of all her energy, yet stayed with me to protect me. Rune is out of contact today and it worries me that she has damaged herself." Two tears ran down her cheeks as she spoke, and her mother leaned close to her and wiped her tears away with her hand.

"Do not upset yourself darling, Rune is fine, she is just very tired and is resting. The Dark One is not easy to defeat, and Rune took a lot of power from both circles just to expel her. She is with the Bowman who is caring for her."

Saff looked up in great surprise. "Rune is with the Bowman, he has arrived, when?"

Mel smiled. "He set out from Loxley just over three weeks ago and was able to prevent the snake from taking the crown. He now seeks to combat the snake, and return the land to the people. Rune is his love and has been by his side since they left."

Saff somehow seemed downhearted. "Rune is his love," she whispered in quiet disappointment, as she fingered the sword pendant round her neck.

Meanwhile back at the castle in Caerleon, Scarlet was trying to hold in her growing temper. "Robbie it is not your task! Why will you not listen? You must find the sword." Scarlet's eyes burned with her frustration.

Robbie turned from the table now covered with dots of green and red. "He is slaughtering everyone along the coast from Canterbury to here. There will be no point to a sword no one can wield."

Scarlet slammed her hand down on the table. "IT IS NOT YOUR TASK!" Her eyes flickered red as she stared at him in anger. She took a deep breath and tried to clam down. "Robbie, Phillip is drawing men down from both Gloucester and Warwick to help make up the numbers. We have attacked and killed four bands of Cutters in one day. Please let us deal with Mason from here; the sisters of knowledge will soon depart for York. You must be in Loxley when they arrive. Skip and Bear will be with you; they are already putting your plans into action, and preparing a meeting of all the leaders for Loxley. You have started the ball rolling; now you must find the missing sword as without it all our work will be in vain."

Robbie nodded. "I am sorry Scarlet, I hate the fact people are dying because of me, and it makes me feel so helpless as I cannot prevent it." Scarlet came around the table, and put her arm around his shoulder.

"You have already achieved more than any thought possible, but listen to me Robbie for I have wisdom that will benefit you. You are still so young, and there are great lessons for all of us still to learn, but please open your mind to the wisdom of others. I have spent years fighting Knox, let me do just that, you must learn to share the responsibility Robbie, for it is the mark of a great leader. Many great men have fallen because they shouldered too much, and it clouded their judgement."

He understood her and smiled. "You sound like your dad."

Scarlet smiled at him. "I will take that as my greatest compliment, my father has always been my hero, and to be likened to him fills me with pride." She patted him on the shoulder. "Go to Rune I feel her stirring, we will talk later."

Rune's mind swirled in darkness; Opal had placed a charm on her to help her sleep free from the dreams of the Dark One. The huge force required to expel her had drawn the last of her strength, and now she floated inside herself in calm darkness. She felt the soft kiss and warmth spread through her body, she became aware of her arms and legs. She moved as his lips moved softly away and then back to hers. The blackness began to fade in to white as the lips broke away and she opened her eyes. Two dark eyes filled with care and love looked down in to hers. "Hey beautiful."

He looked down at her eyes still very violet on which floated the two most beautiful sapphire blue pupils. She was so very pale and drawn, yet she smiled at him and the life and love she held twinkled back at him. "Hi gorgeous."

He stroked her soft red hair back from her face. "Nice to have you back, I missed you." He looked very tired and somehow, she knew he had not slept much, she had been aware all night he was there holding her in his arms as she slept.

Her voice was quiet as her throat was dry. "I love you too," she moved to get up and he slid his arm under her and pulled her into a hug. She was still very weak and enjoyed feeling his arms around her as she slid her head on to his shoulder.

"You really frightened me Rune," she squeezed him softly.

"I was fine, I just used a lot of strength, and I am still learning Robbie." It was nice just to sit and be held in his arms, and she nuzzled into him. He fluffed up the pillows and helped her sit back. He had a tray of food at the side of the bed, and she smiled as he buttered her some toast and jam, then poured her out a coffee with sugar. Her throat felt like card, and she soon finished the cup, which he refilled, as she coughed. "Oh, that's better, I could hardly talk I was so dry."

It was later in the day when Rune reappeared downstairs; Steph and Pete, both hugged her as she came to the table for the evening meal. Robbie stayed close, he knew how tired she still was, and she was paler than he had ever seen her.

Everyone was sat around the table tucking into the food. John and Bear were devouring most of the beef and the potatoes, Robbie looked at their smiling faces as they ate. "We leave for Loxley the day after tomorrow, prepare for a journey and let's get the cart ready." Robbie looked at the crestfallen Jett. "Flash and Jett you will be coming along with us, so sort some travelling things, Jade show them what to pack."

Jett punched the air. "Yes!" Her face lit up with joy as she smiled at Jade.

Rune put her hand on Robbie's and he turned to see her radiant smiling face, he gave her a big grin. "I think it is time we went home." She leaned over and kissed him as Jade and Jett bobbed about excitedly. Alice sat beaming up the table as Robbie pulled Rune close, and looked at the happy smiling faces of his men. He winked at her and she nodded happily. Blades beamed by her dad's side and Robbie leaned over to her. "Now you will see where you really belong, and meet all your family." Her eye's danced excitedly at him and Harry pulled her close.

"Hey baby girl, you will love it. Home is like a really happenin and cosmic place. Wait until you see my pad, it's like totally radical."

Robbie laughed, he had not been in Harry's cottage much, but on his last occasion, he had found two stripped down motorcycles in the kitchen. There was also one in the hall, and one in the front room. The whole upstairs had, been filled with boxes of moonshine. The thought of home was infectious; John and Martin's delight was more than apparent and Jade was over the moon as she sat telling Rowan a million and one wonderful things about Loxley. Fish slipped down next to Robbie. "If you are going home Robbie, what do Hog and me do? We don't really have a home, Sister Mary raised us two."

Robbie placed his fork on the side of his plate, and turned the fold of Fish's cloak that revealed a Loxley Bowman coat of arms. "According to this Fish, Loxley is your home; you are in the service of your lord are you not?"

Fish gave him a huge smile. "I am My Lord."

"Then you are a man of Loxley and that is now your rightful home, I will make sure that Hog and yourself are both taken care of." Rune leaned forward and smiled at Fish who looked very happy.

"You are now one of us Fish, and we all stick together." She leaned against Robbie and sighed a long contented sigh. He smiled and pulled her close.

"Happy?"

"Very, it will be so nice to see grandfather, and get on my loom."

"I must admit I have missed the smell of the greenhouses; it will be nice to see mum again, and listen to John pounding his hammer... Mind you?"

Rune looked up to see Robbie looking at Alice. "John is going to be mad, isn't he?"

Robbie looked back at her, a worried look on his face. "If he ever gets hold of Billy he will kill him, his temper is bloody awful, and Hearne help any man that crosses him. I want to be with Alice when she tells him, although I will have my bow ready. An angry John is something even I am not stupid enough to get in the way of." Alice seemed happy, yet as Rune looked toward her and smiled, she could feel the apprehension growing inside her.

After the meal, Rune was very tired, and Robbie whisked her off her feet and chuckling with her, he carried her up the stairs. Bear sat down watching Rune giggle as Robbie kissed her repeatedly all over her face whilst carrying her. Alice who was off in a dream suddenly realised someone was there and looked up at him. Bear motioned to Robbie and Rune who were just disappearing around the corner. "They are a very nice and very happy couple?" Alice nodded.

"They really love each other and have for many years."

Bear grunted as if trying to cough up a stone in his throat. "Lady Alice, would you consider me rude if I was to ask you to walk in the garden with me?"

Alice began to blush a little. "I would like that very much Bear."

He smiled a huge smile. "My close friends call me Mickie."

"They do, why?"

"My full name is Jacques, Michael, Giles, Phillips. Mickie is short for my middle name and simpler."

Alice grinned at him. "I see. Well Mickie I would love a walk round the garden."

Rune was soon fast asleep and Robbie sat high on the edge of the battlements looking out over the miles of green forest, the sun was sinking low and the day cooling as he breathed the air. The sound of laughter brought his eyes down to the garden. Far below John was running with Jade on his shoulders at Martin who had Jett on his, the girls both had broom handles with large padded pom poms on the end and were bashing each other trying to unseat each other.

Their laughter was wild, as Harry appeared sporting Blades, and they ran into the midst of the battle. Robbie laughed as Rowan walked along the wall and put Robbie's bow and quiver beside him. "You should not be unprotected Robbie." He sat beside him and dangled his legs off the tower.

Rowan looked down and smiled at Jade who had successfully unseated Jett and was now bashing Blades, as the two of them squealed with laughter. "The time we have all spent together has been good for us Robbie; I think we will all return to Loxley better people." Robbie raised his arm and squeezed Rowan's shoulder.

"I think you are right my friend. I am fortunate in the people who surround me." He laughed out loud as Jade toppled off John's back, and both of them fell backwards into the pond. Harry ran around the garden with a victorious Blades on his shoulders, as Jade sat in the pool howling with laughter and splashing Jett who seemed hysterical, as she held her sides.

"You have been a great strength to me Rowan these last few weeks; I hope you know I appreciate it." Robbie looked quite serious as he turned to him. "I value your friendship most, Billy took a great part of me away with him, and you have restored some of my faith."

Rowan put his head down. "You honour me greatly Robbie, I am your true friend as I know you are mine."

Robbie patted his shoulder. "You will love Loxley; we have woods there that go beyond anything I have seen since leaving, I look forward to walking the paths I love with you and Jade. You will love Joe; he is like us in many ways, and one of the best woodsmen in the area."

He slid off the battlement wall and stretched. "I am going to see how Rune is; I would imagine your service may be required with a certain wet Lady Pebbles."

Rowan smiled as he slid down off the wall. "She does seem to be making a habit of getting wet these days." They laughed and joked down the steps to the corridor, where high pitched squeaks announced Jade's arrival. She ran smiling down the corridor and leapt up into Rowan's arms, and threw her arms around his neck and kissed him, as she dripped all over the carpet. Robbie opened his door and stepped into his room.

He stood in the doorway and looked at the bright white pillows and sheet turned over the blanket. Her fiery red hair lay down each side of her pale white face, and spread on to the blankets. Her eyes were closed and her long red eyelashes seemed to rest on her cheeks. He leaned back on the door and watched her sleep; she was to him a picture of complete beauty.

It was still dark when he woke up. Rune was curled in his arms crying in her sleep. He sat up with a jolt hearing her whimpers and rubbed his eyes, and looked down at her in the moonlight. Rune sat bolt upright in bed and the room blazed with deep violet light, Robbie jumped back with surprise at the speed with which she had moved. She turned to him and seeing him breathed a sigh of relief. Her eyes slipped out of focus and then came back burning purple. "Robbie they are in the castle." He felt her hand close on his.

He jumped out of bed and slid his pants on. "Warn Ruby, Jett, and Jade, get Steph and Scarlet up. I will try to warn the others. He pulled his belt and sword on, and then picked up his bow as Rune's eyes flared and she got out of bed, and slipped her pants on. She turned pulling Robbie's shirt over her head.

"Robbie please don't leave me alone tonight." She pulled her belt with a sword on it round her waist. She came up to the door at his side as he slid it very quietly open. Two green eyes blazed in the dark at him, Rowan stood behind them with his bow and sword, Robbie and Rune slipped out.

They walked down the long corridor and saw Jett appear with a long sword at the bottom of it. Rune tried Blades door, it opened and she slipped in, Robbie tried Martin and John's room, as Rowan slipped into Fish and Hogs room. Jade slipped into Alice's room and was a little surprised to find her sat up with Bear, who had his knife out waiting. It was lucky she was invisible otherwise he probably would have attacked her. She faded into view with a finger to her lips. "Shush!" She pointed to the corridor and Bear opened the door to a rather surprised looking Robbie. Steph and a half dressed Smokes came out and signaled from the bottom of the corridor.

Jade slipped into Harry's room and freaked out Maggs, who was already very jumpy considering her mother's recent demise. Jade slipped out of the room followed by Harry with his two long silver swords, he heard the door behind him click.

The group headed down to the end of the corridor that led round to the top of the steps into the large hall, and the side of the balcony. Flash, Jett, and Blades, scuttled along the top of the balcony, Alice, Steph, and Smokes, took up position with their bows. Robbie moved to the top of the steps; he could hear whispered voices near the doorway.

He pulled back on the bowstring and took aim with the arrow; Blades slipped with Jett silently down the steps on the other side keeping very low. A figure in black slunk into the hall close to the steps opposite Robbie; he saw the glint of silver off the sword blade. He slid down the wall slowly and everyone followed his lead.

More figures appeared, as a large group followed into the hall with drawn weapons. The lead figure came level with the end of the opposite steps. Robbie's arrow whisked across the room, and there was a loud squeal as the arrow pinned him to the wooden rail. The figure slipped and hung limp. Blades and Jett erupted over the rail and into the group. Flash flickered her eyes and lit the whole scene.

Swords drew rapidly, as Harry and Bear who had come down the back steps met Scarlet, they roared in from behind cutting off the intruder's retreat. Harry's swords flashing in the light from Ruby's eyes, piled into the throng as arms and legs left their owners, and screams of agony wailed into the air.

Rune closed her eyes and a huge ball appeared as if the sun had erupted in the ceiling and daylight spilled into the room. Robbie and Rowan brought their bows up and fired at the intruders in amongst the sword fighters. Scarlet was ferocious as her blade swung round with speed and skill. Jett whooped and screamed, as she wove like a ballerina with a sword of fire, attacking and slicing at the enemy with surgical precision.

Five broke free, and clambered on to the steps in front of Jade. Rowan swung his bow across, but with the speed of a thunder flash, Jade unleashed a scathing attack of silver daggers, and the men fell backwards knives in their throats. She winked at Rowan as she moved down towards the dead men to recover her daggers.

The alarm bell was sounded, and the huge gates at the end of the courtyard swung shut trapping in those who were loose in the grounds. A large group rushed the steps where Robbie stood, and all of them fell several feet away as the archers on the balcony and behind him let loose their arrows. Noise from outside announced more arriving, having realised they were stuck. Robbie drew out his long golden sword; as a huge man with a large silver sword waded, into the crowd and came right at him. He brought his sword crashing down at him, and Robbie swung his sword upwards.

Rainbows glistened on the walls as he twisted and the swords met with force. The silver sword sheared into two pieces as the sword of truth rung out with a loud chime. The golden sword swept into the air, and as Robbie sidestepped, he brought it crashing down on to the huge man lunging at him. The sword met him and sunk in with ease, and with shock in the eyes of the huge man, he reeled sideways, and fell dead and bloody on to the floor.

A crossbow fired and Robbie felt the instincts of a woodsman kick in, as he swiped the sword in front of him, knocking the arrow away from him. Four longbows sung out, and the crossbow man leapt backwards on to the table pierced in four places.

Rowan was now on the floor with his sword swinging against a Cutter. Blades with both swords now blooded, pranced cat like towards the doors, as she took on one after the other side by side with Jett, both wore huge smiles as they whooped and jeered at their inferior opponents. The fight was spilling out into the courtyard, as Cutters appeared everywhere, Flash was now in the centre of all the action spinning like a top, her white pole barely visible, as she hit each person close to her at least eight times, breaking their limbs before they even realised.

A Cutter ran into the crowd with a long silver lance he caught the inside of Jett's jacket and with all his might, he rammed into the wall pinning her to the wooden beam of the side door. He was a big ugly dirty sweaty man, with matted hair and he drooled as he smiled a nasty evil smile at her. Jett pulled on her jacket as she tried to get free. The lance was up at an angle and she could not swing her sword arm over it. He smirked as he pulled out his sword and moved forward towards her. "Like sword play do you missy? Well let me show you what one can do to a pretty like you." He laughed a horrible sick laugh; Jett flattened herself against the wall.

"Ok big boy, show me what you got." She winked at him as he moved toward her, a small flicker of blue appeared in her eyes. As he raised the sword, Jett's eyes exploded with blue light, and the huge Cutter dropped the sword and clutched his head. He fell to his knees, and screamed in pain shaking his head violently as his nose and eyes started to bleed. The blue in her eyes intensified, and he rolled on the floor thrashing out in agony.

His eyes exploded out of his head and he fell limp. Jett's eyes flickered back to normal as Jade appeared, and heaved on the lance pulling it out of the wood, she looked at the dead man on the floor and screwed up her face. "Yuk, what happened to him?"

Jett stepped over the body and glanced at Jade. "He got a really bad head ache, too many dirty thoughts I guess." She swung her sword into the air. "Now where was I...? Oh yeah." She swung back into action slashing her blade.

The main hall was now full of the fighting mass and the fallen, a crossbow fired and Hog swung out over the balcony on to the steps. He landed at the side of Rune as she aimed at a man behind Robbie. Her bow fired as Hog slipped on to her with a grunt. "Sorry My Lady."

The arrow sliced through his arm, and he groaned as he pushed Rune to the floor. She caught her breath as she realised what he had done. "Hog!" He rolled in pain, the arrow completely through the top of his arm, and he grabbed the rail pulling him back up in front of her. Two more arrows struck him in the back and he slumped slightly onto her gasping in pain.

Rune's eyes widened as he smiled and fell back on to the rail gasping. "Don't move My Lady." His large arm pushed her flat against the step, and she heard the other arrows impact on him, Hog went limp. Robbie glanced up, and seeing Hog in front of Rune, he screamed. His bow swung from his shoulder, under his arm as he dropped his sword. As the bow came up it was loaded and he fired, the first crossbow man had turned to aim at him, but the arrow hit with huge pace and lifted him off his feet. Robbie was already releasing his second arrow and the second man fell.

He turned and ran towards the steps, jumping clean over a man with a sword, and landing five steps up, the man behind him fell as Rune released her arrow. He made it to Rune, and grabbed her in his arms, and ran up the steps, she was trembling with shock. Two arrows bounced off the wall behind him, Alice alone now on the balcony twisted and fired at the man with a double loaded crossbow, and he fell backwards into the throng.

In the courtyard, Scarlet covered in blood, screamed at the Cutters who backed off as she moved with speed. Jett at her left side and Blades at her right, the three of them were like a wall of savage aggression. The Cutters were starting to panic as nothing could stand before the three women whose blades moved so fast, they were barely visible. Harry, Skip, and Fish, swords flashing in the moonlight pushed the Cutters back to the garden, where Fuse and Smokes with Steph picked them off with arrows. All over the castle were screams in amongst the bedlam of clashing swords. Rowan and Philip, with Matthews covered by Alice, were now overcoming the mass in the main hall. Alice moved with precision cleaning the edges with her arrows, and taking out anyone within four feet of the men. Flash and Bear both armed with poles cleared the main doors to the courtyard.

Rune trembled with shock, as she pushed her head into Robbie's shoulder. He held her tight just around the corner backed into a doorframe out of sight of others. She burst into tears shaking violently. "Why did he have to do that?" She wept into his shoulder. Robbie knew the sick feeling of seeing someone die to save your life, and the face of Eric returned to his mind as he held her tight.

There was a sudden scream and everything went silent. Robbie looked across to the balcony but it was empty, a strange voice spoke. "Lower your weapons or she dies." Robbie stepped back releasing Rune, she felt his fear and looked up. He moved swiftly and quietly, loading his bow to the corner of the stairway, Alice was held tight and struggling in the arms of a tall heavy man, who held a dagger in front of her. "Lord Knox wants her, and she is coming with me, but if any of you make a move she will die."

Robbie rolled on the wall around the corner his bow raised and aiming.

"Unhand my cousin, and you will live through this night Cutter."

The man jumped back against the wall dragging Alice with him. He looked up into the eyes of Robbie, and he knew he would die. His hand trembled. "William Knox wants this one, and I am leaving with her, so don't try to stop me Loxley or she will die."

Robbie's voice was cold and calm. "Move one more inch Cutter and your life will end, now take your filthy hands off my cousin and you may well live."

The dagger glinted as his hand shook; two green eyes slid up the wall at his side. "I am death, and I am here for you Cutter." The man screamed and jumped. The arrow hit passing into his shoulder and killing the dagger arm dead, it fell limp as the arrow passed into the wood panel behind him, Alice broke free and Jade grabbed her, and dragged her up the stairs.

The anger in Robbie, who had already loaded his bow, was raising fast, his eyes blazed with fury. "YOU DARE COME INTO OUR HOME, AND PRESUME TO ORDER ME." The arrow whipped through the air and pinned his other arm to the wall, the man howled in pain and his legs slid on the step.

Rune touched Robbie's arm as he raised his bow for the kill. "Enough, you are better than him, and do not kill those who cannot defend themselves. This man is beaten Rob, your name is Loxley, not Knox." Everyone in the hall watched with some fear at the rage in Robbie's eyes. He lowered his bow and looked at them. "Get this filth out of this castle, we have a good man fallen to attend to."

Fish came in slowly and glanced up at Robbie, he noticed the fallen shape of his brother, and his face broke in the pain that suddenly swept through his body. John pulled a big arm around him as he screamed in grief, and brought him into a huge hug. "Alright lad we got you, let it out." Fish wailed the pain into John, who shouldered it as Robbie crouched down and closed the open eyes of Hog.

The whole group lifted Hog, as Rune sat on the top step with Alice and wept; Jett approached the Cutter pinned to the wall. She smiled as Bear came up the steps. "This is going to be very painful, you know that don't you?" Bear grabbed the arrow pinning his arm to the wall and heaved, the man screamed in agony, as the arrow snapped and his arm slipped off. Jett winced remembering her own pain back in the Cathedral.

Bear looked at the sweating, shaking man. "Every moment of pain you now feel, is an innocent you have killed, think about that as I tear your other arm free."

The man's eyes widened as Bear grabbed the other arrow and pulled down. The Cutter screamed louder as the arrow snapped and he slid into Bears strong arms, he lifted him up and walked out to the gates. The man whimpered in pain, as he bounced on Bears large rounded shoulder. Harry was tossing bodies on to the back of an old cart. Bear heaved the Cutter up on to the driving seat, and climbed up at his side. "You are the only one who lived tonight, Lord Loxley has given you life, although you do not deserve it for the women and children you have slaughtered. I would rather cut your throat now, but you have been spared on his orders, think of that as you ride back." He pulled the reins up and tied them to his useless wrists. "It will be painful to control these horses, but life is pain."

Harry threw two more on to the top of the cart of stacked dead, Bear jumped down and slapped the horse, it lurched forward pulling the reins and the man screamed in pain as the cart sped off. Bear spat at the floor, turned, and came back through the gate.

The body of Hog was laid in the small chapel at the back of the castle. Rune insisted on taking care of him, and when Fish came to see his brother, he fell to his knees and cried. Rune had shaved him, and washed him, and combed his tangled matted black hair. She had found some clean brown clothes, and with some help from Jade, she had dressed him.

Fish stood up and thanked her, and with tears in her eyes she hugged him as he wept. Hog looked so different; he was quite handsome with the beard removed and his face washed. He looked at peace and asleep, wrapped in his Loxley cloak with the bowmen crest on his shoulder. Jett stood silently watching tears in her eyes, for Hog was a gentle giant, who she had seen many times with the animals, and noted the care he had taken. There had been a few fights now where it had been Hog, who had watched her back, and for all of her jokes she had been very fond of him.

Extra woodsmen arrived from the barracks up the road and helped clean up the dead. Jade sat on the stairs cleaning her daggers and putting them back in her belt. Rowan came up and slumped down beside her; she leaned over and kissed him. "That's three I owe Billy boy now. He showed them how to get in and told them when, I just wish he had been with them. He would be dead now if he had been."

The undertaker arrived a little later with a white satinwood casket, with a good quality finish, and large brass handles. He had placed a small carved plaque of the Loxley crest on the top. Robbie was touched at the craftsmanship and paid the undertaker thanking him. The entire group helped lay him in his box, and carried him out to the trees as the sun rose into the sky. They stood together around the grave next to Eric's. Robbie stood before Fish who wept onto Jett's shoulder. He cleared his throat.

"I know Hog was raised by the Sisters of Good Hope, and I have very little knowledge of their god. I feel he will treat this man with the same reverence, as I know my Lord Hearne would. Anthony was a good man, and a true man of Loxley, for that is his adopted home. I owe him the debt of my future wife's life, and I will honour it and repay it by fulfilling the tasks he wished to do. I know he wanted to aid Sister Mary more than anything else, and I will ensure it is done on his behalf. He was true and valiant, honour him." Robbie saluted the white casket and all the others followed, and his body was slowly lowered into the ground.

The soil was pushed in by each of them, and then Rune crouched down, and touching the soil yellow primroses appeared and covered his grave. Fish hammered a carved cross into the grave and they silently departed the hallowed site. Rune wept on Robbie's shoulder as they crossed the garden, as Hogs polite apology sounded in her ears. Inside the cleaned main hall, Robbie poured out the glasses, and leaving one on a plate at the end of the table, he turned to the group and saluted the lonely full glass. "To Anthony, our fallen friend." All of them turned and saluted Hogs glass and drank his toast. Robbie placed his glass on the table. "We leave for Loxley first thing tomorrow morning, use the time until then to prepare." He took Rune by the hand and led her up the steps, and back to their room, she was still very upset and he put her to bed and sat beside her. "Will you be alright?"

She quietly nodded. "Don't leave me Robbie, stay here with me." They lay together and she sniffled. "He fell in front of me and apologised for startling me Rob. He knew that arrow was for me, and he apologised." Robbie pulled her close and held her tight.

"He was gentle, even though he was big and tough; his spirit was as kind as a small child's, he honoured you Rune by saving you. I still find it hard to deal with Eric, I just know I will find a way to repay him for the sacrifice he made, and you will for Anthony." Rune snuggled into Robbie and pulled the sheet over her head. He held her tight as she wept, for there were no more words to express the inexpressible.

Robbie left her to sleep a little later on, he came down the stairs looking tired, his shirt undone and his bow and quiver on his shoulder. John and Martin sat talking with Rags. She had delivered several letters and had just returned and yawned. Robbie smiled as he approached the table and poured a tall glass of water. "How are the roads Rags?"

She stretched her arms looking up at him. "A bleeding pain, I am sticking to cross country, it's impossible with all those people moving north."

Robbie pulled the glass from his lips. "What people?"

Matthews came in and placed a hot plate in front of Rags. "Miss," he turned to Robbie. "I am glad you are up Sir, Lady Scarlet would like to see you, My Lord."

Robbie nodded. "Thanks Matthews. I will be there shortly."

Robbie looked back at Rags as she tucked in to her steaming plate; she looked up and nodded as she swallowed. "There are hundreds of people leaving the south and heading north. It seems Knox is burning everything along the coast. His men are now pushing northwards clearing the villages, and everyone is getting out before they meet them." She took a huge bite of a large bread cob and chewed.

Robbie put down his glass and walked to the conference room where Skip and Fuse stood with Bear. He looked at the long line of red across the south coast of

England, and looked up at Scarlet. "This cannot be happening, he is insane."

She nodded slowly. "It looks like he is going to start at one end of the country and work his way north killing anyone who does not support him." Long lines of blue dots had now been placed on the map. They all snaked their way across to what was the old M1 motorway, a long stream of refugees now headed north by the most direct route.

Robbie looked at Skip. "How the hell can we look after all these?"

Skip looked serious. "That I think is his plan, any who will not join him are murdered. Those who escape are now our problem; we need a plan before we reach Loxley."

Bear leaned over the map, and pointed to a thick black line that now divided the country level with Lincoln. "It appears to us Robbie that we are stronger than Knox north of Lincoln. We have made that our front line, and if we can get everyone behind it, we can prepare and face him on the edge of this line."

Skip nodded in agreement. "I think you should now declare yourself as in command north of this line Robbie. We have sent riders to all our commanders north of the line and we are hoping to organise everyone when we meet at Loxley. Knox is making slow progress Robbie, so we have plenty of time to get things in place."

Bear saw his look of anguish and patted him on the back. "Don't look so worried, York will come to your aid, and we have Warwick and Gloucester behind us keeping Wales protected, so he only has half of England for now."

Robbie dropped into the chair and stared up at them all. "This is bigger than all of us. He is trying to stretch us and break us, what chance do we have of making this work?"

Skip smiled at him. "Relax this is just a case of strategy, it's about time you gave me a job I am fully qualified for. Robbie, leave the politics to me, and you focus on making his life hell. Get me to Loxley and give me the authority, and I will organise a relief effort. There are many men mixed in with this lot, so you now have the making of an army. That I believe is one mistake Knox has already made, he is sending you men, give me some time and we will solve all the problems."

Now the war had really started as Robbie had predicted at Canterbury. The country was going to be torn into two and a north, south divide created. In many ways, it came as a little bit of a relief. Robbie now knew where he stood, and finally he could come to terms with what was expected of him. His focus had to be to find the lost sword, and then begin a search from Kirklees with all the facts, and seek out the true heir to the kingdom. Getting back to Loxley was now a priority.

CHAPTER FOUR

THE PAST AND THE PRESENT

It was early morning, and Robbie sat at the long table in the hall writing letters, he had not been to bed and his sword lay across the table at his side. His bow stood up against the table an arm's length away; he sealed each letter with red wax, and pressed his ring into it to give the Loxley Seal. The letters were piled in order of delivery ready for Rags, and then he staggered wearily up to his room and slipped in through the door.

Rune lay on her side fast asleep, he slipped into bed slowly snuggling up to her; and lay his head down on the pillow and relaxed. His whole body ached, and he felt the relief of just slowly sinking into the comfortable bed. Robbie closed his eyes, Rune moved and rolled over to face him; she rubbed the sleep out of her eyes and looked at him. Somehow, he knew she was looking at him and he opened one eye. She gave him a huge smile and her eyes twinkled. "Hi gorgeous."

He smiled at her. "Hey beautiful," she slid up close and pushed him on to his back as she kissed him, her warm body curled around him and he knew sleep was going to be a long way off.

Robbie flopped down at the table next to a bright smiling Jade. "Robbie, you look awful." He leaned forward and rested his head on his hands. Rowan looked pretty much the same, Jade beamed. "You should get more sleep, has my sis been keeping you up all night?" There was something in the way that Rowan glanced at him, that told him Jade had done something similar to him. Robbie reached for a mug, and dragged it across the table and lifted it to his lips.

Jade jumped up and bounced off looking for Jett. Rowan lifted his cup and looked at Robbie. "Is it something to do with their line... you know, the power of Opal?"

Robbie rubbed his eyes. "I don't know, I am too tired to think, Rune has powers of endurance that go beyond me." His head slid down to the mug.

Rowan placed his head slowly down on the table and smiled at the thought of rest. It was an hour later when Rune in her woodsman attire came to the top of the stairs, and saw Robbie and Rowan fast asleep their heads on the table. She smiled at the sight, and came down the steps feeling alive and filled with energy.

Everyone gathered around the cart, which had now been loaded with supplies and extra arrows. The blacksmith had made some further additions, and repaired the hoops over the top, and fitted a new canvas. Two large baskets had been attached to the sides, which helped them carry more food, leather bound cushions had been fitted to the seats, to make them more comfortable to sit on.

Philip also let them have some more of his fine horses, and Skip and Fuse sat ready as Bear mounted with Martin and John, four were still tied to the back of the cart for Robbie and Rune, as well as Rowan and Jade. Jade looked at the horse for her and climbed in the cart; she was not a horsewoman, and was quite happy to let Blades use her horse. Harry and Maggs sat up front. Rowan handed his horse to Alice, as for the start of the journey he would accompany Jade in the cart.

Fish sprung up on to the back and sat with his back to Harry; he had visited his brother's grave early in the morning and said his goodbyes. Rune sat on the tailgate as Robbie came out through the doors with Rags and Scarlet.

"Ok Rags once you have seen Sister Mary head straight to Loxley, we will be travelling to Stratford and then head north to Loxley, I will see you there, if you need to return talk to Len Rimmer, he will know just where we are alright?"

"Ok Robbie, I got you, Sis Mary and home." She gave him a huge smile. "Home sounds sort of cool, don't it?"

Robbie ruffled her unbrushed hair. "Home is cool... Go on get going and keep your head down."

Rags pulled herself up on to her horse and waved to everyone. "See ya guys," she pulled on the reins and Bags turned. With a kick of her heels, she bolted like lightening out of the yard, and through the gates to the road that would lead her to the Sisters of Good Hope.

Robbie looked at Scarlet. "Thanks for everything, you and Philip have been very kind to all of us, and I appreciate it."

Scarlet pulled him into a hug. "You are going to be a great leader Lord Loxley, remember what I said. Trust those you have here and use their talents, and we will have a king. I will stay in touch with Rune and if you need us, we will come." Her Hug was tight and Robbie could barely breathe. She released him and smiled. "Watch over my children for me Robbie." Jett and Ruby came clattering around the corner on their own horses.

"I will you can be sure of it." He walked over to the cart where Rune sat smiling, her bright blue eyes sparkled. He slid his arms into hers as she sat swinging her legs on the tailgate. "Ready to go home?"

"Oh yes please." She kissed him and slid backwards into the cart, as he climbed up. Steph smiled at her excited daughter's pleasure as she sat with her arm around

Smokes.

Robbie climbed up to the front and leaned over to Maggs, who he had not seen since leaving Canterbury. "Nice to see you Maggs, how are you feeling now?"

Maggs rattled as she moved around in the seat. "I am calmer, and my aura is mellow now thank you."

Robbie smiled. "Cool, good to have you back." He slapped Harry on the back. "Harry you old maniac, take us home."

"Hey man like that is completely cosmic and very radical, let's mosey on home real mellow like." He whipped the reins, and the four horses pulled the cart, it lurched forward, and they all waved at Scarlet as they passed under the archway and through the gate on to the long road to Gloucester.

Martin and John rode up front, and the rest fell in behind, Alice and Bear rode side by side and talked quietly. Robbie slid down next to Rune and noticed how Rowan, who's eyes were still very heavy, had pulled his hood up and was already half asleep. The cart trundled along the road and began to pick up speed; Stratford was going to be their first stop as Smokes returned to his old home for a few things. It would be their first overnight stay on the road home.

The previous day as Robbie and his men had cleaned the castle of Cutter bodies, Una and her party had departed towards Windermere on their journey south towards York. They rode down the long road at the side of the lake where no one was to be seen. The whole place was completely deserted, and as the sun shone bright, the trip seemed very pleasant, although Mel felt exposed so far away from any other life. It had been a long day with few breaks and as the sun started to fall in the sky, they headed into the outskirts of Settle. Una knew of a woodsman camp, that she had been told about, and slowly wove her way into the trees towards it. The challenge had come a mile into the heavy woodland.

A hooded figure walked into the pathway from between two trees. "Who wanders this realm without leave of our master woodsman?" He stood with his bow up and his brown hood over his head.

The party halted, and Una urged her horse forward slightly. "I have leave to enter here, as I seek the woodsman Lee Sherman, do you know of his whereabouts?"

The woodsman moved uneasily. "That woodsman is about, but how do I know you are not spies of the enemy?"

Sapphire's eyes began to glow lilac as she looked at the woodsman. "We are kin to the Lady Runestone, who is allied to Robert of Loxley, your master of all the woodlands." Sapphire's eyes exploded in violet light and the cloudy image of Rune appeared before him.

"Hear me woodsman, for I am Runestone Lady of Loxley and your hooded man. My kin have business here and you will escort them to the woodsman Sherman, for he is aware of their imminent arrival. They are on business of high value to the hooded man, and to waylay them would be at your peril." The violet image of Rune walked towards him. "My high grandfather is your Lord Hearne, and it would not do to displease him."

The woodsman fell to his knees. "Forgive me My Lady for I have to check."

"You have not displeased us, go about your duty and guide my kin safely." Rune's violet image faded, and Saff closed her eyes for a moment as the woodsman got to his feet and turned back on to the path.

"My Ladies and Gents, please follow me and I will guide you to the camp."

Una looked back at Mel and winked. "She is very handy to have inside us is Rune." Mel smiled and kicked her horse forward, as they followed the woodsman through the woodland towards the camp deep inside the dark trees.

Lee Sherman was a tall slender man with a drawn face. His hair was thin and white, and the wrinkles on his face showed he was a great age. He smiled his pipe smoking from his lip, as the horses approached and the young woodsman spoke quietly to him. Lee nodded and walked over to greet his new guests. "My Lords and Ladies welcome to our humble camp, I am Lee Sherman and master of these woods, please step down and find comfort while my men care for your mounts." Lee flicked his wrist and two hooded men came forward to steady the horses.

Lee wore the cloak of a Loxley woodsman, and he smiled a kind smile as the party slid down. He waved his arm in the direction of a log hut set back in the trees. "I was informed of your coming and have prepared you a safe haven for your night's stay, please come inside and make yourselves comfortable, and I will arrange a meal. We will talk later on matters concerning your journey." He slid the foul smelling pipe into his mouth and gave a small cough as he smiled.

Una looked at the old cabin. "We are grateful to your hospitality Master of the woods; I am pleased my grandmother sent us here. You are known to Loxley I see." Una looked at the faded crest on his cloak as they walked across to the cabin.

"I once lived and served in Loxley My Lady, I was friends with the lord's grandfather. I travelled here many years ago to find my family, for my eldest brother lived in these parts with his children."

Una stepped up to the door and Lee opened it. "It is a great comfort to know that we are amongst men of Loxley," she stepped inside followed by the others and Lee stood in the door.

"Every man here is loyal to the hooded man; we guard this realm and keep it free of the filth from the south in his honour. Please make yourselves at home, and I will bring you food." Lee pulled the door shut and made his way across the camp. They heard him bark out his orders as he walked. Mac dropped down at the table and lit the lamp; Saff looked at the beds in the back room, whilst Mel and Una sat down at the small table. Jaz stood by the window and watched the camp.

It was late in the evening as Mel sat with Una out on the front of the cabin; Lee came up with three steaming mugs and offered them to the two women. He sat on an old log and packed his pipe, the match flared as he puffed the foul smelling tobacco. The glade was almost in darkness, and the fire at the centre of the camp cast a yellowy orange glow across the trees. Stars peeped through the gaps in the canopy and the breeze gently stirred the ferns and cow parsley that grew beside the cabin. Lee took a large swig of his drink and looked at the two women. "Your journey will take you to York, and then Loxley I take it?"

Una nodded. "We have business at York and intend to travel with Sir Giles down to Loxley to meet with the lord and our kin."

Lee looked at the floor in thought and then spoke. "There are safe paths across the moor that you can use, but you will need a guide. The road from here is still watched from the east and could be dangerous for you, with your permission I will send my son Keith with you, he knows the paths well, and you should reach York within the day safely."

"Any help you could offer us Lee, would be gratefully accepted, stealth and speed are our priority. Lord Loxley will be returning home soon, and we must meet with him on a great matter of concern for the entire realm of this land." Una spoke quietly not wishing for others to hear her, and Lee nodded as if he had some idea of her quest.

"I have important business first thing in the morning, but my son Keith will be outside waiting when you are ready to travel. It will be a long day's ride so be ready early. I will go and speak with him now and organise things, have no fear you are watched and safe here, sleep well."

Lee wandered back to his men, and Una noticed the two guards in the trees, she patted her sister's arm, and got up and went inside. Mel sat out for a while longer, and gazed at the stars that were the same as the ones above her stones back on Callanish. An owl hooted in the trees somewhere above the cabin, and in the distance, a fox screeched its call to its mate.

Robbie and Rowan had slept all the way up the road along the river and past Gloucester. He felt the motion of the cart and opened his eyes to see Rune watching him. She had lowered him down and rested his head in her lap. She smiled sweetly at him. "Feel better?"

He stretched his arms and sat up put them around her. "Oh, I was tired, I have not slept much recently, where are we?" The cart was rumbling along at a good speed, and Robbie lifted the canvass to peer around at the passing trees.

Smokes looked out with him. "We are on the road to Stratford, this is a short cut Harry and I used to take, we will get to my old home a lot quicker."

Robbie looked around, the roadsides were thick with trees and brambles, and the bank either side of the road was so high, it was impossible to see where they were. The group on horses followed behind talking quietly. He dropped the canvass and slid back next to Rune, Rowan was still fast asleep and so was Jade. Fish dozed in the corner and Steph leaned over the front talking to Maggs and Harry, Rune put her arm around him and pulled him close.

"The Sisters of Knowledge have set off for York, they will meet us at Loxley, you must see them alone Robbie." Rune stared ahead as she spoke as if she was seeing something in her mind. "Their news will help you; I am sure."

"Well, if they happen to have a huge gold sword with them that would help."

Rune looked at him in a strange way. "They have information that will help you in your search Robbie, was that just a guess or do you know something?"

"Just voicing my thoughts, I have no idea at all how to even begin to look for the sword. Even Scarlet who is the guardian cannot give me any idea of where to look. All I know is that Knox is searching every religious shrine across the whole country."

Rune thought for a moment and then looked at him. "Why every religious shrine?"

"It would appear that Lancelot was a very Christian man, he even spent some time preaching, I would think that it's Mason's plan to search any religious connection first."

"What I don't understand Rob is why he even wants a sword... You know, this is a man, who is still in love with the past and wants to rebuild it. Why bother with a sword when you can make cannons and other weapons of evil?"

"I don't really know Rune." Robbie shook his head slowly. "The ironic thing is that this is the sword of Honour. That is the one thing Mason has none of; maybe he thinks it will give him some."

Steph sat back and looked at both of them. "Or maybe he knows that without all the sword holders present you will never be able to crown a king."

Robbie looked up at her. "How do you mean?"

"Robbie it is said in the old tales that for a true heir to be crowned and accepted as true king to the kingdom, all five of the mystical swords of the land must be present. If you find your king, and the true owners of the swords, then they will all have to be present in order for that arrow you shot into the crown to be released. Talk to my father he will tell you of the deep magic that exists in this land."

Rune seemed confused. "But that cannot be right because Mason almost had the crown on his head, if we had not stopped him, he would be king now?"

Steph smiled. "And yet he isn't, is he? Events conspired against him. Only three of the swords were present and they were drawn against him."

Rune looked at Robbie, and then back to her mother. "Are you telling me that this magic guided us to stop him?"

"I am Runestone, and you should know better, and understand." Steph smiled at her. "Tell me my daughter what did you do in your sleep last night?"

Robbie looked at Rune. "I dreamt we were being attacked and woke Robbie up."

Steph nodded, "that was the night before, I meant last night?"

Rune looked puzzled. "Nothing I slept."

"So, you did not appear in a wood in front of a woodsman and your new sisters to find a man of Loxley on the edges of Yorkshire?"

Rune looked more and more confused. "No not at all, if I had dreamt that I would have remembered it."

Steph gave a slight smile. "Yet it did happen Rune, I spoke with Una this morning, and you appeared in a wood and told the woodsman to take them to Lee Sherman... The power you hold works through you always Rune, even it appears, when you sleep."

"Hey man is that old goat still alive? Wow he was a radical being he was, him and my Pa would hunt boars in ways that would jangle your vibes man, they were cosmic and very happenin dudes."

Rune looked over to Harry. "This man is real?"

"Whoa yeah, he was my Pa's best pal, he went looking for his brother when I was younger, cosmic guy I tell you man."

Rune looked lost for words. "I have no memory of it at all; I didn't even know I could project myself that is grandmothers' ability not mine."

Steph leaned forward and touched Rune's hand. "You have great powers Runestone, but you are still young. Sometimes the magic will help you, do not worry about it. One day you will have full control, it is early days, you still have much to learn."

Bobby Thorn stood above the gate and yelled. "Rider coming!" Sister Mary looked up at him. She could hear the hooves clattering down the shale road outside the gates as she walked towards them.

The hooves slid on the shale as Bobby yelled. "It's Rags!" Sister Mary smiled and hurried. She pulled back the three bolts and swung the old black gates open. Rags cantered inside on Bags and slid off the saddle on to the floor.

"Hey Sister, how's the habit?" Rags beamed as Mary threw her arms around her and Rags gave her a huge squeeze. "I missed you all; it's nice to be back."

"Oh, Rags my child it has been so long I was starting to worry."

"Michelle... Michelle!" A small girl with long blonde curly hair ran up the yard with tears in her eyes. Rags broke into a huge smile, and went down on one knee and held out her arms.

"Lucy!" The little girl swept weeping into her arms. Sister Mary smiled as Rags hugged her. "Hey Sis, didn't I tell you I would be back." Rags squeezed her tight as she turned with tears in her own eyes to Sister Mary. "Thanks Sister for taking care of her."

Lucy wept as Sister Mary put her arm around Rags. "Come my child tell me of what is happening on the road, and we shall have some tea."

Rags held Lucy in her arms as she walked down the long yard towards the shade of the balcony, and the three old chairs. "It's been a real breeze Sister I tell you; I don't work for the postie's any more, I have a full time job riding for Lord Loxley."

Sister Mary stopped and looked at her with excitement in her eyes. "You work for Robert?"

Rags nodded. "Yeah Sister, I am now his official private despatch rider, I am off to Loxley now, I have a note for you here, from him."

Sister Mary's excitement almost boiled over as Rags awkwardly rooted in her bag whilst still holding Lucy. She pulled the large white letter with the red seal, and handed it over. Sister Mary sat down, and broke the seal and began to read as Rags sat down and gave her sister a big kiss. "Hey what's that on your wrist?"

Lucy waved her hand to show Rags the small woollen woven wrist tie. "Rowan of the woods gave it me."

Rags looked astounded. "When was Rowan here?"

Sister Mary put the letter on her knee as tears ran down her cheeks. "That poor boy, oh Anthony your heart was always so big," she dabbed her face as she wept, and Rags began to realise that the group she had spent the last ten days with, were known to the sister.

"Sister Mary did you know Hog?" She placed her hand on the old Sisters knee as she wept. Sister Mary sniffled and tried to dry her eyes.

"I raised him and James from small children; they were the first two children we ever took in. They are like my own sons." Sister Mary's tears flowed and Rags pulled the old nun over to her and hugged her.

"For what it's worth Sister, he died to protect Rune. He is a hero and braver than I could ever be, and that's the truth." Rags held Sister Mary close as she wept long sobs.

Jade stretched in Rowan's lap and smiled at Rune. Rowan's head bobbed in rhythm with the cart, she looked up at him and stretched up and kissed him softly. She giggled as he jumped in his seat and looked about. She slid on to his lap and put her arms around him, Rowan smiled at her and pulled her close as she snuggled her head into his shoulder. He yawned and looked up at the smiling Rune. "Where are we?"

Robbie looked up from his thoughts. "Hey Harry how long now?"

"Hey man we are like totally on time."

"Great Harry what time is arrival?"

"Well cosmically, it should be like real soon, I think we need to mosey a little longer in this happenin sort of way, and then hey, it will be like, lets mellow we made it on time."

Rowan looked at Robbie who smiled. "You heard the man, it's almost mellow time."

Smokes started to laugh at Rowan's completely lost expression. "Harry says not much longer." Rune, giggled with Steph, and Rowan smiled and nodded at Smokes. He had only just woken up and was still a little groggy, and Harry was difficult enough to understand when he had been awake for hours. Smokes looked over at Rune. "Are you excited at going to your place of birth?"

Rune looked surprised. She had completely forgotten; she had always been introduced as Runestone of Avon in the past. She had become so use now to being referred to as Lady Loxley that it had slipped her mind. Steph smiled at her. "Both you and Jade were born at the house; I must admit it will be nice to see it again. I used to love this cottage; it was hard leaving it to go to Loxley." She squeezed Smokes arm. "This was our first real home, do you remember Pete?" Her eyes twinkled and some special memory seemed to hatch between her and Smokes. He gave her a huge smile and grinned.

"And you call Rune and me for always being at it. God that is such a we were at it like rabbits look." Jade gave her mother a shrewd stare and Steph giggled with Smokes. She looked at Jade and smiled.

"It was a very happy time for me and your father." Jade winked at Rune and pointed with her thumb.

"At it like Rabbits... see, that's what you and Robbie look like when you come back from being alone." Rune burst into laughter with Robbie, and Steph squeezed Pete's arm and laughed with him. Although she did look a little pink around the edges of her cheeks.

Martin lifted his arm and Harry pulled on the break. "Hey man we got like guard dudes."

Robbie grabbed his bow and pulled out an arrow. Jade moved to the backboard and slipped off into the bushes followed by Rowan. Jett and Flash's horses were empty and Skip and Fuse were on the floor as they pulled their horses to the cart and tied them on.

Fish dropped off the back and followed Fuse up the bank into the trees. Rune, Mother and Smokes loaded their bows. Alice slid off her horse with Bear and crept off into the trees as the cart slowed to a crawl. Robbie sat low behind Harry and Maggs. "If there is trouble Maggs, drop off the seat and get under the cart. Don't worry Harry will be safe I am with him." Robbie looked back. "Where is Blades?" Rune pointed into the trees where Jade had disappeared.

"Wherever Jett is, Blades will be." Robbie nodded. The two horses in front slowed to a halt, John already had his bow fitted and was ready to roll backwards off the horse. Robbie heard the call.

"Halt, who goes in this realm without leave?"

Martin gave two flicks of his hand; Robbie looked back. "They are friendly."

A woodsman held his bow up at Martin who pulled his cloak down off his shoulder. "I would look behind you woodsman, for you ask us to request permission when it is you who is the trespasser on our land." The woodsman saw the Loxley crest and glanced back to his commander for advice. His commander stood with his empty bow up in the air with his troops surrounded by a ring of hooded men in green. The lone woodsman lifted his arm in the air and held aloft his empty bow.

Martin looked at the group. "Who is in command here?" The captain at the front stepped forward as Robbie climbed up on top of the cart and stood on the metal poles.

"Are we secured Martin?" Martin looked back and smiled.

"Yes My Lord we are in no danger."

Robbie stood on top of the cart with his hood up and his bow held low across his front. Back lit by the sun he made an impressive sight. "Who stands before the hooded man and waylays his journey?" The whole group of surrendered woodsmen fell to their knees.

The captain at the front looked up. "My Lord Loxley we had no idea, we are honoured you have chosen to pass here. We will delay you no longer." He moved to the side of the bank, and Robbie jumped down on to the road as Rune and Smokes appeared down the side of the cart. He walked towards the group.

"Off your knees woodsmen, I am a man as you are." Robbie approached the captain and offered his hand. "It is good to know that our roads are watched, tell me Captain what is your name?" The captain blanched.

"My name My Lord is irrelevant, I am a servant of your kingdom, and we guard the roads on your behalf."

"Nonsense, every man has a name and I would care to know it." The captain stammered.

"I... I ... I am Rafe My Lord, Rafe of New Avon." Robbie grabbed his hand. "Robert of Loxley. This very wonderful lady here is Runestone, and around you is my most trusted group of friends and partners in obstruction," he smiled as Rafe bowed to Rune.

"My Lady Runestone we are honoured." She took his hand and smiled sweetly at him.

"We are all delighted to meet you Captain Rafe." Robbie walked into the group of woodsmen and shook their hands and patted their shoulders.

"Nice to meet you all, you are doing a fine job, don't be put off by my friends here they are specialists at what we do. So, does anyone have a pot we can boil?

It's been a long journey and we could use a little refreshment?"

The group of woodsmen looked so bewildered it made Jett and Jade laugh. Jade looked at Jett. "You have to admit it, there are times his style is so cool?" Jett grinned.

"Let's check out the talent," and she winked. Blades smiled as Jade gave an evil grin. The cart was pulled off the lane into a small wooded area, and Robbie sat on a log and talked to the woodsmen, who were now getting over the fact that the legend who had blown up Tintagel, and destroyed Windsor, as well as preventing Mason Knox getting his crown, was actually sat amongst them, and drinking Dandelion coffee with them.

Harry and Blades with their crossed swords drew worried looks, and Jett was enjoying being menacing, especially as she was targeting one rather handsome young man. "Hi lunchbox, what's your name?" She winked at him and he swallowed deeply. Her golden brooch on her collar of a scorpion with its tail raised, made him wonder if he was her next meal.

"I am Bowman Ramsey Miss."

"Hi Ramsey I am Lady Jett Amber of Caerleon." She winked. "Got any quiet woodland round here?" Ramsey turned paler.

John nudged Martin. "Hey Jett, don't play with your food." He started to laugh with Martin, as Ramsey physically withered in front of her. Jett flashed her eyes blue and he jumped back a pace. She smiled and pulled him back forward.

"Don't listen to them; I am only playing with you." She winked at him. "I devour my prey on the third date." John and Martin burst out laughing as she walked over and grabbed a coffee grinning. Ramsay gave a weak smile, but stayed where he was.

The cottage was only two miles down the road, but much to Steph's distress the captain informed Smokes, Cutters had burnt it to the floor several years ago. Most of the old barn was intact and a few of the out buildings. The farmland around it had turned to seed and was now a thick meadow. Robbie looked across at Smokes who shrugged. "Well Robbie at least we can still use the barn for the night."

Just over an hour later, the cart pulled on to the weed covered rubble that was once the home of Steph and Pete, and the birthplace of Jade and Rune. The old brick barn stood across the grass covered yard, and there were three small out buildings with burned out roofs.

Harry heaved on the reigns and the cart stopped. Steph was out in a flash, and walked slowly around the start of her life with Pete and her children. Her eyes filled with tears as she remembered the happy times before Pete had been caught and taken prisoner. Pete put his arm round her as she wiped her eyes on her sleeve. "I was truly the happiest I have ever been here Pete." He pulled her close and put his other arm around her.

"They knocked down the bricks, and burned the wood, but here?" He put his hand on Steph's heart "Here this cottage is still a home of love and our children. Knox taught me that sweetheart and it kept me alive." He pulled her close and kissed her. Steph smiled and pulled herself into his embrace.

"I love you Pete." He smiled as he held her.

"Knowing that kept me alive as well."

Jade and Rune walked around their place of birth. "Do you remember this Jade? It feels sort of familiar but I cannot remember it all."

Jade looked at her mother. "Hey Rune link me to mum, she will have the pictures."

Rune's eyes flickered and Steph looked across at her and smiled. Jade closed her eyes and watched a small Jett running about with her in front of a large clear barn. Jade turned to see her mother who looked a lot younger, and behind her was an old stone cottage covered with wisteria and bright lemon and red climbing roses. It had small wooden windows and a polished brown wooden door with a latticework arch in front of it. Jade looked up at the thatched roof.

"Hey Mum I remember this place now. I had a swing and a slide over there." Jade opened her eyes and pointed at a pile of trees and weeds. "It was yellow with a blue seat, and I used to hold Rune in my hands when I sat on it." Her eyes sparkled with delight and Steph laughed as more tears ran down her face.

Rune felt the joy rise in her mother and smiled, as Steph came over to her and hugged her. "Thank you sweetheart, that was a really nice thing to do for your sister." Rune beamed as Jade rooted around in the bushes and pulled out an old faded blue wooden seat. "Hey look?" She waved it above her head. "See I told you."

Two thirds of the barn was dry and Robbie pulled the horses inside with Harry, Maggs found an old metal tub and got a fire going. It was not long before a meal was cooking, and as Blades and Fish took first watch, they all sat around for a meal. Rafe had put guards at each end of the road, and had told Robbie he would let him know if anything was seen prowling around, so they all relaxed and laughed and joked as they ate. Robbie took a plate up to Fish who was sat high in the hayloft watching from a window. He handed him the plate and sat beside him as he ate, Fish had been very quiet, and Robbie knew how much he was missing his brother. "How are you doing Fish?"

"I will be fine Robbie; I am over the shock."

"That's not what I asked Fish." He put his plate down and looked away to hide his tears.

"I miss him Robbie, he has been by my side all my life, and he has gone, and I miss him."

Robbie put his arm around his shoulder. "I wish there was something I could do or say James, but there is nothing. He was without doubt a brave and loyal friend to us all, and we all feel his loss with you."

Fish wiped his face on his cloak. "He didn't say much I know, but Robbie with you and everyone else was the happiest I have ever seen him. He loved Rune and you; he told me you were the kindest people he had ever known, and we were raised by Sister Mary."

Robbie patted his back. "Don't cut yourself off from the others Fish, they loved Hog and they love you too, be a part of them, they are your family now and they feel for you." Robbie came down the ladder and they all looked up at him. John nodded at him and Robbie nodded back. "He will be fine." Martin smiled a sad smile. Robbie walked over and sat next to Rune, she slid her arm round him and pulled him close.

"Do not worry I am watching out for him." He smiled and lay back in the old straw.

Darkness faded into the barn and the flames in the tub flickered. John and Martin, climbed up to keep Fish company, and after not very long, chuckles could be heard. Robbie heard the phrase, 'Rune sick.' He knew they were remembering Hogs funny little moments. He walked out into the dark and spotted Fuse sitting on a barrel in the moonlight. Fuse looked up as he approached.

"I love nights like this when you can see all the stars. When I was a kid there were so many street lights it was hard to see them."

Robbie looked up at the millions of twinkling little lights above him. "What was it like Fuse, why is Knox so obsessed about bringing it back? I don't understand him, and without that I will never beat him." He sat on an old wooden crate at the side of Fuse.

"You show great wisdom Robbie, I must admit I did wonder when you would get around to asking."

Robbie looked down from the sky and into his old eyes. "You have seen or know of the things he is doing, don't you?"

Fuse nodded. "I was born in 1983 and I am 55 years old, I lived a long time before the red death came. I learned a lot at school and saw a great deal on the television."

"The telly what?" Fuse laughed.

"It was a box filled with talking pictures that showed you things that had been in the past fifty years." He leaned forward. "Robbie this life today is very hard, but believe me it is worth it, because people have become connected again. Look at this group and how they feel the loss of their man, I believe it has touched everyone in one way or another." Robbie too felt the loss, and it struck a chord with him.

"In the old days, most people would not have noticed. Life then was so far removed from this that I doubt you will ever fully understand it. I suppose if I had to say it in an easy to understand way, I would say life back then was about power, money, and labels." Fuse noticed his look of confusion and smiled.

"People became hard and unfeeling. They ignored their neighbours most of the time and just concentrated on money. Back then, you were judged by it, money bought you the right clothes and the right house, and you could drive the right car. If you had what was considered right, you did well in the world. Those who did not never got anywhere." Robbie was starting to understand and Fuse could see it.

"I would imagine Mason had the right kind of everything. It was all to do with status, you fought constantly to be bigger, better, and richer than your neighbour, so you moved to somewhere else which was considered better than the rest. People became cruel and exploited each other just to get higher up in status. We invaded other countries in the name of peace, but it was really for their minerals or oil, and we raped and destroyed their lands. In this country, we built more and more houses that cost more and more to buy, even though they were not worth the money." It made sense to Robbie as he listened to Fuse, who carried a sad expression of his remembrance.

"If you lived in one, well you had status so what did it matter? You were better than the rest, so you could abuse and condemn yet more people, and those who were once your neighbours, became lesser than you did as you moved up the status ladder. Nobody grew their own food, my dad did, he had a plot in the garden. I used to help him pull the carrots and pick fresh peas, everything was made so you could eat quickly, and throw away the wrapping to avoid cleaning anything. People were driven into buying more and more things, and the mad thing was, we were told all the time if you do not buy this, you are worthless, and so you bought it. Within a year, a newer and better version was released and it all started again, so you bought the better one and threw the one you had away, and you kept your status." Fuse looked out into the darkness and stared.

"Under this land, there are huge piles of buried things people threw away, because to own them lost you status. You would not believe what we have buried for years upon years, some of it has poisoned the earth for years to come. The rest rots with the remnants of a cruel life, it was all a big con driven by money and the greed for more. There were people in my time that had so much money that they could live a hundred lives and not spend it all, but they still wanted more, it was madness, and people got more and more lazy and forgot the ways of the past." Robbie watched as the old man smiled and the lines appeared on his face.

"They forgot the important things like how beautiful a flower is, or how graceful a silver birch can be. Simple but very important things, because it is those things that connected us to the world, we live in." Fuse spoke with awe, and looked back up at the sky. "Look at the wonder up there, is that not the most wonderful sight?

In the old days Robbie, very few people would have noticed." Robbie looked at the blackness littered with thousands of twinkling stars.

"You know in the short time I have travelled with you; I have marvelled at what I have seen, and if I die tomorrow, I will consider myself blessed. Because in the last weeks I have seen the wonder of nature as it has come back to this world. In my day the pests and the weeds were killed, birds starved from lack of food and died, many of the wild animals were pushed into smaller areas of green and almost died out. Today I know they have survived and returned to the world, and that is how it should be. We all have to live together and respect each other; you know that without being told because you have been raised in amongst it. He does not remember the pain and suffering, because he was part of the cause. You must stop him, Robbie; your way of life is the only way, and I would rather die than return to that old way of life."

Robbie looked down to see Fuse watching him. "I am an old man compared to you, but I have been made very happy watching the love around me. I see Rune and you, for which I think there is no greater example, but with Mother and Smokes and Jade and Rowan, and I think maybe Alice and Bear have a flower between them yet to blossom, it brings me joy Robbie to see it. I had forgotten how very important love is in life, if not the most important thing." He lifted his arm and squeezed Robbie's shoulder.

"You have it all in the palm of your hand my dear boy, if you want to see how to defeat Knox, do to this country what you have already done around you, and you will succeed. Be fair and loyal, and show the love in your heart, for it is great and does you such justice." He looked back up at the stars and smiled. "That is worth fighting and dying for."

He stood up and patted Robbie on the shoulder. "You are a good man Lord Loxley, I will leave you with your thoughts, I am tired, and alas age comes to us all." He walked to the door where Rune stood smiling at him and watching Robbie. Fuse smiled and touched her arm. "Always watching My Lady, that is love, I have seen it before." He walked past her and into the barn.

Rune crossed the yard and sat down beside him. She rested her head on his shoulder. "Hi," he put his arm around her.

"Hey beautiful." Robbie pointed upwards. "Look how beautiful they all are, I have read the stars a million times, yet it just took an old man to point out how wonderful and beautiful they are. Fuse is pretty cool Rune."

She kissed his cheek and slid her arms around him. "You are pretty cool yourself you know? So has Fuse filled in the gaps for you?"

Robbie gazed up at the sky. "Do you remember the picture in the corridor outside our room in the castle?"

"The one of Tintagel, as a ruined old castle?"

"Yeah, I looked at it every day. It was that picture that gave me the idea to attack." He looked down, and turned to her, Rune's eyes sparkled in the starlight and he smiled. "The whole coast around it was filled with birds and flowers, there was thrift and wild pea, and all sorts of plants I did not recognise. Rune that place was so beautiful we could have lived there and been happy. But the night we attacked him, did you see what he had done?"

"I felt it in you; I felt the sadness that came over you as we came around the bluff."

"He poured concrete over those ruins, and removed the birth place of the king he was supposed to be related to, that would be the same as me burning Loxley to the floor. How can any man be so mindless to the importance of his own roots? If he will do that to somewhere so important to him, what the hell has he got planned for the rest of us?"

"He is blind Robbie. You heard what Fuse said, he would never understand the power of love; he is filled with the love of power, which I believe were your words also. Robbie, Mason Knox has no feelings for what is nice; when he looks at the trees, he can only see the value of the timber. The life contained within is not relevant to him." Rune took his hand and opened it, she put her finger on his palm and a small perfectly formed violet appeared. Robbie smiled. "Mason sees something there to walk on and kill. What do you see?"

"I see life and beauty, because this is a part of you Rune, and you are the most beautiful thing in this world and also my sole reason for life."

Rune's eyes filled with tears. "Oh Robbie." She slid her arms around him and held him close. He lowered the flower to the ground, and it settled on the floor where more grew around it, he pulled her close and kissed her. Robbie and Rune sat quietly in the dark holding each other in their arms and watching the stars twinkle above them.

"Rune?"

"Yeah Rob?"

"I really love that thing you do with the violets."

"I know."

"Oh, please don't start that again." Rune giggled.

CHAPTER FIVE

THE ROAD NORTH

The small boat docked, and the three figures came out in the darkness, and up
the damp slimy steps towards the top of the harbour. All of them wore long cloaks
of the deepest green, as they hurried across the weed littered street to the remnants
of the old church.

The lead figure stopped at the rusty old open gate and looked around; seeing all
was clear she slipped inside followed by the others. The dark shape of the church
covered in ivy loomed out of the dark; its crumbled porch leaned supported by
a twisted tree that had grown up by its side. The old door creaked as she pushed,
and it opened enough for them to squeeze through. The door closed behind them
with a gentle thud, an old owl hooted in the graveyard, but all around for miles was
still and dead, no one had been here for twenty years.

The leader walked quickly down the centre of the old church to the small
room at the back, she took out a small key and unlocked the door, then slipped
inside as the other two followed. Inside the room was dark and suddenly light
illuminated the room as she struck the match and lit two candles. It smelt musty
and everything was dull from years of dust.

She lowered her hood and rested a bow of white wood against the table, as
she now looked at the other two. "We will be safe here for tonight, all is not as it
seems here." She turned and moved to a chair, and throwing her cloak back over
her shoulders she opened her bag and took out some fruit, which she handed to
one of the other two.

"Merci." She turned back fast on the figure.

"We speak only English now Treen, we cannot let anyone know from where we
have come."

The figure dropped her hood, and golden blonde hair spilled on to her
shoulders. "Sorry mama."

The woman passed the other a bottle and she took it, as she lowered to the
floor, and throwing off her hood she pulled a black wide brimmed hat out from
under it, and slipped it on her head. "This place looks like fun, why here and not
somewhere a little nicer?"

The woman turned. "Alley we must stay out of sight and this place is special as you will see later. This was once a very old holy place for worship; it is still a very sacred place." She wiped the chair and sat down on it, and pulled out a book and started to read by the candlelight.

The time passed slowly and Alley dozed in the corner, as Treen snuggled up close to her. The woman on the chair turned the pages slowly as her pale watery blue eyes read each line on the paper. Her eyes flickered blue and the pages lit up, she lifted her head and looked at her two daughters. "It is time she is coming; hurry she will not have long."

The two girls got up, and stretched, brushing the dust off their cloaks, and followed their mother out through the small door and into the old dark church. A faint white light appeared at the end of the aisle near the old doors and as it moved up towards them, it formed into the shape of a woman dressed in long white robes with a blue sash, and a long white cloak. Gwendolyn lifted her arms and the woman ran to her, and threw her arms around her.

"Oh Mother, I have missed you." Gwendolyn smiled and embraced her daughter.

"Madeleine my darling," she smiled at the two girls. "Have you no love for your grandmother?" The two girls smiled and ran to her, and she embraced her family. "Oh Citrine you have grown up so much, you are quite the young lady now, and Alexandrite you too are so beautiful and grown. The last time I saw you, you were just tiny babies."

She hugged them both and turned to Madeleine. "I have so little time my darling, and so much to tell you. She will be here soon to tell you of what you must do; Opal is with her now and will give her the knowledge she needs. In the short time I have, you must know that the Dark One took not all my powers. Some of those that remained I passed to Runestone, for she will need them. Tonight, I will pass forever into another realm and I will not be able to return. My place now my darling, is beyond this realm, where I have other tasks to perform. You have the box for Lord Loxley?"

"Yes Mother."

"He must be alone when he sees it, Rune can be there but no other, Oh my darling I wish I could tarry longer, for I have seen and done much that you will never know of. In time you must go to my table and use the power of the star to teach your children, for there is much to do to recover all that has been lost. Time is so short; I can feel her she is coming my daughter."

Everyone was asleep except Robbie, his mind was too full and he could not rest, his eyes flickered but as he fell into sleep, his mind would jolt and wake him up. He jumped awake and the white figure in front of him bowed. "You should sleep woodsman." She waved a hand, and his eyes closed.

Opal knelt down to Rune and she placed her hand on her shoulder. It glowed a silvery white and Rune disturbed in her sleep, Opal stood up, and turned and looked at Jade fast asleep in Rowan's arms. She smiled and knelt down, and placed her hand on Jade's head, it glowed lilac. She then placed a hand on Rowan's head and it too began to glow lilac. "You both have a job to do for me my children of the wood."

Madeleine stood with her mother and children, as the lilac figure walked up the church and smiled a sweet and loving smile. "Hear me my sisters, for I am Runestone, and you are part of my circle." She smiled at Gwendolyn. "I shall miss you Grandmother of my line it has been nice talking this past week."

Gwendolyn embraced Rune and then placed her hand into Rune's. "My final gifts are yours Runestone," as she squeezed her hand Rune's eyes glowed deep purple and Gwendolyn faded away into silver light, and a small butterfly brooch fell to the floor. Rune bent down and picked it up then turned to Madeleine.

"I have a guide for you, my sister." She lifted Maddy's hand and placed the brooch in her palm. Maddy looked down as Rune touched it and its wings began to flap, the butterfly fluttered into the air, and Alley laughed as she watched it land on Maddy's shoulder.

"This will lead you to water; wait and my messengers will collect you and bring you to Lord Robert. War is coming and we have little time, you are with us all now, and part of all the joining circles. You have protection Madeleine, but keep yourself secret until we all meet on the road. You will find horses in the morning, travel fast."

She turned to Alley and Treen. "My sister's welcome home." Rune smiled as she embraced each of them and the church was filled with violet light. The rows of dusty and decayed old pews glowed in the dim light, and the old tarnished candlesticks ignited' and the candles flickered as they burned.

"My hooded man has done well my sisters, he has made great gains as the prophecy of old has told, but we must now use our circle to help him with his task. Una and Melanie are already on their way to Loxley, you will meet Robert of Loxley sooner, and once we are all together, the puzzle of the lost sword will be solved."

Maddy looked into the violet eyes of Rune. "What of the Dark One, it is true then, she has returned?"

"I have faced her twice already, but her power grows with her new life as mine does, and Opal is starting to slowly fade, she too will enter the other realm, and then I will face the Dark One alone. Without the swords of power, we will fail and the land will fall."

Rune turned. "I must return now, but we will meet again shortly." She embraced Madeleine and smiling she walked slowly towards the doors. "Hearne is with you and will protect you, my sisters." Rune faded away into darkness. Alley looked at her mum.

"She looks very young for one so powerful." Her mother smiled.

"Wait until she is as old as Opal, you will know the true sense of power then. Although she is more powerful than even I realised."

"Good morning Lord Loxley, I have good news." Captain Rafe smiled as he walked up the yard towards him, his long brown cloak flapped in the soft breeze.

Robbie smiled. "Good morning Captain, what brings a smile to a man's face on such a chilly morning?"

"I have been ordered to Loxley with my men, all woodsmen have been ordered back to defend the new lines that divide us from Knox, if you would permit I would accompany you?"

Robbie nodded. "It will be nice to have the company of other woodsmen along our road. There is danger for everyone now; it will be safer to move in numbers. We will leave in an hour if that is convenient?"

"My men will be thrilled My Lord to escort you, already your own men have greatly impressed mine. I hope they will use this opportunity to learn a great deal from your group, they certainly know their way around trees."

Robbie patted Rafe on the back. "The woodsmen of Loxley lead by example, I am certain your men will learn much."

Robbie watched as Rafe headed to assemble his men, and looked across the fields and trees. The mist swirled and wove in and out of the tree line, and the wood pigeons cooed as they took flight. It was cold but fresh, and he breathed in the freshness of the morning and felt alive. Rune was talking to Rowan and Jade over by the old tool building. "Do we have to ride Rune; I am not made for horses?" Jade rubbed the inside of her legs as she spoke.

"I am sorry Jade but speed is essential." She looked up at Rowan. "I know you know of this place Rowan; it has been made sacred by the Lord Hearne for it protects three treasures of his realm."

Rowan was unsettled. "How can you know of this Rune?" She touched his arm softly.

"My Lord has kept his promise, and they are in his good hands my friend, be happy Rowan for they have joy in knowing of your love for my sister."

Rowan's eyes glistened. "I have no way of knowing how you know this Rune, but I am touched by your words, for it has been in my heart for many weeks now. Have no fear your party will see a safe road." Rune embraced him as Jade watched. Rowan turned and went to prepare the horses.

Jade looked at Rune with a shrewd look. "What was all that about?" Rune smiled sweetly at her.

"Soon you will see all you need to know about your future husband Sis. Trust me for it is his place to show you, now hurry, I have much to prepare as others are all moving towards us."

High on the wild moor on the road to York, the heather seemed to run for miles, broken only occasionally by small groups of silver birch. The track was wide and dusty as the horses slowly pounded the dry earth. The yew bow sung, and the rabbit fell with the white tipped arrow sticking out of its side, Keith handed the bow back to Jaz who was smiling.

"You are right it has a lot of power; you are fortunate to have such quality of trees in your land. We use the rowan bows, as they are supple and give us great power, but you're right about Yew."

"I find it more than a coincidence that both trees hold the power of the spirit world. Maybe that is why the bows of the north are feared so much." Jaz slowed as Keith dropped from his horse and lifted the rabbit up, and tied it to the other five.

Mel came up with her sister. "Tell me Keith, we are curious, why does a man from Settle wear the colours of Loxley on his cloak? I know your father was a bowman there."

Keith smiled as he pulled himself up on to his horse. "I was born in Loxley My Lady and therefore when I earned my cloak, I had the choice, only a fool would not want to wear these colours. I am a true man of Loxley and proud to carry the colours of my Lord Robert."

Una nodded and smiled. "I cannot say fairer than that, so how old are you if your father left twenty years ago?"

"I have served twenty three summers My Lady; I was but three summers when I left my home. I am trained by my father who was trained alongside Lord Robert's Grandfather, I know the ways of a true woodsman, and one day I will return to Loxley and serve my lord from his side."

Saff cantered alongside him. "You have great love for a man you have never met."

"My Lord Loxley is a great man My Lady, he is the centre of our world on this earth, I love my place of birth and therefore I love the man who is the symbol of that place. Lord Loxley is the hooded man returned, and to a woodsman that is very sacred. He is my leader and my example, and I will follow him wherever he needs me."

Jaz smiled at Keith and nodded as he spoke about his lord, he looked back at his mother. "I must confess I am looking forward to meeting him, they say his skill with a bow is unrivalled."

Keith looked across into the eyes of Saff. "When he aims for the head of a rabbit, his arrow will hit the eye; he can guide an arrow to any mark over any distance. He truly is a remarkable bowman." He smiled at her. Saff smiled back at him, and her cheeks turned a little pink. Mel smiled.

"York is there in the distance My Ladies and Gents shall we pick up our pace and be on the doorstep for an evening meal?"

"Well, my trusted Pebbles, I hope you have protected yourself this time?" Robbie smiled at Jade.

"I got two pairs on this time," she whispered, and both Robbie and Rowan laughed aloud. Rune giggled. Robbie took Rowan's hand.

"Take good care of yourselves and be swift my friend, I shall miss you."

Rowan nodded at the gesture. "We will be back quickly Robbie. I will catch you on the road just past old Leicester at some time later tomorrow." He shook Robbie's hand and kicked into the horse, and Jade and Rowan sped off up the lane heading east.

Rune smiled. "Don't look so down they will be watched over."

"They have both become very precious to me Rune. That silent man we met in the woods of Loxley has become a very reliable friend, I must confess, I value Rowan above all the others."

"I see the hole in you has been closed by Rowan, and I am happy to see it Rob, he is truly never going to desert you, and somehow I think neither will Pebbles."

Robbie smiled. "Finally, a few days of quiet." Rune giggled.

"You think so?"

"HEY ROBBIE!" He smiled as Jett came along side wearing her usual big smile. "Is it true your uncle is an undefeated swordsman in Loxley?"

"It is Jett. John is a true master of his craft, and a ferocious warrior; none to date have stood the test of his blade."

"Cool, will he fight me?" Rune smiled.

"I think cousin you should see him fight first, and then decide, there are few who will spar with him."

Robbie pulled up his horse as they came to the top of the hill. Rafe was already at his side, as Martin and John galloped up the hill towards them. He was completely unprepared for what he saw, everyone gasped. The old motorway that had once joined the south and north, and been a busy highway during the times of old modern man, had once again become a connecting corridor. Rune felt the tears in her eyes as she looked across miles upon miles of slow moving carts, and endless streams of tired and exhausted people on foot. Robbie's anger was swift to the surface. "WHAT THE HELL IS THIS RAFE?"

Skip came up at his side and placed his hand on Robbie's arm. "Yelling Robbie is not going to help, this if I am not mistaken is what I expected. These poor people are being driven north by Knox as he clears the south for himself."

Rune looked heart broken. "These are woodsmen... Robbie, we must help them."

The northbound side of the old motorway was full. The south bound remained empty where every so often a guard on horseback in a black vest rode up or down, jeering and shouting at the endless line of refugees. Robbie looked to his men.

"John, Martin what have you seen?" Robbie eyed a man on horseback, as he rode along the line. He pulled out his telescope and pulling it apart, he placed it against his eye.

Martin looked back at the road. "We pulled up under a tunnel a mile up the road, and had a word with a few of them Robbie. All of these people have been cleared from the woods in the south, as they burned everything for building. It appears that about twenty miles up there is a checkpoint, where they are looting all the carts and a lot of people are being killed. They are all afraid of it, but have little choice, going back is not an option for them."

"Really. So, Knox thinks he will hurt my people and destroy the woods does he?" Robbie turned to Rafe. "How many horsemen do you have?"

"I have about six My Lord."

"Skip we need a plan for these people, you take the cart and join the convoy, work out what you can. Rafe I need to borrow three of your horses, and two of your best bowmen, as well as yourself. Harry, Blades, Fish, Smokes, Mother, mount up. Rafe would one of your men drive the cart?"

Rafe gave his orders, and Bowman Ramsay rode up to him. Jett winked at him and he smiled very sheepishly at her, another of his bowman galloped up with three empty horses. Robbie turned in his saddle and viewed the countryside around. "Rafe get all your footmen into the carts in the convoy. It will be slow going but that will give us time to get up to this checkpoint and have a look at what they are doing. Let your men know to hold their bows until they see our attack; I do not want them having any idea we are here until the very last moment, stealth will save our people."

All the horses moved off the road into the field, as the cart with Skip and Fuse inside made its way along the road towards the junction that joined the convoy. The woodsmen of Avon slipped down through the trees and crept up to the side of the road. They slipped quickly in amongst the convoy, and joined the refugees who smiled and welcomed them, the word Robin Hood was in the area soon spread up the line. Many in the convoy pulled hidden bows out from under seats or from the insides of bedding in the carts.

Robbie turned on his horse and smiled at Rune. "Well, My Lady Loxley, your wish will come true, let's try and help our people." He winked and she beamed at him.

"You are a good man My Lord." She blew him a kiss and everyone smiled. He kicked his legs, and his horse raced north across the fields, as everyone fell in behind him.

On the edge of Misterton across the road, a large barricade had been built. Long rows of huts lined the south side of the old motorway where a barracks had been set up. There was a set of stables and a long row of wooden carts, which were being used to store the looted goods. Men in black vests laughed and jeered as they stopped the carts, and threw people off on to the road. They searched the carts, and took any precious items out of them, and threw them into the long line of empty carts. Women cried as they were robbed, and any who tried to stop them were beaten or stabbed and thrown off the road and left to die. Down the embankment was a gully, filled with the dead and dying, wounded by the Cutters. The carts that passed through were filled with women who cried and sobbed, as they drew away. Young women were dragged from the carts, and raped in front of their families as their relatives, were powerless to stop them. They were surrounded by laughing and taunting evil guards. Rune wept as she sat in the trees with Robbie and waited for their cart to appear.

Rune could feel the anger starting to boil inside him, as Robbie watched in horror and he clenched his fists. There was a rage building inside him, as he saw the slaughter and brutality inflicted on the people of his realm first hand.

Progress was slow and the cart had taken almost two hours. Robbie looked through his scope as it appeared, and he smiled. He gave the hand signals and his people moved into action. Harry, Jett, and Blades, slipped with Rafe, Pete, and Ruby, into the low bushes that skirted the barrier along the old motorway. Bear signaled with Ramsay and Bowman Peters from across the other side.

Alice and Steph dried their eyes, as they took up position in the trees to Robbie's right. Martin and John nodded as they raised their bows ready to the left. Rune fitted her arrow and stood next to Robbie. A young woman screamed, as she was pulled by her hair across the road by a laughing Cutter. He pushed her on to the floor tearing her clothes. She scrambled and fought to hide her nakedness screaming with terror. He forced her down with his foot as she punched and wailed, her mother watched helpless and wept, sobbing in grief from the cart, as another Cutter drew his sword and threatened her. The Cutter undid his pants as the girl below fought with horror in her eyes.

Robbie glanced at Rune. "You do the honours." She smiled, and raised her bow.

As he slid down his pants and laughed, the arrow struck deep, and he screamed with all his might as he collapsed to the floor. "Won't be using that again." Rune breathed as she reloaded. John and Martin winced in the trees. The Cutter who was threatening the mother met Robbie's swift arrow and fell back on to the road.

Robbie looked back at the satisfied smile on Rune's face. "You know you have quite an evil side, don't you?"

From all directions, arrows sung. A loud bell rang out as the swordsmen moved swiftly under the carts and into the centre of the road. More men in black vests appeared, they met the onslaught of Jett and Blades, with Harry, who had been forced to sit and watch for over an hour. Their fury was unmatched as they worked with speed and hatred. The people in the carts huddled together and watched with shock, yet they knew also they were about to be saved. Armed woodsmen rose up out of their hiding places in the long row of carts, and fired covering the swordsmen in support of the hooded man.

Blades bounced, somersaulting into the air and landed in the centre of four Cutters. She whooped and screamed, with each surgical movement of her two flashing swords that glinted like lightening with her strokes. She spun to a standstill and looked at two others who approached her, as four lay dead, her cold blue eyes radiated her anger, and fear rose in the hearts of the Cutters.

Men in the carts were pulling weapons from any hidden storage space, and they dropped on to the road and screamed with rage, as they ran to the aid of the Specialists. Guards in the trees ran down to the road and met the onslaught of woodsmen who had suffered the inhumanity of days on the road. They fought hard and with pride to know that although their life in the south was no more, they had a future in the north with the hooded man.

Harry ran screaming into one of the barrack huts. There were bangs, smashes, and terrified screams, windows smashed as Cutters came flying through them. Bear dropped down off the roof and wrung necks as he walked along finishing Harry's work for him. Harry came out of the door wiping his blades and smiled at Bear. "Hey man, it's like totally cool how they built these huts. Man, they have hardly used a screw."

From the hut beside them, a huge mountain of a man in black leather stepped out, with a sword double the size of Harry's. He leered, as he looked round to see who was disturbing the camp. Bear smiled and pushed Harry in the chest, shoving him back. "This one's mine, they let the freak off the leash." He smiled at Harry.

"Whoa Bear dude, that is like funky and most totally cosmic, but whoa he is one big ugly dude, dude."

Bear drew out the sword of courage, and walked slowly towards the monster of a man. Alice in the trees swung her bow to cover him. "Oh, Mickie please be careful," she whispered as her bow trembled. She flew down the bank and on to the road and climbed up on top of one the carts and took aim covering him.

Bear bowed to the huge man, which completely threw him, and he stopped. He thought for a moment and then he bowed back. "I do like manners with sword play, don't you?" Bear smiled with bright white teeth. He waved his palm low. "Shall We?" Bear flexed his arm and the golden sword spun in his hand.

The giant leather clad Cutter gave a huge roar and Alice cringed, as he raised his long sword and swung it with all his might at Bear. The giant brought down a smashing blow with his sword, and Bear sidestepped out of the way. It angered the huge man who swung his blade angrily at Bear. The sword of courage chimed loud as it made contact, and deflected the massive sword away, he spun on the spot and the sword flashed in the sun, as it whipped up slicing the shoulder of the huge man. He screamed a roaring scream of anger and pain.

"Whoa man, you makin him very unkarmic, his vibes is not happenin." Harry wagged his finger stood far to the side of Bear.

The huge man lunged at Bear as his rage intensified; he swung wildly from left to right and up and down, as he tried to hit the weaving Bear who deflected each stroke with his bright golden sword. Alice watched from the cart holding her breath. "That's more like it my beast of a friend now we are fencing." Bear laughed, and for a large man he was surprisingly very agile. The blows crashed on to his blade, but his own strength absorbed the impact and he smiled with the pleasure of a good strong opponent.

Two men ran round the corner of one of the huts towards Bear, they met Harry and fell dead. "Hey man I am like totally watching this, don't be un-peaceful like."

Jett's whoops and screams echoed across the roadway, as Rafe and her, headed into the crowds pouring out of another two billets. Arrows streamed across from the carts as the bowmen of Avon picked off any guards not close to a swordsman. Her dark eyes shone brightly, as with each scream her blade shot into an opponent, and shot out as she dealt her surgical strikes of death.

Robbie and Rune rushed out of the bushes with John and Martin. They ducked under the barrier at the side of the road shooting as they went, and into the centre of the road. Robbie snatched the young crying girl off the road, as John and Rune took out two men running at him with swords. He ran to the carts and passed her up to her mother, he slipped off his hood. "Care for her, she has had the fright of her life, but she is lucky."

The older woman looked down as he pulled back his hood. "Are you him?"

Robbie nodded. "I am my good lady."

Tears ran from her eyes. "Bless you Robin Hood, I owe you her life."

"You owe me nothing; honour my men by living your lives, for they have spilled blood to ensure it." Robbie turned and pulled up his bow and fired at a Cutter lunging towards Flash. He fell dead and she beamed as she spun like a top her white pole a blur.

"I love you Robin Hood." Black vests folded either side of her as her poles snapped and battered in the middle of the circle of Cutters.

Jett's sword moved so quickly it was hard to tell who had been hit and who had not. Cutters fell in her path as she moved with the force of a twister across the plains. Bodies flung out either side of her, and screams of delight, cheers, and whoops emitted from the centre. Her hair rose in the air as she spun round on her golden heels, the sword glinting like a star above a ballerina of death. Blades pranced cat like, across to her side, and covered her left. Rafe who was surprisingly good with a sword covered her right, and the three of them worked with pinpoint accuracy together towards the billet.

Robbie and his bow team now slowed the pace as they singled out targets from the ever decreasing crowd of Cutters. There were quite a few who ran into the trees and the arrows of Ramsay and Peters sent them falling back down through the scrub, and on to the road. The men of the carts took the rest, and the guards tumbled down out of the leaves and through the grass on to the cold hard road.

Most of the Cutters lay dead or dying, Robbie looked coldly at the man who rolled on the floor blood pouring down his legs as he writhed in pain. "Finish me!" He screamed at Rune. She looked at the young girl who was now wrapped in a blanket to hide her nakedness. The young girl nodded, and Rune looked him in the eyes.

"Before you die you will remember the pain you have caused in this world." Rune's eyes flared a bright deep purple. The man snatched his head in his blood-covered hands, and screamed as if every terror and pain he had ever caused was inflicted on him at once. Robbie felt a cold shiver run down his back, and his goose bumps rose as he saw for the first time, the side of Nature that can devastate and destroy.

The Cutter jerked on the floor, and with one last blood curdling cry, he flopped limp to the ground. Rune's eyes faded back to blue, and two tears dropped from her eyes to the ground where violets instantly sprung up. She walked silently back to Robbie and slid her arms around him. "I took no pleasure from that." He pulled her close and held her tight as she wept into his shoulder. Robbie stared at the man who still wore a look of total fear in death.

Jett and Blades leaned on the wall watching Rafe as he fought off three Cutters. Jett smiled. "I find him quite sexy with a sword in his hand."

Blades chuckled. "He is kinda cute, I must admit." Rafe spun round as the last Cutter fell and he smiled, Jett and Blades grinned back and clapped. He walked slowly over a little breathless and gave a slight bow.

"Thank you my good ladies, I am honoured to have fought beside such truly gifted blades."

Jett seized him roughly by the front of his cloak, and kissed him hard. "God that was sexy."

Rafe was suddenly lost for words, and became a little embarrassed. He smiled. "I am glad you appreciated it My Lady Jett." He looked across to Bear who was still fighting the huge monster of a Cutter with a huge smile on his face. Martin and John appeared out of the billet next to Harry, who was sat with his feet up on a box, watching Bear fight.

"Brew time everyone." Martin put down the tray on a large barrel, and handed Harry a mug. Jett and Blades scampered over, and grabbed a cup and sat crossed legged on the floor next to Harry. Flash sat on Harry's knee and sipped her tea.

Rafe looked very concerned, as Robbie walked over with Rune. "Shouldn't we help him?" Robbie looked surprised.

"Oh, Hearne no, it would really upset him." He pointed to Alice who still held her bow up. "He has cover should he need it." John handed Robbie and Rune a drink, Martin passed one to Rafe.

The casual way in which they worked was difficult to understand, Rafe looked round at the devastation they had caused in wonder. The speed and efficiency at which they had worked had been something he had tried to train his woodsmen to do for years. Here was a small outfit that had done the work of a hundred men in less than an hour. It was staggering. Rune touched his hand and smiled. "These are the best of Loxley, you will get used to it, relax and enjoy your drink, we will have a lot of cleaning up to do when Bear has finished."

Bear swung high and fast; another large gash appeared on the roaring mountain of a man in front of him. He stepped back as the huge man lunged, and Bear went for the kill. The sword of courage sunk deep on the end of his upper cut, and the massive man let out a surprised groan. Bear drove the sword deep, and then pulled back with the blade. The huge Cutter swayed as Bear stepped back, and then fell backwards on to the dusty road with a heavy thump, his sword clattered to the ground. A round of applause broke out as Bear smiled and bowed. Alice shot down the road, and ran at high speed towards him, and leapt into his arms, and he pulled her close and held her as she trembled looking very pale indeed.

The huge figure suddenly sat up behind them with a roar. Two cups smashed on the road, as two arrows swished through the air. Both hit the Cutter in the head and he slammed back into the floor. Alice's head snapped round as Robbie and Rune stood side by side their bows still raised and reloaded. Two broken cups of tea lay on the floor, Rafe had a huge look of surprise on his face, never in his life had he seen such speed with a bow.

Jett came up smiling with two more cups. "Close your mouth, and chill out Rafe, you are with the hooded man and his love now." Rune smiled and took her cup and sipped it.

Robbie walked down the centre of the road, and surveyed the men stood either side of the high banking. "Are we secure?" The men of Avon now lined the trees either side of the road, and signalled the all clear to him as he walked, Robbie looked at all the frightened people in the carts. He climbed up on to the barrier, and shouted down the long line. "We will escort you to safety, but first we must clean this area up, any man who can lift we need your help please come forward."

Robbie walked back up to the huts as men came down the road; Rune and Alice directed the operation of having all of the bodies dragged into the huts. Harry and Bear fitted teams of horses to the empty carts, and Blades and Jett organised the women to collect all the used arrows, then the weapons that were thrown into a large cart.

Two dozen empty carts sat teamed with horses and Robbie arranged all of those on foot to climb in. He allotted drivers, and then when they were almost ready, he pulled Skip, Fuse, and Maggs, in their cart to the front of the queue. Harry climbed up as Maggs smothered him in huge wet sloppy kisses. She struck a heavy tune on her rattling bracelets and bangles. "You are such a huge big brave Harry pops." Rune and Alice roared with laughter behind the cart.

"Whoa thanks Chicken." Harry went a little red.

John, Martin, Fish, and Rafe lit their arrows, and fired them into the huts filled with the dead. The flames leapt into the air as the checkpoint roared into flame, and everyone in the carts cheered. Ramsey and Peters walked up with their horses and the whole group mounted up. Robbie looked down the long line of carts, he sat on his horse as the flames roared behind him; Rune came up at his side.

Robbie gave the signal, and Harry flicked the reins, and the carts all rolled forward. Robbie turned to Rune. "Don't ever tell me how you did that to that Cutter." She smiled a sad smile.

"He saw everything evil through the eyes of those who he had done it to, it was not pleasant for me or him, but he died knowing how responsible he was."

Robbie shuddered. "Remind me never to anger you." She smiled at him.

"You are the one person in this whole world I have not got the power to hurt, I love you too much." Robbie gave a warm loving smile to her.

"Come on beautiful, we have homes to find, and people to house."

Rowan and Jade reached the edge of the trees and slowed to a halt. Rowan slipped down on to the ground and looked around; he crouched as he checked the path for signs of others. His horse walked to the lake edge, and began to drink from the gently lapping water. Jade slid down on to the ground and stretched her legs "Where is this place Rowan?"

He stood up, and looked across the lake and then turned to her. "This place is special to me Jade. This is Rutland, and this was until recently, my home."

Jade was very surprised. "This is your home?" She knew that Rowan was finally going to reveal the truth behind his sadness, and she was suddenly very nervous. She slid her arms around him and held him tight; he gazed at the old oak stump as he squeezed her. Rowan then took her hand in his and walked into the trees. She noticed how similar to Loxley wood they were, her heart beat faster as she felt the tension in Rowan rise. He wove through the trees knowing every inch as well as she knew Loxley, and she saw the excitement of being back home in his slate grey eyes.

Rowan led her down a path that arched as the trees met above her, to the clearing that was surrounded by a curtain of white light; she felt the power of Hearne in the air as he stopped. Jade looked across the clearing at the burned down wooden house, and three mounds of earth with wooden crosses. She felt his tear as it dripped on her hand, Jade squeezed it, as tears ran to her own eyes. Together they stepped through the curtain of light and into the clearing, Rowan's pace was slow as they approached the graves. He sniffled as he stopped before them, Jade looked at the three carved crosses bearing the names of his family. Rowan's voice was strained and soft, and Jade felt her heartbreak as he spoke, and she squeezed his hand.

"Father, Mother this is Lady Jade Opal from Avon. I have asked her to be my wife."

Jade looked at the two large mounds. The carven crosses bore the names of Ben Shires and Rose Avalon Shires. Rowan fell to his knees at the small grave beside them and wept. Jade slowly lowered herself down to the tiny grave with a small bow, and two small arrows lay on it. The small cross bore the name of Willow Shires. She pulled Rowan into her arms as he wept and as her own eyes poured tears, she rocked him gently in her arms. How long she was there, she was not sure, she just knew that Rowan had opened his world to the woman he loved, and she was overwhelmed. Now she understood the sadness of the quiet man of the woods, who had attracted her from the moment she had met him. She had felt his pain many times, but seeing the reason was heartbreaking.

Her love for him was huge, and yet as she sat there, she felt it grow stronger, and as he fell silent, she held him close. Jade noticed the two small violets growing in the grass, next to the ring of white daisies. "Rune has been here with Lord Hearne, she protects your family Rowan."

He lifted his head, and wiped his eyes on his sleeve and looked at the ground where the two violets grew. "I knew she had, when she told me of this place."

The breeze blew past him and whispered to him. "I am Runestone and your family are blessed, and in the care of our noble lord." He looked up at the trees, and Jade smiled as the breeze passed her face.

"That is a pretty cool sister I have Rowan."

He smiled and turned to her. "My real name is Dirk Shires of Rutland, and I have become Rowan of the woods, in the service of my Lord Hearne." He raised himself up on one knee. "I love you Jade Opal, and as both Dirk and Rowan I would have you to be my wife and share a life of the woods with me."

The smile on her face could not be wider, and the love in her smouldering green eyes could not be more. She slid her arms around him and kissed him. "I love you Rowan, and will have you by my side always, yes I will marry you." Rowan's face broke into a smile and he pulled her close and held her tight.

They spent the day walking around the woods, Jade shot four rabbits, and dug up earth apples, and soon they sat by the lake, cooked a meal, and talked. Rowan told her the story of his life and how he grew up here in the woods, after his family had fled from Egleton when he was just two. His father had been a military man, and his mother a natural history teacher. His family line was ancient and his uncle had fled at the same time, although he had no idea where.

He undid one of the woollen ties on his wrist, and tied it around Jade's. "My mother made these for me; she made me one for every birthday." Jade smiled as she looked at the thin woven band of red threads on her wrist. She pulled him into a huge hug.

Rowan still found it hard to talk about Willow. He felt huge pain that something so pure and so beautiful could have been slaughtered by anyone. Jade sat quiet and listened, a warm soft smile on her face as she watched his every facial movement while he spoke. His long shiny black hair with two fine plaits in front, hung as he spoke in quiet tones, his head slightly lowered. He had not said so many words in all the time she had known him, and she loved the sound of his voice as it washed over her.

The day seemed to drift away as Jade was absorbed into the life and the land of Rowan of the woods. Sat with her legs crossed by the crackling fire and the bubbling pan smiling, as she listened to the softly spoken man, she would spend the rest of her days with.

The sound of horses brought them to attention. A small butterfly landed on Rowan's shoulder and his tension eased. "They are here." He stood up as the party of three came around the corner, Rowan bowed. "My Ladies, you have made good time."

Jade smiled at Madeleine. "We have a meal ready if you are hungry?" Maddy gasped and slid down from her horse, she walked round to Jade and embraced her.

"You look like your sister, Jade of Avon."

Jade shrugged. "Her bums smaller than mine," and she smiled at Alley who gave her a broad grin. "Nice hat, got one just like it at Loxley."

The two girls dismounted and Jade made all the necessary introductions, especially since there were three very good looking women around her, she introduced Rowan as, 'my intended' just to be sure everyone understood. He smiled and placed his arm around her.

Rowan discussed Robbie with Maddy, as Jade and Alley washed the wooden plates in the lake after the meal. She could see the family connection with herself in Jade and both of them laughed about it. Alley had long sleek blonde hair and the same green eyes, whereas Jade's hair tended to be the same length and colour, just very curly with her sheep dog like fringe. Alley wore a pale lilac silk top with a long tan waistcoat and tight fitting leather pants, her cloak was a very dark green and her hat like Jade's was stiffened velvet. She was witty and fun and Jade could not help but warm to her.

Alley loved the fact that Jade wore the uniform of a Loxley woodsman, and especially loved her cloak with the Loxley crest. "I get away with the pants, but mother always wants me to wear dresses. I hate them." Jade giggled.

"My mum gave up trying years ago." Treen was quieter, but as she got use to Jade, she began to open up a little more. As they sat on their horses and followed Rowan, she began to ask questions in her heavy French accent.

"What eez the hooded man really like? I believe that he and Rune are together are they no?"

Jade smiled at her. "He is my best friend and I have grown up with him. Robbie is pretty cool, all the woman fancy him like mad, even I did until I met Rowan. He is very kind, and really clever. Everyone around him loves him; you would not think he is a lord because he is so cool. He loves Rune and it does not half show, you should see the way they look at each other. I reckon he is sex mad, they spent days alone in bed together back at the castle."

Rowan could not help but laugh, as he heard Jade making sure that these women stayed well clear of her sister's man. Treen seemed suitably put off, and Jade was pleased with her work. Alley smiled at her, it seemed she understood Jade's protection of Robbie and Rune.

As the sun fell and darkness increased, the long line of wagons trundled on. Horses were tied to the backs of carts, and the group took it in shifts to sleep.

Harry and Maggs curled together in the back of their cart, and Bear and Alice sat up front and drove. Robbie and Rune slipped under the heavy cover of a cart loaded with boxes of tinned food, and made a bed out of blankets and cuddled up, Jett talked endlessly to Rafe as she drove.

The slow movement and extra guards gave them the opportunity to keep moving, and so as the night wore on the convoy of refugees moved on following the road north. By dawn, they were past Leicester and moving towards Nottingham.

Maggs had the steel basin in the back of the cart stood on four thick wooden blocks. She had rolled back the canvass and lit a fire in it. Steph sat on the backboard swinging her legs as Maggs fried deep chunks of salted boar, and made thick bacon like sandwiches. She poured out the coffee and Steph slipped off the back and took the tray. Robbie leaned down as Rune drove and lifted the tray up, as Steph swung herself up on to the seat beside him. "Talk about fast food." She smiled at Robbie. "Modern world joke, you won't get it."

They took it in turns holding the reins, so each could bite their sandwich in turn and Robbie sat back feeling full, he waved to Maggs and patted his stomach, she gave him a huge horsy smile and nodded rapidly, they could hear her jewellery jangle. "She is very sweet really, isn't she?" Rune smiled trying to swallow without laughing. Steph put her head down.

"Maggs is very much an acquired taste Robbie, I have known her for a long time and she is without doubt one of the kindest people I have ever come across. She has been a good friend in the past, you have no idea how important to her Harry is. I know he is not everyone's cup of tea, but he is your uncle and you love him as much as I do, so you will at least understand her."

Robbie smiled and nodded. "He is completely bonkers, but yes I love Harry dearly."

"Well then Robbie, you understand how easy it was for him to fall in love with Maggs."

Rune leaned forward chuckling. "You mean Harry loves her because he thinks she is bonkers, how can he think that, has he not looked in a mirror lately?"

Steph shoulders shook as she looked across at Rune's look of utter disbelief. "Harry thinks calling him Mad Harry is a joke darling. He does not realise that everyone actually believes he is. Harry cannot see anything similar in his behaviour compared to Maggs, he loves the fact that she is wacky, he thinks it is cute."

"No offence Mum, I know he is your friend, but even you have to admit the man is a total loon. How can he not see it?"

"We all see the world through different eyes Runestone, whose eyes would you prefer to look through, those of Robbie's, or those of Knox, because both of them think their world is better. Harry is Harry and he loves Maggs, you go and tell her Harry is mad, and you watch a woman defend her man. Love brings out the best in all of us Rune." Rune sat back in thought, Maggs waved to Bear and Alice as they rode past to relieve the front guard. "Good morrow darlings."

Bear waved. "Good morning good lady." Maggs beamed from the back of the cart and Rune smiled.

Jett woke up next to Rafe under the cover and smiled, she leaned over him as he slept and kissed him softly on the cheek. She scrambled up the crates, and pushed her head out of the top of the canvass and looked down at Robbie, Rune and Steph. She leaned over, and took the coffee out of Robbie's hand, and took a big swig. "Erg no sugar!" She passed it back. "HEY MAGGS, ANY MORE COFFEE?" Robbie almost jumped out of his seat, and Rune and Steph laughed. Jett looked down. "Sorry Rob... any of you lot seen my pants?" Robbie reached under the seat and passed them up to her. "Cheers Rob."

"Please tell me Jett that my Captain is still alive." Jett smiled down at him.

"Told you, I don't eat them till the third date." She slid back under the canvass.

Robbie looked at Rune; her eyes sparkled with bright radiance. "There is definitely some link between your lots powers, and wild sexual behaviour."

She beamed at him. "I hope that's not a complaint Robbie pops?" He smiled at her and slid his arm round her.

"Oh, I can assure you it's not." Steph winked at Rune as she slipped off to get Jett and Rafe their coffee. Muffled giggles came from under the canvass, and Robbie banged on the side of the cart. "Time for duty Captain."

Rune giggled. "Spoil sport."

Robbie leaned back and smiled, as happy memories passed through his head.

CHAPTER SIX

HOMECOMINGS

David Williams walked slowly along the top of the gate, his blue eyes scanned down the valley at the approaching cloud of dust. Henry leaned forward with his telescope. "I think sir it's that scruffy cheeky kid who brings the letters, she has another scruffy kid with her."

David Williams smiled for the first time in days, as he slapped Henry on the back. "She is called Rags, and I think she is a little marvel... OPEN THE GATES!"

He spun on the ladder and slipped down into the compound, as the large gates swung open, the sounds of hooves grew louder as the horse belted into the compound, and slid to a halt. Rags beamed a smile at him as she threw her leg over the back of the horse and slipped off. "Hey Davie, you saw me comin I see?" Rags opened her bag and smiled. "You getting popular Davie, there is two today."

He pulled her into a huge hug as he smiled. "I am happy to see you my little scruffy friend, it was a bit hairy last time you left."

"Don't tell me you were worried about little old Rags here?" She gave a cheeky grin.

"Who is your companion? I thought you only delivered letters?" He looked up at the small blonde girl sat up on the horse.

"That's my sis Lucy, I am training her as a postie." David looked concerned.

"She is very young Rags, should she be out on the road on her own?"

"Don't be silly Davie boy, she rides with me, I am not letting me only family ride off on her own, you mad or what?"

David laughed, and grabbed her and threw her back on the horse. "Get yourself up to Jess she has quite a surprise for you." Rags smiled at him and pulled her horse round to the inside gates that had now swung open.

"See ya Davie boy." She kicked the horse and with lightning speed she flew up the road towards the fourteen cottages and the Lox Farm.

Bags clattered on to the cobbled path at the farm gate, as Rags slowed him down and she came up to the side of the house. The kitchen door banged, as Jess came running out to greet her. "Oh Michelle you made it safely, I was so worried."

Rags slipped down, and Jess pulled her into a hug. "Hi Miss Lox, I told you not to worry, I am the best Lord Robert demands it."

"And who do we have here?" Jess helped Lucy down off the horse, and looked down at the shy scruffy little blonde girl.

"This is me sis Lucy, I am keeping her with me, she is all I have for a family, so I thought I would train her up as another postie for Lord Robert."

Jess smiled as she crouched down. "Hi Lucy, my name is Jess, welcome to Loxley."

Lucy made a little curtsy, and said very quietly. "Good day My Lady." Rags beamed at her sister and back at Jess.

"I taught her that, thought it better she was more refined, and not rough like me."

Jess smiled. "Well I think baths and meals are required, but first I have a surprise." She took Lucy by the hand and led her and Rags round the corner of the house and over towards the barn where a new log cabin stood. Rags stared at the sign above the door. 'Loxley Postal Service.'

Jess opened the door and led Lucy inside. The front room was very small, there was a counter of highly polished wood, with a hatch to lift and walk through. The wall behind was full of pigeonholes for sorting the post, and there was a small desk with red tallow candles and an official looking stamp, Rags picked it up and looked at it. It had the seal of Lord Loxley on it with 'Loxley Postal Service' written around the edge.

Jess opened a little inkpad and pulled a clean sheet of paper on to the desk, and holding Rags hand she pressed it into the ink and them stamped the paper. The postal crest of Loxley was printed clearly on the paper. Rags felt the tears rise in her eyes. Jess smiled. "The people round here will bring you their letters and pay you one brass to deliver it, you stamp as proof of payment. When your riders come in you will have enough money to feed them."

She pushed the door in the back of the wall, and Rags looked into the small room with a table and chairs and a brick fire. "You will live here when you are not with Robbie, and there are two extra rooms with bunk beds to rest your riders." Rags stepped through and looked at the small house with pictures on the wall, and a cupboard with a large vase of fresh flowers on it.

Lucy ran across to a comfortable chair and sat down. "Is this home now Michelle?"

Rags turned to Jess and buried her head in her apron as she wept and sobbed. Jess patted her softly on the back. "Come on now Michelle don't be upset love."

Rags lifted her tearful face. "Robbie is the nicest man alive and now I know why." Jess bent down and hugged her.

"No one should live on the road Michelle; we all need a place to call home. It's not much but it's a start."

"It's beautiful, it's the most wonderful home a girl could have." Jess smiled and kissed her on the head.

"Settle yourself in with your sister and I will sort out a bath, when you're ready come over to the house and have something to eat, and tell me about my son."

Rags sniffled as she nodded. "Thanks Miss Lox." Jess smiled as she left them to discover the wonder of a new home.

A very clean and well dressed Lucy sat smiling at the table as she spooned yet another bowl of stew into her mouth. Rags sat smiling, as she talked with Jess and Robert. Len sat quietly listening and Beth chuckled with delight as Rags described in every detail the attack on the cathedral. She waved her arms about and made a deep voice as she impersonated Robbie. "You dare put a murderer on the throne of England? Speak quickly my arrow grows impatient." Beth put her hands to her mouth and Robert smiled with pride, and Jess just sat with a soft contented smile on her face glad to know her son was alive.

John walked in and Rags hesitated, she looked up at him nervously as she slid a letter across the table to him. "I want no trouble Mister; I just deliver em." John roared with laughter as he took the letter.

"I promise you postie, I will kick the cat if needs be, you are safe, have no fear."

Rags recounted the story of Billy's ear and John roared with laughter. "That's my girl," and he slapped the table. It was a long night, and John carried the small sleeping figure of Lucy across to the Postal Office, he laid the small girl on the bottom bunk and smiled as he came out of the room. "My Alice was always the same, good meal and fast asleep. I put her to bed every night and tucked her in, I miss it."

Rags smiled. "Thanks John." He patted her on the shoulder.

"You done good Rags, Jessie misses him a lot, you set her mind at rest and I appreciate that, she will be fine for a week now." He put two brass bits on the table. "That's what I owe you for the last two letters. I will have more tomorrow; good night Rags sleep well."

The large frame of John Lox walked out of the room through the counter, and pulled the door quietly behind him. Rags sat by her flickering new fire and looked around at her new home. She got up and walked to the small door of her bedroom. There was a little bed with a thick quilted duvet and small pillows. A small wardrobe stood open in the corner. Fresh new clean clothes hung on wooden hangers, and on the back of the door was a blue cloak with the embroidered Loxley Postal Service crest on it.

Rags sat on the bed, and pulled a small neatly folded hand drawn picture of two people out of her shirt. "Mum, Dad, we are safe now." She pulled the picture to her heart and she began to weep.

The little house on the cliff top had its windows rattled as the wind and rain drove against it with a fierce power. The geraniums down each side of the small path danced and bobbed about fighting the bad weather. The sea roared and crashed as it pounded onto the beach far below the cliff, the small white gate banged as she ran through it dripping wet, and hammered on the door with her tiny fist.

"Uncle Seth... Oh Uncle Seth please let me in." She thumped heavily on the wooden door.

The door swung open, and light spilled out past the tired old face of Seth Hargreaves. He looked at her with surprise. "Judith sweetheart, how the hell did you get here?"

She flung herself into his arms and cried with long bitter painful tears of grief. "My mother is dead; I have run away." Her small shaking body dripped on the mat as he pulled her tight, a look of surprise and pain mixed on his old lined face. He lifted his weeping niece as she sobbed into his arms and she dripped, soaked to the skin and shivering, and he kicked the door shut with a loud bang.

Mason slammed down his fist on the table. Lance jumped with fear. "WHAT DO YOU MEAN RUN AWAY?"

Lance shook nervously, his pale eyes wide. "She just went in the night father, we searched everywhere, but we could not find her."

Mason glared at the tall man stood by the door. "YOU WERE SUPPOSED TO PROTECT THEM, WERE THE HELL WERE YOU?"

The house servant shook with fear. "My Lord, I can assure you." Mason pulled out his revolver and fired, the servant slumped to the floor. He turned to Billy.

"We must find the ungrateful bitch; she was always trouble just like her bloody mother."

Mason put down the smoking revolver, and poured a glass of scotch with his bandaged hand, and scowled at the shaking figure of Lance. "Get out of here, go with your older brother and see if you can find her." Lance scuttled across the room, and Billy put his arm across his younger brother's shoulders as he left the room.

"Come on bro, he is in pain, he will calm down in a bit."

"I didn't know honestly Billy. I was so scared I looked everywhere."

Billy pulled his brother close. "Don't worry kid we will find her, she can't have gone far in five days."

"In coming riders." Robbie turned back on his horse as five horses galloped across the fields towards the road. He smiled and kicked his horse on to meet them, Robbie clattered up the slip road towards the point where he knew Rowan would enter the road. Rune spurred her horse forward, and followed and beamed as she saw Jade next to Rowan waving madly as they approached the bridge.

Robbie dropped off his horse as Rowan came to a halt and dropped down smiling. "You said outside Leicester, this is way past Nottingham." He threw his arms around Rowan and greeted him with joy.

Rune ran up and threw her arms around Jade. "Why were you blocking me? I was so worried about you."

"Hey Sis, we got stuck across the other side of Nottingham, we think the Dark One was there, so Maddy and me blocked you to keep us safe from her."

Rune hugged her tighter. "Smart thinking, I am glad to just have both of you back." She turned to Rowan and hugged him as Robbie pulled Jade close.

"Won't you introduce your guests Pebbles?"

Jade turned and smiled. "Oh yeah this is Maddy, Treen and Alley, they are from France and can talk to each other funny."

Madeleine came forward and held out her hand. "Lord Loxley, I am so honoured to meet you at last, I am Madeleine Du Luc of Morbihan, and these are my daughters, Citrine Chalcedony, and Alexandrite Topaz." He took her hand and kissed it, he found the effect rivalled that of Bears.

Robbie nodded to the two young women who smiled shyly, and they came forward and kissed him on both cheeks. "Oh yeah Robbie, watch out for that, they do it a lot." Jade looked cautiously at him.

Rune walked up and smiled at Maddy. "Aunt Madeleine." She pulled her into a hug. "Welcome to our family, it is nice to finally meet you in person."

"Runestone my child you cannot know what this means to us." Maddy turned to the two women. "Come girls and meet your cousin Runestone." The two came forward and Rune smiled and hugged them, their eyes glowed on contact with her. They too kissed her on both cheeks.

Jade looked at Robbie. "That worries me a lot more than you would think." She smiled.

Robbie pulled himself up on to his horse next to Rowan. "We have food and drinks you must be tired and hungry." He turned and slapped Rowan on the back. "Tell me of your journey my friend." Rune and Jade walked with the others to the long stream of carts that approached them as she explained what had happened. Harry slowed the cart as the women boarded, and John and Martin slipped off the back and tied their horses on. The cart moved on with a small lurch, and Robbie and Rowan rode on ahead as they talked.

A rider in a black vest came galloping down the other side of the road towards them. He suddenly realised the riders were not Knox soldiers and slid to a halt, as he turned, the arrow hit him and he fell to the ground. Bear galloped up with Fish on the back of his horse, he cantered up to the side of the rider less horse and Fish jumped across on to the back of it. He pulled the reins and the horse came around. He ran at the barrier and the horse jumped over, he came smiling towards

Robbie and Rowan. "We are getting quite a collection, nearly every woodsman has a horse, you would have thought by now the message would be out."

Robbie chuckled at him. "I am sure Fish soon they will know, but I feel it is too late, the divide line is only twenty miles away and then we will be in woodsman controlled territory and I will feel relieved."

It was several hours later when the long line of wagons pulled to a halt. There was a large bridge across the motorway, which had been fortified with heavy wooden gates. Bowmen lined the top of the bridge. Harry looked left and right to see hundreds of bowmen stood in the trees, all of which pointed their bows at him. Martin came up on his horse. "What is the problem Harry, why are the gates closed?"

"Hey man some dude up there told me to stop and stay still." Harry looked from left to right. "This aint cosmic man I don't like heavy attitude when I was feelin mellow and peaceful."

Martin turned to the gates. "Open in the name of Lord Loxley." Bear came riding up with John as the voices above jeered; he looked up at the bridge as he passed Martin slowly.

"Who here is in charge, I would speak with him on a matter of his own personal safety." More laughter came down from the bridge as Bear slid off his horse. He walked towards the gates and he felt the bow strings tighten as he approached. A large window was cut in the heavy wooden gate; he looked through at the face of a woodsman. "Who is in charge here?"

The man looked up at him, down his long arrogant nose. "That would be me."

"I am Jacques Michael Phillips the Ambassador to York and I travel with my lord to Loxley, open these gates and allow passage, these people are tired and have suffered on their journey here."

"I have my orders, and I do not open the gate to any, this land is now sealed at the orders of Loxley."

"Please Sir you miss understand me, My Lord is asleep which is good for you at this moment, but believe me, you will not want to waylay these people. My Lord will be angry if I wake him and tell him that his land is closed to him because some arrogant fool has neither the wit nor intelligence to see his grave error."

The woodsman at the side of the arrogant chief saw the crest of Loxley on Bears cloak; he tapped his chief on the shoulder. "Sir?"

"Not now Haden can you not see I am busy." He scowled through the window at Bear. "I could just drop my hand and you would be dead; how dare you talk to me like that."

The clatter of hooves sounded on the road behind him. "What is the problem Bear?"

There were murmurs above on the bridge. "My Lord this fool will not open the gates, and he says he has orders."

"Tell him to override them."

Bear turned to the arrogant woodsman. "My Lord demands entry; I think you should listen to him and fast."

A small door opened and the arrogant looking woodsman stepped out. Haden tried to pull him back. "Please Sir you really..."

"For god's sake Haden not now!" He strode down the road towards Robbie. "Now look here sonny, lord whatever the hell you are, I have my orders and you cannot enter so why not take your caravan of riff raff turn it around, and bugger off."

Robbie's eyes smouldered and Rune touched his arm. He very slowly dismounted off his horse and stood face to face with the chief woodsman. "IT'S LOXLEY!"

"What is?"

"MY NAME." Robbie looked like he was about to kill the man; the rage in his face was so blatant. Rune slipped very quickly off her horse, ran around and stepped in between Robbie and the gate commander.

"Woodsman you address your Lord of Loxley, I would suggest you very quickly order the gate open, and then run from his sight, you have angered him enough and I assure you, there is no need to bow... Just run like hell." She smiled and turned to Robbie. "Rob calm down he just made an honest mistake, one I feel he will never forget."

Bear roared with laughter as the arrogant woodsman flew past him screaming. "Open the gates ... open the gates for Lord Loxley."

Rune stretched up and kissed him. "You are so funny at times." He smiled as he calmed down a little.

The large gates swung back, and Robbie lifted Rune up to her horse, he swung up into his saddle and nodded to Harry. "Take them in Harry." Robbie and Rune sat at the side of the gate as the carts began to slowly pass in; Robbie looked down at the woodsman who stood proud at the side of the gates.

"Woodsman, what is your name?" He bowed.

"I am Haden My Lord."

Robbie smiled and leaned down and held out his hand. "Robert of Loxley." Haden swallowed and then wiped his hand on his cloak and shook Robbie's hand. "Where is that fool now?"

Haden looked back up the road. "He ran off as your good lady instructed My Lord." Rune started to giggle behind Robbie.

"He has learned wisdom finally it appears. Haden the people in this convoy have suffered greatly on their journey, is there a large area around here that may house them?"

Haden rubbed his chin as he thought. "I suppose there is the mill My Lord. That has a very large area around it which is still quite clear, and it is surrounded by woodland and there is plenty of game to hunt, I would think that could be useful."

"Do you have a man who could lead us?"

Haden turned and barked at a young boy. "Ned, grab a horse and lead Lord Loxley to the mill at Stainsby." The young lad jumped up and with a smile on his face, he vaulted on to the horse and rode up to the front of the convoy.

Robbie smiled. "Now Haden, there will be more coming, the enemy is clearing the south of all woodsmen and they have no choice but to flee. I will leave you here in charge, and I tell you now, it is my express wishes that any person, who is in need of our protection, should receive it. Is that quite clear to you?"

Haden bowed. "You have my word My Lord; there will be no more turning away."

"Good man. You keep up the good work, and if you're chief returns tell him to report to me at Loxley." Robbie nudged his horse forward, and with Rune at his side he rode up the side of a convoy filled with happy smiling faces.

Skip sat on the backboard as Robbie rode up. "Well, my good friend, I have my people and a place for them to stay, I will need your powers of negotiation to help organise the camp are you ready for it?"

Skip smiled. "Let me have the woodsmen of Avon and we will soon have it organised my friend."

Robbie smiled. "Use all the men bar Rafe. He is too good with a sword to leave behind, and I feel he may survive longer than three days with Jett." Rune smiled at him as he kicked the horse and rode back down the line to organise his own group.

Seth Hargreaves sat in the room in an old rocking chair by the fire, as his wife came back into the room. "She is sleeping now poor little love."

"I have lost our Zandra, I told dad what an evil bastard he was, but he never listened either. Looks like we are all that is left of the Hargreaves now. Poor mite, losing her mum so young, it aint right."

She patted his arm as she sat down by the fire. "Zandra loved you Seth, it was him who kept her away." She stared into the flickering flames as her mind thought. "He will come looking you know that don't you? Mason will never let her go so easily."

Seth looked tired; his eyes were filled with sorrow. "I know love, he will not find her though, we will move and keep her safe from his poisoned hands. If it is the last thing I bloody well do, it's keep her away from him. Our Zandra would have wanted her protected."

He closed his eyes and felt more tired than he ever had. His wife sat and watched by the flickering fire and gave a soft smile to herself. Seth was a proud man and strong in his day, she knew he would do everything to protect his small niece. Opposing Mason Knox though was a tall order and she worried a little.

The grounds around the old mill had been divided into large square bays, that had in their time served as car parks to the once tourist attraction. The mill was now just a hollow shell, stripped by the Cutters for scrap metal. Skip had seized the small offices at the end, and within hours he had made it his headquarters for the organisation of the relief effort. The yard outside the back had been turned into a series of fire pits and the kitchens raided for the few remaining pans.

Hunters went out, and food was brought back, and now the long task of finding and feeding the hungry began. At the top of the car park was a smaller bay, and here Robbie set up his camp. The two large carts of food were sent round the back of the mill, and the two carts of weapons were pulled across in front of Robbie's camp. A gap of ten feet was open between them to give access. A wide green sheet was hung across it. His camp was set at the top, in the middle, and as he leaned against the cart with his shirt open, and with bare feet, he stared down the long line of bays either side of the road where hundreds of families now set up a make shift camp.

Robbie breathed a long sigh and took a swig of his drink. Two slender arms slid round from behind him, and her head rested on his shoulder, he closed his eyes and leaned against her, as she squeezed closely to him. "What you thinking about Rob?"

He opened his eyes and looked down the long line of makeshift camps. He sighed and rubbed against her as she nuzzled into his neck. "All these... Look at them Rune, lost, hungry, and homeless. How the hell can I help them?"

"I don't think you have done so badly for one day Rob." She kissed him softly up his neck. He closed his eyes, he really loved the way she did that, and he felt calmness wash over him.

"Mason knew what he was doing when he sent them here. He plans to swamp us so that we defeat ourselves from the inside, we are going to be so busy that we will not have time to fight him."

"Or maybe Robbie that is what he thinks, there are a lot of woodsmen here Rob, all of them like you, know how to live off the land, with the right organisation they can be sorted into groups who can live in communities and defend themselves. I think you are being too negative; you should talk to Skip he has some very good ideas. I also think that after you have eaten, we should go visit our new neighbours and give them a proper welcome, I think it might surprise you."

Rune slid him round to face him. "But before all of that, I think you should see our tent and maybe relax a little." She opened his shirt and slid her arms inside, and kissed him softly.

In the back of the mill, there had been some huge rolls of dark fabric, John and Martin wasted no time, and had now built a long row of tents for each of the group, the rest of the fabric was being passed around and more tents were springing up all over the site.

Robbie slid in and was surprised at how roomy it was, he slipped off his shirt and flopped on the blankets, the hard surface of the floor seemed to ease his aching back. He lay back, and closed his eyes and drifted; his head seemed so full of the things that were now happening so fast that he felt over loaded.

She slid in and cuddled up to him and he pulled her close and felt the warmth of her against him. She calmed him, and relaxed him as she softly kissed him. It was over an hour later and he was fast asleep when Jade coughed loudly outside the tent. Treen came walking down as Rune wrapped in a blanket leaned out.

Jade, had a small tray with two steaming plates on it, she looked at Treen. "Got to stop em or they won't eat, its madness." She smiled at Treen as she walked past quickly. Rune looked shrewdly at Jade.

"What was that about?" Jade tried to look innocent, something she had never been able to quite pull off.

"Just girl talk between Treen and me, it's nothing really." Rune narrowed her eyes at her. "Well got to rush got my own man to feed you know?" She ran off along the tents. Rune slipped back in with the food.

It was several hours later when Robbie and Rune emerged from the tent; Robbie's shirt still flapped open in the warm breeze, although he had put his boots back on. His hair hung loose and straggly, and he walked with Rune across the campsite and nodded to Steph, Smokes, and some of the others as he walked up to the fire. "I think all of you should introduce yourselves to the people around camp and give them some encouragement, I intend to go around tonight and speak with them, you should do likewise. You will see then what you fight for." They all nodded and agreed.

Robbie walked with his hands in his pockets with Rune on his arm. "Rob are you going to tuck your shirt in and fasten it up?"

"Why, it's a warm night."

"You are Lord Loxley; don't you think you should set an example?"

"I did today when I attacked a Cutter outpost and stopped the persecution of these people. My shirt was not tucked in then... Rune I am a lord, and this is what this lord looks like, I will not pretend to be something I am not."

Rune smiled. "You are hopeless, you know that?"

"I love you though, don't I?"

Her eyes danced as she smiled at him. "I love you too."

The small group were all huddled by the fire eating a stewed rabbit, they had been given some tinned veg from the food truck and after some careful knife work, they had been able to open the tins and add them to their stew. They talked quietly as they ate with their heads down. Robbie and Rune walked up to them. "Good evening, how are you all doing?"

The old woman with a thick shawl and headscarf looked up at them. "We have a little left if you are hungry?"

Robbie smiled and pulled his hand out of his pocket and raised it palm up. "Oh no I have eaten a good meal, please share it amongst yourselves." She smiled up at him, and then gestured to the pot.

"A warm coffee perhaps? We have been given a little by one of the men of the camp, it's not easily found these days and quite a treat." He nodded,

"That would be very nice, yes thank you." The group nudged up and made space around the fire and both of them sat down, as they were passed two cups of coffee. Robbie sipped it and smiled. "Where are you all from, I do not recognise your accent?"

The old woman looked up. "Deal... What's left of it? We walked for two days, and then got picked up by Mr Watkins there in his cart." Robbie leaned forward, and nodded at the dark faced figure in an old torn cloak.

"That was very decent of you Mr Watkins." He nodded back as he chewed. The old woman looked at him.

"I am Martha by the way, that's Jed, Tom, and Alf, those are just me kids, Mr Watkins you know. Then we have Bernie, Kay, Lillie, and that is Stevie." Robbie and Rune nodded to each of them as they were introduced.

"Well, it's nice to meet you all, I am Rob and this lovely lady is Rune."

Kay looked at him. "Are you one of the camps organisers?" Rune smiled at Robbie who she thought was enjoying the fact that to these people he was just one of them. She knew how he loved to play down the title of lord, and she watched him with love in her eyes.

"I am involved with the camp, yes. I am going round to see if there is anything more, we can do to make sure you are all as comfortable as possible."

Kay smiled at him. "We are fine, Lord Loxley has no idea how much he has done for us already, bringing us here in person to make sure we are safe is the kindest thing anyone has ever done for us. He is so loved by his people; I just hope he knows that."

Robbie looked down at the fire. "But you have so little, there must be something more that can be done to help?"

Martha watched, as Rune put her hand on his shoulder, she saw how deeply the remark had affected him. Rune knew the feelings of hopelessness he had at the plight of these people being persecuted. Martha looked up and caught Rune's eye. "You can tell Lord Loxley he should not feel sad for us, he has given us our lives back and all of us owe him."

Robbie looked up. "You owe him nothing, it is he who is grateful, for his people teach him the true meaning of what this country should be, and he is honoured by it."

Martha smiled. "We all love him dearly and we will stand by him to the end if needs be, won't we?" They all smiled. "Aye, bless him."

Rune nodded at Martha as Robbie stood up, he placed his empty cup on the stone. "Let any of the guards know if you require anything at all... Goodnight my good people, may Hearne watch over you all."

Robbie turned. "And you, My Lord, thank you." Martha smiled at Rune as Robbie turned back to her smiling face. All the others looked up in amazement. He smiled at her and nodded.

"How did you know?"

"You have a real lady by you My Lord Robert, her love of you is well known across the land, and old women like me can recognise true love when she sees it." He smiled as Rune slid her arm round him.

"I meant what I said, anything I can do, I will." Martha nodded.

"We already know that My Lord, and we meant what we said, take good care of him for us Lady Runestone."

Rune looked at him with a smile. "Oh, I will don't you worry."

Robbie and all the group wandered through the camp all night. There were dozens of different ways of creating a home space, and fires burned in each of them. As the night wore on Robbie began to feel the strong sense of unity in the air, wherever they went, they were greeted with love and made welcome.

Most of the people did not even realise who he was, and yet both of them were welcomed. The noisiest group by far was a large bonfire area surrounded by children, and in the middle of them, was Harry, Maggs, Blades, Jett, Rafe, and Jade. Robbie laughed as Harry struck a chord on Maggs guitar and all the kids sung out as loud as they could baa, baa, black sheep.

Robbie watched as Rune giggled in the firelight, her eyes sparkling and filled with love, as Jade and Jett conducted the children, and Maggs bashed on an old tambourine. Rune sat down, and pulled two small children on to her knee and bounced them, in tune with the music. All the parents smiled as they watched Harry pull faces, and play worse than Maggs as he taught them Hickory Dickory Dock. All the children laughed and screamed along with him.

Rowan put his hand on Robbie's shoulder. "You have done well Robbie. This place is filled with life and love as a true realm should be."

Robbie looked at his friend's happy face. "This is a start Rowan; it is something to build on." People soon began to realise who he was, although his name had not been mentioned. Maybe it was the respect shown to him by the men in Loxley cloaks as he walked around with Rune. Maybe, it was the way Rune looked at him. Somehow, they knew, and would walk up to him and squeeze his hand. "God bless you Lord Loxley, Hearne protect you, My Lord. Thank you, My Lord." Each and, every one of them left their mark on him.

The young girl, who had been almost raped, ran across and threw her arms around him. "You are without doubt the bravest and kindest man. God bless you and your family my dearest of all Lords, thank you for my life."

Robbie patted her on the back as tears welled into his eyes. Her Mother nodded to him and smiled. Rune leaned over to the young girl. "Your Lord loves all his woods people and he will protect you all, thank you for your very kind words, I think he needed to hear them."

She stood at his side and smiled at him. "You were right Robbie, never have I seen a more worthy lord than you tonight." Her eyes sparkled with love, and she moved forward and kissed him. "Believe these people if you cannot believe in yourself Robbie." He pulled her close and hugged her.

Jade came past with Treen and Alley. "See what I mean always at it, they are like rabbits."

It was quite late in the night when Robbie walked through the old mill with Rowan. The candles burned bright in the small office at the bottom. Skip leaned back in his chair and smiled as he rubbed his eyes. "Well Robert, it appears our camp is quite a success. The good news is that things are not quite as bad as it seems. We have about fifty small towns between here and Loxley that are deserted, but are in reasonable condition. We think we can move a large amount of these people in the next few days, and relocate them to these towns. All the houses will need some work, but a workforce is not something we are short of. I feel they will bond together quicker if they help establish their communities together. I think my good friend you will be surprised at the way your woodland realm comes together." He smiled as he looked up with his tired eyes.

"Everyone in each of the parking bays seem to be well known to each other so it makes sense to keep them together, and move the whole of each bay into each town. Ramsay here is quite a bright lad so if it is all right with you, I will leave him here in charge when we leave. I would with your consent like to stay on for another day just to get things sorted. I will catch up at Loxley in time for the big meeting; I will of course have more information on what has been achieved here."

Robbie smiled. "Of course, you stay as long as you need. I appreciate what you have done here Skip, I owe you one. You are a true friend Skip thanks."

"I think Robert we are straight; you gave me back something as important to me as these people are to you. I believe it is what friends do is it not?"

Robbie smiled as he nodded. "I believe it is... Get some sleep you look exhausted."

Robbie walked back down the mill floor with Rowan, and feeling a little more light hearted; Skip had come through with the answer to a problem of overwhelming proportions. The two friends walked back to the camp in the moonlight, they arrived at Rowan's tent and Jade popped her head through the gap at the front

"Hey Robbie," her eyes twinkled. "Hey lover." She looked up at Robbie. "Is he mine now?" Robbie laughed at the twinkle in her eye.

"Go easy on him Pebbles, I need him alive in the morning." She giggled.

"Your one to talk, I have heard Rune's giggles for half the night. Ok give him here then."

Robbie walked up the line as fits of wild shrieks, and giggles came out of Jade's tent. He crawled into the tent, where Rune sat in bed waiting and she smiled. "Hi gorgeous."

"Hey beautiful." She pulled back the covers and smiling, her eyes sparkled with happiness.

The sun was up and the whole group looked rough. Robbie walked slowly down the path yawning next to a glowing Rune. "Morning," he yawned, and everyone seemed to follow suit as he took the cup Maggs handed him and took a large swig.

"Right, everyone we leave in an hour on horseback. Harry we are leaving the cart for Skip and Fuse. They will be returning in a day or two when things here are sorted." He took a long swig of his drink and shook his head to clear out the tiredness. "Rune thinks we should make an exit to remember, so it will be hoods up on the way out. I want to reach Loxley by midafternoon, it will be nice to finally be home again, so we travel light and fast, get yourselves ready, and for Hearne's sake wake up the lot of you. We are supposed to be the heroes here." Rune smiled at Jade who giggled with Jett, Rafe looked exhausted.

It was an hour later when Robbie pulled himself into his saddle at the front of the line. Everyone sat alert on their saddles with their hoods up and their Loxley coat of arms displayed proudly. Robbie turned, and smiled at the group. They were all so very different from the group that left Loxley thirty days ago. He turned to face Rune and gave her a huge grin. "Are you ready to go home?" Her face lit up with a huge smile and she nodded.

"Oh yes please Rob." He pulled up his hood and noticed the crowd gathering in rows down the road.

He raised his hand in the air. "Men of Loxley, we ride for home." He kicked his horse as he waved his hand, and at a gallop, all of them shot down the road lined with the cheering crowd. They came out of the gate and down the small lane, and woodsmen cheered as they rode by, a convoy of hooded men, they clattered down the old slip road and back on to the motorway as five carts came up the other side, a young boy jumped up in the cart and pointed.

"Look... Look dad that's him... that's Robin Hood."

Henry stood up fast as he looked through his scope, the watchman above shouted. "Incoming riders, twenty cloaked and hooded."

David scrambled up the ladder, and ran to the observation deck. "Who is it Henry, can you see?"

Henry peered down his scope. "Not quite sure, can't see their faces. Hold up a minute got a flash of a crest they are...?"

David leaned over the wall trying to see. "They are what Henry?"

Henry took the telescope away from his eye. "Well, I'll be buggered."

David gave him a confused stare. "Well...? Who the hell is it, Henry?"

Henry smiled a huge smile and David jumped back. "NO?" He snatched the telescope from Henry's hand, and leaned right over the wall. He jumped back and grabbed Henry with a huge smile on his face. "He is back. HA, HA, he's back, and he is safe." David whooped for joy and pulled Henry into a huge hug. He turned and ran down the steps. "OPEN THE GATES FOR YOUR LORD OF LOXLEY." Everyone looked up in surprise as David Williams slipped down the ladder laughing and cheering.

The huge gates swung open, and David stood almost crying and trembling as the horse party at high gallop came round the corner and up the long road to the square. He danced on the spot as Robbie raised his hand and the horses slowed under the gates and into the compound. Robbie was half way off his horse when David snatched him from the seat with huge tears in his eyes, and pulled him into the hug of his life. Robbie threw his arms around and laughed.

"It's nice to see you too Dave."

"Oh God Robbie lad, I am so glad you are safe." He released Robbie and held his shoulders as he looked at him. "We are so proud of you boy... aren't we lads?" The whole gateway roared with cheers as David took Rune in his arms and hugged her. David went round shaking everyone's hand. He hugged Martin and John and he twirled Jade in the air. He almost broke down when he saw Alice, and wept as he almost squeezed her to death.

David gave Harry the biggest welcome as he hugged and danced with him, everyone laughed and cheered as David's delight caught on. He walked back to Robbie and patted him on the side of the face. "Go see her Robbie, she has missed you so much."

Robbie smiled. "I am on my way now Dave." Robbie helped Rune up to her horse, and then pulled himself up. David patted his leg and turned to the inner compound gates man. "OPEN THE GATE FOR LORD LOXLEY."

The inner gates swung open and the group shot through. Robbie felt the excitement rise as he galloped up the slope with Rune at his side towards the fourteen houses of Loxley Village. The feeling of making it back to the home he had missed so much bubbled over as he grinned at Rune.

Alice Kirk was sweeping the yard, as she heard the sound of cheers from the new wooden lodges built up the roadside. She stood at the gate, and looked down the lane and saw the row of hooded horsemen coming her way. Alice dropped her broom, and put her hands to her mouth with a gasp, and then ran across the yard screaming. Anne came running out and looked at her sister who was pointing down the road "He is here; He is back...Young Robbie." Anne looked stunned.

Twenty hooded figures hurtled past heading for Lox farm, and both of them jumped, and screamed and hugged each other. Agatha Patterdale ran out of the cheese shop and scowled as she missed the long line of riders who had passed at such speed.

Jess slid the door of the greenhouse closed, and turned to go down the steps towards the house. The sound of hooves came up the lane and she looked down between the two farmhouses at the long hedge. Hooded figures came around the corner towards the farm drive, and as tears filled her eyes; her basket of fresh veg left her hand and crashed onto the floor. Beth looked up from the kitchen window to see her sister as the veg spilled everywhere start to run.

Robbie dropped his hood as he came up the side of the house, and saw Jess running down the steps, she yelled his name and he smiled and slipped off the saddle. Robbie opened his arms wide, and Jess leapt wailing into them and he caught her in a huge hug, and spun her round. "Hey mum."

"Oh Robbie. Oh, Robbie you are safe, I have been so worried, oh Robbie my darling, my love you are home at last." She wept and sobbed, and he held her tight in his arms. Beth came screaming round the corner as Alice ran to her, and Beth swept her daughter into the air and pulled her into a hug that almost killed the poor girl. She too wept and wailed and sobbed, poor Alice was almost soaked as she cried to see her mum again. Beth wailed as Robbie slid his mum out of his arms, tears still streamed, and her eyes were red as he kissed her on the cheek. "It's nice to be home mum."

Rune came up at his side. "Hey Mrs. Lox." Jess burst into tears again, and snatched Rune into a huge hug.

The barn door burst open and John stood with a large silver sword. "What the hell... ALICE?" He dropped the sword and thundered down the path as she ran weeping towards him, John snatched her into his large bear like arms and burst into tears. He buried his head in her shoulder as he hugged, and squeezed her, and muttered muffled words of love to his precious daughter.

Harry came through the crowd holding Blades hand. "Hey Jessie love. This is my baby girl Kate." Blades beamed at his side.

"Hi Auntie Jess."

Jess smiled and pulled her close into a huge hug. Yet more tears rolled down her face. "Hello Kate love welcome to your family home." Blades burst into tears as she felt the love in Jess. Harry sniffled and pulled out his red hankie and mopped his eyes. Jess looked up. "Harry Lox! You should be bloody ashamed of yourself; how could you leave this poor sweet girl on her own and go off trying to get yourself killed? I will deal with you later."

Harry put his head down. "Yeah, Jessie love."

Jess took Blades by the hand. "Don't cry sweetheart, it's not your fault your dad is a FOOL! Come and meet your Aunt Beth."

Robbie looked round. "Mum where is dad?"

"He is at the meeting house with Len, Robbie love." He saw the look on Rune's face. "Mum we have quite a few guests, Harry will you introduce everyone to Mum for me, I must see dad and Len?"

"Hey man you scoot; I will like take care of things. Trust me man."

Robbie started to laugh, and he turned to Maddy and her daughters, who were wiping their eyes. "My Ladies, if you do not mind, I have to see my father and Len, if you wish to settle yourselves in, I will bring Len back up with me shortly. I am sure Lady Madeleine you will want to see him as quickly as possible?"

She smiled. "Yes, please My Lord; it has been a long time since I have seen my father." Robbie winked.

"I will be back shortly." He pulled himself on to his horse as Mother, Rune, Smokes and Jade pulled in behind him.

Robert Lox sat behind his desk with Len talking when the door burst open. Robert's hand went for his sword and stopped in shock. "Hi Dad got a hug for your lord?"

Robert bounced out of the chair across the room and pulled Robbie into a fierce hug. "Oh, thank Hearne; you are one hell of a son boy."

"I love you too dad."

Rune and Jade ran to Len and pulled him into a huge hug. Len stood in a state of shock as he stared at Steph with Peter beside her. "Hello dad, this is a little news we didn't send you. Look who's back?"

Peter smiled. "Hi dad."

Len burst in to tears as he pulled both of them towards him and hugged all four. Robert looked dumb struck. "Robbie lad, that is Pete, isn't it?"

"Yeah Dad."

"How the bloody hell did you get him back?"

"It took about half a ton of gun powder, and we blew most of Tintagel away, but we slipped him out, it was quite fun really."

Robert's jaw dropped. "Well, I'll be buggered."

There was a soft tap on the door behind them, and the smiling Robbie turned. He saw the letter in her hand with the Loxley broken seal. His smile fell. "Mrs Tanner?" She nodded. Robbie waved her to a seat. "Please come in will you." Her eyes were watery and Robbie felt the pain rise in his chest. Rune turned and looked anxiously as Nellie Tanner sat down.

Robbie opened the bottom drawer in the desk and took something out. He came back round the side of the desk and knelt down by her side. "Mrs Tanner, I cannot express how sorry I am to return to you one short of my team." She started to cry and Robbie breathed deeply as his eyes glistened. "Your son stepped in front of an arrow shot by Billy Knox that was meant to kill me."

Roberts knuckles cracked as his fists tightened.

"There is nothing I would not give, to have seen it coming and stopped him. I held him in my arms in his final moments shocked at what he had given to save my life. He asked me to tell you that he loved you." Two tears ran from his eyes and his words stumbled. "He wanted me to tell you he was brave, and believe me he was without doubt a very different person from the one who left here. Eric was greatly loved by all of us, as he was very important to the team. He did many things to save his friends." Robbie swallowed deeply.

"We buried him with full honours at Caerleon in a patch of sacred wood. He now has a marble tombstone with the Loxley crest, and he is honoured by all there." Robbie opened her hand and placed within it a golden bow. "There are only five men who have ever received these in the whole of Loxley history. It is the highest honour a man of Loxley can achieve, and it is only given for outstanding acts of loyalty to the people of Loxley, he deserves higher." Robbie put his head down and wept, and Nellie stroked his head as she too wept.

"You are the most noble of all lords Robert of Loxley, to have such love from my son. He did not die in vain and I will honour him." Robbie looked up and she smiled and wiped the tears from his eyes. "I would have died for you too, you are the future of all these people and I am very proud of my son."

Nellie got up and smiled at everyone who was wiping their eyes she smiled. "Soft buggers." Robert Lox grinned at Nellie as she left the room. Rune slid her arms around him and held him close.

It was a happy group, which walked up the lane towards Loxley farm. Robbie walked with his dad at the back whilst Steph and Pete walked at their side. Len walked with Rune on one arm and the very talkative Jade on the other. Jade covered the whole story in graphic detail of the trip, and the explosions, and Canterbury twice at high speed. Rune just beamed and Robert squeezed his son's shoulder as they walked each time Jade mentioned how brave Robbie was. They turned the corner and silhouetted in the yard, was a slender figure. Rune turned to Len.

"Granddad, we have someone else who wants very much to meet you." Rune stepped back and grabbed Jade's arm pulling her back. Len stared up the pathway.

"It cannot be.... Madeleine?" He whispered; she came forward into the light.

"Hello Papa." She smiled for the first time since Robbie had met her, and raised her arms; Len pulled his daughter into a hug and wept on her shoulder. Steph guided everyone round and steered them towards the house. The kitchen was heaving as they walked into a roar, Robbie was home and Loxley had its lord back where he belonged.

CHAPTER SEVEN

THE CHANGING WAYS OF FAMILIES

Robbie sat up in bed and rubbed his eyes, he stared around the strange room at the large comfortable bed festooned with elaborately quilted blankets. At the side of the door was a small dark wooden dressing table with a large mirror, and he blinked as he stared at himself in it.

His eyes wandered around past the two alcove wardrobes, to the wall between them where to his surprise, was three beautifully hand drawn pictures of him. One showed Robbie in his hood firing an arrow, the other was him with his hair tied back sweeping Alice Kirks yard, and the third and largest, was a very detailed close up of his head with his hair around his shoulders. He looked in the mirror and then looked back at the picture, it was very good indeed.

Two small silver hairbrushes sat on the dressing table with an assortment of perfume bottles and what looked like jewellery boxes; a small stool was, pushed up close. A table sat in front of the window that was, covered in clothes designs many of which Robbie thought could be for him. The Loxley cloak hung on the door next to a long deep purple heavy velvet one, Robbie remembered how he had seen Rune many times on the journeys to market wrapped up in it to protect her from the cold. He had always loved the way her hair had stood out and shone on it.

At the side of the bed was a neat pile of folded green clothes. He lay back into the soft bed and breathed in her scent from the pillow beside him. He found it funny that this was the first time, he had ever seen Rune's bedroom. He lay back surrounded by the fresh smell of honeysuckle and sweet violets, and closed his eyes. There was a small tap at the door, and as it swung open slowly, Robbie opened his eyes, Pete entered with a tray. "Rune said something about a royal proclamation from you making breakfast in bed mandatory."

Robbie smiled as Pete came round the bed and sat on the side of it, and passed him the tray. "Rune is right; this has got to be the only way to live." The coffee smell wafted into his nose as he slid the knife and fork off the tray.

Pete smiled at him. "Rob, I want to say something important." Robbie rested his knife and looked at Pete's serious face, Pete looked at the bed for a second.

"I woke this morning in my home with my wife, and two happy daughters, Rob, I have no words to express how important a thing that was to me. I guess what I want you to know is, I feel a great debt to you for planning and executing my escape. You will never know how close to giving up I was... I want to thank you Robbie for saving my life."

Robbie patted his arm. "You have no need to thank me Pete, Rune, Jade, and Steph, mean a great deal to me, to see their happiness has been reward beyond my reckoning believe me." He cut his bacon and smiled as he chewed it. He raised his fork. "You know Pete; I think you are as brave as hell surviving that long." He shook his head slowly as he chewed "I am not sure I could have done it."

Pete shrugged. "You have no choice Robbie. I see a great deal in Rune of her mother, and the one thing I always knew sat in that stinking hole, was I knew she would never give up on me, and neither would my best friend." He gave a smile. "Mad as he is, Harry came through for me; he told you where I was."

Robbie nodded as he chewed. "Rune loves you a great deal; I would die for her Pete. I wanted you back here so Rune could be close to you; it was Rune who saved you."

Pete nodded as he got up. "I needed to say it Rob... Rune says wear the new clothes she made you before she left." He winked and slowly walked out of the room.

The kitchen was empty when he came down the stairs, and so was the back room. Robbie stretched his legs in his new pants, which he felt were tighter than normal, he walked through the shop to the front door, her blue eyes glinted at him from between the clothes rails and he smiled.

"Hi gorgeous, you slept late." She slid out from the rail and walked over as he stepped out. She was dressed all in pale blue, and had a finely woven belt of silver hoops that fastened with a silver oak leaf.

"You look beautiful Rune." He gazed into her dancing blue eyes, and pulled her close and kissed her softly, it was a long slow kiss that took her breath away.

"Oh, what I would give for such a man Stephanie." Robbie jumped at the sudden voice and looked over the low wall to see Steph, Treen, and Maddy, sat at Len's small garden table, Rune smiled as she slid her arms around him.

"This lord is mine forever." She smiled at the group of women.

"Good morning ladies." Maddy nodded her head.

"Lord Loxley, I can see you slept well."

Robbie walked into the yard; Rune had all her goods out on display. "So, what is happening in Loxley today?"

Rune looked around. "It's market day and people are pouring in from all over; I have already sold several cloaks. Jade and Alley, have gone up to the farm for

Jett and Ruby, with Rowan, as you can see Maddy and the girls have settled at granddads. Although I am not sure where he is, Fuse and Skip arrived a while ago they are staying at the farm. Just about, everyone in the stockade wants to know where you are, I did not mention you were asleep in my bed."

He smiled at her. "What a bed it is, I slept like a log." He looked up the street at the people going in and out of the shops. "I suppose you will be here most of the day, so if you don't mind, I would like to slip up and see mum."

"I thought you might." She stretched up and kissed him. "Go on she has missed you, and you have a chance to smell the scent of the greenhouses." She patted him on the bum as he passed through the gate and she giggled. "Nice fit on those pants, see you later sexy." Robbie smiled at her as all the women passing giggled and nodded at him.

There had been a few changes at the farm, Jess had increased production, and now had six lads working in the greenhouse with her, John had four new apprentices, and Robert bellowed orders to a few new field hands. Jess smiled as she walked down the greenhouse path and gave him a hug. "Wow mum things suddenly got a lot busier."

She kept her arm around his shoulder as she spoke. "We have had to increase production of everything just to make sure we have all the extra we will need. People are coming from miles away to buy stuff, and we are trying to store a large amount for the winter. I am, having to ration the coffee for sale, as we cannot grow enough. I could use about another three greenhouses the way we are going."

"I noticed the fields seemed fuller as I walked up, are you double planting?"

Jess sighed. "We have to get the numbers up; I want to get a winter crop in as soon as I can. We have increased the rotation to about five cycles a year now, I have been able to bring in a lot more staff, and it will be good having John back he can help train up some of the new guys. Beth is rushed off her feet, having Alice again will help. John and Rob are working flat out, the demand for weapons is so high, and they have brought in extra staff. Sue and Jake at the pot shop are not too happy, because John is behind with the new pans they ordered, and Agatha Patterdale is moaning because her cheese counter needs repairing and your dad has not had the time to get to it."

Robbie nodded as she spoke. "So, it's busy, well that's not a bad thing, we seem to have a lot more people than when I left, so there will be no shortage of willing hands."

His mother turned and stared at him. "You are very dark under your eyes Rob, you should get more sleep, and you have lost a little weight, late night raids no doubt? I don't know Rob what with Alice looking pale and you looking like you should slow down, it is all too much for the pair of you." Jess seemed to go quiet and he watched her as her hazel eyes followed the staff in her greenhouse. "You will be leaving again soon won't you Robbie?" He felt the sadness in her voice and he took her hand and gave it a soft squeeze.

"I have to mum, my life now is not on the farm, there are others who will need my help and I cannot refuse them can I?"

She gave a soft smile. "I love you Robbie, you are all I have left, I would not survive if I lost you."

"I will always come home Mum, because I miss you more than anything else in Loxley. I am sorry about Billy, I know you loved him, and I know how much he must have hurt you."

Her eyes filled. "You will never understand Robbie until you have kids, but I gave that boy a home and I took the responsibility for him. I raised him as your brother, and as hard as it is to understand Robbie it just does not switch off. I will never believe he is like his father because he was raised here away from that monster. No boy of mine would kill his own brother. In Billy's heart he knows I am his mother." Jess turned and kissed him on the cheek. "Remember what I have said Robbie." She turned and walked up the greenhouse. "No not that one, use the fine sprinkler!" The young boy nodded nervously as he picked up the other hose.

In just thirty days, Loxley had gone from a small stockade to a thriving busy wooden town. All down the road from the end of the village to the gates were row upon row of wooden huts. Hundreds of men worked non-stop to build them and house the people who camped on any spare land. The billets by the gate had already doubled in size, and a new wing of stables had been built under the front stockade wall.

All the shops were busy, except the bookshop, which remained closed. A large new building was being built alongside the meeting hall, which was going to be a boarding house for officials who attended the large meetings. Rags was so busy in her new postal service shop, she barely had time to talk, already riders were coming and going every hour as she sorted the new mail into runs with Lucy.

People constantly stopped him, bowed and nodded, and just buying a cake from Alice Kirk was a real effort as visitors to the village mobbed him. Robbie found it hard work and soon he slipped behind Jade's workshop and knocked on her small flat door. Rowan smiled as he opened it. "I see you too have decided to hide my friend?"

Robbie smiled as he slipped in. "I have had enough already Rowan; this lord stuff is not for a woodsman like me."

Rowan poured him a drink and he sat quietly in the chair as he listened to Jade hum as she worked in her tool shop on the other side of the wall. "This is more like it." Rowan beamed at him and slipped back in his own chair.

After tea that night, Robbie pulled Rune up on his horse in front of him, and he rode out of the farm, up the side of the barn past Rags postal station, and up the road past Harry's house. Maggs waved franticly from the window, Robbie noticed the row of half built motorbikes now up the side of the house.

They passed Hay Cottages, where the farm hands lived and further up the road turned right on to a long dusty road. "I have never been up here Rob, where are we going?" He put his head on her shoulder as he controlled the horse from behind her.

"A very special place I know." She giggled as he kissed her neck and gave her goose bumps. He rode down the long straight road, and soon she could see the large wooden walls that marked the edge of the stockade in the distance.

Robbie slowed the horse as they reached a small woodland track on his left. He turned into the small track that led into the trees and followed the path round, through the old and gnarled Oak trees. The light was dim as the sun began to head down towards the end of the day, and Rune gasped as they came into a clearing and stopped.

Robbie slid down and lifted her gently off the horse. They stood in a huge open glade surrounded by some of the oldest oak trees in Loxley. At the far edge of the clearing was a large lake, it was still like a mirror and the sun glinted off it, and all the trees around it were reflected in the water. "Oh, Robbie this place is beautiful."

"I own it Rune; my granddad left me this place in his will. He made certain everyone knew it was separate from the farm, these trees are older than any in the wood or on the escarpment; my granddad always called it Robbie's Mere." He smiled at the look of joy in her eyes as they sparkled in the setting sun.

"Oh, Rob this place is like paradise." She turned and hugged him.

Robbie took her hands in his, and went down on his knee. "I have to seat a king Rune. Nevertheless, when it is done and I return here, will you marry me and live in the house I build in this spot?"

Rune's eyes clouded with tears, and violets sprung up all around as she lowered herself to him. "Oh, Robbie I will spend every day with you here until we die." She threw her arms around him and wept as she laughed. "I love you Robert of Loxley of course I will marry you."

The wood was silent and peaceful and Robbie lit a small fire and pulled blankets out of his bag. Rune smiled as he rolled them out, and they sat and gazed out across the Mere and watched the sun burning red behind the trees, reflected in the still water.

The last of the bees hummed as they headed back to the hives, and a solitary kingfisher watched for one last meal of the day. Across the Mere on an old log, a stork watched quietly as the fish swam close to the surface. Squirrels ran home to their nests for the night, and birds settled down. Robbie felt a strong sense of inner peace flow over him. It had felt for weeks now, as if he was, filled with turmoil and self doubt, sat alone with Rune at the very edge of the mere cuddled close, and watching the sun as her breathing softly stirred the sound in his ears. he knew true happiness and contentment for the first time in his life. He understood that deep inside; it was nature beside him and nature all around him that was what he wanted the most, he spoke quietly as if not to disturb the world around him. "This is my dream Rune; this is what it is all about, pure and simple this."

She stared in wonder at the beauty around her. "This is a magical place Rob, if this is what you want for everyone, Mason hasn't got a chance."

As the moon came up and lit the mere with a silver essence, a large stag stood in the trees and watched the two figures curled together in each other's arms under the blankets as they slept. Owl's hooted and the bright eyes of foxes and badgers bowed to Nature and her beloved woodsman, as they slept in the glade of Robbie's Mere.

Rune woke up curled around Robbie as the sun broke over the trees. The dappled light coloured the grass around her and she smelt the scent of the woods all around. She felt the joy and happiness inside her, as she slowly slid from under the blanket, and rising up she ran across the grass and dived into the cold water of the small lake.

She broke the surface of the water and gasped with joy, as her whole body and soul felt alive and free. She swam out into the lake and dived below the surface, and turning under the deep clear water, she swam back towards the shore, bursting through the surface.

Robbie sat smiling as she ran giggling up the grass and fell into his arms. "Oh, Rob I love this place, it is alive with life and I feel as free as a bird here." He pulled her close and wrapped a blanket around her to dry and warm her. Her eyes had more life in them than he had ever known, and her happiness filled him with a joy like he had never thought possible.

Robbie had suddenly found his place in the world, and he knew his future would be here in Loxley in Robbie's Mere, and Rune would be with him.

Mel had spent two days waiting for Sir Giles to get organized, and felt her impatience growing more and more as she finally pulled herself up to the saddle to leave for Loxley, Una smiled. "All those years alone with your stones, and yet now it drives you mad waiting for one man."

Mel softened her harsh look. "I really want to see dad, tell me you do not...?

How many years has it been?" She cast a harsh glance up the yard. "My stones were a damned sight better company than that rude old badger, I will be fine when I see dad."

"You always were his girl when we were kids; you always ended up on his knee. I must admit it will be nice to see the old rogue. Do you think he will look all old and wrinkled? I hope he still has that little white goatee, I used to curl it round my finger and make him smile."

Mel chuckled. "I don't care how he looks as long as I can put my arms around him and tell him how much I have missed him." The long line of horses moved forward as Sir Giles finally was ready. Saff rode next to Keith as Jaz and Mac quietly followed. Mel and Una rode at the back, Mel watched Mac carefully. "Is Mac alright, he has hardly spoke a word in three days?"

Una shrugged. "He has never been very talkative, I don't know, I try to get him to chat more, but he seems uninterested. Wait till he gets annoyed at something; you will hear him then."

"He has a temper then?"

"To be honest I think it has been more out of frustration, your Saff has had Jaz, Mac has not really had anyone, I suppose he has just been used to being alone a lot. I am hoping he finds some common thread with Robert of Loxley, maybe open up a bit."

Mel sat back on her horse and thought, she felt sorry for him, as the others seemed to be laughing and chatting up front, whilst Mac just seemed to be plodding on unaware of what was going on around him.

The ride from York to Loxley was long and boring. Endless miles of empty woodland passed before them, Sir Giles said very little and seemed uninterested in them at the back of his party. He talked endlessly to his advisors, and despite several requests to halt, he continued on his journey. Una found him quite irksome, and frowned at him from the rear of the party. "He thinks he is better than everyone that one." She complained after being told they would stop for one hour before riding through the night. Mel smiled as she stretched her back.

"I am just glad to feel my feet on the floor and walk on the ground, I am not a rider."

Una looked at Keith. "How far are we from Loxley? I got the impression from you we would be there in a day's ride and yet Sir Giles is talking about riding all night."

The young bowman glanced back at the soldiers of Sir Giles, his dark brown eyes narrowed, it was obvious he was not keen. He looked back and slid his hand back through his hair as he crouched down to talk to the two women. "To be honest we are going the long way round, as the crow flies, we are about twenty to twenty five miles from Loxley, but his nibs are going to take about fifty to get there."

Una looked at her sister and then back at him. "Do you know the quicker route?"

Keith smiled. "Thinking of slipping off after his nibs has left? If you do not mind a bit of a gallop, we could possibly make it by nightfall. I have a map here my dad gave me that will give me a quick route in through the ancient wood round to the front gate."

Una smiled. "Thank god for that, ok let the old duffer go, and then we will follow you."

Keith stood at the top of the hill watching the party from York leave; he had told them he would catch up. He leaned against the tree as Saff watched from where she sat, he was slender for his age and yet she could see he was powerful. Already she had seen how he handled the horses, and he had obvious muscle. He slid his long brown hair back out of his eyes and turned, his deep brown eyes connected with her bright blue, and she looked down smiling to herself. He walked down the path and pulled his horse off the bush.

"Right let's get ready." He stepped up in the stirrup and pulled himself on to his horse; he cantered to the top of the hill, and watched the group from York disappear under a thick canopy of trees. He turned as Jaz came up beside him.

"Well, my friend it appears we once again follow your lead." Keith patted his arm and grinned.

"Let's ride to a wood worthy of the journey; we head across country to Hearne's Seat and through the ancient wood to the gates of Loxley." He kicked his heels and his horse leapt forward. Jaz smiled back at the others, and they all followed in to the trees and through the wood, in a straight line down Blacker Hill and onto Hoyland Common.

Sir Giles continued down the long road for another five miles. His party headed into the woodland at Rawmarsh, and they were hit under a hail of arrows, and his men fell in seconds as he fought to control his horse. Sir Giles heaved back on the reins and the horse steadied itself, he looked up the steep bank at the cocky smile and long blonde hair of his assassin, his blue eyes glinted, as they looked him up and down from behind the bow.

"Where is your sword man of York?"

Sir Giles knew he was going to die and defiantly stared at Billy. "It's where you will never be able to touch it young Knox." He started to laugh but his voice drained with his blood as the arrow pierced his neck. He fell from his horse and slumped shaking to the ground, and he felt his own sword being drawn from its scabbard. Billy walked around to face the dying Sir Giles. He held the sword up and spun it in his hand. "You have the sword of Justice and you chose to use this piece of rusty tin?" The sword spun in his hand, and as he caught the grip, he twisted it down and rammed it into Sir Giles back.

Billy walked back up to the trees; he looked up at his father. "He has three sons in York, one of them must have it, find me a way into that city and I will bring it you."

Mason gave a cold smile. "Looks like the heirs of this land are becoming as extinct as that log choppers dreams; his so called meeting in Loxley for one thing has become a lot shorter. That old wind bag would have talked for days."

The tall flat terrace of white lime slipped behind them, and Saff looked back at the tall pillar sat on top of it. "The seat of Hearne," she whispered to herself as they wove into the trees.

Keith looked back to check that all were still with him. "Keep close now we have just entered into the realm of the Loxley estates, these are the woods of my lord." The trees here were very old and spaced out, their canopies were wide and the late evening sun was twinkling through the leaves, Saff's eyes flickered blue.

"Mother I feel Madeleine, and she is close."

Melanie turned on her horse to look at her daughter. "Is she here?" Saff nodded and smiled.

"I think she is; I can feel her very strongly."

Mel smiled at Una. "We will have a reunion tonight that will be remembered in this family for years." Una smiled.

"Let's hope we can find a way to make her smile, I hope she has cheered up over the years, I know she can absorb sorrow, but she also bloody creates it with her long face."

Mel looked at her sister. "Don't be unkind; she always was a little quieter than us."

"Don't you mean bloody miserable?"

"Una please don't go upsetting her like last time, promise me." Una smiled as she looked at her sister.

"I will stick with Alley if her wit has improved with age, she will be a right scream... and I promise I will be sweet." Mel started to laugh.

"Why don't I trust you?" They reached the stream and turned south, and followed it right down until it came to the old forest road. Keith led them on to it and turned west, down towards the large gate square. The Sergeant looked down and saw the crest of Loxley on Keith's cloak.

"Who the hell are you?"

"I am Keith Sherman, son of Lee, previous woodsman instructor of Loxley, and this is the party of Rimmer I have led down from York."

David Williams popped his head over the edge of the wall and smiled. "You look like your old man... OPEN THE GATES." The large gates swung open as David slid down the ladder, and they rode into the compound. Keith slipped down off his horse as David came across. "You have been away a long time young Master Sherman, has it been so long that you have forgotten your first sword lesson?" David Williams smiled as he embraced a puzzled looking Keith.

"Davie?"

David smiled and nodded, and Keith now recognising the young teenager who would hang around the gates, and give him practice with a wooden sword, beamed and embraced him with great affection. "You have changed my old teacher, but I am thrilled to see you are still here, is Mad Harry still about? He used to drive me around on his handle bars."

"He is here and as mad as ever." Keith smiled.

"I must deliver these good people to a Mr Rimmer, but I would love to come back later and talk, is there a guest house or place I can pitch a shelter?"

Dave patted his arm. "You can lodge with me; I have three spare rooms and it will give me plenty of time to hear all about your dad." Dave Williams turned to the compound gate man. "Let them through Scott, this one is Loxley born and bred." Keith jumped up on to his horse, and saluted and smiled as he rode through the gate and headed off up the village road to find Len.

It was an emotional reunion for Len, Maddy had felt her sisters, and was already at the gate with Len. He hugged his three daughters and introduced them to Steph who apologised for Rune's lack of presence. Jade smiled and looked across at Treen.

"They snuck off for another quickie I bet, told you, they are at it none stop, he's an animal."

It was a large family celebration much to the delight of Jade and Jett. Ruby joined by Blades mucked in with Alley, and on seizing a case of Joe's moonshine from under Lens stairs, they proceeded to doctor all of the drinks. It was a swinging reunion, that brought most of the town's people out, and as Jade and Jett who staggered offered copious amounts of drinks to everyone, it rapidly became a street party.

Jett slid down the wall giggling. "What's this stuff, my lips are num?" She tried to focus with very wild blue flashing eyes, as she tried to read the label. "Dickily Orange" Blades and Jade laughed hysterically.

"No silly it's Dickingsly orammage." Jade pointed at Blades, and laughed even more and all of them looked at each other and laughed hysterically. Jett's eyes closed and she was gone. Alley gave a huge burp and slid down beside Jett. Jade turned to Blades "Hey let's..." Blades, was laid on the floor fast asleep.

Rowan's head came over the wall and looked down at her, Jade looked up and beamed. "Shush, they are sleeting... Hey, sweep hearf." Rowan smiled and nodded his head. He reached down and pulled Jade up into his arms, she giggled wildly as she slid her arms around him. "I dinked a loft."

By the time he got her to her bed, she was fast asleep. Rowan lay her carefully down and smiled as he stroked her long curly fringe back. She was very special if not as crazy as Harry was at times. He carried Jett, Blades, and Alley into Steph's living room, and carefully lay them down before returning to Jade. He curled around her and pulled her into his arms, she murmured in her sleep, and pushed back into him and wriggled.

The day was underway and the sun was rising in the sky. Robbie and Rune lay wrapped in their blankets in the glade. Robbie leaned back and stretched. "Oh, I needed this, just you and me and no one asking me about bloody Tintagel."

Rune smiled. "It has changed, hasn't it?"

He pulled her close, "I think we all have, I must admit I felt a little pushed out, I guess I always thought I would be helping out on the farm. They don't need me Rune, I am now Lord Loxley and the farm is no longer my concern."

"Don't take it to heart Robbie, they have hundreds of mouths to feed, and they had to reorganise, your task is still to find the sword and the king. They know you love them and want to be here, but you have to face facts Rob. You are the one everyone is now looking to, tomorrow at the meeting it will be you who takes the lead."

He looked downhearted. "I will get the praise, but it will be Skip who has done all the work."

"I don't agree, it was you who brought all the refugees into that mill, you were the one who instructed him to organise them. I thought you acted like a true lord should. You sought advice and listened, and then made a decision, and then delegated the most appropriate person to do it. You showed wisdom and great compassion, I was proud of you."

"You sound like Scarlet."

Rune smiled at him. "My aunt is no fool Rob, she runs Caerleon, Phil just thinks he does."

"Who is running Loxley?"

Rune giggled at him and snuggled into his chest. "I think it's a joint effort, don't you?" He laughed as she squirmed where he tickled her.

It was late morning when they reappeared outside Rune's house. They came round the back and tied the horse to the rail, Rowan sat on the wall smiling. "I would whisper if I were you... Seems like some of Joes moonshine got into the orange last night. We had quite a party, although this time I feel Jade and Jett's little joke backfired."

Robbie walked smiling into the kitchen with Rune. Five heads rested on the table; Steph looked like her head was so heavy she would not be able to lift it for days. Jett looked like death and Blades and Alley had probably died, they just were not aware of it yet. Jade was worse than all of them. Rune breezed up the kitchen.

"Ok who is up for a good fry up?" She pulled the large pan down and turned. Steph sat alone as the other four had fled looking for a bowl, she sat up and her head wobbled, she whispered very quietly.

"It is no wonder Harry is so messed up if he drinks that stuff, the last thing I am this morning is Cosmic."

Rune cracked the eggs and dropped them into the hot fat. Steph retched, and fled out of the kitchen door. Rune looked round and smiled at Robbie. "I know you have an appetite." She winked at him.

After breakfast, Robbie headed to the firing range. He sat back on the benches with the still very white group and watched the new bowmen, his presence made them nervous; Rafe and Fish wandered on to the ground and sat down as John walked up and down the line watching. Jett eyed him carefully. "He is a big bugger your uncle Robbie."

Robbie nodded. "Still fancy a shot at the title?"

Jett looked at Blades. "What do you think, should I go for it?" Blades rubbed her eyes, which seemed sunken very deep.

"You won't be happy until you have tried, will you?" Jett lifted herself off the seat and pulled out her sword.

"Hey John, fancy a little sword play? I need some exercise." John beamed at her.

"I am not sure you got what it takes to fight me."

Jett gave a wicked smile. "Well, if you mean I have to be as overweight as you are... then you are right."

John scowled at her, and drew out his sword. Everyone stopped and turned to watch as Jett beamed. "Cool." She swung her blade and loosened her shoulders.

Fish leaned forward and smiled at Rafe. "My money's on Jett." Rafe nodded at him.

"She is good there is no doubt, but hell he's a big'un... I think it's even."

John smiled and made a sweep, and Jett deflected it. "Don't be a pansy John, I want you to test me." He swung his blade back with a flick, and she brought up her blade and deflected it. The swords chimed loudly; Jett smiled. "Now that is more like it."

She jumped forward and attacked. Everyone gasped to see John defend as Jett with great skill and accuracy swung her blade rapidly at him, he grinned as he realised he was facing a true swords woman, John swung back with rapid speed and the fight began in earnest.

For a big man he moved with speed and agility, his wrist flicked and snapped as he brought his big sword down and across in front of Jett. The excitement grew in Jett, and she began to laugh and whoop as she spun and ducked like a dancer, moving in around John countering all his moves and providing some very expert volleys of her own. Several times John stepped back as Jett came at him with very aggressive moves.

Rune gripped Robbie's arm, as Jett once again lunged in at John and he stepped back, John returned unleashing heavier and heavier blows. Jett was only small compared to John, yet Robbie admired her courage and her skill, he knew how good she was, he had watched her fight off Blades who had two swords to her one in many practice sessions. The whole ground was silent except for the clashing of swords as they worked, two masters of their craft.

Jett back flipped out of the way of John's sword, and came up around him and smacked his bum with the back of her sword. She squealed with delight as everyone gasped in admiration, John was surprised, and spun round with huge power and again came a series of heavy blows. Jett faltered and stumbled backwards, as the crowd gasped and then roared. She recovered quickly still fending him off, and moved in for another assault. John nodded to her in respect and she winked at him, as yet another series of whoops emitted from her. She came at him fast and furious, John was ready for her and his arm moved with skill as she approached at speed.

His wrist flicked sideways and caught the edge of her blade, John gave a huge heave and spun his wrist sideways, and caught her off balance, her sword spun out of her hand and spun into the floor three feet away. He slid his leg and he caught her feet dropping her to the floor, she landed with a thud on her back. John rested the blade on her chest and smiled; Jett grinned and offered her hand. John took hold to lift her up, Jett's arm shot back her foot went up, and suddenly John was flying through the air and he landed with a very heavy thump on his back.

Everyone in the crowd gasped as Jett placed her sword on his chest. He roared with laughter, and offered his hand, Jett winked at him. "Pull the other one John, you are a big boy, get up on your own."

John sat up and laughed. "I never thought I would see the day when I met my match." He stood up and patted her on the back. "You have talent for the blade there is no doubt, I really enjoyed that young lady."

Jett looked up at the huge figure of John Lox. "Don't get polite on me John cause I kicked your butt." She smiled and he pulled her into a one armed hug.

"You fight with great skill Jett, just watch your grip, it might undo you." He took her sword as everyone cheered, and took the measure of it. "Nice blade well balanced." He handed it back and picked up his own sword. He walked over to Robbie as Jade and Blades ran to Jett. "She is good, you have wisdom in who you choose around you Robbie lad." John watched her carefully as she spoke with Jade and Blades. "Can I borrow her and Rafe later for the sword trials? With a teacher like her we could really show our guys a thing or two."

Rune smiled at him. "Take Blades as well, she is Jett's equal, they like a good work out."

John scratched his chin. "I notice she has blades like Harry, is she as good as him?"

Robbie nodded. "Actually, I think she is better."

Jess came out of the greenhouse and sat on the step next to Alice who was gasping for air. She patted her back. "It's been some time since you mixed up that feed, maybe you need to get used to the smell again."

Alice took large deep breaths. "I don't understand it Aunt Jess, the smell has never bothered me before." Alice retched again.

"How is the backache, has it eased?" Alice nodded as she gasped for more air. Jess smiled and put her arm around Alice.

"How long do you think you can hide this Alice; it will soon start to show?"

Alice drew a long gasp and looked very frightened, as she looked at her. "How do you know?"

"I know you my sweet niece, and I am a woman which helps. You will need to tell him soon Alice... I am surprised Beth has not noticed it, but you have been avoiding her, so maybe it has not dawned on her. I take it its Billy's?"

Alice's eyes filled with tears as she nodded, and Jess pulled her close. "Oh sweetheart, I am sorry, come on, let's go inside where it's private." Jess walked down the path as Alice wept at her side.

Three hours later, Beth sat back in her chair as she cuddled her daughter. "Now love don't you fret, we can deal with just about anything, we are Lox."

Jess gave her a smile. "I am not sure John will see it that way, would you like me to tell him?" Beth shook her head slowly.

"No, it will be better if I break it to him in a way only, I know. He will be fine don't you worry my darling." She patted Alice on the back as she spoke.

During the evening meal, Alice was very quiet at the table and Robbie watched her, he had noticed Rune seemed to pick up on Alice's apprehension. Jess looked out of the window as John came steaming down the yard with Beth running after him. "John, don't you dare, I mean it."

The kitchen door burst open and the wild eyes of John stared across the table at Alice, as he slammed his huge fist down on the table, all the cups and plates jumped in the air. "IS IT TRUE?" He bellowed at Alice. He went to move round the table, and Robbie was up like a shot and his sword was out. "IS IT HIS?"

John stopped as he saw the steel look in Robbie's eye. "You will not hurt her

John; I won't allow it." Rune was now on the opposite side of Alice, her eyes flickered violet. Alice clung shaking to Jess.

Robbie could see the fear and the anger mixed in John's eyes but he kept the sword of truth up in front of him, as the rainbows danced reflected from the blade on John's angry face. "THAT'S MY DAUGHTER, GET OUT OF MY WAY!"

Robbie stepped forward in front of Alice and Jess. "Calm down John, you are terrifying her; none of us expected him to be who he is. It's not her fault." John pulled at the table, and it flew across the room smashing against the wall. Pots shattered on the stone floor, and Alice blinked and jumped clinging terrified to Jess. Rune stepped up to Robbie and waved a hand in front of him, as her eyes flared deep purple.

John stared Robbie in the eyes, and Robbie swallowed hard as he felt Alice shaking against his legs. Rune's shoulder touched his, as Robbie faced the terrifying mass that was a hurt and angry John. He understood him, but he could not let him hurt Alice. "I am sorry John but I will not let you near her like this. Please John, she is scared enough."

John hit the chair and it disintegrated into broken pieces all over the floor. "Get out of my way son; this is between me and her."

Robbie spoke quietly and calmly. "She is your daughter John, you know...? Your little girl, don't do this like this, she deserves better and you know it, save your anger for him." Robbie kept his eyes fixed on John and his sword high. John's eyes seem to flicker as he looked to the floor and then to his daughter.

"Alice?" His voice was barely a whisper, as the tears filled his eyes. John flopped like a man utterly defeated into the only standing chair, as Beth ran in and screamed at the sight of Robbie holding his sword up to his uncle.

Beth smacked John across the head, and the slap resounded around the kitchen. Rune flinched. "NOW LOOK WHAT YOU GONE AND DONE, THE POOR LADS DRAWN HIS SWORD ON YOU... YOU SHOULD BE ASHAMED OF YOURSELF JOHN HENRY LOX... AND LOOK WHAT YOU DONE TO THE TABLE, YOU BRUTE!"

She slapped him again even harder and John flinched. Robbie slowly lowered his sword and slid it back in its sheath. John just stared at his little girl as tears ran down his face. "Alice, sweetheart, I am sorry."

Alice burst with huge sobs, and came across the kitchen into his arms. "I am so sorry daddy."

John pulled her into a huge bear like hug, and rocked her with his head on her tiny shoulder as he sobbed with her. Beth burst into tears and leant over them hugging them both. Jess breathed a huge sigh of relief, she looked at Robbie as he turned to her.

"Just what the hell are you doing pulling that bloody big sword on your uncle?"

Robbie reeled in shock. "I was...defending Alice."

John laughed, and looked at the furious Jess. "He done right Jess. He knew I would not hurt him and he calmed me. Thanks Robbie, my anger is not here, it is wherever that sneaking bastard is. I mean it I will rip his bloody skin off."

'SLAP!' John squealed, as Beth hit him again. "Stop scaring Alice, and stop bloody swearing in front of her."

John looked down at his daughter as he rocked her weeping into his arms. "Sorry love."

Robbie relaxed as Rune took his hand, her eyes returning to lilac, they both sat down again.

Beth scurried round the kitchen drying her eyes. "I will put the kettle on; a cup of tea will sort all of us out." Jess smiled at John who grinned up from his daughter.

Rune giggled at Robbie as she slid up close to him. "You are either mad or brave, and at the moment I am not exactly sure."

Jess grinned. "He is brave... a hell of a lot braver than the rest of us, Harry is the mad one in our nest."

Jess put her hand up to his face and softly smiled at him. "You are so like your dad at times." Her eyes glistened as she stroked his long hair. "All this upheaval and change, I worry about all of us."

Robbie smiled and took his mum's hand. "Somehow I think as long as we have you and Beth, we will all be fine Mum, just don't write me off the work rota, I will be coming back to finish learning my plant lore when all this is done."

Jess gave him a broad grin. "I love you Robbie, and I would really love it if you did, I have missed you so much." She leaned over and he gave her a huge hug.

Rune smiled as she watched him with her, "I will always come home mum, I belong here."

Beth stood by the sink and burst into tears again as she watched. Tears rolled down her red face, and she howled at the tenderness between a mother and her son. "Oh, I am so sorry I can't help it, I just love you all so much."

CHAPTER EIGHT

A NEW AGE BEGINS

Alice stood at the gate as Robbie and Rune came out, she smiled at him in his ceremonial clothes. Rune had made him a Lincoln green velvet shirt with silk ties, and matching green canvas pants, she cut them tight, as she liked to see them on him.

His hooded cloak was thick Lincoln green heavy velvet, and he wore a golden belt of oak leaves. The blue sapphire acorn was pinned above his richly embroidered Loxley crest. Rune wore a matching long skirt of Lincoln green with a matching top and her long dark purple velvet cloak. She had a silver belt of acorns inlaid with sparkling sapphires. Alice caught her breath. "You two look beautiful." Rune's eyes sparkled as the golden tiara decorated with oak leaves glistened in the sun.

Alice had her duty as Able Bowman of Loxley to protect Robbie, and she was dressed identical to Rune, Robbie held up his arm and smiling brightly she took it. They walked down the street and everybody stopped and bowed to Lord Loxley, for with his ceremonial guard he looked truly like a lord of high standing. "Is everything alright now?" Robbie was still concerned for Alice; she squeezed his arm.

"It is fine Robbie, dad and me talked for hours last night," she pondered for a bit. "I have never spoken so much with him before; it was really nice." She leaned over to him and kissed his cheek. "Thanks Robbie... That was the bravest thing I have ever seen; I was so scared he would hurt you."

"I gave you my word Alice, I told you at the camp, I would stand by you and I meant it."

Rune smiled as she leaned forward to look at Alice. "I am so glad it has worked out, for a moment there I was really scared, I put a protection around all of us."

Alice nodded. "He doesn't mean it, and he is so sorry about it all, he would never hurt you Rob. My dad is so proud of you, honestly he never stops talking about how you are a true Lox and just like your dad."

They reached the doors to the village hall and walked in as the guards saluted, Rune gave him a shrewd look and he smiled. "Just the guards I promise."

The large hall was laid out so that the tables formed a huge gigantic square. In the centre was a large map of the country like the one at Caerleon, only bigger. Red and green figures stood on it and through the centre were endless lines of blue. Robbie noticed straight away how Knox had moved forward and how south of London was all Knox territory.

Skip smiled as Robbie came down the long hall. "Robert my dear friend," he embraced him. "I believe you were off seeking some solitude when I arrived… Good to hear it, you needed a good rest." Rune smiled at him and her eyes twinkled.

Skip pointed to the map. "As you can see, we have been busy, we are already finding and filling up towns with anyone who comes north. The good news is that there are a lot of woodsmen, I reckon you have an army of at least twelve thousand, and it's growing by the day."

Robbie was staggered. "That many, that is great news Skip." He frowned a little.

"Knox has got at least ten times that Robbie, but it is a good start considering the time scale, more are pouring in as we speak."

Fuse walked up with some papers. "Good morning My Lord." He nodded.

"Hello Fuse, I see you are working hard for my people." Fuse smiled.

"I look at the stars every night and it gives me the drive to work harder." He smiled and Robbie nodded.

The room began to fill as the visitors arrived. Una, Mel, Maddy, and Steph arrived in their best ceremonial robes; they looked like women of high standing as they sat at the tables. Jett, Ruby, Treen, and Alley came up and smiled as they were seated; all of them wore long flowing robes or flared skirts, Ruby leaned back and blew him a kiss. Len walked about with Robert Lox and discussed affairs with many of the leaders. Robbie had never seen so many different crests on cloaks, he was used to the red lion of Caerleon, but now he saw a wide range of symbols from eagles to stone circles and flowers. The whole of the woodsman world had representation here to listen to the words of their leader.

Rowan arrived with Jade on his arm and Robbie smiled. Rowan looked as uncomfortable as he felt, and Jade wore green velvet pants, Alley spotted them and pointed showing her mother who scowled.

"My Lord." Rowan bowed to him and Jade beamed.

He laughed; "You look as uncomfortable as I do Rowan." He smiled.

"I am a simple woodsman; I prefer woodsman attire and damp leaves under my feet."

Robbie patted his shoulder. "We will my friend and soon."

Robbie, Rune, and Alice, were seated in their carved chairs at the head of the room, as everyone else settled down. Robbie noticed Bear looking upset, his frame seemed to sag, and he did not hold himself quite as erect as he normally did.

Alice leaned over to Robbie. "His father was attacked and killed Robbie on the way here; it has been quite a blow for him." Robbie was shocked and looked down at Skip.

"Why was I not told of this?" He felt angry, Alice touched his wrist.

"We only got news half an hour ago." Robbie jumped out of his seat and everyone stared as he walked down the long table towards Bear. He saw him coming toward him and he slid his chair back, and stood up and bowed.

"My Lord." Robbie threw his arms around Bear and hugged him.

"I am so angry; I was only just informed. Jacques, please accept my deepest apology and deepest condolence; I would have come straight away had I known. Is there anything I can do at this difficult time for you, my friend?"

Bear was moved, and weakly smiled. "My Lord, your family have done everything they possibly can, I am deeply touched and thank you for your concern and kind comments."

Robbie looked at him closely. "We will dine together tonight and talk my friend." Robbie patted his back and Jacques returned to his seat, as Robbie headed back to his.

Finally, the gathering of the woodsmen began, Robert Lox called the meeting to order and Skip spoke for an hour pointing out where Knox was and what areas he had cleared, and how many refugees had travelled north so far. He asked all assembled to find space to house those who had been moved from the south into their areas, and help with his relief effort. His report was very finely detailed, and delivered with eloquence, Robbie sat back and smiled to himself; he was proud of Skip and saw in him his true lordship finally displayed. Skip sat down and Robbie nodded to Jacques.

"My Lord, I can give you our guarantee that York will offer its full support, and we already have space cleared ready to receive any who can travel a little further."

An older man rose with white hair. "My Lord I am Michael of Lancaster. We have vast areas of land with adequate dwellings, which are unoccupied. We would happily welcome any to our county that would wish to help us strengthen the region. We have great resources for farming in our area and any with agricultural skills would help benefit not just us, but any who are short of food."

Robbie gave a smile. "I am very grateful to Lancaster My Lord; food will always be a priority." He looked at Skip. "Make sure all who head that way have the skills to aid Lancaster." Skip nodded and gave a smile as he wrote on his sheets.

A tall man in deep burgundy rose from his seat. "I am Ian of Carlisle and I too offer shelter to woodsmen who would help support our efforts in the north My Lord. We have a huge range of woodland to cover, and more people would assist us. We find we are too thinly spaced to provide adequate protection to all."

Robbie nodded. "We are very grateful My Lord of Carlisle. Prepare your towns and I promise we will fill them." A thin man in all green stood up, and Robbie looked across to him and nodded.

"My Lord with all due respect, how can you expect us to do this? We all are under great strain and fear for the lives of our own. It is all well and good for the likes of Caerleon, who flout authority about and dictate the terms to us who have few, how many refugees are under their roof? I see little blue on the map of Wales. We already have a fight at our own door."

Robbie was about to speak when Jett stood up and slammed her sword on the table. "What is your name Lord?"

The man looked amused. "I am Edgar of Liverpool."

Robbie leaned forward and Rune touched his hand, as Jett laughed aloud. "You dare slur the good name of Caerleon and my father's house, when you sit with free borders and the protection of Wales to your side. Caerleon has protected your borders for the last ten years; Liverpool is and has been free of trouble throughout. It has been we, who police all of Wales, we, who have sent out aid to prevent the fall of Bristol. We gave our lives to help Lord Brandon recapture Gloucester. We provided the shelter for our lord, it has, been Caerleon who supported the fall of Tintagel. Our arrows that levelled his castle in London, and our lives that surrounded the Cathedral whilst Lord Loxley dealt with Mason Knox. Where were your men? Sat at home, hiding in the trees protected by the men of Caerleon? I demand you withdraw your statement, or I will seek satisfaction for my father's name now."

Her eyes flared blue and Lord Edgar shrank in his seat, Robbie stood up. "Thank you, Lady Jett Amber. The work of Caerleon has been faultless, and I have nothing but admiration and respect to the massive effort they have given. I think all of us here know of their loyalty and support." He stepped down and walked towards the end of the room, as many heads in the room nodded with agreement, Robbie stopped at Edgar's side. He was a thin weasel faced looking man.

"Lord Edgar by the rules of the woodsman law you must apologise to Caerleon, and knowing this good lady's skill with a blade, I would suggest you withdraw your comments and soon." Edgar looked up at Robbie and then glared at Jett across the table, his apology felt forced through his lips.

"Yes, My Lord, I can assure the good lady we meant no offence to her family, or the efforts they have made on the behalf of all of us." Jett stared at him with malice as he spoke, her hand resting on her golden sword.

"Good. You may sit Lady Jett. Edgar tell me, what problems do Liverpool have? I am led to believe you have good trade with Ireland as it is prosperous, and have no shortage of food." Edgar felt pressured under the bright gaze of Robbie, as he noticed every eye in the room was now on him.

"We have some trade My Lord, but we are isolated and alone since the collapse of old Manchester." Robbie smiled and glanced at Jett who had now sat down and put her sword away.

"That is why I believe your borders are patrolled courtesy of Caerleon who have administered all of Wales and yourselves for many years now. Edgar we are all threatened, and there is not a man here who has not seen loss in his territory, Liverpool is expected to play its part as everyone here will."

"Yes, My Lord, we will do as much as we are able." He looked down at his papers; Robbie patted his shoulder and smiled.

"Good, I will ensure Caerleon is informed to help you supervise your efforts."

Jett smiled as Robbie walked back up the room to his chair, every eye in the room was on him as he turned. "My good Ladies, Gentlemen, and My Lords. Mason Knox means to kill and up root every tree and blade of grass in this country. I have seen his work up close as I walked in Tintagel, and saw the eyesore he had built, there was no plant life left. He is burning all of the south coast, and using machines to level the land, and build his new towns and cities to bring back the ways of the old modern age. This land is threatened and our existence as a race of people is doomed if we do not stop him. We have our plans and we intend to act to stop him, I will personally see to that, my only question here today is this. Who will join me?"

Jacques stood up with Jett. "York, Caerleon." It slowly went round the room as leaders stood and declared their interests "Carlisle, Warwick, Lincoln, Lancaster." Edgar was the last to stand as everyone glared at him.

Robbie raised his hands and everyone sat and looked his way. "Thank you everyone. Over the coming days we will have plans for all of you, in the mean time you are guests of Loxley, so please enjoy your time with us and I will speak with you all in the coming days." Everyone stood and bowed, and then broke apart to discuss with others or offer aid to Skip. Rune watched as Robbie sat back and paid close attention to Edgar. "I don't trust him Rune."

"I trust your instincts, Rob." Robbie winked at Jade and Rowan and they came over towards him, he leaned forward.

"Pebbles, I have a little job for you." She smiled.

"Already one step ahead of you Robbie, Dave tipped me off earlier, he doesn't trust him either, Martin has been on him all day and Fish will be on his tail tonight."

Robbie smiled. "You truly are a woodsman of Loxley my Pebbles." She beamed at him. He sat back and looked across the large hall, Edgar had already left and he turned to Rune. "Stay clear of him, OK? Just to be on the safe side."

She smiled at him and turned to Maddy, who had leaned over to whisper to her. Rune nodded and then looked back at him. "My family would like you to have a meal with all of them later, they need to talk to you." He nodded.

"Oh, I promised Bear... could I bring him along? He is not at his best with the loss of his father, and to be honest Rune I would very much like a talk with him." Rune gripped his hand.

"I should think that will be fine." She smiled sweetly at him. "You have the support you need Rob, and looking at the way Skip has organised things, I really think it will help all the woods folk."

Over the following hours many of the woodsmen leaders came up and introduced themselves, Robbie and Rune spoke with each of them, and they discussed their territories, and he slowly began to build up a picture of the country around him. Robbie stood next to Skip as five woodsmen discussed the strengthening of the divide across the country. Rune sat back with Alice and she warmly smiled to herself as she watched him. "For all his hatred of being a lord, and his attempts to be just himself, just look how like a lord he truly is."

Alice smiled back at her. "He has always had that little extra something that no one else ever seemed to have. Do you think he has realised yet that by being himself, he is actually being Lord Loxley?"

Rune giggled. "He has no idea at all." He smiled and spoke his mind, and everyone listened as Robbie gave his idea of what the country should be. His love of the woods was so evident and all around him agreed with him. Rune noticed Alice watching her and smiled. "I know, I can't help it... He is my whole life Alice." Her voice had dropped and Alice put her hand on hers. "I would die of the pain if I lost him."

"You won't lose him Rune, stay close by him always, and you will protect each other."

The time passed and the room slowly cleared. Rune walked up behind him as he talked with Skip and slid her arms around him from behind and put her head on his shoulder. He held her hands close to him as Skip nodded, and walked away smiling at Rune to gather the huge pile of papers he had written on. Robbie tipped his head to one side and she nuzzled into his neck and kissed him softly. "Let's head back Robbie."

They stepped out on to the pathway with Alice and Bear, a crowd had gathered knowing he would be there. Everyone went quiet as the Lord of Loxley and Lady Runestone came through the door, the crowd smiled at them, and Rune held him close as they approached the throng. A woman stepped out from the crowd and bowed. "Bless you My Lord and Lady."

Robbie and Rune walked slowly through the crowd as the strangers took their hands and shook them. "Hearne bless you both. Thank you for all you have done My Lord and Lady." It seemed endless, and Robbie looked around at all the happy smiling faces of people who were now town's folk. Most of them now lived in the long rows of wooden cabins near the gate; Robbie smiled and nodded his head although his surprise was such that he could not find the right words.

Someone threw flower petals into the air, and they floated down and settled on his shoulders, as the old and the young, and middle aged all wanted to give their own personal wishes to him. They separated as Rune walked on his arm, and at the end of the lane from the village hall, Robbie turned to face them all, everyone stood silent and waited for their lord to address them.

"The Lady Runestone and myself are very touched that you have come out today, and I find it difficult to find the right words to express myself... I am one man of a team that has worked very closely together, with the single aim of saving our way of life, I am, honoured by your praise. Please honour everyone who took part, for they all risked their lives in your cause, there are some very brave men and women in Loxley today, and they deserve your respect and your praise. There are two in particular who will never walk on the good soil of Loxley again, for they paid a very high price for their valour. I beg you honour them above all others, honour Anthony Ashford and Eric Tanner, for without their devotion neither myself, nor my good lady, would be here today. Honour them for they are the true heroes of Loxley."

Rune saw Nellie in the crowd with a smile on her face and a tear in her eye. Robbie turned and with Rune, he walked down the street, Alice and Bear walked at their side and they all looked truly the Lords and Ladies they had become.

Robbie sat out in a small chair in the back yard next to Jade's flat. He smiled as he saw the small blue swing seat attached to the wall that now had been inlaid with silver and read, 'Jade's Place'.

He leaned back in the chair and closed his eyes, it was quiet, peaceful, and free of people shaking his hand constantly and he relaxed. Movement brought him out of his thoughts and he looked at Alice sat on the wall beside him, she smiled.

"Sorry I did not want to disturbed you." She took a drink from her tall glass of juice. "It is very humbling, isn't it?"

"I hate it Alice, they praise me above all others and it is wrong. Everyone risked their life in Tintagel and the Cathedral."

Alice shrugged her shoulders. "You shouldered all the responsibility Robbie. You planned it, and we followed your lead and you brought us out. Do you not think you are being too hard on yourself; your ideas were brilliant and they worked wonderfully, you should be praised for seeing what everyone else did not see?"

"I still could not have done it alone Alice; everyone should be thanked for the bravery they showed alone."

"They are not lords though Robbie, when are you going to accept that you are the figurehead, and the standard that we all gathered with pride below. I sat in that camp the night before knowing I could die the following day. I still cleaned my bow, and sharpened my sword, and not because it meant stopping Knox. I was prepared to die in support of my lord, because I love him and I am deeply honoured to know he is such a man of great worth. You are one of the most precious people in this world to me Robbie, like it or not, I will die to protect you, and I will die happy knowing I did. Everyman at your side that day felt exactly as I did, so I think you should start to live with that fact."

Robbie was lost for words, Alice looked fierce as she spoke, and she reminded him a lot of Beth when she hit John. "You are not going to slap me are you?"

Alice started to giggle. "No, I will save that for Bear if he misbehaves."

"You and he seem to be getting on very well; does he know... you know?"

She smiled at him. "Yes, I told him, and he understands my predicament. He is not concerned and says he will help me through it... Mickie is very sweet when you get to know him, he does remind me of dad a lot... You don't think that's sort of weird, do you?"

Robbie started to laugh. "No Alice, I think it is wonderful, and I must admit I am very happy to see you so happy, no its not weird, if he was like Harry, now that would be."

Alice beamed as she giggled and bent down and hugged him. "I love you, Rob."

He put his hands around her. "I love you too sis."

The afternoon passed slowly as Bear and Rune joined them and they all sat quietly out of sight, and laughed and joked with each other. Rowan and Jade appeared, brought two chairs out of the flat, and joined the group of close happy friends.

That evening they walked back to the hall where a long feasting table had been set up, and the two circles of knowledge and life joined with the Lox family and Len Rimmer. Fuse and Skip had been included, and he was especially pleased to see Fish, Rafe, Big John and Martin with his family. Rags and Lucy seemed to have been adopted by Jess who had brought them along saying 'you are family to me.' It was a grand affair as the table was laid with a wide range of foods all cooked by Steph, Maddy, and Mel.

Robbie sat at the head of the table flanked by Rune and Alice, and the families laughed at their exploits and recounted the stories of life in the woods to and from Canterbury, of which Jett and Jade seemed to lead the conversation. Harry told the tale of Bear and his encounter with the big Cutter, and Bear laughed hard as Harry used many cosmic words about his swordplay.

Robbie watched as half way through the meal Jade and Jett laughed hysterically about the revelation of their ants in the pants caper. John and Martin, who suddenly realised, looked up shocked, he put his knife and fork down and leaned on his hands and smiled as he watched the room of happy faces.

Rune put her hand on his shoulder, as Jess looked at her son and smiled at him with a warm and loving smile. Robbie smiled a happy smile, and although they were ten feet apart and could not speak to each other, Rune could see that there was no need for a mother to express her love and her pride with words.

Len Rimmer tapped his glass and stood up, and he smiled as everyone quietened down and looked at him. He cleared his throat as he looked around. "Ladies and Gentlemen, I am very delighted to have a small opportunity to just welcome all of you to Loxley. I see we have four families here tonight that have joined to share this meal. My children from my first marriage have returned to me, and that has brought me great joy. I have more of my family from my second marriage around me and I too am grateful." He smiled at Jett and Ruby

"I also am very pleased to see we have the members of the team that have formed a family of protection around our lord, you have grown close and bonded in his company, and I am thrilled to have met such honourable people. But there is a family who without them, none of us would be here; I speak of the kind and generous family of Lox." Everyone smiled at John and Beth sat with Robert and Jess. Len gave a big smile.

"You have given shelter and homes to many. You have pulled together as a family, and helped so many who were in need of help, and you have made your home the centre and focus of this world of woodland life. You are the example that has shown us the way to live, and you have given us your son to show us how to stand up and fight for our way of life. Everyone here in this room tonight I ask you to raise a glass and stand in honour of the Noble House of Lox."

Everyone stood and faced the family and raised their glasses. Rune stood and turned to Robbie. "The Noble House of Lox." She spoke with all the others, and smiled as she took a drink of her wine. Jess smiled and leaned against Robert as he lifted his hand to her, and nodded to everyone in the room. Beth wiped a tear from her eyes and Alice beamed at Robbie. Robbie looked at his dad and rose up from his seat.

He looked at all the happy faces as he swallowed deeply. "Thank you for those kind words Leenard. I think all of you know my father, and those who do not, let me tell of how great a man he is. This was the land of my grandfather and his before that; it was my grandfather Jake and my father who built this stockade, it was hard work and they fought hard to protect all that came here. My father like his father is the most honourable man that I know, and if any credit is attributed to me, then it is to him, you should say your thank you. Like him I have learned from my father, as to me he is my example and my hero, I raise my glass to the greatest man of honour I am privileged to be the son of... Robert Lox."

Everyone followed Robbie and toasted him as Jess squeezed his arm. Robert just looked at his son with tears in his eyes, and smiled as Robbie bowed with Rune and Alice to him, he gave a nod of thanks lost for words.

The meal was over and the table cleared, and everyone sat talking in small groups. Maddy walked up to Robbie. "Could I speak to you and Rune privately?"

Robbie nodded and signalled to the small office door, Maddy led the way followed by Rune and Robbie into the room. Maddy sat in front of the large polished desk, and Rune sat at her side. Robbie moved behind the desk, sat, and smiled. "What can I do for you Maddy?"

"Robbie, I have something for you, which Mother gave to me many years ago. Her instructions to me were when the king's seat is safe, and you need to find her sword, to give this to the Bowman who leads."

Maddy pulled a golden box from under her cloak and placed it on the table. It was delicately carved with bright golden runes; Robbie looked at it as it glistened in the light of the room.

"You said your mother's sword?" Maddy smiled.

"My mother made the sword for Lancelot, the sword you seek is her work, and I think that the means to find it are in this box." Rune looked at Robbie and smiled, she knew his greatest worry was knowing where to start his search. Maddy slid the box across the table. "Open it later when you and Rune are alone, I understood a lot of my mothers work, so if you have problems with the runes or its contents I would be honoured to help out."

Robbie nodded his eyes on the box. "Thank you Maddy, I will seek your advice if I need it." She smiled and stood up.

"I hope that you will require a bow to replace Alice and accept mine My Lord." Robbie and Rune both looked surprised and she smiled. "In the olden days when the church burnt witches it was usually because we were midwives who used old methods to help at birth, I know a pregnant woman when I see one, Alice is exceptional with a bow, but I feel her father will not allow her to leave here now. I offer you my bow as recompense for her loss."

Robbie nodded. "It would be gratefully accepted Lady Madeleine." She gave him a large smile, and she turned and walked to the door and closed it quietly behind her. He looked at Rune. "I had not thought of having to leave Alice. It will not be right without her."

Rune looked saddened as much as he was. "She is a good friend and we talked a lot on the road."

Raised voices came from the main hall and someone screamed, Robbie and Rune jumped up and ran to the door; Robbie tugged the door open and ran into the hall. Everyone was on their feet and staring at Mac, who held Alice by the throat. Martin, John and Fish had their bows loaded and pointed at him, as he waved a long black steel sword out in front of him, John and Robert both with swords in their hands, glared menacingly at him as he backed to the door.

Alice tried to struggle but his arm squeezed tighter shortening her breath. "YOU KNOW OF THE SEED THAT GROWS IN HERE AND YOU KNOW IT IS NOT LOXLEY?"

Robbie pulled his sword and moved quickly down towards Mac. "Unhand my cousin and you will not die Mac."

"YOU HAVE NO POWER OVER ME; YOU ARE JUST AN OUTLAW AND GRAIN THIEF!"

Robbie moved carefully forward. "Those are names I have heard before Mac, have you found a new master to guide you? Unhand my cousin and I will let you live long enough to tell me." Robbie pushed his father out of the way as he stepped in front. Rowan slid Robbie's bow from the table.

"I SERVE A HIGHER POWER THAN MASON KNOX; MY GRANDMOTHER'S POWER HAS NO LIMITS." Una pulled her hands to her mouth and gasped.

"No Mac not her?" He smiled as his back touched the door.

"She has taught me more in ten years than you ever have, and you are supposed to be the daughter, her power will crush all of you." He pushed the door as Rowan whistled and threw the bow. Robbie dropped his sword, and caught it in one hand and slid an arrow from the quiver on John's back.

Rune's eyes exploded with violet as Sapphire's burned bright blue, Rune waved her hand and the walls turned violet with a shimmering light. Robbie pulled the arrow to the string as Alice screamed her eyes wide with fear and he pulled back and aimed.

A hideous howl came out of the dark and Robbie released his arrow, a huge black bird swooped down and snatched Alice and Mac into the air, the arrow hit air. Robbie flew to the door seizing another arrow as Alice's screams faded into the darkness. He ran out and pointed his bow up into dark sky, Alice was gone and he fell to his knees and screamed. "Aliiiiiiiiiiiiiiiiiiiiice!" He flopped to the floor and wept.

Rune stood on the path her eyes flaring bright purple and she began to spin on the spot, a violet beam shot into the air and streaked north. She slowed down and her eyes faded to lilac. "Help is with her Robbie; she is not alone."

John screamed into the dark as Beth hugged him weeping. Robert talked quickly to him to calm him; Bear looked at Rune as she pulled Robbie weeping from the floor.

"Which way did she go Rune?"

Len touched Bears shoulder. "She will be safe. The Dark One will not hurt her until the child is born, be calm we need to think, you will not catch her, the Dark One flies fast."

Rune guided Robbie back inside where Una sat as her sisters hugged her and she wept. Rowan looked at Robbie and Rune, as Jade wept into his shoulder. Rune nodded and his face dropped, and he pulled Jade closer, John came in holding a weeping Beth and he put his large hand on Rune's shoulder.

"Why is she not alone?"

Rune turned with tears in her eyes. "The blue jay of hope follows her, and it is the only thing that can fly fast enough to keep up with her. It will reach her and then I can speak to her."

John nodded. "When you find my girl, I will be coming along. If they hurt one hair on her head, so help me there is no magic on this earth that will protect them, Mac will die by my hand alone." His face was fierce and white, but his sudden calmness made him more terrifying.

Rune trembled as Robbie looked up and she nodded at John. "Alright John, I will guide you to her."

"Good." He picked up Beth still weeping, and walked out of the door.

Rune pulled Robbie close and wept, he put his hands around her and held her close, Robbie looked around the room. "Prepare for a trip, we will leave as soon as I can find out where they are." John, Martin, Fish, Rafe, and Rags nodded. Steph and Smokes nodded as Rowan and Jade came beside him.

Jett and Ruby got up and Saff and Alley both stood up with them. Robbie looked at them both, and it was Saff who spoke. "Without the swords you cannot defeat her, you need all of us, we also have a score to settle with that evil bitch, she killed our grandmother. We will be coming too My Lord."

Mel helped Una up off the chair. "We will prepare, Una has great power of protection and I have a few of my mother's gifts." Jaz walked up to Robbie and bowed before him.

"My Lord I am fierce in battle and can communicate in ways that will chill your bones, please accept my sword."

Robbie patted his shoulder. "Thank you, Jasper, I would be honoured to accept your sword beside mine."

Jasper smiled. "Lady Alice has been very nice to me since I arrived as have all your family, I will serve them loyally." He bowed and walked out of the room.

Robert, Len and Jess were all that was left, as they sat down with Rowan and Jade. Robbie kissed the top of Rune's head as he released her from his arms. "I have to find the sword and use its combined powers with the other swords to save Alice, and defeat the Dark One, and then we continue looking for the king. Dad, please help Fuse and Skip and get our army ready, we will need every man we can get before this is all over."

Robert stood up and hugged his son. "You have no need to ask me my son; I will always aid my boy." He patted Robbie on the back, Rune's eyes flickered violet and she closed them. Robbie watched as she nodded as if having a conversation and then she smiled and opened them again.

"Rowan and Jade must accompany us now to the Mere Robbie, Opal awaits us and she wants you." Robbie nodded and turned to his mum; he gave her a hug and kissed her on the head.

"I will see you in the morning before I leave." She smiled, and nodded, and gave him a huge squeeze.

"I love you, my son." Robert and Jess left and the four of them walked quickly up to the rear of Rune's house. Five horses stood saddled and ready to go. Len smiled.

"She does talk to me occasionally you know?" He winked at Rune and she grinned as she pulled herself up. They all mounted their horses and Robbie led the way in the dark, he knew the roads from 17 years of life in Loxley, and as they passed Hay Cottages and turned on to the Sacred Wood Road, he urged his horse forward in the dark. They followed his lead as he slowed and headed on to the fine path that wove through the trees.

Opal glowed in the moonlight, as they came out of the trees and stopped. Len looked over to Robbie. "Can I have a moment alone please; she is my wife and we have been separated too much recently?" Robbie noticed the sincerity in Len's eyes, and he nodded as the others got off their horses. Rune came to his side and slipped her arm around him and she watched as Len took Opal in his arms and kissed her. She could not hear their conversation, but she knew it was deep and loving from Opal's face.

"I have to my darling, things are moving faster, we will not have the time we expected, the strength of the Dark One is too great, and I have given most of my power to Rune. I am weak my love."

"Oh no, Opal please take some of my power and remain near me. I cannot bear to lose you." She smiled and softly stroked his long white hair.

"I have watched Rune with her bowman, and they remind me so much of us in the beginning." Opal smiled as she curled her finger in his long white goatee. "The age is over, now is the eve of the age of dreams my love, you know I am right. How can I send her unprepared?"

Tears ran from Len's eyes, as he pulled her into an embrace. "Goodbye my love, my life will grow paler without you."

"Goodbye my love, I will wait with Gwendolyn in the other realms, take care of our children and help Runestone, your age of dreams begins today." She kissed him softly.

Rune watched as Len walked sadly and slowly across the glade, he approached Rune and she drew her breath. He had aged at least another ten years.

"Go to her Runestone, and take your friends." Len walked past and pulled himself up on to his horse. He looked back across the glade as the lady in all white watched, he blew her a kiss, and she waved slowly back. With tears in his eyes, he turned the horse and rode out of the clearing.

The four of them walked towards Opal who had her hood down and smiled, Robbie noticed how much older she was now, as she smiled at him. Opal opened her arms and embraced Rune. "My dear daughter of the woods, you blossom more each time I see you." Rune smiled.

"It's my bowman." Opal smiled and looked at Robbie and winked.

"Two men of such power and honour for my two favourite granddaughter's, I can see the happiness and the love that surround you all. Listen to me carefully; the four of you must stay together, there is a power between you that nothing can harm, stay close at all times and you will be protected." Opal crossed to Jade and pulled her close. "I have a gift for you my little green eyed wood nymph." She opened her hand and placed a white marble into it. "In times of great need, throw this and you will find a way to get through." She kissed Jade on the head and Jade's eyes glowed a bright and intense green.

Jade sensed something was not right. "You are not leaving us are you grandma, I will see you again?" Opal smiled and cupped her face.

"Do you love me Jade Opal, for you have my name?"

Tears welled in her eyes. "Of course, I love you Grandma, you are Opal who we all love and admire, and you are my hero and my inspiration."

"Then how can I leave you Jade Opal of the woods? I will see you again have no fear my precious child." Opal turned to Rowan.

"Woodsman, you have made two lives complete in the love you hold for my special granddaughter. You have done well in the service of both your lords, take care of her for me and treasure her, for she has qualities no other will ever possess." He smiled at her and she embraced him and whispered. "This is hard for me; take Jade away for a walk."

Rowan nodded and took Jade's hand as Opal turned to Robbie. Rowan walked back to the trees as Jade watched walking away.

"My bowman, where can I begin, I cannot say, you have done so much, and mean so much to so many others. The love you hold for my child is so great I feel it overpower me, I have only one task for you my dear bowman and that is love her, and stay by her side and enjoy the time you have. Make her feel special every day and take joy from your children, but most importantly show her you love her always." She kissed his forehead.

Opal turned to Rune, and Rune's eyes flared violet. "Runestone, I have given you a lot of my power and now I am starting to fade as I reach my true age. The age of sleep ends tonight, it is earlier than planned."

"No grandma not yet, I still need you, please I beg you don't leave me alone." Rune burst into tears and threw herself into her grandmother's arms. "I don't want you to go I love you grandmother."

"Child listen to me... The coming of the age of dreams will begin at midnight and you will have your true power, I can no longer share it with you, it drains your strength. You have to grow strong and help your bowman and his family, that will not happen with two forces at work." She kissed Rune on the head as she held her weeping in her arms.

"I love you dearly my child, take care of your sister and watch over the rest of my extended family. We will meet again in the other realm where I will wait for the most powerful of all this family's line, for you do not realise what you can do my child. I shall leave you shortly and then you must help the bowman discover the answer of Gwendolyn's box. My time here is done, the age of dreams has been written on the Runestone for many generations, fight all the Dark Ones and win for my lord and father. For you are now the true daughter of Hearne, white is finished, now the violet brings death followed by rebirth." Rune wept as Opal squeezed her tightly as she looked at Robbie.

"Goodbye my hooded man, raise your hood one more time and honour me." Robbie raised his hood as Rune wept long sobbing bitter tears, and the glade suddenly lit up with intense white light. Rune screamed out loud as she floated high into the air spread eagled casting a shadow on the floor of a five pointed star. Robbie could not pull back his hood it was so bright, that even under his hood he had to screw his eyes up to stop his eyes from burning.

The clouds parted and violet light funnelled out of the sky and flowed down on to Rune, who screamed with fear as the power totally consumed her. There was an almighty explosion as Jade came screaming through the trees with Rowan, and both of them were blasted forty feet back into the wood. White light pulsated mixing with violet, and streamed out of the clouds and narrowed into a pale beam that flowed into the screaming Rune who glowed in the deepest of purple, and then suddenly, everything went dark.

Robbie crawled disorientated on the floor. "Rune where are you? Rune please say something." He tugged at his hood and it fell back. Robbie jumped to his feet and twisted round looking for her. Rune stood quietly looking at him a smile on her face, she seemed to glow violet in the dark and her eyes were a bright intense blue surrounded with lilac. He staggered toward her and swept her into his arms. He looked at the soft ground and realised he was standing on a white robe.

"Are you alright? I was terrified." She smiled sweetly at him and kissed him softly.

"I am fine silly." He pulled her close and squeezed her. "I am fine Robbie honest, I understand now."

Jade staggered her head bleeding as she cried, into the clearing; Rune rushed to her and pulled her into an embrace. "Oh, Rune I thought you were in danger, I felt pain, so much pain inside me and I could not bear it."

Rune squeezed her tight. "Be at peace Jade it is over now, I am Runestone and the centre of the violet circle. Grandmother resides in the other realm now; you must now help me save Alice and destroy the Dark One."

Jade looked into her sisters' eyes. "You have replaced her? Wow Rune you really have power now." She smiled at her. "Go on walk through a wall for me." Rune smiled at Jade as she beamed up at her.

"Don't ever change my precious sister." Rune hugged her, as Rowan appeared covered in mud and leaves. Robbie smiled as he saw him stagger out of the trees, Rowan looked up and smiled.

"What is it with you lot and explosions?" Robbie started to laugh with Rune and Jade.

As they rode back to the house along the dark road, Melanie walked smiling into the garden as a huge eagle swept out of the sky. She raised her arms and shrieked; the eagle saw her and glided down to the top of the gate. Mel's eyes turned bright blue.

"Greetings my queen, I knew you would not desert me."

The large eagle nodded a bow and shrieked back at her.

"We have trouble with the Dark One. I need your help my Queen of the skies, a blue Jay flies in trail of the evil one, he may need the help of larger birds, let your families in the north know, and ask them to go to his aid should he need it."

The Eagle nodded and bowed.

"Yes, my Queen the small ones may be in danger, you must alert them and have them move to the safe house. She can speak as I do, tell her to go to safety, tell her I love her."

The large eagle flapped her wings on top of the gate and Mel bowed to her.

"Fly true and safe my Queen, I will return to your home one more time before my time here is done and we will enjoy time as before I promise."

The large Eagle of Callanish flapped her wings and lifted into the air, she gave an enormous cry and rose rapidly into the air, and with speed only known to the eagles of the stones, she flew into the darkness. Melanie stood silently watching the sky with a happy smile on her face and sensing her eagle as she flew north. Len put his arm around her shoulder and watched the sky.

"That one has a great respect for you my darling."

Mel turned smiling. "I have spent many hours with her over the years; she is a true friend and a good companion." They walked into the house together. "My children are safe with her as a protector."

They came out of the darkness into the farm at a fast pace, and clattered across the cobbles down the side of the house and on to the hawthorn hedged lane,

Rune's eyes still glowed bright violet as she used her senses to guide the horses through the dark. They reached the end of the Village Street, and clattered up it to the far end, and turned around the end of number fourteen, and headed round the back to the small gate. Robbie pulled hard on the reins as the horse came to a stop.

They slid down, and entered the yard and walked into Jade's flat. Rowan flopped into the chair as Jade dabbed her bleeding head with a damp cloth, Rowan got up and took it off her and started to wipe it clean. Robbie leaned against the table as he watched Rune; she seemed to be looking for something, but not with her eyes.

She turned smiling to him. "I have found her Robbie; I must go to her." Rune stood perfectly still as her eyes flooded the room with violet light. She took a deep breath and closed her eyes. Robbie watched as the room went dark.

Mac dragged her across the hall and on to the stairs, Alice screamed and kicked and punched at him, he turned and slapped her hard; Alice squealed out in pain and went limp. He lifted her up and walked up the stairs with her.

Alice came too as the single candle flickered in the small room. She lifted her head off the bedclothes, and she looked around. The room was empty and she rubbed her face as it smarted when she moved. There was a small wooden table and chair, next to a bookcase, she noticed the pirate novels stacked on the shelf. The velvet curtains were open, and outside was dark and bleak, white bars ran down in straight rows barring any exit on the other side of the glass.

The fire flickered in the hearth and Alice knew this would be her prison for the next seven months, she bit her lip and tears welled in her eyes, the glass tapped at her side. She let out a large sob as the tapping continued, Alice turned and through her blurred tear filled eyes; she noticed a flash of violet. "Rune?"

She quietly slipped off the bed and crossed to the window. She looked back at the door and grabbed the latch sliding it open, and then she heaved on the sash window. It moved very slowly, and would rise no more than four inches. It was enough for the bright blue bird to hop in, it looked around and then flew to the top of the wardrobe where it looked down at her and chirped. A violet mist flowed from its beak and Alice smiled as more tears formed in her eyes, Rune became solid and rushed across pulling her into her arms.

"Alice my darling are you alright, they haven't hurt you have they?"

Alice wept as she clung to Rune. "I was so frightened Rune, she is horrible." She pushed her head into her, and Rune held her tight.

"Alice, I have not got long, but I will visit you every day. Robbie is already organising and we will leave Loxley first thing in the morning, we will come and get you but it will take time, you are very far away from us. Keep the bird close to you and leave the window open he has other friends who can help."

Alice looked up with red eyes. "Tell Bear I am sorry, I love him Rune please look out for him, and tell Robbie I love him." Rune wiped the tears from her eyes.

"Don't you think he knows that, why do you think he is coming? He will not desert you, Alice."

She smiled. "I know, I am just afraid, I watched him face my dad, I know he loves me."

Rune looked at the door. They will bring food and look after you well; they want what is inside you Alice, you are safe until the birth, so do not be afraid. This child will be born in Loxley, like the rest of its line." She smiled as she stroked her hair back. Alice pulled her close. "Thanks Rune, the thought of not having contact is more frightening than being here."

"Someone is coming so I must go, talk to the bird I will hear you." Rune blew her a kiss as she faded back into smoke and disappeared, Alice smiled and waved to her. The key in the lock turned as Alice sat back on the bed, she noticed the door glow violet as it opened slightly, and she knew Rune had placed a protection around it. A food trolley rolled into the room as the door swung open, it rolled a few feet and stopped, the door then banged shut and the key turned in the lock.

Alice slid off the bed and crossed to the table. She pulled the trolley over and took the shiny silver lid off the plate, she smirked. "Well, I am eating for two now." Alice lifted it on to the table and looked at the potatoes, veg, and meat; she picked up the knife and fork and began to eat. She leaned back in her chair and looked at the books on the shelf. "Treasure Island... Oh well it will pass the time." She slid it off the shelf and opened the first page and began to read as she chewed.

Rune's eyes snapped open and she smiled. "She is fine I just sat with her and spoke." Robbie breathed a deep sigh. "Where is she?"

"She is being held at a place called Craigevar, it is a sort of castle west of Old Aberdeen, it's a funny sort of place, all turrets and no castle. She is in the top west tower locked in a room, it looks very comfortable, there's a fire, tables and books. She will be safe and well looked after, they will not harm her while she carries the baby. There is no sign of the Dark One, I think she would risk the child, so she is staying well out of the way." Rune gave Robbie a searching look. "She is fine

honestly, she told me she loves you, Robbie." He slumped down in the chair and Rowan passed him a drink.

"If they hurt her, I swear I will kill the lot of them, Mac is already a dead man, he just hasn't realised it yet." He sipped his coffee as he leaned back in the chair and closed his eyes; it had been a long day. Rune took his cup and leading him by the hand into the house, he walked with her up the stairs. He lay in bed as she slid in at his side and curled around him, he held her tight. "You are sure you are alright?" He looked at the neatly folded white robe on the chair. "She has really gone forever?"

Rune snuggled up. "I have replaced her; Opal has passed in to another realm." She looked up at him and her eyes sparkled as she smiled at him. "I am just the same as I was, it's just that now I can do a lot of things without getting as tired."

He watched her carefully and she lifted her head. "What?"

"You will keep using doors, won't you?"

She started to giggle. "I promise around you I will always use doors." He smiled at her, and pulled her up and kissed her.

CHAPTER NINE

THE WHEEL OF CARNAC

Rune moved, and it disturbed him, he looked down at the mass of red hair and pale skin, her head was on his shoulder and her arm across his chest. He felt her leg lay across his, and pulled his arm across her back and softly stroked her soft white skin. It felt so smooth on the tips of his rough fingers; he ran it into her hair, which was as fine and as soft as silk, as it glinted in the first pale rays of sun as it began to rise.

She murmured and turned her head. He stroked her back slowly which he knew she loved, and she made happy little murmurs from beneath the red hair. Blue glinted at him through the tangled mass of red and gold, he could not see her, and yet he knew she was smiling. "Hey beautiful."

She crawled up him and her hair stroked his face as it passed over. He looked up surrounded by a shimmering curtain of red and gold hair, and into her sapphire blue eyes, she smiled. "Hi gorgeous." He lifted his arm and pulled her smiling face towards him and kissed her. It was long, slow and sweet and as they broke apart, she opened her eyes and gave him a beaming smile.

"That is my idea of being woken, don't ever forget it." She straddled over him, and sat up on top of him and flicked her long flowing hair back. He sat forward and pushed his arms around her and she slid her head on to his shoulder. She smelled of honeysuckle and sweet violets, and he absorbed the scent in his nostrils with pleasure, "I wish we could stay here like this forever Rune."

She ran her hands through his hair. "I know, it is getting harder by the day, and now with Alice being in trouble and the search for the sword, I feel the pressure too. I have no idea how much it must weigh on you."

"I really hoped we would have more time alone when we came back, I think we had more on the road."

"It will work out and we will have plenty of time Rob, you will see." She pulled back, and smiled at him and kissed him. "How about I make us breakfast, and maybe we will have a little time after to be alone before they all turn up." Her eyes sparkled as she kissed him, and slid out of bed and pulled on her lilac robe. She gave him a very big smile as she skipped through the door.

Robbie stretched and leaned back into the pillows. The golden box glittered from the dressing table as he stared at it, and it seemed to shine even brighter as the sun came above the large storage sheds across the fields behind the house.

Robbie slid across the bed to the dressing table and picked it up. He slid back and pushed the pillows up behind him; he smoothed the sheets out and placed the box in his lap. He saw the rune of Gwendolyn on the top of the golden box, which had delicately carved fine oak leaves and acorns on it.

Robbie turned it over in his hands and examined the whole box. It had a lid and no lock, and yet he could not seem to get it to open, as he turned it over and over, looking for some way to open it. He placed it back on the bed and stared at it, it strangely attracted him and his eyes seemed very drawn to it. Robbie looked up as Rune came into the room with a tray; she saw the box and smiled. "Jade is already up and was already making us some." Rune walked round the bed, and slipped the tray on the small table and pulled the sheet back; dropping her robe she slid into the bed.

She snuggled up and passed him a coffee. She stared at the box as he sipped his drink. "It is very beautiful, have you opened it?"

Robbie shook his head. "I can't seem to get it open."

Rune picked it up and examined it. "That is the seal of Gwendolyn, so it will have protection on it so only the person it is intended for can open it. Touch the seal and tell it who you are."

Robbie looked at her as she passed it back to him. "Seriously?" Rune smiled and nodded.

He put two of his fingers on the large rune carved on the front. "I am Lord Robert of Loxley, the hooded man and the Bowman."

The box gave a soft click and Rune smiled. "See?" He stared in disbelief as he put his cup down on the table and picked the box back up. Robbie opened the lid and a small cloud of pale blue mist flowed out and turned violet.

He lifted the lid right up and looked inside. There were two small crystal bottles of pink liquid, which he assumed were something to do with the pink liquid given him in the glade at Caerleon by Opal. He knew it would give him strength and help him resist the Dark One. There was a soft piece of blue velvet in the centre of the box and he picked it up and slowly unwrapped it. Rune gasped as the golden disk was revealed, he looked at her and then back at the disk.

The golden disk was carved all around its edge with ancient runes. In the centre engraved was the five-pointed star, but instead of the pentagon in the middle, was a shape that Robbie did not at first comprehend. Rune turned it in his hand and smiled as she looked up at him.

"It's a butterfly look!" She traced the outline with her finger.

Each of the points of the star had, been engraved in a very delicate and beautifully written hand.

'Truth, Justice, Knowledge, Courage, Honour.'

"It's the five swords look." He pointed to each one in turn, his finger rested on Honour. "The missing sword, how does this help me Rune?" She looked at the disk and slowly shook her head.

"I am not sure, is there anything else?" Robbie placed the golden disk on the bed and looked back in the box. Under the disk was a piece of rolled parchment, and a small barrel made of gold with a hole in the top of it. Robbie picked it up and looked at it. He turned to Rune.

"Any ideas?" She shrugged, as he put it on the bed at the side of the disk. He unrolled the parchment and a small pendant of a dragon holding a lion fell on to the sheet.

"That is nice; it looks like the dragon is holding the lion up, and if I am not wrong it is the Pendragon of old, what does that say on the parchment?" Robbie had not noticed the old writing on the parchment; it was all in the same kind of runes as the ones on his sword. He handed it to Rune who looked carefully, her lips moved silently as she read them.

'He who is from the woods, and wears the woods symbol,

That is made of nature shall bear this token.

As the hand of the bowman, his honour is equal to the sword.

As the bowman seeks, he will bear this protection as fair exchange.'

"What does it mean Rune?" She looked at the parchment and read it again slowly. She shook her head.

"I have an idea, but I am not sure." Her eyes sparkled as she looked up at him. Robbie stared at her. "Well?"

"Well, what?"

"Rune... What is your idea, tell me?"

She looked at the pendent and then back at the parchment. "I know it sounds daft, but I think you have to give this to Rowan."

"Rowan?"

"Yes, I think you have to give him this. He is a man of the woods who wears my symbol... A wooden acorn, he has one on a chain of platted hair round his neck. Jade has told me all about it; she really loves it, and plays with it after they have sex."

Robbie coughed as he sipped his drink. "You two really are close aren't you, what do you say about me?"

Rune smiled and blushed a little. "That's between sisters... Hand of the bowman could mean your righthand man, who he has become more and more recently; his honour is equal to the sword. That fits Rob, if you were King Arthur, then Rowan would be without doubt your Lancelot. The sword of honour was Lancelot's sword it all fits really. Rowan has always been at the side of you, or made excuses for you as he did at Caerleon when you lost Billy. He will protect you to the death, and has repeatedly, so I think this is Rowan's and you should give it to him Rob."

Robbie leaned forward and placed the pendant on the bed and Rune gasped as he leaned over the box, she grabbed his arm. "Robbie the lid?" He sat back and looked at it, it was just engraved golden leaves and acorns.

"What about it?" Rune lifted the box and held it in front of him at arm's length. She lifted the lion pendant into the light in front of the box and its diamond eyes sparkled, and a spectrum of light illuminated the inside of the box lid. Red fiery runes appeared on the surface of the metal.

She pulled his arm up. "Hold it there." She jumped out of bed and ran naked round the room to her worktable; she grabbed a sheet of paper and a pencil and ran back round to the bed and jumped on to it. Crouched at his side she adjusted his arm as line by line, the runes appeared and she copied them down on to the sheet of paper.

Robbie's arms shook and she lifted her hand and turned his happy smiling face back to the box. "Behave this is important." Rune finished copying the symbols and then slid back into the bed and smiled at him. "Really Rob you have a one track mind."

He looked scandalised. "How can you say that? Your whole family are nymphomaniacs."

"No, we are not, we are children of nature, we know the true meaning of enjoying life and our bodies are a part of that. I thought you understood that, Rob?" He nodded and smiled as she deciphered the runes, which took a few moments and then she read back what she had written.

"The wings that mirror the evening light.
The light of the fruit from eyes so bright.
Five swords in a star, the smallest sting.
The spinning wheel of Carnac.
Will the lost sword bring?"

"Gwendolyn liked her puzzles didn't she, what the hell does it mean Rune?" Robbie stared at her writing next to the symbols.

Rune reached over, and picked up the wheel and looked at it. "All sword makers hold a wheel struck from the same metal as the sword, this is Gwendolyn's wheel and it is the wheel of Carnac."

Robbie watched as she turned it in her hand. "How do you know that?"

Rune's eyes flashed as they moved from the wheel to his and back. "That is what it says around the edge of this wheel. Those runes all around it see, they say this is the wheel of Carnac and made from the same batch of metal as the sword."

"Where is Carnac anyhow? I have never heard of it before, have you?"

Rune nodded. "There is a very powerful circle there; it is just outside Morbihan in Brittany. The stones there, match Callanish and Glastonbury perfectly. It is one of the biggest mysteries of the old times; Granddad did a lot of research on how the Celtic worshipers could build identical stone circles thousands of miles apart, yet in a straight line. He never told them about Gwendolyn and her line of course, the old modern people did not believe in sorcerers and woodland spirits."

Robbie slid the paper over and looked at it. "I have no idea what this means, wings that mirror, evening light. Do you think that is something to do with reflecting light, using a mirror, you know like woodsmen do to signal each other?"

"Whatever it is Rob. We have to spin the wheel to move on, so we really need to find out what to do, we are supposed to be leaving today."

"Maybe Rowan will know, after all this is probably his pendant, I wish Alice was here, she is really good at puzzles." Rune slid her arm round him and leaned over, as she noticed the sudden look of anguish on his face.

"We will solve this and get her back Rob, don't worry about her, she is fine and I will visit her again later today... come on let's go and see if Rowan and Jade can help."

Both of them dressed quickly, and Robbie put everything back in the golden box, realising how hungry he was he grabbed the plate of toast and chewed as they made their way down stairs and across the kitchen to the back door, and Jade's flat at the back of her workshop.

Rowan looked at the golden wheel and the puzzle as Jade leaned over his shoulder and read the translation on the paper. "Well, that bit is easy, isn't it?"

Rune looked down as Jade pointed. "Which bit Jade?"

"That... You know the bit about five swords, small yet they sting." Jade looked up and beamed "That's the pendants."

Robbie looked at her excitedly. "What pendants Pebbles?"

"What you haven't noticed? God Robbie, Rune has only had hers since birth."

Rune's hand went to her neck as she suddenly realised, she smiled and lifted the golden sword out of her top on its chain. "Mine is Excalibur, the sword of power that was returned."

Jade grinned. "Treen has truth, Ruby has justice, Jett has knowledge, Saff has courage and Alley has honour. I cannot believe you have not noticed, although jewellery is my trade so I do tend to notice it more." She climbed over Rowan's shoulder and sat on his knee.

"Rune I need to see them as soon as possible at your house and I want all these swords on view, it might help us. Pebbles you are a little wonder thanks." He grabbed her face and gave her a huge kiss.

"Whoa, Robbie baby, not in front of the hubby. Wow I never thought that would happen, hope I can work out more of the puzzle. Although I would strongly advise you control yourself around Treen, gagging for it that one." She smiled at Rowan and kissed him softly. "Your mine don't go kissing her or it will mean big wifey bother." She beamed at him and he kissed her back.

"I only have lips for ladies called Pebbles." She hugged him and giggled.

Robbie sat at the kitchen table; his cloak hung on the back of the kitchen door. He stared at the paper. "The light of my fruit, I keep thinking acorn, but they do not light up. Oh, Rune this is hopeless, I will never work this out."

She sat down opposite him and stared at the paper and the golden box. He rested his head on his hands, and stared at her, she was so beautiful and in the early morning sunlight, her eyes sparkled. She looked up at him and her sapphire eyes glinted, he smiled at her, pictures filled his head of sapphire eyes peeping at him through the clothes rails; she smiled and looked up at him. Her eyes danced.

"Stop watching me it's putting me off." Her sapphire eyes blazed and suddenly Robbie froze. Rune looked concerned as his expression changed, and she became self conscious. "What is it; it's not my eyes again is it?"

He smiled as he jumped up from the table. "It most certainly is."

"Why what's wrong with them?" There was a note of panic in her voice. The last time she had inherited power she had freaked him out with lilac whites, last night she had replaced Opal, her mind ran free as a whole list of possibilities that would make her less attractive to him unfolded in her mind.

Robbie ran over to the door as Rune unravelled, and he grabbed his cloak, he turned back to the table. "The light of the fruit from eyes so bright." He placed the sapphire acorn on the table. "Your tears made this, and the eyes of my lion showed us the words on the box. Gwendolyn was very clever; she must have had far sight to work out that all of us would have the tools to make this wheel work, swords and now a brooch."

Robbie took out the wheel and laid it on the table. "That is a butterfly and who loves sunset more than us?"

Rune smiled. "Evening light of course, he said he loved the sunset, and he gave me the spun ball of silk." Robbie smiled.

"The butterfly hairpin, it is the same shape as the one on the wheel, Rune my love I think we are getting somewhere." Rune pulled the golden ruby encrusted pin out of her hair and looked at it.

"That's odd."

"What Is?"

"You know Rob I have never noticed before; it has no head on it." She turned it to show him. He smiled at her and took it out of her hand; Robbie turned it over in his hands and inspected it closely. There was a very finely crafted tube underneath it. Robbie lay it down on the table, as Rune watched nervously. She loved the hairpin, and she worried what he might do to it.

He picked up the sapphire acorn and turned it in his fingers. Robbie opened the pin and slid it into the tube underneath the butterfly. He lifted it into the light and autumnal colours from the rubies refracted through the sapphire casting a violet light all around the room. Rune looked up and beamed with delight. "Oh, Robbie that is so beautiful, how did you think of that?"

"You."

She looked at him. "What about me?"

"Beautiful blue eyes that turn violet, sapphires at sun set. Look at something red through blue and it looks violet, your power emits violet, so violet must power the wheel somehow."

There was noise at the back door, which could only be Jett and Jade; anyone else would have been quieter this early in the morning. Jett burst in full of the joys of spring, "HEY ROBBIE WHAT'S UP?"

Rune scowled. "Shush, my mum and dad are still asleep."

Jett shrugged and whispered. "Sorry, not thinking, I hope this is important I was about to sneak off to the barn."

Rune smiled. "That Loxley barn will be the cause of ruin round here one day."

Robbie smiled at her. "Not ours, we have a whole glade." Rune giggled and looked down as he winked. Rowan came in with a full kettle and placed it on the stove. Robbie looked at the very tired and yawning Treen, Alley, and Saff who followed Jett and Ruby into the kitchen.

"Ladies I need to borrow your sword pendants." They all looked confused as he laid the wheel of Carnac on the table in front of him, he took out the barrel and looked at it. Rune watched him.

"Do you think it sits on top of that, because it has a hole in it and so does the wheel?"

Robbie looked at the centre of the wheel and then the little barrel. The top of the barrel seemed slightly raised and the bottom was flat. He sat it flat side down, and then picked up the small swords as the girls undid their chains and slipped them off on to the table.

Robbie lifted them one at a time and placed them on the wheel as they had done on the table in Caerleon. "Truth, Justice, Knowledge, Courage, and Honour." He looked carefully at the small sword; this was the closest thing he had to knowing what the real thing looked like. He placed it into its allotted star and it appeared that all the swords stuck as if by magnetism.

The wheel glowed and Rune smiled. "Well, that bits right."

Rowan poured out drinks with Jade and passed them around the table as everyone sat transfixed, watching Robbie assemble the wheel of Carnac, Robbie lifted the wheel on to the barrel and it wobbled. It took a few moments to get it balanced and then he picked up the butterfly and placed it on to the wheel, above the engraved shape making sure it matched perfectly. The wheel balanced and wobbled slightly, he almost thought it moved.

Everyone stared at it; Jett looked up. "What now?"

Robbie sat back confused. "I was sure the butterfly would somehow power it and make it spin." He stared at the butterfly with its sapphire acorn head and its ruby encrusted wings, and the small hole in its back. He looked at Rune.

"You are the centre of all circles." She looked confused.

"Meaning."

Robbie looked at her neck below the open laces in her top. She blushed a little and leaned forward. "Robbie stop staring at them in front of everyone."

He grinned. "I wasn't, Rune you are the centre of all wheels and you have the power to make the wheel move."

"How?"

"It's around your neck."

"The sword of..." Robbie spoke at the same time as she did. "Power." She hurriedly undid the necklace and slipped the sword off the chain and handed it to him. Robbie slid the small golden sword through the hole in the back of the butterfly, and it passed through the wheel and into the barrel below.

The whole wheel glowed violet as the rubies erupted into bright red light that sent beams into the sapphire acorn. The beams split and hit each sword on the wheel and it began to glow, and slowly spin.

"Alright Robbie, how cool is that?" Jett bobbed up and down as the wheel picked up speed. The violet beams began to blur, as the wheel spun faster and faster. The beams now formed a disk of purple light that covered the whole surface of the wheel. Rune remembered the table at Caerleon and somehow she knew what was about to happen.

The wheel was now moving at a phenomenal rate, and slowly a white beam began to form in the centre. It rose slowly up from the wheel and widened, and the shape was slow to form, and Rune had no doubts now, she knew who was going to appear.

The small figure in white robes with a blue sash looked up at Robbie. The voice was loud even though the figure was tiny. "Greeting's bowman, you have journeyed far to this point, I am Gwendolyn White Circle, Queen of the Fae, and the creator of the sword of honour, for it was I with my own hands that made the sword for loyal Sir Lancelot."

Robbie watched spellbound, as did everybody else. "Listen carefully bowman for your task has only just begun. I am forbidden to directly name the location of the sword of honour so all I will say is this."

"Without hope, there is only deep despair, beneath hope lies sanctuary inside. Recovered honour lies at his side. Hope lies in the symbols of life, the shield protects, the lion brings courage, and to help you claw forward, the seed of the wood will lead your king. Bring the five swords together and you will see the path. Your right hand will guide your way."

Rune scribbled hurriedly as Gwendolyn spoke... She bowed. "Good luck bowman, truth and knowledge go hand in hand." Gwendolyn began to dissolve and the wheel slowed down and stopped.

"Got it." Rune finished her last line off and looked at the words on the paper.

She slid it across the table to Robbie, Jett and Alley leaned over to read it with him.

Rune looked at him across the table. "Recovered honour lies at his side. The sword is inside the tomb of Lancelot." She smiled at him. "Might be better to not let Harry know that until the last thing, he might think you want him to do bad things again Rob." She started to giggle and Robbie started to laugh as the others joined in. It broke the ice and gave him a bit of relief.

Alley turned the page on the table so she could read it better. "Hope, deep despair, sanctuary, symbols of life, shield, lion, claw, seed, king, five swords, right hand, and guide. All of these things are relevant the rest are just words. So, Robbie the question is, what does all this mean to us?"

Saff leaned forward as Rune wrote out a list of the single headings Alley had mentioned. "My mum has an eagle's talon as a pendant, and Jaz has a shield with three dragons on it round his neck. That could be your claw and shield, will they work on the wheel like the swords did?"

Treen smiled. "My mama has a Pendragon on her bracelet; in France the King eez always called Pendragon and no Arthur." Rune nodded as she marked them on the list.

"Robbie, you have the lion around your neck." He smiled at her.

"And Rowan has an acorn."

Rune looked up. "Of course, Robbie you have not given Rowan the pendant." Excitement glowed in her eyes. "That first puzzle said the pendant would be a fair exchange. You swap it for the acorn and you have the seed."

Robbie took the lion and dragon pendant out of the box and handed it to him. "You are in many ways my other hand, and the box says this is your protection." He handed the pendant to Rowan who looked carefully at it.

"I could not swap this for my acorn Robbie; I have had this since birth. It was given me by my mother's brother who was also my god father."

Robbie nodded. "Nearer the time loan me your acorn for a short spell, I think Rune is right and we may need it." Rowan slipped the chain with the Pendragon and lion on it over his neck, and nodded. Jade looked at it.

"Nice bit of jewellery, well made and very old."

"You have forgotten something Rob?" Rune looked across the table at him. He looked up at her from the list.

"What?"

"Rob the wearer of that pendant is supposed to be your hand... your right hand... which is Rowan." She crossed it off her list. "Rowan is supposed to show us the way and be our guide; he must know how to get to the sword."

Rowan looked lost for words as Robbie looked up at him. He shrugged his shoulders at Robbie, Robbie sighed. "We are lost before we start then; I have no idea of which direction to travel." Rowan looked at him and gave him a huge grin.

"Directions I can do, thanks to Opal." He ran to the kitchen door and disappeared. Robbie looked at Rune and then Jade, both of them shrugged. Rowan came back in a few minutes later; he walked around the table and placed a white arrow on the table. Robbie picked it up and looked at it.

"No offence Rowan but what does this do to help?" He gave Robbie a grin.

"It is a gift from Hearne given me by Opal the first time I met her. She told me that if ever I needed to know the right direction, I should shoot it in the air and it would guide me."

Robbie's eyes lit up and sparkled. "So, if you ask this arrow where to go it will tell you?" Rowan nodded.

"I think it will ... Yes."

Robbie looked around at everyone and smiled. "Well, that is half the puzzle solved." He took the sword pendants off the wheel and handed them back to their owners. "We may need these again but I think it best if you all wear them. If we have problems on the road, and someone gets their hands on this, they will need everyone to make it work."

Robbie handed the hairpin back to Rune and then fastened the sapphire acorn to his top. He wrapped the wheel up in the blue velvet cloth and then placed it back in the box, he pushed down the lid and it snapped shut with a click. The box glowed blue and then violet. "Right, everyone let's get ready to travel, I want all of you to think about the rest of the puzzle. If any of you have any ideas no matter what they are, please tell Rune or me."

Everyone nodded as he stood up and they all made their way out of the room, Rune came around the table and slid her arms around him, her eyes sparkled and the sunlight reflected and glinted off her eyelashes. She kissed him softly. "See, trust in your instincts and they do guide you. We are already packed; I did it last night which means only one thing my handsome lord."

He gave her a huge smile. "We have some free time My Lady of Loxley." She smiled and started to giggle.

"I really love you Lord Robert."

"I love you too Rune pops." He lifted her into his arms as she nuzzled into his neck and laughed.

Robbie rode into the farm with Rune, Jade, and Rowan. Jess sat in the kitchen at the table as he entered, she smiled as he crossed and bent down to hug her. "Off again, I have hardly seen you I have been so busy."

"I still have plenty of time mum, why don't we walk in the orchard?"

The sun was shining all around the long lines of mixed fruit trees. Cherry blossom blew like snow across them in the gentle breeze as they walked slowly in the dappled shade of the large fruit trees. Robbie loved the orchard; he loved the neatly trimmed grass and the wide isles with thick heavy trunks of grey and red, all set like soldiers on parade in long perfectly straight rows.

Jess put her hand on his shoulder. "You seem very comfy with Rune; I see the closeness between you. She is very much in love with you Rob; do you love her that deeply?"

He smiled at her. "Always the mother checking, eh? Mum I love her more than anyone really understands. I have loved her for a very long time; she will be my wife one day and the mother of my children."

"You are still very young Rob; don't be in a rush to decide your life so quickly, the fear of wars can make people do rash things." Jess stopped and looked at him, her face was filled with love and concern. "What I am saying Rob, is that sometimes we feel that circumstances decide for us. You do not have to let that happen; I hope she is the love of your life because she really is a wonderful girl. Just don't settle on the first if you don't have to."

"Please Mum you have to stop worrying about me, honestly I know what I want and I know what I am doing. I honestly did not want any of this at first, I had no idea how to be a lord or fight the enemy. I was a woodsman who could shoot and had always loved the girl with blue eyes down the street. Now I can see what a difference I can make, because I have already made a difference, I actually think I have found something I can do and do well, please Mum let me try."

She pulled him into a hug. "You are my son and I will always worry about you, I love you Robbie as every mother alive loves their child. All I am asking, is are you happy with what you have? I need to be sure Rob; I need to know."

He pulled her close. "I love you too Mum and I am happy, Rune makes me feel so alive and yet so at peace with myself. When she walks into the room, my life improves and I feel like I want to be the man she wants me to be. I want it because the man she loves is a nice person and works hard at being decent. I feel I belong when I am with her, do you understand that?"

He pulled back and she looked in his eyes. "Then you truly are in love Robbie." She smiled. "You are growing up so fast I can hardly keep up, I mean look at you. You are off to save your cousin from an evil witch, please just be very careful, don't lose your head in all this Robbie, keep your feet on the floor and look out for early signs of danger."

She pulled him close and kissed him on the head. The two of them walked to the end of the orchard as Robbie recounted the story of Harry for her at the graveside in Kirklees, he filled her in on the story of Maggs and the straight line, one legged chickens and she howled with laughter. He laughed with her, but not because she was laughing, but because it was nice to hear her laugh again.

Robbie talked to her of the house he wanted to build at Robbie's Mere when he got back. Of how he wanted to build it like the village hall out of timber, that would last for hundreds of years. She smiled as he described the glass front so he could see the mere at all times, and have the sun shine in at sunset, and Jess began to see that he wanted to return and live in Loxley, she had always thought he would leave, but now her worry began to calm a little, as she understood the change that was happening inside him.

They came around the corner smiling and talking, and Rune smiled to see them so happy together. The whole group was assembled and ready as Robbie walked up. John climbed up on to his huge white horse as Beth sniffed into her hankie. Robbie turned to his mum whose eyes glistened. "I am sorry I can't help it."

He gave her a huge hug. "I will be back, you will see." He kissed her goodbye and after being almost squeezed to death by Beth, he climbed up on to his horse. Rune smiled and hugged Jess.

"Watch my boy Rune, don't leave his side I have already lost one, I could not bear to lose him."

Rune held her tight. "I will never leave him Jess, and he will return safely to you. I promise you that."

Rune pulled herself up on to the horse, and Robbie smiled as he pulled his horse round and rode between John and Harry. "You know John in this outfit we already have a Big John. Harry here started a tradition of naming our crew and I think it is only right we find one for you."

Rune and Blades giggled behind John. "You see John, little Blades here saw you charge at that heifer over there yesterday to get her to move, and it appeared your mooing is quite accurate." Everyone started to giggle as John scowled and looked back at Blades. "So, Harry and I think that because of your vast strength, and ability to moo, we should call you Bull."

Jess and Beth shrieked with laughter as Jade and Jett giggled just up in front, Harry beamed at John. "Hey man bulls are like really cosmic creatures; they emit cool vibes and mellow karma."

Robbie winked at John and he smiled and nodded. "At least it's not chicken."

"Whoa man don't be unpeaceful, chicken is a happenin and a cosmically cool name."

"Bull it is people, ok let's move out and follow Rowan's lead." The group turned as Beth blew everyone kisses and they slowly rode down the hawthorn lined lane towards the village. Rowan's arrow had pointed southwest, and as they slowed in the village for Smokes and Steph with her sisters, Robbie looked at the map with Rowan.

Rowan pointed to the side of Winsford. "We will be going close to Sister Mary's place if you want to call in."

Robbie smiled. "I must admit I would like to see if the five carts I sent to her have reached her safe." Jade gave him a grin.

"It would be nice Robbie." He winked at her and as the group joined together, Robbie kicked his horse forward and joined Rowan up front with Jade and Rune behind him. People waved and cheered as the party galloped down the road towards the inner compound gate, it swung open as they approached, and at the gallop, they passed a smiling and waving David Williams, and rode under the archway and out of the gates of Loxley. The group of twenty five riders crossed the square, as the woodsmen on the walls cheered and they headed down to the road that would lead them to the large reservoir.

Maggs sat with Lucy on the steps of the postal service office; she pulled Lucy close to her. "I think we should like hang out together, it would be groovy, because I am going to miss my Harry man, and you the Rags baby." Lucy leaned her sad head on Maggs arm and Maggs stroked her hair. "We girls have got to like pull our vibes together and think cosmic for our chickens... Did I ever tell you I can like really communicate with chickens? There are some who think I am blessed."

Maddy came up at the side of Robbie, her white bow was slung over her shoulder, and her waist length blonde hair blew free behind her. Robbie noticed how like Gwendolyn she looked, especially around the eyes. She nodded. "I have heard of the wheel, my mother made it and talked of it often. How are you going at working it all out?"

Robbie shrugged. "We have unravelled most of it, but it is putting together hope, deep despair, sanctuary and symbols of life that are holding us back. They all connect we just have not worked them out yet."

Maddy nodded. "My mother made up riddles a lot when we were kids to teach us, I do not know if it will help you much but she was great at making one word mean two things. I think deep despair may lead you to a crypt or burial chamber underground. If I am right my mother knew Sir Lancelot, that is why she made his sword, he was a good friend in his time with the king. Arthur suffered great despair at the betrayal of his friend, as did Lancelot because he knew how much he had hurt the king he loved. I don't know if it helps but think about it that could be a reference to where the tomb of Lancelot is."

Robbie nodded and smiled. "Thanks, Maddy that makes a lot of sense, we will all think about it." She gave a slight smile and dropped back to the side of Mel. Robbie pondered her suggestion; it did make a lot of sense; he said the lines of the clue to himself in his head. 'Without hope, there is only deep despair.' He needed hope to find the deep despair, it did not really make sense but he felt it was the right track to take. Lancelot had been out of sight for a long time, and no one seemed to know where he had been buried, it would have to be underground somewhere very safe and secret.

They kept good pace as the afternoon wore on, crossing the moor and dropping down into the heavy woodland area behind Bollington, life here in the old modern age had been very rural and the fields had quickly reverted to the wild. Small dilapidated cottages would rise out of the green, their crumbling walls smothered with plant life, and what had once been neatly tended gardens were a riot of colour, all spreading and sprawling across what now looked like a meadow of thick colour.

They entered a dense patch of trees and stopped in the cool, the sun was high and hot and Robbie wiped his brow as he turned to Rowan. "How far off are we now?"

Rowan looked at his map. "It's about another twenty or so miles off still, we could easily make it if the ground was flat, but some of the area round here used to be very built up so we will be weaving round buried towns a little."

Robbie looked round at the others who all seemed to be hot. "Ok let's make camp here and get an early start in the morning." He slid down off his horse glad to be back on the floor. "Martin, John, Rafe, Pebbles, secure the area. I know we are still in our own zone but I want no surprises. Keith, Blades, Bull organise the camp, Jett give Rowan and me a lift with the horses. Mother, Smokes, let's get a fire going."

Everyone nodded and sprang into action, as he pulled the reins of the horses and led them over to a ring of small trees. Rowan attached a line along three trees and they tied the horses on as they nibbled at the grass. Soon a good blaze was going and pots were bubbling on the fire, Bull had arranged several tents for the group of women made out of canvass sheets and Robbie leaned against a tree watching, and happy to be back in woodland life again. Rune brought him a steaming cup, her eyes sparkling and her face happy as she approached. "You love it don't you? You should see your face, life in the woods and a happy camp." She kissed him on the cheek and he slid an arm around her and pulled her to his side.

"This is my kind of life; I love the feel of leaves above my head and the smell of damp earth in my nostrils. I might add it is only right when I also have the smell of sweet violets and honeysuckle close by."

"Oh, you can be such a smoothie when you want Robin in the hood."

He held her close and gave her a soft kiss on her neck, he felt her shudder and he smiled; he knew how much it made her tingle. "Rune I have been thinking when you see Alice, could you ask her what she thinks of the puzzle? Alice was always a whiz at this kind of stuff, and we need to work out more before we reach the sister. I need to find that sword and then we can start heading north. I want her back Rune, and I want her fast."

Rune slid closer to him. "I will talk to her as soon as I have eaten." She looked up at him. "Don't worry Robbie we will get her back."

He watched the camp sipping his coffee. John, Martin, and Fish laughed and joked with Jett and Jade as they ate their meal, they would be taking the first night's guard shift. Robbie turned and walked into the woods around the camp, he could see his men taking the guard. Jaz sat quite well hidden and looking alert, he nodded as Robbie walked past, he almost did not see Blades she was so well hidden.

John Lox stood against a tree, his long silver sword in one belt, and his large silver axe in the other, he smiled as Robbie walked up. "You run a good outfit, Robbie. Your men are very good, I am impressed at your command, you have grown up a lot since you first left the stockade."

"I fake it John, I always say to myself what would my dad or John do. Then I copy you two and things seem to work out right."

John laughed and he looked at him, his smile lessoned. "Seriously Robbie it is a sign of a good leader that he can learn from others. You have your father's authority, I see it more and more, it commands great respect, I also see a lot of my old dad in you Robbie, and he was a card I will say. He always found a way to lift everyone's spirits when the going was hard, you have that ability to throw a little humour into things, take the edge off the tension a little. My Alice has told me a lot about your travels, she really admires you for what you are doing. She is a bright one, I always listen to her you know, she has a way of painting a clearer picture than the rest."

Robbie patted his arm. "I miss her too John, she was one of my most trusted advisors. We will get her back I promise, I will not leave Alice to their mercy a moment longer than I have to. Go and get some food, Rune will be talking to her soon, you can be there when she updates me." John smiled and gave Robbie a large pat on the back.

"You are a good lad, Robbie." He walked off through the trees back to the camp. Robbie slid his bow off his shoulder, and sat down with his back against the tree and watched the woods.

Alice sat in a chair by the fire; the embers smouldered red in the grate. The half read book lay open on her lap as she dozed, the empty food trolley by her side. On top of her chair sat the blue bird watching the door, he gave a little chirp and blue mist issued from his beak turning violet.

Rune smiled and crouched down by the chair she softly whispered. "Alice darling are you awake?" Alice mumbled in her sleep as she disturbed and lifted her head. Her eyes blinked open and saw two bright sapphire blue eyes watching her.

She moved quickly, throwing her arms around Rune. "Oh, Rune I must have fallen asleep." The book slipped off her lap and on to the floor. Rune pulled her close. "I have a surprise for you, I want you to close your eyes and empty your mind; you are going on a short journey alright?" Alice nodded, closed her eyes and Rune leaned her forehead to Alice. She closed her eyes and a soft glow began to form and swirl around them.

Robbie and John sat in the little tent waiting as Rune sat motionless in front of them. Both of them looked nervous and agitated, John looked at Robbie who was nervously watching Rune. "She is there is she, with my Alice?"

Robbie nodded his eyes not leaving her. "I don't know how she does it John, I just know like Opal she can appear at will somewhere else." John nodded.

"No offence Rob, but that is a lot weirder than Harry." Robbie smiled and lifted his arm to John's shoulder.

"Hang about with us long enough John, and you will see Harry as sane."

Rune's eyes burst open and violet light flooded the tent. Robbie and John both jumped. Violet light swirled and formed into a mist, Robbie watched, as it began to form into a small shape, his heart began to race as the delicate figure of Alice formed in front of them. John's eyes filled with tears and he sniffled.

"Daddy Rune cannot give me long."

John wept. "Alice love are you alright? I am so frightened for you." She came forward and put her arms around him.

"I am alright Daddy; they are taking care of me, I miss you all, but they have not hurt me. Rune wanted you to see I am safe; she cannot do this for long." Alice kissed her dad and he held her tight in his arms. "I love you Daddy."

"I love you Alice love, don't fret now I will come for you. Me and Rob will get you soon, you'll see."

Alice slid out from her dad's grip and turned to Robbie she smiled. "I miss you too Rob."

"I miss you too sis." She gave him a hug and spoke as she held him and her tears ran down her face. "The five swords have to be the heirs. His honour is equal to the sword Robbie, let Rowan lift the sword, if it glows it is his. Sanctuary has always been in a church, the symbols of life I am not sure about, but Lancelot was a preacher, so ask Sister Mary, it could be the symbols of life in the Christian religion. Good luck and come quickly I miss you." Alice kissed his cheek and turned back to her dad.

"I have to go Daddy; I love you come soon." Alice was already breaking apart into a violet mist and she smiled and waved at them as she slowly disappeared, John heaved a huge sob and put his head down as he quietly wept with relief.

Rune's eyes opened and she smiled, she leaned forward and put her arms around John. "Don't cry John you can see she is safe and unharmed."

John heaved his huge arms around Rune as he wept. "I don't know how or what you just did Rune, but thanks I needed to see she was fine."

"She is and I will keep her that way, so you focus on helping Rob and I will keep her protected until we can get to her." She kissed his cheek. "Go on, you go for a short walk and clear your head while I give this gorgeous nephew of yours a big hug." John laughed and shook his head.

"Thanks Rune love." Smiling, he got up and left the tent as Rune beamed at Robbie. He slid his arms around her and pulled her close.

"You alright, that must have taken a lot of energy."

"I am fine Robbie; it was the sharing with Opal that was draining me, that is why Opal left early and gave me the last of her power. There can be only one force of nature, and she is hoping for a long dark night alone in the woods with her man." She smiled sweetly at him and kissed him.

The sun was setting as Robbie wandered around checking all was quiet. Una stood alone just outside the line of the camp staring into the woodland. Robbie watched her as he walked quietly up, her pale lime green clothes edged with small brown leaves seemed to blend nicely into the background, although her waist length snow white hair shone brightly. She leaned on a long staff of holly, which was her preferred weapon of combat. She turned and smiled as he approached, Robbie nodded. "Don't wander too far out of camp... Just in case."

"I won't... I needed some space alone to think." She lowered her voice. "I have sensed and fought evil all my life Robbie. I have my mother's powers to protect any from evil, how could I not see my own son had been taken over, and had turned against us...? I should have sensed it."

Robbie looked out at the soft green leaves and the moss that grew in a lush carpet over the roots of the old trees. "I must admit I do not have a great knowledge of all your powers as a family, but it seems to me that Mac went willingly. He was not possessed so you would not have sensed evil in him, up until the other night he had not committed an evil act had he...? I do not think you should blame yourself Una, I lived with Billy for ten years and had no idea he was the son of Mason Knox, none of us did, not even your father."

Una smiled. "Thanks Robbie, I feel so strongly I have let all of you down, but that does help a little."

He put his hand on her shoulder. "Una here we're all a team. We are close and we work to help each other and protect each other. You are part of the team so do not isolate yourself, no one here thinks badly of you, in fact, I know for fact Flash wants to know how good you are with that staff, maybe you should show her... I have always found that a display of ability with this lot helps you fit in quicker." He gave her a smile and she nodded.

"Thanks Robbie."

"Stay in sight, although you are protected." Robbie lowered his voice to a whisper. "Jade is four trees up front on the left." Una smiled.

"Really I never noticed." He winked as he turned and walked back to the camp.

CHAPTER TEN

LANCELOT'S REMAINING RELATIVE

They rose early and spent the day riding round the green covered remains of the lost towns of the modern age. As the sun rose high in the sky Robbie recognised his surroundings, as they made their way down the long tall hedged lane slowly. The hedges now grew so tall that their canopy had joined and met above them. The sun shone above them and the day heated up, the group rode through the tunnel of green life in the cool dappled shade.

The floor that had once been a road of concrete was soft under the feet of the horses, as it was now covered with weeds, grass and a thick mulch of fallen leaves. Robbie rode at the back with Rune watching the group up in front. The new members seemed to be fitting; Alley was an instant hit with Jett and Jade as she had their own brand of rebellious humour. Jaz had struck up a good friendship with Bear and Bull. Saff rode with Blades and Flash and they all seemed to be chatting happily.

"Treen still needs to find her feet."

Rune nodded. "She will, she has a strange power Robbie, she has no weapons have you noticed?"

Robbie, had noticed and had meant to ask why, he looked over at Rune. "What is it she can do?"

"I worry about that; she has the power to control the mind and possess the body. Any who attack her will probably find themselves throwing themselves off a cliff."

Robbie looked at her riding beside her mother, and looked back at Rune. "Why do you worry? That could be very useful."

Rune gave him a huge smile. "She thinks that Rowan and you are highly attractive, I have made sure she keeps her thoughts out of your head, haven't you seen how protective Jade is of you two around her?"

"I just thought all those at it like rabbit jokes, was just Jade having a bit of fun."

"Jade is wiser than you think Robbie. She enjoys life and fools around, but she is no fool, Jade was on to her the moment she met. Little Miss Treen may be quiet, but she can be a basket of monkeys when she puts her mind to it. You watch yourself around her."

Robbie laughed. "You never struck me as a possessive person Rune, come on I love you; we are as safe as the sacred oak."

Rune gave him a sweet smile. "I am not possessive; I am the force of nature. There is no woman alive who could face me and steal my man. A little extra insurance never hurt though." She winked at him.

They turned off the road and into the long driveway down to the black gates, and Robbie was stunned at the sight of the convent. The two oak trees beside the gates were huge and formed a massive canopy over the front of the gate. The white walls had completely disappeared; they were now a dense, thick, wall of heavy foliage, filled with every type of fruit. Robbie rode down the side of the group to the front of the line, where Martin and Fish headed the group. Robbie looked at Martin and then up at the large oak trees.

"See I told you we knew what we were doing." Martin looked astounded at the size of the trees before him and Robbie laughed as he spurred his horse on to the gates.

Bobby Thorn sat on a little wooden platform in the top of the oak trees as the riders came around the corner. Sister Mary looked up as Bobby's voice screamed out. "Sister Mary.... Sister Mary he is here... He has come back." Bobby stood up and waved his arm back franticly as he pointed to the road. "It's Robin Hood."

Mary smiled a huge grin as all the children looked up happily, and she ran with all her might to the gates, and heaved on the three large bolts. The gate swung open wide, and there he was riding down at the side of the long line of riders a huge smile on his face. She opened her arms and ran towards him as he pulled up on the reins and the horse came to an abrupt halt. He slid quickly down as Sister Mary came up tears in her eyes. She ran into his arms and he pulled her close.

"Oh, Robert my boy, I cannot tell you how happy I feel to see you alive and well."

"I told you I would be back, hello Sister I have thought of you every day since we left, how is everything going, did you get all the goods I sent from Loxley?"

She squeezed him hard. "I have found faith I never thought I had Robert; you gave me the life to continue. Oh, Robert I am so happy."

He let her go and smiled as she dried her eyes on a small white hankie. "Hello Sister Mary." Rune smiled as Mary burst back into tears, and Rune pulled her into a caring hug.

"Oh Runestone my dear, you look wonderful."

Robbie guided everyone in as Fish slid down off his horse. Mary wept bitterly as did he. "Oh, James my dear, I am so sorry about Anthony, I loved him so much as you know I do you. How are you my sweet child, you must miss him dreadfully?" Fish held on to her as his tears ran down his face, Mary took his face in her hands and kissed him on the head and he smiled at the old nun who was so dear to him.

"I miss him dreadfully, but I am around many others who loved him too, and they have been my strength."

She wiped his eyes and took his hand. "Come and see the tree that the children have planted in the yard for him." Mary led him into the yard and there right in the very centre was a large lilac tree. Robbie and Rune stood by it reading the plaque in front of the tree.

In Memory of Anthony Ashford. (Hog). A loyal defender of all children. Fish stood silently by the tree with a soft smile as he remembered his brother, as all the others entered and dismounted. Screams came from all over the yard as Harry held up his arms.

"Hey baby people. How cosmic is this? I like have totally happened myself back here?" He was mobbed and dragged to the floor laughing and joking as the children jumped all over him screaming "Cosmic!" Rune and Steph laughed and Blades beamed as he sat up his face filled with joy. "Hey this is so cool and cosmic. Whoa, my little people you all look like totally happenin dudes. Your vibes is all full and not hungry."

Robbie looked at Mary. "How is the meat store?"

Mary smiled. "It is getting low."

Robbie turned. "Fish take Rowan, Pebbles, Jaz and Bull, we need to stock the meat store."

Mary smiled. "You truly are my guardian angel Robert."

He put his arm around her and they walked down the yard towards the three chairs. Rune smiled as a little blonde girl came running up with a teddy that had only one leg in her hand. Rune knelt down and looked at the bright smiling face of the little girl, who on her last visit had been so quiet and withdrawn. She ran straight into Rune's tearful arms and gave her a huge hug as Rune lifted her up. "Hello sweet pea. Oh, it is so nice to see you again. I have spent many hours thinking of you, how are you doing my darling?"

"I am happy to see you too Runestone." Tears welled in her eyes, it was the first time the little girl had spoken to her and she looked at Robbie as violets sprung up on the floor. He smiled at her.

"We did make a difference on our last trip." Rune sat with the little girl on the step, and as she curled on Rune's knee, she told her all about the house of hope and her brother. Rune beamed with happiness as Robbie watched sat with Sister Mary.

He turned to the sister. "I can see our supplies have made it through, although I have noticed you now have four times the wounded in here that you had last time. Have attacks in the area gone up again?"

"Your border line passes south of here by five miles. This is not an easy area to watch, there have been many Cutter attacks recently, it seems that they are using round here as a route to pass through, and the people suffer a great deal. We have a steady stream daily." Rune looked up at him.

"Alley is dealing with them with Steph, Alley is a healer she will make a big difference."

Mary looked across at the even longer line of tents and could see Steph with Una and Maddy helping around Alley. "Your little group has grown Robert, you have some talented companions, and I notice Lady Runestone has developed a healthier perspective. You hide your talents to the world, and yet to me, you cannot hide what I seek."

Rune looked at her. "What do you mean, what you seek?"

"Now is not the time child, but I think we need to talk later." Sister Mary gave her a smile and Rune seemed to sense that Mary knew something that was important to them. She smiled back and nodded at her.

Blades and Harry checked out all the electrics, which was not the easiest task as they had about a hundred children following them everywhere. Mel sat with Treen and Saff surrounded by children as they all sang songs and laughed.

Martin and Big John did some repairs around the gates and replaced some of the old wood. The children watched and passed them tools asking hundreds of questions. Jett was having the time of her life as she flew around with the kids laughing and screaming.

Robbie sat back feeling happy and contented as he watched, the change from that first day when he arrived so many weeks ago was dramatic. The children were happy and looked well fed, and they all now wore little cloth shoes. Rune came and slid on to the chair beside him, he lifted his arm around her. "We made a big difference here Rune look at them, they are fed and happy."

"Good men do great things Rob, you have touched the lives of thousands so far, I am glad you can see the proof of who you are, this place is a shining example of the power of the hooded man."

The meal in the large hall that night was a feast of fun, as everyone tucked in, laughed and joked. The hall was decked out in its huge wide rectangle of tables, as all the children sat around and happily chatted as they ate their meal. The high walls were painted white up to the long lines of windows that let the evening light stream in. The thousands of faces of the many who had passed through, all smiled painted in long happy rows all around the room. Robbie still found it very disturbing to see so many that had not survived the brutal legacy of the Cutters.

Robbie looked at the wall at the far end of the room. The wall had the large painting of that first group that had arrived, his eyes looked at the hooded figure with 'Our saviour' written above it. He looked at the small figure of Eric, and then his eyes crossed to Hog, he felt the sadness within him, they like so many of the thousands of faces on the wall were no longer with them.

He leaned over his full plate and rested his chin on his hands as he stared at the two loyal members of his group who had both given their lives to save others. At the end of the wall, the happy face of Alice looked back at him, and he remembered how Billy had teased her about her nickname and Harry had defended her. He stared at the picture of Billy, his long blonde hair and his blue eyes looked back at him. Twice now, Knox had planted spies on him, both in the last ten years, although Mac meant nothing to him, Billy however was a different story, his damage was lasting. Robbie's mind jumbled around as all the things that Billy had caused bounced through his head, Alice was now lost to them somewhere miles away, and Billy was responsible. How could he have managed so much damage right under their nose?

Rune touched his arm and he moved putting his hand on hers. "I am fine." He leaned back in his chair, "I am just not too hungry." He got up and walked out of the hall and down the long corridor to the small steps outside. He sat and breathed the night air, as two silent figures appeared in the shadows and stood guard, Rowan and Pebbles slid into the deep shadows as Rune appeared.

"Are you alright? I thought the pictures would upset you, especially Billy." She slid her arm around him as she sat down on the step.

"I am fine honestly; I suppose seeing them reminded me of the two days we had here. It all seemed so perfect then, I guess I am just relieved he didn't send Knox here after we left."

"Billy wants the swords; there was never any point in attacking here Rob, Sister Mary just helps children and the wounded, Billy knew it would not serve any purpose, and he was more interested in finding out what you knew and what you were going to do." Robbie began to chuckle; Rune looked at him puzzled. "What is so funny?"

He pulled her closer and whispered in her ear. "Without hope, there is only deep despair."

Rune's eyes widened. "It's here?" Robbie nodded.

"Think about it, without the Sisters of Good Hope there would be a lot of despair. Deep despair means a crypt; the loss of Lancelot caused King Arthur a great deal of despair. Maddy told me that Gwendolyn would set them riddles that had words that could mean several things. Hope, deep and despair mean many things and all of them connect here."

"Robbie this is fantastic, but where do you think it is?" Her bright blue eyes danced with excitement.

"Sanctuary and I think Mary knows about it as well, which is quite funny because Billy's picture is probably painted right above it."

"But how do you mean Sanctuary? I know Alice had some ideas but I was so busy focusing on channelling her essence, I did not hear what she said."

"Alice said that Sanctuary has always been inside a church."

Rune looked across the yard at the dark shape of the church spire, lit by the moon and set against a backdrop of twinkling stars. "It was right in front of him and he missed it." Robbie pulled her close.

"Looks that way, don't it? I have looked at the map and there is not a single church in a direct path southwest of Loxley, just that one. I really think it is here Rune, everything fits."

She gave a soft chuckle as she pushed herself closer to him. "Sister Mary wants to see us later; do you think she is to going tell you about it?"

"It won't matter Rune we still have one big problem, we will not be able to retrieve it." She turned and looked at him with a frown.

"I don't understand Rob; if it is here, we should get it and look for Alice."

He turned to her and smiled; he leaned forward and kissed her. Her eyes sparkled "I am two swords and two heirs short, the five swords mentioned by Gwendolyn meant the heirs. They have to be present; Skip is in Loxley and Scarlet has the sword of knowledge, and we do not know who the heir to that sword is."

Rune slumped back. "Oh, why is it never just simple?"

"Well, it's not simple Rune but it is easy enough, if you contact your granddad and get Skip to come here with his sword, then contact Scarlet and let her know she should bring the sword of knowledge here. Then when they arrive, I will worry about an heir."

Robbie sat back as Rune's eyes flickered purple. He breathed the cool night air and let out a long sigh, and looked at the old church almost black in the night light, its old rugged outline visible in amongst the stars. It was a very old church and maybe it was a younger brighter building during the reign of King Arthur, but he knew that it had definitely been around at the time, and that was proof enough for Robbie. He felt a little of the burden he now felt lift a little. In a few days' time he would be able to get the sword and then head off to rescue Alice.

Rune's eyes faded back to lilac. "It's done Rob, Granddad will organise Skip and Scarlet was already on her way, she had decided that she wanted to meet her other sisters and has the sword with her, she wanted to surprise everyone, but as we are the only four who know, it will still be a surprise. She will be here in about two more hours."

Robbie nodded backwards. "You know about those two then?" He smiled; Rune nodded.

"Rowan, Pebbles you are getting sloppy, Rune spotted you." Jade stepped out from a dark corner.

"No way! How did you spot me? I was invisible when I came round the corner."

"I smelt the perfume you borrowed off Rune, I know tonight is special for you two as this is the place you first hooked up together, my sweet little Pebbles you somewhat overdid it, although honeysuckle and sweet violets is one of my favourite perfumes."

Rowan stepped out of the darkness. "Jade you could smell, but how did you spot me Robbie?"

"I didn't have to, I knew wherever Pebbles here was, you would not be far away." He started to laugh at the crest fallen look on Rowan's face. "My dear friends I love you both dearly, but please go and be alone and celebrate the love you share; I will be fine here with Rune. It will take but a moment to let Jade know if there is trouble."

Jade giggled and ran up and kissed him on the cheek.

"You are my best ever friend Robbie thanks." She grabbed Rowan's arm and with happy giggles, they headed back down the corridor noisily out of sight.

Robbie sat up as Bobby Thorn walked up.

"Excuse me Lord Loxley, but Sister Mary would like to talk in her office, could you follow me please?" Rune smiled at Robbie who smiled back.

"Well Master Thorn such a polite request should be so favoured, please my good sir lead the way." Rune giggled as she linked his arm

"That's so cute."

Sister Mary's office was at the back of the hall. She had a large wooden polished mahogany desk that was filled with papers; all the walls were filled with books on history and the religious past. Some of her books were very old especially those on the lines of the Celts, Rune's eyes sparkled as she walked along the shelf reading the spines. Mary smiled at them both. "Your grandfather liked to come here and read quite often, although back then we were a convent only, not a refuge for the injured and starved."

Rune looked surprised. "You knew my grandfather?"

"There was a time when every historian in Britain would seek his advice;

Leenard Rimmer was once very famous. You have a certain charisma that reminds me of him, especially in the way your eyes read people." The old nun sat and smiled; her eyes twinkled.

Robbie grinned he knew what Sister Mary meant; he had often seen it in Steph's as well. Mary pointed to the two chairs in front of her desk. "We should talk the age of dreams is starting."

Robbie was now the one surprised. "How do you know that?"

"The moment I saw Runestone I knew that Opal had finally faded, and the rest of her power was passed over. Opal hung around too long; I do think she should have gone earlier."

Robbie looked at her shrewdly. "You have hidden much from us Sister, what else are you not telling me?"

Sister Mary chuckled. "Robert my dear boy, I have been here for a very long time, and I know what it is you seek, like all the others I had a specific time to reveal to you the tasks set me a long time ago, and so tonight I will fill in a few more gaps. Please be patient and I will let you ask questions as I go."

Rune placed her hand on his as he nodded. "You both have come here in your search for a missing heirloom; we all know that so let's for now put it to one side." Mary leaned back in her chair and her dark eyes sparkled. "Sir Lancelot of the lake was a mighty warrior and the righthand man of Arthur, we all know that. He fell in love with Guinevere and his life became torment as he stayed away from the court and avoided her. Morgan le Fey who was Arthur's half-sister stirred the malice and it was she who convinced Gawain that Lancelot was coveting Guinevere behind Arthur's back. It was at that time a lie." Rune moved a little in her seat. "We all know this sister it is common knowledge."

Sister Mary nodded. "However, it has to be told in the context that it happened. We all know that finally Guinevere went to Lancelot, and they made love and Arthur discovered them. Lancelot lost his honour and lost his ability to use the sword made for him by Gwendolyn in Carnac. He turned to the church, and came here to the remains of an old Celtic site of worship, and on the foundations of an old barrow, Lancelot built the church of Good Hope. It still stands outside today."

Robbie looked out of the window at the church, he was right. "He built it?"

"With his own hands Robert, and he hid a great deal of the secrets of his life here, one of them being his wife."

Rune looked at Mary. "But Lancelot refused any other woman for as long as Guinevere was alive. How could he have taken a wife?"

"Only the order of the sisters, know of Sian, yet he did marry, and he set and built the church of hope. He had lost his honour and his hope and so he brought together all those who despaired, and taught them the love of his God and Christ. It was Gawain, who found him here and told him of the plight of the country, and of the deceit of le Fey." Mary sat back as she watched the attentive couple and gave a smile.

"Lancelot lifted his sword and swore at the very altar of this church that he would defend Arthur the king he loved, and win back his honour. He kept his word, the battle was won in honour of the King, and as Lancelot lay pierced with a sword, Arthur went to his friend and forgave him, and he told him his honour once again had been restored. Gawain brought Lancelot's body back, and here it lies below us in a hidden crypt along with that of Sian, who died in the birth of his son. His line still lives today in his last living relative, for all other lines that have come from him were killed in the Red Death. I am seventy years old and when I die the name of Lancelot will be gone forever."

Robbie smiled somehow as she had spoken, he had begun to wonder, the fact that she knew so much had already made him realise. "The sword can only be passed at the final moment of his line, just as he only earned back his honour in the final moments of his life. Now Sister Mary I am truly starting to understand the way all of this works." He looked at her and she seemed so frail and yet so strong at the same time. The life in her eyes shone brightly at him.

Sister Mary gave him a huge smile. "You are a true lord there is no doubt Robert and you have the skills to recover what was lost, but there is another you will require before you can."

Robbie smiled at her. "I believe that I am one step ahead here Sister, Lancelot was the right hand of the king, and it can only be my right hand who lifts and wields the sword, am I right? You thought Billy was my righthand last time, and that is why you were silent about this. You knew he had no honour."

Sister Mary leaned forward on to her desk, she nodded as she thought about that time, and then she looked at Robbie and Rune both sat watching her. "I am sad to say Robert you are right. I was very concerned about that troubled young man. When you left here without the sword, I had many great worries."

"The time was not right, we did not know of the sword then, tell me Sister if it is my righthand man that can only lift the sword, does that mean he is an heir to this kingdom?"

"Rowan is from a noble line; you can tell by his features and his manners. Since the red death, many children have not been educated very well. Work is more important because it means survival, even though all of us have to fight for life each day, the noble have still ensured their children are educated and given manners. I can spot those children a mile off. Billy Thorn is one and I might add yourself and Rune are shining examples."

Robbie nodded as he remembered the lectures his mum gave him about being polite and learning his lessons. Robbie suddenly realised, he knew in Loxley what job their parents had before he asked by the way they spoke. Even Harry, had spent a lot of time educating Blades while he had been away, it made good sense.

The frail Sister smiled at them both. "You have to understand both of you, that there is more to all of this than you first see. Powers have been at work here for many generations; you of all people Runestone should understand this. The true lines are buried very deeply and will only come to the surface when the time is right. Robert many things are happening that you know of, but there is also a lot that you are not yet aware of, and as your search continues more will be uncovered. All of the hidden lines will give you signs to guide you until such time, as it is right for you to know all of the truth. Have a little faith in the deep magic that weaves around from the world that you live in." She gave a knowing smile to Rune.

Robbie sighed. "Sister you know a lot more about the line around me than you first let on. I realised a little when you spoke of Hearne, why are you a nun in a church when you understand and believe so much of the Earth Faith?" Rune looked at Robbie and then back at the sister, she too had often wondered about the sister's dual understanding of the two faiths. Sister Mary laughed.

"You would be surprised young Robert, and you too Runestone how alike they are. The church was built on the stones of the old ways. Harvest, Christmas, Easter all share similar dates and events of ritual. Christianity runs alongside what was called Paganism, although I do prefer Earth Faith it has a nicer feeling to it. I can follow both easily because in my mind my god is the same. I am not alone in my thinking; all over this land in the modern age of man there were many who worshiped Christ and yet still kept the traditions of the old ways alive, although back then they called it superstition. There was too much emphasis put on religion in the old modern ways, it became obsessive and caused all sorts of problems. Understanding and tolerance have to be the way now for everyone; we must stop fighting amongst ourselves and work together for the good of man."

She stood up and shuffled around the desk. "It is late my dear children and I am old. Get some sleep because tomorrow will be a busy day, I have a lot to prepare and you have much yet to work out, there are still a few missing puzzles. I am happy now to know you understand that you are not alone in this quest which was why I wanted to talk to you, go and sleep well my children." Mary took their hands and stretched up, kissing them both softly on the cheek.

Robbie walked arm in arm down the corridor with Rune, he seemed to be getting the answers and now he felt a little excited about the fact that he was closer, and had all the answers almost in his grasp. They reached the door of their room and walked in; Scarlet jumped up off the bed. She had the long bundle with her and she walked right back out of the door. "My father is almost here."

Robbie spun round. "What Len is here?" He looked at Rune and then raced after her with Rune. He caught up with her as she paced with speed to the yard. Bull was pulling open the gate as the cart with its canvass top rolled into the yard. Len waved as Fuse turned the cart into the area near the horses, white foam and sweat dripped off the horses onto the floor. He jumped smiling from the cart and walked towards them.

Rune gave him a hug. "Grandfather how did you get here so quick?" He hugged her and winked at Robbie.

"Little trick I learned from the Green Lord, plus a few of my own." Scarlet handed him the bundle and gave him a long huge hug.

"Oh, Dad I have missed you so much." Len smiled as he embraced his eldest daughter of Opal.

"I have missed you too my darling, I am sorry that you felt such pain at the passing on of your mother, it was her time and we could not continue without Rune at full powers." Rune put her head down; she already knew her mum had cried all night, as she had heard her, Rune felt the pain of her aunts especially Gwinne who had not seen her in years.

Len took the sword and unwrapped it, he pulled it out of the sheath and Rune smiled at the fine blade. Len turned and handed it to her. "Here hold it, this is the finest blade ever made and it was made by your grandmother, this is Opal's work."

Rune looked at it as she turned it in her hand, the sword was etched with runes, and had many incantations etched upon it. It glistened in the moonlight, and had small butterflies and daisies engraved on the guards of the hilt. She smiled and her eyes sparkled as she looked at it, Len looked at Scarlet and nodded. "Do it, kill her."

Robbie screamed as Scarlet screamed, he pulled at his sword as Scarlet lunged forward towards Rune slicing her long golden sword high. His sword glinted rainbows as it came up in front of Rune, and there was a resounding clash of steel and ringing of metal.

Robbie looked at the three swords locked together. At least two of them were swords? Rune's eyes flared bright violet and her sword blade was a bright red and orange flame that burned from the hilt, and yet Robbie had felt the metal as his blade had struck at the same time as hers. Len smiled as Scarlet stepped back. Robbie's eyes flared as he stepped in front of Rune. "WHAT THE HELL ARE YOU DOING SCARLET?"

She slid her sword back into its sheath. "Making sure it had gone to the right heir. Truth and knowledge walk hand in hand."

Robbie's head spun, he looked at Rune and then Len and then back at Scarlet in confusion. "What?"

Scarlet went to put her hand on his shoulder. Robbie brushed it off, and raised his sword toward her chest; Scarlet stepped back and raised her hands. Robbie's eyes flared with anger and fear. "You better talk quick Scarlet, because if you threaten Rune again, I will kill you."

Rune put her hand on his shoulder; she could feel the anger in him and the deep fear. He trembled slightly as he fought to hold down inside him the shock and terror he just felt as he thought Rune would die. His eyes were wild with emotion as he turned to her to see if she was all right. The sword was now a golden blade again; Rune pulled her arm round and kissed him softly. "Please Rob calm down I am safe. Scarlet had to know whom the sword belongs to. The flame of knowledge will only burn in the hand of its rightful owner and that's me."

Scarlet touched his shoulder. "I am so sorry Robbie, it would only ignite if attacked, I could not explain that, Rune had to believe I would kill her because of my mother's death, if she did not think she was in danger the sword would not have protected her."

"GOD SCARLET YOU TERRIFIED ME. I THOUGHT I WAS GOING TO LOSE HER, HAVE YOU ANY IDEA HOW CRUEL THAT WAS?"

Robbie turned and stormed off down the yard towards the bedroom. His heart was still pounding, and he shook with anger and fear, for a moment, he thought every reason he had for living was gone. Scarlet looked upset and turned to go after him, Rune gripped her arm.

"Leave him to calm down; he will be fine; I will explain to him later."

Skip walked over all smiles. "I am assuming I can come out now?" Rune smiled and gave him a hug.

"How are you Skip? We have missed not having you around; Rob will be pleased to see you later. Let me show you all to your rooms."

Rune slid her arm around her grandfather. "That was dangerous, Robbie will defend me to the death, he could have killed Scarlet. What if he had lunged instead of blocked?"

Len gave her a smile. "Scarlet is protected from the swords; she is the guardian and therefore cannot be hurt by one. A little something, I placed on the blades many years ago when she became the guardian. It gave me the peace of mind in knowing that no one could steal them by killing her, the sword of truth knows that, Robbie's hand had a little guide."

"He loves me more than I think you realise Grandfather, you have no idea, I have never ever seen him show fear. Tonight, the fear in his eyes hurt me deeply."

Len pulled her close. "I am sorry my dearest Rune, but it was the only way we could all be sure. The sword can only pass if challenged; you will do the same one day when you pass it on."

Robbie lay in the dark room as he calmed down. The fear at the thought of loss of Rune had shocked him; he closed his eyes and tried to not think about it. It was just a test kept pounding through his brain, the door opened and Rune came in. She placed the sword down at the side of the bed and sat down. He could see her eyes glistening in the dark as she looked at him. "Are you alright Rob? They really are sorry and would like very much to make it up to you." She slipped off her top and skirt and slid under the sheets next to him. He let out a long sigh.

"I have never been as scared in my life as I was then, I cannot handle the thought of losing you Rune. That almost broke me; I never want to feel like that again."

Rune slid round him and kissed him softly. "You won't, I promise."

Robbie woke to the sound of laughter through the window; he opened his eyes and sat up, Rune was already up and out of the room. He slowly dressed and stretched as he yawned. His head felt cloudy, from a disturbed night's sleep, he had suffered awful dreams and had woken up several times in the night. He dropped his shirt over his head and dragged his feet as he wandered up the corridor.

The children were running wild around the yard with Harry and Jett. Una he was pleased to see was using her holly staff to dual with Flash. She spun like a top but amazingly so did Una, neither seemed to be able to outdo the other. Robbie watched fascinated, he had never really mastered the pole, Una was very light on her feet and her long plaited white hair which looked like a thick white rope, was also very effective as she flicked her head, and it whipped like a lash. Flash broke her pole apart and deflected it expertly, and Una laughed with delight to have such a worthy opponent.

Rowan sat down beside him on the step. "Heard about last night, are you Ok?"

Robbie scratched his head. "Yeah, I am fine, Scarlet scared the hell out of me but I understand what she was doing now. Just wish they could be a little more tactful about things."

Rowan squeezed his shoulder. "We have a busy day my friend; we have an heirloom to find." He patted Robbie on the shoulder and got up. "I will find the whereabouts of my good lady Pebbles, no doubt she is up to something with Blades or Alley, I can see Jett which is usually my first point of call."

Rowan wandered off in search of Jade and Robbie headed to the fire in the yard in search of coffee. He looked at the church as he walked, which was very old. The stone seemed blackened with age, and the edges of the brickwork were very rough looking. The spire was high and at the top was a large Pendragon weather vain. There were ugly looking gargoyles all around the higher walls, but what caught his eye was the green man's face in the centre of the high wall just below the spire.

Lancelot knew about Hearne. It surprised him and yet he was not sure why,

Sister Mary had preached tolerance the other night about other religions, and maybe Lancelot felt the same way. The wooden doors were heavy and thick, and he could see they had been built in a time when a church truly did provide protection. The church looked like it had been made to keep out those who would hurt the innocent.

Robbie picked up his cup and filled it. He stood and watched as the others all trained or played with the children, he spotted Rune with Sister Mary by the large doors, Robbie walked over to her, and she slid her arms around him. "Good morning." She kissed him and he smiled at the feel of her lips on his.

"Hey Beautiful."

Mary smiled. "Good morning Robert, I was just saying to Runestone that there are services this morning up until midday, then the church will be empty until this evening, so if we all gather just after noon, we can look for your relic."

"That will be fine sister." Mary nodded and began to walk back to her office.

"Sister Mary!" Robbie walked after her and she turned. "Sister what are the symbols of life in your church?" She gave him a big smile.

"In my church there is no greater symbol than that of the mother and child. Mary and Jesus, we worship the life. I might add it has always been a bit of an in house joke, you know Sister Mary and all her children," she chuckled at him.

Robbie nodded. "It all makes sense to me now Sister thank you."

Robbie sat back on the bed with Rune and all her sheets of paper; he looked up at Rune. "If I am right inside the church of hope, somewhere around a statue of Mary and Jesus, there should be an entrance, which will lead to a crypt. In there is the tomb of Lancelot and in his tomb with him is his sword. All five sword bearers must be present, and Rowan alone will be the only one who can lift the sword. If it glows, he is an heir and I do not want to think of the consequences if he is not and I am wrong. The wheel must play some other part so we must have the holders of the pendants with us."

Rune looked at him and nodded. "We must be right it fits so well. Gwendolyn wanted to protect the sword, but she has made it hard enough to fool anyone who does not have the items required. This has to be right Rob."

Robbie laid back; his head was pounding, from lack of sleep and too much thought. Rune leaned over him. "I can cure that for you." Her eyes glowed as she touched his temples and he closed his eyes feeling a strong sense of peace flow through him. His whole body seemed to lighten and he felt the calmness of Rune inside him. Surrounded by her love and her happiness he drifted.

It was just gone midday when a much revived Robbie stepped out into the yard. The five sword pendant holders had assembled. Jaz, Una, Mel and Rowan were waiting as Jade walked across to join them, he had the golden box and Rune held his arm.

"Great you are all here, right everyone I believe we are standing above the crypt of Lancelot." All of them gasped. "Sister Mary is going to take us into the church and help us find it, we know it's here, we are just not sure where. If we are lucky when we come up we will have the final sword." Everyone beamed excitedly. Jett fingered her pendant and grinned at Jade.

Sister Mary appeared round the corner with Len and Scarlet, and they all walked together toward them. "Good afternoon my children are we ready?" She pulled a large brass key out of her pocket and unlocked the door, it swung back and they all stepped inside. Scarlet touched Robbie's shoulder; he patted her hand.

"It's alright Scarlet, Rune has explained, sorry I threatened you with my sword."

Scarlet looked really upset. "I would never hurt either of you Robbie, you do know that don't you?"

He smiled. "Honestly Scarlet forget it, I am over it, come on we have a sword to find." She gave a small smile as he turned, and she followed him into the church.

Robbie looked up at the old church of dark heavy wood. Light streamed in many colours through the stained glass windows and he marvelled as he looked at them. Each window had a knight of the table on it. Galahad, Tor, Gawain, Perceval, even Lancelot himself.

Above the altar was the largest window which had a huge coat of arms on it and below it was written, 'Honourable men with honourable duty.' Robbie's eyes gleamed with wonder at the golden candle holders and the sheer beauty of the church. A huge crucifix hung in gold from the ceiling above the altar and he marvelled at the wonder of the detail on the body and face. Everyone was pointing out aspects of the church and gasping in amazement.

Sister Mary smiled and walked up the centre aisle of the church to a small altar at the left hand side at the top. A tall stone statue of a woman holding a child in her arms smiled sweetly down, it reminded him a little of Rune and he smiled at her. Sister Mary looked at him.

"This Robbie is our symbol of life, and I think this is where we begin." Robbie took out the golden box, as everyone crowded round and smiled with excitement written all over their faces. He looked up at Rune's bright shining eyes as she watched holding her breath. He smiled as he looked at everyone.

"Are we all ready?"

The wooden door swung open. "Hello Alice."

She jumped on the bed. "What the hell do you want traitor?"

Billy stepped into the room. "I want to talk to you." He stood dressed in all black, his long curly blonde hair flowing down his back.

"Bugger off I've heard it." She scowled from behind her book.

"Please Alice won't you listen just for a minute?"

"Don't keep your girlfriend waiting on my behalf Billy Boy, I would hate her to feel as neglected as I did, tell her you were mapping the place out, did you? Make sure you didn't get lost. You Git. Leave me alone."

Billy shrugged; his blue eyes fixed on her all the time. Alice scowled at him with hate in her eyes. "How's the ear? I hope it is still painful. Another inch or two and I could have done your nose."

Billy gave a long sigh. "Alice you are having my baby, we really need to talk about this."

"The father of my child is called Avalon, not Knox." She lifted up her book and began to read. She looked over the top of the book. "You still here?"

Billy looked at the floor. "I am sorry, it was never my choice you know?"

"What's that Billy boy having sex with me or planning your brother's death? Because to me it looked like you were there on your own without daddy forcing you? How could you Billy...? How could you hurt him? He loved you and you still did it."

Billy still stared at the floor. "I had no choice, I tried to back out but they told me Oscar would kill me if I said anything. I loved you Alice please don't think I didn't, I was caught in a trap I could not get out of."

"Robert Lox and my dad could easily protect you so do not waste your stories

on me; I hate you and despise you for what you have done. Jess gave you a home
and raised you as a son. She gave you love and happiness and you tore her apart.
Robbie was heartbroken. I will never forgive you for the pain you have caused. I
think you are a bigger monster than your father is."

Billy looked up a tear in his eye. "I am not a monster; I am nothing like him.
You are having my child Alice; I want to be there when it grows up. Let me help
you."

"You haven't a hope; Robbie will kill you, if one of the others doesn't get you
first. Billy, you tried to kill him... You know how they feel about him, you are a
dead man, you just have not realised yet... and if you want to help me tell that
moron Mac, I am pregnant. I need to pee more, and I need to exercise. You
have to sort me out some sort of toilet that I can use regularly, and at least give
me a chance to walk around more, even if it is only up and down the stairs more.
Exercise is good for our baby."

Billy nodded. "Alright I will arrange everything for you. I will be visiting once a
week so if you need anything tell me."

"How about my freedom?"

Billy smiled. "I wish I could Alice, honestly I would."

"Billy Avalon would have found a way, which is why we called him Smooth Billy;
he always protected me that's why I loved him so much."

The door closed and the lock clicked. Alice smiled; at last, she had the chance
she was looking for. She could give Robbie her map of the building and see how
Billy liked it, she lay back on the bed and stared at the ceiling her mind drifted
and she rubbed her tummy as she thought. Billy walked down the stairs with Mac.
"She is angry but she will calm down." He stopped and turned on the step. He
looked into Mac's black eyes. "I know this does not seem like a very good job, but
she is very precious to me. I want her taken care of and protecting with your life, if
anything happens to her I will never forgive myself, do you understand me?"

Mac nodded. "I understand you, have no fear she will be safe here."

Billy patted his shoulder. "Thanks, I am glad I found out about this, I owe you
one Mac." Billy carried on down the stairs and lifted his black hat off the post
at the bottom. He grabbed his long black coat and headed across the hall to the
large doors. He slipped out through the rain past the guards, and jumped into the
waiting carriage.

CHAPTER ELEVEN

THE LAST DAYS OF SIAN

Harry, Skip and Bear walked into the church, and down the aisle towards the group, who were gathered in front of the statue of Mary and Baby Jesus. Sister Mary smiled at them as they joined the group. Robbie was looking around the statue for any clues as to where an entrance could be, but it was Jade, who spotted the small carved edge to the wooden surround of the lady altar.

"Look at this Robbie?" She bent down and followed the edge of carved oak leaves and acorns to the floor. Robbie watched as she ran her finger over the soft dark finely carved wood. Every so often, there was a carved face of the Green Lord wearing a crown of acorns. Jade looked up and smiled. "This one has an acorn missing from his crown." Robbie and Rune both lowered themselves down and looked closely, Rune looked at Robbie, her eyes glinted with excitement.

"What do you think? It looks very like the one Rowan is wearing?" He shrugged at her.

"Not sure, it's not easy to spot it's so small, I suppose though that's the point. Only one way really to find out." He looked up at Rowan; "I need to borrow your pendant now if that is alright?" Rowan nodded and slipped the chain of white hair off his neck, and handed his precious pendant over to Robbie.

He passed it to Jade, and she slipped it into the gap in the crown. Nothing at first seemed to happen, and then suddenly a dull rumbling below ground began to grow louder and louder, Jade smiled up at them. "Not sure what, but something is happening, should we step back or are we Ok here?" Everyone looked at Sister Mary. She shrugged her shoulders.

"I have never opened it." The rumbling stopped and without warning the whole of the Lady Altar began to slowly slide backwards. Rune and Jade stepped back from the edge, as a black hole appeared under where the altar had been, Robbie leaned over and peered down.

Stone steps led down into the darkness. Mary handed him a candlestick with a large white burning candle in the top of it, Robbie took Rune's hand and looked at the others. "Rowan and the sword bearers first, the rest of you follow." Robbie led the way as the others gave each other an excited glance and got into line. Mary got

Harry to lift down more candlesticks and pass them round. The wide heavy stone steps wound down into the darkness, Robbie held the candle high to light the dark dusty walls of what looked like a very old stone. It was very dark and different from the stone used to build the church, and he wondered, if this was the remains of the original Celtic barrow that Lancelot had built the Church of Hope on.

He could feel Rune's hand squeeze his as they descended lower, and the temperature began to fall. The sounds of the others behind him on the steps seemed dull as he spiraled downwards, the steps ended and the chamber began without any warning at all. Suddenly he was aware that the walls had disappeared through a tall carved archway, and his single candle lit a vast room of stone. It was cool and Rune shuddered, Skip and Bear arrived with another candle, and the glow parted the darkness a little more and Robbie began to make out the outline of vast shapes. Something glinted as he moved to his left, and he walked slowly holding Rune by the hand at his side towards it.

The armour of Sir Lancelot still shone as if new, as it stood on its stand against the wall, Rune gasped at the size. "Wow he was a big one." His shield hung on the wall; it was bright silver with a thick blue diagonal stripe, and had a glittering golden dragon on it, Robbie looked at the silver suit, which bore the dints of a few heavy blows. He could not imagine how wearing it could be at all comfortable; it looked heavy, and was a clear sign of the strength of the man that wore it.

More candles were arriving with each pair in the group, and slowly the light grew brighter and Robbie turned with Rune looking up and down the crypt of Sir Lancelot of the lake. The vast chamber seemed to be the size of the underneath of the church, and compared to the steps it was remarkably dust free. The armour shone like new, and the walls were decorated with banners and flags, which had hung unseen since the times of Arthur, and were elaborately decorated with the crests of Lancelot, and the coat of arms of the king. At the far end of the chamber was a large bronze statue of Sir Lancelot. He stood tall and proud holding his sword, Robbie thought for a moment that it was his real sword and hurried down the long room to look at it.

The sword was bronze, and he looked at the impressive figure of the man himself. It was not hard to work out how he had become the champion of King Arthur; he was a big and formidable looking knight. Behind the statue on the wall was a heavy canvass tapestry, it had a large circle of black and white segments and in the middle was a large and colourful coat of arms. It was the same, as the one on the stained glass windows, above the altar in the church, he had remembered seeing it many times, but could not quite remember where?

Robbie turned round and looked down the long room to the bottom; the others were wandering around and looking at all the banners and flags. Most of the group stood in front of the armour, and he could see Sister Mary staring at the banners as she walked slowly along. This for her was family history; especially the banner that had a picture of a handsome blonde woman on it, which he suspected, was probably Sian.

"What now Rob?" Rune's voice seemed puzzled as it echoed around him.

"Not really sure, I thought there would be something to give me an idea of what to do." He slowly turned scanning all the walls. "Can you see anything that might be a sign of something to do with the sword?"

Rune shrugged. "There is nothing just this statue, and I cannot see anything on it or round it that might give us a clue."

"Hey Robbie?" Jett waved from the far end where she stood next to a small column of stone. He started to walk down the room in her direction. "Robbie this looks like you should use that wheel thingy on it." He quickened his pace and all the others looked round and started to walk towards it. The group parted as he came up at the side of Jett and looked at the top of the stone column.

The column was carved from a white smooth stone; it rose up from the floor about four feet. The top of the column had the five pointed star in a circle carved into it. In the centre of the star was a small round hole, and around the outside of the circle where each point of the star ended, were small sunken shapes of a shield, lion, claw, acorn and a dragon. Around the edge of the circle were old runes, and Rune leaned forward and began to read them. Her lips moved silently as she sounded each rune to herself.

"Let the wheel echo the past, and it shall lead you to the heirloom hidden." Jett beamed at him.

"Well then get the wheel out and set it up... Echo the past Robbie, do it again."

Robbie smiled and looked round at the gathered group, as he undid his chain around his neck. They all watched with excitement in their eyes, in the candlelight. "Alright Jaz I need your shield pendant, Una your dragon off your bracelet, Mel your claw, and I have the lion and the wooden acorn." They all pulled their chains from around their necks and began to slip the pendants off and pass them to him. He placed each of the pendants in each of their designated places, and then he took out the golden box and touched the lid. "I am Lord Robert of Loxley, the Hooded Man and the Bowman."

The lid of the box gave a soft click, and as he opened it, a small cloud of pale blue mist flowed out and turned violet, and everyone gasped with anticipation. He lifted the wheel of Carnac out of its blue velvet wrapping and placed it on the stone pillar. Robbie lifted the shining golden barrel out of the base of the box and fitted it, into the sunken hole in the middle of the carved star. He balanced the wheel on top of the barrel and looked at Rune.

"I need your butterfly and your sword," he looked at the others. "I need the sword pendants again ladies." Treen, Ruby, Jett, Saff and Alley handed their swords over as Robbie placed them in their specific places on the wheel. He smiled as he noticed the excitement in Scarlet's eyes, as he fitted the blue sapphire acorn to the butterfly and placed it in the centre. He took a deep breath and looked up at Rune as she smiled, her bright blue eyes dancing in the candlelight. "Here goes."

The whole group now gathered in a circle and he could feel the tension of expectation in the air, as all of them watched almost holding their breath. Robbie slid the pendant of Excalibur the sword of power through the butterfly and the wheel into the barrel. The wheel vibrated and then slowly began to spin, the rubies erupted into light as the wheel spun faster as the red beams fired through the sapphire. Violet light spun into the wheel and it began to increase in speed, it spun faster and faster as everyone crowded around their faces lit by the violet light.

Scarlet smiled as she began to understand, she was now looking at a smaller version of the wheel of knowledge and she nodded as she watched. A beam of white light grew out of the violet disk of light, and began to form into the shape of Gwendolyn. She opened her arms, smiled up at Robbie and bowed.

"You have done well Bowman, listen to me carefully, as I show you the way. Heirs and four swords stand firm on the floor, before the second table, that opens the door. Place your swords on the table and you will learn, the secret of Lancelot as the table turns."

Robbie looked at the stone floor where he saw a second ring. It had four triangles each with a crucifix carved into it. "Rune stand here." He placed her on a small square of stone in front of the triangle. He pushed the others back as he grabbed Bear by the wrist. "Bear you on that one, Skip you there. Robbie stepped on to the last small square of stone and looked down.

The wheel spun faster and the voice of Gwendolyn began. "Honour rises, honour blessed, honour the man and receive his guest." The stone circle on the floor began to revolve, and as it did, it rose slowly into the air and came level with the top of the column, creating a large stone table.

Robbie smiled at all the others. "She was a pretty cool woman don't you think?" They all gave him a big smile and nodded, hardly anyone spoke, as their eyes were, drawn to the wheel of Carnac.

The wheel spun into overdrive as violet light lit the whole inside of the room and flooded out over the second table. "Place your swords for a rest, send your man and honoured guest." Robbie drew out the sword of truth, and all the others followed. "Alright follow my lead in order." He placed his sword hilt first onto the table and it fitted into the carved crucifix perfectly. "Truth, now Justice... now Knowledge and finally Courage."

Gwendolyn bowed to him. "Select your man. The man of honour whom you bring, receive our gift and find your king." The old torches along the wall burst into flame lighting the whole room, and the large bronze statue at the far end of the room vibrated and began to turn slowly. Everyone turned with the movement and watched fascinated. The floor in the centre of the room slowly slid away and a large rectangular white marble stone tomb rose slowly upward. They all gasped in amazement, Harry gave a small whimper, the wheel slowed to a soft pace and Gwendolyn faded away so all that remained was violet light flowing round the top of the wheel and across the swords of power. Jade squeaked with delight as she smiled.

"Wow Robbie this is so cool." Everybody laughed. Robbie stepped away from the table and walked with the others toward the white tomb. Harry shuddered as he approached.

"Hey man this is like not peaceful and I forgot my glasses, my vibes won't hack this man."

Jaz touched Harry on the arm and he jumped. "Harry do not be afraid here, this is a site that was built on love and peace, I know because I can hear them, and they are happy."

The colour drained from Harry's face, as he looked at the roof and the walls. "Hey man don't mess with my karma, my vibes aint hacking this, you aint too cosmic at the moment man."

Saff gave him a warm and friendly smile. "Harry do not be afraid it's all fine, my brother can talk to the dead." Harry made a small quiet screaming sound and waved his hands around his head.

"Hey... whoa don't you do that man, it aint karmic, it jangles your vibes, honestly man." Harry shook as Robbie approached the tomb and Harry shook his head violently.

"Please man no... no don't make me do bad things again. Hey man please don't be unpeaceful and make me do it again, it aint cosmic dude." Robbie grinned at Harry, who now had his fingers in his ears and hummed loudly as he danced on the spot. Jade faded behind the rest of them and disappeared into thin air.

Robbie walked along the tomb and looked at the heavy lid, Harry closed his eyes and screwed them up tight. Robbie looked along the seal as Bear came up and examined the sides of the tomb. "This is going to be heavy; we will have to slide it back Robbie."

Jaz placed his ear to the top of the tomb, Harry opened one eye, and saw him listening, and he snapped his eye shut and jumped back two steps. "Oh, whoa this is like so not cosmic; I am goin to the land of uncosmic monsters' man and none radical mind benders. It will like, be evils forever dudes, this aint happenin."

Bear and Jaz placed their hands on the top lip of the tomb and heaved, as they pushed. Harry took three steps back towards the stairs. He felt the tap on his shoulder. "Shush man, I aint going to let Robbie jangle my vibes anymore." He slowly turned to see two large green evil eyes glowing at him.

"ARRRRRRRRRRRRRRRRRGH!" Harry hit the floor in a dead faint,

Jade appeared in hysterics as Jett exploded in laughter. Harry lay on the floor completely out cold.

Rune smirked at Robbie. "Jade leave Harry alone, it will take weeks to calm him after that one." Jade giggled as Jett rolled around on the floor in hysterics.

"Sorry Robbie, I could not resist it, not in here." She pulled Harry's glasses out of her pocket and put them on. "Whoa cosmic."

Robbie helped, and the tomb lid began to slide back, Rune held the candle high as Alley and Saff looked down into the tomb. Robbie looked back. "Nobody touch anything, it has to be Rowan only." They all looked up at him and then over to Rowan, who seemed as surprised as the rest of them.

"Why me?"

The large lid stopped and Bear and Jaz took the weight, Robbie came up to Rowan's side. "You are a man of great honour Rowan; the sword has chosen you to wield it. It must be your hand that lifts the sword from the tomb, and you are the one wearing the pendant."

Rowan looked at Jade and Rune, both of them smiled. "Are you sure?"

Robbie put his arm on his shoulder. "You are the most honourable man I know my good friend; take it you deserve it." Robbie looked over the edge and down the side of the knight's body. He wore full armour, chain mail gloves and his helmet. There was no sign of a sword and he looked across the body, but it was empty.

Rowan looked over the side and scanned the insides of the tomb. He lowered his hand into it, and a pale blue light shone around him, he lifted a small carved tablet of stone out of the tomb and looked at it. Rune came up at his side, and read the inscription and looked at Rowan.

Harry sat up and moaned, he slowly got to his feet, and stared in fear at the sight of Rowan and Rune beside the open tomb.

"Return the tablet to the tomb and reseal the lid, and then go to the table of swords." Rowan slowly lowered the tablet into the tomb and violet light flowed all around him, as he let go of the tablet of stone, the iron covered hand of Lancelot jerked and suddenly snatched Rowan's hand. Ruby squeaked with surprise, everyone else jumped back startled, and Harry gave a horrendous scream of fear and passed out again. The hand held fast for a second, and then released its grip, much to Rowan's relief, he withdrew his hand fast and Bear and Jaz heaved the heavy lid back on to the tomb, as the body of Lancelot crumbled inside his armour.

The group gave a giggle of relief, Rune let out a long gasp looking a little shaken. "Don't know about you guys but that got my heart racing."

Giggles echoed with relief as the five heirs turned and walked to the table with the swords and the spinning wheel, Robbie looked strangely at Rune. "What was that all about?"

She turned to him and quietly spoke. "I wish I had known about that in advance.

That was the test, if he had not been honourable, he would be dead now. I think Lancelot just passed through him and took the measure of him, he has won the sword and it has passed to him, you will see in a moment."

The four sword bearers stood on the square stone slabs, and the wheel spun faster, and Gwendolyn rose from the centre of the wheel. "Bowman you have chosen with great wisdom, take the hidden sword of Lancelot and your task will change." The four swords slid up and out of the holes in the table. They all seized the hilts as the large table began to slide towards the floor, it fitted back into position and as the wheel whizzed faster, the tomb behind them began to slowly sink back into the opening in the centre of the floor, and the large floor slabs moved back into place, the wheel increased its speed again and violet beams of light spun out from the wheel and hit the four heirs in the chest, their eyes glowed lilac.

The wheel began to rotate as the column below it turned slowly. The carved star with the wheel rose into the air and below it could be seen a bright golden handle, as the golden Sword of Honour rose into view out of the stone column.

Gwendolyn's voice filled the air around the room. "Step forward chosen one and wield the sword of Lancelot and do honour by his life for your king."

Rowan stepped forward and grabbed the hilt, his hand glowed violet, as he pulled it away from the column and held it high in his hand. The sword shone like the sun lighting the whole room, Jett fell to her knees; her eyes flickered blue. "All my life I have waited to see it." Her voice was, filled with awe, Scarlet smiled her eyes sparkling with delight, Sister Mary bore a huge smile and everyone bowed to Rowan and spoke in unison. "My Lord."

The column slowly sank and the wheel slowed down and the lights faded as it stopped. Jade pulled her arms around Rowan. "All that to see if you are honourable, all they had to do was ask me." She gave him a huge smile and he bent to her and kissed her.

Light appeared at the far end of the room as Robbie packed the wheel back into the golden box and snapped the lid shut. A bright flowing mist of white and blue light swirled around the room and then in front of the large bronze statue, the mist separated and formed two towers of light. Rune pulled her hands to her mouth and tears flowed into her eyes.

The figures formed, and hand in hand, Gwendolyn and Opal walked down the room. Jade leapt off her feet as she ran with Rune and into the arms of their grandmother. Opal smiled and pulled them close and hugged them, Gwendolyn caught Saff, Treen, and Alley and she wept as she hugged them. Una and Mel walked forward tears in their eyes and hugged their mother.

Opal looked at the weeping Jade and lifted her face to hers. "Did I not tell you we would meet again my dear little nymph? Dry your eyes my precious child and rejoice in our time here, for this is a very old and sacred place of our true ways."

Jade sniffled. "I thought I had lost you forever grandma." Opal smiled at her.

"Forever does not exist in our world Jade Opal. You will see one day you will pass from this realm and into another, and all the love and all the joy you feel will pass through with you. The other realm is a wonderful place with many I have known and loved in this life, and when it is your time to come, I promise you I will be there waiting to welcome you." She gave her a huge squeeze and kissed her on the head.

Opal turned to Rune. "I must talk with you and the Bowman." Opal walked down with her arms around her grandchildren towards Robbie and Rowan who now stood shoulder to shoulder. She gave them a big smile. "My woodsman and my bowman, how you two have grown in stature, I am proud at what you have achieved. Are you ready to bring this world back from the brink and fulfil the age of dreams I wonder? The seeds of the future will be sown in the years to come; yet one seed already grows. You must make haste and free her from the prison she is in. The Dark One cannot enter that realm for her power is poison to the child; she will corrupt the young child from birth, as she knows the powers she has stolen will not keep her indefinitely. Bring her out and keep her close and she will not be able to come near to you. This task you must do before any others for it is of the highest priority."

Robbie nodded to Opal. "We have already planned to leave here to go for Alice."

"Your wisdom has grown Bowman and you have used the skills of your heirs to good advantage. You must remain together, as you will now find others will have tasks of their own to perform, and your group will lessen. Your road will be dangerous, but five swords and bows will be a saviour in disguise. Stay true to yourselves and true to each other, the Dark One has stolen one of your numbers forever, he will never return so he remains now your enemy. Traitors will be abundant so trust to whom you know. Kin will always be there in need, good luck my children." She smiled and turned to Scarlet, Ruby and Jett.

Scarlet burst into tears and threw her arms around her mother. "I thought you had left me without saying goodbye." She sobbed into her mother's shoulder and Opal pulled her close.

"How could I leave my first born without telling her how proud I am of the warrior daughter I raised? I love you my darling and I will miss you most, we have had many hours together in this life time, and it has been the hardest of all the threads to cut for me." She hugged her tightly as she spoke and kissed the weeping warrior in her arms. "Do not cry now my love for I will be here in your heart always and waiting to greet you in your time of return to me." Scarlet sniffled as Opal pulled her back. "I must go soon let me hold my grandchildren one last time."

Jett and Ruby were pulled into a tight embrace and both wept as Opal talked quietly to them. Gwendolyn wept as she broke apart from her Granddaughters and hugged Jaz. Una and Mel wept at her side as she withdrew. Opal pulled Steph into a loving embrace. "My dearest daughter, your seeds and you will change the world forever. How little time we have had, stay close to your father and keep him safe for me."

Steph wept as she slid her arms round her mother. "I love you mum." Opal softly stroked her daughter's hair. "I love you too Stephanie Moonstone, watch your children and guide them, you have the wisdom of your father and it gives me rest knowing you will be by their side. Runestone has taken my place, guide her as I would."

Pete pulled Steph weeping into his arm and slid his other arm around Scarlet who wept with her sister. Opal turned and blew them all a kiss, and walked back down the room. They both stood side by side and Gwendolyn spoke.

"Runestone you are the centre of the age of dreams. We are your sisters of the age of knowledge and sleep, fare you well for you have two powers to aid you. Heirs of the kingdom, I bid you luck and wish you well in your tasks... My family be brave and follow the tasks I have given you."

Leenard stood by the bottom of the steps and watched his wives with a smile. Gwendolyn turned to him and smiled. "My husband you will be revealed as I leave you, the seeker of the truth is ready to know all. Goodbye, my love." Her shape broke and Gwendolyn the last true Queen of Fae broke apart and was never seen in this world again.

Opal smiled. "Goodbye my dearest children remember my words. Sister Mary we will wait for you soon, Leenard my love now is the time. Runestone enjoy the pleasure I have seen for you. Lead well bowman of the Woodland Realm." Opal faded and Robbie felt a twinge in his heart, she had guided him well and he had become very fond of her, Rune rested her head on his shoulder. "This will really surprise you."

Rune walked forward and stood in the centre of the room. Leenard walked to his granddaughter and embraced her, Rune's eyes glowed bright purple and violet light spilled out of her. It spun round the room like a twister and then shot into the back of Leenard. Her voice thundered around the room. "I call upon you Albanlin, master of the white lines of time and creator of space, bring forth into the age of dreams our master from the powers of the creation."

White light exploded and Rune walked back with a raised arm, the words in white light leapt out from her hand. "LEENARD RIMMER." They shot into the spinning cloud of violet light and it turned white, the words spun out into the air glowing purple and Rune screamed at the cloud. "REVEAL YOURSELF MERLIN DREAMER!" Violet sparks exploded out and Robbie gasped with all the others as an older version of Leenard walked out of the cloud of light and it faded. Sister Mary fell to her knees clutching her mouth.

"Merlin, you have returned."

He smiled and looked down at her. "I never really went away my old friend." He lifted her up and hugged her. Robbie looked at Rowan.

"Am I dreaming?" Rowan smiled.

"I cannot believe we missed that. Leenard Rimmer, Merlin Dreamer crafty old bugger just rearranged the letters of his name."

Rune walked up and slid her arms around Robbie and smiled. "You look a little shocked my darling."

"You are the granddaughter of Merlin?" She nodded. "Why didn't you tell me?"

Rune shrugged. "I only found out when Gran arrived, she spoke to me in my mind as I hugged her. I have some of his power mixed with Opals. It now explains why my powers are so strong. Nature and the powers of the Whitelines in one, should at least give the old Dark One a run for her money now." She gave him a sweet smile and kissed him.

Harry moaned and sat up from the floor, he stared groggily around at everyone and looked up at Merlin. "Whoa Len how long was I out man? You like aged a hundred years, man you need to shave that beard it like aint happenin or cosmic." Merlin looked at his long white beard that reached his belt.

"Actually, Harry dude, I think it's quite funky."

Harry shook his head. "Funky man is for chicks. You need to get cosmic."

Jade pulled Harry up from the floor and handed him his glasses. "Hey Harry you should have seen the dead guy when he came at you, it was awesome the way he sucked on your vibes man."

Harry jumped back with a scream, and slid his glasses on; he patted his legs and his chest. "Whoa girl, which bits did he jangle?" He bent over and stared at his body as Jett sniggered behind Alley.

The group came back up the steps and into the church. They all reattached their pendants and Robbie pushed the small acorn back into the slot in the crown of the green man. The statue of the Virgin Mary and her child slid back over the stairway and closed. He handed the necklace back to Rowan who slid it back over his head and dropped it down inside his shirt. Jade beamed at Rowan and patted his chest where it hung.

Sister Mary took Rune's arm as she walked down the centre aisle of the church. She looked up at Rune and smiled. "You know my time here is over don't you Runestone? Take me to my room I feel it coming." A very sad look crossed Rune's face as she nodded to Robbie and Alley. As everyone headed into the light of the day Robbie swept the sister into his arms and carried her quietly to her bedroom, Rune and Alley made her comfortable and then opened the door to him.

Robbie came in quietly and sat on the bed as the old nun smiled. "Do not be sad my most noble of lords, I have had such a wonderful life, and I had the chance to finally meet my guardian angel."

Tears welled in Robbie eyes. "I can't bear the thought of this place without you my dear Sister."

She raised her weak arm to his face. "I am the last of his line, and my time here is done. You have the sword and you are the saviour of my children Robert, I never would have made it this far without you. Paint my picture on the wall and I will never leave this place, my spirit will be in every child who comes through those gates."

Robbie took the old frail hand and kissed it as he smiled down at the old nun who had taught him so much about trust and compassion. "I will never forget you Sister; I am the man I am because of your words of faith. You are my symbol of hope."

Rune sobbed loudly and leaned over and kissed the sister on the cheek. "I have come to love you so much my dear Sister, I am going to miss you terribly." Mary gave a soft smile.

"Runestone Sapphire you are a great power and you have the greatest gift of all, you have life and you have love. You have my guardian angel, look after him he will need you." She looked at Robbie and she winked, he laughed through his tears. "Don't forget young Robert, when you have lived for as long as I have, we will have notes to compare."

He smiled and leaned forward and kissed her on the head. "Good bye my dearest friend, I love you." Robbie leaned back and the Sister's hand went limp in his. His tears dropped on to the pillow as Rune threw her arms around him and wept bitterly. The old nun lay silently smiling.

The church bell rang out across the yard, which was swept clear and empty. No children were anywhere to be seen, behind closed doors, children and adults alike wept and mourned the loss of Sister Mary of Hope.

Robbie dropped the brush into the can of spirit. He looked up at his work, and felt the strong pain of loss in his heart, as he turned and walked out of the hall and up the corridor towards his room. Rune sat alone and weeping on the bed, she wore the plain black robes of a sister and held her hankie to her mouth.

Robbie pulled her into his arms and hugged her, it had been a long sleepless night of tears, and Rune was exhausted. Robbie had barely slept and at five in the morning, he had risen and gone to the great hall, and there he fulfilled his promise to the sister. Sister Carla had made all the arrangements, she had run the convent by Mary's side since the red death, and now she assumed command of the order. Her face was heavy with grief as she organised the service.

"It's time Rune; we have to see she is given the best." Rune nodded as she sniffled and she rose from the bed and with his arm around her, they made their way to the church. The long coffin made of red mahogany stood on the tresses as Robbie and Rune bowed to her. Rune touched the top of the coffin and flowers sprung up across it.

The nuns conducted the service, and they all bowed their heads in respect. Steph turned and buried her head in Smokes arms. Blades sat on Harry's lap and he cradled her as uncontrollable sobs came out of her. Rags wailed into Jett; Rowan's eyes streamed as Jade wept into his shoulder. Martin and John stood with Fish and all three lowered their heads as tears filled the floor. Rune turned to Robbie and he pulled her close. The sounds of her sobs in his shoulder bringing him yet more pain as the tears dripped from his silent cries from inside.

Sister Carla finished her prayers and looked up at him, as she dried her eyes she nodded, Robbie released Rune and looked back to his men. They came forward and standing beside the long wooden box made by John and Martin, they lifted the sister on to their shoulders and began the slow walk of Sister Mary's last journey into the yard.

The quietly weeping party walked into the yard. Mel, Maddy and Una stood with Scarlet, Treen, Alley and all the children. The small children wept as the funeral party walked slowly passed, and the yard was filled with the sound of weeping and sobbing for the last heart of compassion passed them by, Jaz bowed his head in reverence.

The hole was dug and the bars set across it. Slowly the box was lowered on to them and Robbie faced the assembled crowd. He took a deep breath and swallowed his tears. "My dear friends... Here lies a true angel of heaven. I have little understanding of her faith and yet I know that her god will be waiting to bless the hand of the kindest of all of his children." Muffled weeps scattered across the yard.

"All of us here have been touched by the spirit that was in blessed Sister Mary. She was the last of her line and the kindest of all of us. She taught me a great deal in the few conversations I had with her, as she taught me compassion and humility, she gave me my honour and I earned her respect. I once told her I was unworthy of praise, because compared to her I had achieved nothing, she argued with me about that and even now, I find I was unable to convince her."

Robbie swallowed hard to control his tears as he looked at her coffin. "What I know is this much; Sister Mary was old and had great difficulties. Her job was the hardest of all as each day she faced the worst of humankind's actions. She gave love and compassion to all; her hand of friendship was long and met everyone who needed it. The hall of this house has the faces of all that she helped and loved. I loved her for she taught me the meaning of love and life and how to be a decent human being. There will be no other quite like her for they make few of her kind. We will lie her to rest here in her garden where she will be forever close to the children she loved. She has earned her time of rest, so say farewell to the kindest and most loving person you probably will ever have known."

John, Martin, Fish, and Bear stepped up, the bars were removed and the box lowered as loud wails of loss came from the crowd. Robbie lowered his head and his shoulders shook in grief. The ropes were pulled out and Robbie raised his shovel, and with the other men, he filled in the hole. Jade and Blades carried the large cross that Harry had made in the night, Jade had taken two of her silver daggers and melted them down and made a plaque that she had engraved and screwed to the cross. Harry helped fix it in place, and Robbie wiped his eyes as he read it, Rune came up and leaned on his shoulder.

Sister Mary of Hope. The heart of us all, and the love of the world. No child was ever left, no adult ever turned away. Learn from her.

Rune bent down and touching the earth a garden of flowers sprung out of the soil. Sister Mary was now laid to rest beside the lilac tree, and she could watch over her children forever.

Robbie sat on the bench in the garden beside the lilac tree as the sun began to set. He felt a loss like he had never known; grief and sadness surrounded him in every area of the convent. His mind wandered and he did not notice the sister at the side of him. Carla looked tired and she bowed to him.

"My Lord this was on the good Sisters desk, it is addressed to you."

Robbie looked at the envelope and took it slowly from her hand. "Thank you, sister, won't you sit a while, I would like to know how you would cope. I hope you know I will still support the efforts here to the fullest so that Sister Mary's work will continue."

Sister Carla smiled. "Sister Mary spoke of you often My Lord, she had a great fondness for you, and she admired you for the role you had undertaken at such an early age. I can see what she meant, your words for her today touched me deeply and she would have smiled. I do not have her strength or energy, but her work will continue. Lady Alley has offered to stay and help run this place with me, she I feel has the strength and energy of the good sister. It pleases me to know."

Robbie nodded. "Alley has no stomach for death or inflicting pain, all her energy now is for healing, it will ease my mind knowing she is helping you. My support of this House of Hope will continue have no worry, for I will be a frequent guest Sister. You have my word... I feel the world has lost a fragrant flower."

As the evening moved towards the night, Robbie sat in his room and opened the letter. Rune knelt beside him and read over his shoulder.

My Dearest Robert,
You knew tonight that with the recovery of the sword the last of the line of
Lancelot would end. I almost lost the fight sooner, but you saved me just in time.
I want you to know that in you are the powers to bring a world anew, and it has
worried me that you doubt this.
I am old and have seen much of life so please trust me when I say to you, that
when this world is at its darkest and you find yourself overwhelmed think of these
words.
There is a light within you. It burns with the power you hold for Runestone. It
is a force so strong it could destroy the world. In times of trials think of her and
release what you feel. It will always bring you through. It is known as the torch of
the angels, let it light your way, as it did mine.
Take care my dearest of Lords
Sian Mary Lancelot.   (Sister Mary of Hope)

Rune gasped. "She was his wife; how can that be? It would make her over a
thousand years old."

He looked up at her. "It's funny you know, but when she recognised Len as
Merlin, he called her old friend. Merlin was sent into the age of sleep before
Arthur and Lancelot died. He must have known her then... Sian is an old Celtic
name that means god is gracious."

Rune sat back on the bed. "It has been a weird few days, Rob. So much has
happened it feels like months since we were at Loxley."

Robbie slid the other sheet of paper out and looked down at it.

Here are stated the last final words of Lancelot given to Gawain,
SEND FIVE SWORDS THAT SHOULD RISE OVER THE WALL
THE WISE ONE MUST RETURN TO HIS HOME
THE BLOOD THAT WILL FLOW FROM NOBLE VEINS
WILL BE BROUGHT TO THEIR WATERY HOME
MAKE HASTE FOR DARKNESS IS RISING IN THE AIR
LOOK FOR THE SIN IN HER NEST AND GUARD THE EGGS
A TRUE HEIR WILL COME TO A WOODLAND SHRINE
ONLY WHEN THE DARKNESS RESTS
ONE HEIR ALONE CAN WIN THE DAY
ONE HEIR WHO SEEKS THEIR OWN FATE
BUT THAT MOMENT WILL TRULY ONLY BE KNOWN
WHEN THEY ARE STOOD BY THEIR GARDEN GATE.

(The last gift of Sian wife of Lancelot to a noble Lord.)

Robbie read it several times over, as Rune sat back up. He handed it to her and leaned back on the bed, he rubbed his eyes and relaxed, he felt tired and weary as exhaustion mixed with emotions of grief. He closed his eyes; Rune read it several times over. "You know what this is don't you Robbie?"

He gave a long sigh. "I think it is Lancelot speaking from the grave telling me how to return the King of England and true heir to the throne. I am just too tired to work it out now, oh Rune I am so weary."

Rune folded the letter and slid it into his pocket. She pulled back the sheets and slid off his boots and trousers. "Come on get your shirt off, and get a good night's sleep." She dropped his shirt on the floor and blew out the candle, he lay in the dark aching with exhaustion, Rune slid in beside him and curled around him. He lifted his arm and pulled her close.

"I will be glad when all this is over and we can go and live at the Mere." She kissed him softly.

"It will happen, trust me I know stuff." She smiled as he drifted away into a deep sleep.

Rowan and Jade sat in the dark silently keeping watch as the mist appeared around the gates. Rowan leaned forward as the mist opened and the old man walked silently into the yard. The breeze blew across the steps and into the corridors, as the sound of creaking bark and rustling leaves filled the air. The Lord Hearne stopped at the grave and smiled. "Well, my old friend the rest you seek has finally arrived. Come to me and be safe and at peace."

Jade's hand slipped into Rowan's as they both watched from the dark. A pale light rose from the floor and formed a column of white, the shape became clear and Mary bowed to her lord.

The old lord smiled. "He has waited an age for you Sian, he awaits you with joy. Come my child walk into the other realm and be happy again." He pulled her into a hug and kissed her softly on the head. "You have done well, my bowman has all he needs to fulfil his task, we can all rest a while and help prepare for the road he now faces."

Hearne turned and with his long twig like fingers on her shoulder, Sian walked smiling with her lord back towards the gates. The tall oak trees groaned as they bowed to their lord, and in a swirling of white mist the two figures were engulfed and the mist rolled into the gates and was gone. Jade slid her arms silently around Rowan and without words, he held her tight as the dark surrounded them on their vigil through the night.

Robbie walked into the yard his shirt flapping lose and his feet bare. He scratched his head and yawned as the activity of the day grew. The gates were open and a steady stream of weary people walked down the road, Sister Carla guided them in and the other nuns helped. Alley looked at each one as they arrived and instructed each nun in their tasks. Rowan came up at his side and watched the new arrivals.

"More and more Robbie, every day more, we have to stop this."

Robbie lifted his arm and squeezed the shoulder of his friend. "It will stop, I know just the two people to do it." He smiled at Rowan. "But first my good friend, we need coffee." Rowan laughed and patted him on the back as the two of them headed to the fire pit and the silently heating pot.

CHAPTER TWELVE

DARK CLOUDS AND VIOLET LIGHT

The line of people stretched before them, and Judith could see the gate not far ahead. "Is this it Uncle Seth? I am so tired and my legs are hurting." Seth looked down at his niece; she was pale, drawn and dirty, yet her bright blue eyes sparkled with hope and the faith that she held for her uncle, which overwhelmed him.

He stared down the line to the large black open gates beyond the two large oak trees. "Yes, Judith love we have made it." His emotions spun with hope, but also the pain of losing his wife. Thirty eight years of marriage, ended on the edge of a Cutters sword. Something inside him had broken, and he had only been able to find the will to continue through his hope of saving his niece from that monster of a father. His feet dragged as the energy to lift his legs was failing.

Robbie stood with Rune by the gate, and watched the defeated faces and hungry eyes shuffle inside. Rune watched with horror in her eyes at the cuts and gashes that the refugees had suffered. "This is not fighting a war; this is butchery of a people already defeated."

Robbie tightened his grip on her waist. "This is not his army that has done this Rune, they are disciplined. No this is the action of his Cutters; there is a difference between the two."

There was a commotion in the queue as an old man fell and a young girl screamed for help. Robbie ran up to the old man who lay on the ground moaning incoherently, he knelt down and lifted the cut head of the old man up. His eyes rolled around inside his head and lost focus, he mumbled to himself unaware of where he was.

Rune crouched down to the weeping blonde girl and put her arm around her. "Don't cry sweet pea, we will get him help, is he your family?"

Judith looked up into the smiling face of Rune and her eyes met hers. "He is my Uncle Seth."

A cold icy shiver ran down her spine as Robbie lifted the old man in his arms. Rune looked up, but Robbie was already moving to the gate with the old man. "Come on sweetheart, let's go and see what we can do for your uncle." Rune took her small hand and led her down to the gates, where Robbie spoke to one of the nuns. Rune felt the cold chill running through her as they followed the nun and Robbie to a tent that had four beds in it.

Alley came over as Robbie lay the old man down on top of the bed; Rune guided Judith around the side of the bed to a small repaired old wooden chair. "You sit here with your uncle and we will get him help alright?" She smiled at the little girl, as Alley leaned over the old man.

"He is not good Robbie, another case of very bad malnutrition and dehydration, and all the usual signs of shock from beatings and seeing something horrific." Alley turned to the nun in a large white apron. "Give him that tonic I made and lots of liquid; we need his fluid levels up and then some food."

"Will he be alright Alley? This is his niece." Alley smiled down at the young girl beside Rune, and crouched down to her.

"Your uncle is very sick, but we will do everything to bring him through, so do not worry. It might take a few days, but with hope he should be fine." She slipped a large red apple out of her pocket and put it in her hand. "Eat this and in a while, we will get you something better." She winked at Judith and she smiled back at Alley.

Judith bit down hard on the apple and chewed as she sat holding her uncles' hand, Rune walked away from the bed with Robbie and stopped. "Rob you should know, that young girl is a Knox."

"What?"

Rune nodded. "Look at her eyes, they are Billy's. I just got a very cold feeling off her as I walked her into here; she has traces of the Dark One in her and some power. She is still very young and may just be on the edge of developing more."

He turned and looked back at the small skinny blonde girl who chewed on her apple as she held her uncles' hand and softly spoke to him. The long blonde curls did remind him of Billy and maybe the blue eyes. "It has to be a coincidence Rune; you know Knox would never let his daughter get away from him."

"I know what I felt Rob, and I am telling you that potentially the future Dark One sits four feet away from you."

"Rune she is just a young girl, even if she is a Knox, what do you want me to do, kill her because she could turn bad one day?" He watched the girl who seemed very compassionate with her uncle.

"I know what I feel Rob, I will be talking to her uncle in a while, and I am not leaving here until I know who she is and where she is from." Robbie smiled; he leaned over and gave her a soft kiss on the cheek.

"Alright, you sit with her until her uncle comes round, and find out what you can, then we will talk." She smiled and her eyes glinted at him.

"Thanks Rob."

Preparations had begun for leaving, Rags was going to head for Loxley with letters, but would spend her first day riding in the group; Robbie wanted her to stay with him until they were level with the moors. He had a few ideas and if needs be he would send extra information. Skip was to accompany Robbie as a sword bearer and for the first time in many years, it would mean separation from Fuse. Robbie needed him back at Loxley to finish off Skips work with his father.

Scarlet was preparing her return to Caerleon and her father was to ride with her, Robbie found it confusing as he talked to Len and he looked up at him from the seat. "What the hell do I call you now? I have called you Len Rimmer all my life, should I now call you Merlin?"

He laughed and stroked his long beard. "Let me see now, I have been many things for many years, but we are in the age of dreams My Lord, and I am after all Merlin Dreamer." His eyes danced with excitement. "I would like to be given my real name again. Yes, my boy, call me Merlin."

Robbie smiled and nodded. "Ok Merlin it is... So, Merlin what will you be doing whilst I am away up north?"

"There is much to prepare if we are going to find ourselves with a new king one day. I also want to have a good look at what is going on in the south. It has concerned me that no one has been able to get behind his lines and see what he is up to. I know ways of walking amongst his people without detection, I will find out more than any woodsman in his realm."

Robbie stared out across the yard as Merlin spoke, and he watched the stream of people wandering in. It seemed to be lessoning now as the sisters ran around with bandages and food. "I have to find a way to stop him, Merlin; I have to find something that will kill his dream forever. All these people suffering it has to stop."

Merlin patted him on the back. "You will my young lord, you are the seeker of truth and you now have the five swords together. That in itself will invoke powerful magic."

Alley stretched, as she walked out of the tent. She looked across at Jade and Rowan sat by the fire. "Jade!"

She looked up and smiled. "Hi Alley. Busy morning?"

Alley looked at the long line. "Yeah, not too bad though, most of them will rest up a while and head back out in a day or two." Alley looked back down at Jade. "You know I am staying here, don't you?"

"What you are not coming with us?" Alley smiled at Jade's startled expression.

"I am more use here. My skills are the powers to heal not hurt; I could not raise a sword or shoot a bow and kill someone, I live to heal the pain of the world. My place now is here with Sister Carla." She lifted the chain from round her neck, Jade seemed so disappointed; Alley took off the chain and handed it to her. The small sword of honour hung glinting in the sunlight. "There will be a time when only sword bearers will be able to stay together. Rowan has the sword and you will now be his sword guardian, this will keep you together at all times."

Rowan gave a smile as he watched Jade. "That is a nice thing to do Alley thank you." She nodded to him.

Jade beamed as she slipped the chain over her head, and she jumped up and pulled Alley in to a hug. "Thanks Alley. I am going to miss you."

Alley hugged her back. "You must be a regular visitor, and send Rags with loads of letters telling me all about the havoc you and Jett cause."

Jade gave an evil grin at her. "I will cousin; we have got loads of stuff planned for Harry."

Alley started to laugh. "Poor old Harry, he is so sweet and yet such an easy target, you two should cut him a little slack."

Jade beamed an evil smile. "Nah... he is way too much fun."

Big John stood up and looked down the driveway, he shaded his eyes and stared at the trees. "I am not certain Bear but I think you should close the gate and warn Robbie."

Bear gave him a strange look. "What is it?"

"I think we have guests; I only got a glimpse but I would prefer it if we did not let em in on my watch."

Bear whistled loudly, then dropped to the floor, everyone was up on their feet as Bear swung the large gates shut. Rowan ran up to the gates calling across to Harry. "Get the cart up against the gates to strengthen them, and round up all the crew." Rowan leapt up and grabbed the top of the wall. He heaved himself up on top, and wove his way into the large oak tree to John's side. John pointed to a patch of trees just short of the corner of the road, and Rowan followed his finger.

"I could be wrong Rowan but...?"

"You're not... I see one too."

Harry rolled the cart against the gates, and then pulled heavily on the break lever. He lifted four large sacks of grain out of the cart and dropped them under the wheels to act as chocks. Martin, Skip, and Fuse came out from behind the stable with ladders. They propped them on to the walls and scrambled up them. Blades ran up the drainpipe of the large accommodations block, and swung her legs on to the slates. She sat high up with Robbie's telescope and scanned the tree line.

Maddy and Steph climbed on to the ladders and made their way slowly on to the wall. They ran along spacing out and peered through the large fruit trees. Pebbles, Smokes, Fish, Mel, and Rafe scurried along the left hand side of the wall and spaced themselves. Saff, Keith, Rags and Jaz followed Steph to cover the right. Fourteen bows waited hidden in the fruit and oak trees. Nine sword men organised the children and cleared the yard as Robbie and Rune came down the yard with Carla. Robbie spoke quickly as he glanced up at Blades in her look out.

"Keep all the kids in the main hall Carla, and do not come out, Alley has sufficient nuns to do first aid if it is required." He jumped on to the ladder and ran up it and into the overhanging canopy of the large oaks. "What do we have Rowan?" Rune slid in a few feet away and loaded her bow. The long golden sword of Knowledge hung from her belt of golden oak leaves, and her dagger glinted on her other side.

"We are not sure how many yet Robbie, John is watching Blades to find out how many she has seen."

Robbie peered out across the rough grass to the tree line seventy yards away. "They will still have to cover dead ground to get to us. Aha, what do we have here?"

A solitary Cutter walked down the road towards the gate. Robbie signaled to everyone to hold their fire, he had long black curly hair, and dirty brown clothes, and wore the now familiar black vest and red dragon of Mason Knox. A large sword hung from his belt, and Robbie watched him closely with Rowan. Rowan whispered quietly. "Does he know we are here?" Robbie shrugged.

The Cutters eyes never once looked at the walls or the trees; he walked right up to the gates and rang the bell. A small window in the gate opened and Bull pushed his face to it. "Yes?"

The Cutter seemed surprised to see a male face. "I thought this was a convent, who is in charge here?"

Bull looked at him. "I am the caretaker and servant of the sisters, what would a soldier be doing here? We are a refuge for the weak and wounded."

The Cutter sneered at him. "We know what you do here, and we want to talk to the sister called Mary who runs this place." Jett's voice echoed from behind Bull. Rune suppressed a giggle as the high pitched impersonation of Sister Mary echoed under the tree, as she watched from above, her bow pointing right at the Cutter.

"What is it Samson? Do we have more wounded?"

Bull looked behind himself and tried not to smile. "Err no sister it is a soldier who wants to talk to you."

"What would a soldier want here Samson?" Bull looked at the Cutter.

"You heard the sister what do you want?"

The Cutter, seemed quite annoyed at having to use Bull as a go between, he raised his voice louder. "I have been sent here on the order of Mason Knox the Governor of Britain. He has been led to believe his daughter Judith Knox is here. She had some difficulty on the road and I am to escort her home."

Bull stared at the Cutter. Jett's voice came back through the gate. "We have no one of that name here, I am sorry but you must be mistaken."

Robbie felt the tension rise as the Cutter shuffled his feet. "She was seen coming in here, and I have to search this place on Mason Knox's behalf. Please Sister open the gate and let my forces conduct a search, I cannot be responsible for the outcome if you refuse."

"This is a haven of safety and is neutral, you know the Christian Church has rules and you cannot enter. We have no member of the Knox family here." Bull stared a hard threatening look at the Cutter.

"You heard the sister."

The Cutter shuffled his feet and looked back at Bull. "I have orders which I cannot disobey, it would be easier to let us come in, you do not want to refuse the wishes of Mason Knox. Tell the daft old nun to open the gate and stop being silly."

Bull glared at him. "If the sister says no mate, she means no. You had better be off then." Bull shut the window and Jett sniggered. The Cutter kicked the gate and turned, four bows in the tall oak trees followed him as he stormed down the track.

Twigs snapped and cracked in the tree line seventy feet in front of them, as they prepared for the Cutters to come. Six Cutter archers appeared in the trees, their arrows were lit and burning as they pulled back on their bowstrings. Robbie's hands moved rapidly, as his orders were silently given. Rune and Rowan pulled back on their strings. Martin and Rafe took aim, and Steph and Pebbles brought up their bows. Robbie flicked his wrist and the Cutter bowmen fell dead into the grass. Flames leapt up in the dry grass, and shouts bellowed from the tree line in front of them.

Black and grey smoke swirled into the air around the trees, and suddenly a volley of red feathered arrows shot into the sky. "Heads up," yelled Steph as the arrows shot past her and over the wall. The sword group jumped back with their backs against the wall, and the arrows rained into the yard landing rapidly and standing upright in the hard earth. Two pierced one of the hospital tents and there was a violent scream.

"Spot em and shoot!" Robbie yelled, as he put his bow to his eye. Blades whistled, and John shouted to the left of Robbie.

"Four O'clock." Robbie's arrow flew side by side with Rowan's and Rune's. There was a scream and a Cutter fell out of the trees, Blades gave three shrill whistles, everyone prepared, and Rowan gritted his teeth.

"Here they come."

Yells and jeers rose above the trees, and the sound of trampled undergrowth filled the air, the trees parted and the Cutter raiding party of at least two hundred surged forwards. Sixteen bows sung out, and those in front crumpled to the ground, Blades slid down the drainpipe and sprinted up the yard. The Cutters surged forward as each bowman pinpointed their target and shot, Cutters fell as they stormed forward yelling and screaming, waving their swords and axe's.

"Bull we need swords! There are too many to stop before they reach the gate.

Bull placed a large hand on Robbie's shoulder.

"Keep shooting lad we are on it."

As the Cutters lunged towards the gates through the trees, and down the road, ten hooded figures dropped from the oak trees at the gate, and drew their swords. Bull smiled at them all and slid out his huge silver axe. He nodded to Scarlet, and they walked towards the running hoard in a long straight line. The sun glinted as Harry and Blades drew their twin shining swords, Jett swung her long golden blade with a smile, and Una raised her long holly pole as Flash spun her white pole above her head ready as she froze in the road, and kicked her heel into the ground. Jett prepared as she slid her long golden spiked heels into the ground below her black boots ready for the clash.

Bear, Fuse, and Skip picked up their pace and made their advance behind Bull who roared like a lion with Scarlet, and lunged into the mass. Cutters broke in several directions as Bull's wide axe came around full circle, wiping out five feet of Cutters around him. Blades spun up into the air as Jett whooped, and together their swords spun like flames, and the Cutters began to fall.

Scarlet's screams caused panic as the fierce red clad warrior of Caerleon drove hard into the ranks slicing and killing with power and aggression. The bows continued to clear the far edges and protect the swords. Flash spun as Una deflected and hit Cutters into her path. Flash hit them several times before they fell to the ground broken and dying.

Maddy put down her yew bow and picked up the white bow of Gwendolyn. A large group of Cutters had broken away from the rest, and were making their way to the far right of the wall. She took aim with the long white arrow, and it flashed from the bow as she released it. The arrow was a swift flame of bright fire.

It hit the Cutter who instantly ignited and screamed, he lunged at his fellow Cutters screaming and they caught fire as he touched them. The three at the back stopped and turned to run back to the trees. A second blazing arrow followed them, and as they reached the safety of the trees, the last man ignited and ran screaming into the wood. Rune watched Maddy's bow and nudged Robbie. "That is Gwendolyn's bow, it shoots flames, and she is rather good with it don't you think?"

Robbie released his arrow and turned to see a flame whiz at high speed into the trees, screams erupted under the leaf cover. "Wow! I got to get me one of them."

Rune smiled. "Be sweet and I will see what I can do for your birthday next year." She released an arrow with huge pace and a Cutter close to Bear was lifted into the air and fell backwards, Robbie nodded.

"Not too shabby Rune. What about him over there with the funny eye, could you hit his top button?" She drew the string back, and breathed out as she released the arrow.

"Dam!" It hit just below and he flew back into the trees. "Ok, clever clogs, what about that really big one over there? Could you copy Alice, and put a white feather in his earring?"

Robbie smiled as he lifted his bow. The arrow exploded out of the bow, it flew at an immense speed and passed straight through the earring, shearing the white feathers off the shaft as it passed through and killed the man behind him. The huge Cutter jumped in fear as his hand came up to his ear. Rune's arrow hit him straight in the chest and he fell.

Rune smiled at Robbie. "You are such a show off at times, you know?" She fired at the same time as him and two Cutters heading for Jett fell dead as she spun on one golden heel and took out three Cutters with a deafening scream and a whoop.

Bear found himself another big one as Harry ran past slicing his way to the back of the pack. Bear grinned and wiped his forehead as the big Cutter waded towards him with a sword and a small axe. Bear blocked the sword and stepped to one side as the axe swung round. He brought up his sword with savage aggression, and the axe arm fell to the ground, the big Cutter roared in pain. "That's for cheating and using two." Bear moved on to the next Cutter.

Keith and Saff knelt side by side on the top of the wall; their bows almost touching as they loaded aimed and shot. "You know Miss Sapphire; I would be very honoured if you would take a walk in the woods with me."

"Why Master Sherman are you asking me to walk out with you?" They both fired and reloaded their bows. They came back up to the aim.

"Well Miss Sapphire, I do indeed believe I am, I cannot stop thinking," they fired. "Of you and I have to know if there is any hope for my affections." They took aim.

"I believe you may have hope Sir." They fired. "I would very much like to walk in the woods with you."

"Really?" He dropped his bow and beamed a huge smile. She fired.

"Yes, Keith really." She gave him a very beautiful smile and her cheeks pinked up a little.

The trees parted and five Cutters flew through and landed on the smouldering grass. Bull steamed out behind them, and brought the edge of his blade down on the one trying to crawl off. Harry came out a few feet across and smiled. "Hey man it was like pain vibes back there, they is real peaceful now."

Bull nodded, and looked round at Bear as he came up towards them. "It is clear right through to the road, that's the lot. Jett spun to a halt and wiped her face of blood on her sleeve, she grinned at Blades. Flash did one final spin and brought the white pole down on the neck of a Cutter, and he slumped and lay still. A leg twitched next to Scarlet and an arrow hit the body, which jumped a little and lay still.

The swords crew looked around at the field between the wood and the convent walls. The grassy area was black and smouldering, and covered with the bodies of

Cutters. Small flames licked the ground every now and again, and the trees to the far right end of the field smoked and smouldered.

Robbie dropped out from the oak tree and walked up the road his bow still loaded in his hands. He looked from left to right as the sound of the cart rumbled behind him. Bull leaned on his axe. "About time we had some exercise." He stretched his shoulders back.

Robbie looked across at the others as they moved slowly towards him stepping over the dead. "Let's get this lot cleared out of sight, I want no traces they were ever here. There is a deep depression over there, get them in it and burn the lot."

The gate swung open and the others walked out. Keith and Saff took point and watched the road as all the others lifted or carried the dead to the hollow. Over two hours later, Blades and Flash had collected up all the spent arrows and took them back to the cart. Fuse and Skip had carried all the swords, knives, and bows back to the cart, and Maddy loaded her white ash bow. The arrow swept into the midst of the pile, and huge flames burst into the air, the crew turned back and headed for the gates.

Una touched Rune's arm. "I feel her." Rune's eyes were already going violet. Una turned to Robbie. "GET EVERY ONE BACK BEHIND THE GATES!"

Robbie looked up at the sky and the dark clouds rolling their way. "GO NOW, RUN ALL OF YOU!"

The party headed back to the gate, and as they flew inside Bear pushed the gate too. Rune stood silent her eyes glowing and her head twitching as if she was reading some signs. "Heirs follow me." Rune opened the gate and turned to Bull. "Lock the gates and do not open them until I say so, no matter what happens... Do you understand me?"

Bull nodded. "Yeah Rune." She smiled.

"Alright Bull, keep everyone in and they will be safe."

Rune waited until the gate was shut, and the bolts had slid across, she turned and raised her hands. Bands of thin violet light seemed to flow from her fingers on to the floor, like a long snake, it crept along the base of the wall. Robbie watched as it headed to the far end of the compound and disappeared. A few moments later, it came round the end of the opposite side and wove its way back towards them; the two ends met and lay still on the floor.

The five heirs stood in a line across the front of the gate; they all placed their hands on the hilts of their swords. The black cloud was becoming thicker and the light faded as it surrounded them, consuming the sunlight. Rune waved her wrist and a faint violet mist surrounded the swords men. "Say nothing, and do only as I say."

Lightning struck the road up ahead and a blast of thick cloud wafted across the path, as the smoke cleared the black figure of a woman stood before them. Robbie remembered the face with the thin pale lips and the pallid complexion from his dream. "You dare to keep my family from me?" Her voice was soft and yet cruel and cold.

"Return the family of ours and we might talk." Rune was equally as cold in her tone of voice.

"So, we finally meet face to face, give her to me wood child or all of you will die."

"I am the Runestone, Morgan le Fey; I am the life of this land and these people. You have no power here for the land is sacred." Her eyes flickered from violet to deep purple.

The Dark One laughed a hideous and evil laugh. "I have the power of your line Runestone; I stole all the power of Gwendolyn precious wife of Merlin, before I imprisoned both of them. Do you really think you are a match for me?"

Rune smiled. "I am not your equal Mother of a snake, I am your superior, now leave this place."

The Dark One screamed with delight, her laughter echoed right up into the clouds and back. "YOU... YOU... The child of the useless dried up old prune Opal. Look child you may have had a little power from granny before to keep me at bay, but now you are just out of school and still have lessons to learn."

Rune drew her sword and the others all followed, Le Fey stopped dead as she saw the five swords glinting in the dim light. Rune whispered quietly. "Lower your blades and touch them together."

The five blades came down and all met at the tips, the Dark One lifted her hand and Rune's eyes exploded in dark purple. The violet snake on the grass around the walls, shot up into the air in a solid wall of purple light. Morgan le Fey screamed with malice, and a bright red ball of fire emitted from her hand.

Light spilled out of Rune's eyes and onto the sword blades. They glowed white and the two lights mixed, and a ten foot circle of spinning violet light jumped off the blades of the swords, and shot towards the ball of fire. As the convent blazed purple behind them, it hit the red ball of flames and wrapped its self quickly round it. The ball of flame smothered and went out.

Rune stared defiantly at the surprised look of the Dark One. "Your kin have deserted you Le Fey, she will become my student now, we have an even balance, as one of mine deserves payment of one of yours. The balance is now restored; leave here for you do not have the power to defeat us."

She raised her large cloak and black wings came out. Her scream of frustration was terrifying as bolts of lightning fired in every direction, her eyes burned with an evil malice and her face shrivelled with hate. "Step off sacred land Runestone and I will have my revenge, this is not over wood girl." She burst into the air as lightening exploded in every direction and the black clouds thickened as she entered.

They rolled back with speed and the sunlight sent its first rays on to Rune, she smiled. "Wait a moment longer." A massive burst of lightening shot down from the sky and bounced off the violet walls, and then very quickly the cloud rolled back out of sight and was gone. Rune pulled back her sword and slid it back into its sheath. "I need a coffee." Robbie dropped his sword into its sheath and smiled at her.

"That was pretty cool Rune." He winked. "And real sexy."

Rune looked up at the sky as she slid her arms around him. "You know, I must admit I do love that cloud thing she does. I wouldn't mind getting a white one." She kissed him.

Rowan smiled, "I am not sure what we just did, but I really hope Jade hasn't peed herself again." Rowan began to laugh as he banged on the gate.

Rune looked at him laughing. "Bull open the gate."

Jade jumped into Rowan's arms and squeezed him with tears in her eyes. Rowan looked down. "Pebbles sweetheart, we really need to sort this pee thing out when she is about."

She buried her head in his shoulder. "I try honestly but she scares the pee out of me Rowan."

Bear and Skip chuckled at Rowan's face, as he held her in his arms and he kissed her. With her arms round his neck and her legs round his waist, he carried her back in through the gate and went in search of dry pants.

Robbie looked into her bright blue eyes, now surrounded with violet, as he stroked her hair behind her ears. She smiled at him and he smiled back. "You alright... you know full strength and all that?" She kissed him softly.

"I am here in your arms. I love you, Robbie."

He nodded. "I love you too Runestone Sapphire."

She squeezed him tight as Bull coughed loudly. "Shall I leave the gate or will you two love birds be wanting to enter today?"

She slid back from Robbie slowly never leaving his gaze. "Leave it John; we will be just a moment longer." She smiled and her eyes danced at him. He felt a surge of joy slowly pass through him as he lost himself in her eyes.

"I SAW THEM YOU FOOL. THEY HAVE ALL FIVE, HAVE YOU NO IDEA AT ALL WHAT THAT MEANS?"

Mason looked up at his mother. "Oh, for god's sake Mother calm down, you act like it's the end of the world or something. I have told you, I have it in hand. The sword maker will be brought here soon and then all you have to do is work on the blade with him."

She clenched her fists at being lectured to by her son, and swung round and scowled at him. "You had better be right because if you come up against those blades your little empire my dear son will crumble." Morgan le Fey looked out across Canterbury and the miles of stone buildings that had now appeared. Right in the centre stood the collapsed ruins of the Cathedral, surrounded by a circle of green.

"WHY WONT THAT DIE?" Mason rolled his eyes as he buttered his toast.

"What does it matter everything else has?" He took a large bite of his toast and lifted his coffee cup. "I need those factories Mother, without them I cannot progress; you did say you would sort them this week."

She spun round with a look of pure hatred on her face. "ALRIGHT I AM DOING IT!" She stormed down the room and out of the door. Mason sipped his coffee and swallowed.

"Needs to relax a bit, think things out in a calm way, I keep telling her, she never listens and that is how we ended up here in the first place." He smiled at his son. "Come on Lance eat your breakfast and I will take you north, and show you the new wall. It is over a hundred feet tall and set in a two mile band of burned earth. Let's see that wood chopper cross that without me seeing him."

Lance chewed on his toast. "So is that it Father, do we give up looking for Judith?"

"I think so son, she was always a disappointment to me. Kept doing nice things for people, not what a Knox is about at all."

Lance looked at his father. "We are about force and power." He banged his fist on the table and smiled, his bright blue eyes shone below his sleek blonde fringe.

Mason smiled at his son. "That's my boy; spoken like a true Knox." He leaned back in his chair and breathed a long sigh. "Maybe I will get your grandmother to find me a new wife. You could have another baby sister then. That would be nice wouldn't it?"

Lance smiled. "I would like that Father."

Mason got up out of his chair and threw his napkin on to the table. "I suppose I should go and see how your brother is doing, that bloody girl is causing all sorts of problems. I have no idea why he had to choose her. A stupid one would have been much easier to confine."

"She is pretty though dad."

Mason gave a shrewd grin at his son. "That is your brother's weakness. They bat their eyes and his brains fall right into his pants, it will be his undoing, you remember that. I hope you learn to use them for what they are needed for, and keep your brain separate. We all need an heir and it has to be female, remember that. It's just for an heir, don't go like your brother and go all daft on them."

"I won't dad, I hate women, Grandmother drives me mad at times." Mason ruffled his son's hair.

"You get more like your old man every day."

Rune stood in the doorway of the large hall; she leaned against the doorframe and stared at the painting on the wall. Steph smiled at her. "See what I mean?"

Robbie had come into the hall in the early hours the night after Mary had died and he had painted her picture on the wall. Rune looked at the hooded man and his group all in a line with their names painted underneath. Above them, he had depicted Mary as an angel.

She floated high on the wall with her arms open in a welcoming pose; Rune had seen her do it many times. The face was painted with love and skill and she marvelled at how talented he was. It was a beautiful and very life like picture. Small nymph like children sat at her feet, all with happy smiling faces that looked up to Mary. Steph leaned on the wall next to Rune and gazed at the picture. "To be honest sweetheart I never knew he had such talent, I doubt I would do as good a job. The guardian angel of the house of hope that really is a lovely caption and a very fitting tribute to her."

"It's so beautiful" Rune's voice was almost a whisper, Steph turned and smiled at her.

"It sort of captures her spirit, doesn't it? I really hope he paints one of you, I would love one."

Rune looked back at her mum. "What I don't understand is Mary told us Sian died during child birth, and yet she didn't because she was Sian."

Steph followed each line of Robbie's brush stroke with her eyes. "Carla told me that was the moment she decided to become a nun and follow her husband as a preacher. I suppose that is where Sian stopped and Mary began, in a way it was like Sian died because from that day onwards she was always Sister Mary."

"I suppose so; it is just such a shame she had to die because we had to get a sword. The children have been so sad today, I can feel their loss."

Steph put her arm around her and kissed her cheek. "Mary is still here in spirit, talk to Jaz, just don't tell Harry." Rune giggled. "I am off to bed sweetheart, go and find that gorgeous boy of yours and tell him you love him because he is a great artist."

She gave her mother a big smile. "I think I will, if we are setting off tomorrow, he will be busy, I think I will steal him for the night." Steph patted her cheek.

"That's my girl," and she walked off down the corridor.

Robbie was fast asleep when she arrived in the room; she slid gently under the covers, and lay beside him and watched him sleep. Rune snuggled into him and he disturbed in his sleep and pulled her close to him. She laid her head on his chest and closed her eyes, Rune felt a great happiness as she drifted off into sleep.

CHAPTER THIRTEEN

PAINFUL LESSONS

Lance looked out over the wall at the wide expanse of burned and black land. Smouldering tree stumps lay strewn as if some mighty hand had just swept down and smashed them flat. It was a scene of total devastation; large machines drove across in the distance pushing the burned debris into the far off tree line creating a mound as high as the trees themselves.

Mason patted his son on the shoulder. "See what can be done if you have a mind to do it?" He turned back to the sprawling building site behind him.

Hundreds of machines lifted, carried, and worked as they rebuilt the cities. "I will soon have them banging on the doors to come back in and beg for my forgiveness."

The wall now ran east, from the south of Birmingham to Lowestoft on the coast. One hundred feet of towering black, smooth stone. From the walls back towards London, buildings were springing up with factories and engineering plants. A southern wall was in production running down the side of the Old M5 motorway, and Knox planned to join it to the wall in Devon. He was cutting the country completely in half and filling his section with the sprawling monsters of industry. Nothing green remained to be seen, the whole area was now becoming a hard cold baked desert of concrete.

His long white hair blew in the breeze as he stared out across the concrete wasteland, and placed his arm around his sixteen-year-old son. "My lad, this will all belong to Billy and you. When I have finished, we will slowly move across the water and rebuild Europe. It will be yours for the taking, and between you both, you will rule the world, no wood chopper will have the power to stop you. People will beg you to give them space in the New World of Knox."

Lance smiled at his father; he liked the idea of being king of a new world. He felt a sense of power emit from his father, and he liked the feel of it. This would one day be his; the thought of sharing was not something he had in mind at all.

Scarlet hugged Robbie. "I will see you soon enough." She clasped his shoulders and looked at him. Her jet black eyes tinged in the whites with lilac, burned brightly as her eyes met his. "You are very special to all of us Robbie, I am sorry that I had to threaten Rune; I did not enjoy bringing fear to your heart. I see how deeply you love her and I hope you understand."

He smiled back at her. "I do understand, it's forgotten honestly, ride home with a happy heart my friend, and please be careful, there are many dangers for us now." He pulled her close and gave her a big hug.

Scarlet turned to Jett and Flash; she gave them both a hug and kissed them both. "I am so proud of you my warrior daughters, remember my love and protect Robbie and Rune for me." Jett hugged her mum.

"We will mum, we love you." Scarlet wiped a tear from her eye and pulled herself up on to her large black stallion. She smiled as she turned the horse slowly round. "Good bye and good luck my friends." She blew a kiss to her children and bolted out of the gate, a long, bundle of cloth on her back. Robbie looked down at the golden belt of oak leaves, and the golden handle of the sword of knowledge round Rune's slender waist.

"What has Scarlet got on her back?" Rune smiled at him.

"History... she has taken Rowan's and my sword back to the table of swords. They are now heirlooms of these times, and will one day contain power as these do."

Robbie nodded. "I really get lost in the ways of your family at times Rune. All this constantly preparing for the future, I am just glad to know if each day when I wake, it will be your eyes I see as I open mine."

She pulled him close and kissed him. "Robbie that is so sweet."

Judith ran out of the tent crying as Alley ran after her, and caught her in her arms and held her close, Robbie knew that Seth was dead and the only family she had left she had run from. He looked at Rune who wore sadness in her eyes. "It's weird isn't it, he is even hurting his own?"

The team was making all the preparations to leave, Harry, Blades, and Flash were saddling up the horses, and John and Martin were checking out their supplies of arrows. They were faced with a long journey, and they wanted to be sure they had enough.

Merlin smiled as Rune approached. "I have been looking for you Grandfather."

"I have been out in the forest with my old friend in the glade, I was watching you." He pulled her into his arms and hugged her. "My beautiful Runestone, how much you have grown in strength and power. I watched, as you faced her again, you did superbly well. I am very proud of you my darling, although I feel the credit should be Opals. You have adapted to your new role very well indeed and I am relieved to know that as I head south and you north, our hooded man will be in good hands."

"I felt you for the first time in a long time when I faced her, is that because you are now revealed to us?" Merlin stroked his long white beard.

"I gave you the extra powers last of all, I have been hidden for a long time, but now is the time to come forward and fight. The Dark One has drawn a lot of power to her Runestone, so do not underestimate her, she has tapped into other powers than Gwendolyn's, I feel her build more strength and you will find a time when your powers will be almost equal. That will be the time to show her your most powerful force; it is one she will not easily withstand."

Rune frowned. "What force is that grandfather; I thought my strength was that of nature?"

"It is my darling, but there is something you have encountered that even I had not foreseen; the love of nature combines all of the power you hold and it is increased by those who love you, and your hooded man loves you in ways none of us could see. There is a purity to it I would love to study, for I believe you two have discovered a power beyond the knowledge of man and wizards." He gave her a loving smile.

"I do love him grandfather. He is my whole world, and I am happier than I have ever known or thought possible."

"Stay close to him Runestone, for you are each other's protection." Merlin turned to see Harry and Blades leading the horses into the yard. "Go now my precious child, and prepare for your journey, I have a little work to do to help you on your journey."

Robbie and Rowan were bent over the map with Skip and Bear. Rowan traced his finger along the line of the steep valley. "This will get us past the wall, and into Kielder Forest, we have strong support there. It's pointless even considering the east coast, as Skip has pointed out, Knox is very much in control there."

Skip nodded at Robbie. "The frightening thing there is, they welcomed him with open arms. From what little we get from there, he is building at an alarming rate and has been for some time, all of Old Newcastle and Sunderland is completely rebuilt. He has factories already pumping smoke into the sky day and night."

Robbie looked down at the map as Rune slid her hands round him.

"Ok we have cover over the border and into the forest, that should bring us safely to Roxburgh and that has good cover by the look of things what about above that." Rune pointed to Aberdeen,

"There is some very exposed area across these mountainous regions. That is not going to be easy, would it not be better to plan each day as we see what we are confronted with, after all news from the Scots has been very thin and I know that she is up there somewhere."

Bear frowned. "She is in Scotland?"

Rune nodded. "Yes, she has somewhere up there of her own, Opal told me to look to the far north and my greatest enemy, it has to be her."

"I must admit the further I am from her, the happier I am, walking towards her is not my idea of fun."

"I will keep you hidden Bear, do not concern yourself, the five swords will be cloaked until we need to announce our presence, I have the power to hide all of us." He nodded and she noticed that all of them seemed reassured to know she could to some extent keep the Dark One off their backs. She kissed Robbie on the cheek. "I am going to go and get changed into my woodsman clothes; will you come and get me when you are all ready?" He turned and kissed her and gave her a smile as she headed off for the room. Robbie turned back to the map and studied his route.

"Rune we are taking Judith, prepare her."

She turned and looked back surprised. "Is that really wise Rob?" She was not keen on the idea and gave him an anxious look.

"She has no one here, and she is a threat to this place as long as she is here. I will not let these people suffer again; if she is with us, the Dark One will know she is not here."

Rune nodded. "Alright Rob, I was going to send her to Loxley, but if that is what you want, I will get her ready."

It was two hours later when Robbie handed over a large bunch of letters as he spoke to Rags. "There has been a slight change of plan, you travel with Fuse. There are four local woodsmen going to lead you, but keep your head down Rags, do not take any unnecessary risks."

"Ok Robbie, I promise I will be careful." She winked at him and smiled. "I love it when you worry about me." He gave her a big smile.

"Go on and get Bags ready."

Robbie walked over to Merlin. "So, what is the plan for today?" Merlin gave him a big smile and his eyes twinkled.

"I have a trick or two that could assist you in your journey north; when you are all assembled, I will show you." Robbie gave him a what are you up to sort of look, but Merlin just smiled and his eyes shone like crystals.

Rune hugged Alley and then Carla and Robbie helped her up on to her horse. He hugged Alley and then he took Carla's hands in his. "I wish you my very best Sister, I know with Alley here, Mary's dream will continue."

Carla nodded and smiled. "I think I will miss you Lord Robert; your people have been so good to all of us. Please take care of yourself, I will ask both Gods of both faiths to guide and protect you."

"Now you are starting to sound like Mary. Good luck Sister, I will return have no fear." He climbed up and swung his horse around and looked at his crew. All of the circle of knowledge were now in woodsman clothing and wore green hooded cloaks. Jett still wore her usual black with lilac trimmings and Flash as ever was in grey. They both had Loxley cloaks and as he rode down the line towards Merlin, he felt the mantle of hooded man return.

Harry waved goodbye to all the children, who screamed, shouted, and waved, at him as the party made their way to the gate. Robbie looked down at Merlin. "So, my dear old friend what have you got to aid my journey?"

Merlin raised his hands. "Whom will you head for first?"

"We head for Carlisle why?" Merlin closed his hands and white light streamed out of him. A twenty foot orb of pulsating white appeared in front of him. It vibrated and then stretched into a long tube.

"Ride through it My Lord." Robbie looked at Rune; she shrugged her shoulders and pushed her horse forward. They rode into the tube of light, it was very bright and felt damp, and Robbie could hear rain falling on leaves. The tube ended suddenly and Robbie with Rune rode right out into dense woodland in the pouring rain. He pulled his hood up and looked behind, as the others came through and passed him.

John and Martin came last with odd looks on their faces, it felt like they had only travelled ten yards, but the scents in the air and the rain said different. Robbie watched as the long white tube faded away and he could see only trees. Una slipped out her compass.

"North is that way Robbie." She pointed ahead of them.

"Lead on Una." She kicked the horse and it made its way forward, and slowly the others fell in line. This was a strange land and he could feel the subtle differences in the trees and ground, they followed the dirt path as the rain grew heavier and harder.

The surroundings were very similar to Loxley, but there were far fewer oak trees and more beech trees, alder and birch were abundant and the floor around was filled with thick grassy hummocks. The trees were very close together and, in some parts, they dismounted and wove their horses through them. Tracks started and then suddenly finished without a trace. Robbie watched Rune to see if she was sensing anything, but her eyes remained their usual lilac as they moved forward.

The ground was rising all the time, and the trees seemed to thin as they entered large areas of pine and larch. He signaled for them to have a break, as they got under several very tall larch trees that had a canopy so dense that they could stand in the dry for a while.

Steph and Mel lit a fire and made hot drinks; they were not cold but somehow the wetness seemed to feel much better with a hot drink. Rowan, Pebbles, and Bear slipped off for a look round to see what they could discover, and Rune leaned her back against the tree with Steph and Jett. Una and Maddy stared into the woodland where nothing moved and sipped their drinks. Keith sat quietly with Saff.

"When I suggested a walk in the woods, I was hoping it would be dry and somehow nicer." She laughed at him.

"This is not so bad; we have a few places to dry off, and once the rain stops it could be quite nice."

He looked around. "It's funny we have not encountered any woodsmen; I would have thought here there would be quite a few."

"It is odd, isn't it? It would help I suppose if we knew where we were." Saff looked back at Robbie who sat talking to Harry and Rafe; it seemed he too felt a little disturbed by the fact that no one had challenged them. Rune closed her eyes and sensed around the woods for any sign of life, her eyes opened and Robbie was watching her, she smiled and shook her head, there was nothing.

Rowan and Jade came up the path after about forty minutes. Bear walked slowly behind them, Rowan slipped down on the floor and poured a cup as Rune and Robbie leaned into him. "The whole place seems deserted. The wood rises up to a bluff about four miles north, but I could not see smoke or any signs of life at all. I am not sure I like this Robbie, a wood without woodsmen is a worrying thing, I would like to get out of here as quickly as possible and find the reason why."

Robbie patted his arm. "Good work Rowan, and don't worry my friend I usually find that if there is a mystery as to why there is no one around, we will no doubt stumble in to it." Robbie looked up at Rune who shrugged.

The rain began to ease up a little as midday crossed and they set off again heading north. Robbie was still not completely sure of where Merlin had sent him, but he began to start thinking that maybe there was some reason why he had been sent here. They plodded slowly along through the endless miles of dense green feathery leafed larch trees, without a sight or sound from anything. It gave all of them an uneasy feeling as they rode slowly watching the woodland around them. They moved on for almost two hours, when Big John rode back towards them from scouting ahead with Rafe and Martin, he looked very white and shaken. He pulled close to Robbie and looked very upset. "What is it John?" Big John looked back at the others and then back to Robbie.

"I think you should come and have a look Robbie; I have not got the words to describe such a horror." His face was very white and he looked visibly shaken, it worried Robbie, as he knew John was not someone you could easily worry.

Rune looked up the track and back to the white face of John. "What is it John, you can tell us?"

John's eyes glistened. "I cannot say the words Rune, please don't ask. You should not come; this is not for delicate eyes."

Robbie kicked his horse forward and Rune came up at his side a stern look on her face. They followed John at a gallop down the long track weaving through the trees and out on to a wide track, which must have been some sort of wood road.

John slowed as they came round the bend and up to two horses tied against a tree.

They dismounted, and Robbie with Rune holding his hand walked behind John into the trees. Robbie could see what looked like a small wooden town, through the leaves. Rafe came out of the trees looking desperate, his eyes were wide and his face was as white as a ghost. "Do not go in there Rune please I beg you." He looked at Robbie. "I know why the wood is empty and I really wish now I didn't." Robbie looked from his horrified face to the trees and what looked like the small town.

Robbie walked through the thick undergrowth and stepped out into the town built in amongst the trees. The first thing to hit him was the smell, which brought an instant retching to his stomach, his eyes could not understand the pictures as they registered, his hand came instinctively to his mouth as the contents of his stomach emptied.

He turned to stop Rune but it was too late. The horror in her eyes was a picture he was never going to forget for as long as he lived. She stepped out and a thick cloud of flies exploded into the air, Rune squealed and stepped back, turned, and was sick in the bushes. "Oh god!" She gasped and was violently sick again, tears streamed down her face. The whole village of women, children and men hung from the trees with their stomachs cut open, their entrails dangled to the floor where Rooks and Ravens feasted on the hanging remains, scattered bodies lay on the floor with long red arrows sticking out of their backs.

Robbie grabbed Rune, and staggered through the trees to the track back to the horses, where the others were starting to arrive. He crouched down next to Rune who was weeping as she retched, he tried to swallow large mouthfuls of air and breathe. He shook his head as Rowan approached him, as if to warn him, it took him a few minutes to gain his composure. John, Rafe, and Martin all remained silent as Robbie stood up and checked Rune was all right. She wiped her mouth and nodded as she stood up, Rune put her head on his shoulder and cried,

Robbie held her close, as he spoke to Rowan.

"John is right the only way to understand what has happened is to see, but I do not recommend it. There has been a deed here so vile I will not describe it."

Rowan looked at the white face of Robbie and the distress of Rune, but he knew he had to see for himself, he walked into the trees as Robbie looked at John.

"I cannot leave them like that John, it's not right." John nodded at him; an understanding look on his face. It took Robbie a few minutes to explain as Rowan came back looking very distraught, he trembled, as his look of disbelief seemed to frighten the entire group.

"I want them taking care of, but I will not ask any who cannot face this to do it." Robbie pulled a rag from his bag, and he tied it around his face, and turned and walked into the trees. He quickly ran up one of the large trees, and taking out his knife he cut the ropes as John and Rowan appeared to help lower the bodies to the ground.

He looked down tears in his eyes, as the body of the young girl of around twelve slowly descended to the ground, which was already a dark rich red colour from the congealed blood that had spilled out. Jett and Pebbles went in each house grabbing all the bedding; John spread the sheet on the floor as Robbie lowered the young girl. She slipped on to the ground with a splat; John heaved and retched as maggots spilled out all over the sheet. He turned and ran into the bushes. Judith wept bitterly as she grabbed the sheet and gently folded it over the young girl's body, Robbie watched her head shake violently as she retched and cried.

Rune stood in tears and raised her hands, and a long wide trench opened in the ground. The group helped, wept, and sobbed as they worked, Rowan and Pebbles lowered the small bodies of the children into the hole. Rowan's eyes streamed as he relived the horror of his own past and Pebbles pulled him sobbing into her arms.

He stared over her shoulder at the two tiny feet of a baby that stuck out from a fern; he moved over and picked up a tiny shoe. Pebbles sat sobbing, as he tenderly fitted it back on the tiny foot no longer than his index finger. Rowan lifted the tiny mutilated body and walked sobbing back to the grave. With the tenderness of a mother, he laid the baby in the grave. Rowan stood up and walked from the glade into the trees.

It took several hours and the afternoon passed sadly, as each member of the team, faced their own demons that all of them thought could never exist. Silly little things like a wedding ring, or a necklace somehow brought home the pain of these lost people. Rune picked up a wooden rattle, she looked at Robbie, her eyes were red from her tears; her blue eyes seemed somehow dulled with pain. She slid it into her pocket; it was a symbol of the evil that had taken place. His heart seemed to almost tear as the pain filled him, Robbie knew how much she dreamed of her own children, and how easily this could be Loxley and hers.

It was late afternoon before all of the dead, were cut down, and laid in the long grave. There were muffled weeps and out breaks of retching. Saff and Maddy were affected more than the others were, Treen's first sight was enough, and she had returned to the horses and was violently sick. Robbie stood with his head bowed, as the others gathered around sniffling and weeping.

"Hearne take these poor members of your woodland family and treat them with care." He looked at all the group. "Remember this always, we have to stop this ever happening again. This is the hand of Mason Knox and we have to stop him." He nodded to Rune, and she raised her arms and the hole closed, Robbie looked at Judith who was watching him carefully.

Robbie stared at her momentarily, and then turned away and walked into the trees. "Rowan find me a camp close by, it is pointless going on now." Rowan and Pebbles moved off into the trees, as Judith knelt next to Rune and stared at the long grave. Rune noticed and she crouched down to her.

"Are you alright Judy?" Her face was very pale.

"The hooded man hates me because I am a Knox, but I could not do this Runestone, I could never hurt anyone in this way."

Rune pulled her close. "Robbie does not hate you Judy, he is very upset. These are his people; he is a woodsman and their leader. He does not understand the spilling of innocent blood, he would never harm a child; do not forget, it was Robbie's decision that brought you with us, so he can protect you. Judy your father is his enemy; it is hard for him to understand why your father could allow this to happen. You should talk to him."

Rune touched the soil of the long grave. "Sleep with peace my children of the woods." The whole grave filled with the small strawberry looking leaves of the wild Potentilla. She waved her hand and they all burst into a thick carpet of deep red bell like flowers. "Innocent blood will be forever marked so." Rune stood up and took Judith's hand as the young girl stared at the thick mound of deep red blooms.

Rowan and Pebbles arrived back a few minutes later. They led the party into the woods and travelled for about fifteen minutes to the edge of a river, there was a small glade and the camp was soon set up. Robbie put extra watches on to ensure they were safe; he did not fancy a Cutter party wandering into the camp.

He still wore a haunted look as he sat by the fire and stared at the flames. Steph and Maddy sat down beside him and passed him a cup. He nodded as Maddy touched his shoulder. "You cannot shoulder the guilt of this Robbie. He is evil and will stop at nothing to get what he wants; this is going to continue and you must stop him that is your task." She rubbed his shoulder as he nodded.

He sat quietly until his watch came up; he rose and walked into the woods as the darkness descended, he touched Rafe's arm. "Go and get something to eat, and then get some sleep." Rafe stood up and patted Robbie's arm, he walked back to the camp as Robbie sat down.

The pictures in his head haunted him. Wave upon wave of emotion crashed over him, the brutality and pure evil of the actions disturbed him in ways he had not thought possible. He could not imagine any of his group doing such wicked things, and he found it hard to understand what would drive anyone to commit such horrific acts. He stared into the trees lost.

He had been sat some time watching when Judy walked up with a plate; he looked up at her as she offered the food. "Runestone says you should eat." She crouched down and offered him the plate and a fork. "Do you hate me, because he is my father?" It reminded him very much of his conversation with Rune back on Honey Hill, when she had asked if he could handle it being around the child of Billy's. Robbie looked into the same blue eyes of Billy; Judith was a young teenager, her face was softer than Masons, but her hair and bright blue eyes bore the distinct characteristics of Knox. She watched him intently.

"I have no feeling good or bad towards you Judith; I do not know you or know what you are like. I hate what your father orders others to do, but I do not blame you for it."

She sat on the grass and peered at him through the ever increasing darkness. "Did my father really order that?"

"I take no pleasure in telling you Judith, but yes that is the work of his Cutters, the red arrows are their trade mark. Those people did not deserve that; my people would never do that to any supporter of your father. We have killed his men I do not deny that, but all of them have been in black vests and armed."

"One of your men killed my mother." The words resounded around Robbie's head. He knew this moment would eventually come and he closed his eyes and leaned back against the tree, Judith watched him through the dark.

Robbie took a deep breath and sighed. "Your mother jumped in front of an arrow meant for your father... She was never meant to die." Her voice seemed to soften as she asked the question, and he heard the pain in her words. He turned as she looked up and her eyes filled with tears and glistened in the darkness.

"Were you there when it happened?" He knew he could avoid it no longer.

"Judith it was my arrow that took the life of your mother. I have regretted it from the moment I released it, she jumped up to save your father, and I have an innocent life on my conscience."

Judith sniffled in the dark. "I think I knew already, but I needed to know."

"Believe me when I tell you, I truly am sorry. I have to stop your father Judith and I will, but your mother's death was an accident and I would take it back if I could. I can understand it if you choose to hate me, I would hate and want to kill anyone who harmed my family."

Judith wept quietly. "I miss her; I never understood why she loved my father. He was horrible to her and treated her terrible, I begged her not to go but he forced her." Robbie stretched out his hand to her, and she lunged forward and threw her arms around him and wept. Robbie was taken a little off guard, and very surprisingly put his arms around her and held her in his arms as she wept. Rune stood in the darkness with Rowan a few feet away and watched. Rowan slid his hand off his knife, and Rune wiped the tears from her eyes.

Robbie carried the sleeping Judith into the camp when his watch was over, and gently laid her on a blanket by the fire and wrapped her up. He slid down beside Rune at the side of a large fallen log, she turned over and faced him in the dark, her bright eyes shone through the moonlight of the night. "She is not corrupted by the Dark One or her father Rob, we must protect her she is very frightened at the moment. She seems to have some trust in you, Seth told her you alone were the only one who could protect her, so will you?"

Robbie stared into her eyes, his feelings were so mixed up with anger and pain he was no longer sure how he actually felt. "I will protect anyone who opposes that monster. I am very aware of who she is though Rune, it is his blood in her veins." He closed his eyes and layback on the deep piled up soft leaves, Rune watched him for some time, and then cuddled round him and put her head on his chest.

They woke together as Keith handed them both drinks. Robbie sat up, and leaned on the log, he had not slept very well as pictures of tortured and mutilated people filled his dreams. Zandra Hargreaves face screaming had flitted in and out of the dreams, and he felt exhausted and restless. Rune could feel the conflict inside him and looked at him concerned, he smiled. "Bad dreams all night."

She leaned on him. "I felt them; I am not sure anyone slept very well last night. I know mum used her sleeping charm on Jade and Ruby."

Robbie took a long sip of his coffee and stared around the camp, everyone seemed out of sorts. Their morale was very low as they trudged around the camp; no one was ever going to forget the sight of the previous day. Two riders came into the clearing it was Martin and Rafe, they pulled to a halt and dropped off their horses. They spoke to Rowan as Keith led their horses off into the trees.

He nodded and looked across towards Robbie. Rune stretched and groaned. "I need a wash." She stood up, and grabbed her bag and headed for the river.

Robbie got aching to his feet; too many nights sleeping in beds had softened him and he ached all over. He crossed the camp towards Rowan who nodded as he approached. "Well, my good friend we appear to have found out where we are now."

Robbie looked at the map in his hand, and Rowan moved to his side to give him a clearer view. "Looks like Merlin has sent us here." He pointed to a small town on the outskirts of Carlisle.

Robbie stared at the town Hornsby. "Wow Merlin really knows how to travel, we did five days' worth of travel in a matter of minutes, pity he didn't just send us straight to Alice though isn't it?"

Breakfast was slow as everyone slowly came around. They had spent a great deal of time, out of the woods and Robbie noticed how they had lost a little of their edge. He pulled himself up on to his horse and faced everyone. "We are losing our sharpness, snap it up guys, I don't want to find us all surrounded by Cutters, let's get it together, the country ahead could have anything in it. Intelligence from these parts is low."

John and the group nodded. They set off at a gallop; Robbie wanted to put the woods and Hornsby behind him, the group was very subdued all morning; even Jett and Jade were quiet. Rune rode alongside of Robbie. "I can sense others close by Robbie, slow the pace a little, will you?"

Robbie watched as her eyes flickered lilac to violet, he dropped the pace and everyone slowed to a halt. Rowan and Bull came riding up. "Why are we stopping?" Robbie looked at Bull.

"We may have company; I want to know who and where before I move forward."

Rune sat very still as she focused. Her eyes faded back to lilac and she smiled at Robbie. "There is a group about half a mile in front, they are not moving so I am assuming they are camped out." Robbie nodded and pulled round to the others. He slid off his horse.

"Martin, John, and Bull go have a look but stay well out of sight. If we are lucky, it will be the band of Cutters from back there, I would very much like to pay them my compliments." They headed off on foot as Robbie turned to all the others. "This could be the band of Cutters from back at the village, if it is I want you all to know now, I do not want them killed, shoot only to wound." Rune put her hand on Robbie's arm.

"Please Rob you cannot, do not become what you fight." He turned on her and snapped. Rune looked shocked.

"I WILL NEVER BE LIKE THEM!" She recoiled from him and her face coloured as her eyes filled. Robbie softened to her.

"I am sorry Rune. I want them to live, because I want them to remember what they have done for the rest of their lives. Death is easy and too good for these; I will not let them off the hook so easily." Rune nodded with her head down, as two violets sprung up in the grass. Robbie pulled her to him as he spoke to the others. "You heard me, no death just wounds they will remember, knees and arms, hands and feet, right let's move off on foot. Judith will you be able to handle the horses, I can leave Treen with you if you want?"

"I will be fine, but I am not sure about being alone." Jett stepped up to Robbie,

"I prefer to look em in the eye, as I push my sword in, I will guard Judy, I am better with the sword than bow." Robbie nodded and smiled at Jett.

"Thanks. Alright everyone have your bows ready, let's go hunt some Cutters."

The group passed slowly into the trees fanning out on Robbie's signals, it was not long before Martin rose out of the brush and sat with Robbie. "They are just over the bluff Robbie, I am glad you are here because they are watching another small village, and it looks like they are planning to attack."

Robbie crept forward with Rune and Rowan, John and Bull lay in the grass watching the large group. He surveyed the scene and looked beyond to the village, where the women and children were working and playing. Robbie slid back and whispered. "We need three teams. One behind, one in front, and one in the village." Robbie looked at Rowan. "Take Pebbles, Mother, Keith, Jaz, Skip and Blades and get round the other side. I will give you ten minutes, Ok." Rowan nodded and moved off. He looked at Bull. "You fan out here with John, Smokes,

Fish, Bear, Mel and Flash, anything running back, take it out." Bull smiled and nodded.

Robbie slid back into the trees and called Martin, Rafe, Saff, Una, and Harry towards himself and Rune. They gathered closely as he instructed them. "Ok we have to get into that village and secure it without anyone seeing. I need you swift quiet and at the peak of your woods skills, you all up for it?" They smiled and nodded. "Ok, let's even the score for the woodland."

They swept wide around the Cutters, and moved with silent speed and agility. Robbie came out under the low trees and pointed his people around to the huts where there was cover. Each of the group slipped into the houses and took up their positions. The villagers seemed alarmed, their husbands were away, and to suddenly see woodsmen from a different area was frightening, especially as they were armed more than any woodsmen they had ever seen.

Rune slipped in through an open doorway with Robbie. She lifted a finger to her lips as the woman with a child jumped. She slid up her hood and pointed to it. Rune then pointed to Robbie as he snuck out of the back of the hut and carefully crossed to the other hut. The woman suddenly realised what Rune was signaling and her eyes widened, the hooded man himself had just passed through her house.

She put the baby down on the bed and slid a bow out from underneath it. Rune smiled and pointed her to the window; she grabbed a piece of cloth off the back of her chair and placed it on her head to look like a hood. She knew her people would see the hood and see it as a 'friendly'. Rune loaded her bow and moved to the door. She saw Robbie giving signals from the hut across the way. She nodded and waited for it all to begin.

Rowan's group fanned out in a wide arc, as Bulls expanded to cover all of the rear. The trap was set as the Cutters made their way forward. The villagers seeing Robbie's men had sensed something was wrong, and had slowly and very casually, pulled their children in doors. The village was now empty as the Cutters came quietly down the hill.

Rafe rolled back into the doorway; he looked at the woman who sat terrified in the corner. "When he comes through the door scream for all you are worth." She nodded wide eyed, Rafe winked at her. He pulled his long dagger out and rested his bow against the wall, then pushed himself as flat against the wall as he could. The large Cutter entered and the woman screamed for her life, Rafe pounced on the unsuspecting Cutter and his throat slit fast and he buckled to the floor gurgling.

The scream set the attack rolling; Cutters charged into the village in a wide line. They screamed and yelled doing everything they could to instill fear. Hooded figures rose out of the grass and the trees, Cutters fell screaming in pain and agony as arrows whizzed into knees, elbows and shoulders. Rune slipped into the doorway and took aim, her shot took the thigh of a Cutter who folded and fell to the ground. The woman across the room looked, not understanding their rule and shot one through the throat. "Why are you not killing them, do you know what they have done in these parts?"

Rune fired and hit another in the knee, he screamed as he rolled under himself and crashed to the floor. "It is the order of the hooded man; he wants these men to suffer the same pain as those they have hurt." The Cutter on the floor drew out his knife and raised an arm to throw it at Robbie. Rune fired and the arrow sliced deep into his knuckles, he dropped to the floor writhing in agony and the knife fell harmlessly in to the grass.

Cutters in the street realised it was a trap, but they could not head for shelter of the huts as they were filled with hooded men, they turned to run back and fell with the onslaught of arrows now coming from every direction. Some of them dropped their weapons and ran blindly at the woodsmen; they fell impaled with arrows, and screamed on the floor.

Soon the whole village rang to the sounds of pain and fear, Cutters dragged their useless legs as they tried to get away across the leaf strewn floor. The circle tightened as they were, rounded up, and they huddled together in agony as long white feathered arrows stuck out of them. The hooded men dragged them screaming into the centre of the village, Bull walked around them giving them menacing looks as he pulled the white arrows out of them as they yelled and screamed. Maddy and Mel turned away as they saw the pain he inflicted as he stood on their limbs and tore the arrows free.

The leader had arrows through both hands; he was unshaven, rough and now covered in blood. Bull gripped him roughly and snapped the arrows pulling the shafts slowly through, the hole in his hands; Rune turned her head on to Robbie's shoulder. He screamed at Bull. "KILL ME!"

Robbie walked calmly through the men as the Cutter cradled the bleeding hands in his lap. He stood in front of him and looked down at him; his voice was quiet and very calm, although Rune felt the power of the rage building inside him. "Do you know who I am Cutter?"

The bleeding leader looked up at him. "Who cares kill me and have done with your fun."

Robbie stared him in the eyes, and the Cutter began to feel real fear at the anger in the eyes that looked at him. "I am Robert of Loxley, you have made my people suffer, and now like them you too will suffer. You will not die today Cutter, none of you will."

The man looked up at him and shook with terror. "Kill me, do not leave me like this unable to defend myself, let me die."

Robbie shook his head slowly. "Not today... Drag yourself off and kill yourself, but you will not die by the hand of my hooded men. Every moment of pain you feel is equal to the pain you have caused my people, I will not deprive you of those moments, I want you to understand what you have done for Mason Knox. I want you to experience the pain and the fear you have brought to my people. Now go, you are free to leave and die or live, the choice is yours, just remember my words Cutter."

He shook violently as the words of Robbie sunk in. "You are a colder bastard than him."

"No Cutter, I have given you what he wouldn't, a chance to reflect and change. If I meet you again, I will kill you, now take your men and leave."

Robbie stood up and walked away from him. "JUST KILL US, DON'T LEAVE US LIKE THIS, HAVE PITY."

Rune looked down at the Cutter. "You have been given what you gave the women and children of this area, you left them alone to die, the slate is equal, now go."

The hooded men all walked away and left them bleeding and in pain, and dying of blood loss. They huddled together and moaned, some even cried as they slowly slid out of the camp. Those who could walk supported those who could not; it was a long agonising journey just to get a mile away to the riverside, a trail of thick blood marked their route out. Fifty six Cutters started out from the village outside Fenton, only nine ever made it home. Michael Benson the Cutter, who had led the raids, who had crawled for days in agony told their story.

Most of them had crawled into the river screaming in pain and had simply allowed themselves to drown. He had staggered back to his camp, his hands infected and swollen, and his mind on the verge of breaking as the horror of his life had returned to him. Hallucinating he had seen the disemboweled dead return to life and hunt him down, he lay in a hospital bed for a further seven weeks before he could speak of his meeting with the hooded man.

Michael Benson on release from hospital packed his bags and his wife and children and headed across the water to Ireland. He never fully regained the use of his hands, but never forgot the hooded man and lived a life of quiet and kindness to others.

Robbie sat on the wooden porch as a woman handed him a plate and a drink. Rune sat at his side and watched him a worried look on her face. "Rob... Please talk to me; you have not said a word in four hours. I am getting frightened."

He slowly turned to her and smiled. She relaxed and beamed back at him, she burst into tears and dropped her plate flinging her arms around him. "Oh Rob please don't ever do that again, I was so scared, I thought for a minute you had broken inside."

He slid his arms around her. "I am fine, I needed to calm down Rune... come on do not cry, I am sorry." He held her tight as she sniffled.

"I was not sure what to think, I felt all this anger and hate inside you and I thought you had been overcome to a point, where you had snapped or something. I have been talking to you for hours, and you have ignored me. I thought you didn't love me anymore." Rune wept as she spoke into his shoulder between gigantic sobs. He stroked her long red and gold hair and pushed his head into hers as he spoke quietly.

"Rune, come on... how could I stop loving you so quickly? I have been in love with you since the moment I first saw you. Many things will change in this world, but me loving you will not be one of them."

He lifted her head and looked into her sapphire blue eyes washed with lilac, and very red from her tears. He kissed her softly and smiled at her, she gasped and gave a short giggle, as she sobbed. Robbie wiped the tears from her eyes and kissed them, he drew her into a hug as her lip trembled with her small sobs. "I love you with all that I am Runestone Sapphire, never ever forget that." She pushed her head into the side of his neck.

"I love you so much Robbie, I think it will over power me." He held her tight as she calmed back down, and finally he pulled her back and kissed her again.

Robbie held her curled on his knee for a long time, his mind wandered as he thought of the day. It was a cold and cruel thing he had done, but had he acted for the sake of the truth. Was there honour in his actions, he did not know? All he could hope for was that one of them would have learned enough to realise what they had done, and it would be enough to create fear that made every man in the service of Knox question their actions.

He had no idea of the way in which the story would spread, but it did, and over the coming months, Cutters sat in wait would look all around them and hope the hooded man was not about. Robbie had acted coldly, and yet in doing so he had placed the seeds of doubt in the minds of the Cutters. Fear had also become his weapon of truth; the nine survivors had made sure of that.

The men of Fenton, returned the following day and found the trail of blood. In panic, they raced into their own camp and found themselves at the knifepoint of the men of Loxley. There was a great deal of joy and thanks from the men as they heard the story from their wives. The woodsman who led them approached Robbie as he sat on the porch of the woman who had helped Rune.

She had an extra room and had offered them it for the night, and now as the sun rose Robbie sat with his bow on his lap and his sword on the floor, his shirt open and his boots under his chair as he sipped his drink. The woodsman bowed. "My Lord Loxley, I am honoured and relieved to find you in my home village."

Robbie looked up at him. "What is your name woodsman?"

"I am Jenner My Lord, Richard Jenner."

Robbie sipped his drink as his eyes took the measure of the man before him. "Tell me Richard Jenner, is it customary in these parts to leave women and children unprotected?"

"My Lord?"

"The question is simple enough woodsman, why do you leave your village with no protection when you go away, in what I consider my service?"

"My Lord every man here wants to fight to aid your cause."

Robbie watched as the woodsman shrunk before him. "They would have had quite a fight here; I can assure you Jenner, my men here gave a good fight to protect your wives and children. Surely it should have been your men who saved them?"

"My Lord we are honoured and grateful, that you were here to help our families."

Robbie leaned forward. "We fight to protect our way of life and the world we do it in Jenner, what is the point, if all that we hold dear is slaughtered? I will inform Ian of Carlisle, that all villages must have adequate protection first, and spare men for the fight second. I will have no more repeats of Hornsby."

Jenner looked up at him. "Hornsby My Lord? My sister lives there." The colour ran from his face. Robbie stood up and put a hand on his shoulder.

"Then I truly am sorry, for none survived the Cutters, we buried every member of the community." Rune watched saddened as Jenner rose with tears in his eyes and silently turned away, he walked like a man utterly defeated down the row of trees and disappeared behind the huts.

Rune slid her arm around Robbie and leaned on his shoulder. "That poor man, he arrives to find his wife is safe, and then hears of his sister's death. How long can this go on Rob?"

He squeezed her waist. "The day Knox is stopped is the day this will all end forever, and not a moment before, although some how I feel even though he has had ten years to prepare, he is wishing he had prepared more. We have defied him every step of the way Rune, and we must not stop. I have to push him until I break him, for that will be the moment when I kill him."

CHAPTER FOURTEEN

SORROW, TREES, CONCRETE, STONE

Rune rode at the side of Mel, Maddy, and Una. "Ladies I need to talk to you."
She looked at her three aunts, who looked a little concerned. They had been
riding for most of the morning and they were all feeling the heat, and the pace
had slowed down, Kielder Forest was now not far ahead. "We are heading in the
direction of the Dark One, as we make our way towards Alice. I am not sure if you
are aware, but at some point, Mac will feel your presence."

Maddy looked at her sisters and then back across at Rune. "I knew in Loxley
that Una and Mel were not far away, I think we understand you Rune, what do we
have to do?"

"Nothing it is done. Last night I removed Mac from the circle of knowledge
and flung him adrift from all of us. I felt him, he has become dark indeed." Rune
looked at Una who still at the mention of her son became guilt ridden.

"Madeleine, Melanie I have to replace Mac on the wheel of knowledge, I cannot
have an empty spot, it will weaken all of you. I need you to agree to replace him
with Una."

Una looked surprised, as she stared at Rune. "With me?"

Rune smiled. "Yes Una, if you had remained childless you would have been
seated at the table with your nieces, you had Mac so the task fell to him. We now
know he has turned, and so I want you to take up the seat, as you would have
done. You have great power Una to defend against evil; you will enhance the
wheel greatly as a member of the Circle of Knowledge."

Maddy gave her sister a smile, which in itself was rare as Maddy seldom smiled.
Melanie beamed at her. "I think you should say yes Una."

Maddy nodded and Una gave them both a grin. "If I can undo some of the
wrong of my son, I will gladly do it."

Rune nodded. "Great, you will pass on to the seat of the circle at midnight
tonight, if you feel any strange sensations, it will just be me placing you in the right
placement of power." She kicked her horse and moved forward to Saff and Judith.

The large forest loomed in front of them, Rowan looked back at Robbie. "That's
the forest, we have about 120 miles to go to the castle, we are doing between forty

and forty five miles in a day so far. If we pick up the pace, we can be there in two and a half days."

Robbie smiled. "It's at times like this we could use old Merlin's help, another of those strange tunnels would be great about now. It will not be easy in the forest, once we reach moorland, we should pick up our time and speed." They headed down the slope and approached the trees, Robbie felt a sense of relief, he was happier with protection from the skies above. The dapple shade cooled him as they passed under and into the old and famous woodland of the border.

Mac came up the stairs and passed through the steel gates he had finished fitting earlier that morning. He walked down the corridor locking the doors of the two spare rooms and unlocking the third. He walked back to the wooden door, and slid in his key and turned it. He pushed the door open. "Where are you? Talk so that I know."

"Find me, you are the expert." Alice sat in the chair by the fire reading her book; she looked up and grinned, she liked the fact that Mac was so nervous around her. Mac frowned his dark brown eyes glaring at her, Alice turned over the page. "Jumpy little ferret aren't you Mac, what do you think I will do make a bow out of the bed springs and shoot you?"

Mac looked at the bed just to make sure, it was very neatly made; Alice made it every morning as she cleaned her own room. It gave her some exercise and relieved some of the boredom. "You can use the toilet whenever you need to; I have been told to leave your door unlocked. There is a cage at the end of the hall now so you can walk about more and exercise for your baby."

He turned and walked very fast to the bottom of the corridor; he slipped through the steel gate and locked it behind him. Alice peeped through the open door and smiled, she walked into the corridor and tried the first door opposite which was locked. The next door up was the bathroom, and she was pleased to see a large bath and towels.

At the end of the corridor was a large window; she looked out at the different view. Trees, and mountainous countryside surrounded the castle, but at least she now had the ability to plot her position in relation to the tower. The movement of the sun would give her an indication of North, which would make things a lot easier for Robbie.

Mac watched her through the steel cage, as Alice turned. "Well, if it is alright with you, gaoler I will have a bath. I have been here over a week and that bowl in there is nowhere near sufficient." She wandered back into the room and gathered a large bathrobe off the back of the door.

Alice walked back down to the bathroom with the robe on her arm. "Leave the door open." Alice looked back at Mac.

"Bugger off, I am not having you sneaking up and peaking at me through the gap in the door, what am I going to do escape down the plug hole?"

Mac looked annoyed. "I would not do that; I am not that sort of a person."

Alice scowled at him. "You sold us all out to her, you are capable of anything and I for one will never trust you. Your words mean nothing to me." She walked in through the door and started to hum to herself. She shut the door and applied the small lock; Mac sat and watched an empty corridor, whilst listening to Alice hum and the sound of water running. Alice enjoyed herself and had no intention of rushing; she smiled at the large white bath, and the large selection of bath products.

The castle had obviously been owned in the modern times and still had many of the old products of that time. There were big fluffy sponges and large bars of scented soap, some of the products she had never heard of, and read the labels carefully. Alice soon discovered the wonders of conditioner, the bath filled with a thick foam of many scented bubbles and she lowered herself down and relaxed with a satisfied smile on her face. It was the nicest thing to happen since she had been kidnapped.

Hesketh knocked on the large doors, and then turning the large brass knob he slipped in. He coughed politely. "The sword maker is here your Ladyship."

The dark brooding figure of Morgan le Fey stood by the tall arched windows, she stared out through the mesh of lead design, and watched the wind and rain beat the trees below, as it hurtled in off the sea. Her figure was slender and draped in black velvet silhouetted against the panes of glass, her dark jet black hair swished as she moved. She turned and stared with dark foreboding eyes. "It's about time, where is he?"

"He is outside waiting your Ladyship."

She raised a thin white pallid hand, and her black rings sparkled. "WELL... bring him in."

Hesketh nodded and slipped back through the door. The Dark One moved from the rain streaked window, and faced the door at the top of the window step. The fire roared in the large black marble hearth and cracked as the logs split, the door opened and an old man was shown in. His long wet cloak dripped onto the dark blood velvet carpet, he looked up at the dark figure that now faced the room, yet her silhouette had not changed. The man looked down at the floor, and he noticed the lack of a shadow.

She smiled an evil simpering smile. "You are the sword maker Victor Thornson?" He stood before her, and had the look of a man who was once very strong, his face was lined and his hair was thin and pure white. He stood tall and proud and his bright green eyes burned with authority, his accent was strongly

Scandinavian.

"I am he."

She looked him up and down; her face carried the disappointment she felt, and her dark malicious eyes burned in to him as she saw his defiance. "You know of the swords of power do you not?"

He looked from her around the room of old antique polished furniture, his eyes fell on the book case, and then the desk where a large and ancient book lay open, its pages filled with dark ornate runes. "I studied their power and the designs at Caerleon before the red death yes." His voice was clear and carried his authority, his eyes wandered to the elaborate and ornate spiral stair that led to her lair. She smiled a forced looking smile.

"You are unafraid of me I see; it makes a change I must admit. Most people snivel and crawl before me, and yet you do not." Her words seemed cold and devoid of feeling, they were usually used to instill fear, and yet with Thornson they did not. She almost respected it.

"You need me to make your sword; I assume when you have it, you will kill me then. I have lived my life and have just the boredom of age; to make one more sword will satisfy me. I will die a happy enough man."

She laughed a cold laugh. "Make me the sword and you will live; I can assure you."

"The sword will only have the power poured into it; I am presuming you have power to fill the blade?" He seemed unconcerned in her prowess and more concerned about wasting his time. She was irked and found his comment insulting.

"Do you know who I am, and what I alone have achieved? I have the power of Gwendolyn." Her eyes burned brightly as she spoke, and yet he was unaffected by her.

"Gwendolyn made fine blades; the sword of Honour was her finest work, which should be effective... You have a furnace I take it?"

"HESKETH!"

The door shot open. "Yes, My Lady"

"Take him to the forge, I find him irritating." She stared at him and he was uninterested in her completely. Thornson followed Hesketh out of the door and it closed behind them, she turned to the window and watched the rain streaking down, as the almost hidden sun began to fall. "I will have you now bowman, even the sword of truth will not help you."

Alice felt cool, clean and refreshed as she walked up the corridor with her hair in a towel and the clean robes around her. She smiled at Mac. "I have washed my clothes and left them to dry, a change of clothes would be nice if dear Lord Billy the sleaze comes around." She walked happily to her door and stopped. She gestured with her thumb towards the bathroom. "You should have one I can smell you from here." She walked through the bedroom door and kicked the door shut behind her. Alice jumped out of her skin at the sight of Rune stood behind it.

"Rune you scared the hell out of me." Rune smiled and hugged her.

"How are you doing, are they still treating you well?"

Alice smiled. "I am making the best of it. It is quite good fun winding Mac up, I think he was under the impression the Dark One would give him a powerful position, babysitting me is a bit of a disappointment to him." She gave Rune a cheeky smile.

"Pebbles will be pleased to know you are creating trouble."

Alice sat on the bed and rubbed her hair with the towel. "How are they all? I really miss them. Is Mickey all right? I think of him out there alone and I worry about him."

"Alice he is hardly alone, there are twenty three of us on route as we speak."

She smiled but Rune could see the sadness in it, she moved over and sat on the bed beside her. "We have just set up camp outside a place that was called Selkirk. There is nothing there now just large woods and fields, but it is just over eighty miles away Alice. Robbie is coming with your dad as fast as he can, sit tight and it won't be long now before we get you back."

"Robbie is taking a very big risk for me, isn't he? Oh Rune, you must keep him safe, please promise me you will not let him do anything daft. I could not bear it if I was the cause of him being hurt."

Rune pulled her close. "Alice, Robbie has the best there is with him, he is the one person who will get you free. Do not worry he is being very cautious, and I am with him at all times, I will protect him."

She smiled at Rune. "I love our chats; I really look forward to them. Thanks Rune, I was so afraid on my own, knowing you will come each day keeps me going."

"It is funny you know; Smokes is really looking forward to it, I think he sees it as returning the favour after you helped him escape. They all love you Alice, you are one of them, and as you risked your life to get one of them free, they will for you. I am not sure there is anyone out there who could stop them."

Alice put her damp hair on Rune's shoulder. "You don't have a hairbrush on you, do you?" She started to giggle. "I have washed my hair, but I haven't got a brush, it's at home on my dressing table."

Rune stroked her hair and the tangles fell out, she winked at Alice. "I do that with Rob, he hasn't realised yet I am not holding the brush. He looks gorgeous with his hair brushed properly." The keys jangled out in the corridor and Rune knew she would have to leave. She kissed Alice on the cheek. "Same time tomorrow."

Alice smiled. "Keep safe." Rune dissolved into a cloud and was absorbed by the blue bird sat on the wardrobe top in the shadows. There was a knock at the door.

"What now?" The door swung slowly open. "I am on the bed and trying to dry off and sort myself out in private, what do you want now?"

Mac stepped into the room with a tray. "You will need these, you have none."

He placed the tray on the desk and quickly walked out. Alice walked down the room and saw the brush and comb, and clean pairs of underwear. "Oh god fresh knickers how wonderful." She opened her robe and slid the clean pair on. Alice looked down at her tummy, it was small but definitely bigger, and she rubbed it and smiled. She picked up the brush and ran it through her hair. There was not a single tangle, but it did feel good just to be able to brush it.

Rune opened her eyes and Bear and Robbie sat impatiently waiting, Bear smiled. "How is she?"

"She is fine Bear, and she misses you, she told me to tell you she has done nothing but think of you."

He gave her a huge grin. "I miss her too, now I know she is fine I will sleep better." He stood up and turned. "Thanks Rune." Robbie patted his leg as he walked off into the camp.

"She is alright then, well fed and properly looked after?" Rune slid her arms around him, her eyes danced as they faded back to lilac.

"Rob she is fine, I have told you, they are taking very good care of her, but no doubt you will find something to complain about when you get there." She kissed him.

He relaxed a little and pulled her close. "I would hate it if it was you; I think Bear is handling it well." He looked across the camp to where Bear sat talking to Bull. Robbie knew the update would settle his uncle and he nodded as he saw the look of relief on his face as he looked over at him.

Rune pulled up the blankets and she snuggled into Robbie. "Hold me Rob, I always feel helpless when I visit her."

Robbie lay down and cuddled up to her. He pulled the blankets round and she snuggled into him. "I will brush your hair tomorrow it needs it, and I know how you like it."

He smiled as he slid his arms around her in the darkness and kissed her on the neck. She giggled as he tickled her.

Rune curled around under the blanket, and slid closer to him. He lay with his head on the bags his eyes closed tight. The sun would soon be up and the early growing light appeared as the birds in the trees sung their songs of life and happiness to their newly hatched chicks. She slowly opened his collar and with a smile, she kissed his neck softly. He moved a little and murmured, she moved closer and kissed him again, his hand twitched at her side. She stifled her giggles and moved up a little, she moved carefully and quietly and placed a soft kiss on the side of his neck.

Robbie burst up from the floor with great speed dragging her into his arms and dropping her on to her back, Rune screamed with the surprise, and Robbie sat on top of her and lowering his face to hers, he kissed her quickly all over her face, making big kissing noises.

The surprise followed by Robbie's wild noisy kissing had her screw up her face and howl with laughter, as he pinned her to the floor unable to move. Rune shrieked out loud, as everyone sat up and looked across sleepy eyed, at the mound of laughing blankets where the two of them had laid sleeping.

Robbie sat back and looked down on her, as she giggled, her hair was fanned in glistening streaks of gold and red as the first light of the day glinted off it. Her white smiling face beamed and her cheekbones shone, she gazed at him with her bright sapphire blue eyes, that floated on a sea of lilac whites and he saw the love she held for him. He smiled his own hair surrounding her face. "Hey beautiful." His dark brown eyes fixed on her blue.

"I love you, Robbie." He lowered himself down and she kissed him. His face was bright and happy as he sat back and let her up off the floor. She put her arms around him and giggled, her heart was still racing, Robbie looked across the camp as he pulled Rune close.

Jett looked bleary eyed as she nudged Rafe. "How come you don't jump on me in the morning?" Rafe sat up hardly awake and rubbed his eyes.

"What?"

Jett looked at him. "Robbie has just jumped on Rune; how come you haven't jumped on me in the morning?"

Rafe shook his head. "What, here in public?"

"Not that stupid, you know, surprise me in a loving way."

Rafe yawned and stretched. "Jett sweetheart I have seen you work with a sword, trust me I will never ever sneak up and pounce on you. Your skills are just too fast and I would like to continue enjoying our relationship intact."

Jett smiled. "I am that good then?"

"Jett you are definitely the best."

"Wow Rafe you can be really romantic when you want to can't you?" She seized him roughly and gave him a huge kiss. He fell over backwards as she released him and he smiled. Rune giggled as Jett beamed brightly.

Blades toddled past on her way to the river in just her underwear; she looked at Jett and the rather rough looking Jade who had appeared bleary eyed from under the blanket. "Fancy a swim you two?"

Jade slid back under the covers as Jett jumped up. "Yeah, I will, I am starting to stink."

Saff and Treen were already in the water, and Mel and Una sat on the bank washing themselves. Blades and Jett came screaming through the trees, ran down to the edge and dived into the water. There was an almighty splash, and Mel and Una recoiled as the water hit them. Jett's head came up above the water, and she screamed. "It's freezing!" Blades popped up and she took a huge breath and grinned, Saff and Treen laughed as Jett dived back under.

Life in the camp began to stir. Robbie had the fire going and Mother and Smokes were making toast and frying thin slices of pork with some tomatoes. "Oh, I wish we had eggs, Hog was always able to find me a few. I would love to know how he always seemed to be able to come up with them." Robbie smiled at Mother as he thought of Hog.

He looked at her. "I never thought of that before you know." He looked puzzled. "How did he always find eggs in the wild?" He snapped two large twigs and threw them on the flames, as Smokes poured out two coffees and handed them to him.

He wandered over to Rune who was sat smiling wrapped in her blanket. "I feel grotty." She took the cup off him and sipped it.

"Why not go for a swim with the others?" The coffee was hot and he blew his cup.

"I have nothing to wear; you know I don't have any underwear."

"So go further downstream, that's what I do."

"I don't fancy it on my own, not here in the wilds, it's not like the mere is it?"

Robbie laughed. "I thought all you children of nature didn't mind, all of you being free spirits and that?"

Rune smiled. "I don't mind, I am pleased with my body, it's just years of mum warning us not to step outside the rules of people and towns folk, I guess some of it stuck."

Robbie stood up and picked up two blankets. "I am starting to stink a bit, come on grab some soap we will look further down for a quiet spot." She took his hand and smiled. Robbie threw the blankets over his shoulder and grabbed the coffee. Rune slid her arm round him and they headed off through the trees to a quiet bathing location.

It was well over an hour later and everyone was now awake as the sun rose in the sky. The day was starting to warm, and the group sat around eating breakfast. Robbie and Rune came smiling through the trees, his long hair dripped on his boots as he carried his shirt and the blankets over his shoulder.

Rune sat by the fire, and brushed her hair, and braided it back into long plaits that dropped right down her back. Robbie shook his head like a dog and she squealed as he showered her. The fire hissed violently, Mother smiled as he flopped onto an old rotting log and poured out a coffee.

"Good swim?" Robbie beamed at her.

"Didn't swim much but it's good to be clean. There is a really private little bay down there, you want to get Old Smokes down there, remember his teenage years a little." He winked at her. "We will be here for at least an hour or so."

Smokes beamed a smile at her. "I am starting to smell honey." Mother pinked up a little, and Robbie laughed as he wandered over toward Rowan and Pebbles. Rowan nodded as Robbie handed him and Pebbles a cup each.

"Alice is doing alright and she is making a map of the building so we will have some idea of where she is in relation to the others. She is a clever girl, and has herself a little more space to move about. She is high up, so has got a good idea of the land around her, Rune will get the map tonight as we get closer." He looked at Rowan who seemed pale. "You alright, you look awful?"

Rowan shook his head. "Bad, bad dreams Robbie, I get to sleep and all I see is people hanging from trees." He looked sorrowful and Pebbles pulled him close.

"Me too Rob, it's really getting me down." Robbie touched Rowan's arm and gave it a squeeze.

"I will talk to Rune and see if she can do anything to help."

Rune watched them all across the camp as they prepared for their day, and she gave a long sigh. "I must admit Rob, they have all been quiet. John hasn't cracked a joke about Keith in days, and Pebbles is quieter than I have ever known her. Even Bull seems to be carrying a lot of sadness; I cannot remember when I last heard him laugh." She looked round. "Up until down at the pool I wasn't sure you would ever really laugh again."

"Can you help them...? You know like you did for me on the boat."

"That was a different kind of pain, you would have come to terms with it eventually, I just hurried it on a little. This is something very different Rob; it is a lingering sorrow that can last a life time."

Robbie looked at the saddened faces around the camp. "You cannot help them then?"

"I can't but Maddy can." He looked at her bright shining eyes and she smiled.

"What can Maddy do that you can't?"

"I did not say I couldn't, Maddy has the gift of the melancholy side of nature. You know the brown leaves and fungi in the autumn that makes you feel the world is going to sleep, and you feel saddened. Like sitting in a greenhouse in the snow yearning for spring?"

Robbie smiled at her and her eyes twinkled. "How do you know about that?"

She giggled. "I always talked to Jess whenever I saw her. The thing is Rob, Maddy absorbs that out of people, and she stores it up inside her. Why do you think she hardly ever smiles?"

Robbie looked across the camp at her as she wiped her white bow. "I did wonder, it mustn't be much fun having all that inside her."

Rune shrugged. "It's one hell of a weapon if used properly, and she is probably the best."

He watched her carefully. "How can that be used as a weapon?"

She chuckled. "She is one of my lot, you know?" Robbie gave her a grin. "Maddy stores it up, and then when faced with her enemy it emits from her and is absorbed by them. They feel all the pain and sadness and lose the will to do anything, most eventually after weeks of sorrow cannot take any more and kill themselves."

Robbie shuddered. "That is sort of creepy, death by extreme sadness, I would rather Bull took his axe to me when I was laughing. Poor Maddy I had no idea, Hearne that's depressing Rune." He gave her a freakish look. "See what I mean about your lot, I just get used to them and then some really freaky thing happens that wobbles my whole head."

Rune started to giggle and she stood up and put her arms smiling around him. "You are funny at times Rob." She gave him a tender kiss. "I will talk to her and get her to find a less head wobbling way of sucking your sadness out." She started to laugh as Robbie shuddered violently.

"Tell her she can leave me." Rune laughed more as she headed across the camp towards Maddy.

Mother and Smokes came walking arm in arm through the trees, Mother seemed to have a glow about her that was not there at breakfast. Smokes beamed, Robbie looked at them both and smiled. "See." Mother smiled even more.

Rune looked at her parents. "You look happy." Smokes beamed at her.

"Been for a swim in the pool Robbie and you went to this morning." Steph kissed her daughter on the cheek, Rune gave her a knowing smile.

After breakfast, Maddy formed a circle as Rune spoke. "The last few days have weighed heavy on all of us, Robbie and I are worried it is having a negative effect on all of you. Maddy has the power to take those nightmares away, and it is Robbie's decision we do it now before it has an effect on the rescue mission." They all looked worried and nodded to Rune.

The whole group stood around as Maddy turned in the centre of the circle. Her long blonde hair fluttered around her waist in the breeze, as her watery blue eyes focused on each of them. "This will look worse than it is, you will see your sadness but do not worry, you will not be harmed in any way. Right after you will feel a great joy, it will last for about an hour."

Maddy looked at Rowan. He gulped as she slid back her long grey cloak, and lifted her pale blue smock clad arms, the sleeve slipped and a bracelet made of metal and onyx weeping sad eyes sparkled in the sun light. Jade gripped his hand nervously as he looked with wide worried eyes at Maddy. She gave him a nod and he prepared for the unknown.

Rowan looked down at his chest, as Maddy's eyes began to glow dark blue. Thin wisps of what looked like grey smoke started to stream out of his chest, he felt a tug and a hideous contorted grey smoky face came through his shirt. He gasped, and Harry leapt back, his eyes wide.

He pointed a very shaky finger at Rowan's chest. "Whoa like that aint peaceful man." The head increased in size and Harry gasped in horror. "See man I told you, all that freaky bad shit Robbie made you do, it's jangled your vibes man."

The Smokey head broke free of his chest and floated in midair pulling grotesque faces, and silently screaming. Harry began to murmur and closed his eyes as the face hovered behind Maddy, Jade was next. Harry opened one eye and watched the ugly head with green eyes float across the ground, he screamed pointing at it. "It's the evils man, that karma chomped Pebbles, and she sucked its vibes out of her." He patted all his pockets rapidly, and then feeling his shirt and shaking violently he plunged his hand down into his pocket and pulled out his purple round mirror glasses. He gasped a large sigh of relief and put them on. "Whoa man that was not cosmic; I feel my vibes like really jangling." He wiped the sweat off his head and smiled. "Hey peace chickens."

Maddy looked at Rafe, he had a very worried look, and looked down as two evil eyes slipped from his chest. He shuddered as the head stretched out trying to hold on to him, Harry trembled; even with his glasses on, he found he had lost control of his legs. The face burst out of Rafe's chest and Jett gasped and stepped back. Harry leapt back four feet pointing his shaking finger at Rafe, as the head with slits for eyes seemed to growl and snarl back at him.

"Whoa man that is an uncosmic monster, they is bad karma man, they sneak up on you and chew on your vibes while you is like totally asleep." It turned and stared at Harry he screamed and jumped behind Judy shaking violently. His purple glasses peeped over her shoulder.

One by one Maddy went round pulling the ugly smoky faced feelings of sadness out of them. The centre of the circle was slowly filling with a very large cloud of pain and distress; Harry shook with terror as it grew in size, Robbie watched with a sort of gruesome fascination that made him marvel and feel repulsed at the same time. Maddy skipped Rune, she looked at him.

"Rune has cleared some I can see, what about the rest?" Robbie looked into her bright glowing blue eyes.

"I need that for Knox, afterwards, if there is any left, you can have it." Maddy smiled and nodded, she turned to a very frightened looking Judith; Harry stood trembling at her side.

"Hey baby girl, if you don't want to be karma chomped it's cool, I won't either."

She looked up at him. "It's alright Mad Harry I have been sad all my life, I would like to be happier." She nodded to Maddy and stood still.

The grey smoke began to form; it was a small ugly face, which looked very much like Billy. The face twisted and stretched as if trying to escape, as it was dragged from Judith. It grew larger and darker in colour, Rune gasped and her eyes glowed lilac; a violet haze engulfed the dark hideous black smoking face.

Maddy's eyes flared even darker blue as if she was struggling to control it; Rune waved her hand across the circle and the violet mist increased around the dark ugly face. Robbie watched in horror, as the cloud was now a writhing mass of hideous faces that had grown taller than Judith was. "What's happening Rune?"

Rune voice sounded distant. "She is safe I am with her." Robbie turned to see that Rune's eyes were flaring the deepest purple he had ever seen. Tears rolled down her cheeks and violets sprung up everywhere. The dark cloud was contained within an orb of purple glowing light as it left Judith, Rune stepped forward into the circle and made Robbie jump and she turned to Maddy. "You will not carry this one, I will."

Harry jumped up and down on the spot his eyes wider than seemed humanly possible. "Hey Rune baby princess, don't like karma chomp it, it aint radical, that will do things to your vibes that none cosmic monsters can't do." He waved his hands in the air and dithered as Rune walked towards the pulsating orb.

"Whoa chicken, be peaceful like and be cosmic." It was too late the orb suddenly shrunk, to the size of a walnut, and Rune snatched it out of the air and pushed it into her mouth and swallowed it. Harry fainted.

Maddy looked at Harry who moaned on the floor as Judy patted his face. "Harry, wake up."

"Do him now before he sees the none cosmic monster in him." Harry opened his eyes and sat up; a small face stretched out of his chest and looked at him, it pulled its tong out at him. "Hey vibe dude that's not peaceful." It stretched out of him and with a snap, bobbed into the air. It was very ugly, but only the size of a tennis ball. Jett grinned.

"Wow Harry you are like the most laid back one here, how cool is that?"

"Whoa man my vibes is ugly though." The face was cross eyed and looked like it had been put through a mangle. It blew raspberries and wagged its tong as it floated towards the ugly cloud above Maddy.

Harry stared a silly sort of smile on his face. Maddy raised her arms into the air as her eyes flared blue. The cloud began to spin above her head and she looked up at it. The cloud dropped like stone and suddenly it had gone and Maddy stood swaying on the spot. Robbie ran to her and grabbed her arm; she swayed as her eyes returned to the watery blue they were normally. "Thanks Robbie I will be fine now. I need to sit for a few minutes." Two tears ran down her cheeks.

"You can feel it can't you?" She nodded and then patted his arm.

"I am fine it is my gift to the world, Autumnal blues." Her eyes flickered for a moment and then returned to white. She sat down and breathed deeply, Harry walked over to her and crouched down looking very concerned, Maddy looked up at him and he pulled out his red hankie.

"Hey chicken, that was one brave like karma chomp." He gently wiped the tears from her eyes and then kissed her on the forehead, Maddy smiled. Harry beamed at her. "Whoa chick you are one weird lady, if it wasn't for my Maggs I would swipe off with you."

He helped her to her feet. "You are a strange man Harry, but thanks knowing you are tempted, has lifted my week." She gave him a very odd look. Harry beamed.

"Hey girl, sometimes freaky should not be passed up. You ever want to pull your vibes, let me know I have contacts." Rune sat giggling, as Maddy looked appalled and seriously worried.

The rest of the day passed with a long trek out of the woodland, and on to the hills and mountains that were now rising steadily in front of them. The group seemed back to their normal spirits, Jett and Pebbles leaned in next to Blades, and whispered and giggled, as they planned their next assault on Harry. Flash and Judy laughed and joked as they impersonated Harry which greatly amused Mel and Una, John and Martin cracked jokes all day with Bull and Rafe and laughed hysterically as they tried to talk and tell their yarns. Mother and Smokes just smiled at each other, Keith and Jaz took the point and talked happily, as they rode forward.

Robbie sat at the side of Rune as they rode side by side and holding hands. He watched with a sense of relief to see the group happy again, Rune's eyes sparkled. "I think mum and dad tried a little natural freedom this morning, I have never seen her so radiant."

"I am so happy for them you know; I will never forget when I walked into that cell and saw him lay there covered in filth with her head over him as she wept. I thought he was dead at first, I am so happy he wasn't."

"Me too." She gave him a huge smile. "You are a cool guy Robbie in the Hood, that is why I love you so much, you really know how to make a girl feel really special in a morning." Her eyes danced.

Rowan pushed them forward to pick up the pace, the ground rose steeply and soon they were high up in the sweltering sun, and galloping along at a good pace. The grass and wild bilberry rolled on for miles, broken by large patches of bright purple heather. It swished as the horses rode swiftly through it, and everyone felt the exhilaration of the cool air blowing through their hair.

They reached the high mountainous top and revelled in the view. Miles upon miles of green grass and tree lined hills rolled up to the huge mountains darkened in the distance. They could see for miles and had a clear vision of anyone who would approach them, so they pushed the horses hard to make up time and get as quickly as possible to Alice. In the distance, they could see the sea rolling in to their right in the Firth of Forth, Rowan pulled to a slow as Robbie came up by his side. "What is it?" Rowan leaned forward on his horse that stood panting.

"Smoke... Lend me your telescope." He stretched out his hand, as Robbie pulled it from his pocket and passed it over. Rowan pulled it apart and peered down it. He passed it back to Robbie. "Knox has been very busy up here it would appear my good friend."

Robbie looked down the scope in the direction of the sea. Right along the whole line of the coast was a high black shining stonewall, behind which he could see the endless sprawling concrete of a huge city, which stretched for about seventy miles. Factories bellowed smoke into the air that rose like an acrid black tongue into the sky, and drifted out to sea. "Looks like we have an idea of what London will look like, Rowan that place is massive, how the hell do we stop that?"

"Well, I think we will need a little more than dynamite." The group gathered around as Robbie handed over the telescope, Rune gasped as she saw the city of stone. Smokes took the scope from his eye and passed it to Skip.

"It's not like before Robbie. In the modern old times cities were spread apart, and in between there was space, where small towns were collected with green space and lakes, he is using every single inch, and just expanding out."

Skip passed the scope over to Mel. "Well, my good friends, I understand why he was burning the trees and the towns, we now know why so many are on the move. His concrete jungle is replacing our woodland, I really do think he plans to push south from here and north from London and squeeze all of us in the centre." Skip shrugged." It would give him the easiest task in wiping us all out at once."

Rowan stared at Robbie; he felt a chill run down his spine as he looked at Skip. "We have to get Alice and get the hell home, he is far more advanced than any of us thought, Skip we need a plan of action and fast, Loxley and York could end up the only two green places in this country."

Skip nodded. "I think Robbie you have just read his mind; I do believe that is his plan. I once read about a man called Hitler, he tried something similar, he did not use walls he used an army to defeat a whole race of people and clear the way for his superior race. This reminds me very much of it."

Rune touched Robbie's hand. "All is not lost yet Rob." She smiled at him. "Those walls are made using power and magic, her magic. We will not need dynamite; I know something much sharper that will cut through that stone."

He looked at her smiling face. "What?"

"Runestone and Sapphires mixed with a little Ruby and Crystal." Sapphire beamed at Ruby and Rune. Ruby smiled sweetly.

"I like Crystal, we talk a lot, it will be nice to see and meet her, she gets lonely like I used to."

Jett snorted. "What old frosty knickers? God, she bangs on for hours, I fell asleep once and when I woke up, she was still at it in my head, she did not even know I had been sleeping." Rune smiled at Jett.

"Crystal will play her part none the less; we are in this together girls, remember? Rob needs both circles behind him." Jett gave a smile that looked more like a wince; Ruby beamed her red eyes dancing behind her glasses.

Robbie looked back at the coast and the new fortress that protected a city of industry, and now he knew why so little information had come from Scotland. Mason had been busy here for years, they had already seen how he dealt with woodsmen up here, and the odds were high now that all of the woodland folk were either dead or converted to city life. Mason Knox appeared to own the whole of Scotland.

They pushed on heading north, Robbie had hoped to cut across east but now it looked very unlikely. Rowan checked the map and slowly began to bend their route northeast. A wide arc would bring them round slowly to the east and a heading for Old Aberdeen. They stayed under cover and followed the old A9 road that would lead them past Old Perth and across the old woodland country. The going became slow as they spotted small groups of soldiers riding along the roads, several times; they took cover when groups passed close by, and Robbie was feeling more and more frustrated as the day wore on.

It was a long day and the horses were tired, they had pushed as hard as they could and now as the sun began it's decent from high in the sky, they looked for a safe camp. It was late evening as they rode down the side of Backwater, the long reservoir shimmered in the daylight and at the northern tip well away from any roads they pulled under the cool shade of a large pine forest and dismounted.

The group sprang into action, as Harry, Flash, and Judith took the horses to the water's edge. The team secured the area, Bear, Bull, Rowan, and Pebbles went off in search of food. Skip sat in the last of the sun with Rafe and tried to sketch on to the map the size of the area Knox had taken up with his new city. Robbie stood by the water's edge, and looked out across the lake, and up the steep sides of what was the start of the Old Cairngorm National Park.

The mountainous region rose high covered with a thick forest of trees. Rune slipped her arm around him and laid her head on his shoulder. "Look at that Rune... Endless miles of green life, it is so beautiful, how could anyone want to bury it under concrete and fumes?"

"That is what man has done for almost two hundred years Rob. They do not see it as you do, remember why it is you have been chosen to lead as the hooded man. Those who will lead the new world will have no memory of those times. They will only know life after the Red Death, just a few years of memory of those times is enough to prevent you from being in power. There can never be a line of men so destructive again. Knox will never win, even if we lost the fight he is still doomed, the forces of nature will destroy this earth before they allow man to run amuck again."

"Even if I had been born a hundred years earlier, and had lived the life of old modern man, I could not do what he is doing, I could not destroy what is good and pure and beautiful, I love my life with you and the woods Rune."

"You are my life in the woods." She squeezed him tight. "You have shouldered much Rob, the time of my circles is coming, Knox will have a fight on his hands then. Keep your dreams alive my darling, do not let him cast shadows on them. You will have your dream, I promise."

He slid his arms around her and held her close. "I hope so... I will die before I will live under concrete and stone."

CHAPTER FIFTEEN

THE BLACK BLADE OF DUNNOTTAR

The book slid off the bed with a dull thud, and its pages opened and spread on the carpet, Alice murmured and turned over, pulling the blanket round her. The room glowed with a soft violet haze as smiling; Rune lifted the book and placed it quietly on the table. She watched her friend as she dreamed in her sleep, and carefully sat on the bed. Rune softly stroked the hair from her face as she slept,

Alice turned in her restlessness. Rune waved a hand across Alice and she settled into a deep and peaceful sleep. She rose from the bed and walked to the bookcase, she slid out the old hard backed copy of 'treasure island' and there inside was the map.

Sat by the lake her eyes burning purple with a pad on her knee, Rune began to draw the plan of the castle. Robbie watched carefully as her hand moved quickly, he saw the stairs, the bathroom, and the little compass pointing north, exactly as Alice had drawn it. She finished the castle, and then began to add the wall that Knox had built around the place with approximate height dimensions on it. Two extra buildings had been added that were now being used to barrack troops, and there was an old wooden stable and a few out buildings.

Rune added the road and the driveway, and all the trees including the stream and the steep run up to the high mountains. She finished the picture and slipped it off the pad. Robbie took her hand and guided it on a fresh piece of paper as he wrote slowly.

Rune sat at the small wooden table across from Alice and smiled. She let Robbie guide her hand on to a small piece of paper and wrote. "I love you Sis and I am almost there. Be patient and I will get you soon. XXX." Rune touched the paper and a small violet appeared as a pressed flower. She slid it inside the map and placed it back in the book on the shelf, she turned and watched Alice for a few more minutes and then walked back to the bed. She leaned over and kissed her softly on the head. "Goodnight my darling sleep well, we all love you."

Alice stirred in her sleep. "I love you too." Rune smiled and walked back to the blue bird as it watched from the high wardrobe. "Keep her safe my father." The bird nodded but it was the voice of the old man of the trees, which she heard.

"I have, and always will watch over my children, she will be safe in my care." Rune bowed and then faded into a pale violet mist and was gone.

She opened her eyes as they faded to lilac, and she gave Robbie a huge grin. "That was sweet of you; she will be so pleased when she finds that in the morning."

He shrugged. "I miss her Rune." She slid her arms around him, and gave him a big hug.

"I know, but it won't be much longer now, will it? Her map will help; you can now start to plan it all out with Rowan and Bull." He smiled at her, and picked up the drawings and looked carefully down at them.

"Good job Steph carries her pad, isn't it? Alice has done really well, these are great." Rune kissed him on the head as she got up. "Do not stay up too late, we still have a long day's travel ahead of us." She walked towards the fire and sat down next to her mum, Steph smiled and put her arm round her and pulled her close and kissed her on the head.

The wind howled up across the top of the cliff and thundered into the trees, driving the raindrops like bullets into the soft earth. The air was, filled with the roar of the waves crashing against the rocks, as the twigs bent back and the leaves flapped vigorously. Sinclair Forbes pulled back his hood and gazed out across the water at the small island of Dunnottar, his eyes narrowed into the wind and he raised a hand to shield the rain from them. He was forty but looked older, as his face showed the signs of the weather extremity of his region, a hooded figure came up at his side and slid back their hood a little.

Rose Macintosh peered through the dark at the island, and the new black structure that had arisen in less than two months since they had been here. "How is it possible to build something so big so quickly? It is barely eight weeks since we were last here." She leaned into the wind as her eyes followed the silhouette of the tall tower and the heavy black stone bridge that ran from the island to the edge of the cliff, at the opening of a new deep cutting.

Sinclair shook his head. "This is the devils work and no mistake, but looking at the soldiers we killed back there on the road, it has to be something to do with him and that Raven."

The whole of the top of the small island, which was once the ruined fortress, had disappeared. Small traces of the red rock remained in small areas, which had once been the famous castle that had almost defeated Cromwell's soldiers. Now the whole island was the tall black and shiny stone that rose into the castle of the Dark One.

The small windows flickered with a pale blue light and on the furthest side of the island; a bright orangey red glowed in the darkness. Rose shuddered as if something had passed through her, her wet black fringe streaked with white stuck to her head and she wiped it out of her bright watery blue eyes.

"Come on love, its evil here, let's get back and let them know of what we have seen." Sinclair nodded his head and slipped his hood back up; he turned and took her hand and moved back into the trees. They disappeared as if just shadows in the darkness.

Hesketh watched as the old man drew a huge white circle on the floor of the large forge workshop. He was slow and steady as he poured the white powder from the tin, connected to the silken twine. He took a long steel measure and unfolded it to make a large pair of dividers, which he used to make small scratches on the dark stone floor. He stood up and looked at his work, talking and nodding quietly to himself.

From his bag, he took out another can of powder, and traced in the lines across the circle to the scratch marks in the floor, and Hesketh saw the red five pointed star take form in the white circle. Victor picked up the tongs and walked to the bright furnace.

He lifted a hot coal out of the burning heat, and walked back to the circle where he dropped the coal on to it muttering incantations under his breath, the white circle exploded into light and the red star burned bright on the floor. He watched as the powder melted and formed, then set into the heavy black stone.

A strange and putrid smell like death rose into the air; Hesketh coughed and covered his mouth, the smoke wafted past and he saw the floor was now marked with a large red five pointed star in a circle of white. Its outer edge was, lined with a wide golden band.

Victor was on his hands and knees as he carved with a blackish purple stone into the gold. The strange runes glowed as he wrote them, and set in thick black on the golden background. Victor completed the circle and looked up at Hesketh. "Help me with the box." Hesketh looked down at the wooden crate in the yard outside the door; he walked down the stone steps as Victor hurried towards it.

The box was heavy and the two men strained to lift it, and staggered backwards through the door and into the furnace, they half dragged and half carried it over to the circle, then slowly lowered it to the stone floor. Victor stooped to his bag and lifted a crow bar; he nodded his thanks at Hesketh, who stepped back and watched, as he slid the bar into the top on the box and forced the wooden lid up.

The lid slipped to the floor, and Victor separated the packaging taking out a heavy golden stand. It was ornate and decorated with golden runes and Celtic patterns; he placed it on the point of the top of the red star. There were five of them all identical, which were placed at the point of each part of the star, Victor returned to the box and lifted a long smooth obelisk of violet stone out of the box, and he slid it into the first golden stand, and returned to the box for another.

Hesketh looked at the violet stone, which seemed to sparkle in the light of the furnace, he bent down and inspected it closer, he felt he could hear laughter and music some way off in the distance. He looked up at Victor who was slipping the last stone into place.

"This is beautiful, what is it?"

Victor smiled and rubbed his chin, and scratched his short white stubble. "It is violet stone. Sugilite and very powerful, these are the stones of life that I have brought from Carnac. They were the property of Gwendolyn White Circle, the fairy Queen who King Arthur fell in love with, and married Merlin." He looked down at Hesketh and nodded sadly to him. "If she could see how her stones were to be used, she would indeed be a sad spirit. They have her essence of healing and all of the power of the fairy land in them."

Victor dragged the empty crate away and pulled a small table over to the side of the circle. He turned and putting his arms under a heavy black steel anvil, he lifted it up into the air, and groaned with the weight as his face turned bright red. He stepped into the centre of the star and gasped loudly as he lowered the anvil down.

He breathed a deep sigh as he stood up and opened his shirt and slid it off. Hesketh gasped as he saw the large sword tattooed down his back, surrounded with strange Celtic runes. Victor lifted a heavy golden hammer from his bag and placed it on the table at the side of the circle. He looked at the forge, which was burning bright red. "I am ready; you have the metals I asked for?" Hesketh walked across to the side of the furnace and pulled an old cloth back to reveal large bricks of metal.

"Gold, platinum, silver, and black steel, everything you requested in the exact amounts, you stated, I believe that is in order?"

Victor nodded as he looked at the metals, and lowered a pot of stone on to the furnace. He picked up each brick and dropped it into the pot, examining each one as he did so. "This is good... It will take most of the night to make this sword, tell your mistress I want her here half an hour before dawn, so she can add her essence to the blade. Now leave me to work in peace."

Hesketh was curious and watched as he walked up the steps, Victor took small tins of powder out of his bag and with a careful measure, he mixed seven different powders into the stone pot in which the metal was melting and mixing. Victor looked up as he went through the door and closed it behind him. He lifted his arm and grabbed the bellow, then began to pump slowly bringing the heat in the furnace up, and he muttered a strange Celtic language and sprinkled the powder into it.

Mason gave an agitated sigh. "Oh Mother, what does it matter, he will be here soon? The girl needs clothes, you cannot ask a pregnant girl to go naked because it does not suit you."

Morgan turned her eyes blazed at Mason. "I wanted him here; the first hand that touches that sword after the incantation will be the owner. Billy should wield the sword."

Mason relaxed in the chair by the fire and sipped his whiskey; he flexed his fingers as he stared through the window. "Lance is equally as gifted with a blade." He gave a small laugh. "I sometimes think he is the only one out of the three that is truly my son." He looked at the long red scar on his hand. It was still ugly as he turned it in the firelight; Morgan walked to her book and turned the page.

"It must go to your first born, believe me it will bring the true power of Knox out in him, this will be a sword of power so filled with devastation, the force behind it will cure his love for the wood choppers girl."

Mason smiled as he lifted the whiskey to his lips. "The Lox have undone a lot with Billy, he is still tainted by them, the mother especially, she has powers of good that will last on Billy for a long time, will the sword cure him of her?"

"You need more faith in my powers, he will remember nothing once he has taken the sword, and will crave only the power to use it. Billy will become the lord of darkness you have always wanted my son, have no fear, no mortal woman will undo the power of the sword. The powers placed into him at birth will be revealed and he will grow very strong indeed. That Runestone bitch won't know what hit her when Billy gets hold of her." Mason watched as the flames flickered, dancing red and orange shadows across his face, his thoughts were with his son, and whether or not the sword would truly bring the Knox back out in him.

The door swung open and Billy walked into the room. Alice looked up from her bed. He smiled, nodded, and placed a large bag on the end of it. "I have some clean clothes for you, there are several sizes as I thought you would in time need them a little bigger, I hope they are alright."

Alice nodded. "Thanks."

His blue eyes seemed dull and he had black rings below them as if he had not slept in some time. He sat on the end of the bed, and looked down at the floor. "I am sorry Alice, no matter what you might think, I would never have hurt you. It is too late now to prove it, but you would have been protected always. I just wish you could understand that."

She felt like she wanted to scream at him, but at the same time she saw a little of the boy she held in her arms in the barn, and it pulled at her heart. Her voice was quiet and calm. "You say you love me, but I am still your prisoner."

Billy looked up at her; his eyes were sorrowful. "Can you not see that I am protecting you from her? Do you think she would let you live like this? She would cut it from you and leave you to die and use her power to grow the life she wants."

"Let me go Billy... Please, let me go and let Jess protect our child. You know the power of her love; she alone has forgiven you Billy." She saw the flicker of pain in his eyes as she mentioned Jess. Billy had adored her, and Alice had always seen the way he responded to her, Billy had experienced love in its purest form, and Alice knew if there were a way into Billy, Jess would be it.

He turned back to staring at the floor. "I would go back with you if I knew it could be possible, she was good to me and I will never forget her. You are only safe here under my care, I cannot risk you or my child Alice, you are all I have left."

"You still have a brother."

"What Lance, he is as bad as my father; he is no brother to me."

Alice stared at the golden pendant swinging round his neck. "I was talking about the brother you gave a silver lion too." Billy looked up at her; she noticed the pain in his eyes.

"I tried to kill him; he will not forget that... I do miss him though." His eyes were fixed on hers and she could see the same haunted look in his eyes she had seen in Robbie's at Caerleon.

"You know Robbie as well as I do, go to him Billy and surrender to him. He will not kill you; he has the loss of the same brother as you have. End this all now and seek his forgiveness, Billy I have always been true to you, I never lied, and you know I am right... Leave here and go to him." Billy smiled at her.

"I have always admired your faith in your family and in me. I wish I could talk to him one more time Alice I really do, but Rob is a leader as am I, he will act for all his people and there is no room in his life now for me. I have killed woodsmen; under their law I am a dead man."

"I am Lady Alice of Loxley; under their laws I can plead for your life. You are the father of my child, they will not condemn you Billy, take me to Robbie and you know he will listen to me, be free of your father forever, let Rune protect you, she will if Robbie asks, and you know he will."

"It's too late Alice, I have done too much damage, all I have left now is to keep you and my child free of her touch and I will."

"It is never too late Billy to turn from an evil road."

"It is if your name just happens to be Knox... no I am stuck here and have nowhere left to hide, I am tired of it all." He looked at the fire burning in the hearth. "I know I have hurt you and that is my own torture Alice, all I ask is don't hate me. I know you will never love me as you did, but I wish we could just be friends and not attack each other as we did. I did love you, that was never a lie... not ever, think about it."

A tear ran from his eye as he stood up and smiled. Alice watched saddened as he left the room and slowly closed the door behind him. A little of the Billy she had loved so deeply had sat with her, and her heart pulled. She saw the pain and torment that was inside him, and she could not help but feel sorrow. She sat in bed and tears formed in her eyes, somehow, she thought it was the last time she would ever see him again. It was a strange feeling that she could not explain. She sniffled and wiped her eyes.

Victor pounded the steel with his large metal hammer as he held it on the anvil. The ring of the metal was deafening, and he smiled as he heard the sound of power forming in the blade. He plunged it back into the hot embers of the forge, and pulled on the bellows as the fire burned a bright fiery red.

Pulling a rag from his pocket he wiped the dripping sweat off his brow. It had been many years since he had made a blade of quality and he was determined this would be a blade to match the five. He slid the blade back from the coals and looked at it; an eerie orange glow ran up and down the blade. He slid it back into the coals and pumped the bellows.

Dawn was not far off, he had a few more hours and he smiled to himself as he pulled the blade out of the fire, and swung it round as it glowed white, and dropped it to the anvil. His large hammer came crashing down and the moment he hit it, he knew he was almost there. The blade rung out a chime that sang of heaven, he hit again, and it sounded a higher and sweeter chime, once more his hammer smashed on to the blade and it chimed like a clock in the halls of time.

Victor laughed with huge joy, as he plunged the sword blade into the vat of dirty water, the golden blade hissed and spat as it cooled. Happiness rose inside him as he pulled it back and examined his work, he kissed it, a lifetime of work and study had come to him in the last moments of his long life. Finally, he had achieved his life's aim and created a work of wonder that could never be destroyed. This was his Excalibur; his sword of power and it was he who would be remembered not her.

He lay the blade down carefully and lifted his mug. He slurped the drink happily, to quench his thirst, banging the cup down he lifted the handle and began to work at it with a file. The end of the hilt still had a large round socket in it and as he finally finished the filing and soft polishing of the handle, he slipped the silvery Moonstone into the end of it and snapped the locking ring into place.

He looked at the long golden blade and pulled out his scribe, he slowly and carefully scribed the runes down the edge of the blade and they glowed silver as he wrote and faded into the metal. He had almost finished; two more runes would complete the spell and open the blade to the power of the Dark One.

Victor Thornson knew he was the last master of the swords, and this would be the last of an ancient way of making them, he fitted the handle and locked it into place. It was a fine sword and he lifted it up and swung it in the air. He swiped left to right, and began to laugh, it was well balanced, and felt good in his hand as he lunged, and swung with extreme skill. He was a swordsman of quality and held a sword that was perfect in every way.

The light danced all around the room casting reflections of white on all the walls, it sparkled and glowed in the dim light and he knew as the sun rose, and the final moment of making came, his sword would become a complete and living magical entity. He lay it down on the table and walked back to the furnace where metal still bubbled in the pot.

Victor looked through the small window at the sky, and then back at the pot. He still had two hours before she would arrive, he had an idea and he looked at his tools and smiled.

Billy stormed across the hall. "I told you I would be here in time and here I am, what the hell is your problem?" He ran up the stairs throwing his wet cloak on to the rail as he passed. He looked up at his father. "If she lived somewhere that was actually possible to get to, instead of this bloody awful rock, things might be a little easier on all of us."

Mason smiled as Billy ran up the last flight. "She has something very special for you, her way of making it up to you William. Be nice to her." Billy scowled at his father.

"I hate the bitch, she should be nice to all of us, the old hag thinks she rules the bleeding world already." Mason smiled at his sons' humour and patted him on the back.

"Good to see you son, how is the girl?"

Billy sighed and smiled at his dad. "She hates my guts, and is having my kid; how the hell do you think she is? I have her in prison, she is as pissed off as you could get."

He chuckled at his son. "Sounds like your mother when I first met her."

They strode down the long corridor along the red plush carpet; the walls were bland with no decoration at all. "God this place is bleak, it's no wonder she is so bloody miserable. How have you put up with her all these years Dad? I am glad I was at Loxley out of her way."

"She is family Billy. It means something you know."

They reached the door and walked in. Morgan scowled at Billy. "I have been waiting for you."

"Nice to see you grandma how are you? I do hope you are feeling well after getting your ass kicked again."

She erupted from the chair her eyes burning at Mason. "SEE ... SEE, what I have to put up with from the ungrateful tyke? I should tear his heart out and eat it."

Billy smiled. "Speaking of food, I have been on the road all night is there anything in this tomb worth eating?"

Mason turned on Billy. "That is enough William; I have warned you about upsetting your grandmother now stop it," his eyes flared a red colour as he spoke.

Billy sat in the chair. "Sorry Dad... I am starving though."

Morgan gave a simpering sort of smile. "We will all eat soon Billy; I have a gift for you that I know you will love, call it an offering of peace between us. I understand your anger with me for sending you away so young, this I hope will make up for it, and we can start over." She walked to the door. "Come on and see how nice I can be if you let me."

Billy looked at his dad who smiled and shrugged. He looked at her stood at the door, and got up and followed, when she was nice, he trusted her less.

Victor Thornson stood in the centre of the ring as they entered and came down the stairs. The sword lay on the floor covered in a deep purple velvet cloth. She walked round the base of the stairs her eyes dull yet excited. "Well... where is it?"

The old man bent down and pulled back the cloth, and she gasped with delight as she saw it. It gleamed and shone like the sun, she crouched down to touch it Victor pulled the cloth back over it. "Not yet, it is not quite ready."

She looked and gave him and evil grin. "You need to pour in my magic?"

He pulled out his scribe and she nodded as he slid back the cloth. "Once you have spoken the incantation and the magic has been absorbed the first to lift it as I add the last rune will be its first true owner."

Billy smiled as he looked down at the blade of quality on the floor. "If that is for me Grandmother you are definitely forgiven."

She gave an evil smile to her grandson. "Good, so we have a new understanding, and new start my dearest Billy."

He gave her a nervous smile, he had never trusted her, but for a sword like that he thought he could wing it for a while. Victor looked at the windows. "It is nearly time." He began to scribe one of the last two runes on the blade.

Morgan le Fey lifted her arms and her eyes began to burn a deep velvety red. Her voice was loud and cold, and made both Mason and Billy shiver. Her face contorted as she channelled a very old and very deep magic and mixed it with that of Gwendolyn's. The words were of a tongue older than man was, and sounded strange to everyone.

"Sard nay destraught. Sard nay POW. Broth surd nay nite. Ant de lit bit devow."

Light of many colours swirled out of her and howled as it spun around the room, the first beam of light came in through the window as dawn started to rise, and the coloured light flew into the blade and it glowed. Victor placed his scribe at the bottom of the blade and it glowed and faded again. He nodded to Morgan and she raised her arms.

"Sard nay destraught. Sard nay dam. Fult in sol eskith. Draw be mitt hanta."

The light exploded out of her, and she leaned back her head and laughed a loud ugly evil laugh as it flowed to floor and into the blade. Sparks and streams of coloured light flew down and then a wail began of a woman in pain, and the light turned black. The power of Gwendolyn had flowed into the blade and now as her wails grew the darkness of the times of old, and a power not spoken of, also flowed into the blade and the pain of corruption could be heard.

As the stream stopped, Victor etched the last of the rune onto the blade, and it glowed a deep blood red colour and vibrated on the floor. The golden blade exploded with light as a second ray of the sun hit the blade and the room was, filled with an intense light that almost blinded them.

Billy covered his eyes in pain. The rattling blade went still and when he opened his eyes, he saw a black shining sword on the floor, the runes glowed down the side of the blade in a sinister red. The sword that should have matched Gwendolyn's sword of power and shone gold in the sun, had been violated, and corrupted by the forces of darkness. Victor stood up and looked at Morgan le Fey. "Who will be its first owner?" She pointed to Billy and he turned to see the excited glint in his blue eyes. "Everyone else step away, you boy, stand in the centre of the star and do not touch the sword until I tell you to."

Mason and his mother stepped back, as Billy walked into the centre of the circle and stood on the red star beside the sword, he looked excitedly at the black blade, Victor stepped back. "You must repeat your grandmother's incantation in your own language to claim the sword. Repeat after me." He nodded at Billy, and Billy nodded back, and turned to his father and smiled at him excitedly. Mason gave him a huge grin.

Victor coughed and crossed himself with the sign of the cross. "Sword of destruction, sword of power. Bring blade of darkness, and let light be devoured." Billy spoke the words and his voice seemed to deepen and boom as he spoke. The sword rattled on the floor and began to glow as the runes on the side of the blade glowed a deep violent red.

"Sword of destruction, sword of damned, filled with my essence, and guided by my hand."

As Billy spoke the last words, the sword spun on the floor and leapt into Billy's right hand, he caught it with a smile, and red light fired out of his eyes. He swayed a little as the power of the sword flowed into, and through him. He tilted back his head and opened his arms and a cold deathly rattling laugh emitted from his mouth, he swung the sword in the air and swiped and lunged, and then suddenly the light stopped and Billy stood quietly admiring the blade. Victor walked forward and nodded. "The black blade of Dunnottar is now yours."

Billy turned to him and smiled. Victor gasped and stepped back, Billy lunged with the sword and it sliced into Victor's stomach. He grinned as he pulled the sword slowly back and raised the blade to examine it; the runes glowed red as they enjoyed the taste of blood, Billy licked his lips as if tasting it himself.

Victor fell to his knees as Billy turned to face his grandmother; Mason took a sharp intake of breath. Billy smiled at him with deep dark black shining eyes.

"Father, Grandmother what can I say it is a gift to rival no other." His voice was cold and dead.

Morgan smiled and walked up to him and stroked the side of his face.

"Welcome back to the family my darling, my heir, my William, my Mordred le Fey." She kissed him on the lips softly, and he smiled at her.

"I love you Mother." She slid her arm round him and smiled as she began to walk him to the steps. Victor looked up as she climbed the steps with Billy. "You said you would not kill me." He gasped holding his stomach as blood spilled on to the red five-pointed star on the floor.

She glanced down coldly at him. "And I kept my word I did not... He did." Billy and Morgan both laughed out loud and carried on up the stairs followed by a shocked looking Mason, the door banged as it closed behind them.

Alice sat bolt upright in bed and gripped her stomach. "Ohhh!" She breathed deeply and gasped and the pain left her, she caught her breath and lay back down. At that very same moment, Rune's eyes exploded in bright violet light and she sat up in the dark.

Robbie jumped up at her side. "What is it?" The sword of truth glowed and sparkled, casting rainbows in the dark. Rune clutched his arm as her eyes burned brightly.

"Something terrible and evil has happened." Her head moved slowly as if she was trying to sense something. "It's gone." She leaned on him and breathed deeply, her eyes faded and the darkness flowed back over them. Robbie pulled her close.

Victor coughed as he knelt in the centre of the circle; he looked down at the blood pool now spreading away from him, it would not be much longer. The five stones in the golden holders began to glow and the room filled with violet light. He watched as a small girl skipped into view, she was dressed in lilac with a hood over her face. A small silver lion with diamonds for eyes twinkled from her neck above her robes. He smiled at her as she slowed and then walked into the circle. "I knew you would come."

She slid back her hood and her brown hair shone with a sparkle of red, her violet eyes intensified her pale face. Victor opened his jacket and took out a role of purple velvet cloth. "Take this to your father; tell him, it will bring back what should be in his line."

She took the bundle and slid it into her robes, and smiled a warm, kind and loving smile. She kissed him on the cheek and a tear ran from his eyes, the small girl walked slowly round the circle and gathered up the violet stones into her arms. She stood at the edge of the circle, and smiling, her violet eyes twinkled at him, she lifted her free arm and waved.

Victor nodded at her and gave her a warm loving smile. "Good bye my angel, my Queen." He blew her a kiss and she turned and skipped away, and faded into the wall. With tears in his eyes, he fell to the floor and was dead.

Victor Thornson the last great sword maker left this realm forever. His final act had ensured that the last greatest blade ever made had an enemy. Only in the last moments of making the sword had he realised whom Morgan le Fey truly was. He had called the sword his Excalibur, and in doing so remembered that the last blood to be spilt by that sword of power had been that of le Fey's first born child of evil, Mordred.

It was then that he had realised that she would use the power of Gwendolyn, who was the queen of the fairies to bring back her son's spirit. He had no choice but to ensure that the last metal left in the pot was used. All he could do now was pray it was enough, and as he watched the spirit of Mordred enter Billy; he knew he had done the right thing.

Sugilite was the stone of healing and the stone of balance, it existed in small amounts because it had been Gwendolyn's gift to the world. Carnac had the biggest site because that had been her place of residence, he had to hope and pray now he had done enough.

Hesketh came into the cellar and gave a sad sigh as he saw the old man dead on the floor. He cleaned up the room and packed away the holders and the tools in the large wooden box. He stopped and looked for the violet stones, he scanned the floor but there was no sign. He hammered the lid on the crate and dragged it into the corner; Victor's body was dragged into the yard and across to the cliff edge. Hesketh looked down at the old man's face. "Sorry old fellow." He pushed with his foot and the body slipped off and landed in the rough sea. Hesketh turned and walked back to the small door collecting the mop out of the bucket as he passed.

Mason left in a carriage without stopping for a meal, he pulled his cloak around himself and shivered, as it rumbled over the bridge and the soldiers fell in line either side. He looked back at the castle stood tall and black in the dawn light. "Billy was right, it is a tomb."

Robbie held Rune close. "Well, what did it feel like, you must have some idea?"

Rune shivered in his arms. "It was cold and evil, that's the only way I can describe it Rob. It frightened me and I woke up... I just know something bad has happened, and it is something very bad indeed. Hold me close Rob."

He pulled the blankets up and held her tight as she shivered violently. It worried him a lot; he had never seen Rune like this before, it had to be something to do with Knox, but what could he do that was so frightening to Rune. He stared at the mountains in front of them across the lake and his mind wandered.

Billy sat back and raised his glass, it chinked on his mothers and she smiled. "Oh, darling I have missed you so much, you have no idea. Mason was never the son you were, I was so hurt to lose you to your half-brother."

Billy smiled an evil smile. "He has gone forever with his blade, and I now have the sword that will rule. Excalibur is nothing compared to the power of this, now we can rule as planned. A new world, a new beginning, now is our time and my so called father can do the work for us. I will let him toil for now, then when the new child comes, we will rule supreme, we will have no need of the weak." He raised his glass to his lips and his black eyes sparkled with delight; he raised his glass in salute as his mother chuckled a cold dead laugh.

CHAPTER SIXTEEN

THE FUTURE PAST, IN THE PRESENT

Robbie sat up and wiped the sleep from his eyes. He looked around the camp at the large lumps of blankets, under which many of the group were still asleep. Mel sat by the fire pouring herself a coffee as she yawned; she saw him and smiled lifting the coffee pot. He nodded and slowly stood up and stretched, Rune was not there and he looked around under the dense thick larch trees of the camp.

His feet crunched on the deep litter of small dry brown needles and old larch cones. He took the cup from Mel's hand, her slate grey eyes seemed fixed on the water, and he turned to see what she was looking at. Rune sat on a large rock cross legged in her green tight trousers and sage green string laced top. "Something is playing on her mind Robbie; I have never known Rune worry like this before. She is talking to my dad, and has blocked us all out. What happened last night?"

Her long wavy brown hair brushed him, as the soft breeze off the water lifted it, Robbie shrugged. "To be honest I am not sure, something woke her up last night and it seemed to frighten her. By the time I woke up it seemed to have passed, although she did not sleep well after that."

He watched her from the trees; he could see the lilac flashes across her cheeks as she talked to her grandfather.

"I am not sure Grandfather, it was so powerful it shook me deeply, but as quick as it came, it went."

"I must admit that far up north I should not have felt a thing, yet I got a slight blast. I agree it was powerful and I think very dark."

"Do you think she has tapped into more powers?"

"I am not that sure she tapped into power Rune. I think she can already do that without any one of us feeling it; she took Gwendolyn's power without anyone knowing until it was too late. No, I think she has passed power on, we got a blast of a transference, be very careful Runestone if you meet any member of that family, one of them I feel will be a little more dangerous than before."

"I will be Grandfather thank you, give our love to Scarlet and tell her the girls are fine."

"I will my darling take care."

Rune opened her eyes and she looked towards the camp where she saw Robbie leaning against a tree. His brown eyes sparkled as he smiled at her. She slid off the rock and grinned as she walked up the slight slope of the bank, and slid her hands around him as he watched her carefully looking for any sign of concern. She pulled him tight and kissed him. "Good morning gorgeous."

"Hey beautiful, how is your grandfather?" She smiled sweetly at him.

"He is fine and enjoying time with Scarlet." She looked at him. "He felt something last night too, he thinks the Dark One has given someone powers."

Robbie looked at her with a note of concern. "Can she do that?

Rune nodded and looked glum. "I am afraid she can, yes." She glanced down at the ground. "Rob promise me you will be careful." She pulled him close and stood on her tip toes as her eyes came almost level with his. "Promise you will be aware of any member of that family. Any one of them could have some of her in them, and you would not see it until they use it."

He pulled her close and held her as he kissed her. "I have and always will be careful with that lot, you know it. I have never once underestimated them Rune and I am not about to start." She lowered herself down and put her head against his chest; he looked down and watched her bright blue eyes as they watched the lake. He kissed the top of her head and held her close.

The camp was coming back to life as blankets moved and scruffy hair with bleary eyes looked out. Blades took advantage of the lake, and ran down and waded out; she slipped under the water and resurfaced twenty feet away. Bull wandered yawning in from the trees having finished his guard duty. Keith carried his cup and plate into the trees to replace Jaz.

Most of them sat as Smokes and Steph handed out cooked tomatoes and beans. Una worked on a flat stone making more bread biscuits, as they were getting low, and soon chuckles and talk wafted into the air. Robbie leaned back and smiled at the camp, Rune was quiet in thought, and the heat of her slender frame passed through into him.

Rowan and Jade walked down the path towards the camp. Two strange woodsmen walked with them, and they talked, Robbie patted Rune on the back and she looked at him, seeing his eyes watching across the camp, she turned her head and saw the new arrivals.

Rowan had a quick talk to Bear and Bull and then looked up as Bear pointed to Robbie. The two new woodsmen turned and looked across the camp towards him, Robbie released Rune and she slid to his side, as Rowan left the others and brought the two new arrivals across. One was quite tall and stocky, and Robbie noticed the tartan sash across his tunic. His head was shaved and very brown, the other was smaller with very close cropped dark hair; he had a mousy look to him, as he squinted through small eyes. They bowed as Rowan introduced them, "Robbie, Rune this is Angus Macintosh and James McFadden, they are members of one of the few remaining groups of woodsmen in these parts."

Robbie smiled and offered his hand. "Gentlemen I am happy to see you, I was starting to wonder if any of the woodland folk still existed this far north. This is the Lady Runestone of Loxley."

Rune smiled as they took her hand and bowed, Angus looked at Robbie. "My Lord we are honoured you have travelled so far north, but I must advise you that from here it is not easy going, the Raven has many men in these parts."

"The Raven, who is that?" Rune looked a little confused, James pulled a black vest out from under his cloak, he unrolled it and showed the crude spread eagle red raven on the front of it. Rune smiled, as she understood.

"The Dark One is her name down south, and her son has men in these with dragons on them."

The two woodsmen nodded. "If you travel north, you will need a guide, we know where all the groups are hidden and lying in wait. You must be known to be in these parts My Lord for there has been increased activity for several days now."

Robbie seemed evasive. "We are woodsmen and have remained unseen since entering Scotland; any extra precautions being taken are not on our account." Rune watched Robbie closely, she had always seen him welcome woodsmen, and this time he seemed a little out of character, she could feel the apprehension inside him. Rowan seemed a little surprised and he looked questioningly at Robbie, he smiled.

"Gentlemen would you care to join my party for breakfast and coffee, Rune please could you introduce our guests to the others?"

She smiled and nodded, then walked with the two men across the camp. She understood that he wanted a private word with Rowan, and Rowan watched as they walked away. "What's on your mind Robbie?"

He put his hand on his shoulder. "Just being extra careful my friend, tell me where did you find them, and have they asked about our direction?"

Rowan shrugged. "They were camping about three miles up, we closed in on them after finding a few dead Cutters. They had no idea we were with you, until I got back to the camp, they just think I am part of a scouting party looking for contact with more northern groups."

Robbie sighed a little. "You have done well; I think stealth even amongst our own for a while will serve us well, this country has been occupied for too long, and I want no surprises."

The two of them walked slowly over to the fire where everyone sat eating,

Robbie slid in next to Rune and she passed him a plate. Over the breakfast, Robbie heard how most of the woodsmen had been attacked and slaughtered by the Cutters. Many were prisoners who laboured with the stone to build the monstrous fortresses of Mason Knox. He had many large sprawling cities that reached as far down as Sunderland all along the east coast, very little of the green wild areas remained intact.

There were small bands of resistance that kept constantly on the move, the Raven shirted soldiers were everywhere, and travel had become very difficult, especially along the eastern side. Like England, most of the wood folk lived in the west of the country, there were quite a few in the woods, and forests on the high mountain plains, the soldiers seldom travelled that high up.

Angus was on his way east to meet up with his sister who had been fighting below Aberdeen, there had been strange rumours about a tall black castle appearing on the old ruins almost overnight. His sister and her lover had planned to observe and meet up in two days at the Tamanverrie stone circle just north of where they were now. They intended to head into the mountains, and work their way across to the highlands to muster more support to resist those now inhabiting the large castle.

Rune could feel his worry as he talked, and she knew him to be telling the truth, she felt the love he held for his sister and her lover who was also his best friend. Robbie watched her carefully, understanding her signals, and he relaxed knowing he was amongst loyal woodsmen. "Well gents it appears our route is joined for part of the way, you are more than welcome to join us, I should think travelling in numbers will be safer for all of us." He gave them both a smile. "I have men to attend to, if you would excuse me, I shall get organised."

Robbie barked out his orders as he crossed the camp to Bear and Skip, who were looking at the map and setting the route for the castle. "John, Martin be extra tidy today, I want no traces when we leave here." They nodded and began the process of covering and clearing any signs that a camp had ever existed.

It was an hour later when the sun was rising and they set off into the hilly forests, heading towards Loch Lee. Angus knew many trails and paths that helped them to cross the country fast. Judith rode with Rune and Flash rode with Harry to free up the extra horses for the two guests.

The air felt cleaner and fresher as they rose higher, it was cool under the dense canopy of the thick rows of pine, which scented the air around them. The pine forests were so dense that nothing grew under them; the floor was just a thick carpet of dried brown needles and old pinecones. Years of needle fall had created a dense thick carpet, which was soft under the horse's feet. They skirted the base of Mount Keen and followed the trail deep into the afternoon weaving around the forest and streams. As mid afternoon slipped past, they reached the high hill above Coull, and saw the stone circle where they were to stop and rest. Robbie sat on his horse and put the telescope to his eye.

He smiled as the castle described to him by Rune came to view in the distance. It was about six miles away, and he looked at the curious arrangements of turrets, with its pointed roofs and chimneys. Now he understood Rune's comments about it being all turrets and no walls. From where he sat, it looked like three giant brick tubes had been placed side by side, it had a roof top observation platform and some very large trees close to it.

He passed the scope to Rune who gazed at it in closer detail. "When do you plan to go in Rob?" Rowan came up as she asked the question, and she passed the scope to Rowan as she looked to Robbie for his answer.

"I think considering last night we should go as quickly as possible. We have the plans worked out; we just need a little more reconnaissance before we make the final preparations. I want Alice back as soon as possible."

Robbie sat and talked about the castle with Angus and James as Rafe, Rowan, and Jade headed off to get a close look at the place. He placed the map on the floor as they helped fill him in on what the towns around contained. There was a great deal of soldiers stationed on the grounds of the castle or nearby. Robbie added all the extra information as he drew his plan of action.

It was mid afternoon, and Judith, Treen, and James McFadden stood watch as the whole group gathered in the stone circle. They formed a wide arc as Robbie laid the pad of Steph's on the floor. Rune, Rowan, and Bull sat close as he lifted the plans and showed it to the group.

"Can everyone see?" They all nodded. "Alright everyone here is the plan of action. There are four walls around the compound. Knox likes his tall walls; these are eight feet and perfect for us because they will not see us until we strike. I have called them north to west." His finger followed the details on the plan.

"The North is where most of us will go over. Mother, Smokes and Mel you will defend from the top of the wall with bows, Rafe and Maddy will be on the roof of the stables, which back on to the North East corner of the wall. There will be two guards on the wall, Rowan and Pebbles, they are yours." Jade gave a grin at Rowan, who was watching the plan closely.

"West wall has four guards and two guards on the doors of the castle. Angus and Harry, you take out the guards on the doors with bows, Saff you take out one of the guards from the shed roof at the end of the wall, Jett will back you up. Harry, Skip, and Blades you get the guards on the wall." Harry gave a serious nod.

"South wall has two long wooden barrack houses on it. Rafe and Maddy from the roof of the stables you should have a clear shot of the double doors of each hut; they will be lit so any movement will be easily seen. Jaz, Bear and Bull, you come in over the roof and wait, anything coming out of those huts that the bows miss take them quickly." Robbie gave a long breath as he looked up at all of them.

"Here is the tricky bit. The west wall has two large steel gates and a guardhouse. John and Martin, you get to clear the guardhouse, there is a set of main doors right opposite so wait for Keith and Fish. You guys will come down the outer walls and shoot through the gates at the door guards. Get over those gates as quickly as you can and into the compound. Cover the barrack house while Flash and Una keep the gates secure. Flash I do not care how you do it but find a way to melt the lock to keep those gates closed."

He leaned back and looked around his men; they all smiled and nodded as they looked at his drawing on the plan. Rune touched his hand; she felt his nervousness and it reassured him.

"Right now, for the crazy bit... Rune is vital to the rescue and I want her protected at all costs. She will be communicating with Alice for us, so she will have her eyes closed. Mother that is your primary task, sit with her and keep watch. I will go over the wall as Mel takes out the guard on this door, he will be in a blind spot so I will drop down and head over to the ivy covered wall and climb up to the window with Alice behind it. The window is barred and Rune will take care of it, I will secure it to the wall to stop it falling. I will then enter the room." Robbie looked at Rowan, who smiled.

"Rowan you will be in this large tree opposite with Pebbles. Shoot your arrow into the room, and I will pull up the rope and secure it, Jade you follow up the rope and take out Alice as I keep watch. When Alice hits the floor, Mel you get her round to Jett and Saff as quick as you can. Rune will move with Steph, Maddy, and Rafe, covered by Smokes. All you defending the West wall drop and pull back as the group passes you. I will come down the rope and descend with Rowan. We will lead everyone round, and over the roof and off the wall into the trees. Judy and Treen will be with James and the horses waiting for us all."

He looked at everyone and smiled. "It's a walk in the woods, but we have to be fast and as quiet as possible, I would like to get her out right under their noses and without alerting them to us, Rune will coordinate all of you together for timing so those of you who are connected keep everyone in sight. Do you reckon we can pull it off then?"

They all nodded and John boomed from the middle. "Thought you were going to give us something hard boss, it's hardly Tintagel." Everyone laughed and Robbie grinned at them all.

"I will leave the plans here, study them we leave in one hour and please all of you, be very careful, we have two losses; let's not make it more, so look out for each other." They all nodded and began to rise up to their feet and move closer to the pad.

Rowan, Rune, and Bear knew the plan backwards they had all put in their own input and now it was just a case of getting ready. Robbie looked at Judy and Treen. "Will you two be alright in the dark with James?"

Treen smiled at him; "Believe me Robbie I ave ways of convincing Cutters we ezz better left alone." He smiled at her.

"Oh yeah I have heard you can win a convincing argument." He winked at her and smiled at Judy "What about you?" Judy seemed unphased.

"I am a Knox; they will not mess with me." She fingered her little Bumblebee brooch. "I can have a sting if I need to." Robbie nodded at her, somehow, he just knew she could look out for herself.

The evening was wearing on as they moved silently into the woodland just over a mile outside the castle. They all dismounted and Harry took the horses and ran a long line along four trees to tie them on. Everyone checked, and double checked their weapons and equipment. Robbie gave the signal and they moved out into the dense trees.

The light was fading as they wove their way through the thick patches of trees in the direction of the castle. The castle loomed up before them through the trees and Robbie felt his heart pumping as he saw it. The high wall was made a lot better than that of Canterbury, and Robbie stood at the southwest tip of the wall and looked at everyone. "Ok you all know what to do, hoods up and good luck, we will all meet here as soon as we have her."

He took Rune's hand and followed Rowan along the high heavy stonewall. Harry, Skip, Angus, and Blades dropped off as they reached their spots, and he hurried along to the far corner. Rowan peered round, it was clear, as quiet as the dead they ran along the wall keeping low and in the shadows. Fish led and as they came to the northeast corner, he stopped and peered round.

Maddy 's hood rose above the top edge of the wall. She peered around and signaled down, Rune's hood rose at her side, below the wall Robbie and Rafe held the girls on their shoulders. Rune and Maddy slipped over the wall and on to the stable roof. Flash and John appeared next, as they slipped flat against the roofline, Martin and Una appeared. They lay flat on the wooden roof covered with tar smeared canvass, John and Martin peered over the edge.

Two guards walked slowly along the inside of the wall, they looked bored from hours of pacing, they looked at each other and then at the guard stood across the yard by the small side door. There was a faint swishing and they saw the guard crumple with a long white tipped arrow sticking out of his chest. They turned to run as two large hooded figures came out of the sky with glinting knives.

The two guards fell silently as Smokes and Rowan dragged them back into the shade of the wall. Flash, John, Martin and Una dropped to the floor in the shadows at the side of the stable.

Maddy and Rafe lay above on the roof, as Jade slipped quietly across and lowered her hand. Rowan grabbed it and she heaved him up to the roof, and the first thick branch of the mighty beech tree. She passed him a huge coil of rope, which he slipped over his shoulder. Both of them began to climb soundlessly, they wove round the heavy trunk up the tree, disappearing into the canopy like two silent squirrels.

Robbie dropped off the wall and ran across the open space to the ivy; he grabbed the dead soldier and pulled him out of sight behind a large potted conifer. Rune watched as he jumped up into the ivy and started to climb. Mel sat low on the top of the wall her bow loaded and waiting; her eyes peered out from under her hood noting everything happening all around her.

Blades and Angus fired their bows as Harry, Skip and the arriving Smokes took out the walking guards. The two door guards crumpled to the ground, and Blades shot across the open space, and grabbed one and dragged him into the shadow and sat him up next to a large weed filled planter. She peered out and Saff nodded the all clear. She scurried across the doorway, and grabbed the other guard and dragged him back out of sight, then ran to the wall and vaulted up on to it. She picked up her bow and ran along the top of the wall to her spot, loaded her arrow and lay down on top of the wide wall in wait.

The pent of the barrack houses were quite low, and as the three guards lent back against the wall three large heavy hands lowered down. Each grabbed a collar and with a massive heave the three guards shot up into the air, there was a muffled grunt and they did not return to earth. John and Martin shot from the side of the gatehouse and the two guards at the gates collapsed. Two hooded figures appeared outside the metal gates and the guards by the main door of the castle fell to earth with long white tipped arrows sticking out of them.

John and Martin entered the guardhouse. Muffled grunts and bangs and thuds came from inside, and then everything went quiet and Flash and Una slipped round and into the house as John and Martin slipped out and across the long driveway to the main doors. They picked up the dead guards and ran to the back of the stables as Fish and Keith hit the floor just inside the gates. Flash ran out and screwing up her eyes, she slipped off her glasses and a single beam of red light melted the gate catch shut tight.

Flash gave the thumbs up and Keith and Fish slipped flat against the dark shadows of the wall as Flash headed back into the guardhouse. Jett sat on the wall and smiled as she heard the word going around through Rune that the compound was secured. The Specialists were out to recover one of their own, and at their all time best, they were swift and quieter than death itself.

Alice sat on the bed reading; she turned the page slowly over. "Psst... Hey Pigeon, you want to fly home?" The book hit the floor, as she saw the hood and recognised the voice; Alice peered through the gap in the raised window. Tears filled her eyes as Robbie slid his hood back and smiled. "Hey sis, how's my nephew doing? Rune's on her way."

Alice tried to heave the window up higher but it was stuck, the room behind her glowed violet and she turned and burst into tears. Rune slid her arms around her.

"Hey come on now. I told you we would be here for you." Alice stepped back all smiles as the tears ran down her face, as Rune moved her back to a safe spot. "I would keep well clear of the window if I were you." She smiled and then kissed her on the head.

Alice watched, as Rune touched the glass, she smiled at Robbie. "Hi gorgeous, watch your eyes this stuff is going back to nature." As Rune ran her hand down the pane of glass it reverted back to sand and spilled on to the carpet. She smiled at Alice who watched in amazement. "I love being Hearne's granddaughter; it can be so handy at times like this." The whole window was now just an empty wooden frame.

Rune leaned through the gap and touched the bolts on the wall that held the bars in place, they glowed bright violet and then red. Robbie pulled and the thick metal frame came away from the wall, he lowered it six feet down on the rope he had tied on to it. The ivy leapt out of the wall, and grabbed it, and held it firmly in place, he smiled as he watched, but more out of concern as it looked a little creepy.

He climbed on to the window ledge, and heaved at the sliding window, it slid up with a grumble, and as quick as a flash he was in the room and hugging Alice, as Rune stood by the door. Alice shook in his arms as she silently wept and clung to him. He smiled as he rocked her from side to side and kissed her head, Rune smiled at the sight of them and the happiness she felt coming from Robbie.

He leaned back and looked at Alice and whispered. "Won't be much longer now and we will have you out and on your way home, we have to be quick Alice, I have about five hundred hugs all saved up for you later, Ok?" She nodded, and smiled and quickly kissed his cheek.

"I love you Rob." He winked.

"Right... duck?" He pushed her down to the floor. Robbie stood by the window and gave the signal to Rowan just below the window. He stood on the branch, and aimed his arrow as Jade held the long cord in her arms. He fired and the arrow whipped across the long yard below, Robbie stepped back and a long white tipped arrow came in through the window and stuck in the ceiling.

Robbie grabbed the thin line and pulled. He gathered it up as a thicker rope came in through the window, he pulled hard on the heavy bed and it did not move, so he took the rope and wove it through the top of the window, and threaded it round tying it in a heavy knot to the bed. He went back to the window and signaled, and the rope went taught.

Robbie slid his bow off his shoulder and walked to the door, he looked at Rune and touched her, she felt solid and she smiled, he leaned forward and kissed her. "That is so weird, and yet so cool." He kissed her again. She faded away into mist and the blue bird hopped down off the wardrobe and on to the table. Robbie took up guard of the door as two bright green eyes came in through the window.

Jade beamed as she faded into view and snatched Alice into her arms. "Hey girl I've missed you, fancy a slide out of here?" She handed Alice a coiled knotted rope in a figure eight. Alice got on to the window ledge and swung the coil over the rope. She slipped her wrists through the hoops of the eight, and slid off the window. Alice swept down and into Rowan's arms in the tree.

"Good evening Lady Alice. Could I interest you in a little nighttime adventure?" Rowan gave her a hug. "Welcome back," and he guided her on to the wide branch, where she moved to the trunk and climbed down the tree to the roof of the stables where Rune waited smiling.

Pebbles came whizzing down the rope with her legs wide open and a huge smile on her face. Rowan caught her and she clamped herself around him and threw her arms around his neck. She gave him a huge kiss. "It's no fun when you can't scream. You will have to make me a big one at Loxley."

Robbie wedged the chair under the door handle, and headed for the window, he flew down the rope and into the tree and Rowan grabbed him and patted him on the back. "Nice work Robbie."

He smiled. "I do like a smooth running outfit; it makes me look so much better." He laughed. "Come on let's get everyone out." Rune's eyes were already violet, and signals all around the place were being given, Alice was already over the wall and on her way round with Smokes and Steph. Rowan and Robbie pulled Una and Flash, on to the wall, John threw Martin up and then Keith and Fish followed. Rowan and Robbie heaved John up behind them; they ran along the top of the wall to the corner. Saff and Jett covered at the far end.

Keith ran along the wall followed by Fish. The door opened and a guard stepped out, he raised his crossbow instantly on seeing Keith and fired, Saff gasped, Fish brought his boot up and fired at the same time. Keith went headfirst over the wall, and the guard took an arrow to the throat. Two more arrows hit him and Fish spun round to see Robbie and Rowan side by side on the wall their bows still held up, with new arrows fitted. He smiled and nodded.

Fish turned and looked down the wall into the blackness; he could just make out the shape of Keith lay on his back on the floor. He dropped down beside him, and knelt down and looked at him. Keith sat up and grabbed Fish by the arm. "I should be dead." Fish smiled.

"Don't worry, we will find a way to cope." Keith smiled at him and nodded.

"Thanks Fish, I owe you big time." Fish patted his shoulder, and helped lift him up.

"Tell you what, you save mine next week and were quits... Come on this place gives me the willies." They ran down to the far corner where everyone was gathering, and Bull held Alice tightly in his arms as she wept into him. Saff dropped and threw her arms round Keith. Fish smiled.

Robbie and Rowan hit the floor. "Great work team now keep your heads and stay tight, let's get the hell out of here." Rowan took the lead and slipped into the woods. One by one, they followed him.

The horses seemed nervous. Judy crouched by the tree and stared into the darkness; Treen was crouched just in front as James paced around the horses. There had been no sounds of shouting or lights going on and so Treen presumed, everything was going well.

The red tipped arrow came from nowhere and hit James in the chest, it ripped through his rib cage and entered his heart and he was dead before he hit the floor. Treen slipped back against the tree and signaled to Judy to stay silent and still. Judy slid back into the trunk of the tree, and the dark shadow.

Two men crept into the area where the horses were tied up, they looked around and the thinner of the two saw Treen pressed flat against the tree. Her eyes glowed orange, and as his eyes met hers, his began to glow. He turned on his friend and grabbed him by the throat, the larger Cutter was shocked as his friend gripped him, and tried to fight him off gasping for breath, as his neck got squeezed tighter.

They fell to the floor and he saw Treen as he rolled with her eyes burning the same orange as his friends. He smashed his arm up and stuck his fingers into the eye sockets of his friend, as he felt his last air running out. He pushed with all the might he had left and his friend screamed in pain. The grip loosened and he pushed back hard and broke free.

He lunged back at his friend, and seized him roughly and threw him backwards at Treen. The Cutter smashed into her, breaking her concentration as she slammed back against the rough bark. He lunged at her and hit her hard in the face, her nose burst out with blood and she slid to the floor out cold.

Judy stared as she saw the big man stand up, and gasp. He kicked Treen's leg, and it rocked but she did not move. "Bitch." He spat at her and looked around and smiled to himself. He bent over and pulled her away from the tree, Judy suddenly felt a cold finger of horror sweep over her as she saw the man open Treen's legs and lift up her skirt.

He looked around again and then knelt down and began undoing his pants. Judy slid the long eight inch hatpin out of her boot and trembling she slowly stood up in the shadow behind him. She was swift and silent, and before he realised he was not alone, Judy plunged the hatpin into his ear and pushed with all her might.

The long pin went in right to the tip of the ornate flowered end. The man exploded up from the floor, and his pants fell down tripping him up. He hit the ground hard as Judy staggered backwards, and watched as he shook with a fierce fit on the floor. His mouth started to foam as he shook violently and then he went very still, except for his fingers, which twitched.

Judy slid backward quickly; horror in her eyes and felt the tree hit her in the small of her back. She watched for several minutes before she realised he was dead, she breathed hard and plucked up her courage; finally, she crawled over to Treen and pulled her skirt back down over her naked legs. She slid up to her face and lifted her head, Judy held her as she wiped the blood from her nose. Treen moaned as she slowly came around, and saw her friend taking care of her; Judy smiled at her. "Hi, you, OK?"

Rowan had heard the scream and ploughed on forward at top speed, he burst through the trees with his bow ready, to see two dead Cutters and the dead James McFadden. Judy sat in the centre with a very bloody Treen and she smiled up at him. "We are fine Rowan."

Rowan looked around and spotted the hatpin; he bent down and looked at it as Harry came up at his side with his two long swords in his hands. Rowan pulled the long bloody pin out of the ear of the dead Cutter, and lifted it up to examine it. Harry shuddered. "Man, he got his vibes skewered, oh whoa that was not cosmic."

Rowan looked at Judy as the others appeared, she was white and trembled a little. He bent over and wiped it on the shirt of the dead Cutter, and handed it back to her as Robbie watched. "That Judith is quite a sting." She took it and said nothing as she slid it into her boot; Robbie saw the bleeding ear and shuddered.

There was a lot of noise in the distance. Dogs barked and Robbie pulled everyone in together. "We are not home yet, let's get mounted, and get the hell out of here, they know we have been so let's move it and fast." He turned to Angus. "I am sorry about your friend; if you want to take him, I will help you get him on your horse."

Angus shook his head. "He will slow us down, we cannot risk it, there will be soldiers all over in an hour."

Robbie grabbed Judy and slung her up to Harry, he lifted Treen up to Jaz who held her tight as her mother passed him a big green scarf, Treen took it and pushed it on to her swollen nose. Alice was on James's horse next to Bull; Robbie leapt up, and pulled on to the reins and trotted up next to Rune. He looked back wiping the sweat off his head; everyone was up on a horse. "Ok let's move; follow Angus he knows the fastest route out."

They kicked hard and rode out of the glade into the thick forest. They charged through the wood lying low on their horses and belting along at terrific speed. Jett whooped a scream. "HEY ALICE WELCOME BACK," and everyone grinned as Alice beamed clutching tightly to her horse. The group burst out of the woods, and on to the fields in the moonlight, dawn was not long off, and Robbie wanted to be as far away as possible before those first rays of light came over the mountains.

Angus turned west and charged across the meadowlands and through shallow streams. After an hour, the ground was rising in front of them and Robbie knew that Angus wanted to get to the safety of the mountains, where he knew the soldiers would not follow. The grass thinned as the ground rose and shale could be seen flashing past in the grass. The first light of dawn rose as the horses galloped with speed.

They hit a stone path and the horses slipped a little, Jett looked behind her. "WE HAVE COMPANY GUYS!" Robbie looked back to see a group of about forty horse mounted soldiers following about half a mile behind them. He pushed his horse on.

The horses clattered up the steep slope of stone, and onto a mountain road that bent and twisted, he looked back and could see the gap had lessoned slightly.

"Angus they are catching us up, wouldn't it be better to stop and fight?"

Angus shook his head, "trust me there is a bridge not far off, if we reach it they will not follow us." The horse was starting to pant heavily as they clattered around a corner. Robbie recoiled slightly as he saw the steep ravine filled with water to his right. The left side rose higher above him as the start of the mountains loomed.

The bridge was about half a mile in front, he could see it slung across a wide ravine. They galloped for all they were worth pushing the horses harder, it grew larger as they got closer and the ravine was starting to look a lot wider.

The horses came to a sliding halt, as Angus dropped down and ran on to the bridge pulling his horse. Robbie stood at the side of the post and slid his bow off his shoulder; he loaded his arrow as one by one they herded the horses across. Fish and Keith grabbed two horses each as Rowan and Rune loaded their bows. Alice pulled a bow off the horse and stood next to Robbie she smiled at him. "Nice to be back."

Maddy knelt down, and pulled a long arrow out and fitted it to her white ash bow. The others scurried across the rope and plank bridge as it swung under the feet of the horses; the group took aim and waited. The soldiers clattered at high speed up the rise and round the corner as the arrows released.

Maddy's arrow ignited off her bow, and as the front riders fell from the groups arrows, the second batch of riders burst into flames, wailed, and dived from their horses over the edge of the fast flowing ravine and plunged screaming into the water.

Robbie looked back at the bridge. It was empty, Rafe, and Keith and the others were on the other side lining up and shooting at the soldiers. Robbie pulled Alice and Bull back. "Go now!" They scuttled back and he saw Judy holding the post of the bridge and shaking, Robbie grabbed Rowan.

"Judy is afraid of heights take her across, Rune, Maddy, let's go!" A hail of arrows came across from the other side, and Robbie loaded walking backward and shot. Rowan grabbed Judy and lifted her on to his back and stepped on to the violently swinging bridge. Alice and Bull were halfway across, as Rune and Maddy stepped on.

Robbie loaded and fired and one of the soldiers fell backwards down the ravine and into the river. Robbie stepped on to the bridge and lunged out for the rope rail as his feet swung from side to side; he shouldered his bow and grabbed the rail on the other side. Arrows whizzed past from both sides as he put his head down and focused on the bridge. He could see the river a very long way below, and tried not to look at it as he focused on where his feet were. The roar of the water was deafening in his ears, and he looked up to see the others struggling as the bridge swung, and arrows whipped past him and he felt a lurch. He looked back and saw some of the soldiers shooting at the ropes.

"HURRY!" He bellowed across the roar of the water, and he began to try and move faster. He could feel the blood pumping in his head, as he pulled with his arms to get forward and catch up with Maddy, he was halfway across and moving faster, he swallowed hard. The floor lurched from under his feet, and he knew without looking the rope had gone. His arms and wrists locked as the bridge slid into the ravine and he braced for the impact. As the roar in his ears increased, he saw the slate grey wall heading towards him at high speed as the bridge left his feet.

"HOLD ON TIGHT!" He screamed upwards. The wall came at him at an alarming speed and suddenly the momentum in his body stopped as he hit the wall with a smash. The shock and pain mixed into one and he gasped a breath as his legs whip lashed back and increased the weight on his arms, he scrambled for a foothold with his legs as stars flashed before his eyes and he blinked to clear his slightly dazed vision.

There was a scream above him and he looked up, Judy had lost her grip of Rowan and fell backwards. His feet went into the wall as he released his right hand and she came hurtling and screaming towards him, he kicked out with all his might swinging wide back into the ravine.

Judy hit him head on, and he felt the tug on his left wrist as his right arm snatched around her, he pulled her close as they swung back into the wall. "I got you." She cried in terror and clung desperately to him. The impact on the wall was harder as he had extra weight now acting as a force against him.

His head spun as he desperately tightened his grip on the rope and on Judy. The pain in his arm was tremendous as both of them swung, and his wrist twisted round. Everything he had in the way of strength now focused on his left wrist, and Robbie began to feel the true meaning of fear as he fought to get Judy above him onto the rope. "Judy I am hanging by a hand; I need you to be brave for me. I need you to climb up like a ladder. Use the rope and do not look down. Please sweetheart, because I will not be able to hold you like this for much longer." Judy sniffled and shook with fear.

Her eyes stared widely down at the torrent of fast moving water, and she pulled tighter to him. He could see the fear in her eyes and the whiteness of her face.

Rowan was on his way down again and Robbie saw him and breathed a huge sigh of relief. Rowan was shouting, and Robbie could see his lips moving but he could not hear him for the roar of the water. Rowan reached down and grabbed Judy, he heaved and her weight lifted off Robbie's arm.

He snatched with his right arm, and slid his feet into the wooden slats and pushed with his legs. The relief was instant as he pushed up and took the weight off his arm. He gasped and pushed his head on to the rope, as his left arm trembled with the sheer strain he had exerted on it, and the wave of relief washed over him as Rowan pulled Judy into his arms and swung her on to his back.

Robbie pulled, and lifted up about nine inches and slid his other foot into a gap between two planks. He lifted his left arm up and saw Rune near the top looking down. He smiled at her, she looked terrified but John was just above her ready to pull her clear. Maddy was now moving and he took a deep breath, as Rowan moved up with Judy on his back.

He breathed a sigh of relief, knowing they were safe. Rune's eyes glinted sapphire blue, and he felt the joy of her and knowing he would soon be up there with her. His head was pounding from the knocks and his elbows hurt, but he smiled to her knowing it was pointless shouting above the roaring water, which deafened his ears to everything. Bull's huge hand gripped Rune's wrist, as she looked down terrified watching Robbie climb. She blinked and the long red tipped arrow hit him. Rune opened her eyes and the scream was lost in the roar of the water. Her grip on the rope loosened as she went to move down, cold swept through her heart as her eyes widened and terror flooded into her at an alarming speed.

Robbie felt it burn in his shoulder, he winced with pain as his head shot back and looked up. Coldness spread across his back and down his arm into his wrist and fingers. He swung his weakened left arm to the rope and missed. His right fingers were going colder and he felt the rope slip. His eyes met hers, bright blue and shining, filled with love and tears as his whole body went numb. He watched her fighting and screaming as Bull tried to pull her up, and she slipped further away from him.

Her screams met his ears as he felt the bridge leave him, and her face was all he could see, her voice all he could hear as the cliff face rushed past and she slipped away, faster and faster from him. The pain left his body and the tightness of his arms and legs seemed to slacken as his body went limp. Flashes of blue flooded his eyes and a feeling of warmth and love seemed to radiate around him.

The water came past his eyes and everything went dark. "Rune."

"Rooooooooooooooooooooooooobbie!" Bull heaved with all his might as she screamed and yelled, as he disappeared below the water. Saff ran to the edge and launched herself into the air. She shot past the screaming, crying struggling hysterical Rune, she saw the spot where he had gone in and as she pulled her arms together, as she dived for the place in the river. Melanie screamed and Fish dragged her back from the edge, as her arms flailed wildly at the edge and she tried to grab a Saff that had already gone out of sight.

Rune's eyes were purple and wild as she fought the bear hug she was trapped in as John Lox wrestled her down to the ground, she kicked and punched and then a huge power exploded out of her with a scream so loud everyone fell in pain. It was so powerful that it threw everyone in to the air. John was thrown forty feet off her as she rose into the air and glowed deep purple. The other side of the mountain started raining rocks on to the soldiers; trees were ripped apart and flung into the air and tossed hundreds of feet.

Rune screamed and shook as she rose in the air her powers flashing wildly as she lost control. The wind erupted with the force of a hurricane, as the pain exploded in her chest, those members of the group who tried to get up and get to her were picked up and tossed backwards into the air, rock and dirt spun round like a twister blinding everyone and they hit the floor. The river rose and fell again as her wild uncontrolled power brought thunder and rain and the ground shook violently beneath everyone.

Her face was hidden in a bright purple glow as thousands of violets sprung, up from the ground and were, torn up and flung in to the wild storm that raged around her. Her whole body shook in agony and pain, and as Steph flew backwards across the floor spinning, she closed her eyes and blocked out Rune from the others knowing the pain her daughter felt and knowing the force that would explode around her.

The explosion of light that burst from her was equal to that of a nuclear explosion. It radiated out in a blinding flash, and destruction and mayhem followed it. The light was seen for a hundred miles as it burst into the sky, and across the valley, Rune was about to self destruct and both circles of Life and Knowledge prepared as they huddled pressed flat against the floor by the massive power of Runestone.

A massive white light exploded in front of her, and Merlin stepped out, he snapped his fingers and Rune collapsed on to the floor. Four miles of woodland laid snapped, broken, and ripped apart, half a mountain had slid, and the pathway that contained the soldiers had gone forever.

Everyone sat up cut and bruised, and looked around dazed and shaking in fear, no one seemed sure what had happened, Rune hung limp in Merlin's arms. Her violet tears had streaked her white face, and her long red hair hung down swinging by her arms. "I will be back wait here." He turned and walked back into the light. Steph scrambled up off the floor covered in dirt and dust, and ran after him, and shot into the white light as it disappeared.

Mel sat held in the arms of Fish as she wept, Maddy and Una rose out of a mound of dirt and shook themselves. They crawled slowly over to her and put their arms around her. Big John stood at the cliff edge tears in his eyes as blood ran down his face, he looked from left to right to see if could see any sign. Rocks still rolled down the sides of the mountain as they settled, and the river was thinner, higher and flowing faster. Jett and Ruby lay unconscious under a huge fallen tree and Bull and Bear heavily cut and bleeding lifted the huge trunk as Smokes crawled with Rafe underneath to pull them clear. Keith sat alone covered in dirt and his head down as he wept.

Rowan staggered up on to the path where Pebbles sat, he was still holding Judith by the hand, and she looked dazed and confused. Pebbles saw him, and jumped up and threw her arms around him. "Robbie and Saff are in the river come on." She kissed him, grabbed his hand and pulled. Rowan released his grip and Judy walked towards the group in shock.

Rowan and Pebbles grabbed their bags and their bows and headed off downstream. They came to the high edge and looked over; the water was fast and filled with rapids that burst round large rocks. Pebbles fought her tears back as she saw them; she turned to Rowan her fierce eyes burned green as the tears ran down her face. "He is not dead, I would know." She started to cry and pushed her head into his chest. "I would know... help me Rowan I can't lose him, we can't lose him, he made us."

Rowan pulled her close and held her tight, as her sobs rose from his chest.

"Don't cry Pebbles he needs us... he is in trouble and we have to find him." She looked up at his slate grey tear filled eyes and he smiled. "Come on we are his best, let's find him." She smiled and nodded. Rowan and Jade turned and ran along the edge of the cliff watching the water and looking for a way down.

Merlin appeared and looked at Bull. "What happened John?" John Lox fell to the floor and looked up at Merlin, tears rolled down his bloody face. "We lost him Len, I lost my brothers boy, I have broken my sister's heart, how the hell can I tell her?" He dropped his head and wept.

Rune sat bolt upright in bed and screamed, Jess grabbed her and pulled her close and hugged her. Rune pushed her face into Jess's shoulder, and wept as Jess held her and cried with her. Alice sat with her head down and trembled as she wept along with them. Rune cried for over an hour, and soon she was so exhausted that she went quiet and just shook as Jess hung on to her as if her life depended on it. Rune looked into the eyes of a broken hearted mother. Her hazel eyes that had always been so bright and sparkled were dull; she had heavy black bags under her red swollen eyes. Rune's voice was quiet and strained. "How long?"

Jess looked hopeless as the tears streamed back into her eyes. "A week, I am so sorry sweetheart." She shook her head. "Rowan and Jade came back today...

nothing." She started to shake and put her head down.

Rune looked at Alice across the room. "HE IS NOT DEAD! I would know, I cannot sense him or find him, but he is not dead. Hearne would bring him to me if he was." Jess pulled back and looked at Rune. Rune looked at her and shook her head. "He is not with the Lord of the wood I have checked, if he had died, he would be, he deserved the highest seat in Hearne's house and it is still empty."

Rune pulled the sheets off the bed, and slipped her legs out, but Jess grabbed her. "Rune it has been over a week and Rowan and Jade who are the best in Loxley have not found him, you have to listen and accept the facts." Her voice dropped to almost a whisper. "Rune he is gone."

Her eyes blazed violet as she flew from the bed. "HE IS NOT DEAD!" She began to cry again and her lip trembled. "He is my life, my Robbie, he is all I will ever be in this world, he is lost Jess, and I am the only one who can find him."

Alice sobbed loud and painful sobs from the chair as her shoulders shook. Jess could not look at her, she wanted so much to believe that Rune was right, but how could she be? "Rowan could not find a trace of him Rune."

Rune pulled her pants on to her legs and slid her feet in her boots. "Rowan is not the best, Robbie is, and I know Robbie, he is alive and I will find him." Rune slid on her top and grabbed her cloak.

Jess jumped up and tried to grab her. "Rune please, you are not strong enough, please wait and let us help you."

With a flash of blue eyes and a flick of long red hair, she stormed out of the room and slammed the door. Jess fell to the bed as Alice slid from her chair and put her arms around Jess. "I am so sorry." Jess hugged Alice who wept and sobbed into Jess's arms. "It is all my fault, if he had not come to get me, he would still be alive."

Jess squeezed hard on Alice. "That is not true and you know it." She pushed her head into Alice and wept with her.

It was raining hard as Rune pulled Robbie's horse out of the barn. She jumped up on to it, and turned the horse into the lane. It clattered up past the cottages and pounded along the Sacred Wood Road, Rune drove the horse on, its hooves splashing through the puddles, and her hair flowed behind her soaking wet, her blue eyes burned as she felt the panic inside her. The rain blasted into her face and mixed with her tears.

The horse charged into the trees and she wove with skill and speed through to the centre and the glade of Robbie's Mere. Rune dropped the reins and sprang from the horse, a week was too long, why had her grandfather wasted such precious time. She strolled quickly into the centre of the glade and her eyes burned brightly.

"Hear me My Lord."

"Runestone I am with you, and I hear you, my child."

The old man of the woods walked from the trees, and smiled kindly at her. "You have grown more powerful than even you realise now Runestone child of my realm." Rune fell to her knees and started to weep.

"Tell me father of my realm that he is not with you." The old man smiled and touched her wet hair; butterflies flew up into the air, and hovered around her, and the heavy rain ceased. Rune trembled with grief as he gave a sad look at her.

"He would sit at my side and relieve my years of quiet, there is no talk in my house Runestone you know this." She looked into the kind old face of the earth and creation and she sobbed a smile.

"I cannot see him father, where is he? Tell me you know he has life?" Hearne creaked like old bark as he lowered himself to her face; her eyes shone with hope and flicked from purple to blue. His face that had a beard like a prairie and skin like damp leaves smiled, he lifted his hand to her face and she leaned on it, desperate for some comfort from the pain that tore inside her.

"He has life, you are life, and you know where life can exist. My realm is creation and death and he walks in neither, although his seat is prepared if you cannot find him. That land is filled with stones that can hide our kind; you know this Runestone. You know how to overcome this put away your grief and use the power you hold."

Her head dropped. "Oh, Father please I beg you guide me as Opal has."

"Runestone Sapphire, Opal had seen this and she has already told you what to do, use the power that is made between you. You are now the child of nature, more powerful than Opal and yet you do not use the thing that binds you. Remember my daughter what your life holds dear." Hearne groaned as he raised himself up again. "Think daughter, bring calm to the world and use your true power."

Hearne turned and walked back into the trees, as she wept violets on to the grass. She fell to the grass as the pain in her heart increased, it was so bad she thought she would die, and she lay shaking and weeping for hours. The sun was beginning to sink as Rune sat looking over the Mere, the rain had ceased and the bright red rays of the sun flooded the water and reflected off her hair. She rested her head on her knees, and she felt hollow and alone and cold. "Oh Robbie, please come back to me, I cannot live without you. I am not Rune; I am not anything without you. Oh Robbie, I love you so much do not leave me." She began to weep again.

The water of the mere turned suddenly violet. "You two have a power not known to man or wizards; I should like to study it." Rune jumped up and looked around, it was the voice of her grandfather, but it was a memory not him. She thought of the conversation with her grandfather at the house of good hope.

"Power between us?" Her voice was almost a whisper as she strained her mind thinking of the words of her grandfather. A small faint smile painted her lips as she looked up at the mere

She lifted her arms into the air. "I love him and he loves me... Oh Robbie, I love you, where are you?" The Mere turned a deeper violet. Then she saw a small glimmer in the back of her mind. The light grew to a picture in her head; she sat with Opal in the glade at Caerleon. Opal looked down with tears in her eyes. "My dear sweet Runestone, I have seen them and they are truly blessed."

Rune suddenly breathed in as she remembered her grandmother. "My children... she has seen them, and yet I have none. Oh Gods, of the world he is alive and I have to find him, we have children." Her eyes sparkled and her smile grew. "Robbie where are you we have children, they are the future, they are the power between us, it's our love."

A violet light glowed in the woods behind her; Rune turned and fell to her knees, as a small girl skipped into view. She wore a lilac hooded cloak over her lilac gown and a sliver lion twinkled round her neck. Rune gasped, as the small girl skipped towards her, and she trembled as the little girl came up in front of her.

Rune gently lifted her shaking hands, and taking hold of the top, she slipped the hood back. Her eyes filled with tears and she gasped, and then smiled at the sweet face. "Oh, you look so like your daddy my angel." Rune pulled her close and hugged her, as she wept for joy knowing that he could only be alive and lost to her. "Oh my darling, my child thank you." Rune squeezed her tight and shook as the joy and pain in her heart mixed.

The long brown hair shone with streaks of red and gold, her violet eyes sparkled in a way only Robbie's could, and she smiled as Rune kissed her. The small girl and child of Robbie's, pushed forward her small hand to Rune, and she smiled as she took her mother's hand in hers.

"Daddy needs you Mummy."

CHAPTER SEVENTEEN

RIVER TO DARKNESS AND CRYSTAL

Saff hit the water at horrendous pace, it was a very long drop and the water was freezing. She clenched her teeth under the fast flowing water, as her eyes burned bright blue lighting her way. She was light and slender and the water tugged and pushed at her like hundreds of hands, she came to the surface and broke through. The gasp of precious air was long and drawn as she swallowed as much as possible. She looked left and right as she thrashed against the current to steady herself, the cliffs on both sides of her were moving rapidly as it dragged her like a small stick, at high speed down the canyon away from the fallen bridge.

Her arms beat through the current, as she had to push with all her might against the power of the water, kicking her legs as fast as she could just to maintain her place. Saff worked her way to the side where the current was not as fast, gasping and getting tired she looked along the long high cliff wall, and felt a panic starting to rise as she desperately looked from left to right. She took a deep breath and plunged below the water, her blue eyes glowing to give her a little more light.

Her hair wafted around her, as the current pulled at it. In the dim water below the rocks, a figure was face down on the bottom snagged on a rock, Saff pushed her feet on the edge of the wall, and kicked as hard as she could holding the air tight inside her. The current was strong and she fought with all her strength to pull herself down to the dim figure.

She stretched out her long white arm, kicking with all her might, as she reached for the figure, she grabbed and pulled, and the figure rolled up to her face. Panic flooded through her with fear, as the burned grotesque face almost touched hers, the shock made her gasp as she recoiled breathing out, and bubbles burst out of her mouth as she shot to the surface.

Her head came through the surface and she coughed and choked for air trying to cough up the water in her lungs. Her eyes streamed with tears as she fought to calm herself, and shivered as the cold took hold of her. She looked into the water and the body of the burned soldier as it swept away in the fast lower current. She took several long slow breaths as she calmed down, and then dived back under; she kicked her feet and paddled her arms to steady herself, as she scanned around the bottom of the deep water. Her breath was fighting in her lungs and she headed back up to the surface. It was then that she saw a glint of gold.

Saff's head exploded out of the water as she desperately gasped a huge drawing mouth full of air. She swallowed and breathed out as she kicked and thrashed in the current to keep her position. She looked across the fast flowing river at the gently bobbing wet red arrow feather, an energy she did not know she had, began to burn in her now numb skin. The glint of gold had been Robbie's sword handle.

She plunged forward going under the surface with every ounce of energy she could muster, she stroked into the fast flowing current of the river centre. She came above the surface dragging in air to her lungs as she heaved back against the current, her eyes now fixed on the red feathers of hope.

Robbie lay face down wedged against a rock. Desperately she stroked faster and harder to pull her from the icy hands of the water that tugged and heaved at her, as she fought the current. Her white hand extended, thin and pale out of the water and she grabbed his cloak that flowed on the surface, rippling in the current as it would in the wind.

Her heart beat faster as she dragged herself toward him clawing her way along his cloak. Gasping and panting with the effort, she reached his shoulder, he rolled over with her weight and the long red arrow hit her in the face snapping. Tears welled into her burning, smarting eye, and as he rolled over, he broke free of the rock. Saff snatched wildly and he bumped into her arms.

She held him tight and breathed a sigh of relief, as the current took hold, and she was whipped backwards in the fast flowing, forceful current. She put her head on his shoulder and lifted his face from the water. "I got you." She gasped with exhausted lungs.

For a few moments, she just clung to him, the symbol of all hope, and the symbol of hers. She shook with fear and the biting cold of the water and breathed the air of life into her lungs, as they sped backwards down the canyon. The air flowing into her lungs cleared her head and she started to think. "I am the Rune of one line," she muttered to herself. "Rune has the power of nature, I have powers I have never used, I must find them I must call Rune."

At that very moment, high up river a force of pain and destruction was unleashed in one deafening and almighty scream of anguish. Sapphire connected to Rune and the pain of grief Rune felt flowed into her. It was overwhelming as the whole river turned violet; Sapphire's scream of, "NO!" was unheard, and drowned out by Rune's. Her whole body exploded in bright violet light as it pulsed in a force that overcame her completely. Sapphire was exhausted and unable to control it, and like a moth in a ball of flame, it consumed her and flowed out into Robbie.

Robbie coughed hard and water retched, and choked out of his mouth as he took a long suffocated gasp and life reentered him. He felt the warmth of another life and kicked out. Sapphire still clinging to him, hung limp on his shoulder. The whole canyon seemed to rumble and shake as he kicked in the water, and tried to push himself and Sapphire to the side.

They floated into a shallow high above the steep falls, and Robbie clawed at the bottom to pull them close to the bank. The earth was shaking violently as with his last strength and one working arm, Robbie dragged them both into the open mouth of a small cave and a floor of dry sand.

He pulled at Saff's hands bending her fingers to release himself as he coughed and spluttered the last remnants of water out of his lungs. He was tired and exhausted, his head pounded from the large bruise on his brow that had blackened from each passing second, since he had hit the rocks at the bottom of the river.

Robbie rolled over and looked at the pale soaked figure of Saff. Her auburn hair was matted across her wet face, her chest moved very slowly and he breathed with relief. The ground shook and pitched; rocks fell from the roof and splashed around them into the water.

He pushed himself to his knees; he was weak from the loss of blood from his wound and his head, which now dripped into the sand all round him. Lifting his head made him dizzy and he swayed, he grabbed Saff's hand and on his knees with his right arm dragging limp on the sand, he pulled her out of the water and on to the bank. The floor still moved and shook and the river outside splashed as large rocks fell into it. A strong sense of urgency rose in him and he summand every last bit of strength he had, in one almighty heave, he shakily rose to his feet and dragged the limp body of Saff out of the water as he staggered gritting his teeth up to the back wall of the cave.

Robbie swayed as he looked down at her, and then at the cave opening and the rocks spilling down into the river. The floor gave an almighty lurch and his legs buckled; he fell backwards on to the rocks with force banging his head. His scream of pain was over powering as the arrowhead came through the front of his shirt, he hit the sand in a faint as the cave mouth collapsed, and everything went black.

"Rowan... There, what is that? No over to your left. "
He waded through the deep water holding the branch, and plunged his hand down into the icy torrent and gripped the mass of swirling brown hair. He pulled back with huge effort. The body floated up and the blackened burned slimy face rolled over. Rowan shuddered and let go with a retch, the current dragged the body off downstream.

The gleam of hope left Jade's eyes as she sat on the rock, Rowan waded back through the waist high water towards her. He stroked her hair and she pulled him close as the tears welled into her eyes. He lifted her up into his dripping arms and held her tight as the quiet muffled sobs leaked from his shoulder.

It had been three days and the sense of hopelessness had grown stronger with each passing minute. His chest felt tight and he gulped back the strong surge of emotion inside him. His eyes ran up and down the water edge, none of it made sense, they had searched a long four mile stretch and found nothing, now in calmer waters most of the dead soldiers were washing up on to the banks, Robbie and Saff were not here.

Jade slid her head up, and he looked down at her pale dirty face and darkened eyes. He smiled at her, but she had lost her ability to do the thing that she had always been able to do. "What now Rowan?"

He gave a long sigh and looked back up stream. "We have missed something; we go back and search again until we find him." She snuggled into him and he squeezed her tight. "Come on let's get started." She slipped off the rock, and tired and weary they began to climb back up the edges of the rock face.

Saff sat bolt upright, her head spun, and she saw little silver specks flashing in front of her eyes. She bought her hand slowly up in the darkness and rubbed the side of her face. It felt tender and sore and her eye hurt. "Ouch!" She pulled her finger back quickly.

She had no idea where she was, and peered round in the darkness, a pale thin shaft of light crossed the cave as a single beam, and she heard the water softly lapping through the stones. The rumble of the river seemed dull though the thick wall of fallen rock that had sealed the cave tight. Saff looked up and her eyes glowed blue, the ceiling sparkled with a coating of crystallized rock, it was dark and glinted like onyx.

The light reflected around the cave and she saw the mass that was Robbie, dull in the darkness. She moved towards him and moaned, she felt utterly weak and spent, and her whole body ached in an overwhelming pain. It was hard and tiring just to cross the few feet that separated them. She collapsed at his side, and stared at his bruised and bloody face. Beads of sweat burned on his forehead as the fever took him, his eyelids flickered and she knew he was delirious and gripped with a fever. The arrowhead stuck out of his shoulder surrounded by thick yellow mucus, the wound was infected and poisoning his system, the arrow had to come out or it would kill him. Robbie murmured as she touched his face. "Rune?"

She leaned closely over him. "I am here Robbie." He mumbled but she could not hear him. She placed her hand on the arrow and leaned across him; her eyes glowed bright blue and she lowered her lips to his and kissed him. She pulled sharply and the arrow came free, his body jumped and she pulled her lips away.

"I love you Rune." He slid back into his dark sleep, and Saff sat up and shone her eyes on his wound.

She pulled out her dagger as she sat at his side in the dark, and felt for her cloak. She cut long strips away and then crawled to the water; she wet the strips and made her way slowly back. Her head pounded inside her skull, using her power to illuminate her eyes was draining her strength rapidly, and she trembled with the weak hollow feeling that grew inside her.

Flashing her eyes as Ruby did, she carefully cleaned away the puss on his wound, and packed it with dry clean strips of dressing. Her hands shook and when she had finished, she slid to the floor and lay on her back staring at the ceiling, as her mind wandered and she drifted back into unconsciousness.

It was five days later when Rowan and Jade appeared back at the rope bridge, their faces were white and dirty and their eyes had black rings round them. They walked with dirty hair and dirty clothes, and an air of overwhelming sadness around them. Merlin looked sadly up at their dejected and depressed faces.

Rowan shook his head as he approached.

Merlin rose from his seat on the rock. "I have lived for thousands of years, and yet nothing has puzzled me more than this. He has not entered the other realm, and yet he appears not to be in this one either, I will not leave here until this puzzle is solved. You two are exhausted, go back and comfort my precious granddaughter, tell her I will find him, I will not deprive her of the life she chose."

Merlin raised his hands and the white orb appeared. "Go in peace, and wait for my arrival." Hand in hand with their heads down Rowan and Jade walked into the tunnel of light. Just a few short steps away they walked into the yard in front of the barn, and the cut bruised face of John Lox. There was no need for words as his pleading eyes spoke volumes as they met Rowan's and seemed to die. He pulled his arm around the two of them as Jade burst into deep heavy sobs, and shook in his arms as she wailed her grief out into him.

Saff sat with her back to the cave wall; Robbie's head rested on her lap. In the long dark hours her mind wandered, as she tried to talk to Rune but could not get through to her. She had not eaten or drank in five days as she had sat alone and lost to the darkness, and now she sat stroking Robbie's hair deliriously seeing Rune walk around the edge of the water towards her.

Saff smiled. "Rune I have been trying to call you, why have you not answered?" Rune raised a finger to her lips, and Saff smiled. "Sorry, I forgot he is sleeping." She turned and looked down in the dark at the swollen burning face of Robbie.

Rune put her hand inside her cloak and withdrew a long bar of purple stone. It glowed and lit the cave sending beams dancing off the crystal ceiling and walls. She placed the bar on Robbie's wound and it began to pulsate, she lifted his dead hand

and rested it on top of the stone and a lilac light flowed through his hand. Slipping her hand into her cloak, she withdrew a second bar of purple glowing stone, and laid it on Robbie's forehead and then took Saff's hand and placed it on top of the stone. Saff's eyes glowed blue as she chuckled. "This light makes your hair look brown Rune." The face of Rune turned and smiled at her. "I am not Rune; she is coming though." Saff blinked.

"Who are you?" She smiled and patted her hand.

"We will meet again when the time is right." Saff watched as the small figure bent down and kissed Robbie on the cheek, he stirred in his haunted sleep. "Iona?"

The small figure walked slowly around the edge of the water and faded away, the cave glowed violet and Saff was happy to have light around her. She was so tired and her eyes slowly closed, as she slipped for the hundredth time into darkness. Robbie burned and trembled on the floor beside her, she was so exhausted and she was starting to give up. Her eyes opened and she stared into the pale lilac light of the cave, the water continued the dull rumble behind the rocks and she gasped a small cry, no tears seemed to come, as she seemed to have used them all. "Oh help me; I don't want to die here." Her voice was dragged up from a dry worn throat, and it hardly made a sound in the dark cave, her eyes closed and she leaned back onto the wall.

She smiled as she took her mother's hand. "Daddy needs you Mummy."

Rune stood up the tears streaming from her eyes as the small girl pulled her gently across the glade and towards the trees. She slid her hand inside her cloak and pulled out a glowing bar of violet stone, she placed it on the ground. She turned and slipped another out, lying it down on the grass. She passed the third to Rune who crouched and laid it down creating a three-pointed star.

Her daughter took her hands and formed a circle with her mother. Violet light streamed up from the stones and surrounded them. Rune felt a strange ticklish sort of feeling and giggled. Her daughter smiled and again she saw her father in her. The light flooded around them and she swayed.

Rune felt the pressure on her feet, and the light flowed back to the floor and it became dark, water lapped in the pale glow of violet, and as she peered around and her heart burst. "ROBBIE!" She raced across the cave, and fell to her knees, tears streaming from her eyes as she pulled him up into her chest and wept. She looked down at his black and swollen face covered in dark matted blood and she kissed him as her tears dripped on to him. He barely moved and he was burning up, his energy was gone and his life force was failing. Rune held him tightly and wept into his neck; a small hand touched her hair. "Hey Rune, are you real this time or is this just another dream?"

Rune looked up into the eyes of Saff, she had not even noticed her, she had been so focused on Robbie; Rune smiled and stroked Saff's face, Saff smiled. "I am real Saff, you are not dreaming. You saved my Robbie I have not the words to thank you."

Saff burst into tears. "I was so frightened, I thought we would die here alone Rune." She found her tears, which flowed as Rune pulled her forward and kissed her cheek softly and hugged her. Saff put her arms around her and gasped a huge heavy sob. "Can I go home now? I miss my mum and Keith." Her tears dripped on to Robbie as Rune pulled away.

"I have no idea where we are Saff, do you know?"

"But you are here Rune, how can you not know?" Rune looked around the empty cave, her small daughter had gone, and she felt a tug at her heart. She looked down at Robbie who trembled as he burned, time was running out; she closed her eyes and focused.

"Grandfather hear me." No response came. *"Grandfather I have found Robbie. HEAR ME!"*

There was a slight rumble and a stone fell into the water, as a flash of white light flowed into the cave. The beam hit the crystal and the whole cave lit in a dim light. Rune heard the voice of Hearne in her head. "That land is filled with stones that can hide our kind, you know this Runestone."

She looked at the ceiling and the peat coloured crystal that coated it. "Cairngorm stone." Everything fell into place, it was a stone like the Blue John near Loxley, and it was used to make containers to contain items of power. The stone prevented the passage of a force, which was why she could not feel him, that was why he was hidden from her, Rune turned and looked at the fallen stones.

Her eyes glowed a deep purple, and the fallen rocks began to vibrate. Deep rumbling sounded in the floor of the cave and the light flooded in, as the heavy stones exploded out and splashed into the river. Merlin turned sharply and looked back down the valley. "Runestone?"

Saff shaded her eyes from the blinding light as the roar from the water echoed around the cave; Rune could now see the crudely dressed wound and his black swollen face. Fresh air flowed around the cave, Robbie was cold, and he shivered, she opened her cloak and pulled him up wrapping the cloak round him and getting him as close as she could. She placed her hand on the small of his back and her eyes glowed bright purple.

Saff watched, as Rune took her own life force, and flooded it into Robbie. He murmured and moved slightly, he opened one eye and stared up at her, she smiled as she gazed down at him, her bright blue eyes filled with tears. "Hi gorgeous."

His voice was almost a whisper as his throat was so dry. "Hey beau...." Saff sobbed to hear his voice; it was the first clear thing he had said in four days, Rune looked up beaming her smile at Saff.

"Rune hear me."

"I hear you Grandfather; I have found him and I am with him. I need help."

She held him close as her life flowed through him, and back to her in a circle. Rune looked at Saff. "Can you walk?"

Saff nodded, her huge black swollen eye looked nasty in the daylight. "I will try Rune." She slowly rose, and cried with the pain in her legs, she had sat still for a week, and her legs hurt with cramps and bad circulation from her stillness. She wobbled and swayed as she leant back against the wall. Sapphire gasped in pain and cried they hurt so badly, she pressed her palms on the rock wall, and gritted her teeth as she pushed all her weight onto her painful wobbly legs.

Rune stood up and bent over Robbie, she pulled his arm round her neck and slipping the violet stones into his pockets to keep them close to him, she heaved him upwards. He was heavy and did not have the strength to stand. Saff grabbed his other arm, and pulled it around her neck and helped lift him.

The two of them swayed and staggered, as they walked down the sand and into the shallow pool of water. It was slow going, and they waded up to their knees out of the cave. Merlin stood at the top of the cliff wall above them, he lifted his arm and waved, Rune looked up and smiled as he raised his arms, and a circle of white light appeared in front of them. The water roared noisily all around them and they stepped into the light, it lessened and the water disappeared from around their legs.

The sound of the river faded, as the sound of singing birds filled the end of the tunnel, Rune and Sapphire staggered out into the overcast skies of Robbie's Mere, they sank to their knees, as Rowan and Jade ran across the grass towards them. Rowan slid down to his knees and grabbed Robbie out of her arms. He smiled at Rune tears in his eyes; Jade flung herself round him and Rowan. She cried and wailed, as Saff dropped to the grass and lay down, she was exhausted, and lay watching the sky and the clouds float past. She breathed the fresh air thinking she would never see or breathe both again.

Rowan slid the golden box of Carnac out from under his cloak. "Len told us to bring this." He passed it to Rune.

Rune took the box and waved her hand across it. "I am Runestone and heir of Opal, and recipient of gifts from Fae." The box clicked open. Rune lifted the bottle of pink liquid out of the box. "Oh, grandmother you were clever." She placed the box on the grass, and uncorked the small crystal bottle, Rowan leaned the delirious Robbie back and she carefully poured the pink liquid into his mouth.

Robbie swallowed slowly, his lips were cracked and split, and he licked them, she laid him back in her lap, and tore his blood soaked shirt where the arrow had come through, the smell from the wound was foul and they all recoiled. Jade ran to the lake and tore a large piece of her top off and dropped it in the water. She lifted the torn cloth and ran back handing the dripping rag to Rune. She pulled the dressing out of the hole in his shoulder. Robbie twitched and breathed in, the wound was badly infected and seeped a thick slimy dark green puss. Rune carefully wiped the wound as clean as she could, and she looked up at Rowan.

"Use your knife and reopen the wound." He looked horrified; Jade slipped out one of her razor sharp silver daggers. She gently slipped it into the hole in his shoulder, and cut away the brown infected mass and blood flowed to the surface. Robbie jumped and moaned, as Rowan held him down. Rune looked at him. "I need life moss." He nodded and jumped up and ran into the woods. Rune cleaned away the infected scabs, and dead skin, and wiped the blood away. She inspected the wound.

"Jade use my cloak, I need bandages." Jade unfastened her sister's cloak and using her knife to nick the ends she tore long wide strips; Rowan came back with an arm full of green woolly moss and dropped to his knees.

Jade opened the wound, as Rune took the lid off the second bottle. She poured the liquid into the open hole in Robbie's shoulder. Grabbing a large handful of moss, she poured more of the pink liquid on to it, and then pushed it on to the wound. Jade folded a piece of Rune's cloak and she poured a little more of the liquid on to it.

Rune lifted him up and tore the back of his shirt away. Rowan took Robbie's weight and pulled him forward. Rune worked quickly as Jade cut away the infected skin, and Rune cleaned it, applying the liquid, she packed it with moss and held it in place.

Jade held the pads on top of the moss as Rune bound the wound with the wide strips of her cloak. Steam rose from Robbie's wounds and he moaned, Rowan watched in awe at the way Jade and Rune instinctively knew what to do. Rune pulled tight on the bandage and then taking her acorn brooch, she fastened the bandage tightly, and laid him back in her lap. She wiped his black cut and bruised face with the cloth, and then taking a small pad of cloth; she added a few drops of the pink liquid and wiped his face down.

Jade slid under him as Rune moved to look at Saff who still lay exhausted on the floor. Jade sat smiling as she softly stroked his hair back out of his face. Rowan moved round and lifted Saff who was too exhausted to move, and carried her to the water edge. Cradling her in his arms, he scooped a hand full of water up, and poured it into her dry and parched mouth.

Saff smacked and licked her cracked and split lips, as the water revived her mouth, Rowan smiled at her as he poured more, she tried to smile but her mouth hurt. Rune wiped her face; her eye was very swollen and one side of her face was black and bruised. Rune took the pad and poured the last of the pink liquid on to it, she wiped the black area of Saff's face and she winced in pain.

Rune smiled at her. "You are very brave Sapphire; I can never repay your act of selflessness. You followed him into the water knowing you could die with him,

I am forever in your debt, as are my children to come." She lowered herself and kissed her on the cheek.

Saff brought her arm up to Rune. "I thought I would die, and never see the sun again, you owe me nothing Runestone sister." Rune smiled and looked up at the dull sky. Her eyes blazed as she waved her arm across the sky, and the clouds parted and a beam of sunlight fell from the sky and bathed Sapphire in sunlight.

"Look with my blessing and revel in it my sweet sister." Sapphire's eyes filled with tears as she smiled at the sunshine illuminating her.

Rune felt tired as she walked across the grass towards Jade and Robbie. She knelt by his side and looked down on him; she stroked his face tenderly. "Oh Robbie I was so scared I had lost you forever." He muttered as his eyelids moved rapidly.

"Rune... Iona?"

She looked at Jade. "What is Iona?" Jade shrugged.

"Who cares he is alive Rune, you found him and brought him back... I love you Rune." She gave her sister a huge beaming smile, and her tired green eyes shone brightly. Rune leaned forward and hugged Jade.

"I love you too sis, come on let's get him home."

Rune sat on her horse as Rowan lifted Robbie on to the horse, and sat him in front of her. She pulled him close and held him tight, Jade held Saff in her arms and Rowan leapt up on to his horse. They turned slowly and the horses walked into the wood and through the trees.

They trotted down the Sacred Wood Road, and turned towards Lox farm, Rune pulled him close feeling the heat flow into his body, the liquid was working and new strength was growing inside him. They trotted through the farm, and Beth screamed from the greenhouse door and ran to the barn, as Rune rode past and onto hawthorn lane.

She had sent word to her mother and to Jett to let Jess know she was taking Robbie to her house. They galloped down the lane and on to the Village Street, Jess stood with her hands to her mouth by the gate, tears in her eyes as she saw her son on the horse in front of Rune.

She gasped, but smiled and broke into a huge sob, as Robert Lox pulled her close. Rune brought the horse to a halt and Robert and Bear gently lowered him down into their arms. Jess leaned over her son and wept cries of joy and pain; Steph looked up at Rune who looked exhausted.

Rune slid down and into her mother's arms, Steph pulled her close. "I am so happy for you my darling, you did well Rune." Rune held her mum tight feeling safe in her arms. Her head spun she was so tired; she had given a lot of herself to Robbie and now she just wanted to sleep.

Melanie wept as she hugged her daughter, and Saff smiled as she felt her mum hold her. She grinned at Rune as their eyes met and she smiled warmly back. Jaz pulled Saff into a crushing hug, and swept her up in his arms and carried her into the house. Melanie turned and grabbed Rune; she pulled her into a hug and softly spoke. "Thank you Runestone, I had lost all hope." Rune pulled her arms around her.

"She needs rest and love, I think she is in good hands, don't you?" She kissed Mel on the cheek. Rune turned to walk through the gate; Jess stood red eyed watching her, and Rune smiled at her, and Jess pulled her into a hug.

"I am sorry I doubted you, I love him so much Rune I honestly thought he was gone, and I could not bear the thought of it."

Rune hugged her tightly. "I was not sure myself for a minute. Grandfather reckons I destroyed half of Scotland when I lost it." Rune giggled, and Jess leaned back and smiled.

"Len always did exaggerate... but next time, just kick the cat, that's what Robert does." She giggled at Rune and she nodded to the door. Arm in arm they walked in and up the stairs, where Robbie lay in Rune's large soft bed propped up on pillows.

It was late morning when the darkness cleared, and Robbie opened his eyes. He felt the familiar warmth of Rune curled around him, as he looked across the room at Judith who smiled and whispered. "Hi."

His face hurt as he smiled back. "Hey Judy." Alice and Jess had been awake most of the night, and now dozed in two chairs by his side. Robbie smiled as he saw Alice holding her tummy as she slept; Judy slipped off the chair and picked up a glass of water. He lifted a heavily bandaged hand, but his arm hurt like hell, and his hand dropped to the bed. Judy held the glass carefully to his mouth, and the ice cold water felt like nectar as it ran down his hot throat. He gasped as he lay back. "Thanks."

Judith leaned over and kissed his cheek. "Thank you, Robbie, for saving me, I was so frightened, and you caught me." Her eyes filled with tears. "I thought you had died because of me." Robbie lifted his painful arm and touched her face with his bandaged hand.

"Hey don't cry, we all stick together here, and we help each other, you are one of us now Judy. You are safe with us." She lifted her hand and held his in both of hers.

"My dad is a fool to try and hurt you."

Robbie smiled at her. "He will understand one day, I am sure." Judy kissed his hand as Rune moved and moaned in her sleep. "I want to see Saff now I know you are fine I will leave you with your family, can I come back later?"

Robbie smiled. "Call anytime." Judy beamed a smile at him. It was the first time he had really seen her smile, and he thought for a moment he saw a younger Billy with a lot of her mother mixed in. She waved at the door and he waved back. Judy closed the door quietly as Robbie looked down at the mass of red hair spread across his stomach.

He looked at his hands. Both were wrapped tight in white bandages; his hands had burned on the rope and he had not even felt it. He looked across to the end of the bed where he saw himself in the mirror. His left eye was very swollen and almost closed; the whole side of his face was black and blue with heavy bruises. There was a cut on the side of his head, which had been stitched.

Rune moved again and he saw two bright sapphire blue eyes staring at him in amongst the mass of bright red hair. He smiled at her, and the hair moved, he could not see, but he knew she was smiling back at him. He slowly and painfully slid down in the bed towards her, she wiped back her hair as he came close, and she curled around him. Her eyes gazed down into his, and he looked up at the love and joy in her eyes.

"Hey beautiful, I missed you."

She beamed at him. "Hi, I missed you too." Her soft kiss was all he needed to fill him with warmth, she slid her head on his chest and he pulled a stiff arm around her. "Oh, Robbie I thought I had lost you."

"I thought you knew stuff...? I was not going to leave you easily."

He looked into her eyes as she looked up at him. "You were minutes from death when I found you."

"Never a hope, I had you for company all the time I was there, you told me you were coming."

Rune lifted her head and looked at him. "How do you mean? I could not find you Robbie, you were hidden from me."

"I had you as a small child with me Rune. You sat and talked to me and kept me alive with your purple stones. I knew you would come, you just kept telling me to hold on you were coming, so I did."

Rune smiled and lay her head back on his chest, his daughter somehow had been with him, she still was not sure how, but she knew that she had done it. Rune closed her eyes and pictured the face in her mind. She was so delicate and cute; with a white complexion and bright violet pupils in her eyes. Yet her eyes were Robbie's, of that there was no doubt, she had spotted it instantly. Her hair, she grinned to herself, it was his thick wavy mass of brown with some of her red and gold streaks. She was so beautiful and Rune filled with happiness as she lay thinking of the first of her children. "What's Iona Robbie?"

He snuggled up to her and breathed a happy sigh. "Iona... it's an island off Scotland, they call it the isle of violets, Angus was telling me about it... Why?"

"Nothing, I just thought it would be a lovely name for a daughter." Robbie gave her a squeeze.

"Iona... It does have a lovely ring to it, Iona Violet Loxley. Yeah, I like that we should use it." Rune kissed his tummy.

"Hurry up and kill Knox, I really want your baby." She giggled as she felt his stomach rise and fall as he chuckled.

"What's the rush we have a lifetime together?" He slid down a little more and looked at her radiant face. "You have to marry me first, and then help me build the house. Seven bedrooms weren't it. Six pink and one blue?" Rune giggled.

"Make me happy and it could be more, I am nature you know?" Jess sat smiling as she watched the bed covers move and listened to her son and her future daughter.

"More, how happy would that have to be?"

"As happy as I am right now Robbie in the hood." She stretched up and kissed him. "I love you Robbie... don't leave me alone again."

"I love you too, and promise you it will be a long time before I step into water again."

"Oh, I don't know the pool in the forest was quite nice."

"Well yeah Ok, calm pools I can do, but fast rivers are definitely out." He kissed her and she giggled.

"It's a deal... are you hungry?"

"What you got in mind?"

"I thought breakfast in bed for my brave wounded future husband." Rune giggled as he tickled her with the only finger that was not bandaged. She gave a squeal, and crawled up the bed, and popped laughing out of the top of the sheets. "Hi Alice. Hi Jess."

Robbie crawled up slowly and popped his head out and smiled. "Hey Mum, Alice. Sorry we were talking, didn't mean to wake you."

Jess smiled and leaned over and kissed his head. She kissed Rune. "You two remind me of your dad and me when we first met." She smiled. "How about I make you both breakfast while you chat with Alice, the poor girl has waited a week to talk to you."

"A week?" Robbie looked at Alice. She nodded at him and smiled; he looked at Rune, "I thought a couple of days tops." Robbie struggled a bit, as he slid back up the bed; Alice leaned over and helped him sit up. She tenderly lifted him on to the pillows and he smiled as her eyes met his.

Alice's eyes filled with tears, a huge sob rose from her, and he lifted his arm and pulled her close. She nuzzled into his neck. "I thought I had lost you, and it was all my fault, I was so frightened Robbie, I am so sorry at all the trouble I have caused." He pulled his arms slowly round her as he hugged her.

"Alice I am here and intend to stay here, I would have come for you no matter what, I love you. Please don't blame yourself for doing exactly what I know you would have done for me." He held her tight as she sobbed, and Rune leaned over and put her arms round them both, Alice sniffled and felt happy to be close again.

Sapphire looked up from her bed as Keith opened the door; her face broke into a huge smile as he stepped in. He grinned broadly, as he lifted the bunch of wilted daises. "I have been waiting all night; they need a little water I think."

Keith sat on the bed, and she slid her arms around him and he hugged her.

Sapphire, held on to him tightly, for a week she sat alone in the damp and the dark, his face in her thoughts had kept her going. Thinking she would die alone without him had been unbearable. She pulled back her eyes clouding up and as he smiled at her, she kissed him.

There was a long line of visitors who were all told to wait, Jess was fierce in her protection of her son, Steph smiled as yet another member of the crew was told to wait until the evening. She went up to the room with a tray of broth for the two of them; she opened the door quietly and looked down at her heavily bandaged son. He was asleep with Rune curled around him, his shoulder and arm still covered with the thick green strips of Rune's cloak.

Steph wandered in behind her and stood watching them fast asleep, Rune wearing a happy smile in his arms. Steph slid her arm on to the shoulder of Jess. "He is so lucky, her faith in him is absolute, I have to tell you Jess for a moment there I honestly thought we had lost him forever."

"They do have something between them, which is stronger than anything I have ever known before. I always thought Rob and me were close, but these two seem closer than any of us."

Jess quietly placed the tray down and Rune opened her eyes. Jess smiled and nodded to the tray, she whispered quietly. "You should both eat. You need to get your strength back." She turned to Steph and they quietly headed to the door, Rune watched the two relieved parents. "Mum?"

Both Jess and Steph turned. "What?" Steph looked at Rune and then at Jess, the three of them all started to giggle.

It was a busy and very noisy evening in Rune's room. Jade and Jett visited together, and after the tears came the laughter. Blades and Rags accompanied by Judy joined in the fun and Maggs and Harry squeezed in with John and Martin. As they left Bear and Alice, with Skip and Fuse arrived, followed by Maddy and Una. Robbie laughed, and joked, his face now turning a bluey yellow as Opal's potion healed his face.

Rune saw the tiredness in his eyes and slowly escorted all the smiling crew to the door. All of them hugged her and smiled as they left. Robbie sat quietly in his bed. He was becoming drowsy, when the door opened and he looked up. Sapphires deep blue eyes glistened as he smiled. "Hey?"

She swept to the bed and threw her arms around him, her long auburn hair splayed across her shoulders and back. He held her tight as she wept. "Hey why are you crying, you saved me remember?" She sat up smiling; her eye was black and very swollen; Robbie softly stroked the side of her face. "Thanks Sapphire, you showed courage I would never have thought you had, and I am very grateful."

She gave him a huge smile. "I think we saved each other. Oh, that place was horrible; I don't think I will ever swim again." He chuckled.

"No, I must admit I will think twice in future." Robbie had not really talked to her before, and as Rune joined them, they talked together quietly for many hours, the sun had set by the time they finished and Saff waved good bye from the door, and closed it quietly behind her.

The following day Robbie and Rune slept until midmorning, they ate a good breakfast and Robbie wanted to get up, he had more colour in his face, and he had just spent the week lay down in a damp cave. His whole body ached and he felt like moving around.

Rune helped him dress and made him a sling for his arm out of the rest of her cloak. He wore some of the new clothes she had made him before leaving, dressed in a very casual lordly style he walked slowly up the village street with Rune attentively on his arm. Many stopped to say hello and wish him well, and he enjoyed being home, and talking to the people he had known all his life. Alf Smith gave him a huge steak, telling him it would give him strength. Alice and Anne handed him a bag of his favourite scones.

It was a happy day, and Rune beamed as she walked along at his side. Her own heart had recovered, and she was starting to relax a little, after the shock of almost losing him. As the afternoon wore on, Robbie sat in the yard of Rune's front whilst Jade and she sorted out the rails of goods. Skip sat with Robbie and brought him up to date with the Loxley plans.

The army of woodsmen now had reached the level of over twenty thousand as more and more sought refuge. The black stonewall now stretched down and met with Devon, more raids had been carried out on Bristol, but the strength of the army there now was so vast that Caerleon had repelled Knox once again.

Loxley was now the centre of the woodsman campaign and fast becoming the centre of the country, it was widely accepted as the new capital as the country changed forever. Angus had been taken back to meet his sister and his best friend, and now Skip was waiting for him to arrive back with news of the north.

More Cutter attacks were taking place and Skip had strengthened the border patrols, Robbie was greatly relieved to hear Skip tell him that he also based forty woodsmen around the house of good hope. Loxley had grown fast, and now had over a thousand new families living within the stockade. Most of them were bowmen with wood skills, so Loxley was now stronger than ever before.

Refugees were being placed all the way up the west of the country and York was now acting as a placing agency, working with Carlisle to ensure that all small towns were scouted out and protected. Robbie was pleased to find his new rule of protecting small communities was now law and in place. Skip had added the extra provision of making sure each town had an extra number of men. He informed Robbie that in his mind, it gave everyone a sense of pride knowing they were playing their part in the war effort.

Robbie slid into bed early that night, he was tired after his day, and Rune slipped in beside him and cuddled him. He kissed her softly as she settled down and lay back. "The world is changing fast Rune."

She looked up and her bright blue eyes shone at him. He looked into them and smiled, he loved her so much, and almost losing her was now starting to have an impact, as the memory of his fall and her fading as he hit the water replayed in his mind. "I want to stay here for a while, and get to grips with everything, before planning anything else; I know we need to find the heir but I am not ready."

"You must follow your instincts, Rob." She kissed his chest and slid close.

"I need to find Billy, I need to settle with him Rune, if I don't Alice will never be safe."

Rune lifted her head and stared at him. "Robbie you cannot be serious?"

He leaned forward as she sat up, and he pulled her close. "There is still unfinished business between us Rune, I want an end to it before I seat a king, he is the heir to Mason, killing Mason will not end this. I have to find him and try to stop him, I need to rest and prepare, and then I will hunt him down."

CHAPTER EIGHTEEN

THE TABLE OF RUNESTONE

Robbie lay awake watching Rune sleep. Somehow in the night she had woven around him, and he looked at the way she had managed to twist under his leg and across his stomach. Her left arm was under his shoulder and her head on his chest with her right arm holding him just under his left arm.

Her soft white skin was warm against him and he stroked her long red hair back, and watched her pale freckled face, as she slept with a small smile. She had taken off most of her bangles, which he could see on a small silver tree on the dresser hanging from each branch. He touched her pale white shoulder and stroked the soft smooth skin.

She was so beautiful and he loved her more than he could possibly say, Rune to him was life, his life. She stirred in her sleep and moved her arm, bringing it on to his stomach, her eyes sleepily opened and he saw the bright blue of them flash as she looked around. She gave a little moan as she slid round and came up to meet his face; her eyes twinkled as she smiled and kissed him, he pulled his arms around her and hugged her. "Good sleep?"

She nuzzled on to his good shoulder and softly kissed his neck. "Yeah, I cannot believe how tired I have been." She sat up on his lap and smiled as she looked at him.

"You look a lot better this morning, the swelling has almost gone, and your bruises are starting to fade, that stuff of Opals has really worked well."

He watched her as she smiled at him, her long red hair glistened as it fell down in front of her, he leaned forward and kissed her softly on the neck, it tickled and she giggled. "I do feel a lot stronger this morning," He smiled and she gave him a knowing smile.

It was a lot later when they appeared down stairs. Robbie sat at the table as Rune made them something to eat; he slowly sipped his coffee as he thought. Rune dropped beside him and passed him a plate. "Oh, that's made me hungry." She sliced her eggs and began to eat. Robbie lifted some toast as he stared across the room. Rune watched him as she ate. "Still thinking about going after Billy?"

He dipped his toast in his egg and chewed it. "Everything seems to start and end with him Rune, he brought pain here to Loxley, and now twice he has tried to snatch Alice. If she has his child, she will never be safe from him, I have to face him and if I have to, kill him. I have no other choice if I want to protect her."

Rune took his hand in hers. "Just don't think you are alone in this Rob, and promise me you will not face him alone." She squeezed his hand as she looked at him. Rune looked at her wrist and then back to his bandaged hand. "Do you know what Gwendolyn means?"

He looked round as she undid the bandage on his hand, she gave him a sweet smile. "What has that got to do with Billy?"

His hand was red but had healed very well; Alice had done a great job. Rune slid the fine pure white bangle off her wrist; it glinted in the sunlight, and seemed to have a bluish sparkle to it. She held it up to him so he could see it. "This belonged to Gwendolyn, her name means white circle." She lifted his hand and rubbed the ring with the multi-coloured star on it. "Our circles are all set within a white circle; it bonds us together in a power that she created. Once joined it protects forever and allows me to stay close." She slid the white bangle on to his wrist. "She gave me this the night I met Maddy."

"Hear me Robert of Loxley."

Her eyes, flickered lilac. Robbie jumped as Rune's voice sounded in his head. "How did you do that?"

"Do not speak, think of me and then think of what you want to say to me."

"This is weird, how the hell can I talk with my head?"

"Obviously with great ease." Robbie blinked. *"You heard that?"*

She smiled at him, *"You are joined to me now Robbie, I will never lose you again, I could not bear it, I will hear you wherever you are."*

Rune leaned over and kissed him. *"Let's go back to bed."* He grinned at her.

Ⅰt was several hours later when Alice appeared and tapped on the door. She slipped it quietly open and peered in. both of them was fast asleep, she came in to the room quietly and sat softly on to the bed. Alice smiled as she looked at her two best friends snuggled together; she examined the bruises on his face and gave a satisfied look. She gently lifted Robbie's left hand. She undid the bandage and looked at the burnt and blistered skin; it was almost smooth and healing very fast. Alice turned to look at his shoulder, and noticed Rune's eyes were open and watching, she smiled at her and whispered. "Sorry you both looked so happy and peaceful; I was trying not to wake you."

Rune smiled at her. "He is getting a lot stronger now." Alice grinned at her.

"You should give him more time, don't wear him out too quick Rune." Rune giggled

"How is the baby doing Alice?" Her stomach showed a little under her top.

"Fine, I am quite lucky at the moment, just a little back ache." She leaned over to Rune and giggled. "I love bigger boobs, but I must admit they are as sore as hell at the moment." She looked back at Robbie. "I need to see his shoulder; this dressing will have to be changed."

Rune reached up and softly kissed him. He opened his eyes and saw two big bright blue pupils looking at him, they sparkled with life, and he smiled. "Hey beautiful," they twinkled as she smiled.

"Hi gorgeous... Alice has come to change your dressing." She kissed him slowly.

"Oh God that is not fair, no one has ever woken me up like that. Do you two practice at making us all seem like we have sad lives?"

Rune giggled as Robbie leaned forward, and Alice undid the pin at the top of his shoulder. She pulled the bandages slowly round and rolled them up as she pulled them gently off him. Alice pulled the pad with the life moss off the wound. "Well, that looks a lot better than I expected."

Rune gasped. "Hey look at the way it is forming a scar, it looks like a runic R" The two knife marks made by Jade with her blade as she cleaned his wound moved out from the hole, one straight down and one angled. It did look uncannily like the letter.

The hole had sealed and was clean and infection free, the liquid given him by Opal had completely cleaned and healed it, Alice looked at his back where the arrow had entered; once again, it was clean and healing perfectly. "I wish I had a few large jars of that stuff; it is fantastic."

Robbie looked down at his shoulder, which was still very stiff; he could see the white scar surrounded by soft red flesh, Rune noticed his face. "What is it Rob?"

He shook his head. "Nothing really." He looked into her bright sapphire blue eyes. "What if I can't shoot anymore?" Alice prodded gently around the scar with her finger.

"Can you feel that?" He Jumped. "Well then that means there is no nerve damage, give it a week and I will take you on, on the range." She gave him a big smile and kissed him on the cheek, Rune smiled at the look of relief on his face.

The afternoon moved slowly on, recovery was becoming boring and Robbie wanted to do something. He sat in the front yard in the sun as he looked at a book he found in his bag. Sister Mary had written the word 'Tolerance' just inside the sleeve.

Rune sat on the wall and passed him a drink. "What you reading?"

He opened the cover and she looked. "I think Sister Mary left it in my bag, there was a marker in it so I thought I would read it."

"Isn't that a Christian book?"

Robbie looked at her odd look at him and he smiled. "This little story here is actually quite good, and I have thought a lot about it." Rune looked at him in an even stranger way.

"You are not thinking of becoming one, are you?" He started to laugh at her.

"Rune I am just reading this one story about a man called a Samaritan who helps a stranger who has been badly hurt. It is interesting because the men of the church walk past him and refuse to help him, This Samaritan is supposed to be this man's enemy, yet he helps him. I think this Samaritan guy is actually quite cool."

Rune relaxed. "Oh, that's alright then." She turned as Melissa Patterdale walked into the yard, Rune smiled and slipped off the wall as Melissa smiled at Robbie.

"Hi Rob." He glanced up at the tall blonde haired girl, from the cheese shop.

"Hey Milly." He looked back down at his book. Melissa's face dropped and she turned to Rune. "My Gran sent me for her new shawl." She seemed quite abrupt. Rune gave her a smile and walked in through the door. Melissa watched Robbie read. "How are you feeling Robbie?"

He gave her a smile. "I am fine thanks, got the best care in Loxley. Rune is keeping an eye on me." She gave him a weak smile. Rune came out with a neatly wrapped package, Melissa slapped the two silver coins into her hand, snatched the package and walked out through the gate.

Rune watched her walk down the street back to the cheese shop. "You know Robbie I will never understand that girl... No matter how nice I am to her, I just feel she hates me and I am so positive I have never done anything to offend her." Robbie smiled at her.

"It's not you, it's me." Rune turned to him.

"Why what have you done to upset her so much?" Robbie began to chuckle as Rune looked at him completely confused.

"I asked you to go out with me and not her." Rune looked back at the cheese shop, and then back to Robbie.

"Is that all? I thought I had done something really awful to upset her." She looked positively angry.

"Well technically you have, you have convinced me I belong in your bed... which in my own defence, I would like to say I am glad you can be so persuasive." He gave her a big grin.

Her eyes sparkled. "You can be so naughty at times Robert Lox." She beamed as she crossed the yard and bent down and kissed him. "I will send Jade for the cheese in future." He chuckled as she giggled and slipped on to his knee.

Rune closed the shop early as Robbie was getting fidgety, they decided to walk up to the farm, and with their arms around each other they talked and laughed as they walked. Agatha Patterdale leaned on the wall talking to Alice and Anne Kirk as they came out of the yard of Rune's house laughing. Rune reached up and kissed him and she smiled.

Agatha nodded to Alice. "She looks more radiant each time I see her, just look at them they are such a beautiful couple." Robbie tickled her, his eyes never leaving her, and she squealed and he laughed. Alice smiled.

"He has stood in my yard for years watching her you know; we use to laugh about it didn't we Anne?" Anne gave a huge smile and nodded. "I am so glad he asked her out, I have never seen a happier man." Melissa jumped up out of her chair and stormed in slamming the door, the three old women all smiled.

Rune and Robbie waved. "Afternoon ladies." All three of them gave the happy couple a huge smile, and all waved back. Arm in arm Robbie and Rune walked up the street. Alice leaned in close to the other two.

"Little Alice says she has never known such love as they have, she said he has asked her to marry him already, wants to build her a house in the woods he does."

Agatha looked impressed. "It is a bit soon isn't it, they have only been dating for a few months, and mind you she does not look pregnant." Alice gasped.

"Oh, Agatha you cannot blame little Alice for her predicament, that Billy was a proper rogue he was. Alice is a sweet girl; he took advantage he did."

Agatha seemed to rise a little as she looked round. "She is not stupid that Alice, just didn't keep her legs closed, I see she has another one on a string already, that big posh one from York is what I hear."

Alice Kirk was fascinated; she had heard nothing about this. "What the one who looks like a pirate?" Agatha nodded.

"The very same. He is staying in her house you know; I am surprised at John Lox; I would have thought he knew better." Agatha looked stern as Anne gave a little titter.

"Well, the damage is done really, isn't it? It is not as if she could get herself in any more trouble. I am surprised to hear that though, she does not seem the type, now that Jade she is a wild one, I am surprised she has not had a few by now."

Agatha looked at the others. "She is engaged you know?"

Alice gasped. "Never, who too?" Agatha was feeling incredibly happy at having now found out two things more than the sisters had. "That tall quiet scruffy one, they say he is the lords top man, which explains it really. You know keep all the top jobs in the family and all that."

Alice smiled. "I served him this morning; Rowan I think she called him. I must admit he is very polite and well mannered; you can tell he is an educated man."

Alice giggled; "He is very good looking as well." Agatha scowled.

"There must be something wrong with him though, he has after all asked her to marry him, and he won't have an easy time with that one, she has always been trouble."

Anne felt a little sad for Jade, after all Jade had actually always been polite to her. "I think the girl looks very happy; she has never really fitted in here, maybe this is the man for her." Alice nodded at her sister; Jade was always nice to them both. "She will have to become a woman one day; it would be nice to see her in a dress, instead of those boots and pants, and her dad's old shirts."

Agatha frowned. "We will see. I won't be surprised if all ends in tears."

Rags beamed as Robbie and Rune walked into the little office. "Hey Robbie, I was gonna come and see you, hi Rune, come on back and see me place, you have not seen it properly yet." Rags beamed as she lifted the hatch and pushed open the back door through to her little home.

Rune smiled as she looked around. "Rags this is really nice, I think it's wonderful."

"Yeah, Jess is just the coolest, Lucy and me love it, we never really had a home of our own." Rags looked serious for a moment as she looked at them both. "You two are like family to Lucy and me, and Jess she is like a proper mum and all, I am dead grateful I met you two." Her eyes glistened. Rune crouched down and smiled.

"Being able to send a message to our family when we were miles away and homesick, and know we would not be let down, because the person who carried it was the best and loyal to us. That was very important to Robbie and I, you did that for us Rags. If we could repay you in full, you would have far more than this." Rags smiled at her.

"I never thought of it that way."

Rune gave her a hug. "There are times when you have been our life line Rags, you have earned this yourself." Robbie smiled and nodded as Rune spoke.

"I never been happy much, but here I am dead happy, and Lucy is an all. She is going to start school in three weeks; an learn more stuff than I ever did."

Robbie looked at Rags. "What school?" She smiled at him.

"Keep forgetting you been away a lot, Miss Maggs has got your dad to let her convert the old cottages up past Harry's place. Said they bin empty for years so he is rebuilding em to open a school. Miss Maggs is going to learn all the younguns their words an numbers like I have."

Rune smiled at Robbie as his thoughts leaked to her. "Great every kid for miles will be saying groovy and wow and cosmic, not to mention learning how to unjangle your vibes."

The bell rang twice and Bobby Thorn staggered in with a large bag. Rags let him through the hatch. "Great Bobby boy, you drop the bag there and go through to the rest room and get your head down, I will get Lucy to sort you a brew."

Bobby Thorn came through; covered in dust and smiled at Robbie. "Hi Lord

Loxley, and Lady Loxley." He gave a quick bow.

Robbie nodded. "You working for Rags now Bobby?"

Bobby smiled. "Yeah, I do the run to Cheshire because I know it so well, I get to see Sister Carla and Mother Alley all the time that way."

Rune gave a little chuckle. "Mother Alley?" Bobby nodded.

"Well, she is not really a nun is she, and we all love her because she is so kind and loving to us all. So, we all call her Mother Alley, bit like your lot calling Lady Stephanie Mother I suppose." Bobby smiled and trudged through to the rest room, where they heard his boots thump to the floor and the bed boards creak.

Rags came in with a tray of drinks and Robbie and Rune sat with her and she filled them in on life in Loxley, Rags was so well known here now, as everyday people flocked to her postal station to hand in their letters. Nellie helped every other day so Rags could take priority letters out herself, Lucy ran the office very efficiently even though she was only twelve years old, and Loxley now had ten full time riders coming in and out of the office.

During the week, Jess and Beth set up a fresh veg stall outside the postal service house, which Blades had been helping on, and Judy was doing a bit on it. It seemed that there were so many visitors that Jess was selling more than at the market. Robbie was very impressed as he sat and drank his Dandelion coffee, and Rags who was thrilled at having the Lord of Loxley in her home chatted freely away. Each time the bell rang, she watched Lucy who was receiving the mail, and stamping it and dropping the brass bit into a small tin, which rattled a lot Robbie was pleased to hear.

They sat for two hours and surprisingly Robbie really enjoyed himself. Rags was fast witted and he smiled as she cracked jokes to him. When it came time to leave Robbie bent down and kissed her cheek, Rags winked at Rune. "Saving the lips for you I bet, well one good snog from a lord is good enough for old Rags." Rune started to laugh as they left and waved goodbye after giving Lucy a hug.

Robbie looked at her radiant smile as they crossed the yard. "What?" She gave him a curious look?

"Fancy a night at the Mere under the trees?" She smiled it was her most favourite place in the world, and she knew he knew it, she nodded as her eyes sparkled. They walked into the barn and collected two horses, Rune wanted to pick some stuff up from home first, so they rode back and Robbie collected his blankets and some food for the morning and his cups and folding pans.

One hour later Rune sat smiling on the grass as Robbie set up a camp just inside the trees, so they could sit under the leaves and watch the Mere across the grass. It was perfect, he was enjoying being alone with her. Over the past weeks, they had spent precious moment's together, but not vast spans of time that was just them. She sat just in front of him, and he leaned on her shoulder from behind with his arms around her.

They talked quietly to each other about the house he would build and they watched the sun slowly fall, as the sky grew a deep and vivid red, and as the darkness rolled in they curled up together by the fire rolled in the blankets, and they kissed and made love. He felt the joy and happiness of being close to her, and he fell asleep with her in his arms and her smile in his thoughts.

"Daddy, wake up... Daddy." Robbie opened his eyes thinking he was dreaming he looked round and rubbed his eyes, Rune was asleep curled around him; the faint blur of violet in the trees caught his eye. The small girl walked towards him with a smile not unlike Rune's, he thought he was still dreaming. She came close to him and gave him a smile. "I told you she would find you."

Robbie realized, and he smiled. "You are real; I thought you were a dream."

"I am a dream Daddy, but not for much longer, Granny Opal and Granny Gwen have helped me."

She handed him a bundle. "Victor died, but he left you this. The dark woman has made bad things and this will protect you. He told me to tell you there is one more who can do his work."

Robbie took the bundle and looked at her as Rune stirred. "Am I really your daddy?"

She smiled and her bright violet eyes shone. "Oh yes I am your daughter, can you not tell?"

"How is this possible when you have not been born yet?"

"I will be... I am in mummy's tummy waiting to grow, Granny Opal showed me how to share mummy's power to help you, I will begin to grow soon, and then we will see each other again."

A tear ran from his eye. "You are Iona, aren't you?"

She nodded. "I love the name you gave me Daddy." Rune opened her eyes and watched her daughter of the future talk to her father. Her eyes ran with tears as she saw the love and the care in his eyes.

"You are very beautiful my precious angel." She smiled and gave him a hug.

"I have to go back now Daddy and I won't see you until I have grown."

Robbie swallowed hard. "Goodbye my darling, see you soon."

She smiled and her violet eyes twinkled as Rune's did, she kissed him softly on his cheek, and he lifted his hand and touched it. "Bye daddy."

She turned, and he watched as she walked away and faded into the trees. Tears dripped from his face as Rune watched him quietly; he looked down at her and smiled. "She is so beautiful Rune; will she really be mine?"

Rune pulled him close and kissed him. "She is the one that will favour you most,

and she will be the centre of the next circle when I leave here. Iona will have
the biggest power ever known, for she will hold her mother's power of two lines,
but she will also contain the power of her father. Pure love makes magic more
powerful my darling and she has such a lot of it."

He held her close. "When will I see her again Rune?" She squeezed him tight.

"Not yet but the time is not far away, I am glad you have seen her and
understood Rob."

He curled around her and gazed into her eyes, they looked almost violet in the
dark, and he could see his daughter looking back at him. "You are a remarkable
person Runestone, I love you very deeply do you know that?"

She chuckled "Of course I do, I told you I know stuff." She kissed the tip of his
nose and he smiled.

Rune stretched as she moved around and opened her eyes; Robbie smiled as
he built up the fire, and put the pan on to it. She lay wrapped in the blankets and
grinned happily, as she watched her woodsman do what he did best. He had no
shirt on and she could see the scar on his shoulder, it was looking better each day.
He came and sat beside her and she sat up, and slid into his lap and put her arms
around him. He gave her a soft kiss. "Happy?"

She nodded. "Very." He gave a long and happy sigh.

"I love this place; it is the perfect surrounding for you." She nuzzled into him
and he held her close. "I am going to go and find something to eat, watch the
pan for me, and I will cook you a true woodland breakfast when I get back." She
smiled at him and gave him a big kiss.

He lifted his bow and his quiver, and smiling he headed into the trees. Rune sat
and watched the sun coming over the Mere; she dropped her long top over her
head, got up, and walked to the mere. She rolled up her sleeves as she waded in to
her knees, and she began to wash. She hummed an old Celtic tune as she cleaned.

Robbie moved through the trees like a shadow, he was a little nervous about
using his bow, his arm was feeling a lot stronger, but it still felt very stiff. He fitted
the arrow as he moved; he knew there were rabbits about and pheasant.

The trees were now in full leaf, and the light broke through the canopy in white
shafts of light that moved as the leaves above him fluttered in the warm early
summer breeze. The bracken was high, as its long fronds had unfurled. The white
blossom of the wild cherries had faded and blown to the winds, and he spotted the
small round green centres of the flowers that would become the soft dark fruits of
mid-summer.

He felt a new lease of life as he wandered in amongst the undergrowth looking
for his prey. He crossed damp patches of soil and yet he left no prints or traces

that he had ever been there, he was a true woodsman and now realised how much he had missed the freedom of being amongst the trees. He saw the flutter of wings and silently he raised his bow, he took his aim and released his arrow. It shot like a speeding bullet and as the group of pheasant lifted in the air; his arrow took its mark with pinpoint accuracy. He breathed a long sigh of relief, his bow skills seemed unaffected.

Rune sat on the grass watching across the lake. "Runestone Sapphire."
She turned and smiled as her grandfather walked across the glade towards her.
"Grandfather, what are you doing here?" She pulled her top down over the tops of her bare legs.
"I must talk with you Runestone and your hooded man on matters of great importance. He is feeling well I take it?"
She smiled. "He is recovering quickly and his strength is returning quicker than any of us expected." Merlin nodded.
"This is good." He put his hand around her, and they walked to the fire. Rune crouched down and poured her grandfather a coffee. He swept his hand across the grass and three large stumps appeared. "Sit child I must talk with you." Rune felt some concern in his voice, and watched him carefully, his tone was soft but she heard the concern and it worried her. "Runestone my child, I have repaired the damage you caused with your outburst, it has taken some time and a lot of power."
She put her head down. "I am sorry Grandfather, I just lost control and it came out of me."
Merlin leaned forward and looked quite sternly at her. "It was irresponsible and foolish, you are lucky your party survived; have you any idea of what you could have done if that area had been populated, as it was twenty years ago? You are very lucky you did not take thousands of innocent lives. You acted without care or responsibility, for what... a boy?"
"What?" She stood up and her eyes flared at him. "I love him, he is my life."
Merlin stood and faced her as he raised his voice. "He is mortal; he is only a part of your life. You are the force of life in all living things; you cannot just decide to destroy an entire area because you feel hurt. You have a responsibility to all life not just his."
Rune started to cry. "How can you say that when you pleaded with Opal to stay knowing it was draining my life force and killing me? Was her life more important than everyone else's?"
"She was my wife for two hundred years."
"And you have lived for thousands, she was but a small part, and yet you risked my life and everyone else's for a few more years with her, you are a hypocrite."
Merlin flopped back to the tree stump he looked sad and hurt. "Losing

Gwendolyn was painful, I loved her dearly, and when I met Opal, I never thought I would feel love so pure again." He lowered his head and pulled at his beard. "Oh, Runestone I am sorry, I was overcome at losing love again, I was wrong to have you suffer, I have thought of it many times."

Rune sat and took his hands in hers. "You know the pain I felt, I am sorry Grandfather. I am only now finding ways to control all this force within me. It is hard for me at times, my love for him is as strong as the force of nature within me, I have to fight all the time to balance them, it will not happen again, I promise."

Merlin looked up at her and raised his hand to her face, and softly stroked her. "You are the youngest ever to carry this power, even Gwendolyn the most powerful of all was twenty before the force came to her. You must understand Runestone you have two lives now. That of your circle with your woodsman, and the one of life and creation throughout all the world. You must now start to focus, and harness the power to do good, if you do not it will turn you on to the path of darkness, and you would become my enemy. I love you my child, I could not bear to face you and kill you."

Rune's face paled. "Grandfather how can you think such things I am your granddaughter?"

"The Dark One grows more powerful, and you have proved yourself vulnerable Runestone, you must now focus and control what is in you or she will overpower you, and you will turn from the white path, I will have no choice but to protect the white circle of life... Control your power and aid me."

Rune looked at the floor and fear filled her heart. "I will never turn dark; I would die before I turned against Robbie and his dream of bringing back life."

Merlin smiled as she spoke, he knew he had made her understand, and his granddaughter's reaction pleased him. He saw the power within her and he saw the strength she had not yet found; he knew now she would search deep and become the force she was destined to be. "I hear your woodsman returning let us speak no more of this. I will talk as you two make me breakfast."

Robbie smiled as he walked through the trees and on to the glade. He held up the birds and Rune beamed knowing the relief he felt at being able to shoot his bow without loss of performance. Merlin talked happily about life in Loxley, and the joy he felt for Jade, knowing she was so happy with Rowan. Rune and Robbie prepared a meal and smiled at the joy of a proud grandfather. They sat and ate a good meal, as they did Merlin looked up at Robbie. "The Dark One has a new weapon Robbie, it has great power and you will face it alone one day. I know you already seek to meet this power; you have been given the weapon to aid you have you not?"

Rune watched as Robbie lifted his head. "I have the knife yes."

"May I see it?" Robbie looked at him.

"You cannot touch it, for it must only know my hand, you know that don't you?"

Merlin nodded to him, Robbie handed it over to Merlin who lay it on his lap and unfolded the cloth to view it. The golden knife gleamed, and the moonstone in the end shone brightly in the light, the runes on the blade glowed violet.

"Draw the poison from the sword, and handle me no more." Rune read the words and looked at Robbie. "What does that mean?" Merlin looked up at her.

"What that means my dearest granddaughter is that the force you felt when you were in Scotland was the Dark One pouring pure evil into Billy via what has been called for many years the black blade. I had not thought it possible, but now I finally know where the book of black runes lies."

Rune looked up in shock. "But the black book is a myth, like Sequana's Bridge, you told me so yourself." Merlin looked sadly up at her.

"Gwendolyn always argued that she was sure she had seen it, I never believed her, I honestly thought it was a myth, but she found the sword maker against all odds, and her power is growing quickly, I am now sure it is the only way that she could trap Gwendolyn and drain her powers. She has the black book."

Robbie watched and listened uncertain on what they were talking about. "Excuse my ignorance but what is so special about this book?"

Rune smiled at him. "Sorry Rob, it is something my lot has been searching out for a long time, and it was never certain that it existed. The black book contains all the spells needed to soak up dark power, legend says that whoever owns it will rule the world and be unstoppable, you will also have the power to make a sword that cannot be defeated, it is said there are only two other swords to rival it, one is Excalibur which is its equal, the other is the Sword of Destiny which was Excalibur's sister sword."

Merlin looked at him. "Gwendolyn made Excalibur for Arthur and gave it to the keep of her sister in the lake; the metal that remained was made into another sword. It was named Destiny and she used the secrets of four other sword makers to make it, no one has ever seen the Sword of Destiny, Gwendolyn alone knew of its whereabouts, and that knowledge has now gone forever to the other realm."

"So, the Dark One has this sword no one can defeat?"

Rune sighed. "Before the sword can be defeated the evil must be drawn from it, and that must be done with the dagger you have there. As I understand it, if you can trap the sword in the hilt of the dagger, it will draw the evil out and trap it in the dagger. The black sword will turn gold and the dagger black, only then can the sword of devastation be defeated, using Destiny or Excalibur, both of which appear to have left this world forever."

Robbie looked bemused. "So the sword of honour is not the lost sword of Carnac at all. We should be seeking the lost sword of Destiny?" Rune shrugged,

"It now looks that way Robbie."

Merlin looked at them both. "That is not all; the power that is poured into the sword must be from an evil source that has committed a most evil death. I cannot be certain, but I am right I think in saying that the source of such evil will be Mordred."

"No?" Rune looked shocked and frightened. "He was killed by his father; it cannot be so."

Merlin nodded. "The feeling you described to me can only be that of the evil that robbed this world of the purest thing ever, King Arthur first and true king of the Britons. If she has brought him back, he will be contained within another and that I think is Billy."

Robbie looked at them as he finally began to understand their conversation. "So, you are saying Billy is gone and what looks like him is really Mordred, Morgan le Fey's first child seeded from Arthur himself?"

"I am very sorry to say young Robbie, but I fear that is correct."

Robbie leaned back and picked up his cup. "Well thank Hearne for that. I was always going to find it hard to kill Billy, he was my brother, but if it is not him anymore, that will make it a hell of a lot easier."

Rune looked at him with surprise in her eyes. "Robbie this Mordred is evil and nasty."

Robbie smiled and winked at her. "Me too when I am pissed off."

Merlin laughed out loud. "I will give you this Robbie lad; you have a Loxley heart and spirit that is for certain." He gave Merlin a huge grin.

"Of course, I have, that is why I am Lord Loxley, it is my destiny to find the sword and finish him off." He sipped his coffee and smiled at Rune.

Merlin carefully wrapped the golden dagger up in the cloth and handed it back to Robbie. "It will not be an easy task, but you have the heart, and you have the skill, I can only hope you will succeed My Lord." He rose and bowed to Robbie; Rune stood up and hugged him, he smiled at Rune. "Cross words soon fade, where love winds its merry way."

She smiled at him. "I wrote that to you when I was seven, I cannot believe you remember it Grandfather." He hugged her tightly.

"You are my precious Runestone, of course I remember, I love you my darling granddaughter. The truth is always remembered." He winked at her.

"I love you too grandfather." He kissed her on the tip of her nose and her eyes sparkled as she giggled. Merlin strode off and raised his hand, his longer white hair and black robes billowed behind him. "Take care my children I will see you soon."

Rune sat down next to Robbie. "What do we do now Rob? We still need a sword and we have to defeat the very dark power, I thought we were almost there, you know if we could just get the king and put him on the throne, we could begin to live here and be happy."

He slid his arm round her and pulled her on to his knee. "I don't need a house to be happy, I just need you." He pulled her close and she giggled as her eyes twinkled at him.

"I will live in the trees on the floor with you Rob. My home is your heart and as long as we are side by side, I am at home and happy." He kissed her softly.

Robbie held her tight as she sat in his lap, her long red hair flowed free all around him. "I want you to take sword lessons from Jett. She has been trained since birth to wield a weapon of power, I think Loxley needs a table of swords; somehow, it feels these blades share the same fate. Can you use your power here instead of Caerleon?"

She nodded "I think so, Opal lived at Caerleon, and the glade was her home and the centre of her power. Mine has to be here I belong to Loxley, in theory my power should be stronger here than anywhere else. Scarlet is the guardian of the swords I will have to talk to her first, there is deep magic in these tables Robbie, I am not sure one can just be built and used."

"The centre of power of the woodland folk has been shifting to Loxley for some time now Rune. The more I think about it the more I am now beginning to think it is because of you. You are the centre of all circles of life; power will be drawn to you. This is your centre; Loxley is becoming the focus of this whole country."

Her eyes sparkled as she looked at him. "That is because of you Rob. It is Lord Loxley that draws the eye of all in this country not me."

"I am not sure Rune." He stared out into the lapping water of the mere. "I am without doubt the standard bearer of the campaign, but that is what I think the magic wants everyone to believe, you have said before, the magic weaves its way through the things in ways not easily spotted. I think your power draws everything through the actions of the hooded man, I am your diversion."

"Rob that is silly, you are brave and have fought hard to quell Knox and bring your people together. I have not done that."

He leaned back and looked at her. She had such conviction and belief in her eyes and he loved her for it, her eyelashes glinted as she blinked at him. "You have been by my side from the start. You saved me from the Dark One; you found the cave I was stuck in. You have been my strength and support. I have only ever achieved the things I have because you believed I could do it. Your magic has been there always helping me. Do you not see, without you I could not have done any of it, I am close to the centre yes, but it is you whom we all revolve around, you are the Runestone, the centre of everything." He lifted the white bracelet on his wrist. "Even me."

"Your wisdom has grown my Bowman." Rune looked up, her eyes turning vivid purple, Robbie smiled as Rune slid off his lap smiling. She ran across the glade violets springing up where her naked feet touched the grass. Hearne embraced his favourite daughter with a smile, and Rune squeezed him hard. "Oh Father of all creation, I am happy to see you again."

He stroked her hair and wild Cranesbill flowered in it and fell to the floor. "I am happy to see you have found the hole from your heart my sweet child of nature. He grows strong in your care."

She looked up at the tall figure of the woods and his old face dark and lined like bark, her eyes illuminated love. "My father I am so happy, I have found my love and seen some of my future with him."

Hearne gave her a smile. "I see it my flower of the forest, I was not certain that Opal was right, but Gwendolyn was always one for strong argument, and how could I refuse the queen of the fairies. Your seed will become a mighty and beautiful tree in my garden Runestone Sapphire." He stroked her cheek softly as he spoke.

Robbie walked up and bowed to his lord. "My Lord Hearne you honour me again with your visit."

Hearne extended his arm and placed it onto his injured shoulder. "Opal has served you well my Bowman and son of my realm; you are ready to face yet more challenges in the coming of dreams. I have a gift for you two, which will aid you in your battle; the darkness that has been brought back is the vilest of that line. You two must now look deep, and find your true power and bring together the five swords, for destiny awaits them. Come my children walk with me to the centre of your glade."

Hearne walked into the centre of the glade with Robbie and Rune on either arm. He faced the woodland before them, with the Mere behind them, Hearne pulled them close together and put Rune's hand in Robbie's. "The age of dreams is almost here my sweet children, and I think now is the time for the Lord of Creation to place the first stone of its foundation, and give you your own dream to start the flow."

Robbie and Rune stood side by side holding hands as Hearne placed one hand on each of their shoulders. The edge of the forest, where they had their small fire, and had spent the night making love began to shudder. "You have brought more magic and power to a place long known for its own power, here will be the centre of all things."

The trees slid backwards as if walking out of the way and the ground opened up into a huge rectangular pit. It sunk down twelve feet and white stone rose around it lining the walls and floor. Robbie stared in wonder as a huge granite stone table rose up from the floor, it glowed and began to spin, and lightening in beams of black and pure white struck it followed by red and green and violet. The table spun like the wheel of Carnac had, and the light mingled as it spun. Little flashes of colour shot up into the air as it built up speed, and then a streak of violet flowed into the table like swirling ink. It mixed in the light and burned brightly.

Very slowly, the table stopped spinning and Rune chuckled with glee as she saw the heavy stone table with a five pointed star of bright colours on a white background and surrounded with a thick black edge rimmed with gold. She looked at the flabbergasted Robbie and her eyes danced with delight. "Look at the centre."

He leaned forward and saw the usual sparkling sapphire blue pentangle that held the points of the star together. In the centre of the pentangle, shining brightly in silver was a large and decorative Celtic rune. Robbie looked at his shoulder and then at the table. It was the same letter 'R.' Rune beamed with delight. "Robbie this is my table, it is the table of Runestone." Hearne chuckled as she turned and threw her arms around him. "Oh, father of all things I am filled with joys I had no idea I could hold."

Hearne patted her gently as she hugged him hard. "Now my children we must hide such a thing of great power, for there is only one other table that has greater power, but sadly that has not been used for a great age." He turned Rune back to face the rectangular hole and again placed her hand in Robbie's. "You have the gift of the age of dreams, now receive mine. Close your eyes and think of your love for each other."

Robbie smiled as he opened his heart and felt Rune enter it, her eyes glowed and tears ran down her cheeks as she felt him inside her, their love for each other was a huge power that mixed and mingled and flowed as one. There was a blinding green flash of light and Robbie and Rune opened their eyes. The trees moved to the centre of the hole and cast themselves over it. Robbie and Rune watched as the bottom floor of a house started to appear, bricks jumped out of the earth and climbed into a tall chimney with fireplaces, and the walls grew up the sides as a house of wood and stone built itself before their eyes.

Rune wept with joy, as all she had ever imagined her home would be appeared before her. Robbie wore a happy smile as six bedrooms built themselves, and the front grew before him with large glass windows, so he could watch the Mere at sunset. The huge wooden house shuddered to a halt and Rune jumped with delight as flowers sprung from her feet and shot across the glade and formed a bright and colourful garden. Twigs shot into the air and landed around them forming a small wooden fence. The glade fell silent as Robbie and Rune saw their own first home.

Rune spun round, but Hearne was gone, a breeze blew across the glade, and lifted their hair and whispered in their ears. "Be happy my children."

Rune bounced up and down on the grass her eyes sparkling brighter than Robbie had ever seen them, and she shouted at the top of her voice. "I love you my father of all creation." The breeze blew around her.

"I love all of my children, but you are nature and special to me."

Rune leapt into Robbie's arms and wept with joy, never had he seen her so radiant and so happy. She pulled back and grabbed his hand. "Come on let's see it." She ran laughing across the glade and up on to the wooden porch and in through the open glass doors.

The house was big and very spacious everything in it was wood. Polished beams held the roof high above them and carved wooden rails of acorns and oak leaves ran up the side of the stairs to the bedrooms. The largest room looked out over the Mere and again had large glass windows and a small balcony. A large wooden bed was set against the wall, so that when they woke, they would see the Mere.

The corridor had six rooms set down it and at the end was a beautiful and ornate bathroom of silver. A small pump brought filtered water from the Mere, driven by the two wind turbines on the chimney and the water was heated by the rows of solar plates on the roof. Rune loved it and she threw her arms around him, and laughed and giggled as he held her. "Oh, Robbie I love you, I have never been as happy as I am now."

They walked arm in arm down the stairs and looked at the large spacious living room and back kitchen with a large black metal wood burning oven and stove. Rune squealed with delight as she looked around and ran out into the passage; and there on the side of the wooden staircase was a small plaque with an 'R' on it. Rune waved her hand over it and it glowed violet, a small door appeared and swung open. White stone steps led down to the room below and she hurried down them tugging Robbie behind her. The candles in the golden brackets flared into life as they entered, and Robbie's eyes widened at the size and the quality of the table.

Rune walked round it beaming with delight as she ran her hand over the surface, small violet sparks jumped from under her hand as it swept along. She stopped and bent down and lay across it and touched the large silver 'R' shaped rune.

Violet light jumped into the air and spun round in a coil, Rune's eyes turned violet as she smiled. *"Hear me."* Her voice echoed in his head.

"My sisters and circles, I am Runestone centre of all circles, come to me at midnight, and join with me on the table of the Runestone."

Robbie smiled at her as she beamed with joy, and she slid into his arms. "We have our home at last, oh Rob I am so happy." Her eyes sparkled. "It is hours before midnight."

He gave her a huge smile. "We have a new bed." She started to giggle.

CHAPTER NINETEEN

THE FIRST DREAM COMES TRUE

Rune swung open the door and Steph and Jade walked in. "Wow sis that has to be the coolest loom I have ever seen." Rune beamed with happiness as her mother sat down, and ran her hand along the smooth polished wood of the loom, already strung with hundreds of fine sage green threads.

"Oh, sweetheart I am so happy for you, although I must admit, it will feel strange not having you at home weaving beside me." Rune gave her a hug and kissed her.

"Mum look at how much space I have, you can sit here with me and embroider or paint, this home will always be open to you, this is going to be my life, and you are a very big part of it." Steph wiped the tear from her eye as she hugged her daughter.

Robbie sat with Smokes and Rowan and watched, as Alice walked around with Bear at the edge of the Mere, Rowan watched him carefully. "You have recovered have you not, Rune is without doubt my friend good medicine, and so why is it I see a task forming in your eyes."

Robbie smiled. "You know me so well my friend, yes we have a task or at least we still have the same task. That jewel on your belt is not the lost sword of Carnac."

Rowan and Smokes both sat forward looking very surprised, Smokes looked from Robbie to Rowan and back again. "That cannot be possible, what about the wheel and all the clues?"

Robbie sighed. "We have missed something my friends and tonight we must find out what, because news has come to me that is disturbing beyond a doubt. The Dark One has created a sword of power, and without the lost sword there is no chance of destroying the sword of devastation."

Rowan sat back with a gasp. "That woman has blighted our path every step of the way. Can we not just kill her and have done with her."

"I wish it was that simple, but she is not my concern at the moment, the one who wields the black sword is not as all seems, there is darkness so black there it could blot out the sun forever. That is our first concern."

Smokes lifted his glass of blueberry and lemon grass and sipped it slowly. "So, what do we do now Robbie?"

He leaned forward and patted Rowan's leg. "First we see this one spliced to his bride of green, and then we prepare again to find the sword."

Rowan smiled and looked into the house where Jett and Jade laughed with Rune and Mel. "She is really looking forward to it, she is usually excitable but today she is wild."

They all chuckled. "I don't suppose she will be wearing a dress?"

"That my good friend is an argument I would never have begun."

Rowan shook his head. "I think to be honest I will wait and see what Rune and her come up with."

Tables were laid out on the long lawn; Rune had invited the whole Lox household and all the members of the circles, as well as Robbie's loyal group. It was Rune's intention to bring everyone together and celebrate her new home and the coming marriage of Rowan and Jade. The carts began to role in by midafternoon as Beth and Jess arrived with food, John came with a boar, which was set to roast in the fire pit and Harry and Maggs turned up with Rags, Lucy, and Bobby Thorn, who was not delivering and tagged along.

Harry uncorked a few bottles under the wary eye of Steph, and soon the glade was filled with joy and laughter as everyone sat at the table on the edge of the Mere and enjoyed the feast. Martin walked up to Robbie with a very stunning young woman and two four year old girls. "Robbie this is my wife Hanna, and these are my two precious daughters, Pamela and Melody." The little girls curtsied and Robbie smiled and bent down to them.

"Hi, I am Robbie and I am most pleased to meet you both."

Hanna smiled as they both gave him a small kiss on the cheek, which seemed to delight him. He stood up and took Hanna's hand. "You have a good man by your side. I have come to rely on him greatly, I know how quiet he can be but believe me when I honestly say, you have a very brave and highly honoured man."

She smiled, as she looked at him. "Thank you, My Lord, he holds you in great esteem, and our house has been honoured to help protect you." Robbie smiled at her.

"You are amongst friends here Hanna, please call me Robbie." She gave a quiet laugh

"Matty told me you would say that." Robbie placed his arm around both of them and walked them to the house.

"Come and meet Rune, she must be exhausted showing everyone around our new home, but I am sure she will delight in giving you the tour."

The party wore on and laughter filled the air as the sun settled in the sky, Robbie came down to the water's edge with Rune on his arm as his mother watched the red ball of the sun reflected in the water. She looked up and smiled as they came up to her side. She slid out her arm and pushed it round him.

Robbie stood between the two women he loved most, and Jess sighed. "I have always loved this place; it is very special to me." She started to giggle and Rune smiled as she looked across at her. Jess blushed a little. "Do you know why it is named Robbie's Mere?"

Robbie smiled with Rune and shook his head. "No."

Jess looked out across the lake. "This is where Robert and I would sneak off to when John and Beth got together." Her eyes twinkled brightly. "Oh Robbie, you are so like your dad. He was young and wild and very romantic I might add, I loved him from the moment I first saw him."

Jess seemed to stare as if seeing the pictures from her past before her. "We came up here one night and we made love in this very spot." She chuckled. "Your grandfather was a little old fashioned in his views. We fell asleep in each other's arms under the moonlight it was wonderful. Your grandfather caught us both here and went mad, there we were lay on the grass completely naked, he gave Robert such a slap."

Robbie gasped, he was not so sure he wanted to hear about his parent's sex lives that much, but he was surprised at his grandfather. "What did dad do?"

"Oh, Robbie I loved him more than ever after that night. He caught your granddad's wrist." She began to laugh. "It was funny in a way; can you imagine it? Your dad has always been a big man, and he stood there completely naked in front of your grandfather holding him by the wrist. He bellowed at him. I love this woman and she will be a Lox, turn your back you dirty old bugger she is undressed." Jess started to laugh harder.

"The fact that we had been caught making love just didn't bother him; all he was concerned about was my embarrassment as I curled up and tried to hide myself. Your grandfather had a look of shock on his face as I never saw again. I knew then I would stay with him forever, he put me above everything." She turned to Robbie and stroked back his hair from his face. "That was the night you were conceived, right here in this spot. Your grandfather kept Robert working late every night after that until we were married. I was two months pregnant on my wedding day."

Robbie looked at the ground and remembered the first time he had spent the night alone with Rune here, it had been on this very spot where they had watched the sun fall and rolled up together in the blankets.

Jess smiled. "After we were married and I told Jake I was pregnant, he told me he had always thought of it as a place of magic; he also told me my son would do great things. He had a map made a few years later and when it had been drawn out properly, he wrote Robbie's Mere on it. He changed his will so that it belonged to you who began here, I am so sorry he died so soon after you were born, he loved you Robbie, I saw a kindness in him I had never encountered." A small tear ran from her eye. "I came to love him dearly."

Rune sniffled and wiped her eyes, and Jess pulled them both into her arms. "I am so happy this special place will be your home; I hope both of you feel the joy I have here in Loxley. This place is especially magical, but I think you both know that."

As midnight approached and some of the guest started to leave, Rune gathered the members of the circles and the sword bearers. Alice and Smokes sat together, as Rafe squatted on the front porch steps. She led the others down to the large room below the house and they gasped in awe at the size and beauty of her wheel.

Every one stood around the walls waiting to be invited to seat themselves at Rune's wheel. She smiled as she looked around. "Welcome to the wheel of Runestone, my sisters you have seen many wheels, but even this one will be new to you, for it is the centre of all circles and can do many things."

Rune raised her hands and waved them across the table. Golden triangle shapes flowed on to the white spaces between the coloured points of the stars. "This table will seat few or many, please sword bearers come forward and place your swords on the table."

They stepped forward in order and withdrew their swords, Robbie lay his first placing the tip of his sword in the point of the star. Rune sounded out the name of the blades, as they were lay down. "Truth and Justice." She lay her own sword down. "Knowledge, Courage, and Honour. Be seated gentlemen and heirs to this kingdom."

All of them sat in the deep burgundy chairs in front of their allotted spaces. Rune looked to the group. "Pendant wearers sit on the right-hand side of your sword bearer." Treen, Ruby, Jett, Saff and Jade took their seats in front of one of the golden triangles on the right of the sword of their pendants. Jade smiled at Rowan, knowing that she was not excluded from the table as Alley had passed the pendant on to her. Rune looked at the others. Some of you belong on other wheels; some of you no longer occupy seats, but all of you belong on my wheel."

They all smiled as she approached them, Rune led Jasper to the triangle between Robbie and Ruby. Maddy sat between Skip and Jett. Steph was next to Rune's seat and Mel was placed between Bear and Jade. Rune sat down in her seat.

"Remember where I have placed you, for when we meet you will sit in the same seat. Tonight, we begin the fight of darkness, we have the five swords of the heirs, but we still need the one sword from Carnac."

Everyone looked confused and glanced at each other, Rune gazed across her table. "The sword of honour was never lost; a sword can only be lost when the one who knows of its existence is gone from us. Sweet Gwendolyn is lost even to this wheel and cannot return, I believe she has left us the clues we need, so using my wheel of brothers and sisters, we must now find the lost sword of Carnac. The Sword of Destiny is the only weapon we can use to remove the darkness that grows on the black rock in the north."

Rune's eyes began to glow, and Robbie noticed how all the eyes of the women's eyes flickered as their power was drawn into the circle. He felt his white bangle vibrate as he watched a violet mist began to swirl out of the centre of the table. "The wheel of Runestone will show what has passed and what could pass; we now must decide our path." Her lips did not move but her voice bounced off the walls. It contained great authority and power, and Robbie felt like he could hear a little of Hearne in the way that she spoke.

Everyone watched as the pictures began to appear in the mist. A tall black castle rose from the sea, sat on an island just off the coast, they watched as Victor drew a circle on the floor and marked out a star. He made the sword and etched the runes on to it, Robbie watched as he held it with a cloth as he laid it in the circle and then began to make the knife. "The golden knife of Dunnottar is unknown to the enemy." Her voice carried above the pictures as they watched, Victor put on his shirt and tucked the knife into his belt below it.

The Dark One entered and stood before the circle, her face showed disapproval of the symbol of her enemy. Billy came forward and Robbie gripped the edge of the table, Jade watched Robbie, concern in her eyes as he saw Billy lift the sword. Billy's fear and pain showed as the words of the ancient runic language were spoken.

Robbie gasped as he saw his eyes turn black and his features harden, a tear dripped on to the table. For all the pain he had caused to Robbie, he still saw a brother in agony, Jade filled up as she watched his face show the sadness. Victor was stabbed, and fell to his knees as the others left. Robbie's heart skipped a beat as once again he saw his daughter. Jade turned and saw the small girl with violet eyes and looked back at Robbie understanding what she was seeing, her hand slid to Rowan's.

Victor smiled as Robbie wept silently watching his little girl take the dagger, and collect the violet stones; he knew would save his life and bring Rune to his aid. Sapphire sniffed as she too recognised the tiny girl that had saved her, the picture faded and Robbie looked down, joy and pain mixed within him, the violet mist swirled once again and more pictures appeared.

Gwendolyn pulled a golden sword out of the flame and pounded it with a hammer; she dropped it in a vat of water and withdrew it. It shone like the sun, and was a mighty weapon, she lay it down on a red velvet cloth and using the tip of her fingernail she carved its name on to it, 'Excalibur'. The whole room gasped, this was a sword none had ever seen as it had returned to the other realm, Jett leaned forward and studied it closely. "Oh, wow that is a mega cool sword."

Rune smiled as they watched Gwendolyn pour the last of the metal into the same mould of Excalibur. They watched it cool and then she placed it into the fire and heated it, four others stepped forward and pounded it with hammers as Gwendolyn held it on the anvil, Opal was first to work the blade, then two others came forth, Robbie noticed their lips moved while they worked, they were speaking enchantments as they wove their magic into the blade, the last man to work was Victor Thornson, how could it be? How could a man who worked on the sword make another today? They all left the room and Gwendolyn finished the sword alone.

She lifted it out of the vat of water; it was the identical double of Excalibur, except it had a fine line of platinum running down the centre of the blade. She slipped a white bracelet off her wrist and snapped it apart; Robbie leaned forward and watched carefully. Gwendolyn broke off a piece, and spun it in her hand, three moonstones appeared, two large and one small. She placed a large moonstone into the top of the handle and fastened the holder tightly into place. The other two she wrapped in a piece of pale blue velvet.

Using her nail as before, Gwendolyn engraved five words in old runes down the side of the blade, they glowed silver and disappeared. Then she turned the sword over and wrote in clear letters all could read. 'Destiny will prevail.' Hurriedly she covered the blade with velvet and then wrapped Excalibur in bright blue velvet, and as Opal came in with Victor, she handed it to her; Robbie knew Opal would take the sword to the lady of the lake.

Gwendolyn called Victor back and handed him the small cloth with the moonstones in, Robbie looked at the hilt of the golden dagger in his belt and saw the moonstone pulsate, Gwendolyn had known of the Dark One's intentions. As he left the room, the picture faded and the lights in the room glowed brighter.

Rune looked up and smiled at everyone. "Drinks?" Golden goblets had appeared on the table and everyone seemed to jump back in surprise, she giggled. Robbie took a large gulp and stopped, he looked into the cup and saw a bright pink liquid, it smelt of roses and had the taste of elderberries as it soaked his lips, he looked up at Rune who gave him a huge smile and winked. He raised his goblet in salute to her and drank heavily of the ice cold liquid; her eyes sparkled at him across the table.

Rune looked around the table. "Now we have all seen what has taken place, the sword of destiny is not a myth, and we all know what it looks like, that is the true sword of Carnac and sister to Excalibur. We all know now that the sword of devastation is no longer a myth and is in the hands of Billy, although Billy is no longer in command of that body. For those of you who did not understand that ritual, the Dark One poured a vile and evil power into the blade that has now possessed Billy completely. He has been taken over by her son returned."

Una gasped at the same time as Maddy. "It cannot be, Mordred was taken by Arthur, I saw the body." Everyone turned to Una and looked with surprise.

"Aunt Una how is that possible, it was a thousand years ago?" Jade looked a little surprised and very confused.

Una smiled at Jade. "I am a very old woman Jade. That happened one thousand, and one hundred and forty two years ago, I saw the dead body of Mordred as they carried him off the battle field, I was one of the sisters who lifted the body of our most beautiful King..." Her words stumbled as tears ran down her face. Maddy continued.

"We took our most noble of lords to our aunt, and we sat with him as we passed into Avalon, and washed and bathed him and laid him to rest. He was our king and we loved him." Maddy started to weep as Mel raised her hand to her mouth and cried at the memory.

Rune continued the story. "Jade my dear sister, your aunts are the daughters of Gwendolyn, they were but our age when all this took place. The Dark One seized Gwendolyn and her daughters and imprisoned them surrounded by crystals that contained them. They were put to sleep and did not age, when Gwendolyn fought the charm during what was called the age of sleep, she managed to free her daughters and place them in circles protected by her."

Mel touched Jade's arm. "My mother saved us and she died fighting the Dark One, we have lived on this isle and started again from where we left off, I was sixteen when I last saw Arthur... He was something to behold, and we all loved him dearly, my last task before I was taken was to protect Guinevere. I took her to the convent of church hill; she was pregnant by Arthur although she had not known it at the time. I could see his seed in her tummy, and I was glad that his line was not broken."

Una wiped her eyes. "I was with Arthur the night that he visited Guinevere. She was broken hearted and when he forgave her and told her he would do the same for Lancelot, she broke down. He lifted her into his arms and told her of the love he held for her, I cried and left the room for it was the most moving thing I have ever seen. My Lord King spent the night alone with her, and in the morning, he smiled as he left and told me he felt more love than ever before. I was happy for him and not looking what I was doing I fell and twisted my ankle. Arthur cut my staff from a holly tree with one swipe of Excalibur, and handed it to me to aid my walking. It was a royal gift to my household and I never leave it more than a few feet away."

Jade turned and smiled as she looked at the wall where Una's holly staff stood leaning on the wall. "Oh, Una that is the coolest story I have ever heard."

Rune smiled, as did everyone else, Jett flopped back in her chair. "Wow I would be glad to have a baby if I was forty, but Aunties, you guys are the coolest, kids at a thousand has to be the coolest thing ever." She beamed as Una and Mel and even Maddy laughed.

Rune looked around at the group gathered. "My family of the circle we have more to see, for knowledge will aid us in the future, I cannot explain what we will see now for I have no understanding of what is to come, but watch and draw your own conclusions."

The violet mist rose from the table and began to spin as everyone watched as pictures flashed by them at speed. A war with Romans, and Vikings at sea. Robin Hood ran through a wood and was hit by an arrow, Robbie leaned forward thinking for a moment it was him, the likeness was uncanny, it was when he saw him lean out of the very window that he had stood thinking about him at the priory as he fired his arrow, that he understood he was watching the past.

The Dark One spoke commands to a bishop, and women were dragged, tied and bound by men in black clothes, and tied to poles above huge piles of sticks, they screamed as they burned. Cannons fired across fields as men in bright reds and blues fought bloody wars.

Steam trains whizzed up the train lines belching out smoke, factories with huge monsters of metal spun fabric, and guns fired in huge fields of mud where soldiers lay rotting and dead. Hundreds of people were herded into huge rooms and screamed as gas came out from the ceiling. A huge mushroom shaped cloud flashed and exploded into the sky as the wind from it tore up trees and flattened buildings.

Robbie felt sick, as he watched a war in the desert where oil burned casting black smoke into the sky, and men with beards chanted happily waving pictures with strange writing on it as two huge silver towers fell to the earth. Forests were torn down and buildings replaced them, seas rose and flooded a small island blasting all the wooden huts into the sea and killing the people. Large piles of cattle were piled high in fields and burned by men in white suits.

Robbie felt despair rise inside him. Men with money passed people in rags sat in doorways in the street, streets of large houses stood in rows as men in metal boxes with blue flashing lights dragged a screaming scruffy boy into the back of it and beat him, he felt his heart was breaking, the despair from the pictures was too much.

Hearne walked across the top of Hearne's rock with Gwendolyn and Opal. He held their hands as he reached into the sky. The pictures shot up into the air as if being carried higher by a bird and Robbie watched Britain as the green disappeared and was replaced with roads and houses; most of the country was concrete, as the green shrunk back. As the pictures fell back to earth, somehow, he knew what was coming, Hearne opened his mouth and a stream of red flowed into the air. He sat dazed, as he watched his Lord Hearne, breathe the red death out and begin the destruction of humankind.

The pictures that followed were hard to watch. People coughed and sneezed in the street, and soon they turned red as blotches appeared on their skin and spread. The horror in their eyes frightened him and all around him, he heard small weeps.

A man staggered into a large square with a fountain, he was red and blistered all over, and people screamed and dropped their belongings and fled. He fell to his knees as the rash turned bright red and he died as he hit the floor.

The pictures changed as cities burned and houses collapsed, bodies lay everywhere and a man who ran with a tin of food in his hand was shot and fell dead, another man holding a smoking gun picked up the tin and ran off.

People moved out as the towns and cities burned and collapsed behind them. With small bags on their shoulders as they carried little, they made their way into the green spaces. Violent earthquakes shook what was left of the cities, and the earth opened and swallowed the buildings. Robbie's heart skipped a beat as he saw a tall and stocky old man with white hair lowering a winch that contained a mighty tree trunk, it was his grandfather building the wall round Loxley.

The picture turned to a large man stood in front of the Sacred Oak at Loxley in the moonlight. He held up a small baby to the moon and with tears in his eyes and a smile on his face his huge voice boomed around the room. "Hear me My Lord, my life is complete, see my boy for he is my future, take him to your realm and love my precious son of Loxley." Robbie's eyes filled as he watched the pride in his father's face, and heard the joy in his words. He put his head down and swallowed hard, a soft hand touched his shoulder and he turned to see Treen with tears rolling down her cheeks, she smiled.

He looked up and the pictures had faded and everyone sat with their heads down, Rune smiled at him through tearful eyes. There was a long quiet moment as everyone reflected on what they had seen, Rune pulled out a small hankie and dried her eyes as the others swallowed hard and wiped their faces.

She looked round the table. "You have seen what was the world of man. It was harsh and filled with pain; I cannot, and will not reveal your futures because I cannot influence your decisions. You know what we fight and we will look to the hooded man for his leadership, one thing I will say is this. No other from this room can be a part of the last fight. You have all been chosen for the final task, when the lost sword is found and the king comes, you will stand his corner and fight. Think of tonight and talk of it only amongst this circle."

The room moved as she stood up and walked round the table, she stopped at Treen and hugged her, Treen still cried as Rune embraced her. Rune kissed her on the head and them came round to Robbie as he stood up. She slid her arms around him. "Will you hold my children up to the sacred oak with such love and pride?"

Robbie pulled her close. "I had no idea he did that; I have not told him in so long how much I love him Rune." He lowered his head and she squeezed him tight.

"Maybe you should before we leave again."

They all made their way up the steps and back into the house. All wore the same look of deep thought and all were quiet, Alice was fast asleep on the long wooden seat filled with large cushions, she held her hands round her tummy that was sticking out a little, and Rune smiled as she saw her.

Bear lifted her gently in his arms and carried her upstairs, with all the extra space they had, Rune had told everyone they could stay if they wanted to. Steph and Smokes busied themselves in the kitchen as they made drinks and extra snacks. Robbie walked out into the moonlight and stood by the Mere. It was as clear as a mirror and he watched the moon and all the trees reflected in it.

He felt his bow touch his hand and turned to see Rowan. "You never listen to me Robbie; this must not leave your side." He smiled and patted him on the shoulder and took his bow. Jade and Rune sat on the balcony of Rune's new bedroom, they watched their men stood by the lakeside.

"I really do love him Rune, and Robbie; those are the two most precious people in my world apart from you."

Rune smiled at her sister. "I am so pleased to see you find your place Jade. I know you will be happy I have seen things that made me rejoice." Jade looked at her sister's happy face. "You have seen my future." She smiled at her.

"Just small flashes, but yes I have seen some things."

Jade looked fearful. "My biggest fear and promise you won't tell, please?"

Rune leaned forward and took Jade's hands in hers. "I am your sister Jade; I would never betray you to any. You know this." Jade smiled at her.

"Rune I am a woodsman and a fighter, what if Rowan falls for another who is elegant and beautiful? Someone like you, you know he got on really well with Alley."

Rune giggled. "Oh Jade, my darling you have no fear there. You are of the line of Opal creator of all things beautiful and elegant; do you not see you have all the qualities of nature in you? Jade you are beautiful; you are my sister and believe it or not we do look alike."

"I have a big bum, you don't." Rune laughed at her.

"It's not as big as Treen's is it?" Jade started to giggle

"Oh, Rune that's naughty, you are the centre you should be sweet."

"I am truth Jade... believe me you are so very beautiful under all that hair. Ok I tell you what we will do, what do you plan to wear for the wedding, because I have three days and if you will let me, just this once we will show the world the stunning beauty and elegance of Lady Pebbles of Avon. Mum will help."

Jade threw her arms around Rune and hugged her. "I love you sis." Rune held her close. "You need not fear parenthood either Jade, Rowan's children are wonderful."

Jade slipped back and looked at Rune her eyes were wide. Rune smiled and nodded. "I have seen you with them, as you tonight recognised mine." Jade smiled as a tear ran from her eye.

"Did you see Robbie's face; I cried it was so beautiful. That was your daughter then? Oh, Rune she was so like Robbie and so beautiful like you. He knew then?"

Rune nodded. "She came to him in the cave and he thought it was me, I have no idea how they did it, but she came again last night and she spoke to him. Oh Jade, he was so overcome as he spoke to her, I could see the love around them and it was vast. He wants to call her Iona when she is born. It can mean Isle of violets or violet stone."

Jade beamed as she saw the happiness in her sister's face. "She has violet eyes like Una, which is a sign of the power to protect isn't it?" Rune nodded.

"Jade we both have a life worth living, we are so lucky."

Jade looked at the floor. "I will be happy if I can get Treen laid."

Rune giggled "Oh Jade... Stop worrying about Treen. Look at the power of the rose, it blossoms all over." Jade looked out across the glade where Treen stood talking to Skip. She smiled and giggled as he spoke.

"God, she hasn't fallen for that limp lettuce has she...? He loves being boring and talking about refugees and politics, I bet he talks in bed as well." Rune giggled and shook her head.

"We all like different things, and she likes a strong mind, Skip's greatest asset is his mind, even you must see he has helped Robbie organise a lot of things Jade... well Treen admires that, maybe she will bring a little of the wilds of nature out in him, we will see."

Jade watched. "God I never realised, she must be as dull as him if she finds his jokes funny, I have never laughed at one yet... Mind you if she really does like him, that will keep her away from Rowan. I don't trust her she can make them do stuff by thinking."

Rune sat back and smiled. "The more love we have around here the better."

Robbie walked under the moonlit trees with Rowan. "I love this place Rowan it has a power that draws me to it, I feel calm and can think here." The trunks loomed out of the darkness and yet Robbie instinctively knew where every tree was. He walked as if walking in daylight, his feet sure of the path, Rowan admired his gift of the woods, for he knew of no other that could navigate the woods as quietly or with such instinct. Rowan thought that somehow Robbie's mind guided him.

Robbie came to the edge of a wide glade and sat on an old tree stump. He patted the one at its side without even looking at it. Rowan stepped back, another step forward and he would have fallen right over it, he smiled and sat down. "Your woods skills even now Robbie amaze me, how did you learn such craft? I try so hard and yet I cannot match you."

Robbie shrugged, "I love the woods and they love me back; I seem to have a feeling about them, that's all I can say." Robbie looked across the glade at the large fat trunked and immensely tall Oak tree. The pictures of his father holding him up to present him to the forest were still bright in his mind. He looked forward to the day when he lifted his children up and showed them to the world.

Rowan sat quietly in the dark, he felt he knew what Robbie was thinking of, and he did not want to disturb his thoughts, he peered into the darkness surrounding the large mighty oak tree. The place somehow felt magical and restful, he felt a wave of calmness flow over him and he relaxed. Robbie sat still at his side, the same calmness bringing him peace, he could hear Robbie's soft breathing at his side.

The moon came out from behind a cloud and lit the floor of the wood, light danced in the glade before the tree and Rowan touched Robbie's shoulder and whispered quietly. "Are those spirits I see?"

Robbie blinked, and looked into the dark. A figure of white that shimmered was knelt before the tree as if praying, Robbie rose slowly uncertain of what he could see, his bow slid silently round from his shoulder to his hand. He pulled an arrow from his quiver and Rowan followed his lead.

Robbie scanned the tree. The figure was tall and slender, and seemed dressed in white with long flowing tassels that ran down her sleeves and into her long flowing white skirt. Her hair was as white as her clothes, and she wore a cloak of the purest white. He stood not moving, and watched as she nodded to the tree and rose. Was this a fairy, or some spirit he knew nothing of? He had never in his life, seen anything like her in the woods before.

He looked at Rowan who shrugged. The figure bent down and lifted a silver bow from the floor, seeing the weapon, his bow came up and he fired. The arrow flew silent and landed right at the feet of the figure who jumped back in fright. Rowan knew what that was like, and marvelled as he held his bow high. Robbie already had another arrow fitted and trained on the stranger. "Who walks in my woods at such time of night, without the leave of the Hooded Man?"

The figure froze holding her bow with a silver arrow pointing at him, Robbie pulled back on his string. "Announce yourself or I will shoot to hit."

The figure seemed torn between running and talking. "I am no enemy of Loxley or its lord; I seek to speak with him on matters of importance."

Robbie took a pace forward. "Then speak quickly, for you face him."

The figure in white lowered her bow. "If you are my Lord of Loxley, lower your bow and come speak with me, show me the proof of who you are."

Robbie lowered his bow, Rowan did not, he stayed several feet behind Robbie as he crossed the open towards the figure in white. The moon shone on her fair face, and as he came forward towards her, he could make out more detail of her appearance. Her clothing was a dazzling white, as was her hair, even in the moonlight it shone brightly; he noticed the small silver snowflakes that decorated her clothing, and the silver snowflake pendant around her neck. "Who are you and why are you here in the woods at this time of night? How did you enter Loxley without notice?"

"You ask many questions for one who has not proven their own identity woodsman." Her eyes caught his attention and he stared at them almost transfixed. She had no pupils, her eyes, were just black circles with a black dot in the centre, there was no colour.

Robbie pulled on the chain round his neck and the lion with diamonds for eyes dropped down the front of his waistcoat. "I am Robert of Loxley, now name yourself."

She saw the lion with the diamonds for eyes and relaxed. "I am Crystal Onyx of Avalon; I seek you and my cousin Runestone Sapphire." Robbie raised his hand to shake, and she jumped back quickly and screamed. "DON'T TOUCH ME!"

Robbie pulled his hand back quickly. She pulled a long pair of white gloves out of her silver belt and slid them on to her hands; she offered her gloved hand to Robbie. "I am sorry My Lord, but my gift without gloves is fatal, you will be safe now. Will your friend lower his bow now?"

Robbie raised his hand and Rowan lowered his bow, he bent to the floor and picked up Crystals bow, Rowan nodded as he handed it to her. "I am Rowan, nice bow is it metal?"

Crystal smiled as she took her bow from him. "It's titanium, light as a snow flake, but brings the coldness of death quicker than winter."

Rowan smiled. "How cheerful."

Crystal smiled. "I am sorry where are my manners, greetings Rowan, I have heard of you from my cousin Ruby, she seems quite a fan of such a famous double act." She held out her hand and Rowan checked she was gloved before he took it.

"Ruby is quite a fan of a lot of things; she is a sweet person and loved by us all."

Crystal looked back at Robbie. "Is Runestone close? I have travelled a long way and had to cloak myself to avoid detection; I cannot remove my cloaking until I am with her."

Robbie smiled. "She is but a short distance through the trees, if you follow me, I will guide you through. How are your mother and sister?"

Crystal smiled. "You know of them My Lord?"

"I am the hooded man and seeker of the truth, there is very little that does not go unnoticed by me."

"You certainly have keen eyes in the dark My Lord, I cannot see the trees before me, and yet you walk as if in daylight."

Rowan laughed as he followed. "I think he thinks his way through the wood; I have never known any who walk this fast in the dark amongst trees."

Rune sat alone on the balcony waiting for Robbie, most of the group were in bed. Jett sat with Rafe and Jade below her on the porch. She saw the glimmer of white coming through the trees. Jett seemed surprised. "Hey look it's Frosty Knickers."

Rune stood up and stared through the dark. "Crystal?" She turned, and ran through the bedroom and onto the landing and down the stairs. She flew out of the house and down the steps and across the glade to the trees, where Robbie walked out with Rowan, talking to the white clad figure of Crystal.

Rune smiled as she wrapped her hands around her. "Oh Cousin, why did you not let me know you were coming?" Rowan wanted to warn her about the gloves, but it was too late. Rune beamed, as they broke apart. "Long have I waited for this moment, come on into the house and we can talk."

"You live in a wonderful place cousin Runestone." She looked at the wooden house, and the woodland, and the lake it was beautiful.

Rune sat at the table with Crystal as Robbie sat and watched while he drank. "Tell me of Amethyst and Gwinne, how are they? It is so hard to talk as they are hidden, and I would so like to welcome my family around me."

"We have left Glastonbury; it was not easy and we have shared a difficult road. Mother and Amy have carried on north under their protection; mother feels it is not wise for her to talk to you yet. They seek the heir and wish to protect him, darkness has come that mother knows of, and she has sent me here to bring a gift that may aid you." Crystal looked from Rune to Robbie.

"The south is no longer safe; the black wall is almost complete and when finished we would have been trapped forever. Mother's gift proved useful and she smiled her way out and passed the wall. We tried to get to Scarlet but they have quite a war on their hands and we had to skirt round them. We reached North Wales only to find another wall although it is hidden by magic because it appeared that the locals could only see trees, it was strange."

Robbie put his cup down on the table. "Where is this wall of magic?" Rowan sat up in his chair and looked at him.

Crystal shrugged. "It ran from North Wales right around to old Huddersfield where I left it and came over the moors to Loxley, why do you not know of this wall?"

Robbie looked at Rune with a very worried look as he stood up. "Edgar, I knew he was a snake.... SKIP!" He turned and left the room.

Crystal looked at Rune. "Was I not supposed to mention that?"

Rune patted her hand. "It's fine, you just gave Robbie the excuse he has been looking for, just let the boy's sort it out and do not concern yourself."

Robbie ran up the stairs followed by Rowan, he knocked on the door and stepped in "Skip I ne.... Oh, err, sorry Treen." Treen pulled the sheets over herself as Skip smiled.

"Little busy Robbie, just give me a moment." Rowan leaned against the wall of the landing and chuckled, Robbie stumbled for words.

"Are yes... right fine." He closed the door and looked at Rowan who was fighting the laughter inside him. "Did you know about this?" Rowan grinned as he fought the laughter down and shook his head. Robbie smiled. "I had no idea, to be honest I wasn't even sure he liked women." Rowan tittered and gasped as he walked away trying not to let his laughter out. Robbie headed back down the stairs.

"These women are going to wear out my whole bloody army before long, Rafe is forever running off, Jett barely wears trousers these days, I noticed Saff snuck Keith off earlier. Jade kept you in the tee pee for almost a day, and drags you anywhere soft enough and private. Hearne knows what Ruby will get up to when she is older. Even Steph and Smokes have rediscovered their youth since Scotland, and Hearne knows what's happened to Harry, I have hardly seen him since I got back."

Skip came down the stairs tucking his shirt in his pants. "Sorry about that Robbie, it was quite late and I thought we had finished so I thought I would."

"Yes, Skip I saw exactly what you thought you would do."

Skip looked worried. "I have not stepped out of line, have I? Robert my dear friend if I have offended you, I am very sorry."

Robbie raised a hand. "Who you d... what you do in your free time Skip is entirely your own affair, I am sorry to have interrupted, had I known I can assure you I would have left you."

"She is a very lovely girl, Robbie." Rowan chuckled.

"We did notice." Skip smiled

"Can we get on gents please...? Skip what do you know about an invisible wall that runs from North Wales round to Old Manchester, and up past Old Huddersfield?"

Skip looked surprised. "Absolutely nothing at all, why is there one?"

Robbie sat back in the chair and rubbed his tired eyes. "It appears my friend that there is, and only gifted magical people can see it, which I think will explain the reluctance of Edgar to have anyone check out Old Liverpool, he is working for Knox."

Skip looked angry. "I knew it, you could tell by his slippery words. I should have let Jett separate him from a few of his major limbs."

"How much does he know of our plans?" Robbie looked at Skip and yawned.

"Not that much, he left quite quickly after you challenged him, at most he will know who is supporting us."

Rowan looked at Robbie. "Like Carlisle and its surrounding towns?"

The pictures of the hanging woodsmen and women and children passed into his mind, and Robbie felt anger in him like he had never felt before. "Skip our first task after the wedding is find that snake so I can peel his hide off, then we destroy Old Liverpool completely, I will want to know just how many men we have surrounding that wall, Liverpool is about to feel the anger of Loxley."

Skip nodded. "I will get right on it."

Robbie looked up at him as he rose from his seat. "Skip late tomorrow will be fine, you have a young lady who I feel requires your attention, take a night off for once."

Skip smiled. "Thanks Robbie."

Robbie walked back into the empty kitchen; he turned and walked back to the stairs. The house was empty and it was the very early hours of the morning, he climbed the stairs very weary and walked into the bedroom. Rune sat brushing her hair and humming happily. He slid into bed and lay back exhausted; she curled up around him and smiled. "I love our house." She kissed him as she snuggled up close. "I want at least ten children now."

He smiled. "We can start tomorrow Rune darling; I will let Hearne know we will need an extension." He closed his eyes as she giggled.

"Poor Robbie darling I have worn you completely out." He breathed deeply feeling her warmth around him as he drifted into sleep, and a little girl with the most wonderful violet eyes gave him a very beautiful smile, and called him

'Daddy'.

CHAPTER TWENTY

A DAY OF THREE RINGS

It was midmorning when the sound of Ruby drifted into Robbie's ears.

Crystal stood by the Mere, and Ruby ran screaming down the grass her arms out stretched, she jumped smiling into Crystals arms and she swung her in the air and laughed with joy. Robbie flopped back on the bed, as Rune slid round him and kissed his tummy and worked her way up to his face, her two bright happy blue eyes peered at him surrounded by red hair. "Hey beautiful."

She smiled. "Hi gorgeous." She kissed him.

It had been a very late night for all of them, Harry had been very generous with the wine made by Joe and there were some very heavy heads around the place, as Robbie walked in bare feet with his shirt over his shoulder, down the wooden stairs and into the living room. A new rug had appeared overnight that had the large multi coloured star on it surrounded by white with a black edge.

Rowan yawned. "Steph and Smokes left it before heading off; it's their house warming gift."

Robbie nodded as he looked out across the glade where Ruby sat cross legged with Crystal talking by the edge of the water. "Where is everyone?"

"Jett and Rafe are still in bed, they drank a bottle of Harry's wine between them. Skip left earlier with Treen." He smiled as Robbie did. "Jade is making something to eat, Maddy and Mel have gone to the gate, I am not sure why. Una has a hangover and is back in her room wishing she had died. So is Bear, Alice is medicating him as I speak, and Jasper has gone to buy some more cheese." Rowan sat and looked at Robbie, and frowned slightly. "He is an odd one that Jasper, he is always buying cheese, the man must live on it."

Robbie smiled at Rowan. "It's very good for you cheese, especially if it comes with liberal amounts of Melissa." Rowan smiled as it dawned on him, the tall good looking blonde obviously had caught Jasper's eye.

Jade trundled in beaming a huge smile. "Good morrow." Robbie turned expecting Maggs, and started to laugh as Jade placed the tray down. She passed him a coffee and he smiled at her.

"That was a very good impression, you had me fooled completely."

She gave him a big smile. "I miss her a little; we had loads of fun with her on the farm."

He flopped down in the chair. "So, what are we doing today?"

"You two can disappear and leave Rune and me alone, we want to sort some wedding things, and I don't want any of you to see, I want it to be a surprise on my best day."

Robbie smiled across at Rowan. "Come on we need to see what Skip can find out; we will be more use there than here."

Robbie and Rowan walked into the large Village Hall, which was now the centre of all activity in the country. Skip stood at the far end of a very busy room, young woodsmen and women ran around passing sheets of paper to each other. Several lines of desks lined the walls, where young women wrote letters and instructions, which would be despatched to various units around the country.

The large map in the middle of the room showed all of Mason Knox's activity. Both of them stood at the side as a young girl leaned over it pushing red pins in. A large wall was now set on the map and Robbie stared at it. Hearing about it was one thing seeing it on the map was completely another.

The wall stretched from Lowestoft on the east coast and ran right across in a straight line across the map to the farthest tip of southern Birmingham. From that point, it headed south to Chippenham where it joined the wall of the top of Devon. The whole of the inside of the wall was coloured grey. A small area in the centre of Canterbury was green, and it was the only green in the whole section of the map.

Robbie looked at the equally shocked Rowan. "How the hell is he doing all this so fast?"

Rowan slowly shook his head as he looked north. A second wall ran from Scarborough across to the far side of the York moors and then bent north and headed up to the furthest tip of the Firth of Tay and Perth. All round Aberdeen contained another large city, once again the entire area was grey with not a patch of green to be seen anywhere.

Most of the north of England and most of the south was now under the control of Mason Knox, a dotted line on the map marked a large section that ran from what was Deeside and down the old M56. It came round Old Manchester, and looped across to circle the edge of Huddersfield before heading back to Fleetwood. Robbie studied it carefully, there were large patches of green inside it, and most of Liverpool centre was grey.

Robbie felt the anger inside him rise, he looked up at Skip and nodded, Skip smiled at the tall woodsman he was dealing with and then came down to the table where Robbie and Rowan stood. He barely had a chance to say hello, when

Robbie pointed to the dotted line. "Is that where we think this hidden wall is?" Skip nodded.

"It cannot be seen by most of us, but Treen has been able to read back through the memory of some of our scouts, they just see trees, but she sees the wall. By working out where they were at the time and piecing points in from many of the scouts, we now have a rough outline of where we think it is."

Rowan shook his head. "That is a bloody big area to be right on our doorstep guys."

Robbie looked back up at the two of them. "I want this wall down and quickly, we must find a way of making it visible so we can attack it, I want Edgar to deal with personally, we have sent a lot of refugees his way, I hope for his sake they are still alive."

Skip saw the anger behind his eyes. "I have six men inside there Robbie, I am waiting to hear from them, and as soon as I know anything I will let you know."

Robbie patted Skip's shoulder. "I must admit Skip, you and Fuse have done an incredible job here, this must be a nightmare to organise." Skip gave him a big smile.

"There have been tense moments I must admit, but I was trained for this Robbie, my dad always wanted to establish a new government in the country. He gave me the tools to do it, only now can I see why he did what he did."

"Keep up the good work I really appreciate what you have done for the woods folk of this country, believe me when all of this is done with, you will be honoured for what you have done."

"I serve a lord I love and respect, he has been my inspiration." He gave Robbie a huge hug and Robbie embraced his loyal friend. "You gave me the chance to prove myself Robbie when I thought I was not able, it is you who has faced him and fought him at all points. I have followed your example of what a true lord should be."

Robbie smiled at him. "Those are kind words my friend, you honour me."

"They are the truth Robbie, and you deserve the honour showed to you, everyone in this room thinks as I do, and they work hard on your behalf." Robbie looked around at the bustling room and smiled as some of the workers looked up at him.

Robbie and Rowan had a most enjoyable time walking round the room and talking to everyone as they followed their tasks. Most were very shy and Robbie in his usual way came across as just being a normal woodsman who had genuine interest in them. They smiled, and bowed and told him what work it was they did, and how things worked. Rowan smiled as he observed him talking, Treen brought a tray to him and sat beside him, she seemed a little nervous.

"Eez Robbie angry with me Rowan?" Rowan looked into her pale brown eyes.

"Why would he be?" Treen blushed as she looked at him hoping she would not have to explain, Rowan realised. "Robbie is not your keeper Treen. He was just a little surprised and a little sorry he had walked in on you; he saw how embarrassed you were."

She nodded and smiled. "I was much unclothed, normally I would not worry, I ave a good body, but with him I felt bad about myself in front of im." Rowan smiled at her.

"Robbie has a very open mind, he does not stand in judgement of anyone, and you should not feel bad about it honestly. In a way he was pleased to see you both have found someone."

She gave him a bright smile. "That eez good, Brandon eez a very nice man and I really like im. He eez very clever you know?" Rowan nodded at her.

"He is very important in our team; Robbie thinks very highly of him."

"Thank you, Rowan you ave rested my mind, I must get back to work now. I ave to speak with my Auntie Scarlet." Rowan watched as she headed off across the room and sat down. Her eyes glowed an orange colour, and she sat still as she focused.

It was later in the afternoon as the two of them, found themselves sat on the fence of the market ground watching all the new faces of Loxley, as they mulled around the stalls talking to the traders and haggling for better prices. Robbie was in very high spirits as Maggs wandered around with a large pot pouring hot drinks for the traders.

"Good morrow My Lord, would you care to partake of a hot pot?" She smiled as she poured a hot steaming Dandelion coffee out. Robbie noticed Blades and Judy, stoking a fire in the large metal tin Maggs had used to cook on the carts. He smiled at Maggs as she handed him a drink.

"Maggs sweetheart, I am Robbie, you are family now." She smiled and nodded her head vigorously, which made her rattle and jangle in tune. Robbie smiled as he felt he had missed her.

"I hear young Lady Pebbles is preparing for her nuptial bliss. That is so groovy and cosmic." She gave a horse like gasp as she laughed, and her huge front teeth looked like gravestones. Robbie put his head down to his cup and tittered, Rowan fought to keep his face straight.

"Yes Maggs, she is very excited as am I." He grinned and nudged Robbie with his elbow.

"Oh, weddings can be so radical and romantic, it makes you feel sort of herbal all over, don't you think so Rowan?" She jangled as she spoke and Robbie who was fighting an unexplainable fit of giggles slipped off the fence, and stretched as he turned away from Maggs.

Rowan smiled as he suppressed the laugh. "I think it will be a very herbal day."

Maggs eyes opened wider. "Oh my, how totally groovy."

Rowan nodded. "Very." She gave him a big smile and her teeth popped down her front lip, he smiled as she gasped a braying laugh like a donkey. Robbie walked into the stalls quickly, his laughter rose into the air.

It was a fun day and both of them laughed and joked as they walked back through the trees into the glade and across to the wooden house, Rune sat with Crystal and Jade on the front porch, it was a warm day and Rune had opened the glass doors wide. Rune gave him a huge hug and a big smile. "Had a nice day?" He smiled

"Actually, it was nice just to hang out and wander around Loxley, I really enjoyed it." She gave him a sweet smile and kissed him.

Most of the guests had left and the five of them sat down to eat on the porch, Una who was just about recovering came down to join them. It was a gentle and quiet time, the sun sunk slowly over the Mere and the bird song ceased as they settled down for the night, everyone seemed in a quiet mood, and Robbie closed his eyes and lay back on the steps next to Rune who had brought a huge pile of large and colourful pillows out.

His thoughts drifted around inside his head; the sword had been on his mind all day. He had been so sure that now he was ready to face the Knox Empire and destroy it. How could he have missed something, he knew the words by heart, and he had found Lancelot's sword, so where had he gone wrong?

Without hope, 'there is only deep despair.' That had to be the sisters and the vault. 'Beneath hope, lies sanctuary inside. Recovered honour lies at his side.' That was the tablet, which led to the sword. The lion and all the other items were the wheel, bring the five swords together, and you will see the path.'

Robbie thought about it, and he was convinced it was the heirs; Gwendolyn could not possibly have meant anything else. His head spun and Rune could feel his internal confusion. Crystal smiled as she noticed Rune watching him.

"He will work it out, you know he is half way there already." She smiled

"I forget at times that I am around others, and I just pick up on something inside him and I want to dive in and help."

"You love him that is natural. We all felt it the night of the barrow, mother was so moved she cried, and Amethyst bawled like a baby." She began to laugh. "You are lucky Runestone to have such a power to aid you. He loves you deeply."

She smiled as she looked down at the steps where he was now fast asleep. "I would not survive if I lost him."

"You won't... Come on it's late, let's go in and sleep, take your Bowman to bed he looks exhausted. I will talk to him tomorrow and give him the gift from my house."

Rune nudged him and softly kissed him, he slowly woke and opened his eyes and smiled. "Come on sleepy, get yourself in bed." They cleared the pillows and closed the glass doors. Arm in arm they walked up the stairs and slipped into bed in the moonlight.

The following day was hectic. Preparations for the wedding were now at fever pitch. Robbie found himself surrounded by women who all seemed to find him in the way. Beth ran about moving things, and Jess ran from one room to the other with needles and pins. Rune was busy with Jade all day and Steph was running about organising Alice and Jett who were the maids of honour.

Robbie walked into the woods and up to the Sacred Oak where his dad and John were building an arbour under the mighty tree. Bear and Martin laid out rows of chairs with Keith and Rafe in a large semi-circle around the arbour in front of the tree. Judy and Blades helped Maggs with ribbon, as they decorated the woodwork with lemon and lime green.

He once again felt like a spare part, everything was in hand and he sauntered into the trees and enjoyed the feel of leaves above his head. The sword lay heavy on his mind as he walked without thinking. He stepped out of the trees on the opposite side of the lake and looked across at his home way over on the far side.

The glass windows sparkled. Rune stepped out of the house into the sun and he smiled as he saw the light shimmer in her hair. He sat on the grass and watched her as she organised the tables, three of the farm lads had been sent up with a cartload; he saw her glittering in the sun as she walked down the grass. He closed his eyes.

"Hey beautiful." She stopped and he laughed, as he saw her look around.

"Where are you gorgeous?"

"I am watching Loxley's most beautiful woman."

This far away he knew she was smiling, and her eyes would be dancing.

"I see you, what are you doing all the way over there?"

"No way Rune, how can you see so far?"

"I told you Rob, I will never lose you again. Trust me I know stuff."

"I am on my way round, see you in a bit."

"I will be here waiting."

He stood up and he could see her facing him, he started to walk along the edge of the water, round towards the house. Rune organised the tables and then walked down to the trees near the water's edge. He could see her and crouched low, without a sound, he crept up on her. He moved slowly round to her side as she watched the trees smiling.

His arms shot out of the trees and snatched her into the bushes and into his arms, she squealed with laughter and he held her low and looked down at her. She giggled, "I could feel you near me, but I could not see you, you are good."

"I am the best." He pulled her to his face and kissed her as she slid her arms around his neck. They walked back up the grass arm in arm; most of the wedding duties had been done, and almost everything was set for the following day. Robbie looked up at the sky. "I hope it doesn't rain."

"It won't." She gave him a reassuring look.

"Sorry, sometimes I just forget." She gave him a bright smile.

That evening Rowan left for Steph's house. Jade would be spending the night at Robbie's house, as Rune would be dressing her in the morning. Steph had sorted out some new lordly attire for both Robbie and Rowan, she was going to do a last minute fitting of Rowan to ensure he would look perfect.

Robert Lox had gone to check the house on the end of Sacred Oak Road was now finished; it was a special surprise, and his men had worked flat out to finish it in time

Robbie walked into the glade of the Sacred Oak with Rune. She smiled as she saw the ornate arbour decorated with lime green and lemon ribbon.

"All we need now are the flowers." She touched the chair at the end of the row, flowers sprung along the wood decorating every row with lime green roses, surrounded with baby's breath and pale ferns. Yellow lilies and pale evening primrose interwove with the roses, and all the seats bloomed. Robbie watched her fascinated as she walked down to the arbor and white roses wove all around, entwined with white summer jasmine, the perfume wafted all around the glade.

She raised her arms and small acorns with clusters of fresh pale oak leaves wove in and out of the roses. The whole appearance changed and it looked like an enchanted garden. He smiled at her satisfied look, every now and then, she would touch a spot and a small daisy would blossom and fill a gap, her eyes twinkled with pleasure as she looked around. She smiled at him. "She is my sister and I want it perfect."

"It is Rune it is really beautiful; Jade will love it."

"Oh, Rob she is so excited, I thought today she would explode. It has been impossible to get her to stand still while I pinned her dress."

"Her dress... we are talking about Jade?"

Rune put her hand to her mouth. "Oh, please Robbie you won't say anything will you? I promised." He smiled and kissed her.

"I would not do a thing to spoil Lady Pebbles day." She smiled and a small tear ran down her face.

"Oh, Rob she is so beautiful. Every time I think of her, I cry." They happily walked back to the house as the sun set, Una had found some left over wine and half a glass full, had given the desired effect of sedating Jade enough to make her collapse exhausted into sleep. Robbie smiled as he lifted her up in his arms; he carried her up the stairs as Rune opened the door and he crossed and laid her gently on the bed.

Robbie headed down stairs as Rune undressed her and put her into bed; she stroked the hair out of her sister's face and smiled. Jade looked like an angel to Rune, she was Rune's older sister and yet she looked, and acted like her younger sister, Rune loved her very deeply.

Robbie lay looking at the moon through the window, as his sword glinted next to the bed. Destiny was on his mind again, Gwendolyn's words pounded in his head. What had he missed, where was the lost sword of Carnac? Everything in the crypt had gone to plan, what was so plain he could not see it.

Rune came in, and undressed and slipped into bed. "Thinking of that sword will drive you as mad as Harry." She curled round him and he put his arm round her.

"I have missed something. Crazy as it sounds, I know we got everything out of that crypt, if we hadn't the wheel would have continued to spin. We have it, or know where it is without realising it. I just feel it is in my grasp but I do not know where to put my hand." He looked at the blue eyes twinkling in the moonlit room. "Rune it is driving me crazy."

She smiled. "You need to relax and try not to think of it." She stretched up and kissed him. "I can help you sleep if you want... close your eyes." She straddled over him and her eyes glowed violet as she made the connection to him. He felt her in his heart and warmth seeped around inside him as she spliced into him.

He lay back as every muscle and bone in his body relaxed, and he felt he was floating, wave after wave of her love surrounded him and happiness and joy rose inside him. Rune felt him inside her as his love flowed into her, everything he had ever felt about her flowed through him as they connected and their spirits joined as one. There was joy, happiness and bliss, he was at one with her free of doubt and free of worry, he drifted like a free spirit in the universe wrapped in her love.

Robbie woke feeling a powerful sense of relaxation. He felt strong and vigorous, Rune sat at the mirror with her hair tied up, as she put a little makeup on. She used very soft and subtle shades of blue around her eyes, it was so faint it was hardly noticeable and yet it highlighted the sapphire in them. Robbie loved it, and smiled as he sat behind her and watched.

"Rob get dressed you are putting me off." She smiled. "I feel all silly with you staring over my shoulder like that." He kissed the side of her neck and she closed her eyes. "Oh god I love that, it's not fair, I have to get Jade ready." He smiled as he kissed her cheek, he loved the fact he knew just where to kiss her and raise her goose bumps.

He looked at the velvet emerald green pants and open neck shirt with laces, they looked very regal, and she had placed out a golden belt with a cluster of oak leaves as a belt buckle. She looked from the mirror and nodded. "Rob today is the wedding of your two closest friends, you will be Lord Loxley in the full for the day. Jade made you that belt specially to match your golden dagger and sword, I know you hate anything that isn't woodland and smelly, but please for them look the part."

"I don't just like woodland and smelly, I like light and comfy." She got up and came across the room to him.

"Please be good, Jade is a bag of nerves this morning and it gets me going. She wants so desperately for everyone to like her today." She kissed him softly and he pulled her close.

Robbie came down the steps and Una looked up as she fixed Jett's hair into braids and wove soft lilac flowers into it.

"Corr Robbie, you look hot." Jett beamed and winked.

He smiled, Jett was in a long flowing lilac top and skirt edged with black and with her raven black hair she looked very attractive. He was so used to the oriental style black jacket and tight pants edged with lilac, that somehow, she seemed completely different in a skirt and top. Una finished and she stood up and laughed as she twirled and the full circle skirt lifted and flowed round her. "What do you reckon Robbie; do you want me with passion and lust?" Jett giggled as she spun again on her golden spiked boots.

"I think Rafe will when he sees you; you really do look very beautiful Jett." Jett stopped spinning and looked at him.

"Honestly Robbie, you wouldn't lie?"

"If I wasn't with Rune, you would definitely be top of my list." She gave him almost a shy smile.

"Wow Rob, thanks." She looked down at the long skirt and flowing top. "This girlie stuff works then?" She grinned at him, and he saw the cheeky face he was so use to and loved.

Steph arrived and rushed in. "Rowan is ready. He is uncomfortable, but he looks like a prince... Wow Lord Loxley, I am charmed." She gave him a curtsy, he smiled as she blew him a kiss and shot up the stairs.

Rune came down the stairs and Robbie turned and caught his breath. He stood and stared at her a picture of complete loveliness. She wore a long gown of violet, which was very figure hugging; the sleeves fitted her arms close and fluted as they reached her wrists. Around her slender waist was the same belt as his, except hers was in platinum. Her hair was braided back and filled with violets, and on her head, she wore the tiara of Loxley. She looked at him, as he stood speechless. "Well?" Her eyes danced.

He walked over and slid his arm around her. "I have never seen anything as beautiful as you today." She beamed and her eyes twinkled.

"You look very handsome. Very like the lord you are, I wish you would accept it Robbie." She kissed him. "Now come on it's almost time and you will belong in the woods at the side of the groom."

Robbie got ready and lifted his heavy green cloak and threw it over his shoulders, he saw the golden wolfs head and two crossed golden arrows and he smiled, he heard a happy giggle and he turned. Jade stood on the stairs looking very nervous, and he gave her a big smile. Never in his life had he seen her look so beautiful, and he now saw how like her sister she was. Her bright green eyes shone brightly with happiness.

Rune had made her a shoulder less dress in the palest of lime; it had very faint and subtle oak leaves embroidered all around it. She had a choker of Jade green on which hung a golden rowan leaf; her hair was brushed back and pinned into place with gold rowan leaf slides. On her head above her fringe was a sparkling tiara of woven woodland leaves, and she wore a cloak of jade green. He was overcome with the vision of Jade.

She gave him a big beaming smile. "I am ready Robbie; do you think he will like me?" Tears flowed down Rune and Steph's face Robbie smiled.

"Our little woodland Nymph has grown into a woodland queen of the fairies. Jade you look beautiful."

She giggled happily. "Thanks Robbie... I am still a woodsman look." She lifted her dress and there underneath were her brown woodsman pants and her black boots. Robbie laughed and Steph buried her head in Rune's shoulder as Rune giggled.

Robbie walked through the trees and into the clearing. All the guests were almost seated in their finest clothes, and Rowan stood by the arbour looking very nervous in midnight blue. Steph was right he did look like a prince; he smiled as Robbie walked up and Robbie patted his shoulder. "She will be here shortly... Nervous?"

Rowan looked at him. "Robbie, I have faced wild beasts and wild men, never a worry. So why do I feel so scared stupid now?"

Robbie patted his face gently. "Rowan you are about to marry a very beautiful woman. It will scare the hell out of me too when I do it with Rune... Women are ten times more frightening than wild boars or wild men; we can kill them, these we just live with." Robbie started to laugh and Robert who stood a few feet away boomed a deep laugh, and nodded his head. Rowan looked very pale; Jess took Rowan's hand and led him to the arbor.

The High Master of Loxley would normally conduct weddings, but Len was not available as he was at Caerleon, he had arranged to watch through Steph and was going to connect with Jade at the end of the service. Jess was High Mistress of Loxley and so she naturally was Len's replacement.

Smokes stepped out of the trees and nodded to Robbie, he pulled Rowan round. "Here goes, you missed your chance to run." He gave a little laugh but Rowan did not move.

Rowan stared down the aisle of chairs and smiled. Jade stood flanked by Rune, Alice and Jett, on the arm of her father. Rune clicked her fingers, and the sun cast a beam of light down on to her, and Jade glowed in the light. She looked almost shy as everyone gasped, and the flute and mandolin players struck up a soft Celtic tune. Rowan gave her the biggest and most beautiful of smiles. She giggled as her father moved her slowly down the aisle in the centre of the wood under the Sacred Oak. Alice wept into her hankie. Steph, Una, and Mel wiped their tears and Maddy smiled.

Her bright green eyes never left Rowan's slate grey, the love between them showed and as she came up by his side and he took her hand, he whispered quietly. "You are the most beautiful thing I have ever encountered in the woods." Her eyes glistened as she beamed her bright smile at him; Rune wiped her eyes, as they both stepped under the arbor of flowers. Jess took their hands and placed them together.

"I am here today under the watchful eyes of our lord of the forest and all creation to bind you with love, so you may be as one in the world. Through me Our Lord will join your union and celebrate the meeting of creator and life. Will both of you love each other, and care for each other and live as one in the realm of green lands?"

Rowan looked into her eyes and both of them spoke together. "We will"

Jess smiled. "We see the love you hold, and feel the commitment you bring, I bring you together as seed and life and may your happiness grow to full bloom through the seasons of life." She loosely tied a green silken band round their hands as she spoke.

Rowan slid a ring of small golden oak leaves on to her finger. "I am a man of the woods simple and true, but in you I have found a meaning to my life that would not allow me to continue without you. I love you Jade of Avon. With you at my side, I know my life will have meaning and contentment. I will take you into my life as my wife if you would have me."

Her eyes filled with tears as he looked deeply into them. She slid a ring of golden rowan leaves on to his finger. "I have spent much time in this world lost and alone. I knew not my place, and I wandered. From the moment, you walked through a woodland glade and I followed your trail, I knew that I had found my path of life. I belong here in the woods with you, for you are my woodland and my path

Rowan of the woods. You are the soil I walk on, the leaves of my shade and the air I breathe. You are my life, be with me from here on in." She smiled and he pulled her closer.

"I love you so much Jade."

Jess raised her arms. "Jade of Avon and Rowan of the woodland realm have vowed their love before you. Take them in your heart and into your lives as one. Hear me My Lord and grant them life, love and seeds of a future."

Jess smiled as they held hands in front of her. She put her hands on their shoulders and Rune and Jett sprinkled petals into the air. "Children of the woods you are one. Go in peace and live in this realm together." Jess pulled the ribbon, and it unravelled from their wrists and she handed it to Jade.

"Congratulations you are man and wife." Jade burst out into giggles, and jumped into Rowan's arms. He spun her round as he kissed her and everyone stood and clapped as the band hit a merry tune.

Two chairs appeared on long poles, and as everyone hugged and kissed them they were lifted into the chairs decorated with flowers, and with the band in front and Jade laughing wildly, and Rowan smiling, they followed the band as they were carried through the trees to the wooden house of Robbie and Rune.

The food was piled high on the tables, as most of the village turned out for the celebration, and they danced, and laughed and ate their fill. Robbie sat with Rune on the porch as she curled on to his knee.

"Look how happy she is Rob; I have never seen such joy in her." She wiped her eyes. She turned to face him, he smiled and he knew what she was thinking.

"Our time will come Rune, we will marry and fill this house with the lives of our children, and you will weave and I will hunt and run the stockade. We will lie in the moonlight every night and make love, and I will never stop loving you. For every moment I am with you I will love you just a little bit more, and when we die our love will be so great it will fill the other realm." He stroked her hair as he gazed into her eyes and she filled up with tears.

"I almost lost you Robbie; I thought I was going to be destroyed. Never leave me alone again, because I now know the pain of being without you and I could not bear it." He pulled her close as she leant on his shoulder.

"It will not happen again Rune. I love you too much."

"Oh, Robbie I was so frightened and afraid without you." He rocked her gently in his arms and just enjoyed holding her close.

The day wore on, and the tempo dropped as good food and Harry's wine took effect. The whole of the glade was littered with groups all gathered and talking merrily on the grass. Robbie walked round with Rune on his arm, and smiled and talked, and joked with everyone. His new home was talk of the town, and so was the cut of his trousers, the women more than most seemed to like the snugness of their fit.

Rune beamed as she caught the odd comment, she liked them very much in deed and under his cloak, she slid her hand down and patted him before giving it a squeeze. He jumped and she giggled as everyone looked up. Jade slid her arms around him as Rune pulled Rowan in to a tight hug. "I love you Robbie, thanks for everything." He squeezed her tight his affection for her showing greatly.

"Oh, Jade I love you so much, Rowan and you mean so much to me and I am so happy he chose you. I wish you all the happiness in the world." He kissed her cheek and held her for some time. Finally, he let her go and he pulled Rowan into a hug and patted him warmly on the back.

"Rowan my friend, we have seen some times together, and no doubt we will see more. I am happy for you and Jade; you are both precious to me... Come I have something for you."

Rune walked through the trees on Robbie's arm at the side of Rowan and Jade, they came out at the end of the Sacred Wood Road, and there set in the trees was the newly built wooden house. Rune had used a lot of magic to hide it from them, and now as she wove her hand in the air it came into view for them.

John Lox had secretly stolen the blue swing seat off Jade's flat and changed the words in silver to 'Rowan and Jade's Place.' Robbie walked up to the white fence that stretched out of the trees and down one of the fields. He handed her the keys. "This is the gift of the house of Loxley, all the land contained within the white fence is now yours, and you are the first none Lox landowner in these parts in over five hundred years. You both have stood by me and fought the cause of these people. Welcome home."

Rowan looked stunned. "Robbie, Rune this is too much." Jade screamed lifted her skirt and ran through the gate and down the path to the house with a large furnace and workshop on the side. Rune looked at Rowan and smiled.

"Shouldn't you run after her and carry her over the threshold?" Rowan smiled, turned and ran, and jumped the fence; he caught her as she excitedly unlocked the door. Rowan picked her giggling up off the floor and into his arms, as Robbie and Rune came in through the gate and walked down the path.

He carried her into the house and set her down. Robbie stepped into the house with Rune, Jade looked all around the beautiful house. The Lox estate men had done a wonderful job and it was perfect. Jade looked across the living room with a small stone chimney and polished floors, and straight into Robbie's smiling eyes. She burst into floods of tears and ran wailing into his arms. Robbie laughed as he pulled her close. "What you don't like it?"

Muffled sobs and words came out of his chest. "I love you and we don't deserve something so beautiful; you are the kindest person I have ever known, and I do not know how to thank you."

Robbie stroked her hair, and pulled her back and looked down into her weeping green eyes. "When you and Rowan spent a whole week searching, you thanked me."

She wiped her eyes. "But we didn't find you Robbie."

"But that did not stop you trying, did it? Knowing you would look for me against all odds, told me enough to keep going. I knew you would not quit easily." He kissed her on the head and Rune pulled her into a hug.

"You always had the flat, now you have a home, and I am only a short walk away... Come on let's explore, I have not had a chance yet, they were still building at midnight last night."

Jade smiled as Rune led her up the stairs. Rowan opened the stove door and lit it, he threw in a few small logs and smiled. "How about the first coffee in a new home?"

Robbie beamed. "I think that will be wonderful neighbour."

Rowan looked up and smiled, Robbie and Rowan began to laugh, and Jade found the bathroom, and squealed with delight. The front of the house looked out over Loxley, and the large wall behind which was Loxley Wood, the back stepped out into the sacred wood of Robbie's Mere. There was enough land to grow food or graze horses, or even keep a small number of livestock. Rowan was thrilled, not only had Robbie given him a royal gift, he had done something far more special and deeper for Rowan.

Rowan was a landowner in the Loxley Farm Estate. He now had a title and identity, Rowan of the woods was no more, he was now Rowan of Loxley. He had a wife, and a home and a new identity, the outcast with no past or present, who Robbie had cornered in the woods, had a future. That future had roots; Rowan could finally lay his ghosts of the past to rest, and move on with a new life and a fresh start. Robbie knew that meant a great deal to his quiet companion.

They left them to settle and headed back to their house, Rune was happy as they stepped through the trees and walked across to their own home. It was very late when everyone had finally left, and just Crystal sat at the kitchen table with them, as they enjoyed a last drink before bed. Crystal slid a small black box across the table towards Robbie.

"Guinevere had this made for Arthur, it was made by Gwendolyn. She never had the chance to give it him because he died before she could get to him."

Robbie picked up the small black box and opened it, Rune gasped as she saw the ring with five swords, held in the arms of a lion, on a small golden shield. Robbie looked at Crystal.

She smiled. "It is a gift from the house of Pendragon to the house of Loxley. It should be worn on the left hand, and if you find yourself without a weapon, raise your left arm and it will protect you. Gwendolyn made it to protect Arthur should the Dark One ever discover the secrets of the black blade."

Rune took it from the box and slid it on his index finger, and it fitted him perfectly, she smiled and looked up at Crystal. "This is made from the metal of destiny."

Crystal chuckled. "You are so like Opal. Yes, there was a small amount of metal left and she made the magical shield of Morbihan with it, for that is what you now wear. Robbie if they come at you with a sword and you have left your defence open, as they strike your arm, a shield will appear and protect you. It will bear the crest of Arthur Pendragon. Three golden dragons on a silver shield, which will frighten your enemies, believe me."

He stared at the ring as it glistened in the lamplight, he knew that Gwinne must have seen something in his future, and he was glad she thought to protect him.

Later on, he curled up around Rune as she slept and his mind wandered for the thousandth time, as he thought of the lines that Gwendolyn had given him. He had made a mistake, and he had the strangest idea ever. However, would it work? He would soon see.

CHAPTER TWENTY ONE

THE ICY WALLS OF OLD LIVERPOOL

A week had passed since the marriage of Rowan and Jade and very little had been seen of them, Smokes had made several journeys up to the house with Jade's tools and equipment, and he had reported how happy they both were. They were spending long mornings lying in, and doing their house up during the afternoons and getting everything organised.

Robbie and Rune found they had a lot of time alone, and although Una and Crystal were both staying in their home, they saw little of them. Robbie spent his mornings riding down to the Village Hall, where Skip had given him a desk, and he sat with his father and other members of the group, discussing the situation at Liverpool. Information was now starting to flow in and Robbie combed over the papers as he worked out a plan to bring the whole area back under woodland control.

The afternoon and evenings were spent with Rune. He looked forward to their time alone and they sat by the Mere or walked in the woodland around their home. Una would smile as she saw them, walking in each other's arms laughing with each other. It was quite normal now at sun set to see them stood by the Mere as the sun set holding each other and kissing. Robbie seemed calmer and more relaxed than he had ever been, and one night when Jess sat with Crystal, she smiled to see her son walking bare foot in just his tight green pants, and holding Rune's hand out of the trees, as she giggled and he smiled.

"There is a radiance to Rune like I have never seen before, and Robbie looks so happy, he has never been so relaxed." Crystal smiled at Jess.

"They really are so happy here, I must admit Jess, I can only dream I will find someone who makes me feel like he does Rune."

"Rune is glowing." Jess smiled as he lifted her into his arms and swung her round, she squealed with delight and fell laughing into his arms.

"The power of Rune has changed; she has spent most mornings at her table and is learning to balance the huge force inside her. She is becoming very skilled in her art. With balance the true feel of nature can radiate out of her." Crystal watched her carefully as she spoke as if seeing the power inside her.

They came smiling on to the steps and Jess hugged her son. "Oh Rob, it's so nice being able to pop in and see you." He hugged his mum.

"It's nice seeing you mum." She squeezed him tightly, and then she gave Rune a hug. Rune smiled, and took her into the kitchen and all the women sat around the table chatting, Jess filled them in on the farm and how good the crops had been, and Robbie sat and watched them all.

Liverpool now preoccupied his thoughts, Robbie had worried that Mason Knox had somehow slipped in under his nose and taken over a large section of the northwest. His first problem was that the wall was obviously a magical wall, getting over it undetected was going to prove impossible. Any attempt on the wall would be instantly be detected, and Edgar would be tipped off and ready for any attack. He had to find a way that allowed for stealth.

He sat back with the laughter and talk in the background drifting into his head. Stealth, bows and swords, there were still green areas, and some woodsmen in there, if he could make it in then he would have a chance. He looked up and noticed Rune watching him; her eyes sparkled as she smiled.

"Can you make snow?" It seemed an odd question to ask her, everyone at the table stopped talking and looked at him, as an understanding seemed to cross between him and Rune.

"I am nature, I can influence the weather, you know this." He smiled and leaned forward.

"The sisters of the circles can see this wall, but the rest of us cannot, if it could be dusted with snow all of us could see it." He smiled, it was that simple, and who would expect freak weather? None, but it would give him the chance to sneak over without announcing his presence.

Crystal looked across at him. "I am gifted with my bow and have many uses where snow lies, can I join you?" Robbie nodded at her.

"We will need stealth so I want to sneak in, and then at the given moment create havoc. I want Edgar alive if possible; he must answer for what he has done. I want to get as many of the woodsmen out as possible, and then we will level it to the floor, although I am still uncertain of how to do that. If you can help Crystal, you will be welcome. I want to see Rowan today and talk with him, I think the sooner I get this done the better."

Jess turned to Robbie. "They were at the farm earlier talking to Rags, and they will be coming to see you later. They looked really happy together, Jade has become quite the talk of the stockade since the wedding, I must admit none of us realised Rune how very pretty your sister is under all that blonde fringe."

Rune gave a big smile. "She was beautiful, wasn't she? Bet she is back in brown pants, and her green tunic today though?" Jess smiled and nodded.

"The black hat of Harry's is back again." Rune giggled.

"He gave her that when she was twelve; it has hardly been off her head since."

Jade loved Harry, he had always been special to her and she was to him, Jade understood Harry more than most, he was an outsider and so was she. Now it seemed one appearance in feminine clothing and she was instantly accepted.

Rowan and Jade had been to the village for the first time as a married couple earlier that morning, and everyone was keen to stop them and congratulate them. Most of the women of the community stopped her and complimented her on her wedding gown; she was stunned as nice thing after nice thing was spoken to her.

Jade looked at them and smiled from beneath her long thick curly fringe, her bright eyes sparkled with delight, and Rowan smiled at seeing the happiness it brought her. She was of course now Jade of Loxley, and in many ways that made a big difference.

They came across the glade towards the house, and Rune smiled as she heard Jade's wild giggles long before she saw her. She sat on Rowan's shoulders and screamed as he ran at the tree line stopping just before she hit the leaves. Her bright happy face was all Rune needed to see of her sister to know that the week alone together had done her so much good.

Robbie slid his hand round Rune's waist as Jade and Rowan approached laughing, he bent forward and she sprang on to the floor, and ran up into Rune's arms. "Oh, Rune I have missed you. I have had the best week ever though.

Everyone in the village seems to suddenly like me, and my house is wonderful. Rowan is fantastic we have laughed all week... Oh Rune I am so happy." Rune squeezed her tightly.

"I am so glad for you Jade; you deserve this happiness." She kissed her on the cheek and hugged her as she looked and smiled at the very happy looking Rowan. They came into the house and Jade spent the next two hours telling Robbie and Rune all about her new workshop and her house. She raved about the new sculpture she was making for the garden, Rowan and Jade had planned to create a big garden like Rune's and Jess's.

Jess sat with Una and Crystal and they all smiled happily as Jade did all the talking, it was later when Rowan sat with Robbie on the steps at the front of the house, and Rowan sipped his iced cranberry juice that Rowan spoke. "Have you thought more about Edgar? Robert did mention you have been spending a lot of time there recently."

Robbie nodded. "I want to get the team back together and set off as soon as possible, I have a few ideas in the office."

Rowan looked up. "What office?"

Robbie grinned. "I tell you Rowan this house is so cool, I found another room.

There is a hidden door next to the bathroom, it leads to the attic; there is a huge room up there with a big desk in it and some empty bookcases. Rune told me I should use it as an office, she has put her design drawing board up there as well, so while I work on whatever scheme I am planning, she sits and draws up all the new clothing patterns. It is fantastic come and look."

Robbie led the way, and soon they stood in the large room with thick beams and another window that looked out into the forest. Robbie's, Loxley cloak with the gold embroidered badge on it hung on a small golden hook on the wall. The desk was solid oak and carved up all the legs with clusters of leaves and fruit. The top of the desk had neat piles of paper on it, and Rowan could see the lines of Gwendolyn written line by line on each sheet.

"What is this about Robbie?" He looked at the first line of 'without hope there is only deep despair.' Robbie had underlined the words hope, deep and despair. In their place, he had written just above them. Rune, dark, and dungeon. His scribbled notes read. 'A land of pain and hurt (The Black Rock) Rune is my hope, must we enter the dark rock together?'

Rowan looked up from the paper. "I thought we had solved this?"

Robbie pulled another chair up at the side of his desk and sat in the large wooden one behind his desk. He patted the extra chair and Rowan sat down beside him. "We worked out the clues and got your sword, the sword of Honour. Think of this Rowan, the wheel stopped spinning so we knew we had got everything out of the crypt under the church of hope."

Rowan nodded his agreement and Robbie smiled. "Maddy told me her mother Gwendolyn used to set her complex riddles where the lines of each riddle could mean more than one thing. Maddy grew up with these riddles and she would find two or three sets of answers all hidden in the one initial piece of text."

Rowan looked a little confused. "So, you are saying there is more than just getting Lancelot's sword in there?"

Robbie grinned. "Exactly... I think the answer to the sword of destiny is hidden here and possibly what to do with it when I find it. I have spent all week trying to work it out. See look at this" Robbie read the sheet "Recovered honour lies at his side... I think Victor recovered his honour by making the dagger, and the dagger lies by my side at all times. It's here on my belt and when I sleep it's close to my bed, if I am in the woods asleep it is in my belt at my side. Can you see what I am getting at?"

Rowan picked up the sheet he had previously read. "How can Rune become hope?"

"That is simple look at this. Beneath hope lies sanctuary inside. Hope lies in the symbols of life." He showed Rowan the sheet and then pointed with his finger as he read the lines to him. "What if Rune is hope. Beneath Rune is the circle with the star in it, and it is under our home inside."

Rowan nodded. "Ok the wheel of Runestone I can see that, but what about the symbols bit?"

Robbie was thrilled his friend could actually see his ideas. "The wheel of Runestone is a circle. Stone circles have protected Rune's aunties until Rune could connect them. The circle has been sanctuary, and Rune's wheel that is below this house is now the sanctuary of everyone, she uses it to protect us all. The symbol in the middle of the table is the runic 'R'. Rune is nature, her power is life, that Celtic rune is the symbol of life Rowan. Rune is hope."

Rowan now understood and saw the genius of Gwendolyn. "Wow Robbie, I think you are on to something. What else have you got?"

Robbie sat back in his seat and sighed. "That's as far as I have got with it, I have spent a week trying to work it all out, I want to ask Maddy to look at it and see if she agrees with it."

Rowan sat back looking at the line about the shield and the lion. "This has got to be about protecting you; I think getting Maddy up here would be a good idea. We really need to find that sword and take care of the Dark One; Knox is building at too fast a rate for my comfort."

Robbie gathered up the papers, and slipped them into a draw and pulled out a map, which he spread out on the table. "Ok the north west and Knox's little new empire run by our sleazy and slippery friend Edgar. We know the wall around it is invisible and it cannot be seen through. I now know there are several miles of woodland on the other side of the wall. I think Edgar is using this as a cushion to hide the centre of his new city, I think the odds are very high that the woods are clear of woodsmen. That will give a clear run and somewhere to plan and hide."

Robbie pushed his finger along the map as Rowan watched, and noticed all the little markers that Robbie had put on the map. Robbie pointed to the large empty area around the city centre of Liverpool. "We know all this area was devastated during the Red Death and gangs went wild destroying the place. Just about most of the area from Old Liverpool to Old Manchester, was destroyed and woodland grew back here quicker than any other part of the country, I would bet my last bit it still is. Knox wants to really hide something from us and he thinks we will not suspect anywhere green, let's face it everywhere else has been covered in concrete."

"What could he have to hide though Robbie; Liverpool never really had that much in value to Knox, most of it was destroyed it would be easy to build from scratch in the south where it would be safer."

Robbie smiled at him, and Rowan gave him a grin. "Rowan my dear friend we know very little about those times, but there are some that are old enough to remember a great deal, and our good friend Fuse is one of them. Liverpool was very well known for one thing the whole world needed back then, and Fuse reckons it was very well protected at the time."

Rowan lifted his hands. "Which was?"

Robbie grinned. "Petrol"

Rowan frowned. "What's that?"

Robbie started to laugh, "I have absolutely no idea, Fuse got so excited about telling me how it was made, I did not have the heart to ask. Although I seem to remember a silly story about a petrol tanker with no tyres, that exploded. So, it seems to me this petrol burns and very easily by the sound of it. So, whatever it is Knox needs it, and Harry and Smokes know about it."

Rowan broke into a huge smile. "If those two know about it, then it must be very important to machines."

"Exactly my good friend. I think it's like the moonshine Harry uses to run his bikes, although I am not going to admit that to him until I know for sure."

"If it will burn Robbie then we already know how to deal with that, the only problem I can see at the moment is getting past the wall, how can we climb what we cannot see?"

Robbie stood up and patted him on the back. "I have already sorted that one, Rune and Frosty knickers will sort that out... Come on I am starving let's go and see if there is anything to eat."

Later that evening, Robbie accompanied by Rowan, Jade and Rune, they knocked on the door of Spring Cottage. Maggs was delighted to see them and whipped open the door with a beaming smile.

"Oh, what joy, I have guests.... Please my sweet darlings come forth, come forth and be welcomed." Maggs bracelets, and bangles and necklaces rattled and tinkled as she moved backwards, and the group stepped in. Rune handed over a pie.

"At Loxley if we arrive unannounced it is sort of tradition here to bring a gift of food, this is wild bilberry and cranberry I do hope you like it."

Maggs beamed with delight. "Oh, my sweet child I am filled with cosmic joy and happy jangles, how absolutely groovy." She took the pie and turned in the hall. "Please be chilled and come forth to our home and be at peace... Harry chicken we have guests." Robbie followed Maggs down the bike free hall, and through into the cottage living room, Harry sat in a large leather chair his huge stocking feet up on the hearth of a large grey stone fire with a thick wooden lintel.

"Hey man, and dude and dudets. Whoa is this cosmic or what, like you totally blew my karma and surprised me. Hey this is really cool, squat and be chilled chickens."

Blades and Judy sat at a table in the corner making a huge jigsaw and both of them gave the group big smiles. "Hey guys." Jade wandered over and looked at the jigsaw.

"Wow I have not done one of these since I was a kid, can I have a go?"

Judy smiled. "Its five thousand bits, so dive in we have been at it all day and look we are nowhere."

"Cool, mum always told us to do the sky first, can I do that bit?" Blades nodded and grinned; Jade grabbed the box and started pulling out blue bits. Rune and Robbie sat down on a long settee filled with shawls and cushions and Rowan sat in a small comfortable chair by the fire. Rune looked around the room.

Maggs had made a lovely home. The ceiling was quite low compared to the farm cottages, but everywhere was bright and clean. The room was a long oblong with plenty of space, the fire was large and the thick black lintel was filled with odd little pot figures. Small tables were scattered all over the room again draped with small embroidered mats, and each had a large vase of fresh flowers on it.

Two large glass doors showed a bright and colourful garden. At the far end was a workshop that had a row of fifteen motorbikes parked in front of it. The cottage felt very homely, and Rune relaxed in the chair at the side of Robbie. "Harry your house is really beautiful."

"Yeah man. Maggs has broken me old bike vibes, I keep them out there now, she like hates oil and stuff on the walls, she is quite cosmic though about it."

Rune looked a little puzzled; Robbie smiled as he thought about his last visit here when he had climbed over three bikes just to get into the living room. He patted Rune's leg and whispered, "I will tell you about that later." Robbie looked back up at Harry. "I have come to see you tonight Harry because I need to know about Liverpool and its petrol."

The sheer mention of the word seemed to get Harry very excited; he sat upright in his chair. "Oh wow man, I mean like I just love the stuff, smells totally cosmic." He seemed to slip off into a dreamy world and Rune sniggered, Robbie nudged her with his elbow. Harry came out of his dream like state.

"Oh man, it like takes me so back to my kid days. Liverpool had this totally cosmic and real radical terminal where they made it. Oh wow man what I would give to get in there, it would jangle your vibes to see." He slipped off into another dream state and had a strange almost hypnotised happy glare to his eyes.

"What is petrol anyhow?" Rune had no idea and asked what she thought, was a quite normal question.

Harry looked at her in disbelief. "Whoa chicken you have suffered un-cosmic thoughts in my home, petrol is liquid life to my most cosmic and radical machines; it fuels the road of totally wild and happenin mellowness. It is the jangle in my most cosmic vibes."

Rune shrugged at Robbie and looked back at Harry. "What we need to know Harry is does it burn fast?"

Harry looked suspiciously at Rune. "What you askin chicken?"

Robbie leaned forward. "Harry, Mason Knox is protecting something in Liverpool; we think it is a lot of this petrol stuff. So, we want to know if we set fire to it, will it burn quickly."

Harry jumped out of his chair. "Whoa man, like hold your totally uncosmic vibes. This place was like the karma of this area, I could run my totally cool machines for about ten thousand very radical years on what's there man. Hey Robbie man you don't go blowing up my liquid road life man, it aint peaceful dudes."

"It blows up then Harry?"

Harry looked stunned, and like he was about to faint. "Robbie dude I love yeah, but you put a very uncosmic flame next to that place, and whoa man, Liverpool will like split forever man."

Rune looked up at him. "How do you mean Harry, split?"

"Rune baby girl, it's like million gallon land, the place will like turn toast... puff, uncosmic land of charcoal monstersville."

Rowan stared at Harry. "A million gallons, Harry Ladybower is not that big."

"Hey man don't hassle my vibes man, I been there and seen, it is my cosmic Mecca man, you dudes aint seen the dreams of the cosmic life of cool machines, I have man."

Robbie looked at him as Maggs jangled in with a tray of coffees, and the pie sliced in neat glass bowls with warm vanilla milk poured on. "Oh sweethearts, I am thrilled, just positively thrilled you cared enough to visit my humble abode." She beamed as she passed the bowls around and Harry sat down with a thump.

Robbie felt a little sorry for him. "Harry, I know this is hard for you, but Mason Knox wants all this petrol stuff for himself. I think he wants to use it to kill all the wood folk and drive machines to tear down Loxley. I have to stop him."

Harry looked crushed. "Hey man I love Loxley and my folks here, I love all you guys, but Robbie man you are asking a hard thing here man, it like blows my karma apart."

"I am sorry Harry, if you don't want to come, I will fully understand, I would never ask you to go against your beliefs to help me. You stay here and watch Maggs, and we will do it."

Harry jumped back out of his seat. "Hey man, that aint cosmic, you come here with your unpeaceful thoughts and jangle my vibes, and then tell me I am like out of it man. You aint being cool Robbie and it aint nice or cosmic, chill out or talk to my blades."

"HAROLD LOXLEY!" Rune jumped, Maggs looked shocked "Harry Lox you make peace with your nephew now." Her face looked very stern, and Rune looked really surprised. Harry sank back into his seat.

"Hey man I am like sorry for chomping your vibes man."

"No Maggs it was all my fault, Harry is a proud man of Loxley and I insulted him, it is I who should apologise... I am sorry Harry; I love you, and meant not to hurt you. I know you will defend Loxley with all of us."

Harry sat forward. "Hey man we are cool and cosmic you know that man?"

Robbie smiled. "I know this will be hard Harry, but we need you. We have no understanding of petrol."

"Yeah man, Smokes and me can deal with it."

Robbie cut off a piece of his pie and slipped it into his mouth. "Oh wow Maggs this is fantastic, he took another spoon full and noticed Rune had finished hers and her eyes sparkled, he held his bowl out and she gave him a sweet smile as she cut a piece of his pie off and ate it.

Maggs beamed. "When I was small, my mother made custard." Her eyes rolled with delight at just the thought. "I cannot get all the ingredients now, so I make this little delight, it is as close as one can get to it... If Rune likes I will give her my secret recipe."

Rune gave her a huge smile. "Oh yes please Maggs."

Maggs beamed with delight. "Oh wow, how so incredibly groovy."

The visit to Harry's had been a strange time, they were an odd couple who made jigsaws, and played very bad guitar and sang absolutely worse. Robbie and Rune had spent the evening in fits of laughter, but not as Maggs had thought because Harry's jokes and tales were funny. It was because no one understood a word of them, except Maggs who rolled around braying and gasping like a donkey. This however was very funny and Rune had to run to the toilet twice she laughed so much.

It was late when they left still giggling and Robbie and Rune gave them both a huge hug and thanked them for a wonderful evening, which was true it had been immense fun. Maggs was quite tearful; as she was so happy her first ever house guests had enjoyed themselves so much. They walked slowly up the lane and turned into the Sacred Oak Road. Rune hung from Robbie's arm and giggled. Jade larked about with Rowan, and Robbie felt a closeness to his three companions, like he had never known before. He loved them dearly; they were his family and his future.

They walked through the dark along the lane and Rowan sensed something on Robbie's mind. "What you thinking Robbie?" Rune and Jade leaned in to listen.

"We will need two teams, one to blow up the petrol and one to deal with Edgar. I want Edgar, can you lead Harry in and blow the petrol up?"

Rowan seemed surprised. "I would prefer we do one then the other together as always."

"So would I Rowan, but the way I see it, the minute that petrol goes up, Edgar will know we are on to him, the two have to be done at the same time, you are my most trusted and best man Rowan, I will relax if you lead them. Rune and I can sort out Edgar, you and Jade blow the hell out of everything else."

Rowan sighed. "If that's how you want it we will lead team two, although I would be happier Robbie if we stuck together."

Robbie patted his arm. "You worry too much, relax Rowan you can have a taste of my job, you will love it, it stinks." He started to laugh and put his arm round Rowan's shoulder. "Only this once I promise."

Rowan smiled and stopped as they reached the fork in the track. "We will talk tomorrow." He hugged Rune as Robbie embraced Jade and with their arms around each other Robbie and Rune entered the wood, and Jade walked with Rowan down the last bit of the track and in through their gate.

Rune lay in bed her eyes sparkling; he could see the fun in her eyes. She had really enjoyed herself, he sat on the bed and slid off his shirt and she rose up behind him and placed her head on his shoulder. She slid her arms round him and he leaned his head back into her. She kissed him softly on the neck. "It's back to normal now, isn't it? More fighting and death." He sighed and closed his eyes just enjoying the feel of her warmth pass through him.

"It is him or me Rune. I can sit here if you want and wait, because sooner or later he will blow up the gates, and burn down this house, and pour concrete all over the place. Loxley will be the last green space to go; I know now what he plans." Robbie turned and pushed her on to the bed, he looked down into her beautiful blue eyes.

"This house will be the last green space in this country. Our home Rune, he will kill me, and you and then when everything is dead and covered. He will build his palace of stones here on my home as a monument to himself. I will not let that happen, not here. My life, my love and my heart live here, and will forever."

He kissed her softly and she curled around him. "I want children too, but not while he lives."

Robbe sat at his desk in the attic; Rune leaned over his shoulder as he studied the map. Rags had dropped some more updates to the maps off; Fuse had got word from his hidden woodsmen in the woods around Liverpool. It looked like the whole city centre, had been completely rebuilt. Liverpool was a large port, and it now looked more as if Mason was using it to ship goods around the coast. Robbie highlighted the harbour area and the petrol terminal. The rough sketches he had, showed a large central building that seemed of some importance judging by the number of guards around it, Robbie knew it had to be where Edgar would be found lurking.

"This is not going to be easy is it, Robbie? What with the harbour and that big building, we will be stretched? Scarlet's men will help but will fifty be enough?"

Robbie turned and kissed her cheek. "If we have ten men on each attack, and twenty to organise the escape of any wood folk we will be fine. Any more will make us too noticeable."

She looked at his detailed drawings. "Mind you if that refinery thing burns as well as Harry says, then at least we will know what direction everyone will be looking in, and that should help."

She slid around and sat on his knee; he smiled and gave her a soft kiss. "We will be fine; we will be side by side whatever happens. Come on everyone will be here shortly we had better get down and prepare." Robbie folded up the map and they headed down stairs to await the arrival of the others.

Rune sat with Crystal and Una on the front porch in the wicker chairs, and Robbie sat on the steps. Rowan and Jade came across the grass, as others began to appear on the edges of the trees.

Out of nowhere, a large white light appeared and Robbie stood up smiling, as it spun in the centre of the glade and he saw the shadowy figure of a warrior queen come through the light and out on to the sunny grass. Her long red ponytail swished behind her and the sun glinted gold off it, as the dark eyes of Scarlet met his and she smiled.

Scarlet walked toward him as the brown clad bowmen of Caerleon walked out in orderly rank, and the captain marched them to the edge of the trees and formed a set of four long rows. All the men stood proud with their hoods up and their bows held tightly in their right hands. Scarlet threw her arms around Robbie. "You are looking wonderful Lord Robert; I think life back home has done you good." He pulled her into a close embrace smiling.

"I am happy to see you again Scarlet, we have missed the clash of your sword on our practice grounds."

Rune came up and hugged her, Scarlet gave her a long look. "My Rune you have blossomed, home life is a good tonic for you both."

"It has been nice being home again Scarlet, and we have had a chance to rest up a little."

Scarlet walked up the steps of the house and Una hugged her half-sister. Scarlet beamed as she saw Crystal. "My child it has been long since I last saw you."

Crystal hugged Scarlet. "Hello Auntie Scarlet I am so pleased you have come; I have looked forward to meeting you for some time now." Robbie and Rowan started to assemble everyone as they arrived while the girls all talked. Mel and Maddy were especially happy to see Scarlet.

Bull arrived with a cart loaded with bows and arrows, and a few extra swords, his large shiny axe stuck in his belt. Bear stood looking at the long line of bowmen his huge golden sword on his belt and Robbie noticed he now carried an axe on his belt next to his dagger. Jett and Ruby rushed into the arms of their mum, whilst Harry and Blades arrived with Judy, who was carrying a long bow and a quiver of arrows. Blades had a crossbow slung between her two swords.

Robbie and Rowan walked the long line of Bowmen from Caerleon. The captain saluted and Robbie nodded. "Stand your men at ease Captain, let them sit and rest until we are ready, it may be some time, Lady Loxley has prepared some refreshment if you would like to send two of your men over to the house."

The captain thanked him and pointed to two of the men who broke free of the ranks and walked over to the house. As the men sat down on the grass, Robbie walked in amongst them, and shook their hands and spoke to them. Rune smiled from the step, as she saw him chatting to the soldiers. The two bowmen walked up and one coughed. "Lady Loxley?"

Rune and Jade both turned. "Yes?" Jade looked at Rune and burst into giggles. Rune smiled and stepped down to the bowman. "I am Runestone and that is my sister Jade, we are both of Loxley." He nodded.

"Lord Loxley has sent us to collect refreshments for the men." She gave him a warm smile.

"Please follow me; they are ready in the house." She walked into the house and across to the kitchen as the two bowmen followed looking around the large wooden home that was the house of their Lord and Master. They entered the kitchen and two large trays were prepared and ready. Crystal slipped off her glove and slowly passed her hand across the top of the glasses, the sides of the glasses misted as they were instantly chilled. She smiled.

"It's a hot day; these will cool you better now." The bowman gave her a strange look as they looked at the ice cold glasses. They picked up the trays and took them out.

It was an hour later when everyone was sat waiting on the grass and Robbie stood flanked by Rowan, Rune, and Scarlet. "Good afternoon, we are gathered today as you know because we have a problem in Liverpool that requires our immediate attention. Mason Knox has very cleverly built an outpost at Liverpool. He has hidden it using the cover of trees, and is using the harbour to ferry goods around the coast to his other outposts. He has also taken over a big plant that produces and stores fuel for his boats and his machines. I intend to take three teams into Liverpool at dawn and destroy everything he has built; I am not sure but we have been led to believe that he has a workforce of captive woods folk. I want to free them and bring them back."

He looked down at his notes in his hand. "The teams will consist of my team, which will be Rune, Keith, Saff, Fish, Mel, Mother, and Hornet with bows."

Everyone looked up and Robbie smiled. "Oh yes I forgot as tradition dictates Judy will now be known as Hornet, it appears she has quite a sting stuck in her boot." Everyone started to laugh and she beamed a huge smile. "Ok swords for my team will be Jett, Blades, Bear and Rafe."

They all nodded as he named them. "Our target is the main large palace like building on the harbour front, it appears this is their command centre; I want all of you to now sit over where Rune is, and I will instruct you all shortly. Captain I would like ten of your best bows to join me, thank you."

The team got up and moved across the grass towards Rune, who moved from behind Robbie and walked to his left. The captain shouted ten names and they rose and walked smiling over to the others. "Rowan will lead team Two; I want all of you to show him the respect you show me. Jade, Treen, Martin, John, Jasper, Crystal, and Maddy you are his bows. Harry, Skip, Smokes, Fuse and Bull, you are demolition squad, and again Captain if you could select ten men, I would be grateful." The team sat ready as the bowmen joined them.

"The last team will attack the harbour and put it out of commission and help free as many of the captives there as possible, Flash and Una could you join Scarlet and the rest of the bowmen and stay close to her, she will instruct all of you. Ok, we will have a one hour group briefing and then you will all be on free time until dusk, we will leave then."

The three commanders of the groups went to work as they pulled out plans and details and instructed the teams on their missions. Robbie had little detail on the inside of the palace so worked up a plan of clearing one floor at a time until the job was done. Only he and Rune knew the final part of the plan, and he did not mention it.

The groups broke apart after an hour and Mother, Rune, Maddy, and Una, all mucked in and served out food for everyone. Jett and Blades warmed up with a little swordplay, which impressed all the Caerleon soldiers who had never seen such a display of skill or ability. The whole group were of course now legends in Caerleon, and the group were very surprised to find that all the soldiers knew them by name.

Judy and Blades had been having bow lessons from John Lox, Blades had finally gone for the crossbow as it was small and compact and had smaller arrows. Maggs had made her a smaller quiver that fitted between her crossed blades and it had a small fastener on it that the crossbow clipped on to.

Judy now had a quiver and a new bow, and full woodsman attire made for her by Maggs. Because she had no Loxley crest and Robbie had mentioned her new nickname, Maggs had embroidered an angry looking Hornet on her cloak; Robbie had smiled when he saw it.

Rune stood on the porch as everyone sat and ate and she smiled at him. "It is about to turn to winter in Liverpool." Her eyes began to change from lilac to violet, and they grew a deeper and deeper purple, she closed them and thought hard. Robbie watched as she stood very still for a few minutes. She smiled and opened her eyes, violet light spilled out as they faded back to their normal lilac whites.

"It is done, there is a raging blizzard covering all of the wall, I threw a little extra high tide activity in just to shake up the harbour crews and tire them out a little, it is going to be a very rough twenty four hours in the north west." She smiled sweetly and winked.

It was several hours later when Robbie called together all the teams. They lined up on the grass in three long rows, Scarlet and Rowan waited as Robbie and Rune prepared. Rune walked to the edge of the trees with Robbie. "I am really excited about this; I have spent all week practicing when you have been down at the hall in the mornings." She gave him a huge smile and stood in front of the trees. Rune raised her arms and her eyes flooded violet light.

The two large trees in front of her leaned over and threaded themselves into each other forming a large archway. Robbie jumped not expecting sudden movement from the trees. Violets ran up around the top of the archway and down the other side, a faint shimmering of violet light filled the centre of the arch, Rune smiled as she turned to face him. "Off we go then." She stepped through the arch and disappeared.

Robbie looked twice and then stepped through. He was stood in woodland, surrounded by snow on the edge of the wall of Liverpool; Rune gave him a huge smile. "The wheel of Runestone has taught me a great deal Robbie."

He slid his arms around her. "So I see. I am very impressed indeed." He kissed her.

The three rows of groups came through and spread out taking cover. Robbie looked up at the huge wall; it was now covered in snow and visible to everyone. Crystal came up to him. "This is my bit Robbie, is it here you want to go over." He nodded as he looked up.

Crystal stepped up to the wall and took off her gloves, and walked along a twenty-foot stretch of the wall and poked it with her finger every few feet.

Ice exploded up the wall creating ladders in shining steps, like thick heavy icicles. Robbie watched them as they climbed to the top, and shot over and ran down the other side. Crystal took off her necklace of a snowflake; she pushed it on to Robbie's forehead. He felt a cold prickle and she smiled. "Now you are lighter than a snowflake, you will feel no cold and leave no tracks." She did the same to Rune and then walked down each line, pushing the pendant into each person's head.

On the signal as the sun fell, they scrambled up the ladders of ice, and over the top and down into the snow laden woods behind. Robbie wished Rowan good luck with a hug, and kissed Jade on the cheek. A snowball hit her on the head and Jett giggled wildly, Jade laughed and launched one back and then scurried off in the snow behind Rowan as they headed southeast to the fuel terminal.

Rune closed her eyes and all the woodland area began to thaw, snow would now only remain where stone lay. Robbie moved off into the woods and headed for the city centre. The harbour and docks were just in front of the large stone palace, and so Scarlet stayed with his team as they made swift progress through the dark.

Robbie estimated that it would take a few hours to get near enough to the city to see the tower, where he could adjust his plans as required. The woodland was quite sparse in places, where it looked like a lot of timber had been felled. With the clear skies, and the moon above them, they made good time, knowing about the weapons plant and Tintagel helped. Mason loved modern life and as with the weapons plant it was not hard to spot where the centre was, as huge bright lights lit the docks and the centre of the city.

It was just past two am when they reached the edge of the city. Robbie placed guards and sat in the trees watching through his telescope as the others bedded down for some sleep. He sat with Rune and Scarlet and looked at the whole set up; Mason Knox had been very clever. The roof of every building was covered in grass and shrubs, from the air or high places; you would not be able to see any stone at all. The tall palace rose in the centre near the front of the docks, it was like a giant set of steps, with each set of steps having trees grown all over the flat tops. It rose hundreds of feet into the air like a giant mountainous forest, covering the stone pyramid like building.

Robbie stared out at the buildings that led up to it; one had a long tree lined walkway that led to the pyramid. Robbie looked at Rune.

"Ask Crystal, if we are as light as snow would that mean we could run on top of a leaf and balance?" He looked at the long walkway hidden under an archway of trees.

Rune's eyes flickered violet; she went still and quiet, and then opened her eyes and smiled. "Crystal thinks so as long as there is some snow on them." Rune waved her arm across herself and suddenly it started to snow again in the city centre, it came down heavy and fast. The city was quiet as most people were indoors and Robbie looked around he saw his chance for Scarlet, and he passed the scope to her.

On the edge of the city was an abandoned railway track; it ran in a sunken line across the city into the docks. It provided a perfect and protected way in and out, Mason obviously intended to bring it back to use at some point and had left it, Robbie was now beginning to understand Mason and in doing so, he was able to find weakness and exploit it. Robbie settled down with Rune and closed his eyes for a few moments, he felt warm and snug with the charm Crystal had put on him and he soon drifted into sleep.

Rowan and Jade sped quickly down the edge of the wall. A ten foot space had been cleared of trees and so they moved keeping close to the tree line on a smooth surface. The snow was just over two foot deep, and to Rowan he felt like he was running on stone, and yet when he looked down there were no footprints or marks in the snow at all. Crystal smiled at him. "It's an odd feeling, isn't it?"

He looked back at her. "I will never quite understand it. I feel like I am running on a road." She laughed

"Don't think about it."

The bright lights of the refinery were now clear far up front of them, Rowan slowed as Harry and Smokes came up at his side, Rowan was uneasy about the fact there were no guards on the wall. His cautiousness rose as he saw the lights, he looked to one side and saw Harry and Crystal. "Why no guards? It seems odd, I would have hundreds of them looking out for this place."

"He did, I took care of them." Rowan looked at Crystal.

"What do you mean you took care of them?"

Crystal walked across and took off a glove. She touched the wall and ice shot up the wall, it cracked and crackled as it rose. She put her glove back on and then gripped the bar of ice and pulled firmly; a frozen body fell off the top of the wall and sank into the deep snow. Rowan stared at the frozen face of fear and the blue skin. Crystal leaned over and looked at the dead guard.

"I am getting slow he saw it coming." She looked at Rowan. "When I sent the ladders up, I sent ice along the top of the whole wall, it is about minus fifty up there at the moment, and none will survive that." Rowan looked at the blue contorted face and shuddered.

"You look sweet in all white, but you're actually quite scary Crystal." She started to laugh and patted him on the back.

"Be nice to me Rowan and we shall not have to worry." She winked at Jade who grinned.

Harry looked across at the terminal with Smokes. "Oh man we are not cosmic doing this, its shiverin my karma man."

Smokes sighed. "Its dry wheels forever Harry old pal." He watched as the rows of tankers backed up to the petrol terminal. "Look at that Harry man, there must be ten million gallons just waiting to be sucked into a carburettor, and bring hot wheels of freedom. You know Harry old dog, one of them tankers would run us for years."

Harry stared lovingly towards the row of shiny silver vehicles all being filled with the liquid life of the motorcycle. "Hey man the 56 is almost clear, and they have tyres man, we could like mosey on over and hitch a ride home. It would be funky and highly cosmic to liberate the goods of the old ways."

Smokes smiled. "I love driving those beasts, and we won't run out of fuel on the way home." Harry gave him a shrewd smile.

Dawn was not far away and Rowan had his plan, Crystal touched the metal perimeter fence and it froze instantly. Jade hit it with the back of her bow, and the metal shattered into thousands of tiny pieces. With bows loaded under the cover of the last darkness of the night, Rowan and his team slipped silently into the terminal.

Scarlet slipped quietly down the bank of the railway through the trees. The line was disused, and had become a corridor of green as the trees reclaimed the land. Small tufts of grass grew through the white lime chippings, and the concrete sleepers were just visible in amongst the tree trunks and weeds that had spread over them like a worn green carpet.

They ran quickly under cover and out of sight along the line. Buildings were high above them on either side, yet with two feet of snow, filling the roads and pathways above them, there was no one to see them as they hurried past deep below in the old railway.

Rune sat in the trees with her eyes closed, and watched through Jade's eyes and Crystals. The snow melted before Scarlet, clearing her path and now in the terminal Rune swirled snow around all the buildings containing soldiers, and blew the snow out of the path of Rowan and his group. Rune nudged Robbie and he woke. "Its almost time get everyone ready." He sat up and rubbed his eyes, Rune picked up a cup of cold coffee, she held it in her hand and it began to bubble and steam. "Here." She smiled as he looked at the cup and took it out of her hand.

"You are full of tricks these days." He lifted the cup and sipped. He slid back into the wood and prepared everyone, and ten minutes later a long row of hooded men slipped out from the edge of the wood, and ran across the rooftops towards the central high stepped building. As they reached the start of the large square that surrounded it, they jumped onto the top of the trees that formed a high arch, and ran just touching the leaves as light as snowflakes across to the building. They scrambled up on to the flat surface of the first step in the building roof, and slipped under the trees that grew all over it. Robbie smiled at Rune as he watched the last of his party cross the tops of the leaves of the trees. "Crystal really is very useful."

She gave him a big smile as they slipped into the trees. There were large windows that looked outwards through the trees in the sides of the building, and the group slid with their backs to the concrete. On either side of the windows, they settled down and waited for dawn to rise and start their assault on Liverpool.

Robbie waited at the side of the glass window, which was the size of a barn wall, as Rune slipped down by his side, he took her hand. "I love you Rune." Her bright blue eyes sparkled at him as she smiled.

"I love you too my darling. This last week has been the happiest of my life."

He leaned over and kissed her. "Mine too.... Let's get ready to move closer to getting the life we want." Robbie slipped an arrow out of his quiver and loaded his bow; he looked down the long line of men all sat with their backs to the wall. He gave a nod to Keith and Sapphire, and they loaded their bows, the others followed suit and waited for his signal.

The suns first rays crept over the edge of the sea and lit the very edge of Liverpool, Scarlet slid out her sword, as Rowan and Jade loaded their bows. Robbie nodded to his men and they all nodded back, Rune touched the large glass window and the glass returned to nature and became sand, it poured out of the frame and formed a large pile on the floor at the side of Robbie.

Robbie stood up and turned into the window, his arrow shot swift as Rune fired. The guards hit the floor not realising they were dead, and with hoods up, they jumped into the building and fired either side taking out more guards. They were inside and ready for action.

CHAPTER TWENTY TWO

THE HIGHEST PRICE TO PAY

Fuse pushed the wire into the bundle of dynamite as he smiled at Harry. "Come on Harry it's not the end of the world, you and Joe got enough moonshine to last your entire life. It's not like you will never ride your bike again, is it?"

"Oh man Robbie has made me do some bad things, but whoa man this is like the most uncosmic." The sunlight spread across the refinery in the pale light of dawn as Fuse worked stacking bundles of dynamite ready to be fitted together in a long series of controlled explosions.

Rowan watched the guards and pointed up to a high gantry. Treen took aim as Jade aimed across to the other side of the gantry, Rowan signaled and John and Jaz prepared to cross the wide expanse of ground up to the storage tanks. Rowan looked up at the huge round silver tanks with a crisscross of metal pipes that ran out of them above his head.

He gave the nod, and the arrows shot into the air, there were muffled gasps and the guards dropped on to the fine mesh steel walkways. John and Jaz shot out from behind the large yellow barrels, and headed across the wide concrete space. They ducked in behind a pile of blue steel containers, with bright yellow stickers depicting a skull. John looked at it and over to Jaz. "Happy bloody place this, everything in here seems to kill you." Jaz smiled as he nodded back to Rowan.

"Don't worry John, the deadliest things here today are us my friend." John smiled back at Jaz and raised his bow. The two guards came slowly round the corner, John held as he let them walk round the corner where they were out of sight of any others. His arrow was fierce, as was the arrow from Jaz; the two guards lifted off the floor and fell back into the snow. Skip and Bull slipped out from behind a work shed, they grabbed the men's legs and quickly dragged them behind the shed leaving a thick red trail in the snow that swept in an arc round across the floor.

Crystal touched the ground and snow blew across it burying the thick red and covering the surface white again. The whole group came rapidly across the wide area, and in behind the large blue steel drums. Rowan pointed his arm moving from member to member, as he positioned them. Figures shot up ladders and in between pipes, they moved silently like shadows. Fuse pushed a large bundle in between the blue cans and stuck the wire in. The wire ran along the floor behind him as Smokes and Harry followed him to the group, they ducked down as a guard came around the corner on a gantry.

There was a glint of silver, and the guard coughed, and fell over the rail, as Bull stepped out from the shadows. He caught the man in his arms and brought his knee up snapping his back, he stepped back quietly into the shadow where there was a dull thud. A quiet whistle came from the spot, there was another glint of silver and Jade caught her cleaned knife, she smiled and slid it back into her belt.

Rowan looked at the hundreds of coloured wide pipes that ran in every direction. There were huge concrete towers and yet more pipes running from them into large storage containers, which were just about the biggest things Rowan had ever seen, he looked at Smokes as he worked quickly on the explosives. "You do know which ones will explode don't you?"

Smokes winked at him. "Rowan, in the woods I take your advice, trust me it does not really matter too much which goes first, the chain reaction that will follow will be poetry to the rising sun."

Rowan smiled as he looked at the high petrol containers. "We will need to be very far away when this lot goes up." Crystal smiled.

"Rune is with me have no fear Rowan we will get you out safely."

Robbie pointed to the stair and Keith and Saff took up their positions, he looked down the long corridor that led back to the open window. There was no visible sign of the way up, the only stairs led downwards. He looked across at Rune as the others leaned with loaded bows against the many dull brown doors. "How do we get up, when the only way out is down?"

She shrugged. "Maybe down leads back up." Robbie looked back at Keith and Saff.

"Nice and easy you two have a quiet look round, Fish, Rafe, back em up." Saff and Keith slid slowly their backs pressed against the wall, as Rafe and Fish followed quietly behind them. Robbie and Rune waited at the top of the stair. Keith slid up to the door at the bottom of the stairs, he leaned on the door as it slid silently open a nick, and peered through the gap at the large open space, and the glass doors that led down the steps to the harbour. Four large guards stood by the door looking bored.

Saff looked at the stairs that continued downwards, she sensed sorrow and pain. Rune, who was watching through her, picked up on her feelings and looked at Robbie. "There are captives here Rob." She looked very concerned.

"What do you mean captives?" He glanced down the stairs waiting for the signal from Rafe.

Keith pulled the door closed and looked back at Rafe. "There are at least four and another set of stairs leading up at the end of the hall. If we can take out the four, there is a way up, let Robbie know." He looked for Saff but she had gone.

Saff walked slowly down the grey stone steps into the dark. The air seemed to grow cooler around her and it felt damp, she touched the wall, and felt the moisture run on to her fingers, it felt cold and slimy. She peered into the darkness; a soft red light seemed to glow faintly up in front of her. Quietly she edged towards it, and the tunnel ahead came to an abrupt end, which she almost walked out of into the long passageway where muffled voices seemed to echo off the walls. She leaned slowly round and looked down the dark tunnel of doors.

The long tunnel stretched as far in front as it did back behind her. To her right in the distance, she could see light and the outline of the ships lit up on the docks, it was musty and damp, and water flowed down the path in large puddles and streams. Saff looked across the tunnel where a large heavy rusty door stood with a big silver lock on it; two sunken eyes set in a white face looked across at her from a small window. She gasped and stepped back into the shadows.

She peered round the corner and looked back at the eyes that stared into the dark at her. The sad lost look told her instantly that these were the prisoners, and slave labour that Knox had been using to build his secret capital. She looked from left to right checking the tunnel was clear, and rushed silently across to the door and pushed her face to the small barred window. The smell inside was foul and she gasped. "Hi I am Sapphire, I am here with the hooded man, how many of you are there here?"

The eyes blinked as if coming to life. "Thousands." The voice was quiet and devoid of all hope. She looked down at the huge silver lock on the door. She needed help and turned to head back. A large hand slammed her back into the door; she jumped with shock her eyes opening wide. She felt the door, which had large iron bolts, sticking into her back and the pain shivered up her spine, her eyes watered with the pain and the shock. A dark unshaven face with very bad breath from a crooked mouth breathed against her face. "What have we here then creeping about in the dark? Up to no good I take it?"

Saff pushed herself up against the wood as his breath turned her stomach, the glint from the knife was fast and quick, his throat opened and he fell back as if dragged on to the floor, Bear looked at her, and smiled. Saff gasped a long sigh of relief as Bear pulled an arm around her. "You Ok?"

Saff shook, she had been frightened, but she nodded as Keith appeared at Bears side. She slid into his arms and he held her close. Robbie directed his men in the dark as they fanned out and sealed the area making it safe. Rune's eyes flashed violet as she scanned the whole tunnel, she turned to Robbie her eyes flickering lilac in the dark. "Rob there is a lot possibly thousands. This tunnel goes back over a mile and comes up in the woodland where there is a road to the gates."

Arrows shot further up the tunnel and Jett's sword glinted in the pale light, she had found the staff quarters for the tunnel prison guards, she stepped in and muffled cries could be heard above her whoops as she lunged and sliced. Robbie looked at the locks and the long tunnel. "We need them out and now Rune, it will take all day to smash these locks off."

She looked at all of them. "Get everyone back in the passage." Robbie signaled and everyone pulled back down the tunnel into the side passage, and they stood silent in the damp foul darkness as Rune stood at the entrance. He looked at Mel and Mother. "Take five of the bowmen from Caerleon and Hornet, get to the end of this tunnel as fast as you can and get into the woods. I want everyone out as fast as possible, Rowan is at work and the clock is ticking."

Rune's eyes glowed bright purple, one by one running the whole length of the tunnel the doors creaked and stretched in their frames. They exploded out as their frames, splintered, and smashed into tiny pieces on to the floor; Robbie covered his ears as the noise rose high in the long tunnel. Dazed looking faces peered into the darkness, Rune opened her hand and three primroses appeared, she threw them down the centre of the tunnel and yellow lights appeared every twenty feet lighting the way. She turned to Robbie as Mother, Mel, and Hornet charged into the tunnel with five of the bowmen, they ran down the long tunnel shouting. "Come on you are free, the Hooded Man has saved you, follow us."

Robbie watched, as pale exhausted faces came out of the darkness, he remembered Smokes the night he had been rescued from Tintagel, and looked at a thousand similar faces dressed in rags and covered in filth. He felt an anger rising in him, as once again he faced the inhumanity of Mason Knox and the people who worked for him. Rune touched his arm, Robbie turned to her bright sapphire blue eyes. "I sent these people here to be safe, and look what that murdering bastard has done to them."

She gripped his arm. "They are free and being taken to safety Rob, do not lose your head. Scarlet is heading for the top of the tunnel; she will bring the others this way. We have to find Edgar and bring him to justice."

He knew she was right, but his stomach twisted as he thought of all those hopeful faces that had left Loxley and headed here. He felt the responsibility of their fate and his insides burned. Robbie turned to the bowmen on the dark steps as a small primrose floated shining in the air. "We go up now, cover the door while we sort out here, we will be with you shortly." The bowmen nodded and sped up the steps.

He watched the old and the young, the men and the women all with drawn pale, hungry, and exhausted looks as their feet slid on the wet floor as they passed. It was a sight, which haunted him and he knew he would remember for the rest of his life. Robbie looked at the others. "Ok let's finish this." He turned and ran up the steps.

The docks were busy as ships docked and captive woodsmen carried box after box off the giant vessels. Men in black bibs stood with long whips, and lashed down hard on any who looked like they were slowing. Una watched from the top of a stack of metal containers, her hood high up over her long white plaited ponytail. She looked down at Scarlet and spoke with her mind giving her the positions of the guards placed high up with crossbows.

Scarlet sent her hand signals and the long cloaked and hooded figures disappeared into the containers, and behind large wooden packing crates. Scarlet worked her way forward slowly taking in each area of the long dock front. Three bridges broke over an inlet that led to the centre of the city, and across the centre bridge, she could see the open gate of the long tunnel that led past the prison cells and up to the woods.

Una and Flash ran along to the first bridge. Una looked around, the guards on the roof on the far side of the dock walked silently along, she patted Flash on the shoulder as she began to slowly edge to the bridge that was about fifty feet long. The guards turned at the top of the roof, their backs turned and Una and Flash shot over the bridge keeping as low as possible. Una slid in between a large pile of wooden boxes stamped, 'Machine parts.'

Scarlet looked at the long ramps that led out of the centre of the large freight ships. They were being loaded and she knew those would be vital parts for Knox, she signalled to three of her bowmen, and rubbed the heels of hands together, and then pointed to the three large ships.

The bowmen lowered below the large boxes they were stood behind and prepared their arrows. Scarlet sent signal after signal round her men as they prepared, she now had men all along the dock front, loaded and ready, the sun was starting to rise and she knew that very soon Rowan would strike and all hell would break loose. She looked across at Una and she smiled. Flash and she were now level with the central bridge and ready to defend any prisoners who were running to safety. On the dockside of the central bridge, two hooded figures rose and fired.

Their burning arrows went into the storage hold, and flames burst up in one of the large ships. Woodsmen spilled out dropping their boxes and ran back down the gangways towards the dock, and men in black bibs lifted their whips and fell with arrows in their backs. The panicked workers flooded back onto the docks as more burning arrows flew into the ship's cargo holds, the soldiers on the docks struggled as the tide of the workers overwhelmed them. Scarlet jumped on to the top of a large crate waving her large golden sword, which glowed in the light of the flames.

"To me and the hooded man!" She screamed, and the workers poured towards her running blindly for the central bridge, hooded men appeared all along the dock and guards fell from the rooftops. The guards on the docks found five and six prisoners charging at them, and punching and kicking, they beat them to the ground; those who managed to escape and run across the bridges fell as the bowmen picked them out and fired.

More soldiers came running out of a large building on the city side of the docks, Una and Flash spun round, Flash as small as she was pushed Una out of the way. "Get everyone in the tunnel; I want to play with this lot." She was tiny with bright white hair and round rose tinted mirror sunglasses. Her soft white silken pumps moved with the precision of a ballerina as she approached the group, which was now slowing seeing the little blind girl in their path.

She struck her white pole on the floor and it sparked as she slid off her glasses, a large guard looked back at the two behind him and sniggered. "What's up with you lot? It's just a kid, kill her." Flash raised a hand and tutted as she wagged her finger.

"I am sure your mother taught you much better manners than that, you should say please." Her squeaky little voice echoed and one of the men at the back pulled his mates jersey.

"I heard stories about a weird freaky white haired kid at Canterbury, come on Sid, let's bugger off."

The Army guard laughed and drew out his sword. "Talk to me of manners will you brat, well let me give you a lesson with this." He ran at her with his sword. Flash slid her silken shoe across the floor as she slid sideways, and raised her pole in a stance ready to spin. The large guard thundered towards her laughing, she spun like a top, the white pole blurred. Flash hit his face, then his arm and left leg, his momentum sent him sideways and she broke her stick apart, and both poles blurred as she followed round her spin, and came out of it hitting him on the right leg and catching him on the back of the knees.

He folded like a paper napkin and fell on the floor staring up at her, most of his bones were broken and he moaned in pain. She placed a small foot on his chest and smiled. "If you had said please as a gentleman should, I would have killed you quickly." Her eyes flashed quickly and his retinas burned, he screamed in agony. Her head slowly turned to the others who were frozen in fear having seen their best man defeated by a child of just five foot tall. Her red eyes glowed and they all stepped back. "You have been very bad boys, you hurt the woodland folk and I must punish you."

They had no time to move as the white light of the sun flooded out of her. Una watched her from behind amazed, she had heard of Ruby and her gift, but seeing it in action was very chilling. Ruby was a tiny albino who looked so vulnerable and harmless, and yet those eyes burned with a force that scared her as she watched. The guards fell into piles of ash on the docks, the light went out and Flash slid on her glasses, and looked at the pain riddled man on the floor.

"Your men are dead and you are now alone and in pain, all you had to do was say please and I would have finished you."

The guard's head lolled on the floor as he gasped through gritted teeth unable to move and in agony. "Please kill me." Flash locked her pole back together, and stepped over him; she took two steps and spun faster than light. Her pole left his throat and he relaxed as he died, she walked back slowly to Una as fifty piles of ash blew across the dock.

Scarlet swung her blade and clashed with a soldier; she spun her wrist, and up came her glowing blade. The soldier fell back a red line up his front where her blade had cut deep. More workers ran down the bridge and into the tunnel, which was now lined with hooded bowmen. They splashed into the long dark tunnel lit only by the small glowing lights that Rune had left floating in the air.

The door to the front foyer of the palatial building burst open, and as the four guards looked up, they looked back down at the arrows now embedded in their chests. They slumped to the floor, and Rune and Robbie headed out covering both sides of the room, two guards at the top of the white marble stairs lifted their crossbows, as Fish and Rafe came through the door. Robbie fired at the same time as Rune; they dropped on to the steps and rolled down their crossbows still loaded crashing on the steps.

Rafe and Fish headed up the steps and covered the long corridor, as Keith and Saff followed. They looked up at the staircase that rose to the top of the pyramid. Golden handrails wound round as they traced the line of the empty stairs, the dull light of the start of dawn lay across the glass roof far above them as the pyramid pointed to the sky. Jett pounced up the stairs as her eyes glowed lilac and she looked down the hall, she winked at Blades from under her black straight fringe.

"I feel a fun time coming." A loud bell rang and doors opened as soldiers spilled out into the corridor, Blades shot into the air and somersaulted into the midst of the soldiers, her golden blades flashing in amongst the screams. Jett raised her blade, and screamed a charging call, and waded in behind Blades spinning like a dancer and laughing like a banshee, as she swung and twisted on her long golden spike heeled boots. Fish and Rafe took aim and cleaned out the strays.

Robbie grabbed Rune as he sent the bowmen up the next flight of stairs, headed by Saff and Keith. Bear pulled his sword and his axe as he menacingly rose to the top of the staircase, the bowmen took the first five running towards the stairs, Bear with a huge roar took out the next five as his sword and axe flew through the air with crashing bone splitting effect. Saff and Keith moved up to the next level followed by Robbie and Rune.

They came around the corner of the staircase and looked up at the two giant guards with huge swords, Saff and Keith raised their bows. "SAVE YOUR ARROWS!"

Rune pulled them apart and stepped through on to the step. She smiled at the two heavy men above her blocking the top of the stairs; they glared at her with menacing eyes dressed in heavy black leather and hard steel edged boots. Her bright blue eyes twinkled at them. "You boys are not going to give me any trouble, are you?" They looked confused and looked at each other as Rune walked slowly up as if she was delivering the mail. Robbie brought his bow up and aimed.

"Rune don't be silly."

She turned and looked back and smiled as her eyes began to glow violet. "It's alright darling these boys will be nice about things." She turned and looked up as their swords just flopped to the floor, and swung like limp rope, Rune grinned. "Now boys over exertion can do that, not to worry though with a little rest they will stand up again."

Robbie started to laugh at the look of horror on the faces of the guards, who lifted their limp swinging swords. Rune waved her hand across her path and they fell backward fast asleep. The slender figure of Rune walked up the last few steps, and stepped over them and looked around at the long corridors as Robbie came running up behind her giggling. He slipped his arm around her as she smiled sweetly at him; he kissed her on the cheek. Saff and Keith appeared at his side. He looked around the long cold stone corridors of grey. "What now Rune?"

Her eyes still glowed as she looked around the place. "We split up and find Edgar, I sense a few around this floor, there is no one above us. They are on this floor, but the place is like a maze."

Fuse worked fast as he fitted together the wires, Alarm bells sounded and doors all over the place were bursting open and soldiers were pouring out. Jade and Treen took aim and held ready, as across the path, Martin and John aimed in preparation. A few feet down to her left, Jaz stood with his bow of yew ready, Crystal stood next to Rowan. "Let me have first shot, my bow has a few added surprises."

She took aim at the central barrack house that seemed to contain all the soldiers, her silver arrow shone in her bow and she released it. Rowan blinked at the speed it moved, there was a glint of silver and it hit the man in the doorway. He was thrown inside and the door banged shut, ice ran up the outside walls of the building as the windows cracked and frost blew out of every floor. The whole building became one massive block of frozen ice, like a huge iceberg. She smiled at Rowan. "Cool, eh?"

He looked back at the building. "I would say more like deep frozen." She started to laugh at the look of shock on his face as she winked at him

"Snow one in there is going to bother you." She gave a giggle as Rowan pulled a long face at her very bad joke. The others released their arrows in a hail, as soldiers ran round into their view. They dropped and others fell over them,

Maddy let her arrow go into the midst, and the whole group ignited, she lowered her bow and looked at Jade.

"Err... Not the best idea I have had.... RUN!"

Jade saw the burning men heading into the metal barrels screaming, she flew out followed by Maddy across to the others. "I think all of you should duck sharpish."

Martin realised what she meant and with a scream of, "Shit." He grabbed John and pulled him to the floor. The first barrel lifted with a deep orange flame about sixty feet into the air, bodies and metal exploded in every direction, as fire rained down. A smouldering figure bounced off the wall, and landed on top of Martin, he squealed as the charred face touched his, and he recoiled backwards, as John grabbed the body and flung it over the barrel.

Maddy lifted her head and peeped over a wooden crate. "Sorry guys forgot what everything here does." She gave a weak smile.

Fuse smiled up at Rowan as arrows shot through the air, he ducked down as five hit the barrel in front of him and a strong foul smelling liquid sprayed out on to the floor in front of them. "We are wired ready; we just need to get to the power box over there with Harry and we will be ready to blow the joint."

Rowan leapt up and fired, then dropped back. "Won't keep you Fuse, give me a second." He cut the flights off his arrows and fitted two on the string of his bow. He shot up, and fired and dropped back loading another arrow.

"You know being around Robbie is really starting to show Rowan." Rowan slid round the barrel and fired, Fuse leaned out and watched the arrow. "Oh, that was nice, caught him quite by surprise that one did."

Rowan smiled. "Nice to be appreciated Fuse." He fired another and a man fell screaming from the gantry; Crystal slipped back into the gap and came up to Rowan's side.

"What's the hold up?"

Rowan pointed his thumb back over his shoulder as he fitted his bow. "Got about six there want to use me as a pin cushion." She peeped over the top of the leaking can.

She loaded her bow. "Count two after I fire and then aim for the one in the middle." Crystal shot up, aimed, and fired; Rowan followed. Her arrow hit the wall behind the men, frost sprayed out of the tail of her arrow like snow and the men jumped up as it hit them, and they instantly froze. Rowan's arrow hit the figure in the middle and with a resounding crack, the whole group exploded into tiny pieces and splintered on to the floor. He smiled.

"That was really cool Crystal."

She smiled back. "About fifty below." Rowan shook his head as he giggled.

Fuse ran out across the roadway and into the trees as he pulled his wire to Harry's electric charge detonator, he pushed the wires on to it and tightened the screws down. He wound the wheel to build the charge and placed his hand on the plunger ready. "Bring them out Rowan we are about to make poetry at sun rise."

Rowan gave the signal, and his men began to flow across the wide road and into the trees as he aimed and fired at anything in black. Jade took out six and then turned to run across the road, she smiled as Rowan rose in the bushes with his bow aimed high, and she ran across the road. The burning sensation rose quickly and her feet seemed to drag on the floor as Rowan dropped his bow and screamed, and she felt her head hit the floor, Rowan's scream resounded in her head and it all went black.

Rune turned as the boats outside exploded, she grabbed Robbie's arm. "I have to leave." Robbie watched as the colour flowed out of her face. "What is it Rune?"

Her eyes filled with tears. "Jade is with Opal." It hit Robbie like a smack in the face; Rune grabbed him and kissed him. "I will be back."

She waved her hand and the wall turned violet; Rune stepped through and was gone. Robbie jumped forward, and bounced off the wall his arrows spilling everywhere on to the floor and he rubbed his nose. "YOU PROMISED NEVER TO DO THAT!" He screamed at the wall as panic rose inside him.

Rowan held her in his arms in the middle of the road; she lay limp in his arms as the tears fell from his face. The others shouted as they fired at the wall of black guards running along the high gantry towards them. He pulled her close the long red tipped arrow had gone deep into her back, he raised his tear filled head and screamed. "Nooooooooooooooooo!"

A violet light exploded and Rune stepped quickly out, she seized Jade roughly out of Rowan's arms. He pulled hard, to pull her back. Rune's eyes exploded and he flew four feet through the air, he landed shocked and looked at her anger in his eyes. Runes eyes burned. "I do not have much time." She turned and looked at the gantry, deep purple flashed out of the eyes of Rune, and the guards grabbed their heads and screamed in pain. She turned to Rowan. "YOU HAVE A JOB TO DO, FINISH IT!" Rune spun on the spot and was gone, with Jade hanging limp in her arms.

Everyone hit the floor under the trees as Smokes grabbed the weeping Rowan and threw him down the bank. "Hit it Fuse." Fuse dropped the plunger and the whole place lit up, as if the sun had crashed landed on the planet. They pushed their faces into the grass as flames roared above them; the heat was intense and Crystal blasted ice into the air above them to hold it off them. Glowing metal shot into the air, flames funnelled at least a thousand feet into the sky.

Harry cried into the grass, Rowan wept in pain as Maddy pulled him close, and held him in her arms as he wailed and sobbed. Treen shook with fear in Skip's arms, as the ground shook violently and fire poured into the sky, and debris rained to the floor smoking and burning.

Five bowmen sat in the grass under the trees as Mother guided the lost the weary and weak up the steps and into the woodland. Hornet and Mel sat either side of the steps as the convoy of the desolate came up into the light of a new day. They squinted and shielded their eyes from the rising sun, ten guards lay dead just behind the entrance, two of which had fine red holes on their necks as if stung by a large bee. They wandered into the wood and Mel showed them the path. "Follow this and the hooded man will catch up with you." They staggered and helped each other as they headed down the woodland path away from the city. Mother looked across at the bowmen. "Stay with them and keep them safe."

Robbie sat with his back to the wall his mind flooded with pain as he thought of his Pebbles. He felt an overwhelming pain tearing inside him, Rune had just left, why had she not taken him? Where was she? Robbie's anger boiled inside him as his mind raced and the pain mingled with his rising fear and panic

A young looking blonde haired boy, came running round the corner at high speed, he did not see Robbie, and before he realised, Robbie was snapped awake as the boy hit his legs and sprawled forward and went flying past him. "HEY!" Robbie screamed in anger. The boy slid on the polished floor and rolled over sitting quickly up; the blue eyes met the dark angry hurt eyes of Robbie's.

The young boys' eyes flared wide as he realised who was sat on the floor. His eyes darted up the passage as he was expecting someone else to appear round it, and Robbie turned and looked at the end of the corridor from where the boy had just run from, it was empty and he looked back at the boy. The boy slid backward on the floor, he rolled, and jumped up, and ran with all his might down the corridor, Robbie looked back at the corner of the empty corridor and remembered the blue eyes of Billy. Suddenly everything snapped back into reality and he looked in the direction of the boy who had now disappeared. Robbie stood up and walked slowly up the corridor towards the empty corner; he leaned on the wall and slowly peered around.

Scarlet was the last into the tunnel as the boat at the end of the docks erupted into flames. She staggered into the tunnel and flew down behind all her men, Flash blinked as the bright light illuminated everything as they pushed the tired workers at high speed. Several of the bowmen turned and fired taking out the six soldiers that had followed; the bowmen jumped up and ran down behind the others. Fire erupted and lit the dock end of the tunnel, Scarlet smiled as she ran and the tunnel shook, she breathed quickly, she was tired and had fought off many, and she took deep breaths in the damp darkness as she saw the white beam of light ahead of her, she screamed at them all and hurried them along, and the light got closer.

Mother pulled them up the steps as Mel moved them on to the path. Flash and Una came panting out of the tunnel and up the steps, Mother hugged them smiling, and they collapsed on the grass unable to speak as they gasped for air. Bowmen appeared and spread into the trees, as the last of the workers came out of the tunnel and a very hard panting Scarlet strode into the light, smiled, and collapsed on the grass.

The six bowmen walked backwards up the steps and knelt at the top to cover just in case any more soldiers came down it. Scarlet, gasped large mouthfuls of air. "That's... the ... last." She lay back and breathed deeply.

Mel smiled at the three all sat gasping on the grass. "We have about two and half thousand, any word from Rune?"

Mother nodded and looked at Mel. "Nothing, what about you?" Mel nodded. "No... it's strange."

The earth began to shake as if there was a huge and violent earthquake; Mel grabbed Mother to stop her falling over. The sky to the south lit up as a blinding white flash shot across the sky over the woodland, they all looked up through the trees and saw the flames billowing into the sky. Mother grabbed Mel's arm as she watched, Mel smiled and pulled her arm around her cousin. "He is safe, you would know if he wasn't." Mother smiled a weak smile, she still worried about him, this was the first time since she had rescued him that they had been apart. She needed to see him to know for sure.

Bull dragged Rowan to his feet. "Snap out of it Rowan, she is with Rune she will be fine, Rob needs you so get with the plot, and let's get the hell out of here before we fry." Rowan wiped his heartbroken eyes and looked at the long tunnel of ice around them, the others were all running down it. Rowan nodded to Bull, he turned and began to walk into the tunnel, Bull grabbed his hand and began to run, water was dripping as the tunnel melted under the intense heat of the flames. They ran hard, and as they all approached the end of the tunnel a wall of violet light appeared, they all shot through it and ran out into the wood and bumped into Mel, Mother, and Scarlet.

Smokes came gasping through, and in to Mother's arms, she clung to him as he pulled her close. Mother buried her head deep into his shoulder as he squeezed her; she kissed him on the neck and looked up as Rowan came out of the violet light.

Smokes, had his head on her shoulder and was starting to cry, she looked just for a second at Rowan and then around the rest of the group, a cold shiver ran down her spine as she pulled back from Smokes and looked into his tearful eyes. The coldness of the moment created a pain inside Steph like one she had never felt, she looked at Smokes eyes and the tears began to well in hers. "Oh God. No!" She shook her head slowly. He just looked and could not answer as the tears fell from his eyes; he had no words to tell his wife that her daughter was dead. The tears rolled down Steph's cheeks as the voice inside her rose up. It was quiet at first and then it intensified. "No... Please Pete...no, no, no. NO, NO NOOOOOOO!" He pulled her tight as she screamed into him and shook violently. All the happiness she had ever held died inside her as the loss of her happy smiling little girl was torn out of her heart. Smokes stood still as the shaking Steph clung wailing into his shoulder. Rowan collapsed on the grass as Mel, and Una both put their arms around him and he wailed in pain.

The boats erupted and then the earth shook with a violent tremor and Mason staggered spilling his whiskey. He staggered swaying under the vibration of the shaking floor towards the window. He stared at the boats burning in the docks, as across the bay, a blinding white flash illuminated the whole room. He pressed his nose to the glass as flames billowed into the sky; the column rose high and was surrounded by thick black smoke. He knew without having to ask his fuel was gone. "EDGAR!" He screamed and Edgar who was only a few feet away jumped with fear. "I WANT HIM DEAD; DO YOU HEAR ME? I WANT THAT BLOODY WOODCHOPPER DEAD!"

He turned to face Edgar his eyes glowing red with anger, his face purple with rage as he slammed his glass down on the table, and it shattered into a million sparkling shards. "I WANT YOU TO FIND HIM AND THEN KILL HIM, DO YOU HEAR ME. DEAD...? DEAD! I WANT HIM DEAD."

Edgar jumped back shaking with fear. "Please My Lord we did not know, we will find him, and we will kill him. Please My Lord calm down." Edgar shook with fear as Mason leered at him.

The voice was calm and quiet. "Yes, calm down Mason, you will give yourself a headache."

Mason's head turned like a flash and he stared with hateful red eyes at the balcony, and the hooded figure sat cross legged on the balcony rail with a bow across his lap. His eyes burned hate into Robbie. "YOU!"

Robbie slid back his hood. "Me, Mason." He slid the bow off his lap and stood it next to his empty quiver against the balcony rail, and then Robbie looked into the eyes of Mason Knox for the second time in his life.

Mason Knox stared with hate at Robbie. Robbie was very calm and almost relaxed, even though the rage inside him was an anger that had built for several weeks. It was strong and forceful yet he held it in and calmly watched his enemy from above, he smiled down at Mason. "I have come for you Mason; you will hurt my people no more."

The wall of the cave on Hearne's Rock glowed violet and the old man stood waiting as Rune burst through the wall with Jade hanging limp in her arms. Rune fell to her knees. "My Lord I have great need of you."

Hearne felt the pain inside Rune as she fought to hold in and control the overwhelming emotions and power together inside her. His eyes were sad as he looked down at Jade who clung to life by the slimmest of threads. Rune's hands pulsated as she pumped her own life force into Jade to keep her alive. Without it, she would be dead, Rune wept over her sister as Hearne placed his hands on Rune's shoulders.

"Child of nature I am not life, you are." She looked through her violet tears into the sad eyes of Hearne.

"I know not what to do my Father, and I cannot lose her, she is my sister and half of me."

The Old Lord bent down and lifted Jade from her arms. "Oh, my happy little wood nymph, you who deserve more than you have been given." He looked at Rune as she wept on her knees. "There is a way. Gwendolyn's daughter used it to save her, but it will cost you life, Runestone Child."

Rune looked up as hope lit in her eyes. "Take it, use my life force and save her, I beg you my Father of Creation, do not let her die." Her head fell into her knees as the pain inside came flowing out, Rune wept as she felt the loss of Jade welling inside her.

The Old Lord turned to the bed of moss in the corner, and very gently, and with great care, he laid Jade softly down on her side. He looked up at the ceiling and his voice grew deep. "My realms, and my worlds respond to your creator."

Gwendolyn and Opal walked in through the walls and bowed. Hearne turned as Rune rose from the floor and flew into the arms of Opal and wept. "Oh Grandmother, I know not what I can do, I am life and yet I cannot save her." She pushed her head into her grandmother's shoulder and she trembled as she cried.

Opal pulled her close and held her tightly, and stroked her long red hair.

"Runestone you are the seeds of all life, you have the power now, I cannot save her she is not of my realm you are."

Rune lifted her face and her eyes ran red with her tears. "Can you tell me what I must do?"

Gwendolyn placed a hand on Rune's shoulder. "Hush my child, there is a way but you will pay a high price."

Rune sniffled and wiped her eyes on her sleeve. "What is the price I must pay?"

Gwendolyn looked at the old lord. "Is there no other way Father Creator?"

The old lord looked down at Jade her white face was cold, and he knew that time was short and they must act quickly. He shook his head sadly, as he looked at Rune. "There has always been only but one way Gwendolyn White Circle, and you know the sacrifice paid for by one of your own children."

Opal raised her arm around Gwendolyn, as she knew of the sadness it could bring her at times, Rune looked up, her eyes begged to know the only way to save her sister. Tears filled Gwendolyn eyes as the pain of the memory came back to her. "Runestone Sapphire you have only one chance... You must trade a life for a life."

Rune looked at the pain in Gwendolyn's face. "What life do I trade?"

"Runestone what I tell you can have only but a moment of thought, because time for your sister is running out, she is already at the border of our realm." Gwendolyn took a deep breath. "You have seen one life destined for you for she is your first, you must give the life force of your last to your sister to bring back her life from the border in trade. A life for a life. You must give your son's life in exchange."

Rune's heart was frozen. "Her son, Robbie's son?" She stared at Jade and the true pain of life came to her. Rune's eyes flooded and Gwendolyn looked down, as she knew how hard a choice it was.

Opal looked at Rune with great sadness. "You must choose now Runestone or the moment will pass."

Rune gasped as her breath came in short bursts, as her chest restricted. The Lord Hearne touched the red tipped arrow and it withdrew slowly. "You must choose before the arrow hits the floor or she is gone."

Rune watched her eyes wide, as it slowly slid out of Jade and her heart fractured, why not a daughter, did it have to be his son? She saw the metal of the arrowhead starting to appear, and she fell to her knee's tears flowing down her face as she screamed in heart tearing agony. "TAKE HIM AND SAVE HER!"

She fell to the floor and wailed. "Oh, Robbie please forgive me." The arrow clattered on to the stone floor and Jade breathed a long laboured breath.

Hearne lifted her weeping from the floor and pulled her close and held her in his arms. She wept into the old lord uncontrolled gasping sobs; he stroked her hair softly. "I am sorry my child, for I know how important a life he was to you and your bowman. It is a high price but that is the price of balance. Without balance we will all be destroyed, Nature is sweet and beautiful, and also nature is painful and destructive, you know this Runestone."

"Rune what's going on?" Jade moved on the bed.

Rune pulled her head from the lord of creation and looked at her sister with a pale white frightened face. Jade's eyes filled with tears. "Rune am I dead, is my Rowan alone?" The tears flowed down her face and Rune fell to her sister, and pulled her close and held her tight as she wept with Jade clinging to her.

"Oh, my poor darling Jade, no Sister, you are not dead, you were hurt and I had to bring you here to be healed. Oh Jade, I love you so much."

Jade squeezed Rune hard. "I love you too sis... Can I see Rowan now?"

Rune smiled and kissed her sister. "Yes, I will take you to him; he is worried about you as is mum."

The old man looked at her as she rose from her sister and turned to him; he cupped her face and smiled. "You have extraordinary power and great internal strength. Your sacrifice is the greatest any can pay, I can show you if you want before he leaves forever."

Rune shuddered as the pain flowed into her, Hearne closed her eyes, and she felt herself float as if on a cloud. Violet light surrounded her and she watched as a young boy walked alone, his hair fell down his back in long wavy brown curls, and she knew he was the double of his father; it was like watching Robbie when she first came to Loxley. Opal smiled as he ran into her arms and she lifted him up and swung him round. Rune almost fainted and she swooned as she saw him. He was Robbie's double with sapphire blue eyes and the faint streak of copper in his hair. Rune sobbed as he looked up at her, then with a smile, he was gone and the light flowed around her and her heart splintered.

Rune opened her eyes and she stood at the side of Jade in the forest, Jade gripped her hand tightly. "Where are we Rune?" Rune dried her eyes and looked up as a long stream of sad and weary people walked like zombies through the trees. She squeezed Jade's hand and smiled at her.

"Rowan is down here, come on sis." They walked back along the line of moving desperate souls and towards the opening of the tunnel; through the trees she could see the group. Steph stood held in Smokes arms and Rowan sat on the floor with Mel and Una. Jade squealed loudly and smiled. "ROWAN!" He looked up and saw the blonde curly hair, and green eyes and a beaming smile running at him through the trees "ROWAN!" Her arms were open wide and Rune watched the tears in his eyes, and the look of disbelief on his face as he rose slowly as if in shock. He ran as if no one had ever run before, and weeping he snatched her into his arms and pulled her close as she wailed into him.

Rune smiled at them as she drew level and her eyes met Rowan's. It was enough for her to see the love she had saved, Steph and Smokes shot past her as they embraced their daughter. Una came up and a tear ran from each of her eyes as she looked at Rune, she lifted her hand and cupped her face. "Oh Rune, my darling, I am so sorry. I know of the price you have paid; I too have paid it."

Rune broke down as Una swept her into her arms and held her tight, the pain she felt was unbearable. "Oh Una, I have robbed him, how will he ever forgive me?" Una held her close.

"Oh Runestone believe me he will never know, and the others will fulfil his life as will those of his sister in law. I am so sorry my poor sweet girl, now you can see why I have one child and my sisters have two, it was the life I paid to return my mother from the Dark One. I do not think she has ever forgiven me for it."

Jett looked down at the two guards with the drooping swords; she smiled at Blades, "too much booze." Blades and Jett both burst out laughing, as Bear clambered up the stairs behind them wiping his axe on a piece of old shirt.

"Any sign of him?" Bear looked at the two sleeping guards. "Well at least we know Rune came this way."

CHAPTER TWENTY THREE

DEATH SECRETS AND DESTINY

Robbie lifted the bow from his lap; he looked down at the empty arrow quiver stood against the balcony rail. He slipped the bow down and stood it against the rail at the side of the quiver, his brown eyes burned into Mason's. He felt a strange sort of calm washing over him, the self doubt had faded, and he knew that now was the moment he had been preparing for. "I have come for you Mason; you will hurt my people no more."

Mason's eyes twitched as Edgar squealed and he went to run to the side door. "Stay where you are Edgar, I will deal with you shortly. My men are outside and if you leave, you will die." His voice was cold and calm, and it contained a cold hand of terror for Edgar, who fell into a chair, his face pale and his eyes wide with terror.

"I am not responsible I was overwhelmed by him; you have no idea of his power."

Robbie uncrossed his legs and slipped off the rail, his cloak billowed up as he dropped to the highly polished table below. He landed with the grace of a cat, as his knees bent slightly; he straightened up his eyes never breaking contact with Mason.

"It is unfortunate Edgar that you have no idea of mine either." Edgar stared with fearful eyes as Robbie took a step forward on the table top. He began to shake as he saw the calm unconcerned power that emitted from Robbie, a slight smile twitched on Mason's lip. His eyes flicked to the shaking and shuddering Edgar in the chair and then back to Robbie's, he smiled as he looked back at Robbie, who had now taken two more soft steps forward on the table. Mason slid his arm to his sword hilt; Robbie's hands remained loose at his sides.

"I like you wood chopper, we are the same kind of men." Robbie stopped.

"We will never be that Mason, you kill and destroy for your own benefit, I will never be that man." Robbie dropped on to the floor his eyes still fixed on Mason. His quiet and calm manner unsettled Mason who was used to confrontation, he was a man of passions and tempers, and yet here before him was the first man who had not showed any fear at all. He swallowed deeply, as he watched the young strange softly speaking boy in front of him.

"You cannot beat me boy, my family will rule and control here, and you have not the strength or the guts for the fight. You cannot shoot an arrow from safety here and blow me up."

Edgar moaned behind Robbie, yet he paid him no attention, he took another short step towards Mason. "I will have no need of an arrow, as I look you in the eye as you die Mason; you know you will die by my hand today?"

Mason burst a loud and raucous laugh, and drew his long silver sword out of its sheath, the light glinted off the polished blade across Robbie's face. His eyes sparkled with the light, and yet he did not blink. His piercing gaze, burned bright and Mason saw the life and the power of his enemy for the first time. "I have no intentions of dying today woodchopper, you face the Cambridge undefeated sword champion of all time, and you have no hope against me."

Robbie smiled for the first time. "Always labels and titles, when will you realise Mason, those days are dead? They are gone it is you who has no hope, you fight for lies of a past that was never glorious." Robbie pulled the long golden sword from his sheath, and multi coloured light bounced all around the room as the blade glinted. "My fight Mason is truth and I have already won; you just have not realised it."

Masons' sword came up swiftly and swiped across the front of Robbie as he stepped forward. The speed of the Bowman showed as Robbie's blade clashed and a resounding note sung out, the two swords met and the force of each of them pushed down the blades as they met and held together. The strain showed on Mason's face as he pushed on the blade against Robbie's. The golden sword of truth cast small rainbows across Mason's face, Robbie kept his eyes fixed on Mason's as he glared up at him.

Robbie stepped back and smiled, he flicked his wrist and his sword ran down the blade of Masons, they broke apart and Robbie saw the anger rise in the face of Mason Knox. He came at him with four crashing blows, Robbie parried with skill and ability, and his movements were fluid and relaxed as his blade flowed through the air. "Think you are clever boy because you hold an old sword? There is not enough magic in that blade to stop me."

He came back at Robbie, who stepped to one side and brought the Sword of Truth singing and ringing across the blade of Knox. Robbie could see the anger rising in his opponent, yet he felt relaxed and calm as he watched.

"FIGHT ME!" Knox screamed, angry that Robbie was just blocking his strikes. His face was now almost purple, Robbie's eyes began to burn, and as he spoke, he sent an avalanche of crashing blows down on the blade of Mason Knox.

"You have murdered my people.... Raped the women... Burned my woodland. Tortured and killed innocent children, and killed my friends... and for what?" He swung the blade and whipped it back fast, and the tip of the sword sliced into Mason's cheek. Mason glared at Robbie as his hand came up and wiped the blood off his face, the four inch red line oozed more blood as Robbie watched him look down at his hand and see it smeared across his palm.

"You see Mason; you bleed just like the rest of us. You think you are so superior, but you still have the blood of a Saxon."

He glared at Robbie. "Is Celtic blood as red or more precious wood chopper?"

Robbie stepped back and prepared for another onslaught. "You should know better than I Mason, you have spilled enough." Rage burst out of Mason, he waved his sword wildly in the air and his powerful blows thundered down on Robbie. "STOP TALKING BOY AND FIGHT ME, LETS SEE THE ANGER BEHIND THE WORDS!"

Robbie staggered back as he fended off the heavy blows of Mason's sword. "You could not withstand the anger of the hooded man; it would crush you Old Man."

Knox staggered back breathing heavily, a bead of sweat ran down the side of his face, he wiped it off as Robbie stood silently watching, his sword lowered. Mason breathed out; the side of his face glowed with the wet blood. "Show me hooded wood chopper, let's see the mighty hooded man show some emotion, and you call me a lover of labels."

Mason stood next to the ornate bookcase, he slid his hand behind the books and pushed, all the books shot out, and Robbie raised his hand to shield himself. Mason rushed him swiping his sword. "Come on boy show me how much I have pissed you off. You talk a lot but you seem pretty calm about it all."

Robbie pulled up his sword as he allowed his true feelings to flow up inside him, and down into his sword. The speed at which he moved was like lightening and his voice raised high, and filled the room with the true power of the hooded man. "WHO ARE YOU TO QUESTION ME OLD MAN? IS THIS WHAT YOU WANT TO SEE? CAN YOU REALLY TAKE WHAT YOU DEAL OUT EVERY DAY?"

The sight of Robbie, his eyes blazing with the Sword of Truth swishing like lightening and glinting through the air, was a scene of terror to behold. Edgar squealed and jumped off his seat, scuttling under the table like a frightened mouse, as Mason staggered backwards fending off the blows of Robbie's. All the fury and anger of the deaths of his people, and the betrayal of Billy flooded into his arm as he piled on the blows. The sound of the blades clashing was deafening around the room.

Robbie's blade battered and smashed down on the trembling and shuddering arms of Mason Knox, as an onslaught of anger and aggression flowed like a torrent out of him. Robbie's eyes burned with rage, and pushed fear into Mason, as he shuddered with the crashing power of Robbie's golden sword.

Mason showed true fear for the first time in his life as the force pounded down on him and his wrists shook, as he gripped his sword with both hands to force his sword up and defend against Robbie. His knees buckled under him and with wide frightened eyes he fell back on the floor as the sword left his hand and flew under the table. Mason fell sprawling and gasping backwards on to the deep blue thick carpet, and the tip of Robbie's sword touched Mason's throat.

Mason lay back on the carpet and smiled as he gasped for air. "You have quite a temper wood chopper." He began to laugh, as he looked up at Robbie. "You have earned your kill boy, finish the old man and face my son's. You have won only a small victory here."

Edgar slid out behind Robbie and lifted the sword of Mason Knox high, he screamed with all his might as he lunged at him. Robbie jumped and the arrow hit Edgar in the chest and lifted him off his feet, he croaked as he fell backwards and slammed into the floor.

Robbie looked up, and Rune smiled as the patch of violet on the wall behind her faded, her eyes contained tears of fear and they burned bright blue as he gazed into them. She looked at Knox beaten lay on his back with Robbie's sword at his throat, Robbie lifted his blade and stepped back, he took three paces backwards as Mason sat up on the floor. His eyes met with Robbie's, and Robbie lifted the sword with the toe of his boot and flicked it towards him.

Mason looked in disbelief as he picked up his sword from the floor; Rune bit her lip as she saw Robbie walk backwards his blade low but his eyes never leaving the face of his enemy. Mason rose back to his feet and looked at the arrow, with its long white tip sticking out of Edgar's chest. He glanced back at Rune, and then back to the dead figure, and pushed his foot under the body and lifted it rolling Edgar with his fear filled frozen face under the table. There was a loud crack as the arrow snapped and broke off under the body; Mason smiled as he gripped the hilt of the sword. "Chivalry can be seen as weakness boy; I will not make the same mistake twice."

Robbie's eyes burned bright. "Neither will I Old Man, but unlike you I do not slaughter the defenceless, so raise your sword and die like a man."

Rune's finger gripped the balcony rail tighter, as she watched Robbie cool and calm, as he stood ten feet back from Mason Knox, his sword lowered, and his eyes burning into the face of his enemy. Knox swung the blade and regained his composure. "Rule keepers always lose wood chopper."

"No Mason, the truth wins, and honour prevails, raise your sword and take your final breath, today is your day of judgement."

Rune gasped as Mason flew at Robbie, his blade swung with speed and precision, and yet Robbie countered his blows and whipped back faster and stronger. Robbie's mind was focused. "For enslaving my people." Five thunderous blows hit Mason and his arms shook as he snatched the sword with both hands to hold it.

"For taking my cousin." Rune shrunk at the power that Robbie inflicted on

Mason. "For the murder of women and children." The golden sword seemed to shine brighter and become more powerful as if driven by Robbie's anger. "FOR BURNING MY LAND!" Mason looked terror stricken as the rage and force and sheer loudness of Robbie, which echoed around the whole room. The force and anger of Lord Loxley flowed out and Mason finally understood that his life would now end.

Robbie lunged back at Knox; his attack was far more fierce than before, Rune raised her hands to her mouth as she held her breath, his blade was swift, heavy and deadly, he came down with a crashing blow on the sword of Mason and the silver sword sheared in half, as Robbie's blade of truth passed through it. His wrist twisted as he cut the blade back and stepped forwards into Mason. "YOU WILL PAY TODAY!" The hate in Robbie's eyes scared Rune as she watched.

They came face to face, and Mason smiled. "Your troubles have only just begun wood chopper." Mason slid backward off the blade and fell on to the floor dead, Robbie's sword fell to his side as he raised his arm and wiped the sweat off his brow.

Rune flew down the steps and crashed through the door, her face was pale as she rushed across the room and into his arms. She swept into him flinging her arms round his neck and he raised his left arm and pulled her close. He held her tight and looked down at the dead body of Knox. The last of his words was sounding in his head. "Justice has been served."

Robbie kissed her on the head. "Come on we are done here." He released Rune and crouched down and wiped the blade of the sword on Edgar's jacket. Robbie slid the glittering sword of truth back into its sheath. Pulling Rune close he walked to the door. "How is Pebbles?" Rune looked at the floor and then back into his caring dark eyes.

"She is alright Rob, she frightened us, but I got to her in good time, she is with Rowan waiting in the woods." He pulled her close and squeezed her shoulder. He noticed the sadness in her eyes, and he smiled.

"Hey, she is fine, don't look so sad." Rune looked up into his bright smiling eyes, and she felt her heart breaking. She gave him a soft smile and looked down at the floor as he pulled the door closed, and left the sight of Mason Knox dead on the carpet next to Edgar of Liverpool.

"Hey ROBBIE where you bin? We have looked all over." Jett stood smiling at the end of the corridor, along with Keith and Saff. Blades wandered up with Bear, who looked at Robbie with an enquiring eye. Robbie smiled at him.

"Mason is dead." They all gasped, as Robbie and Rune walked past them and headed to the stairs. "Come on let's all go home; we have finished here."

On each set of stairs Robbie's group was stationed waiting, two of the bowmen had been wounded and Saff had taken care of them, one had a dressing on his face and the other his arm in a sling, he was relieved that casualties had been minimal. They all wandered slowly down the dark tunnel, he held Rune close in the dark, she was very quiet, not the happy Rune he was use to after a victory. "Rune I know something is wrong, tell me, you are so quiet what is it?"

He felt her shift at his side in the dark. "I was just very scared when I got back and found you alone and fighting him. It really shook me Rob, if I had not got back in time, Edgar would have killed you. I am sorry, I don't mean to be quiet, I was shaken by it all." He felt her squeeze him and it reassured him. "You also really scared me when you fought him; I have never seen you that angry."

Rune stared into the dark with tears in her eyes. She had never thought there would ever be a time when she had to lie to him, she felt the pain rise inside knowing he would never know, and she was the reason, she would never give him the son he wanted, and from this moment on there would be one part of her life she could never reveal. It hurt to know it, but she had moved forward now, and there was no turning back, it was now too late.

Black smoke funnelled into the air and drifted across the docks and the city. The last remnants of Mason Knox's city ran around trying to fight the fires that were burning out of control on the ships. Many of the people who had chosen the ways of Mason now coughed and choked as the acrid black smoke drifted into the city burning their eyes and creating havoc in the lack of visibility.

Una stood alone at the end of the steps as the group came up them. She smiled to see Robbie with his arm around Rune. She embraced Robbie with a warm smile. "You have done well Robbie; many lives have been spared today."

He looked around the open clearing. "Where is everyone?"

"They have headed to the gates and safety; there is too much smoke here." Robbie nodded as the others all moved on to the track, he stood by the tree, and smiled as they passed him. All of them including the bowmen of Caerleon patted his shoulder as they passed.

Una held Rune tightly in her arms. "Are you going to be alright? You look so white; Rune, you must come to terms with it or it will eat you up and break you apart. Promise me you will trust me enough to come to me at times of need."

Rune felt safe in her arms, she could not talk to her mother and Una felt like a tower of strength. "Thanks Una, I have lied to the only man I will ever love, and it has broken my heart to do it, for I have not the courage to face him and tell him the truth."

Una gave her a tight squeeze. "I am here."

She turned and walked past Robbie and Rune smiled at him, he grinned and walked over, he cupped her face in his hands and he kissed her softly. She threw her hands round him and kissed him with love and with passion. "I love you so much Rob, please never forget that." She pushed her tear filled eyes into his shoulder and he held her close.

"We are closer Rune, soon all our dreams will come true." Her tears spilled down his back as he held her, and she hung on to him, as she had never done before.

"I need you to leave me for a moment; I have to finish what I started here Rob, you go on and help the others." She wiped her eyes, and turned away from him as she raised her arms and her eyes glowed a deep purple. He saw the violet eyes streaming light and stepped back into the trees.

Happy and smiling he walked along the path towards Una up ahead. Rune glowed as she rose from the floor, lightening exploded from her and the ground below the city of Old Liverpool began to shake.

People screamed as concrete fell from the sky, and the whole city shuddered violently. Violent explosions blew up out of the floor as large cracks opened in the earth and they lifted and fell casting screaming supporters of Mason into the abyss, the sea rose and swept across the whole city. Buildings washed away as the city crumbled and sunk into the water. The fire of the refinery hissed and sizzled as the water ran in and the earth along the high wall sunk, dragging the wall down into the hole that appeared and filled with water.

The city sunk away into the sea and was gone forever. The refinery, the docks and the palace of Mason Knox, along with his body had disappeared into the ocean. Rune lowered her arms and looked down as her eyes faded back to lilac. She stood at the top of a small cliff, and to her left she could see the rocky edges of North Wales, and to her right was the woodland that was Lancashire, in between was a basin of water and coastline.

The seagulls screamed in the air as the breeze blew across her face. She dropped to her knees and watched them her tears rose and flowed. Rune cried, and wailed, and released her hurt and her grief alone on a cliff top, a slender figure in green so young to the world and to her power, as she struggled to come to terms with the life she had chosen. Her head in her hands she wept, until she could weep no more, and then she sat quiet and watched the sea lap the base of the cliff. When she was ready, she turned and walked quietly into the trees.

Robbie stood by the arched trees surrounded by violets. Everyone had passed through and was now at the gates of Loxley, she walked slowly through the wood of alder and beech, mixed with the silver of birch, and she gazed at the flowers that sprung up at her feet and she remembered the face of Iona.

The pictures of Robbie looking into the eyes of his daughter came into her mind and she smiled, she knew that Iona would be the first of many joys and her heart lightened. Rune walked out of the trees and there he stood waiting, and smiled as she came into view. Rune ran through the forest and leapt into his arms, and he swung her round in the air and she giggled, her eyes glinting in the sunlight. He pulled her close and she kissed him. "Take me home and make love to me my beautiful bowman."

He swept her up into his arms and she clicked her fingers, and the violet arch glowed an intense purple. Both of them stepped through on to the grass of Robbie's Mere and their home, she held him tightly her head on his shoulder and he walked quietly along the grass and up the steps to the house. She kissed his neck softly. "I love you Robbie"

The news of the death of Mason Knox by the hand of the hooded man spread across the country rapidly. In small towns and villages deep in the woodland there was joy and great merriment. June 12th was to be known from that day on as, 'Justice Day' for it was the day when Robert of Loxley, as the hooded man put right the wrongs of an evil man, and justice was served on behalf of every woodland dweller that had suffered. The building of stone cities seemed to halt, and as the summer slowly passed. The world felt for a time like it had begun to change for the better. Robbie and Rune spent a lot of time alone, and Robbie had been concerned for a time, as a state of melancholy had seemed to slip over Rune.

He had noticed how she had spent many hours alone staring across the Mere, and was always sad for many hours after. He spent more time with her and slowly as the weeks passed, she began to be herself again and would be heard humming as she worked her loom, or she would come up from the basement smiling, having learned yet another ability from the wheel of Runestone.

The bond between Jade and Rune was always close, but now it seemed stronger than ever, and Rune would spend many hours at her sister's house watching her work on her sculpture for the garden. Rowan now joined Robbie in Loxley woods, and he became a good friend of Joe, as he admired the wood skills of his two younger woodsmen.

Loxley had grown again as the men and women saved from Old Liverpool, were housed either in Loxley or in the surrounding new villages, of which there were now many. Love blossomed in strange places all over Loxley as the example of Robbie and Rune seemed to affect everyone. Melanie had been seen many times walking along the front wall of the stockade laughing as she spoke with David Williams, even Henry had watched and smiled. One rumour circulated that

Bobby Thorn had early one morning when leaving the postal office, had turned and kissed Rags goodbye, and she had stood in her robe and waved him off.

Blades had many admirers but such were the stories of her fighting ability, which most of the boys who watched her and yearned to be close to her heard. That they were so frightened of her, that they pined from afar. Robbie changed very little; in secret with Rune, he watched and studied the writings of Gwendolyn. He was now convinced that he had the fifth line of her prediction worked out.

'The shield protects, the lion brings courage.' He now believed that to mean that if he raised the ring of Morbihan, on his left hand, the shield with the king's symbol of three dragons would strike fear into his enemy and bring courage to his men and it had to mean war was coming. The Dark One and Billy had not been seen, but Lance seemed to occupy his thoughts. Had the boy with straight long blonde hair, and Billy's blue eyes, been killed in the drowning of Liverpool? If he was alive, Robbie had no clues to his whereabouts, and he spent many hours talking about Lance with Hornet.

It was mid-September, when Robbie sat alone with Rune at his desk, there were several visitors in the house and they had crept off to be alone. Rune curled on his knee and looked at all the papers strewn all over his desk. Rune stared at the line about claws and seeds of the woods, Robbie had struggled to try and find a connection.

Rune stared at the words on the papers as he kissed her softly down her neck. She giggled, and shuddered and closed her eyes for a moment. "Oh Robbie, don't, we have guests and you know how much I love that." She turned on the chair to face him and her sword handle got stuck in the handle of his. She looked down as she went to pull her sword free from his. "Do we have to wear......?"

Robbie watched as her face changed. "What?" She slowly looked up and her eyes sparkled, as they never had before. She turned quickly to the desk and began searching through the papers.

"What... what is it Rune...? Hey don't mix them up I have spent the last week sorting them out."

Rune lifted the paper out of the pile and held it up to read. "Bring the five swords together and you will see your path." She slowly slid back to face him and smiled.

"What?" She leaned forward and gave him a long and slow kiss; he pulled her close and quite forgot all his questions. She leaned back, and smiled again.

"Get the members of the wheel in the basement, and bring the wheel of Carnac."

"Why what is happening...? Rune where are you going...? Hey wait." She had gone. She ran down the stairs to the basement, Robbie looked at the golden box on the bookshelf. He grabbed it and ran down the stairs after her, he came down to the stairs and as he jumped on to the first step, he spotted Una heading out with a tray of drinks. "Hey Una, can you get all the members of the wheel down at the table straight away."

He jumped down the steps and ran to the small door under the stairs. "Right, you are Robbie, just give me a minute."

Rune sat at her table with her necklace resting on it as she read the description Robbie had written from the pictures he had seen of the Sword of Destiny. Rune looked up at him. "Oh Rob, I have been such a fool, I am so sorry."

He was confused. "Why what is the matter?"

Rune pointed to her pendant. "I always thought that this was just the way the light reflected off it, it's not, this sword has a silver stripe down the centre of the blade." He was surprised and looked over at the tiny sword, her bright blue eyes watched as he examined the tiny pendant. "Robbie, Destiny is an exact replica of Excalibur, except it has a fine line of platinum down its centre of the blade. Can you see this pendant is Destiny?"

He wasn't quite there yet as he looked from the small sword to Rune. "Meaning what exactly?"

She looked him deep in the eyes and he saw the seriousness of her. "Meaning Excalibur is lost to all of us, and it was Destiny that powered the wheel of Carnac... Robbie don't you see what that means, Destiny is the centre of a circle... a circle of sword bearers."

Robbie thought about it for a minute. "So, you are the true owner of Destiny?"

Rune shook her head. "No, I still think you are the true owner, and I think the wheel has one more task to perform, you trust me, don't you?"

"What kind of daft question is that? I trust you with my life."

"Good, then wait till everyone is here and I will show you."

It took a few minutes for everyone to appear and take their rightful seat at the table. They all chatted happily and Jett frolicked around joking across the table with Jade, Rune placed her hands on the table and the murmur died to silence. "Sword bearers, please place your swords." One by one and in sequence of Truth, Justice, Knowledge, Courage and Honour they all laid the glittering swords into position, Rune smiled. "Jett change seats with Robbie, I want him next to me, and you are the sword of truths guardian on the table of swords."

Both Robbie and Jett rose slowly and walked towards each other; Jett shrugged her shoulders as she passed him. They sat down and Jett smiled as she leaned forward and stroked the blade of the sword, violet light flashed across the table and she pulled her finger off fast. "Sorry."

Rune took the wheel of Carnac out of the box, and leaned across the table. A thin spike rose from the centre of the table and she smiled and nodded as she slid the wheel on to it. Rune sat back and the wheel began to vibrate as everyone watched Rune as she spoke in a clear voice. "We gather without hope, and there is deep despair, we look down in sanctuary and peer inside. Recovered honour is now by my side; the ring of Morbihan has found another hand. We seek and struggle for future seeds of hope. I have gathered the five swords, I request, you reveal our path. The right hand is here to receive it, we all follow him.”

The wheel began to spin. Light flowed from the table and on to the wheel, it was many colours and soon began to mix and separate. Two bright beams rose up in the air and wove together in blue and violet, the shadowy figure of Gwendolyn formed on the wheel, and everyone looked amazed.

Gwendolyn bowed to Rune. “New sister of our force, new sister of Nature, I bid you welcome for I saw this moment many years ago and I know of your plight. Runestone Sapphire of the wheel in the land of the bow, I have your future. I am White Circle, the hidden powers and tonight you will receive my final gifts, for I have hidden much from the Dark One. My right hand has earned his gift and soon he will know the power he has taken to work for his people.”

“Truth can no longer be held in his hand, and it must pass to the rightful owner who is ready to receive it and has been guided to this night. Black is her colour and the yellow glow in her soul shall purify the dark into power for good. Pass the sword Runestone Sapphire and make way for the new Circle of Swords.”

Rune looked up the table. “Jett Amber my sister, hold your hand above the table.”

Jett looked around nervously as she slowly stretched out her hand above the sword of truth. It spun on the table, and the hilt leapt up and Jett grasped it and held it up in front of her as she smiled. Her eyes exploded in lilac and the sword blade glowed. She shook for a second and the light in her eyes lessoned, Rune smiled. “True owner of the sword of truth, welcome to the table of swords Jett Amber of Caerleon.” Jett beamed a huge smiled.

“Oh, right how cool is this?” Jett replaced the sword and the wheel began to spin faster, as it did, violet light spun out and over the swords. The whole table became a disk of fast spinning violet light. Gwendolyn’s voice echoed from somewhere inside the table.

“Sister and guardian of the lake I call upon you to fulfil your task as set over a thousand years ago.” The wheel spun faster somewhere under the light and the violet turned to a pale watery blue. It sparkled like the water in the Mere and as Robbie watched, he saw movement in the light at the centre of the table. The top of a head with blonde hair appeared as a tall slender figure with bright blue eyes rose out of the centre of the table. She was dressed in the brightest of white long flowing robes with a cloak of the purest white.

She was so dazzling most of them shielded their eyes, her belt was a chain of golden hearts and in her hands, she held a long golden sword with a moonstone for a setting in the handle, and it had a blade of the brightest gold with a thin line of silver platinum down it. The name on the blade was clear for all to see. ‘Destiny will prevail.’

Steph leaned forward and smiled. “Gwinne my sister, I have missed you, welcome to the table of my daughter.” Tears welled in her eyes as Gwinne smiled.

"Hello sister I have missed you too, but we will meet in your world soon." She bowed to Rune. "Runestone Sapphire centre of the circles and lady of the woods renewed, I bring you greetings from Avalon the fair land of the forgotten realm, I have the gift of my world to honour and protect yours, let the White Circle come forth, and as the right hand of Gwendolyn let him take what is now rightfully his."

Rune turned to Robbie who watched transfixed as he looked at the sword. "Robbie take the sword in your right hand."

Robbie nervously lifted his right hand over the table and he saw the bracelet of Gwendolyn glow blue, Gwinne held up the sword, it was dazzling in the bright light. "The truth has served the purpose it was given and has passed over. You are a knight without a sword who will lead the war against the Dark One, seek those who hide under black stones and destroy the lines of the past and rebuild you're future. What was taken will come by other routes, use well your gift and return the true lines of men to us."

Gwinne reached out and placed Destiny into Robbie's out stretched hand. It felt cool and smooth as his hand closed around it, he stepped back and pulled the blade as it burned blue and then purple in his hand. Gwinne sank slowly back and smiled a sweet smile. "We wear the veil Runestone, my mother has seen it fear not."

She sank into the table and the wheel slowed down and stopped. Everyone stared in disbelief as Rune gave him a huge smile. "This blade was made and hidden from all of us; tonight, it has come at a time when war is upon us. Robbie, you hold in your hand the true and only Lost Sword of Carnac. Destiny is the twin of Excalibur, the sister sword, and you are the wheel from which the White Circle wields it."

Robbie's eyes sparkled as the light reflected on to his face. "Oh Rune, this is the finest weapon I have ever seen." He swept it through the air and he felt like he heard fair voices singing in his head. Robbie dropped the sword into his belt. "We have a war coming everyone get yourselves ready. The Dark One is resurfacing and we must prepare for the worst." He looked down at the moonstone in the top of the handle of his sword, it glowed dimly and the he noticed the moonstone in his dagger glowed the same, it was odd but he thought, somehow the two knew each other.

Everyone began to rise from their seats when suddenly Rune's eyes exploded in violet light, she dropped into her seat and the wheel began to spin. Everyone sat back into their seats and watched Rune with a worried look on their faces. The wheel spun at an alarming speed and Robbie slid over to Rune who looked distressed, he grabbed her shoulder as he thought she would fall off her chair. Saff's eyes exploded blue and Steph slipped over to her, Treen screamed and pointed at the table as thick black flooded into the wheel.

A twisted and wretched shape formed, as if fighting to get out in the middle of the wheel; everyone stared in horror as it rose bending and stretching and twitching. An arm sprang out of the black wretched mass. Ruby jumped back with a squeak, and the other side seemed to tear as another long arm slid out.

Robbie recognised the long thin fingers with black claw like fingernails, and he watched as her pallid white head and face stretched and twisted out of the mass. Robbie stepped close to Rune his hand on the hilt of his sword, and the Dark One formed in front of him. Rune's soft warm hand closed round his and lifted it off the hilt of his sword, her voice was quiet in his ear as she stood up. "She has no knowledge of this, keep it hidden until the last moment." She pushed him to one side and her eyes flared violet as she leaned on the table.

"You dare violate my home witch?" There was anger in her words as the Dark One faced her.

"Save it flower girl and listen." Her cold malicious voice echoed around the room; she turned her white unfeeling face to Robbie. "There you are wood chopper, you will answer to me for your crime, long have I searched for the boy you stole from me? I found him today and know the story of his demise."

She turned to Rune. "Look at you still a child with no more power than the love you hold for your wood chopper and leaf walker. He has stolen something of mine flower girl and I will have my revenge." She leered at Rune who stood fast and did not flinch.

"Speak your vile and be gone Witch."

The Dark One smiled a cruel and twisted smile. "I have something of yours, and I want you to know the pain and the suffering will be terrible. Send me your woodchopper alone and I will use him as the vessel to contain my second reborn unto this world and you may not suffer the pain of loss. You have one month from this date and if your leaf walker is not at my doorstep, I will take your grandfathers limp body and burn it on my fire to heat the halls of the rock. Come to Dunnottar and trade life for life and we will see Loxley survive another year." Her laughter was retched and vile as she slid like tar back into the wheel. The wheel stopped and shot off the table and exploded into shattered fragments.

The room was silent for a moment. Robbie looked at Rune who was still, she blinked and turned to him, she drew her sword and pointed it at him. The blade ignited and he recoiled back, everyone gasped with the sudden shock, Rune's eyes burned with deep violet. "You listen and you listen good Robert of Loxley, if you even try to go near her alone, I promise you I will kill you myself. That bitch has my grandfather and we have one month, we free him and then you leave and let me deal with her. Is that clear?" Robbie was completely shocked, there was fury and rage in her blue eyes and she was as scary as the Dark One, Robbie nodded. "Good!" She dropped the sword back into her sheath. "I cannot believe she had the nerve to come here, I will enjoy plucking that black bird, and then I will fry the bitch for supper." Rune looked up at the rest of the room; they all stared at her in utter disbelief as she smiled sweetly. Jade banged on the table.

"Rune... why did you have to do that? I was doing fine until you pulled a sword on Robbie, now look what you made me do." Jade looked up a sad look on her face. "I only peed myself again." Steph leaned over and looked at the floor; she looked up at Rune and smiled. "See I warned you, I said you should have a bucket down here." Jade smiled at her mum; Jett gave a giggle with Ruby.

Robbie lay in the dark watching the stars through the window. Rune came in, and slid back into bed and curled up around him. He looked down and saw her bright blue eyes looking up at him. "You couldn't kill me, could you?" She smiled and crawled up his chest and kissed him.

"I will not let her possess you Rob, I have weapons she has not seen, but if you get taken and filled with Mason, yes I will kill you if I cannot get him out."

"You know Rune you can have a really scary side at times." She giggled and kissed his nose. "You are safe, but that one.... She is in for a big bloody shock when I cross her path, I can hide my powers now. I have learned the secrets of the dark veil; we will be fine." He smiled as she snuggled around him. "I was thinking about Iona earlier." Rune giggled.

"I think of her often, she will come soon enough, if not sooner. We have to sort out the matter of the Dark One first." Robbie breathed a sigh. "Sooner, eh?" Rune started to giggle as he slid his arms around her.

More Author's
From
Violet Circle Publishing

Mike Beale. (Children's Book)
Crumble's Adventures.
ISBN: 978-1-910299-06-7
Digital ISBN: 978-1-910299-08-1

Colin Smith (Play)
Heaven knows I'm Miserable Now
ISBN: 978-1-910299-16-6
Digital ISBN: 978-1-910299-23-4

Ted Morgan. (Poetry and verse)
Wordsmith's Wanderings.
ISBN: 978-1-910299-04-3
Digital ISBN: 978-1-910299-09-8
Peregrinations of the Wordsmith
ISBN: 978-1-910299-18-0
Digital ISBN: 978-1-910299-21-0
Silhouette Soldiers
ISBN: 978-1-910299-19-7
Digital ISBN: 978-1-910299-22-7
A Menu of Memories
Digital ISBN: 978-1-910299-32-6
Digital ISBN: 978-1-910299-33-3

Robin John Morgan. (Fiction/Fantasy/Slice of Life)
Heirs to the Kingdom.
Book One, The Bowman of Loxley.
ISBN: 978-1-910299-00-5
Digital ISBN: 978-1-910299-10-4
Book Two, The Lost Sword of Carnac.
ISBN: 978-1-910299-01-2
Digital ISBN: 978-1-910299-11-1

Book Three, The Darkness of Dunnottar.
ISBN: 978-1-910299-02-9
Digital ISBN: 978-1-910299-12-8
Book Four, Queen of the Violet Isle.
ISBN: 978-1-910299-03-6
Digital ISBN: 978-1-910299-13-5
Book Five, Crystals of the Mirrored Waters.
ISBN: 978-1-910299-05-0
Digital ISBN: 978-1-910299-14-2
Book Six, Last Arrow of the Woodland Realm.
ISBN: 978-1-910299-07-4
Digital ISBN: 978-1-910299-15-9
Book Seven, Bridge Of Sequana.
ISBN: 978-1-910299-17-3
Digital ISBN: 978-1-910299-20-3
Book Eight, The Circle of Darkness.
ISBN: 978-1-910299-26-5
Digital ISBN: 978-1-910299-29-6

The Curio Chronicles.

Part One, Abigail's Summer.
ISBN: 978-1-910299-27-2
Part Two, Curio's Summer.
ISBN: 978-1-910299-34-0
Digital ISBN: 978-1-910299-35-7
Part Three, Curio's Christmas.
ISBN: 978-1-910299-38-8
Digital ISBN: 978-1-910299-39-5

Other Works.

Rise Of The Raven
ISBN: 978-1-910299-30-2
Digital ISBN: 978-1-910299-31-9
The Countess Of Darkness
ISBN: 978-1-910299-40-1
Digital ISBN: 978-1-910299-41-8

Han's Cottage.
ISBN: 978-1-910299-36-4
Digital ISBN: 978-1-910299-37-1

Find out more about our authors and their books at
www.violetcirclepublishing.co.uk